BELIEVE IN LOVE

THE COMPLETE SERIES

AMY SPARLING

First Edition April 2016

BELIEVE IN ME

A BELIEVE IN LOVE NOVEL

CHAPTER ONE

Keanna

Another small town and another craft fair. This time Mom and I are in Texas, somewhere called Lawson. It's dry and hot, but not the scorching, make-you-want-to-strip-in-the-middle-of-the-street heat that was in Phoenix a few days ago. Texas is humid. Hot. Those rumors about Texas having cowboys everywhere are true.

I'm staring at one right now. He's middle-aged, overweight, and wearing a pair of dark Wrangler jeans and cowboy boots. His cowboy hat is black and, goofy as it looks, it seems to be doing a good job of keeping his eyes shielded from the blinding sun. I can sympathize with this man even though we have about nothing in common. He's stuck here just like I am, at a craft fair set up in some church parking lot in the middle of a tiny ass town. His wife is peddling her wares: scented candles in mason jars.

My mother is peddling hers, wind chimes and jewelry made of broken glass. Not that I'd ever tell anyone, but it's mostly beer bottles that she roughs up in a rock tumbler then claims she found the pieces of blue, green, and brown littered on beautiful beaches all over the country.

Dawn is a free spirit. She really has traveled the country, but she's also got to make a living somehow and beaches aren't as rife with sea glass as you might think. I would know, I've spent my entire life trailing along behind her, in matching boho dresses from thrift stores, scouting the sands for that buried treasure. Dawn's ultimate goal is to travel the world but world-traveling is expensive and having another mouth to feed—me—makes

Dawn is my mom. She doesn't like to be called Mom. I call her that in my head though, because as natural as it is for her to pack up our suitcases overnight and shove us into a bus to relocate to a new town every few months, it's also natural for me to call my mother Mom.

I can't say it to her face, though.

I am seventeen. Dawn just turned thirty-three a few weeks ago.

Don't want to do the math . . . it's a little sad.

Dawn never wanted to be a mother but she also didn't want to give me to someone who didn't deserve me, or so that's what she always says when we're at a restaurant, getting a free meal from an attractive guy with gaga eyes for her. She always manages to tell this tale to every man she dates. She'd wanted to give me up for adoption but never got the guts to do it. She reminds me all the time, like I should be proud that she has such high standards for me or something.

I am aware that my life is weird. Every school I've ever gone to has had at least one kid there who made sure to point it out.

There are certain things that non-weird people my age consider normal. Like, having a massive closet full of various articles of clothing that you can mix and match to make a new outfit for each day.

Dawn and I never have more than we can fit into one suitcase each. That leads to a lot of wearing the same thing over and over again. People call it weird. I call it my life.

I look down at my jeans, faded and ripped along the thighs. Cuffs rolled up to look like they're fashionably short and not just high waters because I got too tall for them ages ago. They're too baggy because I can't keep weight on my bones because we hardly ever eat. Luckily for me, these old jeans are in style right now. They call them the "boyfriend cut" at American Eagle. Also lucky for me, so is being thin as hell.

Guess I should be happy, right?

Dawn's thumb and forefinger snap me right out of my daydreaming. "Look alive, kid. Make yourself look desirable. You never know when your prince charming will run into you."

Her eyes are crystal blue, almost completely colorless as she stares at me with that look on her face like she's giving me invaluable advice. My eyes are dark, deep voids, almost like I have no color in them at all, just two big pupils. They're a genetic gift from whichever man decided to knock up a fifteen-year-old. Dawn won't tell me who he is, but I think it's because she doesn't exactly know, not that she's trying to keep it a secret from me. We're pretty open with each other.

I've seen enough TV to know that most parents wouldn't frequently tell their kids how badly they wished they'd adopted them out instead of keeping them.

"I'm not sure why a prince charming would show up here," I say, looking around at the crowd of craft fair goers, mostly older women and a few children walking from booth to booth.

"I'm sure that's what every spinster has said about every place they've ever gone," she says, holding her chin up high as she adjusts one of the wind chimes on our retractable canvas tent that serves as our temporary storefront.

"I'm seventeen you know. I'm not close to being a spinster yet."

Mom flashes me a smile, her small, pouty lips leaving absolutely no question to why so many men find her drop dead gorgeous. "That's also what every spinster said when *they* were seventeen."

I snort and gaze back out at the craft fair. It's a small one this weekend, with only about fifty booths set up around us. There's a little walkway between them all and we're set up between the candle lady and another woman selling knitted baby clothes.

A woman and her husband walk up hand-in-hand, cooing over Mom's wind chimes. I watch as Mom saunters over to them, somehow seeming like an old friend instead of a salesman. She has this charm about her that always ends up getting her exactly what she wants.

In this case, it's three wind chimes sold. The woman buys one for herself and two for her sisters and I ring them up with a credit card swiper attached to my cell phone. At fifty dollars each, we just made enough money to score another week in the motel on the outskirts of town.

It's also enough for bus tickets, should Mom decide to pack us up again. Summer just started, like literally three days ago, so who knows how often we'll be moving around now.

After a few run-ins with the police for truancy, my mother had to agree not to move me from school to school for at least four months in between. The last four months were spent in Phoenix, Arizona. But now that it's summer, who the hell knows how many places we'll stay.

Mom is a wanderer and I'm stuck along for the ride.

Part of me can't wait until I turn eighteen so I can extract myself from all of this traveling and settle down somewhere to start a real life of my own.

The other part of me is terrified of being without Dawn. There is no house in this world that I would call home. There's only Mom and me, and that makes her my home.

Around four-forty-five, Mom extracts herself from the group of people she'd been chatting with and wraps an arm around my shoulders. The dozen fake-gold bangles around her wrist clack against my back.

"Take one of my fabric totes from under the table," she whispers, her breath smelling the like mint gum she'd bummed off of the cowboy earlier. "Go see if there's any leftover food in the church and grab as much of it as you can."

I nod. This church craft fair had provided finger foods for the patrons and craft sellers for lunch. I'd had four mini sandwiches filled with some kind of meat and mayo and two bags of chips. It was the biggest lunch I've had in a while and my stomach still aches from being so full. If they have any leftovers . . . this will be an awesome day.

The church's rec room is empty when I walk inside, well except for the Jesus hanging from a cross on the wall. He's nearly as tall as I am, his expression a little painful to look at. I open the cloth tote bag and make my way to the food table, grabbing a napkin and loading it with the remaining sandwiches. The only chip bags left are of the gross flavors and the healthy low-calorie snacks, but I take them anyway.

Footsteps sound behind me and I jump, trying to look casual. A church wouldn't, like, get me arrested for stealing, right?

"What's taking so long?" Mom says, rushing over to me. I let out the breath I'd been holding, relieved as hell that the intruder was just my mom, and show her the inside of the bag.

"We got a lot of stuff," I say with a grin.

Mom frowns. The tip of her drawn-on eyebrow is starting to smudge off from the heat of the day. "Keanna, do you want to eat for the rest of the week or just for tonight?" She gestures to the meat and cheese tray on the end of the table. "Get the rest of this damn food, girl."

"I didn't want to take everything," I say, feeling a rush of warmth spread into my cheeks. Maybe it's because Jesus is over there dying on a cross and I'm stealing food right from under Him.

"Look around, kid," Mom says, rolling up a stack of sliced turkey and shoving it into a napkin. "This food is free, so take it. Churches like to feed the poor and all of that, and honey, we're poor."

I let out a huff of air and grab the last two bottles of water, shoving them into my bag.

As we turn to leave, a woman steps into the room. Mom keeps walking but I accidentally stop. The shock of seeing someone who totally was close enough to hear our conversation makes me temporarily paralyzed.

"Oh, hello there," the woman says. She seems pleasant enough, maybe about my mom's age. She glances at the empty food table and then offers us a polite smile. Mom hisses my name, wanting me to hurry up, and my legs finally start moving.

"Wait!" the woman says. My heart leaps up into my throat.

Mom turns around, her multi-colored sundress swaying around her legs. "Can I help you?" she asks.

The lady nods. "You're the woman with the wind chimes, right?" She puts a hand to her chest. "They are absolutely beautiful. I know the craft fair is closing down soon but are you still open by chance? I was hoping to stop by and get one."

Mom beams, her attitude going from defensive to cordial in half a second. "Of course, of course. Come with me. My name is Dawn Byrd and I'm the artist."

"Becca Park," the woman says, shaking Mom's hand. "I run this craft fair and I remembered seeing your entry online when you registered. I've been wanting to come get a wind chime all day but," she shakes her head and lets out a breath. "This has been a busy ass day. I had no idea running this thing would be so hard."

"Well you did a fantastic job," Mom says, leading her back into the parking lot toward our booth.

As they keep talking, I start to wonder if the lady heard our conversation or not. If so, she's being nice by not saying anything. But I guess once people are grown up, they don't dive at every chance to make fun of you for being poor like the kids at my old high school did.

Becca Park and Mom talk for fifteen minutes, and Mom works her charm on the woman. Pretty soon, they're laughing and joking as if they're old friends. I envy Mom's innate skill to bond with just about anyone. That's another thing I never inherited from her.

"Listen," Becca Park says, clasping her hands together in front of her chest. I notice the massive diamond wedding ring on her finger and wonder what she did to make sure she didn't end up as a spinster. "I know we just met and this might be a little forward of me, but I just love your art, Dawn. And well, I'd like to invite you and your daughter over for dinner tonight." She smiles wide and bites on her lower lip. "I live just down the road and my husband is making burgers. There's plenty to go around and I'd love to hear more about your wire-wrapping process. What do you say?"

Mom looks at me and I shrug. But I should have nodded because burgers and leftover food in one day just never happens. They say everything is bigger in Texas, and from what I've seen, the amount of free food certainly is.

"Absolutely, Becca," Mom says, reaching forward and grabbing Becca's hands in hers. "We would love to, isn't that right, Keanna?"

I nod, the thought of getting a few hours away from our smelly motel room making me happier than I've been in weeks. "Yeah, I'd love a burger."

"Wonderful!" Becca says. "Come on, I'll help you pack up your booth."

CHAPTER TWO

Jett

The sun blinds me as I swing my bike wide around the berm of dirt, turning to the west. I drop down to third gear, the bike screaming in protest at the reduced speed. I knew it was going to happen eventually, but dammit if I wasn't hoping for ten more minutes of riding before the setting sun blinds the hell out of me on the track. I stand on the pegs and drop to second gear, riding slowly over the massive jump, dipping the visor on my helmet to block out as much sunlight as possible. Then I pull off the track and ride back to the garage.

The garage is a massive metal barn, used to store dirt bikes. Mostly those of paying customers, but I keep my bike here instead of at home, which is just down the street. My parents own The Track, a place aptly named because that's just what it is—a motocross track. They rarely hold races here because it's mostly a practice facility. My dad and his best friend Park are old has-beens in the professional motocross world. They turned their knowledge into a training course and usually it's badass.

But summers kind of suck because now I have to work.

As I hop off my bike and prop it up into the storage space, I can practically hear Dad's words now.

"Son, you're sixteen now. Your lifestyle isn't cheap. It's time you worked for your money instead of having me hand it to you."

Then, of course, Mom had stepped in the last time Dad brought up the topic of me working at his business.

"Honey, he's just a kid. He needs to focus on school work."

"Not in the summer," Dad had said.

And now here it is, the first week of summer break before my junior year of high school, and I'm already working.

Not cool.

I rip off my helmet and sling my head, letting sweat fly off in all directions. After a day of working at the track, I'd only been able to ride for fifteen minutes. Last summer I spent all damn day out here, working on my technique, getting faster with each lap. Now that I'm forced to work for ten bucks an hour, I'm starting to wonder if my dad doesn't want me to go pro when I'm eighteen.

He tells his clients all the time that practice is everything. And now I'm stuck not being able to practice.

I head into the main building and find Dad in his office, staring at his computer screen as if it had personally offended him. "What's up?" I say.

He runs his thumb and index finger across his forehead and shrugs. "Taxes are kicking my ass. I'm gonna have to get your mother in here to fix this."

I snort. "She's going to love that." Dad always tries to do legal tax stuff by himself but Mom always has to bail him out. She's the one who graduated with a Master's in accounting after all.

"Tell me about it," Dad says, rising from his chair. "How was your second day of work?"

"It sucked," I say, grabbing a water bottle from the mini-fridge in Dad's office. "I only got to ride for fifteen minutes."

"Riding isn't part of your job description, kid."

I roll my eyes and he grins. "You're worried about not getting enough practice huh?"

"Of course I am. You always say you gotta ride your heart out to make it pro." I finish the water and crunch the plastic bottle in my hand.

Dad shakes his head. "How about this. You work three days a week, and you ride four days. That's plenty of practice to make it big."

"Thanks," I say, feeling like a huge weight has been lifted off my shoulders. "Can I have tomorrow off?"

Dad laughs. "Nope. It's peewee lock-in night and I'll need your help."

Damn. I forgot about that. The peewees are what they call little kids who ride dirt bikes. Like four to seven-year-olds. The Track has these lock-ins during the summer where the kids will ride all day, then lay out in sleeping bags in our entertainment room and watch TV and eat pizza until the morning when they'll ride all day again.

I used to love lock-ins when I was little. I already practically live here, so sleeping over was even better. Now I have better things to do than sleep next to snoring little kids. I say goodbye to Dad and head down to the front office where I've stashed all my stuff into one of the tiny employee lockers. I'd promised Emma Clarke I'd be off work by six and it's almost six-thirty. The girl hates being kept waiting, but damn if that's not what she does to me all the time.

There are a few parents in the front office, signing up their kids for the lock-in. Luckily, some chick who works the desk is here so I don't have to do anything. I'm still not sure what her name is, but she's kind of hot for being like thirty-something.

I grab my phone and find two missed texts from Emma. One simply says *It's six o'clock, asshole.*

The other is a kissing face emoji.

I really don't get this girl. But I get her lips on mine, so I keep putting up with all of her hot and cold mood swings.

I text back *Just got off work, want me to pick you up after I shower?*

And a phone dings from across the room. Shit.

I look up and my eyes find hers. Bright blue eyes, perfect blonde hair, and one hell of an evil glare.

"Hey," I say, putting on a smile as I cross the room and give her a hug. She remains stiff in my arms, so I pull back. "What do you want to do tonight?"

She folds her arms across her chest, her fake nails sparkling as much as the rings on her fingers. "You mean what *did* I want to do."

"I don't understand."

She rolls her eyes and takes in a deep breath. "Did. As in, the past. Because right now, I am sick of all of your lies, Jett Adams. You are such a prick, you know that?"

The woman behind the counter calls my name. "Take your drama outside, please." She shoos at us with her hand and I grab Emma's arm, pulling her outside.

"Look, I have to work now. I can't be at your beck and call anymore. I still want to hang out, so tell me where you want to go."

Emma flips her hair over her shoulder with such precision that I have to wonder if she's practiced that move in front of the mirror. "I don't want to go anywhere with you, Jett."

Her lips flatten into a thin line and she turns on her heel, digging a hole in the gravel walkway. "Call me when you decide that your stupid dirt bike isn't more important than me."

I should probably let it go, but I'm a little sick of having shit thrown in my face when I've made my expectations clear.

"Listen Emma," I say, moving in front of her so she's forced to stop prancing away from me. "Dirt bikes will always come first in my life. And don't give me that look. I told you this weeks ago."

Her eyes turn up to the sky like she thinks I'm just *so* stupid, and I kind of feel like walking away from her right now. She's not worth the effort. She's hot as hell, with a killer body, but still not worth the effort.

"I told you I'm not settling down and I have no desire for a girlfriend," I say, because she clearly needs the reminder.

"I never asked to be your girlfriend, now have I?" Emma says, hands on her hips.

"Look, I like you and we have fun, but when you start bitching at me like I'm some sort of shit boyfriend, that's when I draw the line." I'm still covered in sweat from riding so I lift the front of my T-shirt and wipe it over my face. Emma's eyes dart to my abs and I get probably way too much satisfaction from that. "I don't want a girlfriend and right now you're acting like one. So why don't *you* call *me* when you're looking for some fun."

She huffs. "Fine."

I meet her stony gaze with a look of apathy. "Fine."

Mom stops me when I walk in the kitchen. "I need a favor," she says over a frying pan. Looks like she's making fried chicken which is one of my favorite meals of all time.

"Can it wait a bit?" I ask, reaching for a piece of cucumber from the salad on the table. "I need to shower."

"Sorry, it can't wait." Mom ducks into the fridge and digs around, emerging with a block of cheddar cheese. She holds it out to me. "Becca needs this, apparently they only have Colby jack and Park hates Colby jack." Mom smiles. She is what my friends call a MILF, but really I just see the woman who raised me, working and going to college full time while somehow managing to tuck me into bed every night when I was a kid.

"Sure thing," I say, grabbing the cheese.

Becca and Park are our neighbors, though their house is kind of a ways away since we both have a ton of land and the Track between us. I hop on the small pit bike in the garage, crank up the motor and drive it over to their house. I've known these people my entire life and they're kind of like second parents to me since they never had kids of their own. Park used to be a professional motocross racer as well, but he didn't have nearly as bad of a temper as Dad did. I'm not really sure why he quit racing, but I think it has something to do with Becca.

I walk up the steps to their massive wrap around porch and knock on the door. The Victorian house is something like five billion years old and although they've renovated the interior, Becca insisted on keeping the outside of the house original with its intricate wooden decorations and huge old windows.

"Come in, come in," Becca says, yanking open the door.

I hold out the cheese. "I just need to drop this off. You don't want me in there, I stink."

She smiles. I notice she's kind of dressed up compared to usual and her make up is all done. She must have done another craft fair thing. "Sorry, you've got another job to do," she says, taking the cheese.

I follow her into the kitchen and out the back door to the patio. Park is standing at the grill, talking to some woman I've never seen before. Another girl, probably about my age, sits on a patio chair, staring at her fingernails which are plain and natural, not all done up with rhinestones and polish like Emma's.

The girl looks up at me and I offer her a smile. She looks away.

Okay then, be a bitch.

"What's up?" I ask Becca. She turns to her husband.

"Which one tastes better?" He asks, holding up two pieces of hamburger meat.

I eat one and then the other. "I don't know, the first one?"

"Told you!" Park says, pointing to his wife. "I am the best meat seasoner."

"Ugh," Becca says, throwing me a look. "Kid, you're supposed to like mine better."

I shrug, wondering if they'll ever stop calling me kid now that I'm no longer one. "Sorry, you should have warned me."

"You want to stay for dinner?" she asks, motioning toward the patio table. "These are our friends Dawn and Keanna."

I'm not sure which name belongs to which person, the hippie or the super thin girl that looks like she wants to burn the place down. Mom's cooking at home of course, but I could eat a burger and then eat Mom's chicken. I'm about to agree to stay for a bit when my phone beeps.

Sorry for the BS earlier. Let me make it up to you . . .

Damn, just a few words on a phone screen and I've practically got a hard on already. I swallow. "Sorry, I wish I could stay but I've gotta head home."

CHAPTER THREE

Keanna

Ugh, rich people. Could this house be any bigger? The furniture any nicer? These people have a full kitchen inside the house and then another one *outside* of the house. We're sitting on a massive wooden deck with extravagant patio furniture, a grill and a granite countertop kitchen outside. There's even a bar and a flat-panel television mounted on the wall.

Our hosts have music playing from invisible speakers in the roof. It really is a beautiful summer night, and the smell of burgers on the grill has my mouth watering, but it's hard not to feel a tinge of resentment that some people get to live this way every single day.

Like that guy who just came over here with a block of cheese. Tasting burgers like it's no big deal, like family and friends and free meals come all the time to him. Hell, having a block of cheese in the fridge like *that's* no big deal—even that is hard for me to comprehend.

Becca just spent the last five minutes talking about him. His name is Jett apparently. What kind of name is that? It's something rich people name their kids, I guess. Becca goes on and on about what a great kid he is. Did she not see that he's around six feet tall and his arms are absolutely ripped? That doesn't exactly say "kid" to me.

I tune out most of the polite chatter after the man of the house, a guy named Park, gives me a burger. Becca had said her last name was Park and now her husband's name is also Park so that's kind of weird. I don't bother asking what the deal is, because it's not like I'll see these people again after tonight.

I load up my burger with extra cheese and mayo, ketchup, pickles, and even lettuce. Screw it, I put everything they have on my burger because it's available and after one bite I realize this is way better than any dollar menu burger I get with Dawn. I even crumple some potato chips inside and then smash the bun on top to hold it all in. The food is so good; I can't even think straight.

And then Mom starts talking and my senses go on high alert. She's got that dreamy look in her eyes and I steady myself for whatever embarrassing thing she's going to say next.

Only, when she speaks, it's not really that bad.

"I am loving Texas so far," Mom says, grabbing another handful of potato chips from the bowl in the middle of the table. "When we moved here from Arizona, I knew I didn't want to settle down in another large city, you know? I wanted something small, more low key with friendly people."

Becca nods along in agreement and it takes a lot for me to keep my mouth shut. Dawn in a small town? Yeah, right. They are the bane of her existence. She's always talking about how we're going to hit up every major city and sell her art there. Why the sudden change of heart?

"That's what I love about Lawson," Becca says. "We're only forty-five minutes from a big city in case we need something, but we're far enough away that we have all this wide open space."

Mom nods. Then her lips turn down and she shakes her head slightly, like she's disappointed in something. "It's a shame, really. I was hoping to settle in and stay here, but it looks like we'll be leaving in the morning."

"Why's that?" Becca asks, refilling my sweet tea from a pitcher on the table.

"Are you gonna eat that, babe?" Park asks, nodding toward the rest of her burger. She shakes her head and slides her plate over to him.

Mom makes this big dramatic sigh. "Well, my art is my way of living, of course, but if we're going to get enough money for a down payment and first month's rent, I need a job, you see."

Oh god… this is where Mom begs these kind new people to get her employed. My stomach tightens.

"And the great news is that I found a wonderful art consulting job that has a generous sign on bonus and it would let me work from home."

Wow. I did not see that coming.

Becca's eyes brighten. "That's wonderful, Dawn!"

Mom shakes her head "Unfortunately, I have to do the interview and paperwork in person, and it's down in Corpus Christie which is about a six hour drive from here if I'm not mistaken. I wish I didn't have to drag poor Keanna with me, but I can't leave her in a hotel alone."

This is the first I've heard of Mom's fancy new work from home job offer. But I'm not about to question her in front of these people. Mom tends to lie about nearly everything, especially when talking to strangers. But I'm not sure what her angle is here. What's the point in lying about something like this?

"Why don't you let Keanna stay here?" Becca says. "That way you won't be dragging her to your interview and she won't be left alone in a hotel. We have plenty of room here."

Ah. So that's Mom's angle.

Mom puts a hand to her chest. "Oh, I couldn't. That's way too much of an imposition."

"Nonsense. We don't mind at all. Do we, Park?"

Her husband swallows a huge bite of food and nods. "Yeah, I don't mind. She's welcome to stay."

My eyes widen. "I . . . No that's . . .I don't need to stay."

Dawn puts a hand on my arm. "Honey, you don't want to spend six hours in the car only to sit in the car while I do my interview and then have to drive all the way back, do you? The interview will take hours and I can't bring you in with me, that would just look unprofessional."

I open my mouth to object, but I don't want to cause a scene. The thing is, we have never gone more than an hour away from wherever we're currently staying only to come right back again. That kind of talk sounds suspiciously like we've found a home in Lawson, Texas and like Mom actually wants to settle down.

I never thought that would happen. But the idea is kind of awesome. I'd love to stop moving around, maybe get a job and earn some money. Maybe even *possibly* consider college after my senior year.

"What do you say?" Becca asks me. "We just got a new TV for the guest bedroom. You'd love it."

TV? My own room?

Even though it's only for twenty-four hours, I can't possibly say no to that. "Sounds great," I say. Mom's face lights up like this is the best thing she's heard all year.

"Excellent!" Mom says. "Thank you both so much. I can tell we're going to become really great friends!"

AFTER DINNER, WHICH CAME WITH A DELICIOUS CHOCOLATE CAKE FOR DESSERT, Becca takes me upstairs to show me the guest bedroom. It's bigger than the last few motel rooms I stayed in with Mom and it takes everything I have not to dance around like a crazy person the moment I step inside the room.

Plush grey carpeting feels like clouds under my worn sandals. The walls are a faint yellow and fresh sunflowers sit in a vase on the vanity. The bed is huge and although I don't plop down on it like I want to, it looks really comfortable. Also, there's a massive television mounted on the wall. These next twenty-four hours are going to be the best of my life.

I walk over to a large canvas painting on the wall. Splashes of blue and yellow paint cover the canvas and there's a quote drawn on in sloppy, paint splattered letters.

"If you want something you've never had, you have to do something you've never done."

Becca catches me staring at it and walks over. "This is cool," I say, resisting the urge to touch it.

"Very inspiring," Mom says with an approving nod.

"Oh, I'm so glad you think so," Becca says. "This is one of my newer paintings, but I haven't put it in my shop yet."

"You made this?" I ask, my mouth falling open. "It's really cool."

She nods. "I run an online shop with my paintings. It's called Becca's Inspirations. I spent the last decade selling my art online but a few years ago I started doing craft fairs. They're a lot of fun."

"You have a lot of talent," Mom says. "We should partner up sometime. Display your paintings next to my wind chimes!"

Becca nods, and then she gets this sneaky look on her face. "Would you like to see my newest stuff? I haven't shown anyone yet."

Mom clasps her hands together in front of her chest. I'm not sure if she's putting on an act so that Becca will like her, or if she's really serious. It's probably a mixture of the two. "I would love to see your work."

Becca leads us outside and then we take a short car ride to a dirt bike track. She drives us around the back of the main building.

"I have a studio in my house, but I tend to store all of the finished products here," she explains as she unlocks a back door and leads us inside. Only the emergency lights in the hallway are turned on, so we walk slowly, bypassing a few office doors. "You have to turn on all of the lights at the light panel on the other side of the building," Becca explains, using the glow of her cell phone to light our path. "Sorry for the darkness, but we're almost there."

We reach the end of the hallway and there's a door ahead of us marked STORAGE. Becca turns to the left and opens a door next to it, flipping on the light. A girl screams and Becca jumps, knocking into me.

"Holy shit," Becca says, putting a hand to her chest. "You scared me!"

I can't help but smirk as I watch the scene unfold in front of me. The small room is filled with shelves of canvas paintings, but along one wall is a couch. That guy from earlier, Jett, is scrambling to button up his jeans. His T-shirt is in a pile on the floor, and the bright lights make a spectacle of his tanned, muscular chest. The girl is in her underwear, a hot pink matching set. It's no wonder that's she's beautiful and blonde, pretty much the picture perfect model of what every guy thinks is perfection.

They're both bright red and mumbling embarrassed apologies. I put my hand over my mouth to stop my laughter.

Behind me, Mom snorts.

CHAPTER FOUR

Jett

"What the hell is this?" Becca says. She holds up her hand. "Never mind. Don't answer that. I don't want to know."

Emma scrambles past me, grabbing her dress from the floor. "You said we were alone here," she hisses, not-so-quietly, as she clutches the fabric to her chest and glares at me. To Becca she says, "Sorry," before running the hell out of here. I guess she'll put her clothes on in the hallway.

I stand up, bite my lower lip. Only my shirt is off, but I feel about twenty times more naked than any human could possibly be. I lift my eyebrows and muster up a smile. "Don't tell Mom?"

Becca rolls her eyes, bends down and grabs my shirt just so she can throw it at me. "You better hope I don't tell *that* girl's mom!"

The hippie woman standing in the doorway is clearly trying not to laugh. I want to tell her to go for it, that I can't possibly be more humiliated than I already am. But I don't say anything because Becca isn't done laying into me.

"Dammit, Jett." She puts her hands on her hips. If she and Park ever have a kid of their own, she will make a terrifying but excellent mother. "I know you're the heartthrob around here, but did you have to choose my storage closet?" Her arms wave wildly around. "Of all the places in this building, you had to hook up around my art?"

Now the hippie woman does laugh. I dart a look over at her daughter. I can't remember her name. It starts with a K. The daughter is smiling, her dark eyes focused right on me. Her face looks a whole lot better when she's not scowling like she was the first time I met her. I give her a quick wink.

Becca slaps my arm and groans. "Get the hell out of here, kid. Why can't ya'll just make out in cars like normal teenagers?"

I give her a sly look. "Because there's a couch in here."

Becca slaps me again, and I know it's warranted. I put my hands together in front of her chest, an overdramatic prayer gesture to beg for her forgiveness. "Sorry, Second Mom. I won't defile your storage space again."

"Good," she snaps, but then she grins and rolls her eyes. "Get out of here. And to think, I told Keanna you would be a good friend to have . . ."

I glance back at the girl and she smirks. Something tells me she'd be down for having a little fun. I tug my shirt on over my head. Becca starts telling the hippie lady about her art, leaving Keanna looking bored by the door. I seize the opportunity to do a little flirting as I walk by her.

"Give me a call if you ever want a late night tour of the place," I whisper, meeting her eyes for just a second so she knows my intentions. I'm being slick as hell, or at least I think so. But my words turn her look of curiosity into a sneer of disgust.

"Never going to happen," she whispers back.

Damn, I struck out.

Oh well, on to the next one.

Emma is long gone by the time I get outside. She'd met me here with her car, parked in the back so that no one would notice it. Who knows how long she'll stay pissed at me this time.

I start walking toward home, debating if I should send her an apology text. I'm trying to decide if that's a decent thing to do, or if it'll seem like something a boyfriend would do. I am not a boyfriend. Boyfriends get held down and chained up in the bonds of a relationship. They only get to be with one girl. That's just not my style. Dad says I'll change when I get older, that I'll wake up one day and suddenly want a real relationship. He's told me not to burn any bridges with the girls I date now because I never know when I'll suddenly grow up and my perspective on life will change.

Dad loves Mom and Mom loves Dad and they're this perfect couple and all that, and good for them. Honestly, I love that my parents still love each other unlike most of my friend's parents who are divorced. But that kind of life isn't for me. I like fun and adventure. I like hot girls and no strings attached. A professional motocross racer doesn't need some ball and chain holding him back. I've heard Dad's lectures a million times. He's always telling me I'll change my mind someday.

And I'm always telling him that "someday" is not today.

CHAPTER FIVE

Keanna

Did that really just happen? Ultra-hot and super-rich guy made a stupid comment suggesting that he and I could make out? There's no way. Guys like that do not even look twice at losers like me.

Becca and Dawn fawn over the paintings for a little while, but I'm too busy being lost in my own thoughts to pay attention to the conversation. The most embarrassing part of the whole two-second event is that I can't stop picturing it.

Making out with Jett.

Sneaking around a business at midnight, looking for couches hidden away in the darkness. Getting undressed and crawling into his lap . . . Yeah, I can't think like that. As if a guy like him would *ever* seriously consider dating me.

But I guess he didn't say the word "dating" . . . he just meant a hookup.

I've hooked up with plenty of guys before—always random flings and never anything bordering on a real relationship. Dating? I feel the blood rush to my cheeks just thinking it. Why would I even *think* that word? I've never been on a date in my life.

Unless you count the time Mom met some guy who took us both out to dinner because I was thirteen and she didn't want to leave me alone. She'd thought it was so romantic that this guy let me come along, like he was already step-father material or something. After the date, he'd hooked up with Mom then found me sleeping in the next motel room over and tried doing the same thing to me. I threw a motel lamp into his face and he ran out of there, cursing and dripping blood everywhere.

I shake my head to clear it of thoughts like that. Once one of them slips into my subconscious, more always follow. And this is a good day, with an awesome place to sleep tonight so I refuse to let any bad thoughts come my way.

"I guess we should head back," Becca says, yawning. "It's getting pretty late."

We drive back to Becca's house and Mom tosses me her car keys, telling me to grab my suitcase from the trunk.

When I walk back into the house lugging my beat up old Samsonite, Mom holds up a finger like she just remembered something. "Honey, why don't you get your bag, too? That way it won't get messed up in Corpus Christi."

I frown. Becca offers her a refill on her wine glass and I turn around, heading back to the trunk. Mom and I each have a suitcase and a duffel bag. The suitcase is for clothes and living essentials, while our duffel bag has all of our personal belongings. It's not much; Mom's has her tablet and all of her business paperwork along with a few knick-knacks I made her as a kid. The wind chimes and craft fair stuff go in the back seat of her SUV. My bag has a teddy bear from my childhood, a few pairs of sandals, two bottles of nail polish, my tablet for getting online, and a stack of DVDs to watch on Mom's laptop.

I don't know why I would need any of that for a one night stay at a stranger's house, but I grab the stupid bag and carry it into the guest room.

From the living room, Mom calls my name.

I slip into the hallway and jog down the stairs, my hand sliding along the banister as if I do this all the time. A fleeting image appears in my mind; a daydream of being a girl who lives in a house like this with loving parents. A girl whose room is filled with clothes and friends and memories.

"You leaving?" I ask when my feet hit the first floor.

Mom nods. "Going to head back to the hotel for a couple hours of sleep. Then I'll hit the road and make it there before noon."

I glance around the room and notice that Becca and Park are gone. "Did you tell them you're leaving?" I ask.

She nods, examining her hair for split ends. "They went to investigate a funny noise on the grill or something. Now come here, give me a hug."

She spreads her arms wide, her bangles dancing down to her elbows. I kind of want to use this moment of privacy to ask about this weird job offer and berate her for not telling me sooner. Are we really settling down in a place called Lawson? Will I graduate high school here? Or is it just another one of her silly schemes to get rid of me for the night? For all I know, she met some guy at the craft fair and wants to get laid without a teenager holding her back.

I sigh and walk into her arms, returning her hug. She grabs onto the back of my head and holds me tightly, squeezing until I'm all out of breath and have to gasp for air.

"I love you, K-bug," she says softly, using my nickname from my childhood.

"Love you too, Dawn."

When the hug finally ends, she pulls back and holds me at arm's length. Her eyes seem a little watery, but maybe it's just a trick of the lighting. Mom doesn't really get emotional about stuff like this. "You be good," she says as if I'm a five-year-old. "Make me proud, okay?"

I lift an eyebrow. "I promise not to burn their house down in the next twenty-four hours."

Her eyes soften, two clear gemstones without a care in the world. “Okay, well, I’m going to get out of here,” she says.

“Good luck with your interview.”

She nods, her lips pressing together in a thin smile. “Thanks, doll.”

She grabs me in another quick hug and then turns to leave. And maybe I’m just crazy, but it really seemed like her eyes were holding back real, genuine tears. It almost seems like she’s sad that she’s leaving me here. Or like maybe she thinks she won’t get to see me again.

CHAPTER SIX

Jett

I stumble into the kitchen the next morning, obeying my stomach like a starving zombie. Since tomorrow is the first little kid lock-in of the summer, and I'll be supervising it, I'm off work today. I guess Dad thought he'd be nice to me before making me suffer at the hands of a dozen kindergarteners.

One thing about my new job at the family business: it is especially cruel how my body decided to wake up so early on my day off. I used to never get up this early unless it was race day. And even then, I'd wake up early only to crawl into Dad's truck and sleep until we got to the track. But now after only a few days of having a real job, my body is up at freaking eight in the morning.

Mom's chatting on the phone in the breakfast nook, her voice more animated than usual. "So you just let her stay over at your house? You're not afraid she's a robber?"

I lift an eyebrow, wondering who she's talking to as I grab a cereal bowl and fill it to the top with Lucky Charms. Mom continues, "Seventeen year olds can be robbers! She could be a lookout, placed there to scope out your valuables and then alert her crew when you and Park leave the house."

Now I'm curious. They're talking about that girl from last night, Keanna. I glance at Mom and she rolls her eyes, pointing to her phone as if to say, *"You know Becca!"*

I pour the milk and then wander over to the breakfast table, taking a seat opposite of Mom. "That girl didn't look like a robber," I say, and I'm not sure why I'm even defending someone I don't know. She wasn't exactly nice to me.

"Jett agrees with you," she says, lifting her shoulders as she talks. "You should invite her over here. Jace is good at reading people and he'd know if there's something shady going on."

I dive into my cereal, mostly ignoring the rest of the conversation and trying to plan my day off in my head. I know there's a party at the lake tonight, so I'll probably stop by there. Maybe there will be someone other than Emma Clarke to kill the time with.

Mom's voice gets higher. "Ooooh, that would be fun! Yeah, yeah, I have plenty of eggs. Give me five minutes to get dressed."

I stand and grab the cereal box, readying to refill my bowl. "Jett, don't eat anymore," Mom says, shooing me away with her hand.

"What? Why? I'm starving."

"Becca and Park are coming over with that girl," Mom says, taking the cereal box and putting it back in the pantry. "We're going to make a big family breakfast so you better still be hungry."

"I'm always hungry," I say, putting my cereal bowl and spoon into the dishwasher.

"What do you think is up with that girl?" Mom says, giving me this conspiratorial look. "I mean, what kind of mom meets a total stranger and then has her daughter spend the night with her? Park and Becca could be perverts for all she knows!"

I laugh. "I guess it's a good thing they're not."

Mom takes the eggs, bacon, and cheese from the fridge and then hands me two canisters of biscuit dough. "There's still something weird about it, ya know? I mean, I'd never leave you with some stranger."

"That's because you're a good mom," I say.

She grins and wraps an arm around me for a quick hug. "Aww, my boy."

I roll my eyes. "What do you want me to do with this?" I ask, holding up the biscuits.

"Grab a pan and bake them, duh!"

Mom smacks the back of my head and then saunters over to the kitchen island to begin cooking.

I'm peeling apart biscuits and placing them two inches apart on a baking sheet when the back door opens. Since the front door is more of the formal entrance, the Parks always come in through the back. They also let themselves in because they're basically family. That's why I call Becca my "Second Mom" and I think she gets a kick out of it.

I focus on the task of setting dough on the pan even though my stomach is suddenly light and airy at the thought of seeing Keanna again. I know Mom will be judging her this whole morning, trying to secretly discover if Keanna is hiding something sinister in her reason for staying over. Though I think Mom is full of shit for being suspicious, I still wonder *why* Keanna is here. It's definitely weird.

Dad comes downstairs when Mom calls for him and he and Park immediately get to talking about work. Becca introduces Keanna to Mom and friendly hellos are exchanged. I don't know why I'm suddenly so freaking nervous to see her, but I also know that standing here staring at a bunch of raw biscuits kind of makes me look like a weirdo.

I turn casually, and I see her, standing there looking exactly as awkward as I'd expected. "Hey," I say, giving her a friendly head nod.

She's wearing cut off jean shorts short enough that the inside of the pockets hangs down the front of her thighs, and a plain black tank top. Her toes are curling on top of her flip-flops, like she's ready to bolt at any moment.

"Good morning," she says, scratching her elbow. Our eyes meet for just a second and then she looks down, but not down to the floor. Her cheeks turn massively red and I realize exactly what she's looking at. My bare chest.

She turns away, tucks her hair behind her ears. I turn back to my biscuits and put them in the oven, all the while hiding a massive grin.

She thinks I'm hot.

And I think she's a mystery.

We'd taken breakfast outside to the patio, which is really like a room that happens to be outdoors. There's a roof that extends across the patio, with ceiling fans and two TVs hanging from the ceiling. Only the long wall that runs along the backyard is open to the outside. The rest is kind of walled in with trellises and the natural stone fireplace and bar. It's not until breakfast is nearly over that Mom decided to dig her claws into our guest.

Keanna had been pretty quiet all during breakfast, but I noticed she ate a lot, sampling from every dish Mom prepared. We had eggs, bacon, toast, my biscuits, fruit, scones and jams, sausage links, coffee and orange juice.

Keanna ate some of it.

I was just about to comment on it when Mom sets her coffee down with kind of a loud clink, and then smiles warmly at Keanna.

"So, Keanna. Becca said you and your mom just moved here?"

She shrugs. "I guess so. I never really know where we're moving next."

"So you move a lot?"

Keanna begins to nod but then she stops herself and puts on a forced smile. "Something like that."

Mom takes a sip of coffee. "What grade will you be in next year?"

"I'll be a senior, assuming my transcripts transfer okay."

"Jett's a year younger than you," Mom says, somehow managing to look relieved for some reason. "He could show you around Lawson High, introduce you to some people."

"Thanks," Keanna says, reaching for another piece of toast. "I've moved so much in my life that I'm pretty good at making friends, though." Her eyes meet mine. "You don't need to worry about me."

"Why do you move so much?" Dad asks. I guess he's finally decided to join the conversation and stop talking to Park about track stuff. "Are your parents in the military?"

Keanna chuckles to herself. She shakes her head as she layers strawberry jam onto her toast. "My mom is the poster child of wanderlust. She doesn't like being stuck in one place for very long. I doubt we'll be here past summer."

My stomach tightens at the thought of this strange girl disappearing before I've had the chance to get to know her. Dad nods to himself and then says, "You don't want to stay with your dad?"

She chuckles again and then she looks straight at him. "I don't know my dad."

Maybe it's just me, but it feels like an awkwardness has descended. I have this sudden urge to rescue her from my parent's questions so I blurt out the first thing I think of. "You're really skinny for being able to eat so much."

Shit. That was supposed to be a compliment (don't girls like being called thin?) but the look in her eyes makes me wish I could rewind time and keep my damn mouth shut. Keanna stares at the piece of toast and then looks up at me, with something like deceit in her eyes. Or maybe it's anger.

"Ignore my son," Mom says, rolling her eyes. "Eat all you want, dear."

Keanna doesn't stop looking at me though. Finally, she pushes her chair back and stands up, shoving the rest of her food into her mouth. "Sometimes I go all day without seeing any food at all. So forgive me for eating when there's actually food in front of me."

A lump forms in my throat and I want to take it all back, rewind time until it's just me and her meeting again for the first time. Her dark eyes are hiding so much more than she lets on and although it's useless, I search them anyway, hoping to learn more about this girl. I suddenly need to know everything about her and I have no idea why.

Dad and Park started talking animatedly at the end of the table so they didn't hear what just happened. At least I don't think they did. But Mom and Becca heard all right, and they're both looking at me like I'm the biggest jackass in the world.

"I'm—" I begin, wanting to tell her I'm sorry.

But Keanna looks at Becca as if I am no longer worthy of holding her attention. "Mind if I go back to your house and watch TV until my mom gets back?"

"Go right ahead, hun," Becca says.

Mom narrows her gaze at me. "Jett." I cringe. She's using her pissed off voice. "Why don't you clean the table?"

I'm in no position to object, so I start grabbing dishes and carrying them inside, loading up the dishwasher. Mom and Becca talk in hushed tones, somehow getting quieter when I walk back out there to finish cleaning the table. It's obvious who they're talking about. It's the same girl who has taken control of my every thought.

Something tells me Keanna is not like the Emma Clarkes of this world. She's unique and worldly. She's like an iceberg, cold and beautiful. But part of her is hidden away.

When the patio is clean and the kitchen is spotless, I know what I need to do. I need to fix things with Keanna in a way that goes beyond just apologizing for calling her out on being poor.

I need to let her know she has a friend here in Lawson, Texas.

CHAPTER SEVEN

Keanna

I am living two lives. Caught up in two drastically different worlds. My real life, the one I've known since I was born, is on a short hiatus, replaced by this shiny new life. And although the new life is only temporary, I make it a point to breathe in a little deeper, to look around me at all times and really take in my surroundings. I am living in the moment, I guess you could say.

And this moment is absolutely perfect.

After a shaky breakfast with strangers where I was left feeling like a white trash loser, I am now back in the safety of this guest bedroom. No one bothers me for a whole two hours.

It's nearly noon now, and I am laying on my stomach on the guest bed, feet up in the air and remote control in my hand. I am watching TV. Cable TV. Like a normal teenaged girl.

A commercial comes on and I close my eyes and take a deep breath, reveling in the peaceful solace that can be found in your own bedroom.

Of course I know it's not mine. Nothing is mine except my suitcase and duffel bag and I certainly can't relax and watch TV inside of a suitcase.

I've never even had a mattress that belonged to me. Mom and I either stay in hotels, motels, or fully furnished rent-by-the-month apartments that are usually about ten levels slummier than the motels. This mattress isn't mine either, but I can pretend that it is. That this one single day is all mine. I glance at the alarm clock on the nightstand behind me and try to do some time calculations to figure out when Mom will get home.

Her interview was in the morning and would probably last until noon. Then she'd be home by six or six-thirty. That means I get a few more hours all to myself.

I try calling Mom's cell from the land line phone on my nightstand but it goes straight to voicemail. She must still be in her interview. Walking over to the window, I gaze out at the sloping Texas landscape. The guest room window faces the front of the house which overlooks acres of untouched land. Could I really get used to living in a small town like this?

Does Mom mean what she said? Working from home in a place that doesn't have public transportation and a dozen shopping malls within walking distance? Maybe she's having a mid-life crisis. Or maybe she's caught up with some mafia type loan shark and we're really hiding out here in Lawson as a last resort to avoid having our heads chopped off.

I chuckle to myself at the thought. There's a soft knock at the door.

"Come in," I call out, keeping my gaze out of the window.

The door opens and a deep voice startles me. "Uh, hey."

I spin around. I'd expected Becca, not Jett.

"Hi," I say, but it comes out sounding like a question. "Why are you here?"

Jett has put on a shirt since I last saw him. The black fabric stretches over his muscular chest, making me want to reach out and touch it. It's a shame that he's wearing it at all. Not that I'd ever tell him, but I kind of liked the view this morning at breakfast.

Jett scratches his neck and gazes around the room. "There's a party down at the lake tonight. I thought you might want to come and meet some people."

"Why would I want to meet people?" I ask. I realize just half a second later that I'm not being very friendly. But friendliness isn't my strong suit.

Jett's eyes bug quickly, but then he recovers. "Uh, well I don't know. My mom just said I should come over here and ask you."

"Wow. Usually the pity invites come after people have known me a few days." I cross my arms. "You know, after they've had enough time to feel sorry for my shit life."

"It's not like that," Jett says, running a hand through his dirty blond hair. "I'm just trying to welcome you into town."

"I don't need welcoming." If Jett's friends are anything like he is, they'll either try to get in my pants or they'll go the opposite way and talk shit about my ratty clothing. I don't need to make friends right now. I need to wait until Mom gets home and figure out what the hell we're even doing here.

Jett takes a step closer, and although we're still several feet apart, I step backward. "Look, Keanna," he says. Something in his voice sounds truly genuine and I almost feel bad for being cold toward him. "Did I do something to make you hate me? Because I feel like you hate me."

I shrug. "I don't hate you. I just don't know you."

"So you should get to know me," he says, throwing on this sideways grin that probably wins him a lot of hearts. God knows my heart starts to weaken when I see it. So I look away. Jett continues, running his fingers across the top of the TV stand. "You'll probably think I'm cool if you just get to know me."

"That's a little presumptive," I mutter. "Maybe you aren't as charming as you think you are."

He smirks. "You'd be the first to think that."

Wow.

I can't even come up with a witty reply here, so I walk over to the armchair in the corner and grab a book off the shelf next to it.

"Thanks and all but . . . no thanks," I say, sitting and opening the book to the first page. "You can go now."

"You should really come. I could drive us."

"I'm sure you'll have so many girls hanging off your arm that you wouldn't even notice if I did go," I say.

He grins and he doesn't even try to deny it. "If you'd like my entire attention for the night . . . well that can be arranged."

"It's killing you that I am not falling over myself trying to hook up with you, huh?" I chuckle and roll my eyes. "I hate to break it to you, Jett, but I'm not some dumbass bimbo whose brain turns to mush when I'm near a hot guy."

"Your point has been made," Jett says. "Sorry I offended you with my invitation."

He turns and lets himself out of my temporary guest bedroom, closing the door behind him.

Even though I might never see him again, I feel the slightest stab of regret for treating him so poorly. Maybe he was just trying to be nice.

But I've known enough guys in my life to know that very rarely is that ever the case.

"Have you heard from Dawn?" Becca asks over a plate of spaghetti for dinner. I shake my head.

"I think her phone probably died. She always forgets the charger. But it's already seven-ten so I guess she'll be here soon."

Becca nods, twisting the pasta around her fork. "I hate how phones don't last very long these days. My battery lasts maybe five hours if I'm lucky."

She's being all nice and welcoming still, but I know we're both wondering what's taking my mom so long to get here. Thoughts of news reports saying she's been in a car wreck scare me, but I know my mother. She's a little unpredictable but she's not a bad driver. She probably met some guy and he's having dinner with her right now. I just hope she hurries back. I hate being an imposition.

After dinner, I help Becca wash the dishes. Her husband had some meeting with the neighbors about their track business stuff so he wasn't at dinner.

"I washed your clothes from yesterday," Becca says, scrubbing the garlic bread pan with a sponge. "They're on your bed. If you'd like to shower before you leave, I figured you could use a clean outfit to change into."

"Thanks," I say with a smile. "You've been so nice to me and I really appreciate you letting me stay here."

"Oh it's no problem at all," she says, adding more hot water to the sink. "I can't wait to hear about Dawn's new job. I think she'll probably be able to get my artwork in some new locations after this."

I nod. "Totally."

"Well, Keanna," Becca says after we've finished the dishes and split a pack of Little Debbie snack cakes, "I have to babysit for a woman from my spin class, so I'll be gone until midnight or so. It's her and her husband's date night. But you make yourself at home while you wait for Dawn, okay?"

"Sure thing."

After a quick shower and about ten more phone calls that go straight to Mom's voicemail, I start to open up the possibility of what I hadn't let myself believe before. Mom won't be back today. She's probably on a mini vacation, taking advantage of the kindness of strangers to watch her kid for her. It definitely wouldn't be the first time Mom promised a day and came back a week later.

I feel like such an idiot. A burden on society and all of that. I call Mom's phone one more time and when the voicemail beep sounds, I leave her a message instead of hanging up.

"Hey Dawn, it's me. Your kid. I guess you thought that Becca and Park wouldn't mind you staying gone more than one day but I refuse to be the kind of person who overstays their welcome. When you're ready to come back and get me, you'll find me at that motel we stayed in two nights ago. Don't worry about how I'll pay for it. I have your credit card in my bag."

She's going to be pissed at me for wasting money on the one and only credit card we have, but maybe this will make her come home quicker.

I clean up any trace of my existence, make the bed in the guest bedroom and turn off the television.

I write a thank you note for Becca. And then I get the hell out of there.

CHAPTER EIGHT

Jett

The sun is beginning to set, which means everyone is already heading out to the lake. Lake Lawson is small, only big enough for some jet skis instead of real boats, but it's about the only place worth going to in this town. At least until I'm old enough to legally drink. We do have plenty of bars.

I'm still thinking about her when it's time to clock out of work. I ride the pit bike back to my house while thinking of her. She's on my mind when I jump in the shower and when I'm choosing clothes to wear, I picture her face in the back of my mind. Not only does this girl seem to hate me, she doesn't even want to get to know me to verify that fact.

I don't know what I did to make her so hostile toward me. She clearly needs a friend.

It would have been fun if she'd come with me to the lake. Sure, I would have had to dodge Emma and a few other girls, but I'm sure I'd be able to park my truck in a secluded section of the sandbar and find a way to win her over.

Maybe she's right. Maybe it does bother me that she doesn't want me. Okay, it's not a maybe. I stare at my reflection in the mirror as I run some gel through my hair. Girls always like me. I inherited my dad's good looks and Mom says I got her charming personality. I'm not trying to be vain here, but it is what it is. I work out, I'm tan, and I look like my dad. Older women love my dad. Jace Adams is still a big name in the motocross world even though he hasn't raced professionally since before I was born.

I've seen the looks my mom gets when other women are gawking over Dad. She always tells me that it's okay to date around now, but when I find a girl I really like, I need to chill out and let her be the only one. Mom is really sweet like that.

But she's wrong about one thing—I may be charming but I do not have her personality.

I don't want to settle down. So why can't I get Keanna off my mind?

Is it because I can't have her?

Doesn't that make me a jackass in every possible sense of the word?

Shit. My reflection grimaces at myself. I am a jackass. I saw a pretty girl at Becca's house and when she didn't throw herself at me, I got upset about it. I spent the last however many hours lamenting over this girl, wondering what I could have done or said to make her like me. I am definitely a jackass.

I draw in a deep breath and let it out. Flex my wrists and roll my head to loosen my neck. Get a grip, Jett. I don't want to be a disrespectful prick. If Keanna doesn't like me then she doesn't like me. It's fine. I'll settle for hooking up with the girls who do like me.

It's not like there aren't tons of them.

Keanna's words replay in my head. *It's killing you that I am not falling over myself trying to hook up with you, huh?* Hearing her say that had hurt, but she was right. I've never been rejected in my life. Guess there's a first time for everything.

ALL THE USUAL PEOPLE ARE AT THE LAKE WHEN I ARRIVE. MOST OF THEM ARE OLDER than I am, but I've known these guys since I was a little kid so they're cool with letting me chill with them. Plus, they bring beer. I park my truck on the edge of the lake, right near the road in case I decide to make a quick exit tonight. I've already made a pact with myself that I'd stop thinking about Keanna and let myself get lost in the party vibe, but just in case it doesn't work, I might want to bail. Nothing kills a party vibe like asking your friends to move their trucks so you can get out.

I grab a beer and fist bump D'andre, one of my buddies from the track. He's a senior this year and has a good chance of making it to the professional motocross circuit if he keeps winning races.

"Hey man," D'andre says, crunching his empty beer can and tossing it into the bed of his truck. "Are you actually alone tonight?"

I lift my shoulders, cocky grin in full force. "Just because I always leave with a girl doesn't mean I have to arrive with one."

He throws his head back and laughs. "I feel you man, I feel you."

We sit on his tailgate and drink and catch up on what's been going on since summer started. He hasn't been out at my dad's track much lately but that's because he's been training over at Mixon Motocross Park, working with a professional scout. I hope I'll be there as well when I'm a year older. All I need to do is keep working out, keep riding, and don't get hurt. Nothing ruins a racing career like a few cracked ribs or a shattered ankle.

"So you and Emma Clarke, eh?" D'andre says, cracking open another beer can. "She's fine as hell."

"We're not a thing," I say, shaking my head. I almost expect her to come bouncing up to me, acting like we *are* a thing, because that's just how shitty my luck is normally. I glance around just in case, but see nothing but sand and water and people doing their own thing around the various bonfires.

"When are you gonna settle down, man?"

I tilt my head back and chug the last of my beer. I've only had one beer tonight so it's definitely too early to be talking about crap like this. "Uh, never?" I crunch up the can and toss it in the back of D'andre's truck. I know he recycles them for something like sixty cents a pound so I don't feel bad for basically littering in his truck.

"You know, some guys would give their left nad to get as many girls as you do, and you don't even want to keep them."

"Dude if you're gonna start feeling sorry for yourself, you're gonna have to do that somewhere else," I say, pointing off into the distance to give him an idea of where he could go. "Tonight's supposed to be fun, not a pity party about why your ugly ass can't get girls."

He clenches his chest in mock pain. "Harsh, Adams."

"Um, Jett?"

The voice is soft, feminine, and catches both of us off guard. I turn around and see Maria Gonzalez standing next to D'andre's truck, a beach towel wrapped around her body.

"Like clockwork," D'andre says, shaking his head. He reaches for another beer. "Girls can't stay away from this dude."

"Shut up, man," I say low enough that I hope only he can hear. Maria is a quiet girl who takes dirt bike lessons from my dad. She's not usually the type to try and hook up with me, and besides, the look in her eyes tells me something is wrong.

I hop off the tailgate and follow her around to the front of the truck, where it's not quiet thanks to the thumping rap music blasting from D'andre's speakers, but at least it's private. "What's up?"

Maria studies me for half a second and then bursts into tears. "I'm sorry."

"Whoa," I say, reaching an arm out to her shoulder. "Don't apologize. What's wrong?"

She sniffles, wipes the tears from her eyes. I can tell it's taking a lot out of her to keep her composure right now. "Maria." I try again. "What is it?"

"Could you maybe take me home?" she whispers, her Spanish accent thicker now that she's crying again. "Please? I'm so sorry. I don't live far away."

"Sure, it's not a problem," I say, doing some mental math. I'd only had one beer. I can drive. "Let's go."

I wave goodbye to D'andre and don't bother offering him an explanation. Maria climbs into my truck, turning to the side to kick the sand off her bare feet before she closes the door behind her. She holds the beach towel tightly around her chest.

"Are you . . ." I begin, not really knowing how to finish the sentence without sounding like an ass.

She shakes her head. "I'm in my bathing suit."

I nod. "Okay. Cool. Where to?"

"County road thirty," she says, holding back another sob. "Thank you so much. I'm sorry to bother you, I just didn't know who else I could ask and you seem like a nice guy so . . ."

"Hey, what did I say about apologizing?" I turn to her and try to lighten the mood. "Party was lame as hell. I don't mind leaving."

We drive in silence for a few minutes. Some goofy pop song comes on the radio and I sing along, totally off key and missing most of the words and this gets a laugh out of her, which makes me feel like some kind of hero. She points out her driveway and I turn into it, a long gravel strip that leads to a small house.

"Thanks again," she says.

"It's no problem. Have a good night."

I wait in the truck until she's safely inside her house and although I'll probably never know why she left the party crying, I hope it's not because of some guy.

I hope I've never made a girl cry like that. A sudden stabbing guilt presses into me, as memories of all the times I've drunkenly made out with random girls around the bonfires at parties come back to me. I've certainly never seen girls cry in front of me, so that has to be a good thing, right?

Maybe it's good that Keanna blew me off like she did. God knows I didn't have the best of intentions in wanting to hang out with her. I kept picturing those soft lips, often curled into a smirk, and imagining what I would be like to kiss them, to run my fingers through her hair, feel her body pressing against mine, wanting more. They always want more.

I've been called a great kisser more times than I can count. I know exactly what to do to make a girl's body tremble beneath my touch. And I hope to God that I've never left any of them the way I saw Maria tonight. Dammit. Keanna made the right choice to deny my offer to hang out. She doesn't exactly seem like the Emma Clarke no-strings-attached type of girl. And those are the only girls I can allow myself to mess around with.

I wish things were different, but I know myself. Even if Keanna was interested enough to actually go out with me, I'd only end up hurting her in the long run. I'm not going to be that type of guy.

CHAPTER NINE

Keanna

The walk to the motel feels a lot longer than I'd anticipated when I left the Parks' house an hour ago. I remember the drive over as being only a few minutes, so I figured I was about four or five miles away. And given what I remember about the gym class I had suffered through in junior high, normally walking one mile takes about fifteen minutes. So shouldn't I be four miles away by now?

Maybe it's because I'm doing more of a lazy saunter than a real walk, certainly not the powerwalking I'd done in that junior high class. With every passing minute, I hope Mom will listen to my voicemail message and come by to get me. She'll want to stop me from spending money on a motel, especially money we don't have in the form of a credit card.

A car approaches in front of me, driving way too fast to be Mom looking around for me, but I look up just in case. It's a black sports car and it doesn't slow down at all as it zooms across the old asphalt county road.

I sigh and kick at a piece of broken road, watching it bounce down a few feet. When I catch up to it, I kick it again and again until I end up at a red light in the middle of an intersection.

I'm getting close. The motel is to the left, next to a brightly lit shopping center. It looks maybe half a mile away and I pick up the pace, no longer caring about wasting money. I need a shower and a nap. Walking several miles in flip-flops is incredibly uncomfortable.

The same cigar-smoking front desk guy greets me when I walk into the motel. Well, if you could call a bored grunt a greeting.

"Didn't you check out?" he says, flipping a page in the celebrity gossip magazine in front of him.

I pull out the credit card from my back pocket. It has my name on it since I'm an authorized user on Mom's account, so there's no funny business here, not like the last time I'd stolen her debit card and tried to buy beer with it.

"I'd like another night please."

"Sure thing," he says, taking the card. I look around the dreary lobby, the stench of cigar smoke lingering heavy in the air. A little machine beeps and the guy grunts and swipes the card again. The second beep makes me nervous.

"Card's declined," he says, dropping the plastic in front of me. "Got another one?"

"Wha—" I begin, then I sigh. That card had a limit of twelve thousand dollars. There's no way Mom's spent it all in the last day. "Can you try it again? Maybe type in the numbers instead of swiping them?"

He lifts an eyebrow and I want to tell him to stop looking so damn judgmental because since he runs a place so shitty that most of his clientele are probably way worse off than I am. Financially and otherwise.

"Why the hell not," he says, swiping the card again. It beeps. "I can try it all day kid, but it's not going to work."

"I don't suppose you'll let me work off the cost of a night's stay?" I ask, widening my eyes in hopes that they make me look like a puppy in need.

He snorts. "And risk getting the place trashed? Sorry kid. No can do."

"Thanks anyway," I say. I turn around and push the door open and try really hard not to cry. There have been many times in my life where I've felt helpless, but I've always had Mom with me. Dawn may never win a Mother of the Year award, but I'd always trusted her to keep a roof over our head. Even when we'd spent two weeks camping in the national forest, we'd had a tent roof to sleep under.

I swallow the lump in my throat and force myself to face the truth, as much as I don't want to. Dawn *did* leave me with a roof over my head. She thinks I'm safe at the Parks' house so she's not exactly responsible for me being stranded right now.

But I am not going back there. I just can't. I won't be a burden on a total stranger, no matter how nice they've been to me. No one actually *likes* taking in stranded people as unexpected houseguests and I am not going to put that on someone as nice as Becca. I refuse to be an obligation.

I stand outside in the dark, watching bugs fly around the streetlamp above me. Next year I'll be eighteen and a real adult. I'll have to figure out how to take care of myself at some point since Dawn has made it more than clear that she expects me to be on my own by my birthday.

I draw in a deep breath and think. What the hell should I do? I have about a hundred dollars cash on me but even these sleazy motel places won't take cash without a huge deposit.

I wonder if there's a twenty-four-hour store nearby so I could hang out in the air conditioning and come up with a plan. Or maybe there's a bridge.

Shit.

Am I really homeless right now?

All I want is a hot shower, some food, and a bed.

I start walking toward the right since I came from the left and know there's nothing on that side of town. Soon, the golden arches of a McDonald's catch my eye and an even more welcome sign underneath it makes me smile. It's open twenty-four hours. Finally, some good luck.

I head inside and order from the dollar menu, then settle into a booth at the back of the restaurant. It's secluded enough that the employees might not notice if I stay for a while, and the cushiony bench seat has been recently renovated and is pretty comfortable.

Plus, from this table I have a view out of the window. When Mom's car pulls into the motel parking lot, I'll be able to see it. She must be on her way back home by now. I'm sure it won't be a much longer wait.

Loud laughter from a group of rowdy football players wakes me up. That's when I realize I've fallen asleep in the booth, but luckily no one sees me. I lean out into the aisle and check the clock on the wall. It's past midnight. Holy shit. I've been here for four hours.

Mom's car isn't in the parking of the motel, and I sit up straighter in my booth, rubbing the lines from my cheek from where they'd pressed against the seam in the fabric. Am I totally screwed? Am I now living in a McDonald's? This can't possibly be my life.

On shaky legs, I walk back up to the counter and order a milkshake. It's a waste of what little money I have, but I'm feeling a tidal wave of depression coming on and the sugar will help.

The guy takes my order and says the machine will take a few minutes to power up. "What's your name?" he says, holding a pen over a receipt paper.

"Keanna," I say.

He writes it down, spelling it *Keyana* and then smiles. "I'll call you when it's ready."

I head back to my seat, ignoring the football players. They're still in uniform and their entire section of the restaurant smells like sweat and fries.

The door jangles open and one of the football players whoops. "Jett, man, what's going on?"

My blood turns cold. Jett's here? What if Becca's already told him that I slipped out of her house without telling her bye? What if they all think I'm a huge jerk?

I guess it wouldn't matter. Maybe I am a huge jerk. But I slide further into my booth and hope that he doesn't stay long.

"Keanna?"

I jump. The cashier calls out my name again, louder this time.

Dammit, dammit, dammit.

Now I have to embarrass myself all for the sake of a stupid milkshake. Before the guy can call out my name for a third time, I grudgingly walk up to the register, keeping my eyes only on the guy holding my milkshake.

"Here ya go," he says, handing it over. "Nice and fresh for you."

If this were any other time, I would ask how the hell a milkshake can be fresh, but it is definitely not the time. Also, luck isn't on my side.

"Hey," Jett says, his voice full of surprise. He's waiting on his food to be ready, the straw from his soda dangling an inch from his mouth. "It *is* you. Small world."

"Small town," I say, turning to leave.

"Wait." Jett grabs his bag of food from the guy behind the counter and then takes a handful of ketchup packets. "Who are you eating with?"

"Myself."

He glances toward the football guys and it's as if he actually considered that I might have come here with them. "But there's only one car in the parking lot."

"What does that have to do with me?" I say. Damn, he brings out the bitch in me.

"Did you walk here from Park's?"

I nod. This time I do walk away. I'm done with his questions and it's already humiliating enough being seen here, alone, and homeless. Although I guess he doesn't know I'm officially homeless right now.

I make it back to my booth and then Jett slides in on the opposite side, dropping the ketchup packets in between us on the table.

"Uh, hello?" I say, scowling. "Can't you find somewhere else to sit?"

"I'll level with you," he says, leaning forward as he removes his food from the paper bag. "You look like you've had a shit day. I've definitely had a shit day. Probably the worst day I've had all year. You're a friendly face, and, okay maybe not *friendly*, but you're sure as hell easy to look at and I'd like to eat dinner here."

My cheeks become raging hot and I stare at the straw in my milkshake.

Jett continues, "So if you really want to kick me out you can, but I'd like to be in your company if only for a little while."

Something I don't quite understand floods into my brain, taking over all rational thoughts. I have been nothing but rude to this boy and yet he is consistently nice to me. I lift my shoulders and take a long sip of my milkshake.

"Fine, but only if you share your fries."

CHAPTER TEN

Jett

Keanna may be the cutest fry eater in the world. Her lips slide to the side of her mouth while she gazes at the fries, carefully choosing one. Then she grabs it and bites the end off. It takes her two or three bites for each fry, when I'm the kind of guy who shoves a handful of them in my mouth at a time.

I'd ordered two large containers of fries to go with my double cheeseburger and after she asked me to share them, I'd happily obliged and dumped both containers onto a plastic tray.

Normally I'd devour them all in a few minutes, but I make myself take my time for this midnight meal. When it's finished, I'll have to leave and I am not ready to say goodbye to her again. The very thought that some girl is stuck in my head like this drives me crazy, but right now I'm just going with it.

"So where's your mom?" I ask after I've watched her cutely eat a couple fries.

Her shoulders lift. "I don't know."

"Can you call her?"

She shakes her head. "I tried that. No answer."

"I'm sure she's okay," I say. Keanna nods. She's not very chatty but I want to keep talking. "So . . . did you walk here?"

She stares at the fry she just selected, then turns it over in her hand. Her eyes meet mine and they narrow into thin slits. "What's it matter to you?"

It's probably the last thing I should do, but I'm exhausted from the party at the lake and this girl is doing something to me that I just don't understand. So when I burst out laughing, it's not a surprise that Keanna's glare intensifies.

"The hell are you laughing about?" she says, throwing a fry at me.

I catch it against my T-shirt and then eat it. "You. I'm laughing at you."

Her lips press into a thin line. "Why?"

I shrug. "You're so mean to me and I don't know why." I shake my head and try to stop smiling, but it doesn't really work. "It's actually kind of a turn on."

This time she doesn't throw a fry at me. She throws her fist, punching me right in the arm.

"Ow!" I say, leaning back into the bench seat and rubbing my arm.

Her eyes widen. "Oh my god, I'm sorry. Did that actually hurt?"

I shake my head and grin. "No, but it's nice to see you showing some kind of emotion other than animosity toward me."

She rolls her eyes and grabs another one of my fries, this time taking a packet of ketchup to go with it.

"Sorry." She places a careful line of ketchup along the length of the fry and then takes a bite out of it. "You don't deserve my wrath. But unfortunately . . ." She takes another bite and it's still adorable. "Everyone gets my wrath lately. That's just the way the world is right now. So I can't stop it so you might as well accept it."

I see her gazing at a fry with crunchy ends so I reach out and grab it before she can. "Why do you have so much wrath to give?"

"I'm homeless for starters."

She flinches right after she says it, and I seize the opportunity to get her to open up. "What else?"

Silence ticks on for a few seconds and I give up on trying to get her to open up to me. Then she lets out a soft breath and gazes out of the window. "Everything just sucks in my life right now. I feel like I'm having some kind of mid-life crisis but I'm only seventeen so what does that say for the rest of my life? Is it all downhill from here?"

"The hill can always change directions," I say, trying to sound philosophical or something, but I'm sure it comes out like I'm some illiterate freak. "You have to stay positive."

"Easy for some rich white guy to say," she mumbles.

I want to object but, she's kind of right and that makes me feel even more like a dick than I did earlier tonight. Now I've realized that I'm in danger of becoming a heartless prick like the one who left girls like Maria crying at parties, and on top of it all, I'm just some *rich white guy* to this girl.

"I'm not really rich," I say. "I make like ten bucks an hour at my dad's track. My parents are kind of rich, yeah, but not me. I have like zero assets. Besides, aren't you white?"

"I'm Puerto Rican." She looks up at the ceiling. "Well . . . half. That's all Dawn will tell me about my dad."

I smile. "My life isn't perfect, you know."

"You say that, but are you going home to a bed that's yours tonight?"

I nod.

Keanna lists things off on her fingers. "Are you positive you'll have that same room a week from now, or a year? Is there food in your fridge at all times? Do you have a phone and a car and a job? Will you inherit the family business after your parents die? Because your answers are all yes and that makes your life so much better than mine will ever be, Jett Adams."

"Wow." I stare at the dwindling pile of fries, no longer hungry after that lecture from this girl I barely know. And then it hits me. And I probably should have realized it the moment I saw her with the crease across her face like she'd been sleeping on something.

"Do you have a place to go tonight?" I ask, trying to sound casual and not judgey.

She hesitates and that's all the answer I need. "I'll drive you back to Park's and you can stay there."

She shakes her head. "No. I can't go back. I already wrote a note saying I won't bother them anymore."

I lift an eyebrow. "Your mom still isn't back, right? You need a place to stay. They won't care, they're nice people."

"I'll figure it out," she says, but she's tracing the patterns on the table with her finger and the way she looks right now, all frail and small and helpless, makes me think of a little kid. I want to protect her. I *need* to protect her.

"You'll come home with me," I say, and it's not a question. It's a fact. "My parents are asleep and I'll just sneak you in. No one needs to know if you don't want them to."

She frowns and I can tell she wants to refuse the offer, probably even punch me again. I put on my charming smile and try really hard to look like the kind of guy she can trust. "I have a huge bedroom. I'll sleep on the futon and you won't even notice I'm there. And my bathroom connects to my room so you can stay hidden if you want."

"You have your own bathroom?" she asks, her shoulders leaning forward.

I nod eagerly, hoping she'll agree to come home with me. And this is the first time in my life that I've thought this without any kind of sexual ideas in mind.

Of course . . . if she wanted to . . .

I shake my head to clear it of unwanted thoughts. I'm genuinely trying to be Keanna's friend here. I can't go all horn dog on her now. Even if I don't say my desires out loud, I'm sure she'd pick up on it.

I hold out my hand to her, palm up on the table. "What do you say?"

She stares at my hand and then at me, her eyes far away in thought. Finally, she slaps my hand in a horizontal high-five. "Yeah, okay. I could do that. Do I get to shower?"

"Of course."

Ohmygod Jett, do not think of her in the shower.

"And you won't tell anyone?"

I mime zipping my lips shut. "Not a soul."

Just when I think she's about to say yes, her shoulders fall and she shakes her head. "I can't. I can't keep mooching off of strangers."

"Hey," I say, leaning over the booth to grab her hand. She flinches, but I hold on. "You're not mooching and I'm not a stranger. I'm your friend. And yes I'm your friend who thinks you're smoking hot, but I can also behave myself."

Her cheeks go bright red at my compliment and I have to resist sending a dozen more her way. I'm used to the way girls act when I flirt with them, but this time it feels different. This time I'm not just spewing line after line of dumb shit to make a girl swoon. This time I mean what I say.

Damn, I might be in trouble.

But then Keanna brightens and says, "Okay fine. Let's go."

And suddenly my shitty night just got a whole lot better.

CHAPTER ELEVEN

Keanna

After I've agreed to go home with Jett, the entire atmosphere in this McDonald's seems to warp into an uncomfortable silence. Jett seems happy with my decision, he stops asking me a million questions, and although I'm glad to be off the interrogation chair, the silence is still weird. I guess I can't win when it comes to these kinds of situations. If I had a home to go back to, then I wouldn't be in this predicament. For the first time in a long time, resentment towards Dawn grows to a level that I can't exactly ignore.

"You ready?" Jett says when the fries are gone. He shrugs his head to get the dirty blonde hair out of his eyes. That's what makes him look different tonight.

"You normally have your hair gelled up," I say as we clear out of the booth.

"I went swimming tonight so it got all messed up," he says, running a hand through it.

"In your awesome pool?" I recall the massive and elaborate backyard paradise from when I ate breakfast over there. It had a slide, a diving board, and an entire rock waterfall on one end. Had that really only been a day ago?

"Nope, at the lake," he says, pushing open the door and holding it so I can go first. "Lake party, remember?"

"Did you have fun?" I ask.

His face warps as he bites the inside of his cheek. "Not really. I didn't feel like getting drunk and that kind of stuff isn't fun when you're sober. Plus, some jackass broke my friend's heart and she wouldn't tell me who, so it's been bothering me all night."

"You're a good friend," I say, hating myself for the confession. I'm trying to uphold this emotionless bitch vibe, if only to protect my own real emotions. I hate that he's seeing me like this, knowing that I'm homeless and pathetic. God, I hate this so much.

We reach his truck, this massive four door Chevy that's taller than usual thanks to the huge tires. Jett beeps his keys and then rushes to open the passenger door for me. Either he's being chivalrous or he thinks I'm going to scratch the door trying to get inside this thing.

"Not rich, huh?" I say with a snort as I climb into the truck, using the handle inside the door to lift myself up into the black leather seat. The interior smells like a brand new car, something I haven't smelled in a long time.

Jett stands there, a little shorter than me now that he's on the ground and I'm sitting up in the truck. His arm holds the door open and I try not to look at the way his bicep flexes beneath his shirt. Motocross guys must work out a lot.

"It was a gift," he says with a smirk. "For my sixteenth birthday."

"I got an ice cream cake for mine," I say, thinking back to the day Dawn brought it home from the ice cream shop she'd taken a part-time job at since craft fair sales were slow. I'm pretty sure she stole it.

Jett studies me and I lift an eyebrow. "You gonna close the door?" I say, but it doesn't have as much venom as I'd like. He's really, really cute. Ugh.

Finally, he closes it and I watch him shake his head as he walks around the front of the truck to the driver's side. It's as if he can't figure me out. I grin. Good. No one needs to figure me out, because once they do, they'll realize there's nothing special about me at all. It's like my existence on this earth was all by accident. My biggest fear is that people will figure that out.

JETT CUTS THE LIGHTS AS HE TURNS INTO HIS LONG DRIVEWAY, THEN HE PULLS OVER to the far right of their three car garage and parks outside of it. "Garage door is too loud," he says. "Might wake them up."

"Do you normally get home this late?" I ask, glancing the digital clock on the dashboard. It's nearly two in the morning.

He shrugs. "Yeah. They don't care, they just don't like getting woken up. Dad always says there's no real trouble to get into in a town this small. Mom just makes me swear to her like once a week that I won't get a girl pregnant."

He laughs and I nod. "That's probably a good idea. I was an unexpected surprise for my mom and that didn't really work out so well."

"Yeah?" Jett says, his face shadowed from the glow of the motion light on the corner of their garage. "So was I, but think it turned out okay."

I lift an eyebrow. "Are those your real parents?"

"Yep. They got married right before I was born and they're still happy to this day."

"Hmm," I say, gazing at his beautiful face. "I guess some people really do have fairy tale endings."

He shrugs and his gaze darkens a little bit . . . or maybe I'm just imagining it. "Ready?" he says.

I swallow down the tidal wave of nervous butterflies that erupt in my stomach and follow him to the back door.

He punches a passcode into the door's keypad and it opens up, and then he immediately turns to the house alarm panel on the wall inside of the kitchen and shuts that off as well.

House alarms are definitely things rich people have. I've never seen one in my life until now.

Jett smiles mischievously and then puts a finger to his lips, motioning for me to be quiet. Then he takes my hand and pulls me into the house.

All I can think about is the fact that he's *holding my hand* as he meanders through the mansion in the dark. He takes me up a flight of stairs that are off to the side of the house, not the main ones that I'd seen when I was over here. I guess these stairs are further away from his parent's room, wherever that is.

I'm still watching our hands in the dark as we walk down a carpeted hallway that smells like fresh lavender. Even though I don't want my brain to think these things, it starts flashing back to the last time someone held my hand. I guess it was a year ago—James. He was just a hookup who hung out in our low-income apartments and he was old enough to buy beer. He always smelled like cigarettes and I didn't even like him. Why did I let myself get into those situations?

I shudder and then realize we've stopped in front of a door with a massive plastic sign on it. It's white with rounded corners and the number thirty in a big black letters is in the middle.

"Here we are," Jett whispers, opening the door. "I apologize in advance for any dirty clothes on the floor."

"As long as I don't step on a used condom, I'll be fine," I whisper back.

He flips on the light when we're inside and puts a hand to his chest. "I am appalled," he says, eyes wide like he's been scandalized. "I can't believe that's what you think of me."

I put a hand on my hip and give him this look like he's not fooling anyone. He laughs quietly. "Okay okay. But you already know I do all of my hooking up in the Track's back building, not here."

"Really?" I say, narrowing my eyes at him. "Never in your room? I don't believe you."

He nods. "I swear. I don't bring girls here. Then they start thinking they're getting close to me and they're like my girlfriend or something." He shorts and shakes his head. "Not happening."

Of course someone as gorgeous as Jett Adams would be a massive player. "I guess that's a good game plan," I say, wondering how many girls go to bed at night wishing they were the one who could pin him down in a relationship.

"I have to pee," Jett says, heading toward a door across the room. "Make yourself at home."

I gaze around Jett's bedroom. It's bigger than the last few apartments we lived in, and that's not even including the attached bathroom or the closet. Jett's room is tidy, with only an overflowing laundry hamper inside the closet that shows he even lives here on a regular basis. His bed must be a king size judging by how impossibly huge it is and it's made up with a black comforter and a few pillows.

There's a flat TV on the wall in the part of the room that's set up like a living room. It has a coffee table, a futon and an armchair, all black. He has a long dresser with a mirror attached, and dirt bike trophies scattered around various places. They're all taller than I am, with golden number one emblems blazing in the center.

He doesn't have any photos in his room, besides a few motocross posters. His nightstand has an alarm clock and a phone charger. He's a simple guy.

"I'm hardly ever in here," he says when he walks out of the bathroom.

"I can tell," I say. I push open the closet door and gasp. The closet is as big as a normal person's bedroom. He has a row of clothes in there, some shoes and tons of dirt bike gear. But the rest of the room is empty.

Jett appears behind me in the doorway. The sudden closeness of him, mixed with his cologne, makes my toes tingle. I stiffen, not wanting to move and have him back away from me.

"Yeah so," he says, gesturing to the empty part of the closet. "There's a ton of room. I was thinking you could hide your stuff in here and no one would even know."

I'd left my suitcase and duffel bag in the back of his truck, but that's something I hadn't thought of. It can't stay back there forever. Especially if it's going to rain any time soon.

"So you're just gonna let me hide out like some kind of hobo?"

I'm regretting this already. This is stupid. Embarrassing. Ugh.

Jett shakes his head and steps back into his bedroom, leaving my body feeling cold without his closeness.

"No, I'm just being a friend, you dork. You can stay as long as you want, until you hear from your mom or whatever, and no one will know."

"Thanks," I say, staring at the carpet, which is gray and feels like a cloud under my flip-flops. "I really appreciate it. Hey do you have a phone? I'd like to call my mom again even though it's two in the morning."

He gives me his cell and I try calling her but I'm met with the stupid voice mail again. I sigh and hand it back, noticing that his phone's wallpaper is a picture of his dirt bike, not some hot celebrity model like most of the guys I know.

"Here," he says, opening his dresser drawers. He pulls out a dirt bike T-shirt and a pair of American Eagle boxers and holds them out to me. "Towels are in the bathroom. Go get that shower you wanted."

I stare at his clothes, at his freaking *boxers*, and then hesitantly take them. "Thanks."

CHAPTER TWELVE

Jett

I lean back against the plush futon mattress and try like hell to focus on whatever show I'd selected on Netflix. Just a few feet away, under the hot water of my shower, was a girl I was going crazy trying to get to know. She'd lightened up a little at the McDonald's, and even more once we got here. Maybe soon she'll be able to have a normal conversation with me. One that's not filled with layers of sarcasm and snide remarks.

Maybe then I can peel back the layers that make up this mysterious girl and see what she's really like underneath the massive wall she keeps up.

A little while later, the shower cuts off and I wait like some kind of nervous idiot for her to emerge. I'm ready to see her again, to hang out and spend time together. Even though, yeah, it's early as hell in the morning and we should probably go to sleep. I'm just not ready for this day to be over. And this might be the first time in my life that I want to talk with a girl and not just get her clothes off so we can make out. I sneak back outside and take her suitcases back up to my room, storing them in the closet just like I'd promised.

When the bathroom door opens, I keep my eyes on the TV, acting like it's not a big deal at all.

"You have good-smelling shampoo," Keanna says. As if to make its point, I immediately smell the citrusy fragrance as she walks up to me and takes a seat on the other end of the futon. She's as far away as she can get, but she's still sitting near me, so I'll take it.

"Yeah, it's green apple something," I say, casually looking over at her. "My mom buys the stuff."

I hadn't thought it were possible, but this girl is even more beautiful in my baggy shirt and boxers. Her dark hair hangs loose and wet around her shoulders and she works a towel through it as she watches the TV.

"Why are my boxers so short on you?" I ask, hoping that that's not how they look when I wear them. I'm way taller than her after all.

She lifts up the bottom of my shirt. "I had to roll them up a few times at the waist so they wouldn't fall off." She smiles and my breath catches in my throat.

She should not have done that. I can see her hip and belly button. The smooth skin of her stomach that makes me want to slide my hands over it. But I just nod and try to regain my composure and she drops the shirt like it's nothing.

I let out a slow breath. I will not get a hard on while sitting next to this girl.

"You gonna shower, too?" she says a little while later.

I'm covered in dried lake water, so yeah, I need to. But I'm not ready to leave. Keanna nods toward the bathroom. "The hot water should be back by now."

"Huh?"

"The water I used for my shower," she explains, like she doesn't understand why I don't understand. "It takes a while for a hot water heater to refill? Why are you looking at me like that?"

I chuckle. "Our water isn't like that. You can take hot showers in every bathroom all at the same time and it won't matter."

She looks impressed. "Nice. Mom and I usually fight over who gets to shower first because the second person never gets any hot water."

"Not here," I say, figuring I better hurry and get it over with.

I shower quickly. Having Keanna in the other room is like Christmas morning, and I can't wait to get back to her. After toweling off my hair and using what's probably too much deodorant, I try to shrug off my nervousness and head back out into my room.

Keanna has fallen asleep and the sight of it makes my heart hurt. She's curled up on the futon, my supercross throw blanket covering her body. She's using her hands as a pillow and although it doesn't seem very comfortable, she looks serene.

I bite my lip. I could go to bed and leave her here but I'd really wanted to be the gentleman and let her sleep in my bed tonight. I sit on the middle of the futon and lightly touch her arm.

"Keanna?" I say softly as I shake her arm. "Wake up."

Her eyes burst open and she throws my arm off her with enough force that I wince in pain. She sits straight up, her chest heaving, but her eyes widen when she sees me and then she relaxes a little. "Oh my god you scared me," she breathes, putting a hand to her chest.

"I'm sorry," I say, standing up. I offer her a kind smile. "You just fell asleep without a pillow and . . . well I was going to give you my bed . . ."

She looks back toward my bed and then looks at me. "That thing is way too big for just me. You take it."

I shake my head. "I'll sleep on the futon. You're my guest, you get the bed."

She chews on her thumbnail and then sighs. "Why don't we both sleep on the bed. It's so big we won't even know the other one is there."

Yeah tell that to my penis, I think. But I certainly don't say it out loud. I can be a decent guy for one freaking night. "Sure, sounds good."

We climb into bed, me on my side with my nightstand and her on the side that's always been empty until this very moment.

My heart thumps like a jackhammer as I plug in my cell phone and set the alarm for one p.m. The lock-in doesn't start until around four so I'll have time to get food for Keanna and me and then leave her here until I get back from work.

When I lie back in bed and turn around, Keanna is already asleep. Her chest rises and falls steadily and a few strands of her damp hair fall in her face. She is so beautiful when she's not scowling at me.

I slide over a little, reach out my hand and push the hair out of her eyes. She stirs, but stays asleep. And then her hand reaches up and grabs mine. I let my fingers lace in between hers and then I close my eyes and fall asleep.

Sunlight streams across my room when I wake up in the morning. I look over and find Keanna facing me, sleeping all curled up with my hand still laced in hers. She's brought it up her chest, and I am so wound up in her arms that I couldn't escape if I wanted to.

Carefully, I slide my other arm out and pat around for my phone. When I grab it, I turn the screen on. Dammit. It's three in the afternoon. How the hell had I slept so late? What happened to my alarm?

And then I hear it, the sound that probably woke me up a minute ago. Dad's calling my name.

"You awake?" he calls out, just a few feet away from my door.

"Yeah, be there in a minute," I shout.

But it's too late.

The door flies open, my dad looking annoyed as hell that I've overslept on a workday. I hold my breath as his eyes land straight on the sleeping girl in my bed.

"It's not what it looks like," I say, feeling Keanna stirring next to me.

Dad puts a hand to his forehead and shakes his head. "It never is."

CHAPTER THIRTEEN

Keanna

Oh my god. I've been embarrassed several times in my life. Getting bullied on the playground in fourth grade because my pants were "high waters" and then getting bullied even more because I didn't know what high waters meant. Going out in public with guys Mom's dated over the years, watching them get rip-roaring drunk at some little café and then having us get kicked out for causing a scene.

None of those instances equal the amount of humiliation that flows through me now. I am sitting at a kitchen table with Jett. His mom is sitting across from us, her fingers laced together on the table. He gives me this encouraging smile like I'm supposed to trust him. Yeah, right.

"So . . . you say you just let her spend the night?" Mrs. Adams asks her son.

Jett sighs. "For the millionth time, yes. I ran into her at McDonald's and she said her mom wasn't back yet. She had nowhere to go and I didn't want her to be homeless so I brought her here."

"Language," Mrs. Adams says. There's a quick knock on the back door and then it swings open and Becca enters and I swear my humiliation gets about ten times worse.

"Honey," she says, walking straight to me. She throws an arm around me and pulls me into a hug. She smells like cinnamon rolls and I've never been more confused. Shouldn't she be yelling at me?

"Aren't I in trouble?" I ask when she finally releases her grip on me.

Mrs. Adams laughs. "My son is in trouble, not you."

"Mom!" Jett says, slapping his hands on the granite counter. "I was just helping out a friend. *You're* the one who told me to be nice to her and help show her around town."

"Yeah, but I can't have my sixteen-year-old having girls sleep in his bed," she says, giving him one of those classic Mom looks.

"So what exactly happened?" Becca asks, squeezing my hand while she takes a seat on the barstool next to me.

Jett decides to tell the story. "I ran into Keanna at McDonald's. Her mom is MIA and I didn't want her to be alone so I told her to come stay with us."

"That was very kind of you, Jett."

Mrs. Adams clears her throat. "It *was* kind, but then Jace found them curled up in bed together this morning."

Becca laughs. "I almost don't believe that," she says, eyeing me. "You seemed to think Jett was a little bit of a jerk last time I talked to you."

My cheeks are so read they're probably in danger of catching on fire. "What can I say? I needed a place to sleep."

"You'll stay with us," Becca says. "I got your note and it broke my heart, kiddo. You're welcome to stay with us as long as you want. Actually," she says, holding up an intimidating finger to me. "I demand it. You'd be safe with Jett but I don't think his parents quite approve."

Mrs. Adams playfully slaps Becca on the arm. "Don't make me the bad guy here! If you had a daughter would you let her sleep in Jett's room with him?"

Becca pretends to consider this. "Didn't we always daydream about having kids close in age so they could grow up and marry each other?"

Jett groans, rolling his eyes like he's heard this story a million times and his mom laughs.

"You're supposed to be on my side," she tells her best friend. "Keanna, you'll stay with Becca and Park until we hear from your mom."

"And no more running away," Becca says, wagging that finger at me again.

"Okay . . . I guess," I say, but it ends up sounding like a question.

Jett looks over at me and gives me this assuring look that makes my stomach flutter. Every instinct I have is telling me to deny their help and grab my things and run away again. But Jett's dark blue gaze has me frozen to the barstool. As much as I may want to leave, I know there's really nowhere else to go. And I don't want to leave Jett.

There, I said it.

Now I have to find a way to make those feelings go away.

IT'S LIKE ANOTHER FREAKING EPISODE OF SOME PERFECT FAMILY TV SHOW AFTER everything settles down. Mrs. Adams, who now insists that I call her Bayleigh since Becca goes by her first name (and apparently calling her *Mrs.* makes her feel old) makes us lunch and we sit around and eat it just like we had for breakfast the other day.

Only the men aren't here this time. They're already working at the track next door. Jett complains a million times about how he doesn't want to work the little kid lock-in tonight because, according to him, kids are sticky and whiney and they're so slow on a dirt bike that it makes the whole thing boring.

I'm really surprised that I'm not in more trouble. My mom is pretty lax about things, hell she'd probably love it if I decided to move in with a guy so I'd be out of her hair, but I'd expected Jett's parents to be more uptight about the whole thing. Since everything else in his life is like one perfect American family movie, I guess I thought he'd be grounded and I'd be escorted off the property like an embarrassing incident they'd rather sweep under the rug.

I guess people can surprise you when you're not expecting it.

"I gotta get to work in about ten minutes," Jett says, taking my empty plate and carrying it over to the dishwasher. Becca and Bayleigh have moved into the breakfast nook and they're both pouring over some magazine that features Becca's artwork. They've gone just far enough away to give us some time to talk, but close enough that we know they're still watching.

"Let me take your stuff over to Becca's for you," Jett says, flashing me this smile that makes my insides tighten up and twist around, like there's a little monster in there trying to fight his way out.

"It's okay, I can do it." I head back to his room with Jett on my heels. As I make my way toward his closet, he dives in front of me and slips inside, grabbing my bags. "Ha!" he says triumphantly, holding my suitcase and duffel bag up in the air. "I win."

I put my hands on my hips. If the flimsy duffel bag rips open and spills all of my pathetic belongings. I might die of embarrassment. "Give it here."

"No, I'm taking it over for you."

I sigh and reach for my bag. He holds it up out of my reach, his muscles flexing under the weight of all of my earthly possessions.

"Don't be an asshole," I say, feeling all of those happy thoughts from earlier slip away. I know he's teasing me, but it's starting to feel a lot like being in school, where guys do this shit all the time.

"I'm taking your bags and you're going to like it," Jett says. He pushes past me and heads outside, all while I'm following him, but failing to catch up.

In the guest bedroom at Becca's house, he drops my bags and then stands, hands on hips as he gazes out at the room. "There. Job well done."

"You're a jerk," I say, grabbing my suitcase and pulling it away from him. Anger fills me up and I latch onto it, preferring the feel of being pissed off to those earlier feelings that were strangely like having a crush. I will *not* let myself feel things like that for this guy. He is not my type at all. He'll only screw me over, or make fun of me to his rich friends, just like every other guy like him. I made a mistake going home with him last night, and I guess I'll just blame that on being delirious from too much fast food, a sugary milkshake, and a lack of sleep.

"Hey, what's wrong?" Jett says, his face falling. He reaches for me and I back up.

"Just get out. Seriously."

"Really?" He looks hurt, but then he replaces the look with a smirk. "Don't I at least get a thank you or something?"

"Why the hell would I thank you? You took my stuff without my permission! You carried it over here against my wishes and you lorded your strength over me like you're superior and I'm just the pathetic girl who has to do what you say. That's not cool. And I'm definitely not thanking you for it."

The hurt on his face is real, and I love the satisfaction I get from seeing him verbally bitch-slapped.

"Wow, um. I'm sorry, Keanna. I was just messing with you."

"Your definition of messing is my definition of bullying."

Jett runs a hand down his face, his brows pulling together in thought. "You're right. I'm so sorry. I really meant no harm."

"I don't care. Just go."

"But I don't want to leave things between us like this," he says, scratching the back of his neck. "Can I make it up to you?"

"Yeah, you can leave and never come back," I snap. "Go make out with girls in supply closets or whatever the hell you did before you met me and made me your charity case. I don't need your help, Jett."

He swallows and his Adam's apple bobs. His chest rises as he breathes in and it makes him look a foot taller. "Okay, then. Bye."

I close the door behind him and twist the lock. Becca had said she'd be back over here in an hour or so. But for now I'm alone, and all I want to do is sleep and pretend I am somewhere far away from here.

CHAPTER FOURTEEN

Jett

I am not all about this summer. This summer actually kind of sucks. I've spent my entire life at this track, all day every day, after school, every holiday. Only now that I'm working here, the place has become my nemesis.

Maybe I'm still pissed off about Keanna choosing to cut me out of her life so quickly. Whatever the case, I am not in a good mood.

I walk around the track, keeping to the areas between the jumps as I bend down and turn on each sprinkler I come across. The entire track is lined with them, massive sprinkler nozzles that shoot water onto the dirt. We have to water the track down a lot during the summer because the hot, dry air keeps turning the track into dust. No one rides well on dust.

I kick at a hard clump of dirt as I make my way to the next sprinkler, holding onto my shirt as I bend down to turn it on. I've been getting somewhat of a "farmer's tan" on my chest and arms from wearing a shirt at work so I took it off and have it draped over my shoulder. I'm not going to let this job turn me into a weirdly-tanned freak. I have somewhat of a hotness reputation to uphold.

What was the word Becca used?

Oh yeah, *heartthrob*.

I am all about girls who are all about me, but ever since Keanna kicked me to the curb a week ago—yeah, it's been a whole week—I haven't quite bounced back.

I glance over at the Park's house as I turn around a jump and twist another sprinkler on. It's so far away I can't really see anything, but that doesn't stop me from wishing I'd see her walking in the backyard, picking wildflowers.

Damn.

Here I am inventing cute little things for her to do, and she won't even talk to me. How the hell would I know if she likes wildflowers? Maybe she doesn't. Maybe she's got a new boyfriend now. I wouldn't know. She completely shut me out and I've been too embarrassed by the whole thing to ask my parents if she's still staying over there.

I really hadn't meant to piss her off so much when I took her suitcase. I was just trying to be a gentleman.

But maybe that right there is my problem. I'm a player. A no-strings-attached kind of guy. I'm not exactly the world's leading expert on all things Mr. Darcy-esque, so it makes sense that when I tried to be gentlemanly, it blew up in my face.

I breathe a sigh, long and slow, as all of the air in my lungs deflates until my chest is at the same sunken level as my heart. For the millionth time since the day Keanna kicked me out of her room at Park's house, I tell myself to get the hell over it. Suck it up, Jett. Move on. Call up one of the billion girls in your contacts list and have one come over to hook up.

But I can't. And this last week might have been the longest I've gone without a girl's lips on mine.

I turn on another sprinkler and curse when the blast of cold water hits me right in the face. I'd been so caught up in daydreaming (i.e.- obsessing) over Keanna's rejection that I hadn't paid attention to where I was standing. And now I'm soaked.

My teeth grit together and I stand up, using my shirt to dry off. That's it. Keanna doesn't want anything to do with me and I will no longer sit around here like a pansy with my head in the clouds. I won't pine after some girl who hates me. I'll throw myself back out there and get a firsthand reminder of why I don't do relationships.

I finish turning on the sprinklers, making sure I'm on the right side of the spray nozzles, and then set an alarm for an hour from now to remind me to turn them off.

Once I'm back at the track, I flip open my contacts list and scroll. Although Emma would jump at the chance to come over, I'm kind of sick of her. After a few minutes of scrolling through girl's names, I hit up Facebook instead. I type: Boreedddd.

And then I shove my phone back in my pocket. With any luck, someone will invite me out to do something. So what if it's a Thursday—it's summertime.

AFTER WORK, I HEAD INTO THE MAIN OFFICE TO GET A SNACK OUT OF THE MINI-fridge Mom keeps behind the front counter. All the riding lessons are done for the day so thankfully there are no customers or kid's parents loitering inside. Thursdays are usually early close days for us so I open a can of Sunkist and plop down on one of the barstools at the front counter. I worked my ass off today. I feel more exhausted than when I spend the whole day riding. Dirt bikes take a lot of endurance and strength, but it's a kind of strength I know by heart. Pulling the throttle and kicking the bike into another gear comes naturally to me now. It's all muscle memory and when I'm riding the bike around the track, it's a full body workout that feels more like playing. I love every second of it. I do *not* love the manual labor I did today.

Dad walks in talking on his phone. He hangs up a second later and then grins at me. "Ready for your first paycheck?" he says, handing me a folded piece of paper.

"Not really," I say in a joking tone as I open the paper. "Now you and Mom are gonna make me buy my own stuff."

Dad laughs. "Yep. That's the beauty of making your kid get a job."

"Wow, two hundred bucks," I say, ripping the check off at the perforated edges. "Not bad."

Before Dad can say anything, Mom calls his name from somewhere down the hall.

"Shit, she sounds like there's some drama going on," Dad says, rolling his eyes before he walks away.

I can hear Becca's voice saying hi to Dad and suddenly whatever drama they're discussing I want to be a part of. Carefully, I slide off the stool and walk down the hallway, making my shoes step as quietly as possible over the black and white checkerboard tiles.

Becca, Mom, and Dad are talking in the kid's playroom. It started out as a daycare when I was a little kid, but now it's kind of a lounge area for kids, teens, and parents. There are couches and TVs and stuff in there. I walk up to the doorway, pressing my back against the wall so I can eavesdrop.

Becca's talking. "It's been a week now, and I just don't know what to do."

"Her mom isn't answering the phone at all?" Mom says.

"Most the time it goes straight to voicemail but sometimes it'll ring, so that must mean her phone is on, right?" Becca says.

"So what are you gonna do?" Dad asks. "Call the cops?"

"What!" Becca sounds offended. "Why would I do that? The girl isn't a criminal, Jace."

"Yeah, but," Dad says, slower now. He's probably trying not to piss her off anymore. "Maybe you should report the lady as a missing person or something. Or turn the girl into child services since she's a minor."

"No, I won't kick her out," Becca says. "I actually like having another girl around. Makes me think of the kid I never had. It's fun having someone to hang out with and she's a sweet kid, Jace. She really is."

"Oh we had a blast when we went shopping," Mom says. "That girl can eat a lot."

What? When did my mother go shopping with Keanna? And why wasn't I informed?

Becca laughs. "I keep telling her my goal is to make her gain ten pounds. Shouldn't be too hard. Every time I make food she acts like she hasn't eaten in weeks, the poor thing."

"I think you should give it more time," Mom says. "She doesn't have anywhere else to go and you don't want the cops involved. They'll just put her in some kind of home."

"Hey, don't give me that look," Dad says and I picture him holding up his hands in surrender to the two women in front of him. "I was just trying to be helpful. God, I don't want the girl in a home or anything. I'm just worried about her mom."

My stomach clenches and I turn away, quietly walking back to the front office. I don't want to hear any more. It's bad enough that I already have a crush on a girl who hates me, so I don't need to add feeling sorry for her to that list. Maybe her mom will come back soon and everything will be okay. Maybe by the time school starts in the fall, she'll have forgiven me and maybe we can be friends again.

I call D'andre on my walk home, but he's already committed to seeing some dumbass kid movie with his little brother tonight. He invites me along but I pass. Sure, I love movie popcorn but sitting through some brightly colored, extra loud little kid movie would be more like torture. I'm not that desperate for companionship. Maybe I'll just play the Xbox all night.

I walk up the two steps onto the back patio and a small cough startles me. I look up to find Jacey Hamilton sitting in one of the patio chairs, a beach towel strung across her lap and a sexy smirk on her lips. She's got long blonde hair and she's a little chubby, but in all the right places. Her ass and tits are amazing, and she knows this judging by the bikini she's wearing under a see-through mesh tank top.

"Can I help you?" I ask, stopping when I'm standing right in front of her, invading her personal space. She peers up at me and pokes her lips out. The thing with Jacey is that she is all about harmless hookups. You never have to worry about this girl sending you a million emotional texts the next day. She's casual. She's fun. And I haven't seen her in a while, not since Emma scared her off at the Spring Fling school dance.

"I saw your Facebook post," she says. "Figured I'd come over and take you for a swim."

I grin. "Without even texting first to see if I'd be free?"

She stands and her boobs press into my chest. She tosses the towel over the back of the patio chair, making sure to let her butt graze up against me when she turns. "I took a chance. So what do you say?"

I shrug. After spending all day in this hot ass sun, the pool actually sounds like a great idea. I don't know why I didn't think of it earlier.

I toss my shirt to the deck and empty my phone and keys from my pockets. I'm already in board shorts so I give her an evil eye wiggle. "Last one in has to rub the other's shoulders."

Her eyes go wide and then we take off running. But I'm closer and faster, my long legs far quicker than her short ones, so when I dive into the pool head first, I know I've won.

Jacey's glaring at me when I bob back up from the water. "So not fair. You cheated."

I gasp like I'm totally offended. "Did not. I can't help it that your little kid legs don't take you very fast."

"Hey, I'm the same age as you," she says, swimming over to me. Her hair looks brown now that it's all wet. I get a sudden flash of what Keanna's hair looked like wet, sprawled out over her face while she laid in my bed. I have to blink it away and tell myself to focus on the girl in front of me. The girl who actually wants me . . . well, as much as you can want a casual hookup.

"So what's been up with you?" Jacey says, treading water in front of me. We're right where the water gets about six feet deep so my feet touch but hers don't.

I shake my head. "Nope. No talking. You owe me a shoulder rub."

She rolls her eyes and then grabs my arm, using my body as an anchor to pull herself around. She wraps her legs around my waist and then grabs my shoulders and starts rubbing them. I close my eyes. "Holy shit, you're good at this."

"Enjoy it cause I'm not doing this forever," she snaps, digging her thumbs into my shoulders. "So, like I said, what's been up?"

"Not a damn thing. I'm working at the track now, so my life has become motocross and then more motocross."

"Hasn't that always been your life?" she says.

"Yeah, but before I had a job I at least had *some* free time. Now it's work work work, ride work ride and then work again."

She giggles while she rubs the tension out of my shoulders. "I bet Emma hates that."

I groan without even realizing it. Jacey stops and leans over my shoulder to look at me. "Uh oh, trouble in paradise?"

"Okay, don't make me kick you out of this pool," I say, giving her my best mean glare. "Emma and I are *not* a thing."

"Yeah, yeah. If she had her way, you would be. I'm proud of you for holding your ground."

"You might be the only one," I say, taking her hand and pulling her around so that we're face to face again. The massage felt great but I feel bad using her like that.

"I don't really like Emma that much," Jacey says. The corner of her lip curls. "She's kind of a . . ."

"Bitch?" I suggest and we both start laughing.

"Actually, I kind of wanted to talk to you about something," she says, pushing away and leaning her head back so that she starts to float on her back.

"What's up?"

Before she can say anything, Mom walks up. Damn, I hadn't even heard her approach. It's a good thing we weren't doing anything inappropriate. Note to self: Keep an eye out for the parents. They're not as loud as you hope they are.

"Hey," Mom says, giving a little wave as she passes us on her way to the back door. "Will you be home for dinner?"

"Yeah," I say and Mom nods. "Jacey, you're welcome to stay, too."

She slips inside and Jacey gives me a look. If we weren't in the pool, her hands would probably be on her hips. "I feel like your mom doesn't like me."

"Mom likes everyone."

Jacey's eyebrows narrow. "But it feels like she doesn't like me."

"That's because your name sounds like my dad's name, Jace. She said it creeps her out."

Jacey smiles, looking as if everything makes sense now. "So it's not because I randomly make out with her son?"

"Nah, she doesn't care about that."

Speaking of, this might be the longest we've been without her jumping my bones. "So what were you saying?"

Her smile fades and even though she's covered in water, she seems to look a little scared. "Well . . . I don't know. Maybe it's stupid."

"Okay, now you have to tell me." I lift my feet and dunk down into the water, tossing my head back so my hair will flatten when I resurface. "What's going on?"

"Okay so, well. How should I begin?" Jacey bites her bottom lip and swims out across the pool, probably buying for time. "So there's this guy."

I lift an eyebrow. "You're interested in a guy?"

She nods and her cheeks flush. "I know I spent my whole life saying I'd never get in a real relationship because that kind of shit never works out for my parents, but . . . I don't know. I kind of like him."

"Do I know him?" I ask. "And are you asking my permission to date him, or something? I mean, you and I are just a no-strings-attached thing. So why would I care?"

"We're not even that anymore," she says, throwing her hand through the water. "Emma made sure to put a stop to it."

Is that why girls haven't been calling me as much?

"So, about the guy," I say, pressing for more info. "What do you need my advice for?"

"Okay, so don't laugh. Because I mean yeah, we make out and all, but you're still my friend, ya know?"

I nod and she seems to relax a little more. "So I guess I want to know . . . do you think a guy would like me enough to be my boyfriend? Like . . . am I worth it?"

"Of course you're worth it, if that's what you really want," I say.

Jacey bites on her lip again and sinks down until just her head is above the water. "I guess I feel like I'm just some slut that no guy would ever really *like*, like. And I know it's stupid but I *like*, like him. I want to tell him that but I'm not sure if I'm girlfriend material."

I walk across the bottom of the pool and take both her hands in mine, making sure to meet her gaze. "You are not a slut. You can't think that about yourself."

She frowns and stares down at the water. "What the hell is wrong with me, Jett? Relationships are stupid! Ugh."

I smile and let go of her hand so I can flick water in her face. She grimaces and flicks water back at me. "Dude, if you like him then go for it. And if he doesn't like you then he's a jackass, okay? You're awesome and I'm glad we're friends."

"Thanks." Her frown morphs into something like a grin. "I may not be as hot as girls like Emma Clarke, but I'm a good kisser, right?"

I nod and give her a wink, "Totally."

"Good," she says, playfully splashing me with water again. "You taught me everything I know, so I should be good."

"Psh, obviously," I say. Then I grab her head and dunk her under water, just like we used to do when we were kids. She screams and tries to retaliate, but I'm too strong.

The sound of footsteps on the deck startle me again and I look up, expecting to see Dad. Only it's not.

Keanna gives me the slightest scowl before she walks up to my back door and lets herself inside.

CHAPTER FIFTEEN

Keanna

I guess I should be happy that it doesn't faze me to see Jett playing around with some girl in his pool. It's not like I have a crush on him. It's not like I *had* a crush on him. It was one night, one kind deed on his part and then his epic ruining of the deed by being a condescending jerk.

Mrs. Adam's house smells like clean linen when I step inside, grateful to put a solid brick wall between Jett and me. Every room seems to have one of those light up wax melter things and that's where the clean scent comes from. There's something really nice about walking into a house that's not only clean and tidy, but that also smells nice. Motels smell like stale laundry and moldy carpets. Low-income apartments smell like weed and fast food grease. Mrs. Adam's house smells like perfection.

(I refuse to call it Jett's house.)

"Hey there," Mrs. Adams says with a kind smile. Becca had just talked to her on the phone and I was told to let myself in the back door and that's just what I did. She's wearing tight-fitting yoga pants with the word PINK written on one leg. Her tank top is neon pink and she looks like she could pass for someone in college and not the mom of a teenager.

"Okay, so Becca needs sprinkles?" she says, joining me near the kitchen island.

"Yep. She only had one jar of Christmas sprinkles and they expired two years ago."

"Ew," Mrs. Adams says, curling her nose. "What is wrong with that woman?" She shakes her head and turns toward a cabinet, her high ponytail bouncing as she walks. "Let's see what we have here."

"I really like your tank top." The random statement startles me and I'm the one who said it.

She gives me this knowing smile. "It's the sparkles, right? I love it. I have it in three colors."

It must be nice to like something and be able to buy three of them. Of course I don't say that . . . I just smile politely and hope that this moment is over soon. I've spent a week avoiding Jett and now he's right outside the door. What if he decides to come inside and introduce me to his date? Ugh.

"So . . .," I say. "Sprinkles?"

She turns back to the cabinet and starts taking out jars and bottles. "Here ya go," she says, sliding four containers of sprinkles across the counter to me.

"Whoa, Mrs. Adams, you're a sprinkle fan."

"Yeah, I'm a little obsessed. Have you tried these silver ones? They look like real metal but they're totally edible. I love them. Here, take them too."

I take the jar of sprinkles that look like silver BBs. She's pulled out star-shaped sprinkles, little dots, stuff that looks like glitter, black and white, pink and purple . . . if it's sold in the stores, I'm pretty sure she has it.

"Let me get you a bag for these," she says, opening another door and pulling out a grocery bag. "Oh, and it's Bayleigh. Don't call me Mrs. Adams until I'm like, forty. And maybe not even then. I don't want to be old."

"Don't worry, you don't look old."

The corners of her eyes crinkle. "Thanks, dear. You keep up those compliments. In fact, tell all of Jett's friends to do the same thing. They're always making fun of me."

I don't really have anything to say to that since I don't plan on talking to Jett, like ever, for the rest of my life. So I focus on putting the sprinkles in the bag and then I thank her.

The walk from their house back to Becca's seems to take a million years. Jett and his friend are still in the pool from the sound of the water moving around, but I make sure I keep my eyes forward and not on the pool.

Becca's eyes light up when I show her the sprinkles. "Holy shit. Bayleigh is insane."

"It does seem like an obscene amount of sprinkles for one household," I say. The jar of silver sprinkles catches my attention. They are pretty cool.

Becca lines up the jars on her kitchen island, from smallest to largest. "Okay so, you're probably wondering why I sent you on a sprinkle errand . . ."

I shrug. "You're having a sugar craving?"

She points a finger at me. "Hell yes I am. I figured you could make some cupcakes with me, yeah?"

I nod and try to look enthusiastic about it. Becca's been doing things like this all week. At first I thought she felt sorry for me and was trying to entertain me as if I were some little kid, but now I think she's just genuinely a nice person.

"I always pictured having a cupcake making night if I ever had a daughter," she says, her eyes far away as she daydreams about what hasn't happened yet. "Park and I can't have kids and I keep trying to accept the fact but it sucks, ya know?"

I stare at her.

"Well okay," she says with a knowing nod. "I guess you wouldn't know since you're still a teen. Anyhow, thanks for hanging out with me."

Now I'm starting to wonder if I feel as sorry for Becca as she feels for me. She's a really nice lady and always seems genuinely interested in anything I have to say. Last night we'd spent hours in her studio while she painted and I watched. It was fun, if not a little awkward. Most of my stay here has been spent in my room, watching TV, but the few times we hang out I end up enjoying myself. Talking with Becca is the only time I'm not thinking about Jett.

Well okay. I'm always thinking about Jett.

Becca and I mix the batter and pour cupcakes into every tray she has, making forty-eight in all. She has two ovens so we're able to throw them all in there to bake at the same time. As the cupcakes cook, I help her clean up our mess.

"What are we going to do with all of these cupcakes?" I reach for another paper towel to wipe off my hands.

She gives me a sneaky grin. "Eat them, duh! We can rent a movie or something and have a girl's night. I'll make Park hang out in his man cave."

"And what are we going to do with the other forty cupcakes?" I ask, laughing.

"We'll give them to the boys. Jett can probably eat a dozen in one sitting."

Though he'd been on my mind this whole time, the mention of his name out loud sends a dark shadow over my happy mood. Becca seems to notice because her smile fades and she tilts her head. "You okay?"

My heart is aching in my chest but I nod anyway. "Yeah, I'm good."

"Is it your mom? Oh honey . . ." Becca frowns. That pitying look I've seen so many times returns to her face. "I wasn't sure if I should tell you or not . . ."

The lump in my throat returns. "What? Tell me what? Did you hear from my mom?"

She shakes her head. "No . . . not yet. But, you know how her phone does that thing where sometimes it rings and sometimes it doesn't? That has to mean her phone is on, right?"

I nod, my throat suddenly feeling like it'll close at any moment. Mom's phone has been driving me crazy. If it were dead, then it'd go to voicemail every time. But when it rings . . . is she ignoring me? That's really the only explanation.

"So, what is it?" I ask.

Becca lowers her gaze and stares at her fingernails. "I hope you don't mind, but I called around. I checked with every police department from here to Corpus Christi. She hasn't been arrested or brought in or anything."

"Oh." I nod. Try swallowing the lump, but it doesn't go anywhere. "I'm not mad."

Three nights ago, Becca and I had called some hospitals to see if they had taken in my mom. No one had heard of her, so I'd been a little relieved. "I haven't thought of that. That's actually a good idea."

She nods, her lips pressing together in a gesture that's both caring and frustrated. "I don't know what else to try."

"She's never done this," I say, going through my memories yet again. Never, ever, has my mom just straight up left me like this. "I don't understand and I swear I didn't know about it. I had no idea she was going to do this."

"I know sweetheart, don't worry about that." The timer dings and Becca grabs an oven mitt. I open the oven door for her and she takes out our cupcakes, which are perfectly baked and already look golden and delicious. The smell fills up the kitchen and makes my mouth water. I am eating like some kind of god over here and I love every second of it.

"I know I've said this before," Becca says as she sets the trays down on fleur-de-lis trivets. "But I'd love having you here for as long as it takes. You really are a pleasure to have around and I don't mind one bit. I hope this doesn't sound crazy, but I kind of feel like maybe your visit is like a gift from fate. I've always wanted a child and lately I've been thinking that if Park and I had kids when we got married, that I'd have a teenager by now and . . ." Her eyes fill with tears and my mouth falls open. "God, Keanna, I'm sorry. Here I am crying like a lunatic! Oh my god, you must think I'm a freak."

"No, I don't. I think you're a lifesaver." The moment I say the words I realize they are true. "I'm a total stranger and you took me in and I'm really grateful."

I'm afraid she's going to hug me, but instead she takes off her oven mitt and wipes her eyes. "Tomorrow, let's go shopping. I want to get you some clothes."

"No way, you can't do that. You've already done too much." She waves her hand at my words but I keep going. "Actually, can I maybe work for you? Do some chores to help pay for my room and board?"

She considers this for a moment. "Okay my first thought is no, because you're my guest but—actually, there might be something you can do. I work a couple days a week at the track but I'm looking at going to Louisiana for a few days to showcase my art at this huge craft fair they have there. You could cover for me. I'll even pay you."

"Working at the track? I don't know if I could do that." What I don't say is that Jett works at the track.

She shakes her head. "Nah, you totally can. The front desk is easy. You can come with me tomorrow and I'll show you the ropes. Cool?"

"Well, I do need to work off my debts here so, I guess I should."

She smacks me with an oven mitt. "You have no debts here! The money you earn at the track will be yours. You can spend it going out with friends or something."

I snort. "I don't have any friends."

"Sure you do. Jett's your friend."

Pain settles into my stomach again. "Yeah," I say, turning so she can't see the anguish in my eyes. "Sure."

CHAPTER SIXTEEN

Jett

I'm off work on Saturday morning and Dad and Park have both taken the day off as well. This is some kind of summer miracle because now it means I get the track all to myself. No dodging around slow kids that my dad is trying to train, or getting into races with idiots who think they're faster than me. No one is ever faster than me on my own track.

I head out to the track's garage where I keep my bike, my heavy riding boots clunking along the concrete floor. The outdoors smells like warm air and wildflowers and since it's seven in the morning, it's just cool enough to feel the last few seconds of nighttime chill before the sun heats it all up.

I grab my helmet off the wall and pull it on, buckling the strap beneath my chin. My heart isn't racing, not exactly, but it's beating with an enthusiastic rhythm because finally, finally, I get to ride alone. Just me and the bike on the track I know by heart.

My bike cranks up with only one kick of the kick starter, which is nice because I haven't been on it in a couple of days. I check to make sure it's full of gas and then I ride out of the garage, feeling all of my stress and anxiety dissipate with each turn of the piston.

The track is supreme this morning. The dirt is wet and tilled up from the tractor, perfect for pinning it around the hairpin turn. A good rider never sits on their dirt bike; we have to be standing, knees and elbows bent, guiding the bike where we want to go. Sit down even for a second and your lap time just got slower.

My muscles throb as I ride. The familiarity of the movements come back to me, but my body has had a break for two days so it screams in protest. I grit my teeth and push harder, faster, letting the racing modified engine of the bike accelerate with all its got.

When I'm on the track, I'm not Jett Adams, the prick who hurt Keanna. I am a racer, an athlete. I am one with the bike. And I know that sounds lame, but it's true. The only time I can forget about the stresses that plague me are when I'm on a bike.

So why can't I stop thinking about her now?

It's been a week. I've ignored every text from Emma, and even ignored the flirty Facebook chats with Ryann and Beth, two girls whose brothers race with me. I've had a flirty back and forth with both of them for weeks now and I've ignored it all. For the first time in my life, I don't want to mindlessly hook up with someone.

I want to have a talk with a girl. Share secrets and feelings. Make her feel special and safe and protected, like I did that night I drove Keanna home from McDonald's. I want to hold her hand and show her off to the world. All she wants is to forget I exist.

I pin the throttle as my bike jolts forward and then I slam on the brakes to take a sharp turn. All of the shitty, horrible things I've done come back to me. All of the hookups that I've never called back, the kisses I didn't mean, the girlfriends I stole from their boyfriends. Those are the things that make me feel like shit.

Carrying Keanna's bags shouldn't be one of them. I wasn't trying to hurt her. I was trying to make her think I'm strong and chivalrous and kind. Maybe make her think she's not alone in this world even though her shitty mother has left her in that exact position. But all it got me was a cruel glare and a warning never to talk to her again.

I push on, riding around and around the track until I am exhausted and my body screams for me to stop and take a break. I need water. I need food. But the pain of pushing myself to my athletic limits makes me feel good in this twisted way. Finally, I pull off the track.

The closest water bottles are in the mini fridge in the front office, so I pull my bike up to the door and hop off, leaning the handlebars carefully against the brick wall. Racings bikes don't have kickstands. My chest is heaving and I rip off my helmet, setting it on the bike seat.

I drop my hands down to my knees and concentrate on breathing slowly. This isn't exhaustion from a lack of endurance. I am in excellent shape. This is something different, something I hadn't known I could experience.

Heartache.

I stand and pull off my jersey, then the neck brace and the chest protector, all of the equipment that's expensive as hell and meant to keep my body from getting hurt in the event of a crash. Too bad it doesn't help at all for what's inside of me. If they made heartbreak protectors, I'd buy fifty of them.

It's hot as hell outside and still humid since it's only around nine-thirty in the morning. Luckily, my chest is covered in sweat so it helps cool me off. I head into the office and the cold blast of air conditioning makes goosebumps prickle across my skin.

"Hey there," Becca says cheerfully.

I nod as I walk and I stop short when I realize she's not in here alone doing Saturday morning paperwork. I swallow, my eyes focused on Keanna. She's wearing a pink sundress with thin straps that make her shoulders look frail and somehow cuter than normal. Her hair is in a messy bun, with strands hanging in her face and all I want to do is push it out of her eyes. Let my fingers trail along her skin . . .

The whole world seems to slow down until it's just a vortex with Keanna and me trapped in the middle. I watch her eyes go from startled to somewhat friendly and then straight back to anger. It's almost like she forgot she was mad at me for a second. Too bad she didn't forget forever.

"How was the track?" Becca asks, her face turned down toward the papers she's organizing. She's too busy to have noticed those few seconds of awkwardness that passed between me and her houseguest just now.

"Good," I say, suddenly forgetting every other word in the universe.

"Water?" Becca asks, leaning over to the mini fridge by her desk. She takes one out and hands it to me.

"Thanks," I say, wondering if I'll ever find the ability to say more than one word now that Keanna is here looking like a damn angel.

I look at her as I bring the water bottle to my lips and she watches me, her eyes gazing down to my bare stomach before she looks down at the front desk.

"What are you doing here?" I ask, trying to sound friendly.

Becca answers for her. "I gave her a job. Since I'll be gone for some craft fairs soon I figured she could do what I do so that I don't have a ton of work waiting for me when I get back."

"Great idea," I say, pulling out a barstool right next to the one Keanna's sitting on. There are only two stools behind the front counter but Becca is standing over by the computer so I had to seize the opportunity.

"Need any help?" I ask her. Hopefully she won't tell me to screw off in front of Becca and maybe, just maybe, I can win back her friendship.

"Not yet," she says, keeping her eyes on the paper. It's a parent's manual that my mom typed up a long time ago because she got sick of explaining the rules of motocross to dumbass parents.

"Hey, I can totally help with this stuff," I say, tapping the paper. My finger comes dangerously close to hers and she doesn't recoil, which must be a good thing. I give her a smile. "I know everything about motocross."

"Everything?" she says, somehow peering down at me even though she's shorter than I am.

I nod, feeling the cockiness return to my smile. "Everything."

She leans back, straightening her shoulders and pursing her lips. "Okay then. What year was the first professional motocross race?"

"Uhh . . ." I bite my bottom lip and then shake my head. "Damn. I don't know. Like the seventies or something?"

Keanna's stern expression softens and I'm reminded of how angelic she looked while asleep in my bed. "Remind me never to call you when I have a life or death motocross trivia question."

I laugh. "When would you ever have a life or death motocross trivia question?"

She shrugs, playing with the pen in her hand, drawing circles in the air. "I don't know. But it could happen."

"It could totally happen," Becca says, reminding me she's still in the room. I look over at her and she puts a hand on her hip, pretending to be disappointed in me. “My own godson doesn’t know the first professional motocross race,” she says, shaking her head. “What an embarrassment.”

“Okay then, when was it?” I ask, putting Becca on the spot. She looks at Keanna and then back at me.

“Hell if I know!”

We all burst into laughter and when I look over at Keanna she’s looking at me. And for the first time in a long time, it doesn’t seem like she hates me quite as much.

CHAPTER SEVENTEEN

Keanna

Laughter feels good, even if it is awkward as hell. Being around Jett is fun and I hate myself for thinking that. I'm supposed to hate him! Especially after seeing him in the pool with that girl. I bet he's spent every day this past week with a different girl, each one more beautiful than the last.

"Damn, I'm out of coffee," Becca says, frowning into her empty mug.

"Want me to get you some more?" Jett offers. "One sugar, no creamer?"

"You're a doll," Becca says, handing over the mug.

I try to focus on the manual in front of me, but I catch the scent of Jett's deodorant as he walks behind me toward the coffee maker in the other room. Okay, the guy is covered in sweat—thinking that his armpits smell good is like the stupidest thing ever.

But damn does he look great in those black and blue dirt bike pants, his abs glistening from sweat. Without his jersey on, the riding pants sit low, revealing the V of his hips, the faint white line of skin where his tan stops. I draw in a ragged breath and try to make sense of the words on the paper.

The yellow flag means to slow down because another rider has fallen on the track up ahead of you.

Yeah, okay, my focus is gone.

Jett returns, walking slowly because he's filled the mug up to the top.

"Ya'll got any food around here?" he says, putting a hand on his perfectly chiseled abs. "I'm starving."

"Ooh!" Becca says, her eyes lighting up. "Key, go take him back home and give him the cupcakes."

Becca has taken to calling me only half of my name. It's like we're old friends after only a week, but I kind of like it. Mom never gave me a nickname.

"Cupcakes?" Jett says, looking more than excited.

"Yeah, we made like five hundred of them last night," I explain, as I think about what Becca just said. She wants me to take Jett over to her house, alone, to give him the cupcakes. Can I handle that?

"Okay that sounds awesome, and I will be eating four hundred of them, but can we get real breakfast first?" Jett says, running a hand through his hair. Because it's sweaty, half of it sticks up. "Too much sugar will make me sick. I need protein."

"You could go to Sherry's Café," Becca says, and I guess she's trying to be helpful but *ohmygod* is she suggesting that I go alone to a restaurant with *Jett*? That's a thousand times worse than taking him to her house.

Jett nods. "Good idea. Want me to bring you back some waffles?"

Becca sips her coffee. "You know it."

"How do you have all of her food and coffee choices memorized?" I say, if only to buy some time before he asks me to go with him.

Jett shrugs. "She's my Second Mom. Also I've been a slave to both of my moms since I was old enough to walk. They're always having me get them crap, the lazy be-yotches."

Becca rolls her eyes and reaches into her purse, which is under the front desk in a cubby hole for employees. "Here's some cash. Ya'll two go have fun."

"Hey, second mom?" Jace says in this overly cool way. "I don't want your money. You're embarrassing me in front of the pretty girl."

Becca snorts and shoves the money back in her wallet. "Suit yourself."

Am I the pretty girl in this situation? Oh my god, why does he do this to me?

Jett turns to me with this hopeful look in his eyes and it hits me now that he's actually worried about me agreeing to go with him. "So . . . wanna get breakfast?" His voice is low, his eyes focused on mine as he stands in front of me, his gorgeous muscled chest on full display.

I swallow. My head tells me to yell the word no and slap him in the face. But my heart says, "Yeah, that's fine."

His blue eyes light up. "Yeah?"

I nod. "Yeah."

He grins. "Cool. Give me like two seconds to shower and change clothes." He holds up two fingers. "It'll be fast."

I nod and he takes off jogging down the hallway to where there's a gym with a locker room. Becca had given me a tour of the facility earlier and it's pretty cool. There's offices, a big lounge area with TVs, a daycare for little kids, and a gym with all of the same equipment you'd find in a real gym. There's also a few storage rooms like the one we'd seen Jett in on my first night here, making out with that girl. She definitely wasn't the same girl in the pool. I wonder how many girls he's made out with in all of the various rooms of this building.

And then I hate myself because I kind of wish I was one of them.

"Thanks for coming with me," Jett says, glancing over at me while we're stopped at a red light. Once again I'm in the front seat of his truck, the scent of leather and hot boy an intoxicating mix that confuses the hell out of me.

"Yeah, well I didn't really have a choice."

He tilts his head. "You could have said no. But I'm really glad you didn't. I want to make it up to you."

I lift an eyebrow. "Make what up to me?"

I can see his Adam's apple bob while he focuses on the road ahead. "You know . . . that night . . ."

Oh, it's fun messing with him. I bring my eyebrows together. "Huh? What night?"

He fidgets with the steering wheel as he drives. "That night I carried your bags and disrespected you . . . you know . . ."

I chuckle. "Yeah, I know. I just wanted to hear you say it."

He leans his head against the back of the driver's seat. "You're so mean to me."

He slows and turns into the packed parking lot of a café that looks like a log cabin on the outside. We park and then he cuts the engine and turns to face me. "Look, I am sorry. And I want to make it up to you. It means a lot that you came here with me today."

He gives me a small but meaningful smile and, dammit, if I don't find myself smiling back at him.

I draw in a deep breath and stare down at the fabric of my new dress. When I'm sitting here, the hem rises to my upper thighs and suddenly I'm very self-conscious of it. "Look," I say, letting out a breath. "I don't know why I'm saying this but . . . maybe . . . I don't know," I say, shaking my head. "Maybe we can start over and like, be friends."

"Yeah?" Jett's face bursts into a smile bigger than I've ever seen. He slaps the steering wheel and then pops open his door. He's over on my side of the truck before I can gain my composure and suddenly he's opening my door and holding out a hand to me.

I take his hand and feel a warmth spread up into my insides as he helps me climb down from his massive truck.

"Thanks," I mumble, running my hands over the pink fabric to make sure it's all down and where it should be. "I probably shouldn't wear a skirt if I'll be riding in this massive thing you call a truck."

Jett closes the door behind me and takes my hand as casually as if we do this all the time. "Don't worry. If someone tried getting a look up your skirt, I'd kick their ass."

I roll my eyes, finding it very hard to walk now that my hand is in his. "You wouldn't need to do that," I say.

He squeezes my hand. "But I would."

When we reach the doors of the café, Jett drops my hand and opens the door for me. I'm glad the awkwardness of holding his hand is gone, but I also miss the feeling of his skin on mine. Maybe it's just the fact that no one really touches me anymore. It's not because it's Jett. Right?

The place is packed, but the hostess finds us a spot near the back in one of those tiny booths made only for two people.

Jett orders a Dr. Pepper and I order a water and when the waitress leaves he gives me a look. "Are you one of those people who hates sodas?"

I shake my head. "I just wanted a water."

Honestly, it never occurs to me to get anything other than water. Dawn and I rarely went to restaurants, but if we did, we had to be as cheap as possible. We always got water and split an entrée. Mom would say it's what keeps women thin and then she'd go off about how being thin is everything.

Funny, because I would have rather spent my childhood without going to bed hungry every night.

"Thanks for coming," Jett says shortly after our food arrives.

"You've already thanked me like three times," I say, stabbing into my hash browns. "You can stop thanking me now. I'm having breakfast with you, not curing cancer."

"I'm just glad you're here," he says, unfazed by my poking fun of him. "Don't take this the wrong way, but I can't stop thinking about you."

My heart seems to seize up in my chest. "What way am I supposed to take that?" I reach for my water because my throat is suddenly dry.

He leans forward, his eyes like deep oceans that lock onto mine. I am in danger of falling straight through to the bottom. "It means I have a huge crush on you, Keanna."

Okay, my heart has definitely stopped.

His lips curl up. "And it means I can't stop thinking about you and wondering what you're doing and kicking myself for pissing you off. And frankly, being forced to spend time away from you is only making me want you more."

I swallow. His words just made me into a molten goo, but I need to gain my straight back, soon. I need to pull back the walls that he's trying to knock down. They need to be reinforced.

I stiffen and sit up a little straighter. "You don't even know me."

"But I like what I do know."

"What about that girl from the pool?"

"What about her?"

His eyes are challenging me, but I refuse to surrender. "You looked pretty content to be playing around with her in the pool."

"She's a friend. She came over to ask me about a guy she likes."

My eyes narrow. "Did ya'll hook up?"

"No."

"Have you hooked up before?"

"Yes."

The openness with which he says it makes me pause. What kind of guy doesn't start babbling and making up excuses and trying to turn stuff around when you ask a question like that?

I point my fork at him. "Why should I believe you?"

He doesn't even blink. "Because I've never lied to you."

Oh shit.

Where are my metaphorical walls?

They are gone, crumbled and broken, while Jett stands on top of them like some kind gladiator who just won an epic war.

"Why are you telling me all of this now?" I ask, my voice barely above a whisper.

"Because I don't want to be friends with you, Keanna." The whole restaurant seems to disappear as his eyes lock on mine. "I want to see if we could be more than that."

CHAPTER EIGHTEEN

Jett

I can't stop grinning on the entire drive back from the café. One glance at Keanna shows me that she's suffering from the same problem. I can't help but look at her at every red light and stop sign and just about every second in between. It's a miracle that I don't accidentally drive us into a ditch.

She is so beautiful, and even more adorable now that I took the epic risk and spilled my guts to her. I was afraid she might slap me or throw her glass of water in my face when I admitted that I had a massive crush on her, but she didn't. She granted me the privilege of pouring out my feelings and she didn't even laugh about it.

In fact, I think she's cool with it.

We reach the final stop sign before my house and I look over at her again. She turns a deep shade of pink that matches her dress and links her fingers together in her lap.

"So where are those cupcakes?" I ask.

"At Becca's house," she says. But we've already pulled into the parking lot at the Track, which is in between both my house and the Parks'.

"Wanna walk over there?" I ask.

"Maybe we should see if Becca still needs work done," she says, playing with the hem of her dress. "I was technically supposed to be learning what to do on the job today."

"Eh, it's easy. You'll just answer phones and stuff."

"Yeah, but what will I say when I answer it?" she says, smirking. "A good employee would know what to say to the customers."

I shrug. "You say *hello*." Then I take off my seatbelt and look at her. "Do you not know how to answer a phone, Keanna? Because I could teach you."

She rolls her eyes and throws a playful punch at my arm. "You're a dork."

"Takes one to know one," I say as we climb out of my truck. It's cheesy and pathetic and I'm fully aware of how one smile from this girl completely wipes away all rational thoughts. She is like a drug and I don't care that's drugs are supposed to be bad for you.

We walk up to the main office and I grab the door, holding it open for her. She looks up at me as she enters, the expression on her face telling me she's enamored with my manners. See, this is what was supposed to happen that night I pissed her off. I wanted to impress her and now I'll do whatever it takes to make it up to her. I'll do it right this time.

We find Becca sitting in Park's lap on one of the couches in the lounge. The TV is on to a Metal Mulita DVD, which is basically just a bunch of badass dirt bike stunt guys performing all of the crazy cool shit they can do on a bike.

"Uh, gross," I say, grabbing a throw pillow off the adjacent couch and throwing it at the two lovebirds.

Becca startles, eyes wide as she whips around and nearly falls out of her husband's lap.

"Dude," Park says. "Cock block somewhere else."

"This is the Track *Lounge*! I say, throwing another pillow at him. "Kids could walk in here."

Becca sits up and fixes her hair. "We're closed today so we're not worried about little kids. Of course I guess we should have been worried about *teen*agers barging in on us."

Becca leans over to see past me and to where Keanna is standing, holding her elbow with her other hand. "How was breakfast?" she asks.

"It was good," Keanna says, putting on that smile that I know is hiding her uncomfortableness. "Um, do you still need me to do any work?"

Becca shakes her head and waves a hand to dismiss us. "Nah, you're good. Ya'll go have fun. And lock the damn door on your way out, Jett."

"Ew, ew, ew," I say, putting my hand on Keanna's lower back as we leave the room. "Don't you two have a bedroom in your own *house* that you can do this crap in?"

The only reply I get is Park throwing a couch pillow at my face while he makes out with his wife.

"That was . . . weird," Keanna says as we walk back down the black and white checkerboard hallway.

"They're grossly in love," I say. I remember the time I was about five years old and I overheard Becca telling my mom about how she dressed up in a whipped cream bikini for Park's birthday. They didn't know I was listening and they laughed their asses off when I spoke up and asked how a bikini made of whipped cream would hold up in a swimming pool.

When we get back to the front office, I notice Keanna staring at my hands. Does she want me to hold her hand again? Should I even risk that bold move for a second time today? It had worked at the café, but I'm not sure how far I can push my luck.

I lean against the front desk, resting my elbows behind me on the counter. I watch her gaze travel down the length of my body and I want so badly to grab her and wrap my arms around her. But I have to take it slow with this girl. I don't want to scare her away. I need her to know that I'm sincere.

"Okay well, thanks for breakfast," she says, giving me a little wave as she turns toward the door.

No. She can't leave yet.

"Wait," I say, rushing to catch up with her. She turns and looks up at me expectantly and I have nothing to say. I just don't want her to go. I'm not ready to be away from her and the scent of her cherry shampoo.

I scratch the back of my neck. "You wanna go see a movie?"

She flinches. "Ah, not really. I mean, I would, but I can't."

"Why not? I'll drive us. We can see whatever you want."

I follow her outside, all but begging to keep her interested in me.

"It's not that, I just don't really want to go out in public, just . . . not right now."

I lift an eyebrow. "You don't want to be seen with me?" The thought alone hurts more than it should.

She shakes her head. "No, it's not that. I mean, maybe it is. I don't know. I just don't think I can handle the movies right now."

As much as I don't want to admit defeat, it might be best to give her some space. I sigh and shove my hands in my pockets. "Okay, yeah. No pressure."

She bites her lip and looks up at me, her eyes like a lost puppy, or like maybe she thinks *I'm* the lost puppy. "You're not pressuring me, Jett. I mean, I *want* to hang out, I just . . ."

"We don't have to go anywhere," I say, seizing the opportunity. God, I want to reach out and hold her so bad, but I keep my hands firmly in my pockets. "We could watch a movie at home?"

"I could do that," she says, a smile playing on the corners of her lips.

"My house?"

She nods.

My heart explodes with all of these new feelings. "Okay, um, walk or drive? Half the time I leave my truck over here anyway."

She glances across the field toward my house and then an evil thought lights up her gaze. "I'll race you," she says, and before I can make sense of her challenge, she takes off running.

I sprint to catch up. She doesn't stay ahead of me for long but I don't get in front of her, maybe because I'm a gentleman or maybe because her ass looks great in that dress. When she runs up the stairs onto the patio she grabs the back door handle and turns, but it doesn't budge.

"Ha!" I say, stopping right behind her. "You can run but you can't get away unless you know the passcode."

She turns around, her back against the back door and that evil grin still playing on her lips. "I think you let me win," she says, panting for breath.

I hold my hands up innocently. "I don't know what you're talking about."

She laughs and it makes her face the most beautiful thing I've ever seen.

"You're really beautiful," I say, the words falling out of my mouth without a second thought.

"So are you," she says.

And then she kisses me.

CHAPTER NINETEEN

Keanna

I kiss him. Like some kind of dramatic airport scene in a movie, I throw my arms around his neck and lean up on my toes and press my lips to his. And he kisses me back. I hadn't realized I was afraid that he wouldn't kiss me back until the moment our lips meet. But it all works out because he leans into the kiss, wrapping his arms around my waist, his fingers digging into my sides as he kisses me back with a force that says he's been wanting to do this as much I have.

I know I shouldn't be doing this.

I know Jett is not on the same level I am. He is rich, I am poor. He is popular and loved, I have no one. He is *so* hot, and I am just me. A homeless girl with a missing mom. A charity case.

My lip quivers as I think all of this and then Jett's hand slides down to my hip and he presses up against me, flattening my back to the door. He smells like woodsy cologne and his lips taste like spearmint.

When our lips break apart, we both gasp for air. Suddenly the whole world comes back to me and I remember where I am. Outside in the open, where anyone could walk up on us.

Jett gives me this devilish grin as he towers over me, seeming even taller now that we're so close. "Wanna take this to my room?"

My throat is dry and my heart is an Olympic gymnast in my chest so I just nod.

He punches in the passcode on the back door lock and we go inside, the cool lavender-scented air bringing me back to reality.

I am with Jett in his house and we just kind of made out on the patio.

OMG.

He takes my hand and pulls me across their massive house, toward the same back set of stairs. We go up to his room and when he closes the door behind us, he twists the lock. That single action makes my stomach flip over.

"So, um, a movie?" I say, still breathless from that epic make out session. Or maybe from the run over here. All I know is that Jett has taken my breath away and I haven't quite got it back yet.

"Yeah, a movie," he says, gazing down at me as he inches forward, slowly closing the short distance between us.

His toes touch mine and now we're so close but not touching anything else besides our shoes. It feels like a static bomb of electricity has exploded in the small space between our bodies. But I already made the first move outside. I'm not doing it again.

Jett's hand reaches out and grazes my arm. "Was that a mistake?"

Yes.

I shake my head. "No."

"Do we . . . wanna. .?" he says, pausing to run his tongue over his bottom lip.

"Keep making out?" I say with a sudden burst of boldness.

He nods.

I draw in a sharp breath. "Yeah."

"Yeah?" Jett wiggles his eyebrows and it makes me laugh. In the moment of silliness, he slides one arm around my waist and cups my face with the other hand. Slowly—so painfully slowly—he pulls my face upward and then kisses me softer than before. I melt into him, returning the kisses and wanting more. More kisses, more Jett, more of this feeling that maybe the world doesn't suck.

When he pulls away again, I groan.

"Does this mean you don't hate me anymore?" he asks, running a finger down the strap of my dress. Goosebumps prickle across my shoulders. If I let myself think of the true answer to that question, it might ruin the mood.

I shrug. "It means you're really hot and I'm tired of over-thinking everything."

He looks like he wants to say something else but I slide my hands up his chest, kissing his neck in a trail up to his ear. He moans when my lips touch the perfect spot on his neck, so I run my tongue across it.

"That's it," Jett whispers. In an instant, he's grabbed my ass and slid his hands down my thighs, lifting me off the ground. I hold on to his neck while he walks me to the futon in front of his TV. He turns to where his back is against the futon and then sits down, leaving me straddling him.

My dress pulls up way too high so I lean forward, pressing our chests together so he can't see anything. I am wearing cheap underwear from Target. Not exactly the sexiest thing for a guy to see on the first day you make out.

Jett's hands find my butt and he holds on to it as if it were his own personal hand resting space. I grip his shoulders and kiss him, letting our tongues explore each other's mouths.

When he groans and lets out a little shudder, pulling my hips into his, I know I've driven him to the edge. And since I don't plan on having sex with him right here, after only one day of not hating him, I pull away.

Suddenly I'm hit with memories of what happens when you piss off a guy who wants more than making out. It is never good and it usually hurts.

"Um," I say, leaning back on his lap. I remember the whole dress situation and then carefully stand up, climbing off his lap so that I can sit next to him on the futon.

"Okay I'm sorry, please don't hate me," I say, unable to meet his eyes. I know he has an erection and he locked the door and dammit, this could ruin everything. Guys do not like to be denied sex.

"Why would I hate you?" Jett says. His head rolls to the right to face me and he reaches out, tucking a strand of hair behind my ear.

I exhale and try to look sweet. Try to look like a nice girl that you don't want to punch in the face. "I'm just . . . I'm not ready to . . ." My eyes drop down to his crotch and my face burns. I can't find it in me to say the words.

"Have sex?" Jett supplies for me.

I nod and brace for the backlash.

Instead of getting angry, he grins and sinks down lower in the futon, spreading his legs open wider as he relaxes. "Nah. Why would I hate you?"

I swallow. Looks like all rational speech has left my brain for now.

Jett reaches over and grabs the TV remote and turns it to the Netflix screen.

"I wasn't going to have sex even if you wanted to," he says, giving me an assuring smile. "You just became my friend again. I want to prove that I'm worth it."

"Friend?" I say with a snort. Damn. Of course. That's all this is. Jett the heart-throb, hooking up with every girl he sees and calling them all "friends". God, I am so stupid.

"Yeah, friends." I nod and focus on the television, but he hasn't picked a show to watch so it's kind of pointless.

"What's wrong?" he says, leaning over and poking me in the arm.

I shake my head. Put on a happy smile. "Nothing."

He narrows his eyes at me. "Am I a terrible kisser? Is that why you pulled away?"

I roll my eyes and can't help but smile. "You know you're a great kisser," I say, feeling warmth from his gaze trail up my whole body.

"Then why'd you pull away?" He reaches for me and takes my hand, lacing his fingers through mine. I stare at our hands on the futon. His are tanned, calloused and huge. Mine are pale, and shaking.

"Honestly?" I say.

He nods. "I only ever want honesty with us."

"I stopped so you wouldn't get pissed that I didn't want to have sex."

"Yeah, but now that I've explained that I don't want to do that too soon . . ." he says, giving me a seductive grin that makes butterflies tickle my insides. "Maybe you should come back over here. I miss your lips."

"It's only been a few seconds, how can you miss them?"

His eyes lower to my lips and he leans over, making the frame of the futon squeak as his lips brush against mine in a kiss so soft it makes my whole body shudder. "Because they're perfect lips, that's why."

I give him a look and he nods. "I'm serious. The best lips ever."

I cross my arms. "I'm supposed to believe that? Out of all of the millions of girls you've hooked up with, I am somehow special?"

He shakes his head and winks at me. "It wasn't millions. Maybe closer to hundreds of thousands."

I slap him playfully. He grabs my arm and puts my palm up to his lips.

This is wrong. This is so wrong. I can't just let him win me over like this. I need to be strong. I have to remember that he is not like me. That I'll leave soon enough and I'll be back in the slums, in shitty apartments and back rooms in seedy dive bars and I'll never step foot in a house this nice ever again. And when I kissed him on the patio, I had told myself it would just be for fun, just a joke, just a way to fulfill my desires without making it a big deal.

But Jett isn't like the other guys. Maybe he's a really good liar. All the rich guys are. But it just really seems like maybe he's being genuine with me. I'd be a fool to think that, though.

"What are you thinking, beautiful?" he whispers, his lips tickling my ear.

"I'm thinking that if all those other girls can have fun with you," I say, trying to mean it even though my heart is crying out otherwise, "Then why can't I?"

CHAPTER TWENTY

Jett

I set two baskets of burgers and fries on the table and slide one over to D'andre. He grabs the massive cheeseburger in one hand and takes a bite.

"So what's up, man?"

My shoulders fall. "I'm in trouble."

He takes another bite, his eyebrow rising. "Like . . . legal trouble? Man, what did your dumbass do?"

I laugh and grab a fry. Even though we're at a Red Robin restaurant and not McDonald's, I still think of Keanna when I eat French fries.

"Okay first of all you can't say shit about this, okay?" I point the fry at him as if it's some kind of weapon I'll use to whip his ass if he talks.

He takes another bite of his burger. "Okay now I'm intrigued. I mean I was interested when I thought you wanted to use my dad's lawyer services to bail you out of some kind of legal trouble but by the look on your face, this'll be good."

"I'm serious, man. No telling anyone what I'm about to say."

He sets down the burger and gives me his undivided attention. "Lay it on me."

I draw in a deep breath. When I'd called my best friend to come eat lunch with me today, I'd known I wanted to tell him all about my dilemma. But now that it's about to happen, I kind of want to laugh and say I was kidding and go on with our day like normal. But if I avoid talking to someone about this, it'll only make the problem worse. If D'andre can't help, then I'll go to my dad. But I really don't want to because that's just embarrassing.

"Yeah so, I'm in trouble," I say again. "With Keanna."

His eyes light up. "Is she pregnant?"

"What?" I sit up straighter. "Dude, no."

D'andre lifts an eyebrow. "Okay so, why are you acting like the world is ending?"

"Don't judge me, but I'm kind of into her."

He takes the bun off his burger and adds a huge amount of ketchup to the meat before replacing the bun. "Uh, okay. You're into a million girls. That's why I hate you," he says with a chuckle. "You get all the hot girls and guys like me get the leftovers."

I shake my head. "No, I mean, I'm into her. Like, we've spent every day this week together."

"Whoa."

I expect him to laugh at me because I'd do the same thing in his position. But even under all of the joking and giving each other shit, he's still a good friend.

"Well, I guess the great womanizer Jett Adams can settle down if he wants, right?" D'andre says with a shrug. "What's the problem?"

"That's exactly the problem. I don't settle down. I've pretty much based my entire sex life on being a no-strings-attached kind of guy."

"And is this chick trying to attach strings to ya'll?" he says, moving his finger around like it's attached to an invisible thread.

I shake my head. "That's another issue. Sometimes she acts like she's really into me too, but the other times she'll do something sexy as hell and then walk off like it's nothing. Like what we have doesn't mean shit."

D'andre lowers his gaze at me. "You mean like how you treat every girl you've ever been with?"

The words are true but they sting regardless. I stare at my burger, counting each little sesame seed on the bun. "I don't know what to do. I keep telling myself to treat her like any other girl, but I can't. I really like her."

"And this is coming from the guy who has promised me numerous times that he'll never fall for a girl," D'andre says with a laugh. "Man, you're screwed."

I draw in a deep breath and sigh. "Yeah, I know. Even if she liked me back, I wouldn't know what to do. I'm not a girlfriend guy, ya know? Like, that in itself would be a nightmare to figure out but that's not the problem. The problem is that I have no idea if she likes me back or not." I sink my forehead into my hand. "Sometimes I think she's just messing with me. Like she still royally hates me and is messing with my head."

"Girl's will do that," D'andre says, nodding like he knows that fact all too well.

"You're not helping at all," I say, trying to get back to eating. I haven't eaten all day so maybe the lack of food is making me even more heartsick.

"Dude, what I am supposed to do?" he says, taking a long sip from his drink. "Want me to ask her?"

I shake my head. Keanna could lie to him just as easily as she lies to me. And just the thought of that girl lying to me makes my heart feel five kinds of pain that it's never felt before. I've promised total honesty with her and I've been true to my word.

It occurs to me now that she's never offered the same promise to me.

"Look, Jett," D'andre says, grabbing three fries at once and dunking them in ketchup. "Why don't you bring her to the lake party this weekend? I'll chat her up and we can get the guys to meet her and then see what everyone thinks."

"Absolutely not. What the hell did I say about keeping this to yourself?" I say. "No one else can know but you, okay? Don't tell anyone."

He holds up his hands in surrender. "Okay, man, chill. You're either completely in love or terrified of this chick embarrassing you for having emotions."

"Honestly, it might be a little of both," I say, feeling my chest constrict.

"So bring her to the party," he says. "Let me meet her and I'll tell you what I think about her feelings toward you. I mean I'm no relationship expert, but it looks like I'm all you've got."

"Yeah okay," I say, wondering how I'll bring it up to Keanna. We've only ever hung out alone, although we've spent nearly every waking moment together this week. "I'll bring her."

AFTER WORK, I RUSH HOME AND HOP IN THE SHOWER. I'VE ONLY SEEN KEANNA ONCE today and it wasn't nearly long enough. She'd been in the front office with Becca, preparing for her first week of working alone since Becca is leaving for some craft thing tomorrow. So all I was able to do is say a quick hello to her since I was with a customer and I had to show his little kid around the track.

Seeing Keanna looking beautiful as hell in a blue tank top and cut off jean shorts but not being able to kiss her was the absolute worst. My heart has been aching all damn day. I kept trying to find ways to sneak back in the office, but my dad had me busy at the track all day.

But it's over now and I'll get to see her soon.

This last week has been a whirlwind of new emotions and experiences. We've hung out every single day without planning it. Somehow we find ourselves in each other's arms, secretly of course. My mom might suspect something but no one else knows. The last three days in a row, I came home to find Keanna waiting for me on the porch. Today she wasn't, but that doesn't stop me. I'll see her soon enough.

I crank up the hot water even though it's hot as hell outside. I let the shower steam up the bathroom and I scrub every inch of my body with the best smelling soap I have. The water hits my neck and I close my eyes, picturing Keanna's lips in that exact spot. She is intoxicating and she has taken over my whole heart. I am in *so* much trouble.

And that's probably why this hurts so badly. I have no idea what she really feels. We haven't exactly talked about it. And I come from a long stream of pointless hookups so I've never had this conversation. I wouldn't even know how to bring it up.

"Uh yeah, are we like, dating?"

That wouldn't be very charming.

I sigh and let my head rest against the side of the shower wall. This is going to drive me insane if I don't get answers soon. I've been trying to be kind and respectful, especially since I know she's worried about not hearing from her mom. But now it's at the point where thinking about Keanna hurts more than it feels good.

Because I've got some major feelings for this girl and if she doesn't feel the same, it'll crush me.

After my shower, I towel off and pull on a blue shirt because two days ago she said I looked hot in blue. I throw some gel in my hair and rush out of my room, almost forgetting my phone. All I want to do is be near her.

I refuse to worry that her not being on my porch today was a bad sign.

Becca opens the door for me when I arrive. "Hey, kid," she says, letting me in. "You here for Key?"

I nod. "Is she in her room?"

"Yep. You staying for dinner?"

I shrug. "I dunno. I might take her out."

"Okay, well let me know."

I smile and head across their vintage house to the guest bedroom. I knock softly, realizing that my entire body is now just a nervous sack of skin and organs.

The door opens and she is so beautiful I can't help myself. "You're hot," I say, leaning against the door frame.

She smiles and steps back, letting me enter her room. "How was work?"

"Work was work," I say, taking her face in my hands. "I don't wanna talk about that, I want to kiss you."

She smirks. "Then do it."

When we kiss, my anxiety melts away. I hadn't realized how scared I was about her not being at my house after work until her kiss takes it all away. Maybe she was running late or something. I slide my hands through her hair and try not to let on to how much I love when her boobs graze against my chest. "I missed you," I whisper between kissing her perfect lips.

"You always miss me," she teases, dropping down to her normal height. She'd been up on her toes a second ago and now she feels so far away.

"Yeah, but you never say you miss me." I make a pretend puppy face and hope to god that she'll tell me something I want to hear.

"Maybe I do, maybe I don't," she says, that frighteningly adorable smile still on her face.

"You kill me, you know this right?" I say, wrapping my arms around her and pulling her close to me. She's still wearing those cut off shorts I love so I slip my hands in her back pockets and revel in the feeling of her being so close.

My heart is aching with all of the questions I have—does she like me? Is she messing with me? But I don't even care right now. I just need to be near her.

"Hey, can I ask a favor?" she says, peering up at me with this serious expression.

"Of course. Anything."

She bites on her bottom lip. "Could I use your phone?"

I take it out of my back pocket and hand it to her. "Thanks," she says as she dials a number from heart. She puts the phone to her ear and turns around, walking to the window that overlooks the fields on the other side of the road.

I follow, giving her some space while she waits. Finally, she lowers the phone and turns back around, holding it out to me.

I take the phone and frown. "Your mom still not answering?"

She shakes her head and looks at the floor. "It's driving me crazy."

"I'm sorry, Key." I wrap her in my arms and hold her tightly, lowering my chin on top of her head. We stand like that for a long time and then she finally breaks away.

"Sorry I'm in a crap mood," she says, her eyes full of sorrow. She points to the bed where one of Becca's old laptops sits. "I've been looking up police news, accident reports, everything. I can't find any sign of my mom. I even looked up craft fairs to see if she was listed as a vendor. I just hope she's alive, you know?"

I take her hand. Here I was spending all day freaking out about if a girl liked me or not, and she's got real issues to deal with. God, I'm a dick. "I'll help you look," I say, pulling her with me to sit on the bed. "We can drive down to Corpus Christi if you want. Ask around for her?"

She considers this a moment and then shakes her head. "I don't even know the name of the company she was interviewing for. For all I know maybe that was a lie."

"Have you called hospitals?" I ask.

She nods. "Yep. I even hacked into her email account and it hasn't been used in months."

I squeeze her hand in mine. "I'm sorry. I'm here for you, though. Anything you need."

Just when I think we're having a moment, she shakes her head. "Don't worry about it. It's not your problem, it's mine."

That hard look is back on her face. The one from the night I first met her. She's built her walls up again and is shutting me out.

"Okay well, I don't care what you say. I'm still here for you."

She shakes her head and stands up, dropping my hand. "What do you want to do tonight? Or are you busy?"

"I'm doing whatever you're doing," I say with a smile that doesn't make anything better. She's still shutting me out and I still hate it. "We should go get you a cell phone."

She snorts. "I can't afford it. Plus, you have to be like eighteen to sign the contract, I think."

"You don't need a contract. They have prepaid phones and stuff. We should get you one because I've been dying to text you. I'll pay for it."

"What would you text me? We're always together."

"Not always," I say, feeling some of the flirty vibes come back in between us. "When I'm in bed at night all alone, I wish I could text you."

"Ah, so you want dirty pictures," she says, glaring at me. "Can't you just use the internet like every other guy?"

I open my mouth, looking offended. "Totally not what I meant. I just want to talk to you. We should get you a phone. It can be camera-less if you want."

She rolls her eyes. "I'll think about it."

"Let's go now," I say, tugging on her hand.

"I don't really want to go anywhere now." She frowns. "I'm worried about my mom and I'm super worried about work. Tomorrow is my first day on the job without Becca."

I steal a kiss on her forehead before I speak. "Well you're in luck because I'm off work tomorrow so I'll just hang out with you."

"That actually makes me more nervous."

"Psh," I say, poking her in the stomach. "I'm awesome."

"Keep telling yourself that."

God, I want to kiss her so bad. I swallow and try to play it cool since she's obviously not in the mood. "Hey, I have an idea. After work tomorrow, some of my friends are hanging out at the lake. We should go."

"Another one of those lake parties where you drive girls home crying?" She says, lifting a skeptical eyebrow at me.

"They're not normally like that," I say. "My friend D'andre wants to meet you so I told him we might stop by."

"I don't know," she says, looking down. She steps forward and grabs my pockets, slipping her thumbs under the waistband of my shorts. "I'll think about it."

But I don't really hear what she says because her thumbs draw a line across my skin and my body is on fire with the need to touch her. Her hands slide up my chest and I grab her, lifting her off her feet as we kiss and for now, all of my worries don't matter. Because for now, she's mine.

CHAPTER TWENTY-ONE

Keanna

There's no dress code for working at the Track. Becca had told me to dress comfortably and I guess that makes sense, for a place whose official business name is The Track. I guess I shouldn't have expected some lame uniform or anything.

I throw on my cut off shorts, the only pair of shorts I have, and a white tank top with little sequin sparkles along the collar. Becca had given me the tank top the other day, claiming that it was too small on her. I think she's just trying to secretly give me stuff in ways that won't make me feel like a charity case. I appreciate it though, even though it *does* make me feel like a charity case. At least I can wear something cute on my first day of work. And who am I kidding? The only person I want to impress is Jett Adams.

Ugh.

I don't even know what I truly think about the boy. Just that I'm crazy about him, about this place, this atypical summer vacation. It's so much better than anything I've ever experienced. Better than stargazing at the Grand Canyon with Dawn. Better than that time my fifth grade teacher invited me over for Thanksgiving dinner because my mom was stuck working and I got to eat not only one plate of food, but two, along with a huge slice of pumpkin pie.

Jett makes me feel alive. I am fully aware that this is temporary. Maybe that's why I like it so much. He is so hot and so nice. He holds open doors and he kisses like some kind of sex god. Sometimes I think he really likes me, *like*, likes me. The kind of like that middle school girls obsess over. But then I have to bring myself back to reality and remember that Jett is a player. He is sexy and perfect and I am just the flavor of the month.

But who cares? I'm along for the ride and I love every second I'm with him. When I'm in Jett's arms I play this game with myself. I pretend I'm his girlfriend and that the guest bedroom is my own room and that Becca and Park are my parents. I feel a *little* guilty about that part, but it's not like Dawn will ever find out about the fantasies in my head.

Every day I spent with Jett erases a hundred bad memories of my shitty life. And I know it's all as temporary as my room at Becca's house, but I hold onto it anyway. I'm embracing each day, every second of happiness. Because one day it'll be gone and all I'll have left is the memories.

I pull my hair back into a ponytail and then stare at myself in the vanity mirror in my room. "You're going to be fine," I say, willing the nerves to dissipate.

It doesn't really work.

Becca left last night, taking a plane to Louisiana and leaving me with a list of responsibilities at the track. It's my first official day of work and I'm getting paid to hang out in the front office and help customers all day. It's a real job and I don't even know what I'll do with the money I earn. I was going to save it and try for a motel on my own, but now that I'm having so much fun with Jett, I really don't want to leave.

I've been making sure to be an excellent houseguest for the Parks since I've been staying there. I keep my room spotless and I do the dishes and laundry even though Becca says it's not necessary. The other day I found her duster and dusted the whole house. Anything I can do to keep myself from being a burden, I do it.

When I can't prolong going to work anymore, I leave my room and head outside. Park is already at work and had asked me to lock the door behind myself, so I do.

My nerves reach epic proportions by the time I make it to the track and I tell myself to freaking chill. I can handle this job, but it's the fear of disappointing Becca that makes me so worried.

I walk inside and a familiar smile greets me front behind the front desk. "Good morning, beautiful."

Jett leans in on his elbows. "Ready for work?"

Happiness spreads from the top of my head to the bottom of my toes. I can't even remember what being nervous felt like now. "What are you doing here?" I say, turning to the left to flip on all of the lights. They turn off half of the lights when they close at night. That's one of the first parts of my job, and I remembered to do it, so yay.

"I told you I'd be here to hang out with you," Jett says, bending down and disappearing below the desk.

"Yeah but it's six in the morning. You didn't have to get here this early." I walk over behind the desk and Jett sits back up, a brown paper bag and two Starbucks coffees in his hand. "I didn't want to miss out on one second of being with you," he says, leaning forward for a kiss.

My lips fits so perfectly on his and the kisses we share are starting to feel a lot like home. "Why do you do this?" I say, pulling out the barstool next to him and sitting down. "Why do you have to be so romantic like that?"

"Uh, because I'm crazy about you," he says, reaching into the bag. He takes out two blueberry muffins and hands one to me.

I hold the muffin under my nose and breathe in the delicious sugary smell. "I'm gonna miss this when it's over," I say softly, turning to look at Jett.

He's looking at me like he's just as enamored as I am, but that can't be true. There's no way he likes me as much as I like him.

"Who says it has to be over?" he says, nudging me with his shoulder. "In case you haven't noticed, I'm trying really hard to win you over."

I roll my eyes. "Is that code for *trying to get you to sleep with me?*"

He flinches. "No. Why do you always jump to that conclusion?"

"Because you're a guy."

He exhales loudly and shakes his head. "I need to turn on the computer," I say, taking a bite of my muffin before moving around him to get to the computer. I can tell he's a little annoyed with me, but I'd rather not dive into the conversation of our pretend relationship, or fling, or whatever this is. I know he's just trying to be nice. But I don't need false hope from a gorgeous guy. Hell, the way things are going, I'll probably sleep with him just for the fun of it. It's not like a guy like Jett would ever want something meaningful with me anyway.

I flip on the computer and rest my hand on the mouse, waiting for it to start up.

A few seconds of silence pass and then Jett is behind me, his strong chest touching my back. "We need to talk," he whispers into my hear. I tense.

"About what? I'm busy."

"No, you're not. You're stalling and trying to avoid me."

His hands cover my arms and slide down to my hands. He turns me around and then steps closer, backing me literally into a corner of the front desk. "Look at me," he says, like it's an order.

I look up and he doesn't say anything. He just takes me in his arms and kisses me hard, deepening the kiss the moment I relent and kiss him back. I hold onto this chest while he pulls me against his strong body, his mouth caressing mine with the energy of someone who can't get enough. His lips pull away and I lean up on my toes, so drunk on his kiss that I want more. "I'm sick of you pushing me away," he whispers, his lips just barely on top of mine. "You can't keep doing it. I'm crazy about you."

"I don't believe that," I whisper back, every fiber of my body needing to be close to him. This is so wrong, so destined to end up in heartache, but screw it, I don't care. "I know you like me," I say, taking in a ragged breath. "I also know this won't last forever. You're famous around here. You'll move on and I'll always just be the loser without a real home."

"Don't say that," Jett says, closing his eyes.

I shake my head. "It's true but I don't really care, okay? So just chill and stop trying to make things better for me. This is a fling and it's fun and I like it, so just chill out and let's have fun, okay?"

My voice had risen a little louder than I realized, and Jett's expression goes from worried to cold. He takes a step back and shakes his head. "I don't think you listen to anything I say, Keanna."

"That's because I don't believe in any of it."

A muscle in his jaw twitches. "What will it take to make you trust me?"

I snort out a laugh. "Jett, please stop. We were having fun. Let's just have fun."

"Dammit, Keanna," he says, his jaw tightening as he runs his hands through his hair, messing it all up. He turns around and holds the back of his head in his hands, staring off in the distance. Then he spins back toward me and shoves me against the desk again, caressing my neck, my ear, my lips with his. I groan at the feel of his hips pressing into mine and he grabs my face in his hands, kissing me hard and then so soft I barely feel it. He pulls back, staring into my eyes for a long moment. "I'll prove it to you," he says, his resolve apparent in his features. "I'll prove it and you'll be sorry."

"I'll be sorry?" I say, trying not to laugh while also catching my breath from that hot make out session.

He grins. "Yep. You'll be sorry because by then you'll be totally in love with me." He puts a finger on my belly and drags it down until it hooks under the waistband of my jeans, he pulls my hips against his and whispers into my ear, "And there won't be anything you can do about it."

Damn, that's hot.

I swallow and try to stand up a little straighter, try to get my head back in the game. And that's when my elbow hits something warm and I knock over the coffee on the desk. It tips over, spilling scalding hot coffee out of the hole in the lid.

"Shit." I flinch and flail, but the damage is done. This pretty white tank top is covered in dark brown, the liquid seeping up the shirt and ruining the whole thing.

"It's okay," Jett says, turning down the hallway. I hear a door open at the end of the hall and I grab a roll of paper towels to wipe up the mess. Most of the coffee ended up on me, so at least the computer and the papers on the desk are okay.

Jett returns with a black T-shirt with some dirt bike logo on it. "Here, wear this. It's a small so it might fit you."

I take the shirt and frown at it. "Where'd it come from?"

"My locker. It's a couple years old. Doesn't really fit me anymore, but it's clean so you can wear it."

There goes my cute tank top look for the day. "Thanks," I say, and I duck into the women's restroom to change. There's a drawer and a couch in here, and I dig around the drawers and find a new pack of hair ties. I use one to tie up the bottom of the shirt in the back and I roll up the sleeves to make it a little more girly. The moment I pull the shirt over my head I am thanking fate for making me spill the coffee. This shirt smells like heaven. I might never give it back.

THE MORNING GOES WELL AND WORKING HERE ENDS UP BEING PRETTY FUN. SO FAR all of the customers who came in have been coming here a lot so their info was in the computer and all I had to do was check them in. Becca taught me the procedure for signing up a new riding client but I haven't had to use it yet.

Jett hangs out with me just like he promised, and he knows everyone who comes in so it takes a lot of the pressure off me.

Mrs. Adams—I mean Bayleigh—calls the office phone around noon and asks what kind of pizza we want. She says it like that, using the word's *what kind of pizza do you guys want* as if she knows Jett planned on being here all day. It makes my head spin but I manage to have a normal conversation with her.

Half an hour later, she shows up wearing short shorts and a tank top with a checkered flag made of rhinestones on the front. I can tell why all the guys around here call her a MILF. She's pretty hot for a mom.

Bayleigh smiles and sets down the pizza box in her hands. "Half cheese, half pep. There's still drinks in the fridge, right?"

"Yeah, thanks Mom," Jett says, opening the pizza box and grabbing a slice.

"Thanks so much for lunch," I say, standing tall and trying to look like someone she should like. I mean, she always acts like she likes me, but I want her to *definitely* like me.

"You're totally welcome, Keanna," she says. She pulls her massive purse off her shoulder and sets it on the counter, digging around for a black plastic bag. There's red Verizon logo check mark on it.

"Okay, so this is the newest model of the phone Jett has," she says, taking out a phone. Then she pulls out a pink phone case and pops it out of the plastic box. "I got pink, is that okay? If you hate it, we can exchange it but they didn't really have many cute options."

"Uh, what is this?" I say, staring at the new smartphone on the desk.

Bayleigh gives a look to her son and puts her hands on her hips. "You didn't tell her?"

"Shit," Jett says, chewing faster to swallow the bite of pizza. "Um, yeah, I forgot. Key, Mom got you a phone."

"What?" I shake my head. "No. No, I can't take that. I can't afford the bill. Maybe after I've had a job for a while, but—"

Bayleigh holds up her hand and gives me this sweet mothering look. "No worries. I added a line to the business phone plan. We all have phones on the business account. They're a tax write off, and since you work here, you get one."

I lift an eyebrow and turn to Jett. "You did this."

He grins. "You need a phone."

"I can't take this, you know that."

"You can and you will," Bayleigh says, taking my hand and putting the phone in it. "Besides, I can't let a teenage girl walk around without a phone. It's just not safe."

"She has me, Mom," Jett says, reaching for another piece of pizza.

"You're not as safe as a phone," she says, rolling her eyes at him. To me, she says, "Don't you worry about this at all. It's unlimited minutes, text, and data so have fun."

"Uh, thanks," I say, trying not to jump into the air and scream for joy. My own phone.

Wow.

Jett has me call him so we can save each other's numbers into our phones. Bayleigh gives me her and Becca's numbers and Jett has to constantly show me how to use the damn thing. It's way more complicated than Dawn's old cell phone. As soon as we're done playing with it, and the customers clear out, I put the phone in my pocket and say I have to pee.

As soon as I'm locked safely in the bathroom, I take out the phone, and with trembling hands, I close my eyes and hope she'll answer.

I call my mom and listen while once again, the phone goes straight to voicemail.

CHAPTER TWENTY-TWO

Jett

I don't know why people get so excited over Friday night football. Friday night motocross should be everyone's favorite activity. The track is perfect tonight, the dirt smooth and gritty at the same time. The warm summer air has a gentle wind that keeps you from getting overheated. I pin the throttle and soar over our ninety-foot-long tabletop jump, closing my eyes halfway through so that it feels like I'm flying.

It should be five o'clock soon, and Keanna will be off work. I'd asked her to come out and watch me ride for a little bit. I told her she should learn about the sport since she's working here and all. But really, I just wanted to show off. I know she already likes me, but if she sees how fast I am compared to everyone else out here . . . I don't know. Maybe that's lame.

Still, the thought of the girl I'm crazy about sitting in the bleachers and watching me ride makes my chest swell up in this totally caveman-esque way. I want her to know that I am strong and fast, that I can protect her and keep her safe. I'm not sure how riding a dirt bike would prove that, but still.

I really want her to see me ride.

I pull off to the side for a quick water break and another bike rides up to me. The bike's number plate is empty so I'm not sure who it is until he pulls off his helmet.

"D'andre, man, what's up?"

He shakes the sweat out of his hair and climbs off his bike, propping it up against the fence post. "Just realizing how out of shape I am," he says while he catches his breath.

"You didn't pay to get in, did you?" I ask.

He shakes his head. "Nah, your dad saw me drive up and waved me in."

"Cool. Keanna is working the front desk so she doesn't know everyone who gets in free yet."

At the mention of her name, his eyebrows rise. "So what's up with her? You still crushin' like some kind of teenage loser?"

"First of all, I *am* a teenager," I say, holding up a gloved finger. "And secondly, yeah."

He laughs and shakes his head like he now realizes the amount of trouble I've gone and gotten myself into. "What are you gonna do with all the other girls lining up to get with you?" he says.

I shrug and reach for my phone, which I had kept in my pocket even though it's risky. Of course, I wasn't planning on crashing so there's really nothing to worry about.

"Dude, I don't know," I say, holding it up like it's some kind of girl summoner. "They keep texting me. I hoped ignoring them all would make them go away but no such luck."

"Oh boohoo," he says, rolling his eyes. "Girls are still flocking to you. How annoying."

"Shit," I say, running a gloved hand through my sweaty hair. "Emma sends me naked photos almost once a day. I finally told her to stop sending that shit and she sent about ten more in reply. Do you know how to block someone's number on here?"

"Block her?" D'andre says it like it's a curse word. "Shit, man. Figure out a way to forward all those messages to me. No one sends me nudes."

I shake my head. "I delete them the second she sends them. I'm trying really hard to win over Keanna and if she saw that, she'd never talk to me again."

D'andre lets out a long breath of air and he's staring at me like I've just decided to sell everything I own and go live under a bridge. "Are you seriously ready to throw away all these hot chicks and settle down with just one of them?"

I grin, not because of what he just said, but because now I'm thinking of Keanna. How cute she is when she smiles, the way she ends all of her texts in an emoji now that I've shown her how to use them. The way her body feels when pressed against mine . . .

"Yeah, man. I am."

"Okay, well I still have to officially meet her if I'm going to give you my blessing," he says, narrowing his eyes at me like he's trying to be serious.

"Tonight at the lake." Now I narrow my eyes at him. "Be respectful and don't say anything that'll get me in trouble.

"Like what? How your text inbox is a powerhouse of porn?"

"I delete it all!" I say and then he laughs. I check the time on my phone. There's still five minutes before Keanna gets off work. "Wanna hit up the track again?" I ask, nodding toward our bikes.

"Yeah, but go easy on me," he says, grabbing his helmet. "Like, if you stay in second gear, maybe I'll be able to keep up."

We get back on the track and although I try going slow for D'andre's sake, it makes riding so boring. Eventually, I let him pull in front of me and then I tail him, urging him to go faster. It sounds mean but the best way to ride faster is to have someone on your ass making you work harder to stay ahead.

I keep glancing over at the bleachers, hoping to see Keanna. On my fifth lap around the track, someone waves to me from the bottom bleacher bench. Ugh. It's Emma.

I try to ignore her but she jumps up and yells out my name and I realize that Keanna will be off work soon and the last thing I need is for her to see another girl calling for me.

So I pull over and ride up to her, keeping my bike on and my helmet over my head. She doesn't get any special treatment.

"Yeah?" I call out over the rumbling of the engine.

"Turn that thing off," she says.

I shake my head. "I don't have time. What do you want?"

She puts a hand on her hip and her lip-glossed lips turn down in a pout. "You never thanked me for my pictures."

"That's because I didn't want them. You need to stop sending shit like that to me."

She scowls. "Why the hell wouldn't you want them?"

"Because I don't."

Her nostrils flare. "Okay, look. I heard the rumors and I figured they weren't true, but you're being a really huge ass right now so maybe they are true."

"I don't give a shit what rumors you've heard about me, Emma."

I rev the throttle and shift into first gear, making it clear I'm about to take off.

She steps in front of the bike. "I heard that you've been spending time with some bitch who isn't even from here," she says, her eyes squinting so she can try to garner something from my expression. She always did that; always went on and on about how my eyes would tell her what I was really thinking.

"Okay, well, since you asked," I say, pulling off my goggles so she can see me better. "I am dating a new girl and it is none of your business. And if you'd like to keep some of your dignity, stop sending me pictures cause all we do is make fun of them."

Lies, of course. Like I'd ever show some other girl's naked photos to Keanna. Still, I know the very idea of it should piss off Emma, and judging by the look in her eyes, it's done just that.

"You'll be back," she says, flipping her silky blonde hair over her shoulders.

I shake my head. "I won't."

"You will," she says, glaring at me. "I know you better than anyone, Jett Adams."

"That's where you're wrong," I say, sliding the goggles back on. "You don't know a thing about me."

CHAPTER TWENTY-THREE

Keanna

As soon as the last client leaves the office, I shut off half of the lights and lock the front door. Then I go through the closing procedures and log out of the computer, turn off the coffee pot, and power down the credit card machine.

Jett asked me to meet him on the bleachers after work, so I head into the bathroom and do a quick hair check, then put on some powder to make my face seem less stressed. It was a pretty good day at work, but standing and dealing with people all day had made my face all shiny and less radiant.

When I'm finally as cute as I can possibly get, I say goodbye to Park who is doing work in his office and then I slip out the front door, locking it behind me at Park's request.

The bleachers aren't a long walk from here and I gaze out, wondering which loud dirt bike on the track is Jett's.

Then I see him, sitting on his bike in front of the bleachers. I stop in my tracks and watch as he talks to some girl. No, not some girl. That same girl he was making out with in Becca's art closet. She's wearing short shorts and a flimsy sheer top that leaves absolutely nothing to the imagination. She grabs his arm and tilts her head up at him and although I have no idea what they're saying, it's pretty obvious she's still into him.

My heart flip-flops in my chest. Warm tears sting at my eyes and I curse to myself. *Why are you so stupid, Keanna? Stop getting sad over a guy you knew would cheat on you.*

But it's not really cheating, is it? We aren't exclusive. We're just a fling, I'd said as much myself. I've spent every single night lying in bed, telling myself not to get too attached to this guy.

So why does this hurt so bad?

Drawing in a deep breath, I turn and head back to Becca's house. I need a shower. A hot, scalding shower. And a good cry.

I do exactly that. Since Becca is out of state and Park is still working, I don't even care when the tears start flowing the moment I walk in the back door. I walk up to the guest bathroom and turn on the water as hot as it'll get and then I just stand there, crying into the shower. Like the loser that I am.

I told myself not to get attached. I knew he was bad news. My whole life lately is like a Taylor Swift song and the most pathetic thing is that I let it happen.

I'm supposed to be smarter than this, stronger than this. Jett was supposed to be the hot guy I messed around with this summer. No strings attached, no feelings to hurt, no heart to break.

So why are my feelings hurt and why is my heart broken?

Why am I so stupid?

When I've been in the shower long enough to feel guilty about all the hot water I'm wasting, I get out and throw on some pajamas. They're also a gift from Becca. Black leggings with hot pink diamond print and a pink tank top with a massive black sparkly diamond in the center. They're really cute and kind of ironic because nothing about how I feel is cute.

I towel dry my hair and then crawl into bed and pull the comforter up to my chin. It's only six in the afternoon on a Friday and I'm in bed. Maybe when Park gets home I'll ask if he'll take me to get some ice cream and then I can truly wallow around in self-pity.

I grab my phone and try calling Mom again, but it goes straight to voicemail as if her phone isn't even turned on.

I don't remember what the five stages of grief are, but pretty soon I sit up in bed and feel nothing but pissed off.

How can I just sit here and cry about some stupid boy? What is wrong with me?

I throw the covers off and I climb out of bed and walk over to the window, my hands clenched into fists at my sides. I am better than this, dammit.

You know what? I deserve an explanation. I should walk right up to Jett's stupid gorgeous face and ask him why he told me all those lies about wanting me when really he's still dating other girls.

I'm sure he'll just tell me another lie, but it'll be pretty awesome to watch him squirm.

Yeah.

I swallow and straighten my shoulders, feeling braver by the second. I'll just go ask him. I deserve an answer. We're friends first, right?

I slip on my flip-flops and catch a glimpse in the vanity mirror. My hair is tussled and half wet, my makeup is all washed off and I'm wearing pajamas.

Oh well.

I'm going over there now.

The long walk between the Parks' backyard to Jett's house starts making me calm down. I start thinking maybe it was all some misunderstanding. I mean it could be, right?

I know the chances of him saying something that'll make me feel better are slim, but I figure Jett at least owes me an explanation.

I cut through the Track's parking lot on my way to Jett's house and there are still a few people in the parking lot which makes me a little insecure about my clothing. But screw what everyone else thinks. I need to find Jett and get an explanation from him. At the very least, maybe he'll apologize.

A car door opens as I'm walking past it and someone steps out. "Man," a girl's voice says, "I am exhausted."

I turn to the right and see the same blonde girl who was talking to Jett on the bleachers. Her hair is tousled and her lip gloss smeared off.

I keep walking.

"Wait," she says, walking up to me. "Are you going to see Jett?"

Before I can say anything, she gives me this lopsided smile, like she's about to confess to a crime. "You might wanna wait a little bit," she says, giggling. "You're that other girl he's sleeping with, right?"

Again she doesn't wait for my reply, not that I can think of one right now if I wanted to. She clutches her chest and gets this dreamy look in her eyes as she gazes off into the distance. "We just hooked up a few minutes ago so if you're looking to get laid, too, you might want to wait a bit." She touches my arm like we're friends and gives me a wink. "Let him get his energy back, sweetie."

And then she turns and gets back into her car, waving at me while she drives away. I'm stuck in the middle of the parking lot, wondering what the hell just happened.

Jett just hooked up with her? He'd said sex wasn't everything and that he wanted to wait with me. My jaw clenches. I guess waiting is easier when you're sleeping with someone else.

I swallow the lump in my throat and turn around. There's a hollow pain in my chest and I tell myself to ignore it. There's really no point in talking to him now. No explanation for him to give me. He's sleeping with that girl and he's stringing me along as well.

I make it all the way back home and I haven't cried yet. I tell myself I am strong and that I'll get over this.

And then I turn off my phone and crawl back into bed.

CHAPTER TWENTY-FOUR

Jett

Keanna never meets me on the bleachers and after another fifteen minutes of waiting around, I go look for her in the office. The door is locked and the lights are off so I press my face to the glass but the front desk is empty. I pull out my phone and text her, letting her know I'm going to shower so she should meet me at my house.

I put my bike back into the storage garage and hang up my helmet.

The overbearing scent of Emma's perfume hits me as I'm closing the garage door. I draw in a deep breath and turn around.

"What?" I ask.

She stands there, arms crossed over her chest, pouting at me. I think she thinks that look makes her attractive but really it's annoying as hell. I like a fun, playful girl. Not a whiney princess bitch.

She cocks her head to the side. "Jett, we should talk."

I step around her. "There's really nothing to talk about."

"Yes there is, oh my god why are you such a jerk?" She rushes to catch up to me and her voice seems to echo loudly in this narrow hallway between all the dirt bike storage rooms. It's like a storage facility but with narrow stalls where people keep their bikes and the last thing I need is for a client or their parents to see the track owner's son back here with a pissed off girl.

I fold my arms over my chest and glare at her. "I thought I made it clear that you and me are done. Why are you still here?"

"Look, I'm sorry I got upset about your new girl, but I realized I'm cool with it, okay? You can have both of us." She grins like she's the greatest thing in the world and then bats her eyelashes at me. "See? I'm not unreasonable. I'm happy to share you. After all, it's no strings attached, right?"

Damn, I almost feel sorry for her. She's so desperate it's sad. I know a ton of guys who would be happy to date her. I'm about to tell her that when she launches forward, throwing her arms around my neck. She slams her lips into mine, forcefully trying to make me kiss her back.

I grab her hands and pull them off my neck, keeping my mouth stiff and unresponsive to her surprise make out attack.

"Dude," I say, trying to peel her off me.

She gives me this seductive look and grins, then reaches for my crotch.

"You know you want me," she purrs, lifting up on her toes to lick my neck.

I'm not trying to hurt a girl but I shove her off, holding her by the shoulder so she can't get any closer to me. "You're getting a little too desperate, Emma," I say, trying like hell to keep my voice down since everything echoes in here. "I don't want it to come to this, but if you don't leave me the hell alone, I'm going to call the cops on you."

She huffs and tries to flip her hair over her shoulder like she always does, only now it's all messed up and not nearly as smooth as before.

"You'll be back," she hisses. She turns on her heel and heads toward the parking lot leaving me wondering what the hell just happened.

I mean I guess I should feel like some kind of awesome guy who is so desirable it makes girls go crazy, but really this is just creepy. Now I'm starting to wonder if Emma has the capability to try to harm me, or worse, Keanna.

I take deep breaths as I walk in the opposite direction, back to my house. I'll have to explain all of this drama to Keanna soon, before Emma does something even worse.

All I wanted tonight was a fun night with my girl on the lake, introducing her to my friends and showing her off like the angel that she is.

As I shower and get dressed, I tell myself to put thoughts of Emma away for now. I'll explain it all to Keanna later. But tonight I just want to hang out with my girl.

KEANNA DOESN'T REPLY TO MY TEXT BY THE TIME I'M READY, SO I CALL HER. IT GOES straight to voicemail. I smile because she probably forgot to charge her phone again. I can't even begin to explain how refreshing it is to be with a girl who isn't attached to her phone like it's some kind of vital body part.

I hop in my truck and head over to Park's house. His truck is still at the Track so he's probably still working. Dad had come home on time and now he's going on a dinner date with Mom.

Knowing that our house will be empty tonight kind of makes me want to bail on the lake party and take Keanna back to my room instead.

I let myself into the house and head to her bedroom. The door is closed so I knock.

"Key?" I say, leaning against the door frame. "Are you ready for an awesome night on the lake?"

She doesn't reply so I tap on the door again. "Did you fall asleep? Are you naked? Because I'm coming in."

The door swings open so quickly it makes me jump back. Keanna is in pajamas and she's glaring at me like I'm a serial killer. "What the hell do you want?" she snaps.

"Whoa." I try to walk into her room but she blocks the door, her fingers turning white on the door frame. "Key, what's wrong?"

"Don't call me that," she says, her jaw clenched. "And if you came over here to get laid for the second time today, you can forget it, okay? I'm not into getting STDs."

"Whoa, okay. What the hell is this about? What happened to my normal girlfriend?"

"I am *not* your girlfriend." She tries to close the door again but I hold out my arm and keep it open.

"Keanna, please talk to me. Why the sudden change? I thought things were good between us."

She looks up toward the ceiling and then shakes her head. "Look. You and Emma can do whatever you want but I'm done being your summer fling, okay? I'm just done."

"Key, I didn't do anything with Emma. I haven't done anything with her since that day you saw us in the closet."

She rolls her eyes. "I thought you didn't lie to me, remember?"

I swallow. "I'm not lying."

"So you weren't the one who got her hair all ruffled up a few minutes ago?"

I falter, because yeah, I was, but it's not like she thinks it is. Also, my fears are now confirmed: Emma got to Keanna before I did. My shoulders fall. "I can explain."

I probably shouldn't have said those words. She slams the door in my face and locks it before I can get it back open. "Keanna," I call out, leaning my forehead against the door.

I can see her shadow at the bottom of the door, so I know she's still standing right there on the other side. "It's not what it looks like," I say. "She came on to me and I turned her away."

"Right, that makes sense," Keanna says through the door. "And that explains why you wanted to wait with me. I mean why bother sleeping with me when you're sleeping with her already, right? I guess I was just your make out buddy when she was busy."

"That's not it at all," I say. Leaning into the door as if I could somehow slip through it and be on the other side. "Please open the door and talk to me."

"No."

"Please, Keanna."

"Stop saying my name. Look Jett, I don't want to be friends anymore. I thought I could handle being your fling but then you said all those lies about liking me as more than a fling. It's my fault for believing it, I guess. Just go away."

I watch her shadow fade away from the door and I sigh. "Please open the door. I'll explain everything. Then you can hate me if you still want to but please just let me talk to you."

She's quiet for a moment. "Have you had sex with Emma?" she finally asks.

My chest constricts. The truth is supposed to set you free but all it does is dig me deeper into this hole. I want to lie, I want to say no and make her like me again. But I promised I wouldn't lie to this girl and even if she hates me, I won't break my word.

I press hands against the door.

"Yeah. But it's been a long time."

"That's all I need to know," she says, her voice sounding soft and far away. "Don't ever talk to me again, Jett. We're done."

CHAPTER TWENTY-FIVE

Keanna

My pillow fills up with tears. There are so many of them, so many painful drops that I didn't know I was capable of crying. I never cry. Maybe when I fell and hurt myself as a kid, but crying over physical pain isn't nearly as earth-shattering as crying from a broken heart. This is way worse. I'd take a million broken bones over the pain in my heart right now.

Why did I fall so hard for this boy?

Part of me really wanted to let him inside and hear what he had to say. I'm not sure what he *could* have said that would have made any difference, but I wasn't quite ready to send him away. I did, though. I kept my dignity and I was stronger than I've ever been. I made Jett leave and now I'll never talk to him again.

I turn on my phone and call Mom's number. She doesn't answer, so I call back again and again. I can never bring myself to leave her a message though. I've been wanting to tell her about my new phone number, send her a text and tell her to call me back at this number. Maybe even tell her I have a job and that we can settle down here. But something keeps stopping me from admitting that I have a phone now. Deep down, I'm afraid that if Mom knows I'm being taken care of here, that I have my own phone and everything, that she'll stay gone longer. So I hang up and never leave a message. I hope she'll start to worry about me, or want to check in. She may be an artist who loves to travel the world, but she's still a mom. Moms have that motherly intuition, right?

And even though it's kind of implausible, I am still holding onto the hope that Mom fell and hit her head and she's in some recovery room waiting for her memories to come back.

Maybe she'll show up soon and take me away and we can go back to our normal lives. I don't want to be here anymore. I don't want to be reminded of the boy who broke my heart and made me feel like the biggest idiot in the world for falling for him.

Sure, my life with Mom was shitty.

But at least my heart wasn't broken.

CHAPTER TWENTY-SIX

Jett

I chug the beer in a few seconds, then crunch the can in my fist and toss it toward the old plastic trashcan. "Hand me another one, will you?" I call out to whoever wants to comply.

The air smells like bonfire and cigarettes and D'andre's lawn chairs in the sand make a perfect place to sit and forget about everything that's gone wrong in my life.

Someone hands me another beer. A girl, I think, and I take it and pop open the top, chugging as quickly as my body will allow. I know I should thank this beer deliverer, but I don't really care. I don't care about anything right now, especially something as stupid as politeness.

All around me people are having a blast. It's a lake party after all. Music is bumping and the bonfire is roaring, warming up the cool night air. Girls squeal in the lake when guys splash them and camera flashes go off every few seconds.

I don't care about any of it.

I'd driven out here after Keanna kicked me out of her life. I had nowhere else to go, except maybe home but home was the last place I needed to be. My parents were out on a date and the house is too big and too empty. I needed to clear my head and fill it up all at once. I needed a distraction.

So I came here.

The third beer goes down easily, and I find the ice chest next to me so I reach in for another one. I can't seem to drink it fast enough. I just need the buzz, the sweet dizzying feeling of being carried away from it all. The girl I love kicked me out of her life, all because of my past. My stupid ass choice to sleep with some girl I didn't even like. It's ruined everything.

"Dude," D'andre says, dragging a lawn chair across the sand to sit next to me. "You look like shit."

"You just noticed that?" I say with a snort.

"Kind of, yeah. I've been chatting up Brittany. I think she's into me but she has a ten o'clock curfew so she had to leave."

I nod and down some more alcohol. "Cool."

"Man, what happened to you?" he says, leaning forward to put his elbows on his knees while he studies me.

I shrug. Drink some more.

"The girl?" D'andre guesses.

I nod.

"What happened?"

I crunch the beer can and reach for another one. A girl in a hot pink bikini is sitting on the ice chest so I touch her leg instead of the lid. "Oh," I say, seeing her there. "Sorry. I need a beer."

"Another one already?" she says, but she's being flirty, not judgmental.

"You gonna give it to me or should I move you and get it myself?"

Her eyes light up in this flirty way. The old me would have lit up too, jumped into the opportunity to hook up with a random cute chick. But the new me just wants another damn beer.

I hold out my hand and she gets up and grabs another can from the ice chest. "Here ya go, sexy."

I nod. "Thanks."

D'andre is suddenly right next to my ear. "You should hit that," he whispers. "She obviously wants you."

I turn to look at him but he's kind of blurry. It's probably a mixture of being drunk and the shadows of the fire reflecting off his face, but he barely even looks like my friend right now.

"Maybe I will," I say.

The girl reaches over and slides her hand up my knee, resting it on my thigh. Had she heard all of that? I don't even know.

I look over at her and she smiles at me. "You're Jett Adams, right? Your dad's like really famous."

"*I'm* like really famous," I say, leaning in.

This makes her smile even wider and she scoots closer to me until she's sitting on the very edge of the ice chest. Both of her hands grab my leg. "You wanna get out of here?"

I'll admit, it crosses my mind.

But this girl isn't Keanna. She won't taste the same. She won't feel the same. She'll just be a warm body that leaves me feeling colder than before. Even drunk me knows that.

I lick my lips and lean closer to her, bringing my mouth to her ear. "You don't want to do that," I whisper.

She presses her forehead to mine. "Yes I do," she says, squeezing my thigh. "Believe me, I do."

I stand. "I gotta take a leak."

"I'll be here," she says, waving at me. I turn and walk back toward my truck, which is parked at the end of the sandbar, near the tree line.

I don't really have to piss, I just needed to get out of there. Maybe I'll become a monk for the rest of my life, because hooking up with a girl who isn't Keanna doesn't appeal to me at all.

My phone vibrates in my pocket and I reach for it, hoping to god that it's Keanna and that she's changed her mind and wants to talk. The phone falls straight out of my hand and sinks into the sand. I grab it and blow off the dirt. It's a text from a number I don't have saved.

But those numbers in that order look pretty damn familiar.

Who is this?

My vision is blurred and my typing sucks but I manage to reply: *Who is this?*

I draw in a breath of warm summer air and lean my back against my truck as I gaze up at the sky. The stars are bright and beautiful way out here and I wish I could reach up and knock them all out of the way. They're too pretty for a night this shitty.

My phone beeps again.

Do you know Keanna?

I grit my teeth. Why does this number seem so familiar? It's not her number, I have that memorized and saved in my phone. In my drunken daze, the only assumption I can come up with is that this is some guy who wants her. Someone trying to take my girl from me.

I type back: *This is her boyfriend.*

If he wants her, he can go through me first.

The anonymous person takes a long time to reply. I've almost dozed off while standing against my truck and when the phone vibrates again, I startle.

Great. I'm glad she has you. Tell her I won't be coming back. I have an opportunity in Spain and I had to take it. She's almost eighteen anyway so she's practically already an adult.

An overwhelming feeling of doom crashes into me. This can't be right. Her freaking mother wouldn't do this to her only child. Right?

I type back: *tell her yourself.*

Followed by: *wtf is wrong with you?*

The reply is nearly instant. *Can't. Don't want her to be mad at me. Tell her I love her. Bye.*

I swallow but my throat is as dry as the sand beneath my bare feet.

Keanna's mom just left her for good and made me become the bad guy who has to tell her. I *need* to tell her though. She may hate me, but I love her and she needs to know.

She needs to know right now.

I pop open my truck door and climb inside, not even bothering to kick off the sand from my feet. I don't even know where my shoes are but I don't care. I grab the keys from the cup holder and start my truck. Then I look ahead and another sinking feeling overtakes me.

I can't drive.

I'm so drunk I can't even read the fuel gauge.

Dammit, Jett.

I lower my head to the steering wheel. I need to get to her. I need to talk to her. I try calling her phone but it's off, just like it has been all night.

Ah, crap.
As my phone glows in the dark cab of my truck, I realize what I have to do.
The phone rings a few times and then he answers.
"Dad?" I say with a heavy sigh. "I'm at the lake. I need you to come get me."

CHAPTER TWENTY-SEVEN

Keanna

When I've cried so much that no more tears come out, I end up curled up in bed, the TV idly on but there's nothing worth watching on a night like tonight. I don't think I could be more annoyed with myself than I am right now. *Get it together, Keanna.*

How could I have let a stupid guy hurt me so badly? What makes it even more embarrassing is that I knew what I was getting into from the start.

I heave a heavy sigh that makes the empty feeling in my chest feel better for only a split second and then I pull the comforter up to my chin. The sun has long since set, leaving me in the wake of dark, cold night.

Becca is gone, my mom won't answer her phone, and although Park had knocked on my door earlier to tell me that he'd ordered pizza, I didn't eat anything.

I'd told him I had a stomach ache so he'd leave me alone. And now, ironically, my stomach does hurt because I haven't eaten anything all day.

I think about venturing down to the kitchen to find something to eat, but the second I look at myself in the vanity mirror, I know that's not a good idea. My eyes are swollen, all red from crying all night. Now I get what people mean when they say they have bags under their eyes.

I don't want Park to see me like this. He'd immediately know that I didn't just have a stomach ache and he'd probably ask what's wrong. The last thing I want to do on a day like this is explain my broken heart to the guy whose house I've been using like a hotel.

Or, more like a homeless shelter.

With a groan, I roll over and face the window, holding on to the comforter like a security blanket.

The bright beam of headlights turns off the road and into the driveway, shining right into my eyes. My heartbeat quickens. Is Mom finally back?

I throw off the sheets and run to the window, my heart thudding with anticipation.

Then I catch the Chevy logo and my chest deflates. It's just Jace's dad's truck. My shoulders fall and I walk back to the bed, tucking myself in like all the blankets might protect me from more than just the cold.

I hear the truck door close and then the lights flash through my window as the truck retreats down the driveway.

A few moments later, there's a knock at my door.

"I'm sleeping," I call out, closing my eyes like that'll convince Park on the other side of the door.

The door softly opens and I squeeze my eyes tighter. Someone sits on the edge of my bed and I stiffen. That's not something Park would do.

"Hey."

The voice is soft, tentative. Like he thinks I might throw an atom bomb his way. And I probably should think about violence but instead all I can do is melt inside. A tear rolls down my cheek.

"Can I talk to you?" Jett asks.

I shrug, keeping my body facing away from him on the bed. "Looks like you're already talking to me."

"Yeah but I want to talk to your face," he says. His fingers slide along my back and I lean into his touch, completely overtaken by my feelings for him.

Damn.

With a huff, I roll over and face him. He's sitting in the middle of the bed, his eyes glazed and hair messy. He smells like bonfire and beer, and this sudden realization brings a bad feeling to my stomach.

"Why are you here?"

"I need to talk to you and I want you to listen and try not to totally hate me for the time being, okay?"

Only his words are all slurred and barely make any sense. I sit up in bed, wishing I could look anywhere else but into his gorgeous eyes right now.

"What do you want?"

He holds up a finger. "First, I want to do something." I watch curiously as he takes out his cell phone and the glow of the screen lights up my room. His thumb slides across the screen and his eyes meet mine. "Just stay quiet, and listen, okay?"

I lift an eyebrow, still not totally sure why I'm even allowing him to stay in here. "Okay, I guess."

He calls someone and puts the phone on speaker. We stare at each other while the phone rings. After a few awkward seconds, a girl answers.

My heart sinks. I recognize the voice the second she says, "Hey there."

"Emma," Jett says. He holds up a finger to me as if to say he's sorry for what he has to do. "Listen, I've been thinking we should get together."

"I knew you'd come around," she purrs.

My stomach tightens and I feel like I could puke even though I haven't eaten anything in hours. I give Jett this wide-eyed look and mouth the words, *are you serious?*

Is he seriously talking to this girl in front of me?

"I can't remember the last time we hooked up," Jett says, staring at me the whole time he says it. "I mean, you ambushed me today and I shoved you away, of course."

"Yeah, like a freaking jackass," Emma says. "But I forgive you. I'm free now if you want to come over."

"Tell me real quick. When did we hook up last? I can't remember." Jett holds out the phone, as if making it a few inches closer to me will make me understand her reply any better.

She sighs. "I don't know, like a few months, I guess? Why does it matter? Let's hook up now."

Jett's face twists into a sinister grin. "It matters because you're on speakerphone and I had to make sure you'd admit that we never did anything today. Now my girlfriend can be sure of that."

"What the hell?" she shrieks.

Jett smiles at the phone. "Don't ever talk to me again."

And then he hangs up and drops the phone on the bed between us.

"What the hell was that?" I say, shocked when I hear the excitement in my voice.

He reaches for my hand and I let him take it. "I needed you to believe me. I didn't hook up with Emma today. Not since I met you. I need you to know that."

I draw in a shaking breath. Relief settles over me in waves. First, the sight of him here next to me, even though I was mad at him just moments ago has healed my heart more than all of that crying did. And now he's pretty much proven that he wasn't lying to me earlier. That Emma's jealous bitch routine had worked, making me run away from the guy I care about.

I stare at our hands as they rest on the bed between us, his thumb running over my palm.

"Okay," I say. "I believe you. Thanks for that."

He blinks a few times and I realize he's trying really hard to sober up from how drunk he is. "How much have you had to drink?" I ask, reaching up and brushing his hair out of his eyes.

He closes his eyes and shakes his head. "Too much. I should have thought of this earlier. I needed you back so bad and I thought drinking would help but it didn't. And now my dad is pissed at me, but I had to call him. I had to get to you."

His chest sinks and he leans toward me. I wrap him up in my arms and we sink down to the bed together. I snuggle against his chest until I can feel the thundering of his heartbeat through his shirt.

He strokes my hair and I close my eyes and everything feels good. He takes a deep breath and lifts up on his elbow. "Babe." He lets out a slow breath and then sits all the way up on my bed, taking my hands in his. "We need to talk."

All of those feel-good feelings I'd had just a second ago disappear into the darkness. My heart pounds and whatever he's about to tell me, I know it's not as simple as the Emma thing.

"What is it?" I say, my voice barely a whisper.

His forehead creases in pain. He squeezes my hands. "It's about your mom."

CHAPTER TWENTY-EIGHT

Jett

She is so beautiful. I love this girl. I love her with all of my heart and I can't tell her that right now. It's totally not the time. And seeing as how I've never told anyone I love them, I'm not sure when it is the time for a thing that powerful. I'm confident that I'll figure it out though.

I want this girl for the rest of my life. I don't care that I'm not even out of high school yet. I know what I want and I'll make sure to keep her happy for as long as she'll let me.

I brush her hair behind her eyes, cupping her chin in my hand. This will be the hardest thing ever, but she has to know.

As much as I want to kiss her and tell her a joke to make her smile, I can't keep this from her anymore.

I try to swallow back the effects of the alcohol and I pray that the right words will come to me as I hold her hand and meet her gaze.

"I got a text from your mom."

Her eyes light up. "Are you serious? What'd she say? Let me call her."

She reaches for my phone but I cover it with my hand. "This isn't easy for me to tell you but, let me talk to you before you look at the texts."

I want to soften the blow somehow, and I'm not even sure that's possible. Keanna's expression is one of total trust and it kills me that I have to tell her something so life-shattering.

"She said she's going to Spain," I begin.

Keanna's eyebrows draw together. "Is she coming to get me?"

I shake my head. I can feel her heart break.

"What else did she say?" Keanna's voice is soft, on the verge of breaking. I can't see her cry. It'll kill me if she starts crying.

I try to smile. "I don't know, I guess she thinks that since you're almost eighteen that you can take care of yourself, so . . ."

"So she left me," Keanna says as tears fill her eyes. She looks down at the bed, at my hand covering my phone to shield her from the coldness of her mother's texts.

I nod. "I'm so sorry."

"I know." Her breath hitches and I dive across the bed, wrapping her in my arms as I hold her close to my chest. Nothing is more sobering than seeing the girl you love crying and knowing you can't make it better.

"But I talked to my dad," I say, holding her tightly as I run my fingers through her hair. "He said you still have your job at the Track and that you can come stay with us if Becca and Park don't want you to stay, but they probably will. They're really nice people and they don't mind that you're here." I keep talking, telling her all about my plans to make this better for her, to lessen the pain and fear of the unknown. "It'll be okay, Keanna."

She sobs into my chest, soaking my shirt with her tears and I just keep holding her.

When I get home, I'll have hell to pay for getting wasted at the lake, but after I'd explained everything to my dad, he'd told me to stay here as long as it takes to make her feel better.

My parents are awesome like that. They know that some things in life are important, and this was one of them.

After a long moment, Keanna turns to the side and plays with the hem of my shirt. I keep my arms around her, my chin resting on top of her head. "Did she say anything else?" she asks.

I swallow the lump in my throat. "She said she loves you."

This gets a snort of sarcastic laughter from her. "Yeah, sure she does. I can't believe she would do this."

"You have me," I say kissing the top of her head. "And you have Becca and Park and my parents, too. We're all here for you. My parents really like you and they're glad that we're together." The moment I say the words I realize the deeper meaning behind them and stiffen. "Well, I mean . . . if you want to be with me, officially. It's no pressure."

She looks up, her tear-filled eyes meeting mine in the darkness.

Overwhelmed with my feelings for her, I can't help myself when I lean down and press a soft kiss to her lips. She kisses me back, her arms squeezing tightly around my stomach. I lean my forehead against hers and take slow breaths. My feelings for this girl are so strong, I worry that my heart may explode inside my chest.

"I love you," I whisper, hoping that this is the right time. That she won't rebuke me, or laugh, or say that she has no feelings for me.

She blinks and then her soft lips kiss mine. "I love you, Jett."

My whole world changes in that instant. The air seems sweeter, the temperature somehow perfect. My entire body is warm and in love and there is no pain and no single thing on this earth that could harm what we have in this very moment.

I can't help but smile as I hold her in my arms. "Everything is going to be okay," I tell her.

She nods. "I know. I believe you."

Thank you for reading Believe in Me! When Keanna's new guardians register her for high school, she realizes there's more to real life than hanging out with your hot boyfriend all day. School sucks, the people are mean, and no one thinks she's good enough for Jett.

Next in this series: Believe in Us

Read an excerpt below:

Believe in Us

Chapter One

Keanna

SHOPPING ON A WEEKDAY IS THE GREATEST THING EVER. ESPECIALLY AT ONE IN THE afternoon when most people are at work. The lines are short and the stores have great sales. It's Tuesday and the mall is nearly empty so Jett and I have circled around it twice already. Each time I find something new to try on, play with, or buy.

I glance over at my boyfriend as we walk toward The Gap.

Okay, I might be going a little overboard. The poor guy is holding six shopping bags in one hand and a big yellow pillow with an emoji face on it in the other hand. Jett wanted to get the poop emoji pillow. I mean, really? I shot down that idea and bought the obvious choice: the two hearts for eyes emoji pillow. It's adorable and snuggly and it was on sale for five bucks so I had to have it.

Of course, Jett whined about the poop emoji so much that I kind of want to sneak back up here and buy it for him one day. I don't exactly have a car though, so I can only go places with Jett or Becca. It's too bad his birthday isn't until December because I'll probably forget about the stupid pillow by then.

"I'm hungry," Jett says, bumping into me with his shoulder. "Does the crazy shop-a-holic want to take a break and get some cheese fries?"

I roll my eyes. "I am *so* not a shop-a-holic. This is well deserved! Your mom even said so."

Hell, she'd given me fifty bucks this morning when I told her we were going shopping for clothes. I believe her exact words were, *"Honey, you need some clothes. I love you and all, but yeah."*

I've been officially living in Lawson for two? Months now and most of those months involved me living out of a suitcase, getting by with hand-me-downs from Becca and stolen shirts from Jett.

Of course, Jett's shirts are my favorite. But I still need my own stuff. Hence, the epic shopping trip. I've got two months of pay from working at The Track saved up and I'm blowing at least half of it today. Who cares about frivolity? It's fun!

A sparkly tank top catches my attention from the mannequin in front of Forever 21. "Ooh!" I say, wandering over to it.

Jett leans over and whispers into my ear. "Cheese fries." He draws out the words so he sounds like some kind of cheese fry-addicted ghost.

I laugh. "Okay, okay, fatty. Let's go get you fed."

"Mmmmm, food." Jett pats his stomach as if it's a hell of a lot fatter than it really is. In reality he's got a sexy six-pack that he works every single day to maintain. (Sometimes it's annoying how much time he spends in the gym, but I don't tell him that.) We order two large trays of the best thing in the food court: Extreme Fries. They're curly fries covered in melted cheese, ranch dressing, bacon bits and jalapenos. I let Jett eat all of the jalapenos because I'm not a fan of spicy things.

"I'm not sure this counts as a real meal," I say, stabbing into a cheesy fry with a plastic fork. "I can totally hear your dad now, talking about how you need to eat balanced meals to become a pro racer."

Jett licks cheese off his fingers and leans in, giving me a quick kiss. He gestures toward the trays of fries. "This is totally a complete meal. We have potatoes, which are a vegetable. Bacon bits, that's totally protein, and it's a really good protein because of healthy fats . . ." He gives me a wink and continues, "And cheese. That's dairy. Dairy is good for you. Strong bones and all of that."

I laugh and stab into another fry. Unlike Jett's grab-it-with-your-fingers approach, I like to keep a little dignity while eating in public. "I should probably stop eating so much junk with you. I'll get fat. I can't believe I had to buy a bigger size pair of jeans today."

I crinkle my nose. Jett pokes me in the arm with a fry, that luckily doesn't have cheese on the end of it. "Babe you're totally hot. You're even hotter now." He takes a bite of the fry and his eyes travel down my body. "You were a little *too* thin when I first met you. So whatever you're doing is working."

I snort as an uneasy feeling settles over me. "You mean eating normal food? That's what I'm doing now."

Now that Jett and I are closer, I don't mind sharing certain parts of my life with him. It had taken a while for me to open up, especially about my shady past with Dawn, but now that I have, it's like I can't ever go back. I reach for another fry and feel Jett's eyes on me. "I hardly ever ate when I was with Dawn." I punch him in the arm. "But you can't point out that I'm fat now, Jett! I'm a *girl*, you can't do that!"

"I never said you were fat, you dork. You're hot. You were hot when I met you and you're hot now. You're hotter now, because I think you look better with some meat on your bones."

I let out a long groan. "Babe! You can't say that!"

He laughs. "Yeah, I realized as soon as I said the word *meat* that I probably shouldn't say that to a girl." He holds up his hands as if in surrender. "Okay, how is this?" He looks me in the eyes with his dark blues and it sends a shiver down my spine. "Keanna, you are the most beautiful girl I've ever seen."

I swallow. Whoa.

"Um, thanks," I mumble, turning my attention back to the food. "Seriously though, I need to stop eating the same crap you do. I do *not* want to buy another bigger pair of jeans in a month."

Jett takes a sip of the large soda we're sharing. "My mom told me something once. We were talking about girlfriends and stuff and she told me about the time she knew that my dad was her soul mate and that she wanted to be with him forever."

My eyes widen. "Oh yeah? Do tell." Jett's parents are the picture perfect example of a flawless marriage. I confidently believe that if every couple on earth loved each other as much as they do, then there would be no war, no divorce or custody battles. There'd be no problems at all.

Jett takes another sip of our drink. "Apparently my mom got fat when she was pregnant with me and she was like freaking out about it." He points a fry at me. "Much like you're freaking out now."

I roll my eyes and he continues. "And I guess my dad had taken her to California to meet my grandparents or something, and she said that at one point he told her he'd love her no matter what, even if she stayed fat or got fatter." He shrugs and eats another fry. "Which is kind of silly because you women are all obsessed with what you look like, but whatever. My mom said that and she knew right then that he was her soul mate and that she could be happy with him forever. When she told me that story, I thought it was—well, you know—dumb, but I guess it makes sense."

"Of course it makes sense," I say, gazing out at the crowd of mall shoppers.

Jett shakes his head. "What I'm saying here is that I understand what my dad meant now. Nothing you can do, short of cheating on me, or like, becoming a serial killer or something, would make me lo—care about you any less."

My heart catches in my throat. Was he about to say *love*? I choke out my reply. "Um, thanks. Same here . . . don't become a serial killer."

He grins and nods toward the half-eaten fries. "Be who you are and don't worry about gaining a few pounds. I mean, who cares? I don't."

"Let's change the subject to something that doesn't make me feel so self-conscious, okay?"

"You're so cute," Jett says with a mouthful of food. "I love everything about you. Even how you think that having serious conversations aren't fun."

"Good, because you're stuck with me," I say, trying to be all light-hearted. In reality, joking around like this terrifies me because I never know if Jett and I will actually be together forever. I just really, really hope we are, but hopes and dreams don't mean anything in reality.

"No, you're stuck with me," Jett says. He leans over and kisses the top of my head and a cloud of his cologne fills my lungs. Even though I spray it on the shirts I steal from his closet to wear to sleep, I don't think I'll ever get tired of the intoxicating scent of him.

"So what else should we talk about?" Jett asks, straightening back up in his chair. The cologne smell goes away and I instantly miss it, but I'm not going to crawl into his lap in the middle of the food court. "School is starting in a few weeks."

I make a gagging sound. "Ugh, no. I don't want to talk about that."

He laughs. "Have you registered yet?"

Since I'm pretty much stuck here for the foreseeable future because my mom has moved to a different country and completely abandoned me, the only logical next step is that I finish out my senior year of high school here in Lawson. Becca has been talking about it lately but I've been trying to avoid the conversation at all costs.

"The other day, Becca said I could look into homeschooling if I wanted," I say, recalling our talk at work last week. "Apparently there's internet programs where you can kind of teach yourself everything."

Jett's brows draw together and his lip curls up. "Ew, no. Don't do that."

I give him a sideways glance. "Why not?"

"Because then you'll be home all day instead of at school with me," he says as if it were obvious.

"You'll be a junior and I'll be a senior so we probably won't see each other."

He shakes his head. "Not true. Have you seen Lawson High School? There's like ten people there. We'll have the same lunch and we can get the same electives and you can ride with me to school, too. It'll be awesome."

"It'll be *school*," I say, pronouncing the last word as if it were a curse. "I've been to dozens of schools in my life and they've all sucked. I get made fun of for not knowing anyone or not knowing how to do anything in the stupid school. My clothes get ragged on for being old and worn out, I—"

Jett stops me with a sharp look. "Babe, that was all in the past. You know people now. You know me, and Jacey will totally be your friend, too. Most of the guys at the track aren't in this school district but a few of them are." He points to the heap of shopping bags on the other side of our table. "And no one can make fun of your clothes anymore."

"Okay, you're right about the clothes," I say.

"And Jacey," he says. I nod reluctantly. It's a little weird that a girl my boyfriend used to make out with for fun is now kind of my friend. She is really nice though, and now she has her own boyfriend that she's head over heels for so it all kind of works out. I'm still not about to call her my bestie or anything.

I sink my chin in my hand. "I don't know. It's still scary. You've been at the same school your whole life, right?"

"Yeah," he says with a little nod. "It *is* easier going back since I know literally everyone. Plus, some of the teachers used to teach my mom and Becca. They don't ever let me forget that, either."

"I know you and maybe a few more people." I give a little exaggerated shudder. "School is not fun for me. It's always scary as hell."

He wraps an arm around my shoulders and gives me a squeeze. "It'll be okay. I'll make sure you have an awesome time. And if anyone tries to be the least bit rude to you, I'll kick their ass."

I smile and reach for another fry. "I don't need a knight in shining armor, Jett."

"Then what do you need?" he asks. There's genuine concern behind his eyes.

I consider it for a moment. "I can take care of myself. But I'd like it if you have my back."

Jett peers at me, a sense of pride in his features. His arm is still around me and he squeezes my shoulders. "Always."

BELIEVE IN US

A BELIEVE IN LOVE NOVEL

CHAPTER ONE

Keanna

Shopping on a weekday is the greatest thing ever. Especially at one in the afternoon when most people are at work. The lines are short and the stores have great sales. It's Tuesday and the mall is nearly empty so Jett and I have circled around it twice already. Each time I find something new to try on, play with, or buy.

I glance over at my boyfriend as we walk toward The Gap.

Okay, I might be going a little overboard. The poor guy is holding six shopping bags in one hand and a big yellow pillow with an emoji face on it in the other hand. Jett wanted to get the poop emoji pillow. I mean, really? I shot down that idea and bought the obvious choice: the two hearts for eyes emoji pillow. It's adorable and snuggly and it was on sale for five bucks so I had to have it.

Of course, Jett whined about the poop emoji so much that I kind of want to sneak back up here and buy it for him one day. I don't exactly have a car though, so I can only go places with Jett or Becca. It's too bad his birthday isn't until December because I'll probably forget about the stupid pillow by then.

"I'm hungry," Jett says, bumping into me with his shoulder. "Does the crazy shop-a-holic want to take a break and get some cheese fries?"

I roll my eyes. "I am *so* not a shop-a-holic. This is well deserved! Your mom even said so."

Hell, she'd given me fifty bucks this morning when I told her we were going shopping for clothes. I believe her exact words were, *"Honey, you need some clothes. I love you and all, but yeah."*

I've been officially living in Lawson for two? Months now and most of those months involved me living out of a suitcase, getting by with hand-me-downs from Becca and stolen shirts from Jett.

Of course, Jett's shirts are my favorite. But I still need my own stuff. Hence, the epic shopping trip. I've got two months of pay from working at The Track saved up and I'm blowing at least half of it today. Who cares about frivolity? It's fun!

A sparkly tank top catches my attention from the mannequin in front of Forever 21. "Ooh!" I say, wandering over to it.

Jett leans over and whispers into my ear. "Cheese fries." He draws out the words so he sounds like some kind of cheese fry-addicted ghost.

I laugh. "Okay, okay, fatty. Let's go get you fed."

"Mmmmm, food." Jett pats his stomach as if it's a hell of a lot fatter than it really is. In reality he's got a sexy six-pack that he works every single day to maintain. (Sometimes it's annoying how much time he spends in the gym, but I don't tell him that.) We order two large trays of the best thing in the food court: Extreme Fries. They're curly fries covered in melted cheese, ranch dressing, bacon bits and jalapenos. I let Jett eat all of the jalapenos because I'm not a fan of spicy things.

"I'm not sure this counts as a real meal," I say, stabbing into a cheesy fry with a plastic fork. "I can totally hear your dad now, talking about how you need to eat balanced meals to become a pro racer."

Jett licks cheese off his fingers and leans in, giving me a quick kiss. He gestures toward the trays of fries. "This is totally a complete meal. We have potatoes, which are a vegetable. Bacon bits, that's totally protein, and it's a really good protein because of healthy fats . . ." He gives me a wink and continues, "And cheese. That's dairy. Dairy is good for you. Strong bones and all of that."

I laugh and stab into another fry. Unlike Jett's grab-it-with-your-fingers approach, I like to keep a little dignity while eating in public. "I should probably stop eating so much junk with you. I'll get fat. I can't believe I had to buy a bigger size pair of jeans today."

I crinkle my nose. Jett pokes me in the arm with a fry, that luckily doesn't have cheese on the end of it. "Babe you're totally hot. You're even hotter now." He takes a bite of the fry and his eyes travel down my body. "You were a little *too* thin when I first met you. So whatever you're doing is working."

I snort as an uneasy feeling settles over me. "You mean eating normal food? That's what I'm doing now."

Now that Jett and I are closer, I don't mind sharing certain parts of my life with him. It had taken a while for me to open up, especially about my shady past with Dawn, but now that I have, it's like I can't ever go back. I reach for another fry and feel Jett's eyes on me. "I hardly ever ate when I was with Dawn." I punch him in the arm. "But you can't point out that I'm fat now, Jett! I'm a *girl*, you can't do that!"

"I never said you were fat, you dork. You're hot. You were hot when I met you and you're hot now. You're hotter now, because I think you look better with some meat on your bones."

I let out a long groan. "Babe! You can't say that!"

He laughs. "Yeah, I realized as soon as I said the word *meat* that I probably shouldn't say that to a girl." He holds up his hands as if in surrender. "Okay, how is this?" He looks me in the eyes with his dark blues and it sends a shiver down my spine. "Keanna, you are the most beautiful girl I've ever seen."

I swallow. Whoa.

"Um, thanks," I mumble, turning my attention back to the food. "Seriously though, I need to stop eating the same crap you do. I do *not* want to buy another bigger pair of jeans in a month."

Jett takes a sip of the large soda we're sharing. "My mom told me something once. We were talking about girlfriends and stuff and she told me about the time she knew that my dad was her soul mate and that she wanted to be with him forever."

My eyes widen. "Oh yeah? Do tell." Jett's parents are the picture perfect example of a flawless marriage. I confidently believe that if every couple on earth loved each other as much as they do, then there would be no war, no divorce or custody battles. There'd be no problems at all.

Jett takes another sip of our drink. "Apparently my mom got fat when she was pregnant with me and she was like freaking out about it." He points a fry at me. "Much like you're freaking out now."

I roll my eyes and he continues. "And I guess my dad had taken her to California to meet my grandparents or something, and she said that at one point he told her he'd love her no matter what, even if she stayed fat or got fatter." He shrugs and eats another fry. "Which is kind of silly because you women are all obsessed with what you look like, but whatever. My mom said that and she knew right then that he was her soul mate and that she could be happy with him forever. When she told me that story, I thought it was—well, you know—dumb, but I guess it makes sense."

"Of course it makes sense," I say, gazing out at the crowd of mall shoppers.

Jett shakes his head. "What I'm saying here is that I understand what my dad meant now. Nothing you can do, short of cheating on me, or like, becoming a serial killer or something, would make me lo—care about you any less."

My heart catches in my throat. Was he about to say *love*? I choke out my reply. "Um, thanks. Same here . . . don't become a serial killer."

He grins and nods toward the half-eaten fries. "Be who you are and don't worry about gaining a few pounds. I mean, who cares? I don't."

"Let's change the subject to something that doesn't make me feel so self-conscious, okay?"

"You're so cute," Jett says with a mouthful of food. "I love everything about you. Even how you think that having serious conversations aren't fun."

"Good, because you're stuck with me," I say, trying to be all light-hearted. In reality, joking around like this terrifies me because I never know if Jett and I will actually be together forever. I just really, really hope we are, but hopes and dreams don't mean anything in reality.

"No, you're stuck with me," Jett says. He leans over and kisses the top of my head and a cloud of his cologne fills my lungs. Even though I spray it on the shirts I steal from his closet to wear to sleep, I don't think I'll ever get tired of the intoxicating scent of him.

"So what else should we talk about?" Jett asks, straightening back up in his chair. The cologne smell goes away and I instantly miss it, but I'm not going to crawl into his lap in the middle of the food court. "School is starting in a few weeks."

I make a gagging sound. "Ugh, no. I don't want to talk about that."

He laughs. "Have you registered yet?"

Since I'm pretty much stuck here for the foreseeable future because my mom has moved to a different country and completely abandoned me, the only logical next step is that I finish out my senior year of high school here in Lawson. Becca has been talking about it lately but I've been trying to avoid the conversation at all costs.

"The other day, Becca said I could look into homeschooling if I wanted," I say, recalling our talk at work last week. "Apparently there's internet programs where you can kind of teach yourself everything."

Jett's brows draw together and his lip curls up. "Ew, no. Don't do that."

I give him a sideways glance. "Why not?"

"Because then you'll be home all day instead of at school with me," he says as if it were obvious.

"You'll be a junior and I'll be a senior so we probably won't see each other."

He shakes his head. "Not true. Have you seen Lawson High School? There's like ten people there. We'll have the same lunch and we can get the same electives and you can ride with me to school, too. It'll be awesome."

"It'll be *school*," I say, pronouncing the last word as if it were a curse. "I've been to dozens of schools in my life and they've all sucked. I get made fun of for not knowing anyone or not knowing how to do anything in the stupid school. My clothes get ragged on for being old and worn out, I—"

Jett stops me with a sharp look. "Babe, that was all in the past. You know people now. You know me, and Jacey will totally be your friend, too. Most of the guys at the track aren't in this school district but a few of them are." He points to the heap of shopping bags on the other side of our table. "And no one can make fun of your clothes anymore."

"Okay, you're right about the clothes," I say.

"And Jacey," he says. I nod reluctantly. It's a little weird that a girl my boyfriend used to make out with for fun is now kind of my friend. She is really nice though, and now she has her own boyfriend that she's head over heels for so it all kind of works out. I'm still not about to call her my bestie or anything.

I sink my chin in my hand. "I don't know. It's still scary. You've been at the same school your whole life, right?"

"Yeah," he says with a little nod. "It *is* easier going back since I know literally everyone. Plus, some of the teachers used to teach my mom and Becca. They don't ever let me forget that, either."

"I know you and maybe a few more people." I give a little exaggerated shudder. "School is not fun for me. It's always scary as hell."

He wraps an arm around my shoulders and gives me a squeeze. "It'll be okay. I'll make sure you have an awesome time. And if anyone tries to be the least bit rude to you, I'll kick their ass."

I smile and reach for another fry. "I don't need a knight in shining armor, Jett."

"Then what do you need?" he asks. There's genuine concern behind his eyes.

I consider it for a moment. "I can take care of myself. But I'd like it if you have my back."

Jett peers at me, a sense of pride in his features. His arm is still around me and he squeezes my shoulders. "Always."

CHAPTER TWO

Jett

My stomach growls. I haven't eaten in over three hours and my body is now waging a war against me in the form of rumbling angry growls until I give it some food. Luckily, my parents and Park and Becca (my other parents) are grilling burgers tonight. It's kind of an unofficial Sunday night tradition that usually takes place at my house.

I throw on some shorts and a blue T-shirt and grab the pair of flip-flops by my door. Not only am I starving, I'm anxious to see Keanna wearing one of the new outfits she bought today. She's been making this slow transition ever since the day I met her. She used to be shy and reserved and a little bit mean. She's had a hard life and I never really know exactly *how* hard it was until her own mother made me tell her she wasn't coming back home. That was a rough night.

And it's been nearly two months since then and we still haven't brought it back up. Mom says it's for the best that we let Keanna work out her issues on her own time and that we should just be there to support her. Dad has similar advice for me. He's drilled it into my head that whenever she talks, I should just listen. I shouldn't try to fix everything for her, no matter how badly I want to.

Every day it's like she becomes more and more of the person she's supposed to be. She's no longer angry at the world, and she doesn't seem to keep so much from me anymore. Her new clothes mean a lot, I know. The way her eyes lit up when she tried on an outfit at the mall—it's like she's trying on a new self. And I love the way she smiles now—like she has something worth smiling for.

Everything she picked out made her look beautiful and I'm excited to see what she'll wear tonight. I'm not exactly a guy who cares what a girl wears, but when it makes her eyes light up and her smile a little bigger, then I'm all for it.

I take the back stairs that lead into the kitchen instead of the front grand staircase. I'm also texting Keanna to let her know I'm out of the shower, so my footsteps are slow to avoid falling down the stairs. Mom and Dad are talking in the kitchen and something Mom says makes me stop in my tracks.

" . . . drunk as hell tonight," she says, giggling. I lift an eyebrow. My parents don't exactly get *drunk as hell,* like ever. Dad chuckles and Mom says, "If I can't drink for the next nine months, I should fit it all in tonight."

My blood runs cold. Nine months? That could only mean . . . I take a step back up the stairs, making sure I'm out of their sight. I probably shouldn't be eavesdropping but this is just too good to walk away.

"It's actually ten months when you think about it," Dad says. "It's forty weeks and all that, which is ten months. Why do they always say nine?"

"Hell if I know," Mom says. "Can you hand me the margarita mix, babe?"

"Don't get too crazy on the drinks," Dad says. There's some shuffling sounds while he digs through the pantry. "Once you get a couple of drinks in you, you tend to pass out."

"Ugh, true," Mom says. Then she yells, "Jett! Keanna is here!"

The back door opens and my parents tell her hello and I quietly walk back up the stairs and then come jogging down them as if I'd only just left my bedroom. If anyone notices that I'm freaked out of my mind, they don't say anything.

"Hey," I say, hugging Keanna. She's wearing a pair of jean shorts, silver sparkly sandals, and a flowy tank top with the words "Follow your Bliss" printed across the front in cursive letters. We'd picked out the outfit today and she looks even cuter than she did in the fitting room.

"Do you need any help in here?" Keanna asks my mom.

Mom waves her hand and pours herself a margarita from the large pitcher on the counter. "No, hun, we're all good here. You brought an appetite, right?"

Keanna nods and reaches for a handful of chips from the bowl on the counter. "You know I did."

"Me too," I say, grabbing some chips. It's funny how hearing your mom talk about having a baby takes the hunger right out of you. I eat anyway, hoping it makes the nerves in my stomach calm back down.

Does this mean Mom is already pregnant? Or that she's trying to get pregnant? It must be the second one because she wouldn't be drinking so much if she were already pregnant. I didn't even know she wanted another kid; she's never exactly talked about it.

Keanna and I take the appetizers and some chips out to the patio table on the deck. I pour us a Coke and take a seat next to her on one of our fluffy patio chairs. My hands shake the whole time.

"You okay?" Keanna asks. She leans back in her chair and a soft breeze blows her hair back. I know it sounds cliché, but I swear it makes her look like an angel. I don't even know how I survived before I knew this girl. Maybe that's why I wasted so much time with other girls. I was always trying to find the perfect girl, but I was looking in the wrong places.

"Jett?" Keanna says, leaning forward. "You look weird."

I snap back to reality. "Sorry," I say, reaching over. I grab the armrest on her chair and drag her closer to me, then I rest my hand on her knee. "I was just thinking."

"About what?" she says, lifting an eyebrow.

I'm just about to tell her about the weirdness I overheard from my parents when Park and Becca walk up. Damn.

"Hey, kiddos," Becca says, climbing the three stairs to the top of our deck. She's carrying a pie in her hands, apple from the smell of it. "Congrats on the win, Jett."

"Thanks," I say, glancing over at Keanna. Last weekend was the regionals motocross race and I'd taken first place in all three classes I raced. Now the racing season slows down for a bit before the winter season which will start after school begins. I know my talent is due to years of training my ass off, but lately it feels like having Keanna there on the sidelines is what helps me to win. That might sound cheesy, but I don't care.

Park and Becca join my parents for margaritas and then they all come out to the deck to start grilling. I can't get a single second alone to tell Keanna about what I just overheard.

I'm about to take her inside and make up some lie about needing to show her something, but then Dad starts talking to me about motocross.

Keanna watches me while we eat dinner. She can tell there's something I want to tell her and I love that we're that in tune with each other.

Becca brings up school again, and the moms talk about how great it will be for Keanna to finish off her high school at LHS. When we've finished eating, I realize Keanna and I are the first two done with our burgers, probably because the adults are yapping away constantly, Becca and Mom talking about school and Dad and Park talking about motocross.

"Let's take our plates into the kitchen," I tell Keanna, flashing her what I hope is a knowing look. Normally I'd take our plates in by myself, but I need her to join me. She gets my gesture and rises to follow me into the house.

"So what is going on?" she says, her eyes sparkling with curiosity. "You look like you've seen a ghost."

I glance around then check out the kitchen window to make sure they're all still on the patio. They are, but I whisper anyway. "I overheard my mom saying she should get drunk tonight because she won't be able to drink for the next *nine* months."

Keanna's jaw drops. "They're going to have another baby?"

I lift my shoulders. "I guess? They've never talked about it, ever."

"Wow, that's really crazy, especially because of Becca . . ." she says, putting a finger to her lips.

I put our plates in the dishwasher. "What do you mean?"

She bites her bottom lip while she thinks. "Well, it might be nothing, but Becca has been acting really weird lately. Like, she's suddenly become obsessed with cleaning out their other guest bedroom, the one with all the junk in it."

"That's not *too* weird," I say.

She nods. "But Becca has been straight obsessed with that room. She's talking paint colors, new carpet . . . and it's weird because she doesn't want to fix up any other rooms in the house. I know it's a long shot, but this morning I got the idea that maybe *she's* going to have a baby, ya know?"

"Whoa," I say, as all of the pieces click together. Why else would you fix up a junk room in the house? Keanna and I must get the same idea at the same time, judging by the look on her face. "Do you think they're both having a baby?"

A look of fear crosses her face and I'm not sure why. She shrugs. "I guess we'll just have to wait and find out."

CHAPTER THREE

Keanna

The early morning sunlight filters in through my yellow curtains, giving the whole room a warm glow. I stretch and blink my eyes. I don't even remember falling asleep last night after watching tons of Netflix with Jett. I yawn and roll over.

And land face-to-face with Jett.

"Oh shit," I mutter. I bolt up in bed and look around. It's seven in the morning, so who knows if Park and Becca are awake yet. My TV is still on the Netflix menu. We must have fallen asleep last night and that's why I don't remember telling Jett goodbye.

I lean over and shake him. "Wake up!" I whisper-yell. "Wake up."

His eyes squish together and he yawns, slowly opening them against the bright sunlight. He smiles when his eyes focus on mine. "Hey there, beautiful."

I throw a pillow at him. "No! This is bad!"

I jump out of bed. The blankets aren't even rumpled that much since we'd fallen asleep on top of them. But this is bad. I know for a fact that Becca and Park won't be too pleased if they know Jett slept over last night. And Bayleigh! Oh my god, she'll be so disappointed.

I shudder as I remember the awkwardly embarrassing safe sex speech she'd given us a few weeks ago. Jett and I have *not* slept together yet, and after the terrifying story of her teenage pregnancy, we might not ever.

I look over at Jett and he grins and it makes my toes tingle.

Okay, maybe we will. One day.

"Get up, you big . . ." I glare at him and try to come up with an insult. "Butt-face!"

His grin stretches into a smile. He sits up and rubs his eyes, then yawns again. "It's so early," he says slowly, blinking and trying to wake up.

"Babe, you have to go," I say, my arms swinging widely toward my bedroom door. "I don't want to get in trouble."

He snorts. "You won't get in trouble. Becca loves you."

I put a hand on my hip. "What about your mom?"

He flinches. "Maybe it's best if she doesn't find out."

My heart races as I crack open my door and stick my head out into the hallway. I can't hear anything but that doesn't mean much. It's Monday morning at exactly the time Becca gets up for work. We have to be at the Track in an hour.

"Oh god," I mutter, turning around and pressing my back to the door. "I don't want to disappoint Becca or Park or your mom." I heave a sigh and close my eyes. "I just want them to like me."

Jett checks his phone then slides it into his pocket. He walks over to me and puts a hand on my cheek. "Baby, it's okay. Breathe. If anyone sees me, I'll just say I came over here early to get you for breakfast."

"Wearing the same thing you wore last night?" I ask, eyeing his blue shirt.

His shoulders sag and he steps closer, his toes touching mine. "It'll be okay, Key." His lips kiss mine, slowly, lovingly, until my heartbeat slows.

And then he wraps his hands around my waist and slides his tongue across my bottom lip and suddenly my heart is back at it, beating insanely fast, but this time it's not out of fear of getting in trouble.

I break away to catch my breath and put my hands on his chest to keep him a few inches away. "You have to go," I whisper against my heart's desire to keep him here, as close as possible, forever.

"Okay," he says, leaning down and kissing me again. "Whatever my girl wants, she gets." He gives me that oh-so-adorable wink and then slips his shoes on.

I rush into my closet and change into a black tank top, but keep the same shorts on. I throw my hair into a ponytail so that I look different from yesterday.

"You want to make sure the coast is clear?" he says, opening the door.

I inch into the hallway and walk down to peak into the living room. It's empty, so I motion for him to follow. We do this same routine until we're outside and I can finally breathe again.

"It's a good thing I walked instead of drove," he says. "My truck in the driveway might have made Park suspicious when he went to work this morning."

Sure enough, Park's truck is gone but Becca's car is still here. She must be getting ready for work, although since the weather is nice she'll probably walk there instead of drive. "Hurry up," I say, pushing him toward his house which is on the opposite side of the Track. It's a fairly long walk.

He takes my hand. "Come with me."

"I—" I begin an automatic excuse but then I realize that I'm already dressed. "Well, I guess I can," I say with a laugh. Now that we're out in the open, it just looks like I'm going to work. I pull out my phone and text Becca that I'm already at the Track so she won't look for me when she leaves the house.

Jett and I hold hands as we walk across the Track's parking lot toward Jett's house. "I wish I could wake up next to you every morning," Jett says, squeezing my hand.

"Maybe when we have our own place," I say, putting a hand to my chest. "That was way too much drama for me. Don't laugh at me! I can't stress it enough, Jett. I *do not* want to get on Becca or Park's bad side."

A stinging fear hits me again, the same fear from last night. If Becca really is cleaning out that guest room for a baby . . . does that mean she won't want me anymore? I'm just a weird house guest that's been crashing in their spare room for weeks. I'm not exactly a perfect addition to a husband and wife who are having their first child.

"Why do you look so sad?" Jett says. "I'd love to have my own place with you. And one day I will and it'll be awesome and we'll sleep naked."

I give him a sideways look. He winks.

When we get halfway between the Track and his house, we stop. "I'm going to work now," I say, turning to face him. He slides his fingers into my front pockets and pulls me toward him. "I guess I'll go change clothes and come to work, too." He drops his forehead to mine and then slowly nudges me backward until my back presses against a massive oak tree. I slide my arms around his neck and hold him close. His eyes gaze deeply into mine, and it's almost like he wants to say a million things at once, but he doesn't say anything. I get it though. I want to say a million things to him as well. Like how he makes me feel like a real human being. Like someone worthy of being loved. I want to tell him how freaking hot he is, like all of the time, and how much I miss him when he's not right next to me.

But we kiss instead, and I put all of my emotions into my actions, letting him know exactly how I feel by kiss alone. Jett presses against me and his body is warm, strong, and *so* sexy. I run my hands up the back of his head and squirm when he kisses my neck.

We both stop when the sound of footsteps breaks the silence. He looks up and glances over, then the alarm on his face softens into recognition. He holds one finger up to his lips and gives me this devilish grin as he presses me closer against the tree.

We're hiding from someone.

His mom's distinct laughter fills the air and then his dad says something I can't quite figure out. They must be walking to work, and if we're lucky, they won't see us hiding on the other side of this huge tree trunk.

His parents talk some more and Jett and I shuffle around the tree as they get nearer. I'm trying not to laugh because I'm not quite sure if what we're doing is stupid or hilarious. My heart pounds in my chest as they get really close, walking right past the tree. We slide over until we're on the other side and we can't see them so I'm guessing they can't see us.

"It'll definitely take some getting used to," Jace says. "I mean, it'll be weird, for sure."

"But," Bayleigh says, sounding a little curious and excited. "You're saying you're totally okay with me having another man's baby?"

My jaw hits the ground.

Jett's eyes go wide and he stumbles backward, the shock throwing him off balance. I grab his hands and hold him still. His jaw flexes and I can tell he wants to run out right now and ask what the hell is going on, but I shake my head and mouth the word *no.*

That would be way too awkward. Plus, with all of our freaking out, we didn't even hear the rest of what his parents were saying and now they're too far away to hear any more.

We stand against the back side of the tree for a while. Jett's nostrils flare and he shakes his head. "What the *hell* was that?"

I bite my bottom lip. "That doesn't make any sense . . . your parents are perfect for each other . . ."

"Why would my dad be okay with this?" Jett says, running both hands through his hair. "This doesn't make any sense."

I put my hands on his chest and look him in the eye. "Baby, you have to calm down. You can't run after them and confront them on this."

"Why not?" His hands clench. "I want some answers."

Having been in the middle of tons of Dawn's drama over the years, I know better than to let him run and confront his parents right now. So I take his hand. "Let's go back to your house and you can change clothes and calm down first."

He heaves a heavy breath and then sighs. "Okay. Yeah, okay. You're right."

I slip my arm around his back and we start walking toward his house. "I know I am," I say, holding my chip up in the air. "I'm *always* right."

Jett tickles my side. "Uh huh, sure you are."

CHAPTER FOUR

Jett

Keanna's hair smells like green apple shampoo that she bought after using mine that one time she showered at my house. Tearing myself away from her is the hardest damn thing ever. But eventually I get back home and take a quick shower, hoping it'll cool my head. It doesn't really help. No amount of hot water rushing over my face will wipe my mother's words out of my head.

Another man's baby?

What the actual ef is that?

My mom would never cheat on my dad—at least, I never thought she would. And *why* is he okay with this? I know he loves her more than life itself but damn. I would be beyond crushed if Keanna hooked up with another guy. Would I want her back? Probably not.

I groan as I get dressed and my pulse races as I walk back over to the Track. Keanna doesn't want me to confront them, especially at work, but I can't help it. I shouldn't have overheard this in the first place, but I did, and it's going to kill me until I know the truth. And if the truth is as horrible as I think it is—I don't know how I'll ever live around my parents again. They are supposed to be much better people than this.

I take the back entrance into the building, walking through the gym. If I came in the front doors, then Keanna would see me and I don't need her trying to stop me. Luckily it's after nine in the morning so she's working the front desk. She won't be able to walk around anywhere else since most of the clients arrive at this time.

I walk to Mom's office and find it empty, so I go over to Dad's. Bingo.

Dad's in his desk chair, looking at his computer and Mom sits on the corner of his desk, wearing one of his old motocross jerseys over a pair of leggings. How can she just sit there smiling and acting like this is a normal day?

"What the hell is wrong with ya'll?" The words fly out of my mouth before I have an opportunity to censor them or make them into something a little more polite.

Dad's expression hardens. "Excuse me, son? You want to try that again?"

I fold my arms across my chest. Sure, he's my dad but I'm just as tall as he is now. "No, I was being perfectly clear. What the hell did I overhear outside?"

Mom stands. "Jett, what are you talking about?" Her forehead creases and she reaches for me. I pull backward. If my mom's a cheater, I don't want anything to do with her. God, I can't even look at her the same way.

"You're having another man's baby," I spit out, unable to meet her eyes. I look at Dad. "What is going on?"

My parents exchange a glace and then they both start laughing. I throw my hands in the air. "Uh, hello? I'm still waiting for an explanation."

Dad's brows crease. "Wait, why were you outside? I thought you slept late?"

"Never mind me, what were you talking about?"

Mom clears her throat and sits back on the corner of Dad's desk. "Okay well, you're not supposed to know this yet, but since you're so mad, I'll tell you but you have to swear to keep it quiet for now."

My entire body trembles with anger. Why is she being so calm about this?"

"Your mom didn't cheat on me," Dad says.

Relief hits me hard and makes me feel a thousand times better. "Then what did I overhear?"

Mom frowns and plays with the hem of her jersey. "You really aren't supposed to know but . . . first of all, I'm not pregnant. Not yet, anyway."

I lift an eyebrow. Mom glances behind me and then motions for me to close the door. I do, and then glare at her for an explanation.

"Becca and Park have asked us to consider being a surrogate for their baby. That means that I'll go to a doctor and they'll put Becca and Park's baby inside of me, and I'll have the pregnancy since my body is healthy for childbirth but Becca's isn't."

My nose wrinkles. I didn't exactly need that many details. "So . . . you'll have her baby?"

She nods. "It's one hundred percent their child's DNA. They'd be using my womb as a greenhouse to grow the baby, so to speak. And then once the baby is born, I'd give it over to them."

"Wow." That's all I can say. I sink into the chair up against the wall to take it all in. "You would do that for them?"

She nods and Dad grabs her hand. "Of course I would. It kills Becca that she can't have her own baby and we've been talking about this for a while. What you overheard was just me joking with Jace. This is a big deal for all of us because if we do this, I'll have to get fat and pregnant and your poor dad will have to put up with my fat, moody ass and he won't even get a baby out of it."

Um, gross. I hold up a hand. "I don't exactly need to know all the details," I say. "But I'm really really glad you're not cheating on Dad."

They both laugh at this, like it's the craziest idea in the world. And that makes my heart feel better because it *should* be the craziest thing in the world. My parents are soul mates. Even when everything else in the world is wrong, I can count on them.

"Okay, well I guess I won't say anything." When I stand up, it feels like I'm back in control of my own body now that I'm no longer falling over the cliff of panic.

"You can't tell anyone, Mom says again. "We haven't done the procedure yet and Becca doesn't want anyone to know until I'm officially pregnant and we know that it'll work out."

I nod, but I must look uncertain because Mom's eyes narrow. "Do not tell Keanna. Don't tell anyone."

I hate lying to my mom but I'm definitely not lying to Keanna.

As soon as we go on lunch break, I slip out of the gym where I'd been serving as a personal trainer for a fourteen-year-old boy I've been helping my dad train. Keanna smiles when I find her at the front desk. She grabs her purse. "Taco Bell today? We haven't had it in a while."

"Whatever you want is fine," I say, taking her hand. We slip into my truck and I blast the radio while we sit in the parking lot. It's not like anyone can overhear me but I'm not taking any chances since I totally lied to my mom. When the music is nice and loud, I tell Keanna every single thing my parents told me.

"Wow." Keanna touches her throat. "So, I guess that's good right?" Her voice gets higher. "I mean yeah, that's awesome for them. Yay for Becca . . ."

"Why are you acting like a crazy person?" I ask.

She shakes her head quickly and reaches for the radio button, changing channels. "I'm fine."

"You don't seem fine."

I have to work on her all the way to Taco Bell before she finally tells me what's wrong. Her lip quivers and she gives me that look—the same fearful face I'd seen the night her mom left her for good.

"I know this makes me a terrible person, but if Becca has a baby . . . she won't want some teenager living at her house anymore."

"Keanna, that won't happen," I say, brushing her hair behind her ears. She shakes her head and disagrees with me and I remember Dad's words to just listen and not try to fix everything.

So I listen, right here in the parking lot of the Taco Bell, as Keanna pours out all of her insecurities and worries. I want to tell her that it'll be fine, but I'm not sure she'd believe me if I did.

CHAPTER FIVE

Keanna

Keeping this secret has been a lot harder than I thought it would be. I spend nearly all of my time with Becca when I'm not with Jett, and it's been completely insane trying to hide what I know. It doesn't help at all that Becca is being overly happy and excited all of the time. Even if I didn't know that she was trying to have a baby, I'd suspect that something was up.

For the next few days, Becca is like a freaking ray of sunshine floating on clouds and spewing hearts of happiness out of her eyes. Nothing at work gets her down—not even when she spills her coffee and it gets all over her white jeans. She just giggles and calls herself a klutz and then runs home to change clothes.

"It's cute but it's weird," I tell Jett during our lunch break on Thursday. Well, it's my lunch break. Jett is working out in the gym and I'm sitting next to his weight bench. "Lately Becca is like some kind of . . . well, I can't even think of an example to compare her to because *no one* is as happy as she is lately."

"I wonder how long she'll take to tell us about it," Jett says, exhaling as he lowers the weight bar. He does another rep and then sits up and reaches for his sweat towel. "You think she'd be dying to tell everyone since she's so excited about it."

I peel off a dirt bike sticker that some kid stuck to the floor the other day. "Who knows? Women are weird when it comes to babies."

I don't really know this from personal experience since my own mother only talked about how annoying babies are, but I've seen enough movies and TV shows to know that baby fever drives women crazy. That's why some of them go off and kidnap babies to raise as their own. I shudder.

"What is it?" Jett asks.

My phone alarm goes off, signaling the end of my lunch break. "Just thinking about baby-stealing crazies," I say with a shrug.

He lifts an eyebrow as he leans over to kiss me goodbye. "You're a weirdo."

I run my tongue over his lips just to prove him right. "So are you!" I say as I head back into the hallway and toward the front desk. I actually forgot to get anything for lunch because once I saw Jett shirtless and working out, I kind of forgot all about food. Now my stomach is growling. *Guh*.

Two teen girls are talking to Becca when I get back to the front desk. "Ah," Becca says, turning to me. "This is Jett's girlfriend, so you should probably ask her."

She gives me a warm smile. Uh, okay.

"Hi?" I say to the girls. I realize now that they're dressed to kill as far as Texas summers go. Short shorts and skin-tight tank tops, perfect hair and perfect makeup.

The brunette speaks first. "You're Jett's girlfriend?"

"I'm Keanna, yeah." I look back for Becca but she's already gone, slipped through the back exit for her lunch break.

"Jett's *girlfriend?*" The other girl says with a pretty Spanish accent.

"Um, yeah." Why is that so hard for them to believe? I put my hands on the front desk. "Can I help you?"

They give me the look over, and it's exactly like in the movies when the bitchy girls are making a pointed example out of the loser girl. "What's wrong?" I ask, suddenly fed up with all of this dumb drama. "You look like you can't possibly believe that I'm Jett's girlfriend. Well, I am. He's in the gym if you'd like to verify."

"It's not exactly the *who* I'm questioning," the brunette girl says. "It's the why. Jett doesn't settle down."

I know they're trying to get a rise out of me, to make me question my relationship. But it's not going to work. "Guess you don't know him very well," I say, turning my attention to the computer behind the front desk. There's nothing on here worth looking at but I take the mouse and pretend to click on stuff. It's only been a few weeks but Jett has promised me he's not the guy he used to be. He's asked me to trust him and I guess I knew this kind of thing would happen one day, so I keep my head high and act like I'm not affected at all. After all, the more I pretend like my life is perfect, the more I'll start to believe it.

After work, Jett texts me that he's helping his dad with a client so he won't be free until later tonight. I go home to shower and Becca finds me when I'm drying my hair. Her brown hair has been curled and is tossed up in a messy bun. She's wearing yoga pants and a tank top but you'd think she's been at the spa all day with how much she's glowing.

It's getting really hard keeping the baby thing a secret from her. I wish she would just hurry up and tell me.

"Where's Jett?" she asks, leaning inside my room.

"Working," I say while I put up the hair dryer. "What's up?"

"Want to help me cook dinner? I'm thinking something easy like chalupas."

"Sounds good," I say. Part of me thinks it's a little dorky to have only two friends—your boyfriend and a thirty-four-year-old woman who is also your caretaker. But the other part of me remembers what my life was like before I met these people. Constant moving around, craft fairs, cheap motel rooms that smelled like urine and cigar smoke. I didn't have a single friend back then; just my mom and I don't count her as a friend at all. She wasn't even that good of a caretaker.

When I was in school, I'd keep to myself or manage to make maybe one or two friends who never really got me. Sure, I had guys who only wanted a hookup, but there was never any kind of connection there. Hooking up with guys gets really, really, old.

Here in this tiny little town, I have two adult friends, Becca and Bayleigh, and one hell of an amazing boyfriend. Even if it only lasts for the summer, even if I have to move away once I'm eighteen and the Parks want their house to themselves and their new baby, it won't matter. I'll still be happy that I got one perfect summer with people I care about.

Becca and I go about making chalupas, which is probably the easiest dinner ever, second only to a bowl of cereal. I chop up lettuce and avocado and she cooks the refried beans. Park comes in when we're almost finished, his hair all sweaty from a day of work. "Smells great," he says as he gives Becca a quick kiss on the lips. "I'm going to shower real quick, will you save me some?"

"Of course," Becca says. Her eyes trail down to her husband's feet. "Those shoes better not be tracking dirt in the house."

Park winces and bends down to remove his shoes. He tiptoes them to the back door and then tosses them outside.

Becca laughs and shakes her head and then she joins me at the dining table, her plate filled high with extra cheese and black olives.

"So," she says after I've eaten a few bites of my dinner. I tense as I look at her. That wasn't a casual so. It had something else hidden behind it. Something she wants to talk about.

"What's up?" My mouth is suddenly dry. I reach for my soda but it doesn't help much.

"We should look into getting the transcripts from your last school. That way we can get you registered for Lawson High next week."

She gives me this encouraging smile. This isn't the first time she's brought up enrolling in school for next year, but it is getting late enough in the summer that I won't be able to put it off much longer. I know I *need* to go to school, so that's not the big deal, I guess. I think the reason I don't want to deal with any of this is because I hated my last school. I don't like thinking about any of it. I just want to float through life being happy and carefree just like the last few weeks. I don't want school and the fear of having enough lunch money, or the right clothes, or friends. I know Jett says all of those things won't be a big deal, and I pretty much believed him until I heard about the baby thing.

Now that Becca will have a baby in nine months, I need to find a way to get out of her house. That means saving money and not stupidly blowing it all on clothes. Looking for a cheap apartment and maybe a car to get around since Lawson doesn't have public transportation. All of this will take a lot of work—a *ton* of work—and it scares the shit out of me so yeah, forgive me if I don't want to talk about enrolling in a new school right now.

"I don't think we have to worry about it," I say, trying to put on a soft smile. "I think I'll just get my GED and—"

"What?" Becca flinches. "Honey, you can't drop out of school."

"I won't be dropping out, I'll be getting a GED." I hold up my finger and try to be convincing. "It's way better than dropping out."

She rolls her eyes. "Keanna . . . you shouldn't be so quick to give up high school. It's your senior year," she says, putting emphasis on the last two words as if they're super important. "You should have fun and take fun classes, do high school stuff." Her eyes light up. "Prom! You can't miss out on prom. And Senior Skip Day is a blast . . . you'll miss out on all of that if you just get a GED."

I stare at my food and try to picture a world where I actually went to prom and had a real date. I never thought that would be possible before now. Now, I can almost picture Jett looking stunningly handsome in a black tux, and me, dressed in one of those frilly, sparkly dresses. We could even pose in front of the fireplace like everyone else does.

"See?" Becca says, pointing at me with her half-eaten chalupa. "I can tell you're thinking about it. High school should be fun, and senior year is the best. You get to be lazy and take blow off classes for the second semester. You should really go, sweetheart."

Things like *honey* and *sweetheart* are terms of endearment that Becca has been calling me pretty much since the day I moved in. I don't deserve the pet names but she gives them out freely, as if she knows they make me feel wanted. Like I belong.

I smile. "You're going to be a great mom one day."

Becca blinks. Her cheeks flush and she reaches for her glass of wine. "Thank you, dear. I don't know what made that come into your mind."

"You're just really nice to me and I'm not even your kid," I say, swallowing the lump in my throat. "Anyway, I appreciate what you're saying but I'm just not sure I should stay here and go to school for another year. I'll be eighteen in November and that's not far away."

She purses her lips but I keep talking. "So I think I could probably get a GED before November and then when I'm eighteen I'll just move out of here and get out of your hair."

"Keanna!"

I flinch. For a second, Becca sounded exactly like Dawn used to when she'd yell at me. Becca sighs through her nose and then drops her food onto her plate and looks at me. "Keanna, don't say that. You are *not* in my hair at all. I love having you here. I—"

She stops and sighs. When she tries to talk again, she gets all flustered. "I just—Keanna, no." Her lips flatten into a thin line. "Just think it over some more, okay? You are welcome to stay here as long as you want, honey. I can't stress that enough. Do not skip out on having a great senior year experience just because you think you need to leave."

The way she's acting, all flustered and weird, makes me think there's more to this than she's letting on. Maybe I'm just reading into it, but I don't think she's being weird because of the baby thing. I think it's something else.

"Is there something you're not telling me?" I ask slowly, not sure if I want to hear it, whatever it is. "You look like you want to say something but you're not. Is it my mom?" My voice trembles but she shakes her head.

"No, there's nothing. I haven't heard from Dawn, have you?"

I shake my head. I haven't even texted my mother from my new phone yet. Becca smiles and reaches for the bowl of shredded cheese. "I just worry about you, kid. I don't want you to make any mistakes. You have a whole future ahead and I'm here for you, okay?"

I nod and I don't bring it up again while we eat dinner, but I'm not stupid. There's something else, something not related to having a baby, and she's not telling me.

That means it must be important.

CHAPTER SIX

Jett

As soon as I'm home from work, I text Keanna and ask her to come over. She writes me back with a smiley face and I feel a sense of relief. Every day that she still wants to hang out with me is a good day. This is the first time I've ever felt this way about a girl—like I can't get enough of her. Usually girls get annoying after an hour or so. Texting, phone calls, lunch dates? Hell no. Not until now.

Now I come home from work and pray that she'll want to come over, that I'll get the little smiley face reply day after day. So far she's never said no. I fear the day that she grows tired of me.

I do a quick cleanup of my room, tossing dirty clothes into the hamper, pulling my bed sheets up so that the bed is sort of made. We usually spend all of our time on my futon in front of my TV, but I want the place to look nice anyway.

Then I jog downstairs and wait for her on the back patio. Her face glows from her cell phone screen as she walks over.

"You should play this game," she says, pointing her phone toward me. The screen is a mixture of colors and shapes. "It's so addicting."

"You're addicting," I say, slipping my arms around her and kissing her neck. That gets her to put the phone away. Her arms wrap around me and I hold her tightly, squeezing her up into a bear hug for as long as she'll let me. I breathe in the scent of her green apple shampoo and then kiss her head.

"So what do you want to do tonight?"

Her lips move to the side and she pretends to consider it for a moment. "How about the same thing we always do?"

"And what is that? I forgot."

She rolls her eyes. "Make out and watch TV?"

"I believe the cool kids are calling that Netflix and chill."

She crinkles her nose. "I don't want to be a cool kid. I want to be us."

We go inside and Keanna says hi to my parents who are cuddled up on the couch, watching a movie on TV. Mom says something back, asking her about some nail salon and Keanna breaks free from my hand and walks over to talk to her.

I make this loud sigh and pretend to stomp over there like a petulant child. "Mother, how many times do I have to ask you to stop stealing my girlfriend?"

"This is your fault," she says, giving me that classic mom look. "You shouldn't have dated such a cool girl and maybe I wouldn't want to walk to her."

Keanna laughs and high fives my mom. Dad takes the remote and pauses their movie. "What are you guys up to?"

I shrug. "We're gonna Netflix and chill."

Dad looks confused and Mom's eyes brighten. "Hey, that's what we're doing!" She elbows Dad. "See Jace? We're still cool."

"Netflix and chill is internet slang for a booty call," Keanna says all matter-of-factly. "Looks like someone didn't tell your son that, though."

My cheeks burn and it only gets worse when both of my parents laugh at me. "Okay, maybe we're not that cool anymore," Mom says.

I grab Keanna's hand. "Can we please leave these two old geezers to watch their movie in peace?"

She grins. "I guess, but your parents are so much cooler to talk to than you." She pokes me in the stomach, a playful smile on her lips.

Mom holds out her hand for another high-five from my girlfriend. As we head over to the stairs, Dad calls out, "Have fun Netflixing and chilling!"

Mom laughs and says, "Be safe!"

"Oh my god," Keanna murmurs under her breath as we walk up the stairs. "Do you think they think we're having sex when we're up here?"

I shrug. "Of course they do. We're teenagers."

She lifts an eyebrow. "Shouldn't parents, like, be mad about that?"

I lead her into my room and close the door behind us. "My parents don't get *mad* about sex. They were teen parents, after all. My mom has practically raised me on a mantra of knowing how to respect women and knowing about safe sex and stuff."

She seems equal parts horrified and impressed. "My mom only ever told me that if I get knocked up she'll kick me out." She snorts and sits on my futon. "Turns out I didn't have to get pregnant to have her leave me."

I sink into the plush mattress next to her and wrap my arm around her shoulders. "I'm sorry, babe."

She leans on my chest and reaches for the remote. "It's cool."

"It's really not cool. What your mom did sucked. But I'm here for you."

Her chest rises as she takes in a deep breath. "Let's just relax tonight and not talk about any of that crap, okay?"

I brush her hair out of her eyes and lean down to kiss her forehead. "Sure."

We cuddle and watch a few episodes of our favorite shows for a while, and it feels good but it also feels like something is on her mind. Her shoulders are tense and she keeps biting her bottom lip. She doesn't laugh during the funny parts and we *always* laugh during the funny parts.

During the credits, Keanna sits up and stretches, then takes off her shoes and kicks them to the side. She faces me while I'm still sitting on the futon.

"What's up?" I ask when she doesn't sit back down.

"You're really hot," she says with a smirk.

The quick flash of desire in her eyes is enough to get me all turned on. I move the remote from my lap to the armrest and beckon for her to come here. She walks forward, leans over and puts a hand on the back of the futon and then straddles my lap.

"You're the hot one here," I say, leaning forward to kiss her. She slides her hands around my neck and I grab her hips, pulling her closer to me. "Especially in this shirt," I whisper into her ear. She squirms and I slide my hands under her shirt, which was taken from my closet the last time she was here. My fingers trail up her sides, her skin soft and prickling with goosebumps.

"Why did I buy all those sexy shirts if stealing one from you does the trick?" she says, cocking her head.

I dip my head into the crook of her neck and trail kisses up to her ear. "To be fair, you're hot in anything you wear," I whisper. My thumbs slide up her chest and graze under her breasts. Her breath hitches and she leans into me, rocking her body against mine.

It would be so easy to take this further—to slip off her shirt, carry her to my bed. There are still parts of each other we haven't yet explored, but the sadness behind her eyes tells me that there's more going on right now than just a steamy make out session.

"You should talk to me," I say, kissing her.

She shakes her head and grabs my lips between her teeth, pulling me back into another one of our epic kisses. I slide my hands back down to her hips, hooking my thumbs under her belt loops. Every muscle in her body feels tense. Her kisses are passionate but off. She's not putting everything into it like usual.

"Key, you should talk to me," I whisper, resting my forehead against hers. "Something's bothering you."

She shakes her head then grinds against my erection, making me moan and gasp for breath. "I don't wanna talk," she says, slipping her tongue into my mouth. "I just want to forget everything and be with you."

I close my eyes as a shudder ripples through my body. She runs her tongue up my neck, her boobs pressing into my chest. All I want to do is rip her clothes off—but I can't. Something is wrong.

I squeeze her hips and pull her off of me, setting her next to me on the futon. Her eyes narrow and her lips form a pout. "What are you doing? Don't you want me?"

"Key, I—" I stop short and exhale. Is now the time to tell her I love her? It's too soon, right? I've wanted to tell her for days now but it always seems too soon. When do you tell a girl you love her in a way that makes her believe it?

Keanna's pout gets sadder and I take her cheek and pull her toward me for a kiss. "I want you so bad, you have no idea. But I'm not stupid. You're hooking up with me right now to forget about whatever is bothering you."

The flash of guilt that crosses her face tells me I'm right. I take her hand. "We're not some booty call couple, Key. We're in this for real, so you're gonna have to tell me sooner or later what's bugging you because I care and I want to help you."

Her shoulders fall and she tucks her feet up underneath her. "Okay, fine. I can't go to school with you in the fall."

Okay, that's the last thing I expected to hear. "Why?"

She shrugs. "I need to get my GED and get a full time job and move out. Find my own place, be on my own."

My heart speeds up. "Why are you saying this? Do you want to leave? You don't want to be with me?"

She smiles sadly and shakes her head. "No, the plan is to keep you as long as possible. You're my rock." She squeezes my hand. "I just can't keep being a burden to Becca and Park. I need to support myself and I can't do that if I'm in high school."

"Have you told Becca this idea? Because she won't allow it."

Keanna's frown flattens. "Yeah, she said I need to go to school and stay with her but that doesn't matter. She's just being nice."

"She *is* nice," I say. "She likes having you there."

"I've been a burden my whole life. I need to support myself."

"You're seventeen. You don't have to do all of that right away."

She swallows and stares at the throw blanket behind our backs. "When that baby comes, I'm not going to belong there."

"Then I'll move out with you."

Her eyes widen and she gives a quick shake of her head. "No way. You can't leave this awesome house."

"I'll leave the freaking planet if it means I get to be with you," I say, sitting straighter. Anger replaces all of my worry and suddenly I need her to know how serious I am. I stand up. My hands hurt like they want to punch something. "You either stay here and go to school with me or you quit and move out and I move out with you. I'm going wherever you are."

She stands. "Not happening. You can't leave your family and school. You're only a junior. It's not happening."

"Good, then you'll stay and go to school with me," I say, folding my arms across my chest.

She groans. "No. I need to support myself, Jett. Why don't you just get that?"

"Why don't you get that people care about you? You can't miss out on high school. What about college? And getting a good job? You need to stay so you can achieve all of that."

She laughs and walks toward my door, then turns to glare at me. "You're talking about stuff that *normal* people get to do. I'm just poor and homeless and no one gives a shit about me. When that baby comes along, there won't be any place for me, Jett. Don't you get that? You deserve better than some trailer trash girl with no life or future."

Tears spring to my eyes and although I'm supposed to be manly and shit, I just can't help it. "I can't believe you would say that." My voice is low and raw. Pain fills my chest until it feels like I can't breathe. "I can't lose you," I say, but it sounds more like a whisper.

"You're not going to lose me," she says slowly. She shakes her head and stares at the floor. I think she's trying to hold back tears as well. "Just let me fix my life and stop telling me everything is okay when it's not."

CHAPTER SEVEN

Keanna

I am a total jerk. From storming out of Jett's house to texting him that I'm going to bed when I'm not—I am a jerk. A selfish, rude, horrible girlfriend. I don't deserve the title, not really.

I just took the only guy who genuinely seems to care about me and I told him to leave me alone.

Why. Am. I. So. Stupid.

I don't want him to leave me alone. I just don't want anyone to see me this way. Especially someone whose opinion I very much care about.

It's one-fifteen in the morning and I'm laying wide awake in my room. Becca's guest room. I still feel weird calling it *my* room even though it's been my home for two months now. I don't own any of the furniture, the TV, the sheets on the bed.

With a heavy sigh, I throw off the comforter and sit up in bed. I am tired of pretending like I'll be falling asleep any time soon. There is a very big, very distinct problem in my life right now and I can't just run away, hide my face under a pillow and hope it all goes away. Running away is what Dawn does and I will be better than her. I'm probably not better than her now, but I can be. I will be.

I walk over to the desk near the window and take out a notepad and a pen from the top drawer. I click on the little lamp and sit down and take a deep breath.

How to fix your life

My handwriting is downright awful, but I stare at the words and try to smile. The first part of my problem is very easy to identify. Money.

It's always money. I can't think of a single problem in my life that couldn't have been fixed with enough of it. It sucks and it's sad and pathetic but money makes the world go around. If I plan to move out by my eighteenth birthday and support myself, I'll need as much of it as I can get.

Using the credit union app on my phone, I pull up my account and write down the balance: $1216

I groan. Why did I spend all that money shopping again? Just last night, out of curiosity I looked up apartment rentals in the area. The cheapest one was nine hundred a month plus *two* months' rent as a deposit. I need at least eighteen hundred dollars before I can even try to rent my own place. And that doesn't include furniture, dishes, a shower curtain—all those things you need in order to live. God knows Dawn and I have had our share of moving into crappy apartments only to not have a shower curtain or the money to obtain one.

Doesn't matter. I'll figure it out. I write: *save every penny, try to earn more and then move on to the next line.*

At three in the morning, I have sixteen full pages written down. An entire plan to fix my life, and it includes keeping Jett as my boyfriend for as long as I can.

A stab of pain hits my chest, like someone just lit a whole box of matches and tossed them inside me. The tiny voice in the back of my head tells me what I spend all day every day trying to ignore:

Jett is too good for you. You are not worth it. He'll never stay with you.

All of these things I know to be true. But like I said earlier, I am a jerk. A selfish jerk. I care about Jett so much that I will do whatever I can to keep him mine. Of course, after the way I yelled at him tonight, maybe he's already gone. God, I hope not.

THE NEXT DAY IS JETT'S DAY OFF WORK, SO IT'S EASY ENOUGH TO IGNORE HIM WHILE I'm behind the front desk. We are swamped with clients and their annoying parents so even when Jett walks in the front doors with his dad, Jace, I'm only able to give him a quick wave and a *"sorry, look how busy I am"* expression as he walks by.

Around noon, Becca bounces in the front doors looking spunkier than ever in a bright pink sundress and flip flops showing off her fresh pedicure. "Lunch break!" she sing-songs as she relieves me from my post. "You can stay gone an hour today," she says, flashing me a grin as if we're both in on some joke.

"Why? I'm just going to grab some cereal at home so I don't need that long."

She smirks to herself and checks her email on the work computer. "Just trust me on this."

The rumble of a dirt bike motor sounds closer than usual and I look over to find Jett parking his Honda up against the front of the building. Bikes are definitely not allowed up here, especially since riding on concrete is dangerous with motocross tires, but being the owner's son gives you certain privileges.

Jett walks in wearing khaki cargo shorts and a Honda T-shirt that matches his bike. He's wearing a black backpack and I have a sudden idea of what he looks like when he goes to school. It's cute, to say the least.

He gives me a half-smile, his hair all messy from the helmet he left on his bike. "Lunch?" he asks.

Something in his eyes lets me know he's worried I'll say no.

"Sure," I say, smiling. I don't exactly want to pretend that last night never happened, since that's how Dawn always handled our arguments, but I also don't want to talk about it. I'd hoped when I finally fell asleep this morning, that figuring out a game plan for living on my own would make me feel better today, but it really hasn't done anything but ensure that I'm exhausted while trying to work.

Outside, Jett shrugs off his backpack and hands it to me. "Can you wear this?"

That's a weird request, but I put on the backpack and whatever is inside is cold against my back, but it feels good in the summer air. Then he hands me his helmet. "On it goes."

"I have to wear this?" I ask, holding it up as if it were toxic. "Why?"

Jett smirks and climbs on his dirt bike. "Because we're going for a ride."

I put on the helmet and climb on behind him, adrenaline coursing through my bones the moment he cranks the bike to life. I've never been on his bike before and I'm a little scared but mostly excited.

He pulls back the throttle and we zoom across the parking lot, toward the track. He turns left and steers the tires into a little trail that runs alongside the main track. I hold onto his waist while we cruise for a few acres, past all of the practice tracks and to the very back of their land, where it flattens out into unoccupied fields of trees and tall grass.

The thrill of being on the bike makes it easy to see why Jett loves this sport so much. The bike slows and Jett cruises up to a massive old oak tree. Its branches reach out tall and wide, its trunk as thick as a car. My heart does a little pitter patter when I see what's been set up beneath the tree.

A quilted blanket lies on the grass in the shade, a bouquet of sunflowers tied in a ribbon rest in the middle of it.

When he stops the bike, my hands are shaking and it's not from the exhilarating bike ride.

We get off the bike and Jett leans it against the oak tree, then he helps me take off his helmet, which he hangs over the handlebar.

I feel like I'm blushing, both from this romantic gesture and from the ride. Two wrinkled circles on the front of his shirt show exactly how hard I was holding onto him while we road over here.

Jett takes off my backpack and slings it over one shoulder. He takes my hand and leads me to the blanket. "These are for you," he says, dropping to his knees on the quilt.

I take the sunflowers and sit next to him. "They're beautiful." I lean over and kiss him on the cheek. "Thank you."

Jett unpacks our lunch and sets it out on the blanket in front of us. He brought bottled water, which was what made the backpack cold, and a selection of finger foods that he lovingly chose and packed into his mom's Tupperware containers.

There's cheese cubes and turkey slices, crackers and chips, various chip dips, olives (black and green since I once mentioned I love them both), chocolate chip cookies, and chicken taquitos.

"Sorry I'm not exactly a good cook," he says, cracking open his water bottle. "But I'm good at organizing random food that's good and calling it a picnic." He winks and my heart melts.

Oh my god, I feel like I might actually cry. *Why, Keanna? Stop being a dork!* I shake my head to gather my thoughts, but no matter what I do, I can't stop smiling.

"I'm sorry for last night," I say. It's not the right time to talk about this but I feel like if I don't clear the air then I won't be able to enjoy this wonderful lunch.

Jett sips his water and then gives me this sweet smile. His eyes gaze into mine. "No need to be sorry. This is a huge life change for you and you're allowed to get mad about it."

"I was such a bitch to you," I say, shaking my head.

"So? It's okay. You're still my girl, right?"

A flash of something like fear flickers across his features and I want to throw myself on him and show him just how much I am his. "Of course I am." I lick my bottom lip. "You're my rock."

He takes my cheek in his hand and places a soft kiss on my lips. "Let's start over. I won't bug you about going to high school and staying with Becca anymore." He tilts his head. "Eh, well, I won't do it for like two weeks."

I grin. "Okay, truce. But you need to know that it's not like I *don't* want to go to high school with you. I'm just sick of feeling like I'm overstaying my welcome at the Park's."

"You're not," he says, handing me the olive container that I'm too far away to reach.

"How can you be so sure about that?" I ask, grabbing a black olive.

"Because I'm awesome," he says, relaxing back on his hands. "Just trust in the magic of my wisdom, my dear."

CHAPTER EIGHT

Jett

After our picnic lunch, Keanna's mood seems better than it's ever been. She doesn't stop smiling or joking around with me. There are still issues I feel like we need to talk about, still a ton of good points I'd like to make to hopefully convince her to stay here and go to school, but I'd promised I wouldn't so I keep my mouth shut.

I'm pretty sure all of this wanting to move out stuff is something she's brought upon herself. When Becca and Park say they don't mind having her live with them, I believe it. They're good people and they wouldn't lie about that kind of thing. It makes me wonder if Keanna overheard them saying something that would make her think otherwise.

Anyhow, I don't want her to quit school and move out. If she did that, she'd probably find a better job, and meet older people and move on without me. Why would she still want to date me if I'm a year younger than she is and still in high school? She'll probably meet some twenty-something guy with a real career type job and his own house and she'd choose him over me.

An ache grows in my chest and Keanna talks for a few more minutes before she stops and frowns at me. "Are you feeling sick?"

"Nah, I'm fine," I say, reaching up and tickling her side. She jerks away and holds back a giggle.

"Well, you look weird. Was my story boring you?"

I shake my head and move the plastic trays of food away so I can slide closer to her. "I was just thinking about how much it would suck to lose you."

She blows a raspberry. "Lame. Why would you think negative thoughts on this super romantic picnic date?"

I shrug and lean back on my elbows. "I don't know. You're right, I shouldn't."

She lays on her side and snuggles up next to me. I brush the hair out of her face, but it's just an excuse to cup her chin and bring her in for a kiss.

That kiss leads to making out, and soon Keanna's hair is all in my face while she lays on top me. I run my hands down her back while we kiss, and I swear the more times we do this, the better we fit together. Our bodies know each other and kissing her feels better than kissing anyone else.

She pulls away and gives me a devilish grin. "You know what I want to do?"

The look she gives me is such a turn on. "Tell me."

She sits up and tucks her hair behind her ears. "I want to take a ride on your bike again."

I can't help but laugh. "And here I thought you wanted some of this," I say, gesturing to my body.

She shakes her head. "Eh I've had enough of you for one day. Will you drive me around some more? It was fun."

"Of course," I say, pretending to be all insulted that she doesn't want to make out. She squeals and then dives on top of me again, giving me one last sweet kiss.

"I'll make it up to you tonight," she whispers in my ear before sitting back up and jumping to her feet. "Right now I want to feel the wind in my face."

I stand up and hand her my helmet. "As you wish."

CHAPTER NINE

Keanna

Why is it that when things seem to be going right, my brain decides to unleash the fury of its horrible imagination during my sleep? I wake up for the third time tonight, breathless and panicked from another nightmare. It doesn't even make sense because I'd had such a great time with Jett earlier this evening. Then we both had dinner with Park and Becca and everything was great. So why did I just dream that Jett sat me down on the bottom bleacher in some imaginary high school gymnasium just to humiliate me?

My cheeks burn as the entire dream floats across my mind. Usually waking up from a bad dream makes them go away. This time, it lingers in my memories, playing over and over again.

I asked him what we were doing at a random high school gym and he just told me to wait. He said he had a secret for me. I thought maybe it was another romantic picnic, but then suddenly hundreds of teenagers came bursting in through the doors, marching across the gym floor and sitting in the bleachers on the other side of the room.

Suddenly I was high up, no longer sitting with my feet on the floor but on the top bleacher seat, all by myself. The entire other side of the room was filled with people, scornful faces, mocking grins.

Jett stood in the middle of the floor, now holding a microphone.

"What's going on?" I asked.

He just laughed, evil and maniacal like some evil villain in a movie. "I wanted everyone to see," he said, spreading his arms out to the crowd. "When I told you that you will never be my girlfriend, that I will never love you, and that you'll never be good enough to date me, Keanna Byrd."

Everyone laughed, all of those faces of people I'd never even met. Jett's normally sexy smile turned evil, angry, as he laughed right along with them until I stood and tried to run away.

Of course, it was a dream, so I didn't get far. I just woke up in my bed, panting and wanting to cry. Now that I'm fully awake and back in reality, I know the dream was stupid. Jett would never do that to me. Even if he decided he didn't like me anymore, it's not like he'd publicly shame me for it, so *why* is my stupid brain giving me these nightmares?

I reach for my phone to see what time it is, and find a new text message from Jett. He sent it at midnight, about an hour he left. I guess I was already asleep so I missed it.

My chest aches as I click on the message, almost worried that I'm still asleep and this is just part of the nightmare.

Jett: *I can't sleep... miss you too much.*

Okay, I'm definitely not still sleeping. I stare at his words until the pain in my heart is gone and I roll back over and tell myself to dream something nice for a change.

I WAKE UP IN THE MORNING TO BECCA CALLING MY NAME. MY EYES OPEN AND I SEE her standing in my doorway. "You're late for work, kiddo!"

"Shit," I curse, throwing the blankets off me.

Becca chuckles. "You'll be all right. It's lock-in day though so get over there as soon as you can, okay? I have bagels in the front office."

"Cool," I say, giving her a smile that hopefully makes her forgive me for sleeping past my alarm.

I throw on some shorts and a black T-shirt with The Track's logo on it and the word STAFF across the back. It's my favorite work shirt because it makes me feel official. The Track doesn't make us wear them since the owners are the coolest people on earth, but I'm wearing mine today since it's lock-in day.

Lock-in day happens every couple of weeks. It's where about a dozen kids of various age groups (tonight is the junior high age group) will bring their dirt bikes and sleeping bags and spend all day getting riding lessons from Jace and Park. Then we order a bunch of pizza and movies and they all pile into the lounge room and have a sleep over, only to wake up and ride again the next day.

I've been registering teenagers all week for this event, and at three hundred dollars per kid, Jace and Park are really raking in the cash. I've never given too much thought to what I want to do when I'm older but I think it'd be really cool to own a business.

"What's up?" Jett says. I jump at the sound of his voice because I was just logging into the computer system and didn't hear him approach from behind me.

"You scared me, you butt." I pretend to punch him in the arm.

"Did you know you were humming to yourself?" he says, shifting his feet until he's standing directly behind me.

"I was not," I say, typing on the keyboard.

He slides his hands around my waist, pressing his palms flat against my stomach as he rests his chin on my shoulder. I can feel his tight chest muscles on my back and electricity runs up my spine. "Yes you were."

"I wasn't humming," I mutter, trying to log into the computer and ignore the tingling in my belly at the same time.

He chuckles and kisses my neck. Okay, no more ignoring the tingling. "You were, too," he whispers in my ear. "What were you thinking about?"

I turn, mostly to break his contact from me because I simply can*not* attempt to get any work done if he's this close to me. Something tells me his parents wouldn't be too fond of me ignoring the customers because I'm making out with their son on the front counter.

I smile. "Actually, I was thinking about how cool it would be to own my own business. I just don't know what that would be."

"I'll be taking over this place when my dad retires," Jett says, tapping the counter. "We can run it just like my parents do."

I put a hand on my hip. "And when will that be?"

He looks up toward the ceiling. "Probably twenty years or so. It'll be after my professional supercross career is done."

He catches my eye and reaches for a bagel from the box Becca left for me.

"That's some long term life planning you got there," I say. I know he's just talking. It's not like we can see into the future to see if we'll stay together that long.

Jett nods and takes a huge bite of his bagel. "I like to think ahead. But if you have another business idea, that's cool with me. We can do both."

The door opens, making the little cowbell tied to the handle jingle. "Hi, welcome to The Track," I say in my welcoming employee voice. "Are you here for the lock-in?"

"I'll catch you later," Jett whispers, giving me a quick kiss on the cheek before ducking into the back hallway.

The woman approaches the desk, eyeing Jett as he walks away. "Is that Jett Adams?" she asks, turning toward me. Her extra sleek brown ponytail swishes behind her. Next to her is a young boy carrying a sleeping bag and a huge motocross gear bag in his arms.

"Yes. He'll be helping with the seventh graders today and the eighth graders tomorrow."

She gives a curt nod. "And you are . . ?"

"Keanna," I say, but it comes out sounding like a question.

"But you are . . ." The look she gives me makes my insides twist into knots.

"Jett's girlfriend," I say, and again, it also sounds like a question. I straighten my shoulders. This lady is way too old to be crushing on Jett so I don't know why I'm letting her intimidate me. "I'm his girlfriend. But I also work here and I'd be happy to get you signed in."

"Oh wow, well my daughter will be very displeased with that news," the woman says. She makes this noise with her throat that could be considered a chuckle, I guess. "She is convinced she'll be marrying the boy one day."

She hands me her registration info and I sign in her son, not really knowing what to say to that. Every teenage girl seems to have a crush on Jett, so it doesn't really matter.

"Well, I guess there's always plenty of time for her to get her chance," the woman says.

"You can take your stuff right down this hallway and to the left," I say, using my friendly employee voice. I will not let this bitch get to me. "There's signs on the wall directing you where to go. Please have a great time!"

It takes several deep breaths to feel back to normal after the woman drops off her son and leaves. Other kids start showing up and I sign them all in and luckily there are no more incidents like the first one.

I'm reaching for my second bagel when the door opens and I drop it back in the box. Eating in front of customers is rude, and I'm still trying to impress my bosses every chance I get.

D'andre walks in, drinking from one of those massive convenient store soda cups. I relax and reach for the bagel again.

"Good morning," I say, spreading some cream cheese on the bagel. "You're here early."

D'andre is one of Jett's best friends and he also rides motocross. He leans across the front counter, resting on his elbows. "Tell me about it," he says, drinking more of his soda. "I'm hoping this caffeine will wake me up. Homeboy made me get here early today to help him wrangle the kids."

I laugh. "Isn't that Park and Jace's job?"

He shrugs. "Technically, but Mr. Adams is paying me a hundred bucks under the table just to help out with lunch. Not bad."

I nod. "Want a bagel?" I slide the box over to him and he takes one. "Jett's already back there in the lounge if you want to go find him.

"I actually wanted to talk to you for a minute," D'andre says.

Panic latches onto my ankles. I worried about the day that Jett's friends would question our relationship, or bring up the fact that I don't deserve to be with their friend. "What's going on? I ask, my voice dry.

His teeth dig into his bottom lip. "Okay so, there's this girl," he says. I lift an eyebrow. He takes out his phone and flips through the screen. "Her name is Maya." He turns the phone to me, showing me a photo of a pretty African American girl wearing a Lawson High School cheerleading uniform.

"She's pretty," I say, noticing the bashful way he's looking at her photo. "What about her?"

"Well, believe it or not, she's actually been on a couple of dates with me." He grins and he's like a little kid, all shy and sweet when he talks about her.

"Aww, you must really like her!" I say, poking him with my plastic cream cheese knife.

"I do. And she is *so* out of my league here." He swallows and shakes his head. "So anyway, she seems to like me and I'm trying not to blow it. She doesn't know anything about motocross but she thinks it's cool so maybe you could help me out?"

"I'd be happy to date your pretty friend," I say, winking.

He laughs. "Oh *ha-ha*. I'm thinking we could go on a double date and meet at the track. Maybe you can help me convince her that I'm worth her time?"

"Sure," I say, giving him a warm smile. "I'd love to."

He points at me. "I knew you were a cool chick," he says, taking another bite of his bagel.

I snort. "Psh. Duh."

When my shift is over at five, I clock out and then begin shutting down the computer system. Jett wants me to hang out with him all night while he's wrangling the kiddos. We ordered pizza for lunch and now for dinner, we're having toasted sandwiches from this delicious shop in town. I can hear all of the excited voices filtering in from the lounge as I go through my closing the shop routine. It'll be fun to be a chaperone with Jett tonight. It'll feel like I'm finally the adult in a situation where I've always been the kid. Plus, in a way, it's like I'm experiencing all the fun stuff that normal kids experience. I can't imagine Dawn ever paying money for me to go somewhere fun like this.

Becca and Park walk in from the back hallway. Becca twists her wedding ring around her finger.

"Hey, kid," Park says. He pats my back as he walks by. "Good day at work?"

I nod. "Is everything okay?" They both look like they want to tell me something, like maybe they need me to stay late and work tonight. "I was just about to go help out Jett," I say, gesturing toward the hallway.

"Could you wait on that for a minute?" Becca says. "We'd like to talk to you."

My blood turns to ice. No. Not now. This can't happen now.

I look from her to Park and back. Their expressions are serious, but not exactly what I'd expect if they were going to kick me out.

"Okay, let's talk." My own voice doesn't sound the same when I say it. I am far too scared to be coherent right now.

Park smiles. "Let's go back home to talk."

The short walk home feels like I'm walking to my death. Becca fills the silence with happy, pointless chit-chat, but I don't hear a word she says. Finally, we get inside and they tell me to have a seat at the dining table.

So this is how I get kicked out.

My hands shake so I close them into fists and keep them in my lap. Every time I blink, it feels like I'm going to cry.

"So," Becca says, giving me this warm smile. "I know this might be awkward and there's really no easy way to talk about this kind of thing . . ."

I blink back tears and wish she'd just rip it off like a bandage. Park clears his throat. They're both sitting next to each other and I'm on the other side of this small table, yet it feels like I've already been cast out into the streets.

Park takes Becca's hand. "Becca and I have been doing a lot of talking and soul-searching, and although we feel like it's the right choice for us, want you to know that you have a say-so as well."

I almost laugh. Right. Like I can choose to not get kicked out.

Becca gives a loving look to her husband and then looks at me. "We know you're seventeen and you're almost an adult, and by then you can do anything you want." She breathes in through her nose and then tilts her head. "But, well—" She grins. "We'd like to adopt you."

CHAPTER TEN

Jett

Between D'andre talking my face off about Maya, and the seventh graders arguing over who gets to set up their sleeping bag directly in front of the wall-mounted TV, I'm having a hard time keeping my thoughts straight. I keep checking the door for Keanna, since she's the only person I care to see right now. It's twenty minutes after she got off work, so maybe she went home to change clothes or something.

D'andre leans against the wall, scrolling through photos of Maya on her Facebook page. He's been talking for the last ten minutes but I kind of stopped paying attention. He's my best friend, but he could use a lesson in chilling out when it comes to being obsessed over a girl.

Today was a pretty good day at the track. Training guys who are closer to my age is a lot easier than it was when I had to help train the five and six year-olds. Plus, the little kids only ride on the little track and that is boring as hell. Today we stuck to the main tracks, and I taught a few guys how to fix their form in the turns. Dad also seemed impressed with me, which is great because I'd love to become one of the official trainers one day.

Of course, I also want to turn pro as soon as I'm eighteen, and that will have me traveling all over the country, racing each weekend. To put it lightly, motocross has been my entire life and it will be my entire future. Luckily, I wouldn't want it any other way.

Dad calls out to get everyone's attention and then he gives the group a pep talk, talking about how great they were in practice today. Usually Park is here for this part too, but I don't see him. Dad tells everyone to enjoy dinner and then get their sleeping bags set up.

Tonight's entertainment is a stack of Metal Mulisha DVDs and everyone is pretty psyched about it. Mom brings in three power strips, asking if that's enough outlets for everyone's phone chargers.

Since they have it all under control, I grab a sandwich from the catering platter and join D'andre against the wall.

"Yeah man, so Keanna said she's cool with a double date," he says, finally looking up from his phone. "Where should we go?"

"Dinner?" I ask with a shrug. I look back at the doors again. Where is she? Yeah, this makes me a douche, but I'm kind of dying for the guys to see my hot girlfriend. I've been hoping she'll get here before they all settle down and watch the movies.

My phone buzzes.

Keanna: *We need to talk.*

Before I can reply, it buzzes again.

Keanna: *now. Like now.*

Me: *Come to the Track?*

Keanna: *already walking over.*

"Hey, I'll be right back," I tell D'andre. "I'm going to go get Keanna. Can you fill in for me for a few minutes?"

"Sure thing," he says, reaching for another sandwich.

I stuff the rest of my sandwich in my mouth and jog out of the building. Things between us are good so I'm not too worried about whatever she wants to talk about. Still, she's never acted this weird. I find her walking quickly across the grass, her eyes are wide and she's chewing on her bottom lip. It almost looks like she's been crying.

"Key?" She walks straight into my arms. I told on tight and kiss the top of her head. "Everything okay?"

She nods, her head pressed against my chest. "Let's go inside. I need to be sitting when I talk to you."

In the front office, we sit facing each other on the two barstools behind the front counter. Keanna's feet twitch and her whole body seems to be bouncing with excitement.

"So what's going on?" I ask, lifting an eyebrow.

She holds out her hands as if bracing me for whatever she wants to say while she takes in a deep breath. "Park and Becca . . ."

Her eyes sparkle and her cheeks go pink. I am literally on the edge of this barstool waiting to hear what she'll say next.

"Babe," I say. "What is it?"

She smiles so wide it reaches her eyes. "They want to adopt me."

"Whoa."

At first it's just words. But then the weight of the situation sinks in. "They want you to be their legal child?"

She nods and leans forward, her foot tapping like crazy. "They said if they legally adopt me then I can get on their health insurance and they'll be my legal guardians. They can enroll me in school and help pay for college and even train me to take over their half of this business one day."

"Whoa," I say again.

She laughs. "Becca said she's wanted a kid so long it's driving her crazy. Trust me, it took everything I had not to mention the surrogacy thing, but they said they love having me here and they don't want me to spend my life without a real family. Park even said he'd love to be called 'Dad', can you believe that?"

"So what do you think about all of this?" I ask her.

She's quiet for a moment but her face stays happy and serene. "Well, at first I'm like yes, obviously. They're such great people. And if they become my adopted parents then I can stay here and go to school, ya know?"

"You could have done that anyway," I say. She rolls her eyes.

"But then I'd feel bad about abandoning my mom . . ."

I think it over first but decide to say it anyway. "She abandoned you first."

Her eyes meet mine and she nods slowly. "That's why I shouldn't feel guilty about this, right?"

"I can't tell you what to think, babe. This has to come from you."

"I want to do it," she says while staring at her nails. "I do feel guilty about my mom, but she's abandoned me and there's also years of neglect on her record when it comes to parenting. I'm not sure she deserves to have me as her kid anymore. I mean she left me by texting *you* . . .she couldn't even tell me herself."

She's quiet for a minute and then she smiles. "Here I was thinking I was a huge burden to them and then they tell me they love having me around and have started considering me their daughter. It's kind of awesome."

I touch her arm and rub my thumb across her skin. "It's really awesome. Becca loves kids and she's always wanted one. There's room for you and the new baby, you know. Their house is huge."

She nods. "I'll have a father figure for the first time in my life." She tosses her arms in the air. "I'll have *parents* who actually *care* what happens to me."

"That's a good thing, right?"

She slips off the stool and takes a step toward me. I open my knees to let her move in closer and she wraps her hands around my waist. "I think it is," she says. "I think it's a really good thing."

CHAPTER ELEVEN

Keanna

The Lawson county courthouse is a small building that somehow managed to stay exactly the same as it was in the eighties. With the exception of a slightly newer set of computers (that are still old), everything is ancient. The wood-paneled walls smell like a grandparent's house but there's a country charm to the place that almost makes you think you're on vacation somewhere remote and desolate.

The entire process goes quickly. I stand between Becca and Park, whose first name is actually Nolan. I know I knew that but since we only call him by his last name, I totally forgot it. It only trips me up a little bit when the judge calls our names.

He's an older man, portly and balding with gray hair and a tweed blazer. He reads over the adoption procedure and we all sign paperwork and swear an oath.

When it's all said and done, his secretary, who looks twice his age but is dressed to impress in a purple pantsuit, steps forward. "Ready to take a picture?"

So we stand there: me, Park, and Becca with Judge Peterson. The dark wood desk is behind us and an American and Texan flag stands on either side. Someone hands me the certificate of adoption and I hold it in front of my chest.

My grin is pretty huge when the camera flash goes off, and I hope it's a good photo. It's our first family photo, after all.

The secretary says she'll email it to us as soon as she gets back to her desk. I look over at Becca as we walk out of the courtroom and she's a total mess.

"Are you crying?" I ask all lightheartedly, because I'm about to make fun of her. But then she nods and her face wrinkles up and she cries even harder and now I'm fighting tears.

We step into the tiled foyer of the courthouse and Park opens the door for us, leading us out into the beautiful cloudless day.

"I'm so sorry," Becca says, wiping at her eyes. "This is just very emotional."

I smile. "Are you going to run back and tell them you changed your mind?"

"Oh no. Never." She shakes her head furiously and Park chuckles while we walk to his truck.

"Okay, girls," Park says, checking his watch. "We have a little time to kill before dinner." He gives me an excited look. "You want to go to the DMV and see what it'll take to get your license?"

"Oh my god, are you serious?" I stop so abruptly, I run straight into the open truck door.

"Well you're seventeen. What seventeen-year-old doesn't want to drive?"

My grin is the size of Texas. "Let's go to the DMV."

It took two weeks to get the adoption all set up. That night when my new parents talked to me about it, I had sent my mother a text from Jett's phone, explaining the situation. I asked her to please let me know how she feels about it. When two days went by without a reply—I was practically glued to Jett's phone the whole time—I sent her a text from mine. The first time I gave my mother my new phone number. I put it off for a long time because I kept thinking I if I gave her the number and she never used it then it would hurt more than if I purposely never talked to her.

Well these two weeks went by without a single text from the woman who gave birth to me. I didn't tell Jett this, but I sent her one text a day. And no replies. So maybe it's harsh on my part, but I am totally at peace with my decision to denounce my mother's guardianship and become the legal child of Becca and Park.

I spend a lot of time reading the inspirational paintings around the house, and they all tell me the same things I need to hear. That moving on is good, okay, and for the best. It's time for me to become the person I am capable of being, without having to drag around the weight of my mother's bad influence.

I can have a future now, a real life. I can make good choices and have solid, loving people who care about me. And it feels really good.

I don't know how Becca did it all, but she got my birth certificate and my social security card reissued. The paperwork has been done and filed and after we leave the DMV, I'm signed up for driving classes and have a paper version of my identification card. It's not a real driver's license yet since I have to pass the class first, but it's a state issued ID. With a real home address. Still pretty cool.

I stare at the paper in my hands. I'm sitting in the backseat of Park's truck while we head home.

Keanna Park

My new adopted parents told me that I didn't *have* to take their last name. But I wanted to. They're sacrificing so much for me already and they've *welcomed me into their house and their lives*, so the very least I can do is become one of them. A Park.

I smile and my chest feels warm. I am a new person now. I've shed the old pain and I'm starting all over. This new girl *can* be Jett's girlfriend. She can have a normal life and stay in the same house for years at a time. She won't ever be homeless again.

"Keanna? Did you hear me?"

I look up. We're pulling into the driveway and Becca is giving me a concerned look from the front seat. In the rear-view mirror, Park glances at me.

"Sorry, I was zoned out. Did you say something?"

She laughs. "I said we should redecorate your room now. Make it more you."

"Yeah that could be fun, but I like it the way it is, honestly."

"No can do," Park says. "You should have *seen* Becca's room when she was your age. There was paint and canvases and *glitter* and all kinds of girlie crap everywhere."

"Um, it wasn't crap. It was *art*," she says, shoving him in the shoulder.

He shuts off the engine and looks back at me. "It was crap," he says with a wink. "But it was a teenager's room, that's for sure. You keep your room way too clean and tidy."

I'm not about to tell him that I keep it clean both because it was never really mine until now, and because when you don't have many things, it's hard to be dirty.

Becca starts talking about paint colors and bedroom themes while we go inside our house. It feels awesome saying *our* house, so I do. I say it in my head all constantly now. I allow myself to think that this is my home, and my room, and my furniture.

I let Becca throw a bunch of ideas out there, even though I don't really care how we decorate my new official room. I'm happy just *having* a room. It doesn't need a theme. As far as I'm concerned, the theme is home.

"Alright girls," Park says, clapping his hands together. "We have an hour and fifteen minutes . . . is that enough time to get ready or should I change the reservation?"

I lift an eyebrow. "Get ready for what?"

Becca's eyes crinkle. "Oops, did I forget to tell you . . ." she says all slowly, giving me the side eye. Then she grins really wide. "We're taking you out to celebrate becoming our kid!"

Park throws an arm around his wife's shoulders. "I'm very sorry your new mom is the biggest dork on earth, Keanna. I really am."

She blows a raspberry and flips her hair over her shoulder. "Keanna, dear. I am *so* very sorry that your new dad is a total dork."

"See?" Park says, looking at his wife like she's a basket case. "She's so dorky, she doesn't even know how to identify a dork."

"Okay I think I can settle this," I say. I'm still reeling over the terms 'mom' and 'dad' but I manage to keep it together. "You're both dorks," I say, putting my hands on my hips.

Becca gazes up at Park with this adoring look on her face. "Well, babe, I'm happy to be whatever you are."

They kiss and heat rushes to my cheeks. I hope I grow up to be just like them.

"Okay, now we have one hour and ten minutes," Park says, eyes wide. He looks at me. "Keanna should be fine, but Bec takes no less than a century to get her hair fixed anytime we go somewhere fancy, so she better hurry."

"I do not," Becca mutters, swatting at him as she walks by. He ducks it and grins at me.

"Wait, we're going somewhere fancy?" I ask.

"Of course," Becca says, throwing an arm around my shoulders. "We're celebrating! So dress nice."

"How nice? I don't really have a lot of stuff," I say, looking up to the ceiling as I mentally think over my wardrobe.

"Wear that white dress," Becca says, nodding in approval. "It'll look great."

CHAPTER TWELVE

Jett

While Keanna is getting officially adopted, I'm sitting around the kitchen island with my parents, snacking on chopped up carrots and broccoli with ranch dip. I'm very excited for her and it's taking everything I have not to text her and ruin her special event with her new parents.

"You know what would go great with this?" I ask, pointing to the carrot in my hand. "Those brownies in the pantry."

Mom rolls her eyes. "Only healthy snacks. We're going out to dinner in a couple hours and you don't want to ruin your appetite."

"Mom," I say, giving her a look. "When is my appetite ever ruined? I'm always ready to eat."

Dad reaches for a carrot. "That may be true son, but respect your mom's wishes."

"Yes sir," I say, casting a longing glance toward the pantry.

"Do you have a dress shirt ironed for tonight?" Mom says. She just got her nails done so she reaches for a piece of broccoli as if the polish is still wet.

"Yeah, I think so. The blue one should be ready."

"Great. We're going to a really classy place, so we all have to pretend that we're even two percent classy, okay?"

Dad and I laugh and we agree to do the best we can but Mom doesn't exactly look convinced.

"I can't believe my best friend adopted a seventeen-year-old after only knowing her a couple of months," Mom says. She sinks her chin into her hand and gazes out the back window.

"Well if things had gone the way Becca wanted them to, she'd have a teenager right now. Hell, she'd probably have three or four kids," Dad says. "Can you imagine how great it'll be when they get their new baby and he drives Park crazy the way Jett used to drive me crazy?" Dad chuckles and shakes his head. "It'll be awesome."

"Hey!" I say, pretending to be offended.

Mom waves away my worry with her hand. "You were a great baby, Jett." Her head tilts. "Kind of a pain in the ass when you were five to seven though . . ."

I wince. "Sorry."

Mom shrugs. "Back then we were only a couple years into the business and we were still working out all the kinks. That kid room at the Track practically raised you, not us." She points a carrot stick at me. "But you turned out okay, so far."

I glance at my phone. "I wonder if they're back yet?"

Dad is closer to the back window than I am, and he gazes out of it. "Doesn't look like it."

"You'll be back with her before you know it," Mom says, rolling her eyes. "Jace, were we as love-struck as our kid? We couldn't have possibly been that bad."

Dad's brows lift. "Of course we were! You were totally in love with me from the start," he says, shaking his head. "Couldn't keep your hands off me . . ."

Mom makes a sarcastic face and looks at me. "So things with you and Keanna are getting kind of serious?"

My parents are cool—way cooler than most of my friend's parents—but it's still awkward talking to them about my relationships. Especially since I've never really talked to them about girls before. Keanna is my first real girlfriend. Simply saying yes, we're serious, doesn't seem like it'd do the relationship justice. But I say it anyway.

"Well I never thought I'd hear my son say that," Dad says with a mouth full of broccoli.

"Okay, you're acting like I'm some kind of man slut," I say.

Mom and Dad look at me. I throw up my hands. "Okay, I'm not anymore. I'm an honest man now."

"Well, while we're on the subject of girls, you should probably brace yourself for dealing with Keanna over the next few days or weeks," Mom says. "She's going through a lot, and she's already been through a lot in her life. You may think she's the only thing you care about, but she has a lot of stuff in her life right now, so don't get upset if she can't dedicate all of her attention to you."

"That's a good point," Dad says. "Don't get upset if she doesn't text you constantly," he says, nodding to my phone which I've been looking at every few seconds. "She'll need you to be there for her but don't be pushy about anything."

The words kind of sting because I want to spend every waking second with her, but I nod. "That's actually good advice. Thank you."

My parents exchange a look. "Our advice is always good advice!" Mom says. "It's funny though," she says, looking off in the distance. "When you were a baby, Becca and I used to talk about having kids close in age and then they would date each other. Now, it's kind of happening."

I smile. "With any luck, Keanna and I will turn out just like you and dad. And Becca and Park."

Mom picks up the veggies and starts packing them away in the fridge. "Maybe you should aim for being like Becca and Park, not me and your dad. Being a teen parent sucks and ages you terribly."

"Aww, don't say that, Mom. You look amazing. You don't look a day over twenty-five."

She pats my head as she walks by. "That's my son. Now go get dressed up nice and show Keanna how lucky she is to have you."

CHAPTER THIRTEEN

Keanna

My celebration dinner is going to be a hundred times better now that my new parents have told me Jett and his family are coming, too. I'm practically dancing around my room as I get dressed. All of this family stuff has been amazing and life changing but all day I've just wanted to share it with Jett. But I need to be here too, at my new house, to experience how wonderful it all is. And now he'll be at dinner so I get the best of both worlds.

My fists shake in excitement, and I laugh at myself in the mirror. Everything is so awesome right now, I'm not even sure how to handle it. My brain might just explode. On my death certificate they'll say the cause of death was too much happiness.

The white dress is part of my new wardrobe. It's dual-layered. The bottom layer is made out of T-shirt material that's sleeveless and very short, like a mini skirt. But then a sheer white layer on top has tank top sleeves and it goes down to just above my knees in the front, but gets long and flowy in the back. I feel like a mermaid or some kind of beach princess in it. Even better, Jett had stepped outside to take a phone call when I was trying it on at the mall, so I'm pretty sure he hasn't seen me in it.

I want to wow him tonight, so I borrow Becca's curling iron and use it to make big, flowy curls around my face. I do my makeup, using a combination of the eyeliner I've had from the old days with Dawn, and the new makeup I recently bought. I don't usually wear any makeup around here, especially since it's so hot outside I'd just sweat it off. But we're going out to dinner and I want my looks to reflect just how beautiful my life is right now.

When I'm satisfied with my hair and makeup, I hear Park call out, "Fifteen minutes, girls!"

Becca calls out, "I only need five!"

And just to join in on the yelling across the house, I say, "I'm already ready! I win!"

The bathroom in the master room is almost as big as my bedroom, and it has a built-in vanity with a mirror bordered in lights just like some Hollywood actress's dressing room.

I knock on the door as I pop my head in.

"Come on in," Becca says, motioning with her hand. She leans forward, looking into a handheld mirror on the counter as she applies her mascara.

"Just bringing back your curling iron," I say, holding it up. "Thanks for letting me borrow it."

She points to a cabinet to her left. "It goes in there, and you're welcome to borrow it anytime, dear."

Becca stops me when I go to leave. "Turn around," she says, twirling her finger.

I spin slowly. Her lips purse. "Hmm . . . you look nice but you need something extra."

She walks into her closet, motioning for me to follow. Inside, it's like a home organizer's dream. Cubby holes and shelves and rows of hanging clothes. Their master closet is spectacular. Becca goes to a tall jewelry cabinet and pulls open the drawers, searching through them.

"Here," she says, smiling as she takes out a silver necklace with a sparkling blue pendant. She puts it around my neck and then steps back to admire me. "Perfect!"

I finger the sparkling jewel and check out my reflection in the tall mirror mounted inside the closet. "Thanks," I say softly.

"Anything in here you can wear any time you want, okay?"

I nod. So this is what it's like having a normal mother. I can definitely get used to it.

I TEXT JETT ON THE DRIVE OVER TO THE RESTAURANT.

Me: *I miss you*

Jett: *I miss you more*

Me: *How far away is this place?*

Jett: *About 45 minutes, if it's the place I'm thinking of.*

I GROAN. THIS DAY HAS BEEN SO WONDERFUL, WAKING UP AND MAKING BLUEBERRY pancakes with Becca, then having lunch with her and Park before going to the courthouse. Even the long line at the DMV was fun, but now that I'm so close to seeing Jett, I'm desperate to be with him again. I'm missing the woodsy scent of his cologne and the flash of mischief in his eyes.

I kind of wanted to ask if I could ride with Jett to the restaurant, but then he said his dad was driving them. There's no point in taking three cars, and since it's my first day as an official member of this family, I need to be riding with Becca and Park. I just miss Jett so much. It really is kind of pathetic.

Inadequate doesn't even begin to describe how I'm feeling when we get to the restaurant. For starters, there's valet parking, so we climb out at the front of the restaurant and someone else drives away Park's truck. The Lantern is a posh place that's on the water of Lake Conroe, so you can see yachts and boats out on the water while you're eating. The hostess is dressed nicer than I am and she leads us to our table.

My stomach tightens with nerves as we walk through the elegant dining room. I am so close to seeing Jett and I need him so bad. I can't even function without him now, as silly as that is. I guess I've just been through so much in the last few days that he is my normalcy. My rock. I need him so I can feel grounded again.

His blue eyes crinkle when he sees me. It takes everything I have not to break into a sprint and throw myself at him. Instead, I play the role of *normal human* and nod politely.

Jett looks like a movie star. Wearing black slacks that look as though they were custom made for him, and a dark blue long-sleeved shirt that hugs his chest and arms just enough to show his muscle definition. He stands, and he reminds me a lot of his dad since they're both dressed nicely tonight.

Bayleigh wears a little black dress that makes her look gorgeous. She puts the rest of us women to shame.

Jett wraps me in a tight but chaste hug. "I missed you," he whispers as he lets me go. Jace and Bayleigh also hug me, welcoming me into Park's family.

Before I take my seat, I notice Becca across the table. She's staring with a confused look on her face. "Why are there two?"

I don't know what she's talking about, but I slip into the chair next to Jett and thread my fingers through his.

Bayleigh clears her throat. "I'll explain in a second, Becca, but first of all, I don't think your new daughter even noticed what's in front of her."

I look up. "Huh?"

And then I see it, a gorgeous bouquet of flowers in pinks and blues and purples. A card in the middle has my name on it. I flush. Yeah, I totally didn't notice that.

"Thanks guys," I say, taking the card.

It says *Welcome to the family. We love you -The Adams'*

I look up to thank them for the kind gift, but then I see what made Becca so confused. There are two bouquets of flowers on the table.

Bayleigh stands up and we all turn to look at her. "This second bouquet is for you," she says, sliding the vase across the table to Becca.

"Me?" Becca says, putting a hand to her chest. "I don't need flowers . . ." She says, rambling on as she takes the card out of the little plastic holder.

I can tell by the look on Bayleigh's face that something else is going on. Something good.

"This is very sweet guys, but—" Becca stops rambling mid-sentence and puts a hand to her mouth. "Oh my god." Her eyes fill with tears and Jett squeezes my hand and everything all happens at once.

"You're pregnant?" she says.

Bayleigh nods quickly and lifts her hands. "The procedure worked!"

Becca tumbles out of her chair and rushes across the table to wrap her arms around her best friend. My heart swells to what I'm sure is capacity but somehow manages to get even more happy as I watch the two men at the table shake hands, the experienced dad congratulating the new one.

Becca and Park embrace and I'm pretty sure they're both crying. I lean into Jett's arms until I'm halfway off my chair and halfway onto his. His strong arm wraps around me and holds me in place and I nuzzle against his neck, inhaling the scent of him.

"This is a good day," he says, kissing the top of my head.

Today I got parents and a new sibling in the same day. "Yeah," I say, smiling at Becca. "It's the best."

CHAPTER FOURTEEN

Jett

The gym is loud today. Normally I can tune out all the noise and listen to music on my earbuds while I work out, but today I'm working out with D'andre so no music. The gym at the track is huge enough to be a regular gym at one of those chain companies like 24 Hour Fitness. Because of this, we sell gym memberships to regular people too, not just dirt bike riders. It's a great source of extra income for the track, which my dad always stresses is important when you run a business, but sometimes it's annoying when I'm used to having the place largely to myself.

The Track is located right between two small towns and there aren't any other gyms nearby. So although today is a Thursday, and it's only two in the afternoon, seemingly everyone and their freaking mom is here working out today.

D'andre sits on the bench opposite of me and focuses on dumbbell curls. He's a lot stronger than I am but he doesn't give me shit about it, which is part of why we're friends. He doesn't get all macho man competitive with me. Of course, I'm faster than he is on a dirt bike so I guess it all evens out.

"That's kind of insane," he says after I've told him more details about the Parks adopting Keanna. "It's like a perfect girl for you just fell from the sky."

I snort and lift the weight bar. "It's a good thing, too, because there are no good girls for me here in Lawson."

"Yeah right," D'andre says quickly. "I seem to remember your ass dating a new girl every week before you met her."

I point at him. "Exactly. There weren't any girls to settle down with before. Now there is."

He shakes his head. "Keanna helps me out, too because now you're not taking all the chicks around here."

"What's up with you and Maya?" I say, sitting up and re-racking my weights. "Is that still going on?"

He nods. "I'm hoping my luck continues until school starts. Can you imagine what kind of cred I'll get by dating a cheerleader first thing? I'll have girls tripping over me like they used to trip over you."

I shake my head. "Don't even act like you're not completely obsessed with this girl, man. You couldn't be a player if you tried."

He sighs through his nose and readjusts the fifty-pound dumbbell to his other hand. "Hey, I only like her if she likes me, okay? At least, that's how I'm acting. That way if she ditches me for some other dude, it'll look like I don't care."

I sigh, suddenly feeling like I'm the Yoda of dating advice. "Man, the only way to pull off the vibe that you don't give a shit is to genuinely not give a shit. She'll see right through you if you're only faking it."

He grunts as he does a few last curls of the weight. "Then let's make sure she likes me."

A sudden high-pitched and insanely feminine ringing bursts through our part of the gym and D'andre grins like he's a kid in a candy store.

"What the hell was that?" I ask.

He reaches into his pocket and takes out his phone, all the while his smile stretches across his whole face. "It's Maya texting me."

I run a hand through my hair that's half wet with sweat, so then I wipe my hands on my shirt. "What the hell is that ringtone though?"

He shrugs. "Last time we hung out she said she wanted a special tone for her number and I let her pick it out." He grins goofily and clutches the phone to his chest. "It's like music to my ears."

I stare at him. "You've officially gone off the deep end."

He reads her message and his eyes go wide. I can't tell if he's happy or terrified. "She said she wants to come see me."

"Tell her to stop by. Keanna loves watching me work out. I'm pretty sure all girls think it's hot. She can see you being all swole and shit."

He nods. "Good idea." I go back to working out while he types out a reply and then when the stupid girlie music plays again, he says, "She's on her way. Do me a favor and don't be charming, okay? I don't want her falling for you."

I put a hand to my chest. "I am a taken man, dude. You don't have to worry about me anymore."

"Keep telling yourself that," he says.

I move over to the leg press and send Keanna a quick text before I put my phone on the windowsill to keep it from falling out of my shorts on this weight machine. She's working the front desk today, otherwise she'd be back here hanging out with me.

Me: *I miss you*

Keanna: *Then come say hi!*

Me: *I will after this set. D's bringing a friend to come watch him work out.*

Keanna: *You mean *bats eyelashes* MAYA!!!?*

I laugh and type back: *Yep, that's her.*

Keanna: *He's so gaga over her it's a little insane.*

Me: *Just like how I'm gaga over you?*

She sends me a thumbs up emoji, followed by: *Bring her up here. I want to meet her.*

When Maya arrives, she's all smiles and anxious energy, and you'd be an idiot if you didn't figure out that she likes D'andre just as much as he likes her. I don't usually care about these things, but I'm happy for him. He's been single a long time and he wants a relationship more than anything. Maybe this will work out for him.

I let them hang out for a few minutes and then when their awkwardness with each other reaches epic proportions, I step in. "Hey, Maya," I say, waving at her as I towel off the sweat from around my face and neck. "Glad you could make it out."

Maya's expression hardens just a bit as she looks me over. "Hi, Jett."

There's a weirdness in the air and then she finally smiles, even though it doesn't feel very genuine. "I'm not really supposed to be talking to you," she says, looking back and wrapping her arm around D'andre's. "But I will for D'andre's sake."

I fold my arms across my chest. "Why can't you talk to me? We've always been cool."

She nods. "*We* have yeah but . . . well, if the girls on the cheer squad knew I was being nice to you then they'd kill me. You're not exactly their favorite person."

"Ah . . ." Like a sack of bricks hitting me in the chest, it all comes back to me. Last year at school, I *might* have dated one or two—or five—of the cheerleaders. None of those flings ended well. How did I forget that over the summer break?

I run a hand through my hair. "Well, I guess my next question is out. I was going to ask if you'd help welcome my girlfriend Keanna to school next week but . . . yeah . . ."

She laughs. "D'andre told me about your new girl. Apparently you got lucky and she just moved here so she doesn't know about your past."

"She knows," I say, feeling the weight grow heavier in my chest. "she's just okay with it. I'm a one-woman man now."

"That's good," she says, giving me a more genuine smile. D'andre has practically frozen in his spot, unable to stop grinning and looking at his arm where Maya has her tiny hand wrapped around it.

She waves the other hand as if waving away the bad vibes from the air. "It's cool. I'll be nice to your new girl. It's not her fault that every girl at LHS hates you," she says with a laugh.

"They don't *all* hate me," I say. Hell, most of them want to date me—but I'm not about to say that out loud. D'andre and Maya exchange a look so I amend my statement. "Okay, okay. *Some* of them don't hate me."

While they share a laugh at my expense, I bite down on my lip until it draws blood. This whole summer was a dream—a whimsical, falling-in-love, dream. Now that school starts next week, I'll be forced to face an entirely different life. High school.

Maybe packing up and running away with Keanna isn't such a bad idea after all.

"So," Maya says, putting her hands on her hips. "When do I get to meet this charming new girl who has stolen your heart?"

I swallow the lump in my throat. "Come on, I'll introduce you now."

CHAPTER FIFTEEN

Keanna

After four days of professional driving lessons followed by driving around town in Becca's Honda Accord, I'm a pretty good driver. Becca and Jett have taken turns studying the driver's manual with me and I'm pretty sure I'll pass the written test without a problem. The excitement of getting a license, even though I don't have a car, is still pretty awesome. I've been saving most of my money from work so maybe I'll be able to buy one by next summer. Plus, I'm pretty sure Becca will let me drive her car around, but I haven't asked yet. I'm not trying to push my luck here.

Becca walks into the living room while she's pulling her hair back into a messy bun. "You ready?"

I nod and turn off the TV. "I'm hoping this doesn't turn into one of those scenes from a teen movie where I make a total ass of myself."

Becca laughs and we walk outside to her car. "You're going to do fine. You've totally got this."

Park walks outside too, and remotely unlocks his truck. "You girls have fun," he calls out as he gives Becca a quick kiss. "I have some errands to run, but let me know how it goes."

"Will do," Becca says.

Park gives me a wink. "Good luck!"

At the DMV, we get to bypass the long line of people waiting for renewals and I'm brought to the back of the building into a small room. Much like the courthouse, this town's DMV hasn't been renovated since it was built. Who cares though? I can handle a little musty smell in an old classroom if it means getting a license.

The test goes by quickly and I'm the only one taking it which helps my nerves calm down. Then I'm brought outside where a thin man with wire-framed glasses explains the driving test to me. It's pretty simple—I get to use Becca's car if I want to, and I do, and so I don't have to get used to driving one of the DMV's loaner cars.

We cruise around the parking lot and he has me make several turns and practice parking. Then we drive up and down the main road a few times and then circle back. In all it takes about fifteen minutes, and absolutely nothing dramatic happens like in the movies. Phew.

"Congratulations Ms. Park," my instructor says. He hands me a piece of paper with his signature at the bottom. "You passed."

Becca sets her e-reader in her lap as soon as I emerge back in the waiting room. She watches me with eager eyes and a huge smile. "Well?"

I hold up my paper and grin. "I passed."

"That's my girl," she says, squeezing me in a hug. I get my paper license and they tell me the real one will come in the mail in a few days.

Out in the parking lot, Becca holds up the keys. "You want to do the honors?"

"Yep!" I say, taking the keys and sliding into the driver's seat. "Let me text Jett and tell him I passed real quick."

"Good idea," she says. She checks her own phone while I send a quick text to Jett.

"Okay, so should I take the highway back home or go to the left?" I ask. I don't really know my way around this area very well yet.

Becca frowns, looking at her phone. "You know what? I don't want to go home yet."

She squints as she looks around the parking lot and across the road where a shopping mall and a few fast food places wait. "Let's get lunch."

I try not to text Jett too much while Becca and I are eating toasted sub sandwiches at a nearby restaurant. It's definitely rude to be on my phone so I keep it to a minimal. Becca however, can't stop texting Park. I'm not sure what they're talking about and it would feel rude to ask, so I just eat quietly.

Becca frowns down at her phone screen when the waitress takes our empty plates away. "I don't feel like going home yet," she says. Her lips slide to the side of her mouth as she thinks. "There's a shoe store just up the road. "Want to go look for new school shoes?"

I agree because admitting that I only want to go home and cuddle with my boyfriend would be lame. Becca and I try on a million shoes and although I assure her that my favorite Chuck Taylors and a pair of sandals are all I need for school, she buys me three pairs anyway. I get a pair of running shoes for gym, some black ballet flats, and a silver pair of flats that are similar but covered in glitter. They make my feet feel like a mermaid.

Finally, Becca decides that we've done enough shopping and can go home. There are only four days until school starts and I plan on spending every single second of them snuggled up with Jett, watching TV. Now that summer is pretty much over, they don't need us to work at The Track since there are no more kids taking lessons during the day.

I'm elated as I grip Becca's steering wheel and drive us home. I am going to cuddle with Jett so hard. I don't even care how much of a dork that makes me. I need him and I hate being away from him.

We near our house and something dark purple and shiny catches my eye. "What the . . ." I manage to say before stopping the car at the end of the driveway. Parked facing the road, is a brand new dark purple Ford Mustang. There's a bright red bow on the hood. My jaw hits the floor and I look over at Becca.

"Surprise!" she says, throwing up her hands.

"That's . . ." I say, unable to find words. "That's a car."

"For you!" She beams. "That's why I had to stall so long. It took Park longer than he thought to get it home."

"This can't be real," I say. My vision blurs and everything seems to move in slow motion. "You can't get me a car."

"We can and we did," Becca says, grinning from ear to ear. "Come on, let's go look at it."

I pull up a little further into the driveway and then turn off Becca's car, nearly forgetting how to put it in park. My legs are jelly as I climb out and walk toward the brand new and totally gorgeous car. I don't think I could close my gaping mouth if my life depended on it right now.

Park walks outside, grinning. "I heard someone passed their test," he says.

I manage to nod and then he hugs me and then Becca hugs me and I still can't close my freaking mouth. "Guys . . ." I say with a heavy sigh. "You can't do this. I don't deserve a new car!"

They both laugh. Park holds out a brand new car key for me. "Yes you do. You're our kid now, and our kid drives in style."

My new parents seem genuinely thrilled to watch me sit in my new car and take in all of its fancy features. It has black leather seats and a DVD player in the dash. I've never been in something so nice in my life and now it's mine. Mine. I'm having a really hard time understanding that concept right now.

I call Jett and he rushes over and slides into the passenger seat. "Sweet ride," he says, nodding in approval as he slides a hand across the dash.

"Can you believe this?" I ask, my voice coming out slightly louder than a whisper. I'm still afraid if I open my eyes too wide everything might vanish, and I'll be back in a crappy motel room with Dawn.

"Yep, I can." Jett leans across the center console and kisses me. "I picked out the dark purple color. Hope you like it."

"Wait." I eye him. "You knew about this?"

He nods and his grin turns from sweet to conspiratorial. "Of course I knew."

My eyes bug. "And you kept it a secret from me?"

"Psh, duh. I wasn't going to ruin the surprise."

I press my lips together and shake my head. "I can't believe I never suspected that you were hiding something."

He grabs my knee and squeezes it. "I can be sneaky when I need to."

I try to make a mad face but it doesn't last very long. I'm starting to wonder if there's a certain level of happiness one can achieve before their entire body reaches a max capacity and explodes. Of course, if that existed, it would have happened to me by now.

"So, beautiful," Jett says, buckling his seat belt and leaning his head back against the headrest. "Where are we going first?"

"I don't know," I say, waving to our parents who are all sitting on the back porch watching while I crank the engine to life. "Let's just drive."

CHAPTER SIXTEEN

Jett

On Friday, I head over to Keanna's house so that we can go pick up our schedules at the high school. I'm so not ready for summer to be over, but I'm glad my girl will be going to school with me. Becca lets me in the back door and tells me Keanna's in her room.

I tap on the door and enter, finding her sitting at her vanity applying eye makeup.

"Hey you shouldn't make yourself look so beautiful," I say, walking up behind her. I slide my arms around her shoulders and lean down, kissing her neck. "All the other guys will try to steal you away."

She snorts at my idea and continues making herself all fancy.

"Scoff all you want," I say, sitting on her bed and leaning back on my elbows. "You're too hot for your own good. I'll be fighting guys nonstop, keeping them away." I sigh heavily and shake my head like it's a task I'm not looking forward to. This wins me a grin from her in the mirror.

She turns around and stands up, gesturing to her clothes. "How do I look?"

I take in her skinny jeans and a white shirt with the Eiffel tower printed on the front. "You'd look a lot better if those clothes were on the floor," I say, giving her a nod. She rolls her eyes. "The correct answer is that I look like a high school senior."

"That too," I say. "But I liked my answer better."

She walks toward me slowly, knowing that it's driving me crazy. I lift a hand and motion for her to come here. She crawls onto the bed, positioning herself on top of me as I lay back. Her knees are on either side of my hips but she holds herself up with her arms, keeping her body entirely too far away.

I slide my hands down her ass and lift her until her lips can touch mine and then she finally sinks down into my kiss, pressing her body against me. I tangle one hand in her hair and keep the other one on her butt, getting the best of both worlds while we make out.

"Mmm," she murmurs against my lips. "As much as I love this, we have somewhere to be."

I sigh and run my teeth along her bottom lip. "Fine, we can go. But you're mine when we get back here."

She wiggles her eyebrows. "I wouldn't have it any other way."

I'M DEFINITELY NOT USED TO BEING THE PASSENGER WHEN KEANNA AND I GO PLACES, but she's so excited about her new car that she wants to drive, so I'm happy to let her. We always hold hands when I drive, but I don't want to distract her since she's still a new driver, so I keep my hands to myself. She's a good driver, though. I get the feeling she'd be good at anything she tried.

Keanna follows my directions as I give her the secret back roads to get to the high school. When we arrive, there's already tons of cars in the parking lot and we're immediately thrown into the fray of bored high school students not quite ready to get back to school.

Keanna grabs my hand and shoves her car key in her front pocket. "I'm scared," she whispers.

"I got you," I say, bumping into her as we walk toward the front of the school. "I'm your rock, remember?"

She smiles up at me but it doesn't reach her eyes. "My stomach hurts. I don't want to do this."

"You'll be okay. No one will even notice you." I lean over and kiss her forehead.

A few guys call my name and we wave at each other but I don't say anything so they won't come over and chat. Having a girlfriend is making me unsocial in the best way possible.

"So this is Lawson High School," I say, casting out my arm in a grand gesture. "Home of the Hornets."

I curl my lip. "They just voted to change our mascot to the Hornets a couple years ago and it's really stupid, I know. Like, pretty much any animal can defeat a stupid insect."

Keanna giggles and leans into my arm. I pull open the door for us and we enter into the main lobby, a green tiled floor with tan walls and the school's brand new concrete hornet statue as the centerpiece.

Teachers mull around and welcome everyone and students filter here and there. Mostly we have to line up at these tables in alphabetical order to get our schedules. Park is far away from Adams. I look down at Keanna. "This is where I leave you," I say, making this over exaggerated frown. "Shall we meet up on the other side?"

She nods. "Godspeed."

We go our separate ways and I stand in line behind some freshman girls who are sneaking not-so-subtle looks at me. I've seen that look before; it comes with the territory when you're a famous guy's son.

"Are you Jett Adams?" one of them asks.

The other one adjusts her bra in this way that can't possibly be on accident. Is that supposed to turn me on? Because it doesn't work.

"Yeah," I say, glancing to the right, hoping to see Keanna. Unfortunately, the tables for B-0 last names are so busy that I can't find her in the crowd.

"We're freshman," the same girl says. She flips her black hair over her shoulder and peers up at me. "I'm Ava. And this is Abbi." She gestures to her friend, a blonde with bright blue eyes and too much perfume. "We love motocross."

"Cool," I say.

"Maybe you could show us around school this year," Ava says, twirling hair around her fingers. "We don't really know how to get anywhere."

"Sure," I say, trying not to smirk. "My girlfriend just moved here so I can show all three of ya'll around."

Her smile falters. "Okay cool."

Something tells me she probably won't be taking me up on that offer. Ha. This must be another sign of falling in love. I no longer care at all when girls try to flirt with me. I used to eat that shit up even if I didn't like the girl who was doing the flirting. It was just fun to flirt. Now I'm bouncing on the balls of my feet, waiting to get back to my girl.

Keanna and I meet up a few minutes later and I pull her into the entrance of the library, so we can get out of the crowd of students. "Okay, show me what you got," I say, holding out my schedule. We compare them and find that we both have biology with Mrs. Smith together last period, along with the same lunch.

"This is embarrassing," she says, dropping her head. "I'm a senior taking junior level science classes. UGH."

"So what? It's not your fault your credits didn't transfer."

"It is my fault I never passed the stupid class. But we moved so much last year it was hard to stay focused on my class work. I did quite a few homework assignments while sitting in the car while Dawn went on a date."

I put my hand on her shoulder. "It's no big deal. Plus, now we have class together."

"Hi Jett!" We both look over to see some girl waving excitedly at me. I lift my eyebrows and nod toward her.

"Adoring fan?" Keanna asks sarcastically.

I shrug. "I have no idea who that is. Come on, let's go find all of our classes."

After a few minutes, I've already had a handful of girls say hello to me in the hallways. It's embarrassing to say the least, but I act like I'm unaffected. I even go out of my way to say hi to all the guys I know, just so Keanna doesn't notice a pattern of only girls talking to me.

We go through both of our schedules and pretend walking to each of our classes so Keanna knows her way around the school.

"And this is where we'll meet after fourth period," I say, stopping at the staircase on the south side of the building. "And then we can walk to lunch together."

I take both of her hands in mine and kiss her quickly on the bottom stair.

She gazes up at me and the look in her eyes is adoring and beautiful and makes my chest ache with how much I love her. But I can't tell her that here, in a school. That would be too lame.

"Ready to go?" I ask, giving her another quick kiss. Only the kiss turns into something more passionate, and we both can't pull away for a second.

Someone clears their throat and we look up. Jasmine Garcia stands with her hands on her hips, watching us for God knows how long. My stomach twists into knots. Jasmine and I sort of dated at the beginning of last year and it did not end well.

"You should run away while you can," she tells Keanna. Then she narrows her gaze at me. "This guy is bad news."

"Come on," I say, taking Keanna's hand and rushing out of there. I heave a sigh and ignore everyone else as we walk back through the school and out into the parking lot.

This is going to be a long year.

CHAPTER SEVENTEEN

Keanna

It's the first day of school. No big deal, right? This is my twelfth year after all, and I've done this way more than a dozen times. After a few years of awkward puberty, junior high wasn't too horribly bad. I got free lunches in the school programs for poor kids and I finally learned how to stop caring about people and their judgmental looks. In fact, I was pretty good at it back in Arizona.

So why am I freaking out now?

I guess because I know this will be my final public school. I am finally living in a place where I know I'll stay all year and graduate in the spring with a group of people who have had nine months to get to know me. These are Jett's friends, and the kids of my new parent's friends. I want them to like me. I can't just duck into the shadows, keep to myself and hope nobody notices me this year.

This year needs to count. I need to be somebody.

I choose a pair of skinny black jeans and a purple flowy sleeveless shirt that has some sparkle designs around the collar. I wear my silver flats and use Becca's curling iron on my hair. I'm going for classy with a little bit of casual, hence the jeans.

Jett thinks I'm over thinking it. "You should be more like me," he says, grinning from the doorway. He bites from an apple and swallows it before talking again. "I just throw on shorts or jeans and a T-shirt and I'm out the door. Sometimes I don't even brush my hair. It's high school."

I sigh and dab some powder on my face. "You're a guy so you can get away with that. I saw the way the girls were dressed when we picked up our schedules. It was like they were going to eat at The Lantern or something." I make a gagging face and turn back to the mirror. Finally satisfied with my *look as good as possible without looking like I'm trying* look, I get up and grab my backpack.

It's brand new and filled with a binder, paper, pens and pencils and highlighters—even note cards and white out. Becca wanted me to have anything I might need so she'd bought all of this crap for me. As I heft the heavy backpack onto my shoulders, I remember my first day of kindergarten when Dawn dropped me off with Mrs. Sparks and when the teacher asked where my supplies were, Dawn said, "You mean the school doesn't provide them?"

For the rest of my elementary life I lived off of free supplies from teachers and borrowing glue sticks and markers from the bins in classrooms. As bad as it sounds, I kind of wish my biological mother had abandoned me a long time ago.

Having new school supplies as a seventeen-year-old doesn't mean nearly as much as it would have when I was five.

Nervous energy threatens to suffocate me when we leave my room. Every foot closer to the back door is one foot closer to starting school. Park is already at the Track, but Becca gives me a hug and sends us on our way as if this isn't something to be worried about.

"Do you want to drive?" Jett asks when we step outside. The early morning air is humid and warm and it doesn't help the anxiety in my stomach.

"Can you drive?" I ask, peering up at him. "I think I'm too scared to remember which pedal is the gas and brake."

Jett's dark hair falls in his eyes and he sweeps it back with his hand. "You don't need to be scared, babe. This will be a fun day. Teachers don't even pass out real work on the first day."

Right, because school work is what scares me. *Not.*

We get to school early enough to have time to eat breakfast, which Jett swears is pretty good at the school. The main food serving part of the cafeteria is shut down, the metal gates pulled down to keep everyone out. But there's a kiosk to the side of the cafeteria just when you walk in. A sign above it calls it "the café" and a little old woman sells donuts, muffins, parfaits, and Pop-tarts. Another woman next to her mans a coffee and hot chocolate cart. I keep my gaze on Jett and let everyone else fade into the background. I do notice a few stares or curious glances as people walk by, but I tell myself it's just innocent curiosity about a new girl. Surely not *everyone* is staring at me, right?

Jett gets three glazed donuts and I get a blueberry muffin and an orange juice.

"So I usually sit over here," Jett says, leading me across the cafeteria, which is filled with the normal long lines of tables. We stop at the back wall which has a bar that stretches from one end of the room to the other. Attached barstools mark each place to sit and the view is kind of cool because it looks out a long window, giving a view of the parking lot outside.

"Is this the cool people bar?" I say, giving Jett a playful smile while we take a seat in the middle of the long seating area.

"It is now," he says, tearing out a huge bite of his first donut.

I peel off the wax paper wrapper from my muffin. "Do you get breakfast every day?"

"Yup," he says with a nod. "I'm not really a fan of eating first thing in the morning. So by the time I get to school, I've had more time to get hungry."

I smile. "I learn something new about you every day."

He leans over and grins back. I want to kiss off the tiny crystals of sugar on his lips.

D'andre approaches and drops down into the seat next to Jett. "Oh no. Look at these two knockouts—already starting drama up in here."

"Who, us?" I ask. I feel all of the blood drain from my face. Here we go. My nightmare senior year is starting.

D'andre smiles and waves his hand like it's no big deal. "I'm just messing with you. I heard a few girls asking who the new girl was."

I lift an eyebrow. "That's not exactly the whole story," I say, desperate to know more. "Who was talking about me?"

Carefully, I glance behind us, expecting to see a sea of eyes staring at me, but everyone seems to be minding their own business.

"I'm just playing, Keanna." D'andre sips from his hot chocolate and I'm worried that he's *not* playing with me. But I shut up about it. No sense in begging him to tell me something he clearly doesn't want to.

Breakfast is over before we know it and Jett walks me to first period. I have math, which is probably a good thing to have first thing in the morning since your brain is more alert, but I am so not in the mood right now. It's remedial math, after all. Plus, it means I have to leave Jett and I won't see him again for four more hours.

Jett lingers at the doorway of room 204, his hands holding mine and his eyes gazing into mine while the whole world goes on around us.

"I'm way more scared than I thought I would be," I admit. My shoulders fall. "I don't know why. This is so stupid. I've been to a million schools before so this shouldn't be a big deal."

"I wish I could kiss you," Jett says, squeezing my hands. "But there are too many teachers around here and I'd get my ass handed to me." His gaze softens as he peers down at me. "We can't have the principal calling my parents on day one. They'd be so pissed they'd probably ground me from seeing you."

My eyes widen. "If you get grounded from seeing me then *I'm* grounding you as well."

"I'll be good," he says, winking. "See you at lunch?"

I nod and let go of his hands. I wish I could lean in and get a good inhale of his cologne, but he's right— there are too many teachers everywhere.

As I walk into first period, it ends up being okay. No one looks at me or says anything and when Mr. Ellis begins his class, he doesn't even bother asking if there's any new students this year. I'm able to blend in just like I'd hoped.

Everything is going perfectly. Until the bell rings.

"Hey wait up," a girl says behind me. I keep walking, assuming she's not talking to me, but then she grabs my arm. "Hey," she says, giving me the fakest of all fake smiles. Seriously. She should win an award for this one. There's even a dimple in her left cheek and a twinkle in her eye.

"I'm Aubrey."

She's a little shorter than I am and she has light brown hair cut in a sharp bob, and she wears black framed glasses.

"Keanna," I say.

We step into the hallway with the crowds of other students. I try to remember which way to second period but Aubrey won't stop staring at me so I get all tripped up and have to reach for my schedule in my back pocket.

"You're dating Jett Adams, right?"

"Ah, there it is."

Shit, did I say that out loud?

Aubrey blinks. "Excuse me?"

It's funny how quickly I can revert back to my old self. The Keanna who didn't give a shit about anyone and who definitely didn't let fake ass bitches like this push her around.

"You heard me," I say. One glance at my schedule tells me I need to find room 450. "If you're going to introduce yourself to be nice, that's great, but I don't need another wannabe motocross groupie trying to complain about me dating the man of their dreams."

Her eyes bug and it feels pretty damn good to put her in her place. "That's not what I was going to say," she blurts out.

"Yeah? Because you sure seemed like I hit the nail on the head." I smile. "Nice to meet you."

"I was actually going to warn you," Aubrey says, scurrying on her tiny legs to keep up with me. "You're dating a total player, Keanna." She gives me this look of satisfaction like she's been dying to tell me this since the first bell rang. "He's going to break your heart, you know."

Her prissy, know-it-all attitude makes me want to punch her in the face. She *cannot* know that what she's saying is pulling at my very own fears of dating Jett. I channel the old Keanna and say, "Not if I break his first."

CHAPTER EIGHTEEN

Jett

By lunch, I've been loaded down with syllabus after syllabus and more first-day-of-school homework than I've ever had in my life. So much for taking AP classes thinking they'd be easy.

But the first half of the morning is finally over, so I walk to the corner between the history and science hallways where Keanna and I had agreed to meet. I'm anxious to see her, to smell her green apple shampoo and say something stupid to make her smile.

It's like I'm an entirely different person this year compared to last year. Last year all I cared about was turning sixteen, getting a truck, and dating girls. Now the only thing on my mind is Keanna, and to a lesser extent, motocross.

I have a girl I love and the best sport ever in my backyard. Could I be any luckier?

My chest warms as I grin and I don't even care if people are watching me with funny looks on their faces. I wait a minute and finally see Keanna's soft brown hair on top of her adorable head. It's all I see, since the crowd of other students are all around, shoved into the hallway like sardines. Everyone is anxious to get to lunch, and I'm probably the most anxious. After all, I have the best girlfriend in the school.

"Hey," I say, when she walks up to me. Immediately, I know something is wrong. Her expression is solemn, her eyes far away. I slip my hand into hers. "Did something happen?"

She snorts through her nose. "Define *something*."

We weave into the crowd and make it to the cafeteria. Keanna doesn't say anything else and I can tell by the look on her face that she doesn't want to talk about it. That doesn't mean she's off the hook. It just means I'll wait until we're somewhere more private to ask her about it.

My friends are already sitting at the bar when we arrive, and D'andre has saved two seats with two of his textbooks. The guy can't be bothered to use a backpack. Every year he just carries around his stuff.

"Are these for us?" I ask.

He nods while taking a bite of his cheeseburger.

"Where's Maya?" I look around for her, but all the seats are filled and her spunky, always smiling self isn't here.

"Cheer practice for the first week of school," he says. "I think they're getting ready for the pep rally on Friday." He wiggles his eyebrows. "The fact that I know that means I'm dating a cheerleader."

Keanna sinks into the chair next to me and stares blankly out the window in front of us. I put my hand on her back. "Are you hungry?"

She doesn't answer, unless pressing her lips together for a split second counts as one, so I ask another question. "Want me to get us some food?"

She shrugs. "I'll get us food," I say, rubbing my hand on her back before I get up and head to the line.

This is driving me crazy. I know she was nervous about starting school, but she seemed okay earlier today. What could have possibly happened between first period and now?

My mind runs rampant with crazy thoughts while I get into the food line and fill up a tray with various things I think she might like. I get a cheeseburger, two slices of pizza, cheesy fries, and a fruit cup in case she's not in the mood for junk food.

D'andre is talking to her when I return, and she's actually talking back, so that might be a good sign.

I set the tray down and her eyes go wide. She looks up at me. "You must be extra hungry today."

"Half of this is for you," I say. I lean over for a kiss and for a split second it feels like she might not give it to me. Then she leans forward, presses her lips to mine quickly and then takes a plate with a pizza slice.

"Thanks," she says, peeling off a pepperoni and eating it.

"Your girl here is having a little trouble from the ghosts in your past," D'andre says over a mouthful of food.

She talked to him and not me? My blood turns to ice. "What exactly does that mean?"

He shrugs and nods toward Keanna. She peels off a piece of the pizza crust and eats it.

"Oh come on," I say, trying not to sound as agitated as I feel. "You'll talk to my best friend but not me?"

She sighs. "There's nothing to talk about. I've just had a hard morning."

"How?"

Her eyes flit to mine for just a second and then she looks back at her food. "Every single class has had at least one girl berate me for dating you. And I'm like . . . how the hell do you even know about that?" Her hands turn palm up. "How does the whole freaking school know that I'm dating you? It hasn't even been a whole day. But by the way that they're talking, you'd think we were caught having sex on the auditorium or something."

I realize I haven't been breathing since she started talking, so I gasp for a breath. "Damn," I say, letting it out slowly. I run a hand across my forehead. "How *do* people know? It's not even a big deal! Everyone is dating someone in this school, right? It's not like dating is some rare insane thing."

"Calm down, bro." D'andre nudges me with his elbow. I realize a little too late that I was probably talking way louder than I should have.

Anger has me clenching my fists. "Who talked to you? What'd they say?"

She shakes her head. "It's not a big deal, Jett. It just seems that every girl in this entire school thinks I shouldn't date you."

Okay, I have *not* dated every girl in this school. I'm not *that* bad.

"They're just jealous," D'andre says. "Trust me. Every girl wants Jett but not every girl gets him. So hold your head up high, girl."

"Thanks, man." I nod toward him but I don't think his comment helped Keanna at all. I put my arm around her back and lean in close, pretending it's only us two in the cafeteria. "You're just something new to look at," I tell her. "They'll get over it in a day or two."

"I hope you're right," she says, leaning into my chest as I hold her close. "If not, I'll be looking into homeschooling and GED classes."

I grin. "If I'm not right, I'll look into those myself."

Keanna is a lot better by the time lunch is over and we hang out in a bay window alcove, hands wrapped around each other, kissing and talking until the two-minute warning bell rings for fifth period.

"Only three more classes," I say, pressing my forehead to hers.

"Thank God," she mumbles, but she gives me a smile that lets me know she's okay. For now. "I'll see you after school?"

"Yep." I tap her on the nose with my finger and her face scrunches up. Now would also be the perfect time to tell her I love her. But I chicken out and head to History class instead.

My teacher, Mrs. Perrone, is the same History teacher I had last year. She teaches mostly AP classes and I like her a lot because she prefers to give animated lectures instead of classwork. You only write one paper per year for her class and she gives just a few tests that are all open book.

I slide into a desk in the back and a long wave of blond hair sits next to me. The hair flips over her shoulder and Ashley Lubbock flashes me her extra white teeth. "Hey there."

"Hi, Ashley."

I pull out my binder and pretend to be searching for something. Mrs. Perrone passes out the syllabus and introduces herself, giving a long-winded story about each of her four Chihuahuas at home.

"Alright guys, now it's time for your own introductions. Partner up with the person sitting next to you. For the next ten minutes, you'll learn about your desk mate and then introduce them to the class. You'll each be speaking for a minimum of three minutes."

Ashley exhales and turns toward me. "I was hoping she'd do that. I'm Ashley, but you already know that, right? I mean, of course you do."

"Yeah, I'm Jett." I ready my pen over my paper. "So tell me enough things about yourself so I can talk for three minutes."

She laughs and puts a hand over her chest. She leans over and wraps her arm around my elbow, leaning in just the way that makes her low cut tank top show everything she's got under there. "Jett, you're so cute," she says, running her hand through my hair.

I jerk backward and she frowns. "Ugh, please," she says, waving a hand at me. "Don't act like you don't want the attention." Her eyes flash conspiratorially. "We both know you love it."

"Are you hitting on me?" I have to whisper it even though everyone in class is talking to their partner. I can't believe what's actually happening right now, especially after Keanna and I decided that the entire school knows about my girlfriend by now. Surely she does, too.

Ashley rolls her eyes and does the hair flip thing again. "Okay, you're acting like you don't remember what happened between us," she says, even quieter.

I lift an eyebrow. "Nothing has happened between us."

"The end of school party last year," she says, watching me for any sign of recognition. She runs a finger down my arm. "Remember now?"

I look up, trying to remember what she's talking about. A bunch of football guys threw a party at one of their houses last year. I remember going with D'andre . . . and I remember getting super wasted. That's it.

"Look, whatever you think happened between us, that won't happen again. I have a girlfriend and I'm committed to her."

Her face hardens for a second and then she shakes her head. "Look. I know I gave you the best blow job ever, and you were dying for more." Her eyes bore into mine and she lowers her voice to barely a whisper. "So if you'd like more fun times with me, I'll keep it quiet, okay?" She winks and leans so close to me that her boobs touch my arm. "I've had even more practice since then."

God. Did that *really* happen between us? Was I even sober enough to let that happen? I was single at the end of school last year, just dealing with the on-again-off-again crap with Emma Clarke. I guess it's possible . . . but . . . ugh.

Damn. I kind of hate myself right now. "Thanks, but no thanks," I say, turning to focus on my paper. "Tell me generic things about yourself so we can do this stupid assignment."

"Okay here's one," she says, pointing to her finger. "I have a cat named Missy. And two," she points to the next finger. "I give really great head."

I palm my forehead. This is going to be a really, really long year. And sheltering Keanna from all of this insanity might end up being the death of me.

CHAPTER NINETEEN

Keanna

Whatever doesn't kill you makes you stronger.

I'm not sure who came up with this saying but it really doesn't make sense, at least not on a reasonable level. But one would think that whoever said this originally, whoever believed it enough to make it into a saying that's universally known, must have felt there was truth to it. So I repeat it to myself every single day in class.

In three days, Aubrey has gone from giving me condescending glares to being a straight up vocal bitch. Every time she gets a few seconds near me, she'll say something about Jett and me.

Are you still dating him? Wow.

I wonder how many girls he's slept with in the last week.

Have you been tested for STDs? God, you must have a ton.

I ignore it. Doing nothing about her bitchy comments is the right move—I know, but it's killing me inside. All I want to do is grab her short brown hair and yank it backward, kick her in the back of the knees and watch her tumble to the ground, begging for mercy. Yeah, I get a little graphic in my daydreams.

By Friday, Mr. Ellis has us doing math worksheets to see where we are in math skills. When we finish a worksheet, we take it to the back table to turn in and then grab another sheet from a stack of five different assignments. I'm turning in my third worksheet when Aubrey approaches the back table. We're the only two students here, and Mr. Ellis is playing music over the speakers so no one can hear her.

"Let me guess," she hisses. "You have Jett's parents locked in a basement?"

"Excuse you?" I say.

She makes one of her fake smiles. "Well I'm trying to figure out what kind of horrible thing you've done to make him pretend to like you. Obviously it has to be bad. I mean look at you, you look like straight up white trash wearing designer clothes."

The worksheet crumples in my grip. I glance back to make sure our teacher is still focused on his computer with his back to us. "Let me take a guess, here, Aubrey." I lean in until her eyes are the only thing I see. "You've lusted after my boyfriend for months, probably even years, and he didn't want you because you're ugly and vapid and now you're pissed because he's taken and you can't harass him anymore?"

Her eyes widen and I nod. "Yeah, that's probably it. I'm sorry you're too much of a troll for my boyfriend to look twice at you."

I turn on my heel and march back to my desk. I can handle this shit. It only makes me stronger, right?

Something in Aubrey's glare tells me that I've moved our little bickering sessions into deeper territory. I can feel her gaze boring into the side of my skull for the rest of class. And when I finish my worksheet, I wait until three or four other students are at the back table to go turn it in. In my old schools, under the care of Dawn, I wouldn't have backed down. If Aubrey wanted to complain and moan until I got so annoyed I punched her, that'd be fine. I didn't care back then.

But my new parents are angels. They're the kindest and most generous people on earth. They look at me like I'm worth loving. I'm not going to get in a fight at school just weeks after I became their daughter. It won't happen. I'm going to be the person they want me to be and not the piece of white trash that Aubrey has so accurately seen buried underneath my good girl bravado.

I keep hoping that Jett will be right and that the girls who say rude things to me will slowly give up and move on to something else, someone else. But I get the stares when I'm alone in the hallways. Some girls ask if I'm Jett's girlfriend and they just sound curious, but others say it just to be mean. Just so they can get the satisfaction of me saying yes and then they can point their smirks and judgmental laughter my way and know that I understand it's meant for me.

I never knew that dating one of the most popular guys in school would be such a curse. It's only been three days of my senior year at Lawson High School and I'm already dying for it to be over. I've considered making a poster board sized calendar to hang on my wall. It'd have the rest of the days of the year written on it so I can cross them off one by one, counting down the days until I'm free and out of this high school drama.

I spend the rest of my time wondering how long it'll take Jett to wake up and realize I'm just some loser. Some pathetic nobody with no fun life experiences and no money and nothing worth loving. He's bound to find out sooner or later. And when it does, it's going to crush me.

Just two weeks ago I'd thought I was the luckiest girl on earth. I had new parents, a new car, a gorgeous house and a bedroom all to my own. My boyfriend is the hottest guy ever and he's caring and loving and doesn't ever pressure me into sex stuff unlike every other guy I've ever known. Just two freaking weeks ago —hell, just four days ago—my life was perfect. I guess I always knew that it would come crumbling down at some point.

I guess I just thought I had a little more time.

After gym class, I hitch my backpack onto my shoulders and walk quickly to my next period. The gym is on the other side of the school, and with five minutes between classes, it's always a close call to get to English class on time. And my English teacher is at least three hundred years old. She doesn't give warnings—she gives tardies. And tardies equal detention.

I round the corner into another hallway near the stairs. My body goes flying forward, my head crashing against the wall. I stumble and cry out in pain but I don't fall, since I manage to grab onto the staircase. What the hell just happened? I rub my head and turn around.

Aubrey stands there, arms crossed, a perfect bitch look plastered to her face. "What the hell?" I yell, starting toward her.

A strong arm slams out, blocking me. That's when I see the guy standing next to her, using his massive arm as a barricade. He has dark black hair and the same eyes as Aubrey. "Is this the bitch who was bothering you?" he asks her.

She nods. "That's her."

With his arm pressed to my chest, he slams me backward until my back hits the wall. There's nothing I can do to stop it; he's way too strong.

His breath smells like spearmint gum as he hovers in front of me, using his forearm to press down on my neck. I reach for his arm and dig my nails into his skin but it doesn't faze him.

"Get the fuck off me," I manage to say through gasps of breath.

"You stay away from my little sister, you hear me?" His lip curls and from this close, he looks like he's thirty. He must have failed a lot of classes to still be in high school.

"I didn't do shit to your sister," I say. I contemplate doing something really horrible—like bad—spitting in his face. I've never sunken that low in my life, but he *does* have me pressed against a wall while he hovers so close to me I can feel his heart beating through his arm.

"You're a cute little thing," he says, his eyes roaming down my body. From the corner of my eye, I see his sister walk away, leaving us all alone in the stairwell. The two-minute bell rings.

"Let me go, asshole."

"In a minute," he says. There's a hunger in his eyes that I've seen on countless other men in my life. With one arm pressed against my neck, he leans in, pushing his body up against mine. I wince and turn to the side, trying to slide out of his grip but every time I move, he chokes me harder, His other hand grabs my boob and squeezes it so hard I gasp.

"Get off me," I say through gritted teeth.

"You like that," he says, moving his mouth even closer to mine. I keep my jaw tight and I turn and twist and fight like hell to break free, even though I can't breathe anymore.

His disgusting hand slides down my side and reaches for my jeans. I manage to lift my foot just enough to kick him in the shin but it doesn't really help. My throat burns and my vision fills with black spots.

I hear a grunt and then I'm released. Oxygen rushes into my lungs and I fall forward, gasping for air like I can't possibly get enough.

Cursing fills the hall, the voice familiar. I sit back on my knees and watch while Jett plummets the guy's face with his fist.

The guy fights back, landing a blow to Jett's eye, but Jett doesn't flinch. He attacks Aubrey's brother again, grabbing his shirt and pulling him to the ground.

Commotion sounds from down the hallway. Doors open and close. I see administrators rushing toward us, talking into handheld radios. I just sit here trying to remember how to breathe, rubbing the sore spot on my neck that's surely bruised, and I watch my boyfriend kick this guy's ass until a teacher pulls them apart.

JETT'S EYE IS SWOLLEN AND BLEEDING JUST ABOVE HIS EYEBROW. THE ENTIRE SIDE OF his face is a purple mess, and I can barely see the blue in his left eye because it's nearly swollen shut. The nurse gave him an ice pack which he holds over it while he walks out of the principal's office.

He had to talk to him first. I went second. After telling the principal the story—leaving out no details—I learned that Aubrey's brother is a college dropout who only showed up to school because Aubrey texted him. This was a planned attack and I was the victim. After hearing this story, the principal called Jett back in. He was in there for only two minutes, according to the clock on the wall.

"Hey," I say, standing up.

Jett holds up a pink slip of paper. "Suspended for a week. It doesn't matter that I was saving you. Apparently I was *more aggressive than necessary*."

"Oh my god," I say, putting my hand on his chest. "This is all my fault."

"None of it is your fault," he says, taking my hand. We leave the office and head to the parking lot. School isn't over but we're sure as hell not going back to class after what happened.

"Jett, I can't believe this," I say, feeling tears rush to my eyes. "Your parents are going to kill you."

"Nah. It'll be okay." It could just be because half of his face is swollen, but it doesn't seem like he believes what he's saying.

He chuckles. "Remember on the first day of school when I joked about getting suspended?"

"Don't remind me," I say, looking at the ground.

"At least I made it three whole days," he says, nudging me with his shoulder.

"You are *not* funny," I say, trying to hide my smile.

He winks at me with his good eye. "Maybe I'm a little bit funny."

CHAPTER TWENTY

Jett

My parents spend ten minutes arguing over whether or not I should go to a clinic for my busted up face. Dad says I'll be fine, that it's no worse than the dozens of dirt bike injuries I get every year. Mom says the busted eye might leave permanent scarring, that I might have a broken eye socket or worse.

Dad rolls his eyes. We're all in the kitchen, sitting around the island in the middle of the room. Well, I'm sitting. Mom's behind me, her hands on my shoulders while she argues with Dad and tilts my chin up to look at me every few seconds. Dad sits on a barstool on the other side of the island. He's working on his laptop and talking to us at the same time since he had to come home early from work when the school called my parents to tell them what happened.

"He could have a concussion!" Mom says.

"He didn't hit me that hard," I say. "It's really not a big deal."

"How many fingers am I holding up?" she says, shifting so she's not directly behind me. I have to turn my head to see her hand with my other eye. "Three."

"Ugh, you can't even see out of your left eye," she says, resting her hand on my cheek. I wince at the pain, but try to hide it. Because she's my mom, she doesn't miss it.

"Honey, you're in pain."

"Of course I am, I got punched in the face repeatedly," I say with a sigh. I turn and step off the barstool. I'm taller than Mom when I'm standing in front of her. "I'm fine, Mom, really. I promise. I'd rather go be with Keanna right now."

"Not until we have a talk," Dad says, his tone serious. He points to where I was sitting moments ago and I take a set again. Lines form in Dad's forehead while he stares at me. "Tell us exactly what happened."

I heave a sigh. "I walked around the hallway, saw a guy pressing Keanna to the wall, so I ran up and grabbed him and punched him. Then I realized he wasn't just pestering her but he was choking her. So I beat his ass until a teacher made me stop."

"He was *choking* her?" Mom says in a high pitched voice. She sits straighter, and twists her ring around her finger. "Jace," she says, staring at my dad like she expects him to do something.

Dad leans forward, his brow furrowed. "So you mean this guy was just attacking Keanna? You two weren't fighting over her or something?"

"What?" I practically choke on my own spit. "Are you kidding me? Why would I be fighting over my own girlfriend?" Anger and something a lot like amusement courses through me, mixing together until I'm not sure if I'm pissed off or if this is all hilarious. "Dad, what the hell do you think I was doing?"

He glances at Mom and they exchange a look. "I guess we thought you might have been up to your old antics," he says, pressing his palms to the table. "I was afraid you were fighting for the wrong reason."

"Oh my god." It's definitely anger now. Anger flows through my veins, warming my muscles and making my heart ache. "Dad, I love Keanna! Some asshole attacked her and it was all because of me, probably, but none of this was her fault. I'm not the person I used to be. You have to believe that."

My parents do that stupid look thing again, like they're talking to each other by gaze alone. It's infuriating. Mom puts a hand on my arm. "How are your ex-girlfriends handling the fact that you have a new girlfriend?"

"I don't have ex-girlfriends," I say before I realize to keep my mouth shut. Way to go, Jett. You just admitted you're a man slut to your mother.

Mom sighs. "You know what I mean. How are they handling it?"

"Not well." I heave another sigh. "That's why Keanna got attacked. Some bitch in her first period class is friends with a girl who liked me last year but I didn't like her back. Apparently this girl has been berating Keanna all week and finally when Keanna stood up for herself, the girl had her brother come dish out a beating."

Dad's fist slams into the table. "This is not acceptable. We can't let this shit happen, Bay."

Mom shrugs. "That Aubrey girl is suspended and they said the brother was taken to jail. There's not really much we can do."

Dad's jaw flexes. "Keanna is our responsibility, too, Bay. Our son's dumbass past is going to hurt her." He casts a quick glance at me and I've never felt so fucking low in my life.

Dad's face falls, and he stares off into the distance. "Keanna is my best friend's daughter now, Jett. If you're going to date her, you can't treat her like the others."

"Dad, what makes you think I would?" I say, desperation filling my voice. "I love her, okay? I won't let anything happen to her."

"Seems like something already has," Mom says, her words hitting straight to the bone.

I open my mouth to argue, but I know there's no point. I am a shitty person. I dated around too much, had too much fun, and now I'm learning that it wasn't fun at all. Those girls meant nothing to me. I only thought I was enjoying my dating around days because that was before I knew what real love is. And now Keanna has been choked, ridiculed, and hassled because of me. Because of my past.

My lip quivers and Mom throws an arm around my shoulder. "Honey, we're not trying to be hard on you right now. We care about you."

"That's true," Dad says. "But we care about Keanna, too. She's not some bimbo girl you bring around for a week and then we never see again. She's a sweet kid and she's here for good. She's the daughter of my business partner and our neighbor. You can't treat her the way you've treated others."

"I won't." It's the truest thing I've ever said.

"Does Keanna know this?" Mom asks. My mom's embrace has always felt comforting, even as I've grown up and gotten too old for that kind of thing. But now, I don't deserve her loving embrace. I'm a shitty son and a bad person and I have embarrassed both of my parents.

"Keanna knows," I say. I bite my bottom lip and stare at the dark patterns in the granite countertop. "Well, I'll make sure she really knows." I look up and meet my parents with a look of confidence. I need them to believe me. "I know I've been a shit person in the past, but I'm not that same person anymore."

"Honey, you were never a shit person," Mom says, emphasizing the last two words. "You're just a free spirit, much like your dad was before he met me."

"Maybe Keanna is your Bayleigh," Dad says.

I make a gagging sound. "Okay gross."

They laugh. "You know what I mean," Dad says. "I was just like you until I met your mom and settled down. I had it easier because I left my past behind in California."

I look at Mom. "Were you able to forgive Dad for dating around so much?"

She shrugs. "There's nothing to forgive. That all happened before he met me." She flashes him a devilish grin that grosses me out. "He's been mine ever since."

"I hope Keanna feels that way," I say, looking down at my hands. Having this talk with my parents should be awkward as hell but I find it reassuring. It's nice to have parents I can go to, talk to, and not feel judged.

"I'm glad I have you guys," I say softly while I stare at my hands.

Dad stands and grabs a beer out of the fridge. "This will be okay, son. It'll work out if you just be genuine with her. But we need to make sure nothing like this happens again. Keanna doesn't need to be in danger."

"I agree," Mom says. "Our first priority is making sure Keanna is safe and that she knows you won't mess around on her. God knows what that Aubrey girl put in her head."

I groan but it almost sounds like a growl. "I need to talk to Keanna," I say.

My parents nod. "Go," Dad says, twisting open the cap on his beer. "I can't believe my son got suspended for a *week* and I'm not grounding him."

Mom chuckles and puts a hand to her stomach. It's still flat, but she does that a lot lately. I guess she's more aware of there being a baby inside than we are. "Have fun," Mom says, waving me away. "Go tell your girl everything will be fine."

CHAPTER TWENTY-ONE

Keanna

Jett has been treating me like a porcelain doll for the last two days. Like he's afraid if he even looks at me wrong, I'll break into a million pieces. I appreciate the fact that he cares, but he's the one person I want to treat me normally. I'm fine with Becca fawning over me and rushing me to the doctor to check out my bruised neck. I'm fine with Park, who gave me a talk Friday night about how he'll kick any guy's ass who tries to hurt me again. In fact, it made me feel awesome and loved that my new parents care so much. But with Jett, my rock, my boyfriend—I just want him to be normal.

We've spent the last forty-eight hours watching Netflix, cuddled in my bedroom. Pretty much the only time I've left my room was last night when Becca and I made cupcakes and Jett watched us, knowing he couldn't exactly help because he sucks at baking. He had decorated some of the cupcakes though, claiming that he was the Sprinkle Master. Last night was fun, but now that it's Sunday, and the fear of going to school tomorrow has fully manifested, Jett is treating me with epically huge kid gloves.

"Can I get you more water?" he asks, gesturing to the empty bottle on my nightstand.

We've piled up all of my pillows to give my headboard some cushion and we're sitting on top of the comforter, Jett's arm around my shoulders, and my head resting on his chest. We're on the final season of Bob's Burgers on Netflix. Jett is only letting us watch happy, upbeat stuff.

I sit up and turn to look at him. "Jett, I'm stronger than you think I am."

He lifts an eyebrow. "That doesn't answer my water question."

The corners of my lips twist into a grin. "I don't need water, but I *do* need you to stop treating me like I'm breakable."

He frowns, and lifts his hand to my cheek. "You are breakable, baby." I catch his eyes flick to my neck, where I know the bruises remain, though they've faded some.

The swelling in his eye has gone down, but it's still purple and red. I shake my head and grab onto his wrist while he holds my face. "I'm fine. I've been through a lot. As long as someone doesn't put a bullet in my head, I'm gonna be fine."

His expression hardens. "Don't talk like that. God, I can't even *think* of that—" He looks away, his chest heaving. "If *anyone* hurts you, or tries to hurt you, or even looks at you wrong—I'll destroy them."

"Apparently they suspended Aubrey, right?" I shrug. "It's fine. I don't have any other enemies, just a bunch of jealous girls giving me dirty looks." Then, because Jett's expression is so painfully angry, I smack my fist into my palm, pretending to be tough. "I'm not worried about those girls," I say, grinning.

He smiles, but it's a sad expression. He leans forward and kisses my forehead, so slowly that his lips linger on my skin for a few seconds. "This is all my fault. If I hadn't been such a fucking player all my life—" He heaves a sigh and then shakes his head, his hand tightening on my cheek. "My dumbass past has hurt you and I'm so *so* sorry, Keanna."

I feel his eyelashes flutter closed on my temple. I lean into him, wrapping my arms around his body.

"Don't blame yourself for some jealous psychopath," I whisper.

He seems like he wants to say more, but he doesn't. He just stretches back and lies down on my bed while I snuggle up into his arms. I wrap an arm over his stomach and his chin rests on top of my head.

"I'm scared to go to school tomorrow," I whisper against his chest. His shirt smells like laundry detergent and lavender, a clean scent I'm beginning to think of as home.

"You could skip it," he says, stroking his fingers through my hair.

"Nah, I'll be okay. It'll just suck without you."

He snorts. "Tell me about it. D'andre and Maya said you're still welcome to sit with them at lunch."

I let out a long breath, closing my eyes while I relish in the feel of his fingers running through my hair. "Cool."

We go back to watching the TV. Becca pokes her head in the door and tells me she and Park are heading to the grocery store. As soon as their car pulls out of the driveway, I watch it through my window while it disappears down the lonely county road. The current episode on TV ends and the credits roll. I lean up on my elbow and look into Jett's eyes.

"Hey there," he says, peering down at me.

"Hi," I say. My eyes narrow seductively and I move until I'm on top of him. His hands slide down to my hips and I lean forward, kissing his neck, trailing my lips up to his ear. He sighs and his hands dig into me, holding me steady while I roam my hands down his chest and just to the edge of his jeans. When my lips meet his, he parts his mouth and runs his tongue along mine, sending a shiver of delight down my spine. He tastes like Dr. Pepper and slide my hand up his chest while we make out, letting my body mold to his and move with him while our hands and mouths explore.

I keep to the right side of his face since the left side is all bruised and I notice Jett makes no move to kiss my neck like he usually does. As much as I want him, we can't exactly make out like normal right now.

I kiss him hard on the mouth, and feel his excitement pressing into my belly. I look up at him and get an idea—risky but sexy—and I decide to act on it before I chicken out.

I lean forward and lick my tongue up his neck. He throws his head back and closes his eyes, his hands pulling my hips into him.

I push up on my elbows and swing my leg around him, until I'm straddling him. I lower myself down to his stomach and kiss the skin between the bottom of his shirt and the top of his jeans. His tanned stomach has a sharp white tan line just beneath the elastic of his boxers and I push it down with my tongue.

I slide my hands down to his zipper. He freezes. "Key," he says, breathless. His hand covers mine. "Don't. You don't—have to do that."

"I want to," I say, trying again to undo his pants.

He shakes his head and sits up. His arms slide around my waist and he pulls me back up to him, holding me snugly around my back so I can't move back down. "We don't need to do that," he says, avoiding my gaze. If anything, his thoughts seem far away.

My lip pouts. "Why not? I thought it would be fun."

He shakes his head. "I don't—that's just—it's too soon, okay?"

Alarms go off in my head. It definitely seems like he's lying to me. But why? And do I really want to know why my boyfriend denies the one thing that guys love more than anything?

I mask my disappointment and worry and roll over to my side, taking the remote control and turning up the volume. "Okay," I say, trying to focus on the television and not my shattered ego. "Whatever you want."

CHAPTER TWENTY-TWO

Jett

The walk home is a lonely one. It's just after eleven and although we spent the last couple of hours watching TV and laughing at all the funny parts, there was definitely something off in the way things felt. I know Keanna is probably upset with me for stopping her advances, but I just couldn't. The thought of her getting sexual with me kept bringing me back to what Ashley told me in class. Flashbacks of getting wasted at parties, flirting with girls—it's all too much. I can't seem to get into being with Keanna when the guilt of my past is killing me slowly.

I'd all but convinced myself to tell her about my past of being a serial dater—to *really* tell her, in detail—but then on Friday after my talk with my parents, I got to her house and saw her angelic face, her kind eyes—and I just couldn't do it.

I can't let her know what type of person I used to be. I mean, I know she has an *idea* but I need her to know the truth, to hear her either forgive me and accept me or kick me to the curb. She deserves better than me. I swallow the lump in my throat as I step up onto the deck by my back door. It's dark tonight, with only a sliver of the moon glowing in the sky. I know deep down that Keanna deserves to know who she's dating, and she deserves to make the choice to keep dating me or not. But god, would I love to ignore it all and just live in the moment with her, allowing myself to have the greatest girlfriend on earth, burying away all the guilt I feel.

The pool glows from the single light that's on near the diving board. That light is always on, and the rest of the pool's lights have to be turned on manually. But it's just enough glow to beckon to me in the darkness. It's close to midnight, but it's not like I have school in the morning. I kick off my shoes, pull off my shirt, put my cell phone on the patio table and dive in.

The water is warm on the surface and cooler the deeper I sink. I dive down until my fingertips graze along the bottom of the pool at the deepest end. Then I lift my head toward the sky and let my body slowly float back up.

I can't stop thinking about finding that guy choking Keanna in the stairwell. The image of it haunts me, mostly late at night. It surfaces in my mind now.

There was actually a split second where I didn't know who he was assaulting. A tiny fraction of time where I saw a guy choking someone else, and I dove forward to stop it. In the very next instant I caught a glimpse of her face, saw that this innocent victim wasn't just any student, but Keanna, and I've never felt so much rage in my life.

It also feels like fate had a hand in it. I don't normally walk that direction and we don't meet there between classes. It was a fluke that I'd happened to be the first person out of my class and therefore I was in the hallways quicker than usual. I took a different route just to avoid seeing Ashley, and it led me to Keanna. What would have happened if I hadn't been there?

Even in the warm pool water, my body gets the chills. I wish I'd had five more minutes with that guy—more time to bash his head in before I was pulled away. I almost wish the whole thing had gone viral—that for once some dipshit with their phone had caught the whole thing on film and posted it for the world to see. I want everyone to know that you can't mess with Keanna and get away with it.

But we were the only ones in the hallway until someone heard the yelling and called a teacher. There are no videos, and I'm suspended for a week. By the time I come back, it'll probably be old news.

At least I hope it will. Violence isn't the option, I know. But high school shouldn't be this hard. It'd taken everything I had to convince Keanna to come to school this year and be with me, hoping we'd be normal high school students with normal high school lives.

Three days in, and that's all gone to shit.

I swim a few laps to get my anger out, and once I'm exhausted, I climb out of the pool and take a hot shower.

I text Keanna that I miss her, knowing she won't be able to write back since she's asleep, and then I try to fall asleep, ignoring the guilt that plagues at me every second of the day.

It's one thing to be haunted by the fact that my past is full of a couple dozen girls who all wanted to be "the one", that's a shitty fact of my life that I just have to deal with. It's not like I slept with all of them—most of them were just casual drunken make outs. I could get over it. I could shove it to the back of my mind and forget it ever happened—call it my old days of being crazy before I settled down.

But it's not that simple.

My past has resurfaced and hurt my girlfriend. She has bruises around her neck to prove it. So even if I *could* forget it all and pretend it never happened, could Keanna?

Would she care about me the same way if she knew how shady I was? How many girls I let text me without ever getting a reply? How many lips have touched mine when I was partying too hard to think clearly?

Would she still love me if she knew this?

Does she even love me now?

CHAPTER TWENTY-THREE

Keanna

My car smells like the homemade blueberry muffin Becca handed me on my way out of the door this morning. I nibble on it while I drive to school, careful not to spill any crumbs in the interior of my gorgeous car. I haven't driven it much since Jett usually takes me to school. I glance down at the odometer: 326 miles.

The small number makes me remember when I was little, when Dawn was bragging that her piece of crap car had just broken two hundred and fifty thousand miles and was still running. She'd gotten the car by trading it for a guitar she'd stolen from an ex-boyfriend, so in all, it was a pretty good deal. I don't think she's had a new car in her entire life, and here I am driving one at the age of seventeen. Funny how that works.

I pull into Jett's parking spot and cut the engine. Holding my hand under the muffin to catch any crumbs, I eat it all and then wish I'd brought a coffee or orange juice with me. Now I'm dying of thirst.

With a heavy heart, I shoulder my backpack and make my way toward the school. *Head down, blank expression.* That's the only way I'll get through this humiliation. Thank God, my bruises are a lot better, and I'd used concealer and a carefully-placed fluffy scarf to hide my neck. It's summer and hot as hell, but Becca had assured me that skinny jeans, a tank top, and this flowy scarf would be in fashion. The fact that they even sell scarfs at all in Texas is a testament to them being worn merely as fashion accessories.

I stop at the café kiosk and get an apple juice, then I make my way to first period, sliding into my usual desk before anyone else is in here, including Mr. Ellis.

I read an eBook on my phone and eventually everyone files into class and the bell rings. Mr. Ellis passes out our test reviews, the ten-page assignment from hell that is meant to prepare us for our first benchmark test, and I'm pleasantly surprised to see a big red 97 on the top of mine. Not bad at all.

The door opens and an office aide hands Mr. Ellis a green slip of paper. You know those weird moments of clarity, where you instantly know something is about to happen? Well, it happens to me now. I don't know why or how, but I know that note is for me.

Mr. Ellis looks up, eyebrows raised. "Keanna? Ah, there you are," he says, walking toward me. He smiles and hands over the paper. It's an office memo telling me to report to the counselor immediately.

Mr. Ellis turns to the board and begins talking about the problems that most people got wrong. Now that Aubrey's desk is empty, there are no more threatening or insulting gazes thrown at me, and that's nice. Everyone else in this class seems pretty chill. I pack up my things and duck out of the classroom.

This is probably just some getting-to-know-you new student orientation thing. At least I hope it is. During our principal meeting last Friday, I wasn't in trouble. Jett was, but not me. Plus, this is a visit with the guidance counselor, so I'm not exactly worried.

The office is big and decorated like some kind of fancy home accents store threw up in here. There's a wax melter on every little end table, burning some kind of autumn scent that smells like orange and cloves. The receptionist looks up when I enter and her gaze goes to the green paper in my hand.

"Counselor?" I ask.

She points to the right and I follow the hallway until I reach the right office. Mrs. Albright is a short, chubby woman with blond hair and an even stronger wax melter scent in her own office. This one smells like linen, I guess, and it has me wishing for the orange and cloves scent again.

"Hi, um," I say, holding up the paper slip. "I was called here?"

"Keanna Park?" she says, standing to shake my hand. I nod, still not used to hearing my new last name.

"New student orientation?" I say, only it comes out sounding kind of sarcastic. Whoops. "I mean, don't get me wrong, I'm glad to be called out of math class," I add with a laugh.

Mrs. Albright's smile flattens. She motions for me to sit in the chair across from her desk and she sits, too.

"This isn't an orientation, Keanna. I've actually called you here to talk about what happened last week, among other things."

I frown. "I feel like I've already talked a lot about what happened. It's over now."

She nods. Her cell phone goes off, her ringtone sounding like birds chirping. She grabs the phone and shuts it off. "Well, then we can only talk about that really quickly, if you'd prefer. I wanted you to know that Aubrey has not only been suspended, but she's decided to transfer to another school."

She leans forward, lacing her fingers together. "You no longer need to fear being bullied by her, Keanna."

The way she keeps saying my name is kind of annoying, and I wonder if it's some therapist type of rule to make a student like you or feel at home, or whatever.

"Okay, thanks. That's cool I guess."

She studies me for a moment. This isn't my first time seeing a school counselor, so I should be used to it by now. And the good thing is that now I am a new person—now I don't have to talk about being homeless, or the endless parade of men in my house, or my mother—my *old* mother.

Mrs. Albright draws in a deep breath. "So I had a talk with your mother this morning—Mrs. Park."

I lift an eyebrow. "Okay?" Becca already knows about the Aubrey thing—why are we still bringing it up?

Mrs. Albright reaches for a pen and turns to a new sheet of paper in the legal pad in front of her. "Your mom shed some light on your situation with me, and I'd like to spend some time discussing it with you."

My arms fold in front of my chest. "What situation?"

"Tell me about your childhood, Keanna. Let's talk about your biological mother and your recent adoption." Her eyes light up like she gets some sick satisfaction in talking about people's screwed up lives.

I sigh and look around her office. There's a ton of family photos filling the shelf behind her desk. One of the girls looks to be about my age and she's often dressed in a Hornets cheerleading uniform like Maya's.

"Tell me about you, Keanna." She leans back in her chair, pen and notebook poised like she's ready to settle back and listen to a long story.

"Do I have to?" It's the first thing I think of, and I don't really care if it's not polite.

"I thought you were happy to get out of math class?" she says, lifting an eyebrow.

I sigh. "Okay sure. What do you want to know?"

By the time Mrs. Albright is done with me, I've lost track of how many times the bell has rung. She's like some kind of psycho, needing to know my whole life from its messed up beginnings of my mother not wanting me and choosing to remind me every chance she got, to my newest development of getting new parents who actually care about me. She takes a ton of notes and I am *so* freaking bored. She probably hopes I'll have some kind of cathartic experience by telling her my whole ordeal, but it doesn't do anything. I am just bored and ready for it to be over.

"This was wonderful," Mrs. Albright says after another bell goes off. The sounds of students filling the hallways can be heard even from deep inside her office. "I'd like to continue these sessions weekly."

"*What?*" I practically fly out of my chair. "What else do you possibly need from me?"

"Keanna, it's not what *I* need from you. It's what *you* need from me. You've been through a lot and you've had quite the hard life. These sessions will help you heal."

"I'm already healed," I say, throwing my backpack on my shoulder. "My life wasn't that bad."

"The fact that you think that tells me we need more sessions." She stands and puts her hand on my arm, giving me this pitying look that's probably also in the school therapist handbook. "This will help you transition into the young adult that you are. You'll be able to work out your issues and be confident going forward and graduating."

She smiles. "I have a feeling this is going to be really eye-opening for you."

As much as I want to say something sarcastic or rude, or both, I hold back. I fasten on a smile and thank her for her time. I have to pretend that I'm okay with this or else she'll force me to come back even more often. Maybe next session I'll start crying and pretend I've had a massive breakthrough. I'll get out of this as soon as possible.

When she finally dismisses me, saying she'll send for me next Monday, I power walk into the hallway, looking for a clock to see how much time I've missed. It's lunchtime. Holy crap, I've spent four class periods talking about my stupid past with a stranger.

So much for having a normal school day.

CHAPTER TWENTY-FOUR

Jett

Okay. My first day of the five day suspension should be a glorious, school-free, vacation of wonderfulness. It should be butterflies and rainbows and fast food and watching TV all day. For the most part, it is, but I'm missing her bad. I hate that she's at school without me, that she's probably feeling awkward around my friends.

I kick up my feet on my futon and lounge back, mindlessly watching television. I texted Keanna earlier, when she would have been walking to third period. She hasn't written back, but I guess she didn't have time or maybe her third period teacher is strict about phones.

My stomach starts begging me for lunch. I reach for my phone to check the time, but at the same time I get a text from Keanna.

Keanna: *What are you doing?*

Me: *Nothin. How's school?*

Keanna: *Come get me please.*

I glance toward my window but it's not like I can see her driveway from here. I type back quickly.

Me: *Didn't you drive to school today?*

Keanna: *Yes, just please come meet me.*

Me: *Be there in ten.*

I throw on shoes and a clean T-shirt and head out the door. Mom says something about staying out of the public eye since being suspended means I'm supposed to stay home. But she's too busy pouring over baby shower ideas on Pinterest to really care, so I slip past her and haul ass to the school.

It's a beautiful September day, the kind where it finally stops being so ungodly hot outside and starts to feel a little bit like fall. I roll down the windows while I drive, the scent of a bonfire in the distance making it feel even more like fall. I hope everything is okay with her. Anxiety over whatever's wrong will only get me killed, so I focus on the road instead and soon I'm pulling into the parking lot.

Her Mustang is parked in my usual spot and she's sitting inside, hands on the steering wheel and her gaze off in the distance. I walk up to her window and tap on it. She opens the door, climbs out, and throws her arms around me.

I twist to peer down at her, but she's not crying. Her eyes are closed, her expression blissful. She breathes in deeply.

"I missed your smell."

"What's going on?" I ask, rubbing her back. "You still have four more days without me here so this isn't a good start.

She laughs. "Tell me about it."

"Did something happen?"

She nods. "Will you take me somewhere?"

I scratch my neck. Ditching class on Keanna's second week of school could get us in a lot of trouble.

Her eyes flutter up at me and she pokes her lip out just the slightest bit. "Please?"

I reach into my pocket for my keys. "Sure thing. Where are we going?"

She shrugs and tosses her backpack in the back seat of my truck. "I don't care, but I am hungry."

We drive to Jack-in-the-Box since it seems the least busy out of all the fast food places along our town's main highway. I think about what Mom said but I'm pretty sure that's not a thing. It's not like police officers will be searching around to see if a suspended student is out having fun.

We take our food to a booth in the back of the restaurant. Keanna frowns when her straw refuses to break through the slot in the stop of her milkshake lid. I take it and do it for her. Her shoulders fall and she breathes a heavy sigh. "Thanks. This is a crap day."

"So what happened?" I ask, ripping off the tops of several ranch packets. This place has the best tacos if you dunk them in ranch. It makes the curly fries better, too. I give Keanna a playful grin. "Do I need to kick someone's ass again?"

She steals one of my curly fries. "Not unless you want to take on Mrs. Albright."

"Who?"

"The school *counselor*," she says, making air quotes around the last word. She screws up her face and sticks out her tongue. "It was a freakin' nightmare. She called me down to her office and made me talk for three and a half freaking hours."

"What?" My soda cup clanks to the table. "Is she allowed to do that?"

Keanna shrugs. "Apparently my new mom told her about my adoption and my hard life growing up so Mrs. Albright decided to make me talk about it. She wants to have *weekly* sessions . . . are you *kidding* me?"

Now my expression matches her disgusted one. "Can she actually do that? Force you to talk when you don't want counseling?"

"I guess so. I mean, she did." Keanna follows my lead and dunks her fries into the ranch. "I feel like I should be all happy that I got to skip four classes for this shit, but I am so *not* all about spilling my guts to a stranger. She kept looking at me with all this pity, like I'm some orphaned kid no one wanted. My life wasn't bad, okay?"

Her voice rises as she talks and I nod. "I know, babe. You don't have to convince me."

Her eyes meet mine and she seems to snap back to reality. "It was just so stupid. She obviously has no idea how a normal teenage girl should act or feel. Her kid is some cheerleader so I'm sure her world is the complete opposite of mine, ya know?"

"Ah, Albright," I say, nodding. "We do have a cheerleader with that last name."

"Let me guess," Keanna says, rolling her eyes. "You've hooked up with her."

I almost choke on my taco. I shake my head in a furious and adamant no. "No. I don't even know her. I just recognize the name."

Keanna doesn't seem to care though. She's too busy staring at her food as if it's the source of her gloomy mood.

We eat in silence for a while. Keanna sighs. "Sorry, Jett. You didn't deserve that."

I lift my shoulders. "Yeah, I did. I have a past. A . . . sordid one."

She looks up at me, her lips wrapped around her milkshake straw. "Is that what's been bothering you lately?"

"Hmm?" *Shit, are we really getting into this now?* I know we need to, but I've been happily ignoring it.

She meets my gaze and gives me this *don't play dumb with me look*. "You're feeling shitty that I know about how many girls you've dated, right? Since I've been subjected to an onslaught of that information ever since school started."

My throat is suddenly dryer than the dirt bike track in the middle of summer. "I, uh—"

She reaches across the table and grabs my hand. "I have a past, too. I have shit that I'm not proud of and I'd be mortified if someone told you all about it." She blinks and shakes her head. "No, I'd be *dead*. I would straight up drop dead if you had to endure people talking about my past."

Funny, because that kind of thing should bother me. It doesn't, and I'm not sure if that's a good thing or a bad thing.

I glance to the right but we're all alone back here. My heart races but I figure we've made it this far. Might as well lay it all out on the table. I lean forward on my elbows. "How many guys?"

"Sex?" she asks.

I make this noncommittal gesture that's supposed to mean yes. Do I want to know? Do I even have a right to dive that deep into her personal life?

Her dark eyes peer up at me, honest and open. "Two."

I swallow. I don't know what I was expecting, but that wasn't it.

She releases her grip on my hand. "Your turn."

I take a deep breath. "I'm a bad person."

She rolls her eyes. "Having sex doesn't make you a bad person."

I take a sip of soda and blurt out the real answer, no matter how much I wish I didn't have to. "Five."

She smirks, but it might just be to cover up whatever real emotion she has. "Okay, Adams. That's not too bad." She laces her fingers together and flexes them in front of her, popping her knuckles. "Should we reveal hookups as well? Because I'm not so angelic on that one."

"Please," I say quickly. "Anything to make me feel like less of a man slut."

She scoffs. "Man slut is such a derogatory term. Saying *man* first implies that the word slut is for women only and that's just stupid." She rolls her eyes. "Anyone can be a slut, you know? It's not even a bad thing, necessarily. Some people are really proud to be a slut." She reaches for a fry and shrugs. "It's only a bad thing if you've done it for the wrong reasons. Or, if you're like me, slutting it up just to *feel* something." Her lip curls while she stares at the fry between her fingers. "I can't even tell you my hook up number, Jett."

"You can tell me anything," I say, almost automatically. But I really do mean it.

She shakes her head, her brown hair falling in her face. After pushing it back behind her ears, she looks up at me with solemn eyes. "I can't tell you because I don't even know the number. Probably twenty, or more."

"Same here. Probably twenty-ish." I gnaw on the inside of my lip. "But none of them mattered and it's all over now and in the past, so who cares?"

Her eyes light up. "You really mean that?"

"I do."

"Good, because I hate judging myself over most of those guys in my past. I didn't even want to do anything with them," she mutters, going back to eating.

"Then why would you?" I ask. That isn't something I can claim—my teenage hormones have gotten the best of me more than once. I've always been happy to make out with someone in the backseat of a car. My dad says that's just how guys are wired—that we're massive horn dogs who want one thing. And for the most part, he was right. It wasn't until I met Keanna that my entire way of thinking changed. Now the idea of randomly swapping spit with some peppy girl who wants to be a motocross groupie gives me the chills. Ugh.

Keanna shrugs. "Well, you know how it is for girls."

"No, I don't. What are you talking about?"

She brushes her hair behind her ears, but it's already back there so the movement is pointless. "You know . . . guys force themselves onto you. They guilt trip you for oral sex—just the usual crap."

A foul taste in my mouth makes me drop my food onto the tray. The lump that had been in my throat earlier is now a hard pit in my stomach. "Are you serious?"

"Jett, chill. It's not a big deal."

"It *is* a big deal," I say, trying hard to keep from yelling. White hot rage takes over every inch of my body. All I can think about is beating the hell out of any guy who ever took advantage of her.

"That is *not* normal and it's not okay. You need to know that." I stare into her eyes, refusing to let her look away. "I've *never* treated girls like that ever. If they didn't want to do something, they didn't have to."

She shrugs. "Babe, seriously. Calm down. It's over and in the past." When I open my mouth again, she gives me a glare that makes me flinch. "Drop it."

My jaw aches from clenching my teeth but I shrug and try to obey her wishes. Still, my hands are fists and I can't seem to eat or drink anything anymore. I want to single-handedly track down every guy who's ever forced her into something she didn't want. I ache to kick their asses. It's all I can think about until Keanna slides into the booth next to me, taking my arm in her hands and wrapping herself around me, leaning her cheek on my shoulder.

"Please don't be mad. My life is starting over, remember? I'm with you and you're with me, and we can pretend that's all there ever was, okay?"

"I'm not mad at you, Key." I kiss the top of her head. "I love you."

She snuggles into me more, the scent of her shampoo drifting up and sending warm fuzzies through my chest. "I love you, too," she says, and suddenly it hits me.

I finally said it. I didn't even mean to—it just fell out of me like it was meant to be here all along.

And she said it back.

And just like that, all of the anger and rage and twisted darkened feelings inside of me are gone. I smile and let out a slow, relaxing sigh.

I guess love really is as powerful as all those old country songs say it is. "Come on," I say, taking her hand. "Let's go do something fun."

CHAPTER TWENTY-FIVE

Keanna

The week without Jett is absolute torture, but luckily it passes by just like every other bad thing in my life. Soon, Jett is back in school and things settle into a routine. I still get a few random glares from girls but I don't have the time or energy to care.

Keep your head high and your standards higher.

Well, that's not exactly my motto, but it *is* a saying that's selling really well in Becca's online art store. She paints it on these small square canvases that have little wooden easels to display them. They're the perfect size for putting on a desk or in a cubicle, and I think women really like the message it projects. I've been trying to keep my head high, too.

Things with Jett are great. I shiver as I think about our night together last night, the romance and the intimacy of making out with him in my bed. We still haven't gone *all the way*, but we don't have to. If anything, the slow anticipation of that big night—whenever it may come—keeps our relationship exciting.

It's Sunday morning and Jett is running laps with his Dad on the track. I'm sitting alone on the top row of the bleachers, sipping from a coffee in one of those paper cups in the Track's break room. Although we're open for business right now, the only client is with Park and Becca is running the front desk so she said she didn't mind if I wanted to watch Jett.

Hanging out at the Track is such a welcome pastime now that school has started. This place was practically my home all summer and it feels good to get back here. I haven't really worked much lately since they haven't been busy, but I'm not worried about money anymore. I have some saved up in my bank account, and my lovely new mother gave me a credit card the other day.

"For essentials and emergencies," she said, wiggling the card before handing it to me. "Park and I will pay the bill, so don't worry about it."

"Essentials like, when you need me to get something on the way home from school?" I asked. "Because I don't mind getting milk and stuff for you."

"Essentials like food, gas, manicures, Starbucks," she said, listing it off on her fingers. "You know. Stuff parents pay for."

I grinned. "Just admit that you're dying to blow money on me."

She batted her eyelashes and handed me the card. "It's my motherly duty, hun. Get used to it."

Even with her permission to use the card freely, I haven't used it at all yet. But it's nice to know I have it. It's nice to finally go to bed at night not worrying about money, or the lack of it. I almost let myself wonder about Dawn, and how she's doing. If she's still getting by with little to no money. But that would be a waste of my time, so I don't think about it.

"Hey girl," Bayleigh says, walking up to the bleachers. She holds onto the railing and climbs to the top, taking a seat next to me. She's wearing a tank top and yoga pants but I still can't see any sign of a baby bump yet. Last week she said it took about four months of pregnancy with Jett to see her belly growing.

"How long have they been at it?" she asks, nodding toward the track where Jett and Jace chase each other on dirt bikes.

"Only about ten minutes," I say, gazing out. Even though Jace is nearly twenty years older than Jett, you can't tell them apart on the track. They're both tall, muscular, and covered from head to toe in gear.

Bayleigh crinkles something—a Pop-tart bag—and pulls one out. Strawberry, by the looks of it. She takes a bite and holds out the silver wrapper to me. "Want the other one?"

I take it and we eat in silence for a bit while we watch the guys ride.

"You ever think about getting on a bike?" she asks.

I shrug. "I like riding on the back with Jett. Not sure I'd be good enough to ride one on my own."

"It's fun, you should try it." She finishes her Pop tart and brushes the crumbs off her hands. "Of course, I'm not any good at it since I started so late. They say getting a kid on a bike when they're too young to know fear is what makes them good riders. Once you're an adult and you get on a bike, you have that fear of death, fear of getting hurt—and you're not very fast."

I nod. "How old was Jett when he started riding?"

"Three," she says, laughing. "My husband fought like hell to get him on a bike. I was scared out of my mind, but it all worked out. I just had to trust him, ya know?"

I nod. I like these little talks we sometimes have. It always gives me an insight into what a perfect relationship is like and how the two people who have raised Jett to be the guy I'm in love with deal with their everyday lives.

"Jett is crazy about you, kid."

"Um, what?" I blurt out just because I'm so stunned to hear those words.

She focuses on Jace as he soars through the air, turning two smaller jumps into one massive jump. As soon as his bike lands safely on the other side, she looks at me. "My son is totally in love with you. I mean, who can blame him—you're adorable and I love you, too." She watches him ride around the track, almost as if she's remembering something that makes her happy.

"I really love him," I say, hoping she knows it's the complete and total truth.

"You two are a lot like Jace and me." Her eyes do that far off gazing thing again and she tells me a little about their relationship, how they started off hot and heavy and how it never faded. "Everyone thought I was stupid for falling so hard so fast, but I didn't care. Getting pregnant was the best thing that ever happened to me."

She laughs and pats my arm. "Not that I'm telling you to do the same thing. Ya'll take your time and do what's best for your relationship."

My shoulders lift. "I don't think I'd be a good mom, so you don't have to worry about that."

"What? Of course you would!" She pulls out the hair tie in her messy bun and redoes her hair. "You can't think like that because I want grandchildren, you hear me?" She gives me this pretend serious look. "I want to be a hot young grandmother, but like I said, no rushing into it." She winks and I can't help but grin.

I'm barely getting used to the fact that I'm in love with my soul mate. I can't exactly think about having a family with Jett. I mean, he's a junior in high school. So yeah—not happening. Still, maybe in the future . . .

"Damn, girl," Bayleigh says. "I can see it in your eyes. You two are the real deal. You're just as crazy about my son as he is about you, huh?"

Heat rushes to my cheeks and I'd almost rather dive off the back of these bleachers than answer her question. This is awkward, after all.

"Yeah," I say, breathless. "Yeah, I think so."

"Well, I can't imagine a better girl for my kid. Just keep him in line, okay?"

"Sure thing," I say, grinning as Jett pulls off the track and rides over to us. "I'll take care of him."

After lunch, I lay on my stomach on Jett's bed, flipping channels on the TV. He's in the shower after a morning of motocross practice and I can't wait for him to get out. Bayleigh and I made grilled chicken and a huge salad for lunch, and we bonded even more while in the kitchen.

I've always liked Jett's mom but after today, it feels like we've grown closer together. Like we're family. I don't know . . . maybe I'm just imagining it. But whatever it is, it feels good. After all, having a guy's parents on your side is always a good thing.

Jett emerges fully dressed and I'm a little sad I don't get to see him walking around in nothing but a towel around his waist.

"Lazy weekends are the best," Jett says, stretching out his arms and diving onto the bed next to me. "We should go see a movie or something tonight."

"Sure," I say, leaning over on my elbow so I can kiss him.

"Nuh-uh," Jett says when I roll back over onto my stomach. "I don't want just one kiss."

Warmth fills my stomach when I see him gazing at me, his eyes full of desire. I roll over to my back and put a finger to my lips. "Hmm . . . then what do you want to do?"

Jett is never one to miss an opportunity of being close to me. He seizes the moment now, rolling on top of me, holding up his weight on his elbows. "I want to do this," he says, dropping his lips to my neck. The stubble on his chin tickles, his breath on my neck sending chills down my shoulder.

I slide my hands under his shirt and up his back, feeling the taut muscles under my fingertips. I lift my head and kiss him slowly, our tongues exploring each other. "Why aren't you closer?" I whisper, whining because he's holding himself too far above me. I want to feel his body against mine.

"I just like to torture you," he whispers, kissing me harder.

I grumble and wrap my arms around his neck, trying to pull him closer. He gets this cocky grin and straightens his elbows, keeping himself a foot above me on the bed.

"You need to be closer," I say, kissing his collarbone.

"Oh, but it's so much fun to mess with you," Jett's raspy voice sends tingles down to my toes.

That's it. I wrap my arms around his neck until my fingertips touch my elbows, and then I swing my legs around his stomach. I'm like a sloth on a tree branch as I pull myself up to him, holding on tight until I'm happily snuggled against him.

He laughs and bends at the elbows, slowly lowering us until my back hits the bed. I keep my legs wrapped around his stomach, feet hooked at the ankles.

"That's hot," he whispers, letting more of his body weight press against me.

My hips grind into his, and his breath hitches.

Then his freaking phone rings.

"Ignore it," he whispers, his hand sliding down my side while he kisses me passionately, his body feeling so damn good against mine.

But three phone calls later and our make out is kinda ruined. He breaks away from our kiss, and leans over on his elbow. "I wonder who that is," he mutters, casting a scornful look toward his phone on the nightstand.

I slide my fingers down his chest, feeling the ripples of his muscles until I get down to the waistband of his jeans. "You should probably go check that," I whisper against his lips.

He kisses me one more time, teasing me with his tongue, and then he leaps off the bed, leaving me cold and aching with desire.

"Ugh, it's D'andre," he says, holding up his phone. "Wonder what he wants . . ." His face glows from the phone screen and I roll over on my stomach, watching him.

His eyes squint together while he reads a message. "Oh shit," he mutters, running a hand through his hair. "No, no, no."

My brows pull together. "What is it?"

He looks up at me and shakes his head. "I'm fucked."

CHAPTER TWENTY-SIX

Jett

My eyes blur as I stare at D'andre's text for the tenth time. Why the hell is this happening to me? I *try* to be a good person. I've turned over a new leaf, settled down. I don't steal or kick puppies. But I guess the sins of my past refuse to let themselves disappear, refuse to let me truly start over.

"Babe?" Keanna says, pushing up to a sitting position on my bed. "Is someone dead?"

"My career, probably." I throw my phone onto the bed and sit, sinking my head into my hands. Keanna reaches for my phone, probably to read D'andre's text.

"I don't understand what this means," she says a few seconds later. The bedspread shifts around as she climbs over and sits down next to me. "What is Girlfriend Beware?"

My fingers curl into my hair. I sit up and then exhale sharply, wishing all of my anger would go out with my breath. It doesn't.

"Girlfriend Beware is this stupid website that some seniors set up a couple of years ago. I was a freshman at the time and it became a big deal when a bunch of senior guys got called out on it. Basically, it's a blog where girls send in stories about guys who are cheaters or liars. It's spread out all over the county now, not just in our school."

D'andre's text wasn't very long, but I know what it means. He'd simply texted: *Shit man, you're on girlfriend beware.*

"Okay first of all, that's really stupid and secondly," Keanna says, pushing off my bed. She walks over to my desk and opens my laptop. "Let's see what they posted, hmm?"

I run my hand down my face. "No way, I don't even want to know."

But when she opens the browser and searches for the website, I can't help but go over there and peek over her shoulder.

The website is rudimentary, set up on some free blog hosting site. The only user who ever makes the posts is someone called *TruthSeeker*, but on the side of the website it has a link for girls to send in their stories to be posted.

And right there on the homepage, is a photo of me, probably stolen from someone's Facebook page. I'm holding a beer and smiling, but not at the camera. It's at one of the lake parties, a couple years ago, judging by the length of my hair.

"Jett Adams makes this week's list of guys to stay far away from," Keanna reads aloud. "Actually, make that guy of the *year*. Ladies, you don't want to go near this handsome bastard."

"Ugh, I don't want to hear anymore," I say, turning around and walking to my window. I stare outside, watching a bird fly between the powerlines.

"It's not too bad, Jett." Keanna scrolls through the page, speed-reading it all. I'm cringing inside, but I've already decided that if we're going to be together, we'll eventually know everything about each other. There's nothing on that website that I should keep from her anyway, so it doesn't matter if she reads it, despite how much I hate the idea.

Keanna clicks off the website and closes my laptop. "It's really not that bad, babe." She joins me in front of my window and wraps her arms around my waist.

"It is bad." I sigh and slide my hand around her back. "This is bad for my career."

She peers up at me. "How?"

"It's still two years before I can go pro, but the motocross world is very much a family sport. Racing teams won't want me on their team if I have drama surrounding me. I've seen it happen to guys before. If a racer cheats on his wife, he's out. Hell, it's what happened to my dad. He got in a fight with some guy and they kicked him off the team."

Her chest inflates. "Hmm . . ." Then she spins around, twisting out of my arms and heading straight toward my computer again.

"What are you doing? I don't like that look," I say, following her.

"No worries. I have an idea."

I watch curiously as she navigates back to the webpage and scrolls down to the bottom. There's some contact information and she searches it on some other website. Soon, she's on a domain hosting page and it says the owner of the website is Jennifer Upton, a name I vaguely recognize from my freshman year of high school.

"If this works, you owe me a backrub," she says, winking.

"All you have to do is ask," I tell her, folding my arms across my chest while she types the number into her phone, after first loading an app that claims it'll make her number private on their caller ID.

"What exactly are you going to say?" I ask.

She gives me a devilish grin. "It's ringing," she whispers. She waits a beat and then, in a super professional voice she says, "Hello, I am looking for Jennifer Upton. Excellent, this is Julie from District Attorney John Fuller's office."

I lift an eyebrow. I'm pretty sure she just made up that name—it's not like we go around talking about DA's all the time. Keanna's lips curl into a smile. "It has come to our attention that a slanderous post involving our client, Jett Adams, has been posted to your website called Girlfriend Beware. I am giving you twelve hours to remove the content from your site or we will be proceeding with a warrant for your arrest, pending serious defamation charges."

I put a fist over my mouth, trying not to laugh. Keanna nods, her eyes focused not on me, but on the task at hand. "I see. Okay well, it's very much appreciated. I'll alert the DA and verify that the content is removed and all charges will be dropped. If it's not, however, I'm afraid there are no second chances. Okay. Mmhmm, thanks. Have a great day."

She ends the call and her professional smile turns into a smirk. "Bitch believed the whole thing. It sounded like she was crying and she promised to remove the post and never mention your name again."

My jaw hits the floor. "You were just bullshitting all of that legal jargon, right?"

She nods, an evil smile playing on her lips. "Yeah, I'm pretty sure DA's don't handle stuff like that," she says, shrugging. "Luckily, I was betting on the fact that a girl who started a website like this in high school would now be just as stupid as she was back then."

Keanna pretends to brush something off her shoulder. "Your problem is solved, my dear."

"I love you," I say. I throw my arms around her and lift her off her feet, swinging her around and around. She giggles and holds on tightly, burying her face into my neck.

When I set her back on the floor, she leans her head back and kisses me. I brush her wild hair back into place. "You are the greatest girlfriend in the world."

Her eyes sparkle. "I know, I know." She snorts and shakes her head. "I can't believe that worked."

CHAPTER TWENTY-SEVEN

Keanna

I hold it in pretty well. I smile and laugh and revel in my victory of pretending to be the District Attorney's assistant and saving the day. Jett doesn't even suspect that anything is wrong, and that's how I know I'm really pulling this off.

Normally he can read me like a freaking book, but tonight he just hangs out, being all romantic and fun and he doesn't even mention once that something might be wrong with me. Maybe he was just too preoccupied with the horror of finding that shit posted online about him. Or maybe I'm just becoming a really good liar.

I hold his hand all the way back to my house, where we kiss at the back door and I tell him I love and he says he loves me, too. It's a normal goodbye for us. As soon as he starts walking back home, I go inside, close the door behind me, and let the tears fall.

"Keanna!" Becca's voice makes me jump, and I realize with humiliation that I'm not the only person in the kitchen, despite the fact that most of the lights are off. Only a glow from a light underneath the cabinets is on, but I see Becca sitting at the breakfast table, holding a package of Girl Scout cookies. She stands and rushes over to me. "What's wrong, honey?"

I wipe away my tears and change the subject. "Are you eating cookies in the dark?"

She shrugs and glances back at the table, where her half-eaten package of Thin Mints waits. "I guess, yeah. But it's not what it seems. I was just too lazy to bring them back to bed with me."

"Can I have some?" I ask.

"Of course, but you're going to tell me why you're crying."

Becca joins me at the table and we share the cookies in the near dark of the kitchen. I'm pretty sure she'll never drop the subject, so there's no point in trying to escape her inquiring gaze. Plus, the tears keep threatening to spill out of my eyes again, so I guess I should talk about it.

"Just some drama happened with Jett today," I begin, biting into another cookie. "Some girl posted a story about him on a website, saying he can't be trusted and then she went on to insult me because I'm his girlfriend."

That's the part I hadn't told Jett about. Since he didn't want to read the post himself, I'd only skimmed it out loud, but I read the whole thing to myself. They called me a *rat face*, and *desperate*. And *anorexic*. Whatever the hell that means, since I eat all the time.

Becca listens intently while I tell her all of this, summarizing all the points of the post for her even though I'd left them out for Jett. He would have just gotten mad and made things worse by trying to stick up for me. Luckily, I can stick up for myself, at least in public. Internally, I feel like shit.

"The post is gone now," Becca says, handing me another cookie. "So you don't need to worry about it anymore. I bet not many people even saw it."

I shake my head. "That's not the problem, really. I just—every single time I start thinking I might be worth it, that I might actually deserve happiness and a good relationship—crap like this happens and it slams me back into the real world where I don't deserve anything good."

"Honey, that is not true." Becca's eyes light up with that fiery mother look. It's a similar look that Jett would have had if I'd told him what the article said about me. Protective. "The girls who post stuff like that online are the ones who don't deserve happiness. And trust me, they won't ever find it. They'll bounce from guy to guy, get divorced a million times, and never be happy. They're petty, jealous, and stupid. You are so much better than that. You can't let them get to you."

I smile, and it's actually genuine. "Thanks, Mom."

The words just kind of come out of me. Becca's smile lights up the whole darkened room. "I like the sound of that," she says, sitting straighter. She grabs another cookie. "We should have these talks more often."

I laugh. "Once that baby is here, you'll be getting called mom all the time."

"And I'll love it!"

When the cookies are gone, I'm feeling a little better from the mother-daughter chat. It still sucks deep down, and I know it'll be hard for me to handle all of this pathetic drama from other girls at school. I still have to endure the occasional rude words or stuck up glare in the hallways.

"You know, you could look into homeschooling," Becca says. "Hell, you and Jett could both do it. He used to beg to be homeschooled so he could focus more on motocross and now that he's close to going pro, it might be a good option for him. That way you two could be happy together and not worry about those idiots in the school."

"Isn't that just running away from the problem?" I ask while I trace the chevron patterns on the placemats.

She shrugs. "Probably. But it could also be argued that you're choosing a healthier way to live your life and be happy without letting the negativity of others get you down."

I give her a pointed look. "That sounds like something on one of your paintings."

She grins. "That doesn't make it any less true. But think about it, okay? High school is overrated and you two could totally homeschool yourselves if you want. They do it all online now."

"I'll think about it," I say. And then because she's the greatest adopted mom in the world, I get up and give her a quick hug before heading to my room.

After a shower, where I let the hot water wash away my tears and the stresses of the day, I crawl in bed and call Jett.

"Hey, beautiful," he says. The sounds of the Xbox roar in the background. "Hold on a sec." I hear him shut off the TV. "What's up?"

I try to sound neutral as I tell him all about Becca's suggestion of us becoming homeschooled. Truth is, I'm not even sure how I feel about it. Part of me thinks it'd be awesome to sleep in late and teach myself, maybe even graduate early. The other part of me says the only reason I even went to school without getting a GED was to appease Jett, so we could have this fun high school experience together. So quitting it all would be kind of stupid, right?

"So what do you think?" Jett asks, when I've finished telling him everything.

I laugh. "I don't know. I was hoping you'd tell me what *you* think."

"I've already said how I feel about wanting to share high school with you," he says, but his voice is strained. "Of course, focusing more on motocross and less on spending eight hours a day at school would be amazing."

"So what do we do?" I ask as my head sinks into my pillow and I stare at the ceiling.

"I don't know. Let's just think it over or something. I think we could be strong and face this together. But if school gets worse over time, maybe we should quit and be homeschooled." His voice turns seductive. "After all, we'd have a lot more time together . . ."

My stomach tingles at the thought of being next to him. "That's always a good idea."

"Okay so, we'll think it over," he says. "And we'll just see where this crazy life takes us."

"Sounds good. I miss you."

He chuckles, but his voice is quiet. "I miss you more."

There's a soft knock on my bedroom door. "Hold on, someone's at my door," I say, hoping Becca doesn't want another long chat right now.

"I'll just let you go."

"No! I'm not done talking," I say, scrambling out of my sheets to go to the door.

"Neither am I," he says. The door swings open and Jett stands there, cell phone to his ear, a cheeky grin on his face.

I hang up my phone and give him a hug. "Becca didn't complain about you being here so late on a school night?"

He shrugs. "She wasn't around."

I lift an eyebrow. He grabs my hips and backs me up until we're inside my room, then he presses his forehead to mine and closes my door with his foot. "I have a house key, remember?"

"Sneaky," I say, feeling blood rush to my cheeks. He smells like he's just showered and his body wash is intoxicating. It's like a magic spell that pulls me under every time.

"So," he says, pulling my hips close against his. "Do you still miss me?"

"Mmhmm," I murmur against his lips.

He kisses me, running his tongue across my bottom lip. "Great, because I've got just the remedy."

CHAPTER TWENTY-EIGHT

Jett

Keanna's jaw drops as I tell her about Ashley's latest assault on my poor innocent butt today. We've successfully made it another week at school, and even though Keanna and I feel like pariahs sometimes with the way a select group of girls leers at us in the hallways, things are okay for the most part. Except of course, for History class with Ashley Lubbock.

"So she just *grabbed* it?" Keanna says, taking a bite out of her carrot stick. Recently she's sworn off fries, because she eats way too much junk food with me.

"Yep," I say, taking a sip of my orange soda. We're the first in our group of friends to sit down in the cafeteria today, so we have a few minutes to talk to ourselves. "I was walking by, holding my poster board and she just reached up and grabbed it."

"Like, the whole butt? Just one cheek?" Keanna asks. Her lips twist like she's trying to hold back laughter.

"Like . . . one handed, one cheek. A full cheek cup." I mimic the motion with my hand.

This makes her burst out laughing. "Wow. Just wow. I feel like I should be mad at her, but it's just too hilarious."

"You should apologize to my butt," I say, leaning over so that part of my butt lifts off the seat. "Tell it you're sorry for laughing at its pain. It was *assaulted* today, Keanna Park!"

She only laughs harder. D'andre walks up holding a tray with his and Maya's food. Maya bumps into his back because she's staring at her phone. "Whoops," she says, backing up. "Wait, what's going on here?"

She eyes Keanna and then me. "Is there hilarious gossip that I don't know about? Spill it!"

Keanna moves her purse off the seat she'd been saving for Maya. Ashley Lubbock grabbed Jett's precious butt cheek in class today."

Maya's hand flies to her mouth. She gasps extra loud and looks appalled, but in this exaggerated making-fun-of-me way.

"You guys are hilarious," I say. I turn to D'andre who is too busy diving into his cheeseburger to care about what the girls find ridiculously funny. "I think our girlfriends should quit their day jobs and go on the road as comedians."

He nods. "If all their material is just making fun of you, they'll probably get rich as hell."

I roll my eyes and focus back on my food. Keanna leans over and kisses my cheek. "You're a good sport, baby."

I give her a silly smile. "You know . . . if you were a good girlfriend, you'd beat up my bully for me," I say, throwing her a wink.

Keanna shrugs. "Eh, I think Ashley would like that too much. The bigger punishment is to just ignore her and let her wallow in the painful realization that she's not the center of attention."

I nod. "Harsh. I like it."

"So, you two thought more about quitting school?" D'andre asks. I've told him all about our possible-maybe-kinda-sorta idea to quit high school and be homeschooled. Of course, I spun it as a way to practice on my bike more and left out the main reason—that Keanna and I are the subject of severe scrutiny from all the girls in my past.

"I think we're waiting until the Christmas break to decide," Keanna says. She eats another carrot stick and then crumples up her face and reaches for one of my fries.

"Cool, cool," he says. "You should stay for senior prom though. "Don't make me go by myself."

"Excuse you?" Maya says, slapping him on the arm. "You'll be with *me* at prom."

"I know, baby. I meant I need a guy friend with me, too."

Maya rolls her eyes and gives Keanna a look. Keanna nods, affirming whatever thing they're saying in girl language.

The conversation soon turns to the epic racing win I had last weekend. D'andre is both impressed and a little envious of my wins, so he's been bringing it up every day this week.

It was the State Championships, which are a big deal in the amateur motocross world, and the fact that I won both of the classes I raced in is a pretty big deal. I'm just trying not to let it get to my head. The best part though?

Seeing my beautiful girlfriend cheering me on from the sidelines.

Of course, she had been standing next to my mom, so that took some of the sexiness away, but I loved it anyway. I love how excited Keanna gets when she watches me ride. I love that she practically jumped my bones after I'd thrown her a sign language *I love you* sign as I flew over the finish line jump.

That little move had been an unplanned last minute decision, but a photographer caught a picture of me doing it, and now all the major Texas motocross websites have a front page article of me and that glorious photo. Dad says it's going to be epic for my career and that all I need to do is keep bringing in win after win and all of the upcoming races. People don't really care about kid racers, but once you're close to being eighteen, people take notice.

In three months, I'll be seventeen and that will start the countdown until I can go pro. Sponsors and teams will be looking at my racing record and it'll be very important that I have my shit together. So homeschooling is starting to look better and better every day.

AFTER SCHOOL, KEANNA AND I HEAD OVER TO THE TRACK, WHERE KEANNA HAS agreed to pick up an extra shift so Becca can go with Mom to get the first baby ultrasound. Mom's only two months along so she said it's too early to see if the baby is a boy or girl, but they'll be able to tell if it's healthy and all of that other good stuff.

"I want pizza for dinner," I say. I'm standing behind Keanna at the front desk, rubbing her shoulders. "Is pizza cool?"

"Are you ever not *thinking* about food?" she says, turning around and poking me in the stomach. Joke's on her because I tighten my abs and all she gets is a finger of pure muscle. She rolls her eyes. I stick out my tongue.

Her silly expression turns into something more adoring. "I love that I can be a dork with you."

"I love everything about you," I say, kissing her.

The bells on the front door jingle and we both jump. The mail guy walks in holding a stack of envelopes over his eyes. "Don't mind me, you lovebirds," he says, slowly lowering the envelopes and winking. He's a cool guy, barely older than we are, so I know he doesn't care that he saw us making out. But it could have been a customer and that would have been bad. I need to keep my insatiable desire to be with Keanna in check, especially when I'm at work.

"Here ya go," he says, handing over the mail.

Keanna thanks him and he leaves. She flips through the letters casually, and I run my finger down her neck just to mess with her.

"Um, Jett?" she says, handing me an envelope. It's tan and the paper feels expensive, like someone's graduation invitation. "I've never seen you get mail here before."

I study the envelope, which has my name written in pen on the front. "That's because I never have."

I rip it open and pull out a few papers that look like some kind of registration form. My heart kicks into a higher gear as I skim over the first page. "This can't possibly be what I think it is . . ." I say, handing the letter to Keanna. "Is it?"

BELIEVE IN FOREVER

A BELIEVE IN LOVE NOVEL

CHAPTER ONE

Keanna

Going back to school after Thanksgiving holiday is like marching into jail on Monday morning. We'd had the whole week off school and it was glorious. I spent every moment with Jett or my new parents or both, and I'd finally met my new grandparents. Becca's dad is the Lawson Police Chief and her mom is really sweet—almost as sweet as Becca. I haven't met Park's parents yet but they're supposed to come down for Christmas. Park said that in the summer he'll take us to California to hang out with them at their beach house and I couldn't be more excited. By then, my baby brother or sister will be here so it'll be even more of an adventure.

Jett and D'andre are having a friendly guy argument about which professional supercross racer is going to win the championship, so I eat my blueberry muffin in silence, preferring to watch the two of them go at it. I still don't know enough about professional supercross to comment. I do know that those guys are all pretty attractive and the girls who hang out at The Track fawn over them constantly. The most popular guys have social media profiles filled with self-taken sexy photos of themselves, usually shirtless and standing near a dirt bike.

My mind wanders off while Jett begins what I'm sure is a well-thought-out argument for his favorite racer. I think about Jett's social media profiles and how he hardly ever used them before we met. (I know, because I stalked through them after we *did* meet.) Now, he still uses them but it's rare. He's not big into posting stuff online and when he does, it's all motocross related.

Honestly, I think it's attractive that Jett isn't obsessed with social media. The guys who post pictures of themselves every single day just come off as arrogant and constantly looking to get laid. It's not very attractive when a guy cares more about taking selfies than being a good boyfriend. Jett doesn't care about any of that. Just another reason why I'm so lucky.

When the bell rings, I groan. Jett wraps an arm around my shoulders and brings me in for a kiss. "You'll be okay, babe."

"I'm not so sure about that," I say, slowly moving to grab my backpack from the floor. "Every time I'm in that woman's office I consider shoving her letter opener through my skull just to end it all."

"Babe, I would be so pissed if you offed yourself in the high school counselor's office," Jett says, laughing as we make our way through the cafeteria. "I'd have to kill myself with the same letter opener so we could come back as ghosts and haunt the high school together."

Maya's floral perfume fills the air as she goes, "Aww! That is so romantic!"

D'andre gives her a look that is both a little adoring and kind of like he's freaked out.

Once a week I have to skip my first period class to join Mrs. Albright in her office for a mandatory counseling session. After she'd first cornered me when school started and kept me hostage in her office for four hours, I haven't been able to get out of this crap. I've tried everything I can think of—pretending to be fine, pretending to be *not* fine but then making a breakthrough and getting better, lying about seeking out a real therapist to see outside of school—nothing worked. If anything, I think she has some kind of creepy fascination with my life story and she thinks that maybe she can be the one to turn me around like some kind of after school special feel-good movie. Gag me.

Two teachers watch everyone as they walk through the main hallway, so Jett just stops by the office and gives me this look. It's the grumpy, unfair look we have when we can't show any public displays of affection because an adult is watching. It's annoying and it only happens at the freaking school. Our own parents are cool with displays of affection. Hell, both sets of our parents are always all over each other anyway.

"We should be homeschooled," I whisper as I grab onto the front of his shirt and peer up into his dark blue eyes.

He grins. "It's almost the end of the first semester—you could probably just graduate early."

My brows pull together. "Is that a thing?"

He nods. "A lot of pregnant high school girls do it. Like they can graduate early in December and not have to come back after the Christmas break."

"Lucky them," I mutter. The two teachers have honed in their focus on us, so we need to break apart soon before they come over here and tell us themselves.

"Well, I'll see you during lunch," I say, releasing my hold on his shirt.

"Have fun being a desolate youth in need of intervention," he says, winking. Then he pulls me in for a quick hug before we go our separate ways. High school is so freaking overrated.

Mrs. Albright's office has transformed into a Christmas-themed oasis since I was in here last week. There are gaudy Christmas statues in front of her desk, Stockings hung on the window and even a fake cardboard fireplace on the wall. Her wax melter now has a distinct Christmas smell in it, but I can't quite place the scent. Some kind of pine mixed with a food spice.

"Good morning, Keanna," she says as I enter. Mrs. Albright's cheeks are too pink from a heavy hand of blush this morning. Usually her makeup isn't so overdone.

"You look nice," I lie. I smile and take my usual seat in front of her desk.

"Thank you, Keanna. That is quite nice of you to say." She takes a sip of her coffee and then laces her fingers together around the paper cup. "Now, what would you like to talk about today?"

It actually hadn't crossed my mind a few minutes ago with Jett, but now I have a brilliant idea.

"I'd like to talk about graduating early," I say, leaning back in my fake leather chair.

Mrs. Albright's eyes widen for a second and then she returns to that classic smile. It's the same kind of smile that the bad guy in a movie has, just before you realize you can't trust them.

"Are you feeling this way because you've spent several months here already and it's a little jarring for you, spending so much time at one school when you're used to moving around a lot?"

Ugh, *enough* with the psychoanalyzing.

"Nope," I say, putting on a cheery smile as bright as the plastic Santa on her desk. "I'm just a little sick of high school and all the pathetic crap that comes with it, and I recently heard that seniors can graduate half a year early if they have enough credits."

"Well yes, but usually those students have a plan." She waves her wrist around as she talks. "Like college classes in the fall, or some kind of problem at home that requires them, like maybe a sick or dying parent . . ." Now comes the pitying stare. "Keanna, honey, do you have a problem at home?"

This poor woman. She is so desperate for me to be screwed up that she's practically begging for me to admit something deep and dark. She'd probably crap herself if I actually had something good to tell her.

I shrug. "Nope. I'm just ready to get out of here and start my life."

Her eyes narrow. "I think we should discuss how you're feeling now that you've spent almost four months here at Lawson High."

"I think we should look up how many credits I have and if I qualify to graduate early."

She stares at me for a beat and when I don't relent, she sighs. "We *could* do that, but you still have so much more to experience this year. You don't want to miss out on all of that."

"Like what? Being the weirdo who has to skip class to talk to the counselor?" I snort. "Trust me, I've been made fun of enough in my life that these little sessions only remind me even more of my screwed up past. They don't help it at all."

She actually looks offended at this. "Therapy works the best when you allow it to help you, Keanna."

"Yeah, probably," I say, glancing over at her SpongeBob themed nativity scene. "But it probably works the best when the person seeks out therapy themselves and it's not forced on them. Anyhow, let's see my credits, shall we?"

I realize I'm getting increasingly more sarcastic as I keep talking, but I don't care. Jett accidentally implanted this idea in my brain and I won't stop pursuing it until I know if it's a viable option for me or not. Sure, I'm still in sophomore biology class, but I might have enough credits. I point toward Mrs. Albright's computer. "Can you check my graduation credentials?"

Her lips press into a thin line and she continues to stare at me, either deep in thought, or maybe she's just trying to convince me to change my mind.

I put my hands on the armrests of my chair and go to stand up. "If you can't help me, I'm sure another counselor will."

"That won't be necessary," she says, heaving a sigh. "If you insist," she says, leaving off whatever else she was going to say. She turns to her computer and types some stuff, and it could be my imagination but it feels like she's taking much longer than necessary to get the job done.

Finally, she says, "There are three types of graduation at Lawson High. The regular, recommended, and distinguished plan. You need twenty-four credits for the regular graduation, which is not recommended. The recommended plan needs twenty-eight credits and the distinguished needs thirty-two."

I wiggle my eyebrows. "So how many do I have?"

"Twenty-two and a half."

My chest falls. "So I don't have enough."

"Not at this very moment, no."

Something in the way she says it makes me wrinkle my nose. Then it hits me. Jett had said those girls graduate in December after the semester is over. "How many credits will I have in December?"

She flinches and obviously she was hoping I wouldn't ask that question. "I can't answer that accurately," she says.

"Why not?"

Her shoulders lift the slightest bit. "Because I have no idea what your current grades are, or if you'll be passing any of your classes at the end of this semester."

"So all I have to do is pass all my classes and then I'll have enough credits to graduate?"

She looks away and her lips press into a thin line. "I suppose."

Warmth floods into me as the reality of being able to graduate early hits me. That's only three and a half weeks away. This could totally happen. I could be out of here and be done with these stupid therapy sessions, the glares in the hallways from pathetic jealous girls—all of it.

"How do I graduate early?" I ask, trying to contain my excitement, which is hard because all I want to do is jump around and praise SpongeBob Jesus for making this become a reality.

"You would need a parent to apply for early graduation if you are a minor—"

"I'm not," I say eagerly. "I turned eighteen a few days ago."

I glance down at my wrist, at the beautiful gold bracelet that Jett had given me for the occasion.

"Well then you'd just need to apply."

"How do I do that?"

She shakes her head. "In my professional opinion, you are not of the maturity level to graduate early, Keanna. I am recommending that you stay in school and see it through to your real graduation date in May."

Can she do this? Surely she can't do this.

"You know what? Thanks for all your help," I say, standing up and shouldering my backpack. “If you won’t assist me in graduating early, I’ll just have my mother come up here and do it herself.”

Mrs. Albright’s eyes widen and her lips press together but she doesn’t say anything. I walk into the hallway and then turn back to her. “This will be our last session,” I say, flashing her a smile. “Now that I’m eighteen, I won’t be forced into counseling that I don’t need.

I keep my head high while I walk through the hall and out into the office that leads me to the main hallway. I have no idea if I can actually call off the sessions myself, but I did and I’m going to pretend that it worked. After all, I’m officially done with this school. To Mrs. Albright’s chagrin, I know I’m passing all of my classes and I will have no trouble acing the final exams in a couple of weeks. I’ll have enough credits to graduate and I’ll be done with this place. I don’t need the *full high school experience.*

There are way better things in my life than dealing with all this pointless drama.

CHAPTER TWO

Jett

I can't even describe what it's like to be the newest member of Team Loco Racing. Well . . . the newest *intern*. I'm not a full member yet, but you wouldn't know it based on how much free Team Loco shit I've been given in the last few weeks. My closet has two extra feet of hangers now, all filled with the free T-shirts with their cool lightning bolt logo.

And all the craziness is just getting started. They only recently added me to their website, doing a profile and interview of me as their newest intern. My social media profiles freaking blew up after that. Five hundred new friend requests in one hour. It was insane.

Now I'm stuck going to school every day and wishing I was home so I can get back to practice. My first official race as an intern for Team Loco is in two and a half weeks at Oakcreek Motocross Park and I've been busting ass to be as fast as possible.

Too bad school keeps getting in the way. I wish it was still summertime where I could ride all day every day and make out with my girl in the afternoons.

When the last bell of the day finally rings, I head out of class and power walk until I get to Keanna. Her hand slips into mine easily and we face the throngs of people together.

"I'm so glad this day is over," she says squeezing my hand. Her hair was down and curly this morning, but now it's thrown in a messy bun on top of her head. Looks like the stresses of the day got to her, too.

"You say that like you've just finished the walk to Mordor or something." I nudge her with my shoulder.

Her tongue runs across her bottom lip in that way that usually says she's hiding a smile. "Well . . ."

"Well, what?"

She gnaws on her bottom lip and ducks under my arm as I hold open the door to the parking lot. "Well . . . I might have just completed a long journey." She blinks and shakes her head. "Well, not at this exact moment, but come Christmas break —" She chucks her thumb to the right. "I'm out. I'm done."

"Done with school?" I lift a brow. "And when did this development happen?"

Now she can't hold back her grin. "During my stupid counseling session. I'll tell you all about it later."

We're at my truck now, so we climb inside and I crank the music. She holds my hand while we drive home, and although the sudden news of her quitting school should shock me, it doesn't. This has kind of been building for a while now, for the both of us. I know I'd fought for her to stay in school and have a senior year with me, but that was before my Team Loco deal. Now, I think I want out of school more than she does.

I pull into Keanna's driveway to drop her off, but as soon as her hand grabs the door handle I stop her.

"I need a kiss first," I say, giving her a look. "Preferably two or three."

She rolls her eyes but she's smiling. "You'll see me again in like fifteen minutes, you horn dog."

"Now you owe me five kisses," I say.

She lowers her gaze and then scoots over, leaning across the center console. The way her hand grabs my shirt and tugs me closer sends a ripple of desire coursing through me. She's normally so timid and I freaking love it when she takes control. Her lips melt into mine and our tongues graze, our mouths melting into each other.

Just when I'm about to throw her into the backseat of my truck Hulk-style, she pulls away.

"I think that makes me all paid up," she says, flashing me wink as she steps out of my truck.

I know I have a goofy ass grin on my face as I watch her walk around the front of my truck toward her front door. She turns around and mouths *I love you* and then blows me a kiss.

Damn, I love this girl.

My mom is in the living room, wearing only yoga pants and a hot pink sports bra as she works out to a kickboxing DVD. Her stomach pokes out with the baby bump from being a surrogate for best friend's baby.

"Ew, Mom," I say, just to do my duty as an annoying son. "What if I'd brought home one of my friends? Can't you wear real clothes?"

She scoffs and waves a hand at me before high-kicking along with the man on the television who is completely ripped. Talk about false advertising—no amount of kickboxing will make you look like that guy.

"I'm pregnant, Jett. None of your friends would look twice."

"All the more reason to cover up," I say, rolling my eyes as I head into the kitchen and get a snack. When I was a kid, it was kind of a big deal when my mom would dress less than mother-like. All of my friends were obsessed with her, calling her a MILF and the likes. It always grossed me out when I was growing up.

She's my mom, so I didn't get what the big deal was about, but when everyone else's parents are fifteen years older than your own, your friends can't help but want to talk about it.

I'm making my second Hot Pocket when Mom walks in to refill her water cup. "Dude, when's the last time you checked the PO box?" she asks, her voice panting from the workout.

"Friday," I say. I'd had about fifty letters from fangirls who had seen the news of me joining Team Loco. "Why?"

She gulps her water and then walks over to the dining table where a garbage bag sized tote waits. The post office logo is printed on the fabric. I lift an eyebrow.

"Friday was three days ago."

She hefts the bag off the table and shoves it in my arms. "That adorable mug of yours seems to have a fan club."

In my room, I dump out the post office bag on my floor. It's mostly envelopes with girly handwriting, hearts and stars and little decorations drawn all over. Some appear to be written by guys, and if they're anything like my mail from Friday, it's teenage guys writing me for advice on how to get their own internship.

What's ridiculous is that this isn't even all of the messages. My email is blowing up as well. It was probably a terrible idea to give Team Loco our PO box address when they did my initial interview, because that's what they used for fan mail and, damn people are using it.

I grab my phone to text Keanna.

Me: I got a shit ton of fan mail. Wanna help me read it?

Keanna: You know I do. I'm gonna shower first, okay?

Me: Shower here . . .

Keanna: K. You want some of Becca's lasagna?

Me: Yesssss

It's kind of funny how I asked her to get naked and shower in my bathroom and she only said "k".

I guess part of me feels all puffed up and important as I gaze out over the mountain of fan mail. In reality, these girls don't even know me—they're writing out of a desire to get close and personal with a "famous" person. I don't feel that famous, not really. I'm just a guy who's good on a dirt bike. I guess these girls think they'll get some kind of famous themselves by knowing me? I don't know. But I do know that Keanna was into me before she knew who I was. She didn't grow up knowing my dad's name in motocross, or idolizing professional racers. She just knew me for *me*, and that's what she liked. Because of this, I trust her to be my girlfriend for the long term and I know she won't screw me over just to get something from me.

Taking one of the thicker envelopes, I rip it open. Keanna walks through my bedroom door at the exact second I slide out a handful of naked photos.

"Holy shit," I mutter, dropping them to the carpet.

She peers at them and wrinkles her nose. "Girl needs some serious razor burn gel."

I grab the photos and flip them over so we don't have to look at it, then I skim through her handwritten letter that smells like some kind of prostitute's perfume.

"She's sixteen. Are you kidding me? That shit is illegal."

Keanna nods, tossing the new outfit and towel she brought over. They land on my bed and I catch the sight of her cute purple thong and get an array of dirty thoughts floating through my mind. But then I look back at the overturned photos and scowl.

"We need to burn these," Keanna says, kicking at them with her foot. "If that girl's underage, you could definitely get in trouble."

I nod and run a hand through my hair. Is this my life now? Screening fan mail for illegal photos? "Ugh," I say.

She kneels down to my level and kisses me. "You don't need these gross photos, babe." She does a little shimmy and runs her tongue across her bottom lip. "You've got me, and that's better than photos."

CHAPTER THREE

Keanna

I haven't always been very lucky in life, but that might be turning around. All I had to do was corner my parents in the kitchen during dinner the next day and explain to them about the pregnant teenagers.

After their initial looks of shock wore off, I told them that no, I wasn't pregnant, I just heard that pregnant seniors can graduate in December instead of waiting until May if they have enough credits. My parents were immediately on board with the idea. Becca was cool with it because she knows how much I hate going to school and Park was excited that I'd be around to work full time at The Track again, since one of their employees just quit to move out of state.

After making a few calls to the office to figure out my graduation status and set up an application, (and one call to the principal to complain about Mrs. Albright's treatment of me) Becca has all the info I'll need.

Two of my teachers agreed to let me take the final on Friday instead of waiting one and a half more weeks until the day before Christmas break. They both essentially said that no real work is done or taught in those last two weeks so it wouldn't matter if I took the exams early.

Have I mentioned how much I love my English and History teachers?

My final exams are scheduled for Thursday and Friday mornings at six freaking a.m. since they can't interfere with school hours.

I don't care about the early hour though. I'll walk barefoot through miles of snow if it means getting out of here early and with a real high school diploma, not the shame and regret of being a dropout. And let's face it, at one point in my life I thought I'd actually end up in the dropout boat.

All of my graduation talk has sparked Jett to consider becoming homeschooled or maybe getting a GED. Of course, the second idea probably won't happen since his mom is hugely against it. I really hope he does get to become homeschooled, and it's almost entirely for selfish reasons. I can't stand the thought of Jett sitting with other girls at lunch or walking with other girls between classes. I don't think he would, but with how popular he's been lately, maybe he wouldn't exactly have a choice. Sometimes Jett is too nice for his own good.

He's been talking to his parents about homeschooling but they keep telling him to wait until the Christmas break to figure it out. I know he's angsty and annoyed about it, but I'm pretty sure they'll let him do it. All we can do until then is wait.

After dinner, I text him.

Me: Something is really wrong in my bedroom…

Jett: What is it?

Me: There's no boyfriend here…

Jett: haha. I have a shit ton of history homework but I'll be there as soon as I'm done.

I TURN ON MY TV AND STARE AT THE PHONE. THE GOOD GIRLFRIEND THING TO DO would be to give him my blessing to take as long as he needs to get his homework done. Homework is important, after all.

But maybe I'm a terrible girlfriend because I text him something bad.

ME: COME OVER AND I'LL HELP YOU!

Jett: I'll bring cookies.

THE BOY GETS HERE IN RECORD TIME—LIKE, I HAVE A FEELING HE WAS ALREADY ON his way over before I told him to come over. I hear Becca talking to him in the kitchen, so I run out to meet him. Yeah, I *run*. Like it's been years since I've seen him instead of just a couple of hours. Pathetic? Yes, but who cares.

Jett's strong arms circle around me, warming up all of my cold parts. It's especially cold in here today since Park is working from home and he always cranks the air conditioner. I bury my head in Jett's chest and he hugs me tightly to him, his hand on my head.

"You guys are ridiculous," Becca says, waving her hand at us. "I mean, Park and me were like that, too, but seeing it from the eyes of a grown up makes me want to make fun of you."

"It's not my fault your daughter is so perfect," Jett says.

Becca brightens. She always does when someone calls me her daughter without adding the word "adopted" before it.

When he pulls away I notice his dark brown hair is all messy, probably from pulling at it while working on his history assignment.

"Come on," I say, tugging on his pocket. "Let's go do that homework."

"Shall I bring the cookies?" he says, holding up a plastic container of what looks like Bayleigh's famous chocolate chip cookies.

"Not without letting me raid them first," Becca says. She swipes three cookies and then shoos us away.

Jett and I settle onto my bed and I help him with his homework by reading all of his vocabulary words and quizzing him on them. Part of his final exam will be to know these words so I hope all of this studying will help him pass and move into homeschooling.

When we've studied until Jett knows the words before I've even read the whole definition, we finally close up the textbook.

"It's only eight-thirty but it feels so much later than that," I say, rolling over to my side to check my phone off the nightstand.

When I turn back around, Jett is laying down, his head propped up on his arm, the other hand reaching for me. I grin and roll over until we're facing each other on top of my plush comforter.

"Thank you for studying with me," he says, his voice low and sexy as hell. I slide closer to him, matching up our bodies until my toes touch the tops of his ankles.

"That might be the first time two people have actually studied instead of making out," I say. I reach up and touch his chest, letting my fingers slide down his pecs.

"Oh I have every intention of making out," Jett whispers, sliding his hand around my waist and tugging my hips closer to him. He kisses me full on, not building up to it with slow, innocent kisses. I tangle my hands into his already messy hair and shudder when his weight rolls on top of me as we make out.

This is good. We are *so* good at this. But we still haven't taken it much further and part of me wonders why. The other part of me says it doesn't matter if we take it slow, because we'll be together forever.

Jett's hips press into mine and I feel his erection, his need, both from the feel of his body and the way he kisses me. I shudder from the sensation and then pull away.

"Babe," I breathe. Jett immediately lifts up on his elbows, worry stitched across his gorgeous face.

"What's wrong?"

"Nothing," I say, shaking my head. "I was just thinking about how we haven't . . . you know . . ."

"Had sex?" He kisses me on the cheek and then locks his gaze on mine again. "I guess I've been waiting until it felt right."

"It doesn't feel right now?" I ask, trailing my fingers down his cheek.

He grabs my hand and kisses the inside of my palm. "I guess it always *feels* right. But you know what I mean." He glances toward my closed bedroom door. "Maybe when your parents aren't here . . ." His gaze turns sultry. "That'd be a terrible time to find out if you're loud in bed."

Then he winks and my cheeks are probably so red they could pass for a street light. "I agree," I say, biting the inside of my lip. "We should probably wait until we're fully alone."

"So does that mean we're ready for it?" His hand slides down my arm, leaving a trail of goosebumps on my skin.

"God, yes," I say, only to blush even more when I realize how freaking eager and dorky I just sounded.

He chuckles. "Here, roll over and I'll give you a massage so you're stress free for your exam tomorrow."

I do as he says and I close my eyes.

Best boyfriend ever.

CHAPTER FOUR

Jett

My alarm blares, nagging me over and over again as I repeatedly tell it to sleep. It's five forty-five in the morning—why the hell is it going off? I need my sleep. Sleep and I are lovers and I would like to get back to her.

Then it hits me. Keanna.

I sit up in bed and yawn, reaching for my phone. That's why I'd set the alarm—so I could send her this text.

Me: Good luck on your final exam, baby! I know you'll do great

I fall back onto my bed and close my eyes as sleep beckons to me again. My phone buzzes and I read her reply.

Keanna: Thanks, hon. Now go back to sleep!

She knows me so well. I reset my alarm for the same time tomorrow when she'll be taking her second final and then I fall back asleep.

In just two days, everything has changed. Keanna passed both of her exams and got an A on each one. I'd known she could do it, but she apparently didn't have the same belief in herself because she had burst into tears when she got her results. Silly girl. She's so much smarter and better than she'll ever give herself credit for.

The greatest part of Keanna's early graduation though, is that it convinced my parents to let me pursue homeschooling. My dad was all for it but Mom has her reservations. She seems to think I'll spend all of my time riding my dirt bike, hanging with Keanna, and studiously ignoring my school work.

To give her credit, she might be right. But an education is important, and I do want one, so I had to convince them that homeschooling is what's best for my career. Since my parents are too busy and (according to my mom) not *teacherly* enough to homeschool me themselves, Mom found a program online that she thinks will work the best. It's an online high school diploma program, but it's partnered with the local branch of Texas State University, so I'll have an actual professor to report to and I'll take all of my exams at the college with him. The rest of the work is done online. There are even video lectures that I can watch online as if I were in a real classroom. The best part? Some of the classes will get me college credit. Awesome.

Since The Track was busy as hell this past weekend, we've all decided to go out tonight, Monday, to celebrate Keanna's graduation. So today, although I get to skip school because I'm about to drop out anyway, I'm busier than usual.

I have to shower, work one hour at The Track's front office because Mom and Becca have a baby doctor appointment, and then I have to go to the college which is an hour away and meet with my new professor. Then it's a quick trip back home, shower, and go find the prettiest flowers money can buy because I want to surprise Keanna for her early graduation. She doesn't think it's a big deal, but it is. Especially since she started school this year as a girl who had hopped around so much she really missed out on a lot of good grades in her past. I knew she was smart, and now she'll have the diploma to prove it.

I'm falling asleep at the front desk when Mom and Becca come bouncing in the doors, talking animatedly in a way that makes them look like teenagers.

"How was the doctor?" I ask.

"So perfect," Becca says, giving Mom a wide-eyed smile.

"How's the baby?"

"Also perfect," Mom says, tapping her belly. "This time we had two other couples assume we were lesbians. It's annoying how people feel the need to point out your sexual orientation when they don't even know you." Mom rolls her eyes and Becca meets me behind the front counter, relieving me of my work duties.

"I'd be damn proud to have you as my wife," Becca tells Mom.

"Hell yeah you would," Mom says, shaking her hips. "I'm a trophy wife."

"Excuse you?" Becca says, putting a hand on her hip. "*I* would be the trophy wife."

Mom throws an arm around her shoulders and flashes me a smile. "Becca, dear, you are the best trophy wife of all."

They've always been this weird. It's not a new thing. Growing up with my mom and her best friend since childhood has been fun for the most part, but sometimes they get a little *too* weird and I have to extract myself from the situation. Now that Mom's carrying Becca and Park's surrogate child, they're even closer, and I hadn't realized that was possible. It almost feels like I'll be getting a new baby brother or sister myself, since Becca is like a second mom to me.

"So, do you know if it's a boy or girl yet?" I ask.

"Not yet, but they said by our next visit they'll be able to tell." Becca logs into the computer. "But you'll all find out more at the party."

I lift an eyebrow. "Like a baby shower? Because men don't go to those things."

Mom punches me in the arm. "Men go to whatever supports the women they love, you little punk. And she's not talking about the shower. She's talking about the baby gender party!"

I check the time on my phone. I need to get out of here to make my appointment on time but I *have* to know more about this. "What is a baby gender party?"

"It's where we gather all our friends and family and reveal what the sex of the baby will be," Mom says. "Becca won't even know until the party. We're going to keep it a secret until then. It'll be a fun surprise."

I nod sarcastically. "Okay . . . ya'll are weird. . . but I love you both. I gotta go."

"Have fun at college, sweetie," Mom says, shooing me off my barstool so she can sit next to her best friend.

I wish Keanna could come with me, but she has one final meeting at the high school to get all of her graduation stuff completed. She might actually be the first girl to graduate early who isn't knocked up. Funny, because I've already heard some rumors going around that people think she must be pregnant. Those people can go screw themselves. Why does everyone have to get into other people's business? What Keanna and I do in our relationship has nothing to do with them.

She's been right about one thing though—high school has entirely too much drama. I'm so glad we're almost officially done with it.

I crank the stereo in my truck and make the drive north to the university. I've been here before for football games, and for when Mom graduated college, but never as a potential student. It all seems a little scarier now that I'm alone. Of course, I'll never admit that. Not even to Keanna.

I follow the signs and find the Humanities building, and then make it to Mr. Walker's office. He's a younger guy than I expected, probably in his mid-thirties.

"Welcome," he says, shaking my hand. He gestures to one of the chairs in front of his desk and we sit. "So tell me why you want to be homeschooled?"

"I'm a motocross racer and I just got an important internship on a professional racing team," I say, trying not to sound too braggy but also trying to let him know this is important. "If I'm homeschooled then I can concentrate more on my career and hopefully go pro in a year or two."

"Impressive," he says, nodding. "Most kids come in here and say they're too lazy to get up in the morning, or some other crap. You actually have a good reason. How are your grades now?"

"A's and B's," I answer honestly. "I'm in advanced classes as well."

His eyebrows shoot up. What, does he think a dirt bike racer can't also be smart? "Sounds like you've got a good head on your shoulders, Mr. Adams. I'll be happy to be your homeschooling professor."

Relief hits me and I'm floating on cloud nine for the rest of the meeting. He gives me a ton of paperwork, shows me how to log into the online learning center, and tells me his expectations of the classwork. Although I'll have other teachers for certain subjects, he's the main professor who will determine if I pass or not. He's a progressive kind of guy and doesn't require too much busy work. If I understand the lesson, then that's all he needs. Awesome.

He shakes my hand again and walks me to the door. The only process left is for my parents to pay the fee and to get all the textbooks I'll need.

Mr. Walker suggests that I spend some time walking around campus to get oriented. "I may or may not get a bonus for the amount of students I refer to apply to the college their freshman year," he says, giving me a wink.

"Thanks," I say with a chuckle. "I'll definitely check it out."

I head toward the cafeteria to grab something to eat before going back home. The moment I step in line, two girls walk up to me. They're in short shorts and tank tops and don't look like they're actually taking classes, although their backpacks would suggest otherwise. Can you really dress like this in college?

"Hi there," one of them says. She's almost as tall as I am and looks like she lifts weights. "I'm a big fan."

"Me too," her friend says. This girl is shorter but still looks pretty athletic. I don't think they ride bikes though, or I would recognize them from the local motocross scene.

"Thanks," I stay, looking back up at the food menu. I already know I want a cheeseburger, but they don't know that.

"I didn't know you go to school here," the first one says. "I'm Belia, by the way, and this is Sara."

"I don't go here yet," I say. "But I'm about to start their homeschooling program to get done with high school."

"Oh my God, you're still in high school?" Belia says, putting a hand to her chest. "That is so freaking adorable."

"Um okay," I say, furrowing my eyebrows.

Sara scoffs at her friend. "Dude, she should know that. We both follow your Instagram," she says to me. She bats her eyelashes and I hold back a groan. Why does this always happen to me? Why can't girls simply say hi when they recognize me and then move on?

"So, you want to come to a party tonight? I can get you all the beer you'd like."

I take a step forward in the line, wishing the three people ahead of me would hurry the hell up so I can get out of here. "No thanks. I'm busy tonight . . . celebrating with my girlfriend."

"How old is she?" Belia asks.

"Why would that matter?" I say.

Belia smiles. "Can she buy you beer? Because I can."

"Are you really trying to put down my girlfriend based on her age?" I ask. I put my wallet back in my pocket, planning to leave and get out of dealing with these idiots.

They must see the disgust on my face because Sara gives Belia a look. "We're sorry. We didn't mean to insult your girlfriend. She can totally come to the party, too."

"Thanks, but I'll have to pass."

Sara bites her bottom lip. "Do you think maybe you'd take a selfie with us?"

I draw in a deep breath. "Sure."

The girls flock to my sides and Sara holds up her phone. I give a polite smile because this will be all over the internet and I don't want to look like a dick.

As soon as it's done, I get the cheeseburger and eat it on the way to my truck. Keanna calls.

"Hey, beautiful."

She snorts. "Why do you always answer the phone like that?"

"Because I know it makes you smile."

"Whatever . . . so yeah, I was calling to tell you something."

I unlock my truck and climb inside. "And that is?"

"I am an official graduate!" I can hear the smile in her voice.

"Awesome, babe. I'm proud of you. We'll definitely have to celebrate tonight."

"Eh, it's no big deal," she says. "I'm just happy it's over."

She can say it's no big deal all she wants, but we'll see if she's thinking differently when she gets those flowers tonight. I grin. "Can't wait to see you."

"Same here. I need to know all about your fancy college experience."

CHAPTER FIVE

Keanna

The most beautiful bouquet of flowers graces my vanity, filling the air with a delightful fragrance of roses while I get ready. We're all going out to dinner tonight to celebrate me graduating and Jett's transfer into homeschooling. In my old life, I would have thought having a fancy dinner with Dawn and a boyfriend's parents would have been lame and awkward. But now these people are my favorite people on earth. Jett's parents and my new parents aren't at all like normal parents. They're young and hardworking people who don't judge others and are always pleasant to be around. I wonder how much better of a person I'd be if I had been raised by Becca and Park.

I ponder the effects of some alternate reality where Becca could have children and I was her real daughter while I apply my eye makeup in front of my vanity mirror.

Tonight I'm wearing a black dress with a lace overlay that has silver sparkly sequins all over it. The sleeves come down to my elbows but the skirt stops mid-thigh so it's still sexy. I'm keeping my hair down and just straightening it so it's sleek and simple.

My parents get a ride with Jett's parents and since we can't all fit into anyone's single car, I'm going to ride with Jett. Like I said, our parents are awesome to be around, but I still like having private moments with my boyfriend.

Jett meets me in the driveway. My parents have already walked over to the Adams' house so we're all alone.

"Damn," he says, scratching his neck. "You look hot."

Jett's wearing crisp dark jeans, black leather shoes and a gray long-sleeved button-up shirt. The sleeves are rolled up his forearms, showing the sexy muscles and veins that pop out when he flexes.

"You look hotter," I say, walking up to him until our bodies are touching. He lets his hands roam down my back and to my butt.

"Maybe we should skip dinner and lock ourselves in my room instead." His voice is deep, almost a growl.

I slide my finger down the buttons on his shirt. "As much as I'd love that, this dinner is specifically to celebrate *us*."

"Okay, but you're mine as soon as we're home."

I look up into his eyes. "Deal."

IT'S STILL EARLY DECEMBER, BUT YOU'D THINK CHRISTMAS IS TOMORROW BY THE WAY this town decorates. I'm in awe as we drive back home in Jett's truck, the lights and decorations a beautiful backdrop to our wonderful dinner.

"I'll have to take you to the fancy neighborhoods," Jett says, reaching over and grabbing my knee while he drives. "They take decorating their houses *very* seriously."

"Awesome." I smile and put my hand on top of his.

Slowly, he wriggles his fingers under the lacy hem of my dress, and lets his hand slide up my thigh. His warmth is always a welcome touch and I try to keep a straight face as his fingers go higher and higher. When he reaches my panties, he turns his hand down and slides it between my legs, then squeezes my thigh.

All while driving.

I gasp and grit my teeth. "Such a tease," I mutter, trying to regain control of my body. Warmth spreads out in all direction from his touch.

He grins, keeping his focus on the road. "Just paying you back for all that teasing you do to me every day."

I cross my arms over my chest. "I do not tease you every *day*."

He nods. "Mhm. Just by being around me, wearing that cute grin and smelling like a damn angel."

"You're a charmer, you know that?"

He lifts a shoulder. "You bring it out in me."

When we get home, my parents have already gone back home and are getting ready for bed. Jett's parents tell us they plan on watching a movie and we politely decline their offer to watch it with them.

Jett laces his fingers into mine as we walk up the stairs and toward his bedroom.

"You know, when it was summer I was dying for the heat to go away, and now that's it's getting colder each day, I wish it was still summer."

He snorts. "Yeah, for as hot as it is in Texas, it also gets pretty cold."

I shiver and press into him. "I wish we had a sauna or something."

He stops just inside his bedroom door. "Well . . . we do have a hot tub."

My eyes narrow. "Could we use it?"

He gives me this cocky grin. "Of course."

In the cold night air, I shiver as I pull off my clothes, revealing the yellow and green bikini I keep in Jett's pool house. "This better be hot," I say, as I walk over to the bubbling hot tub at the edge of their pool. The lights inside are turned on, LED bulbs that switch colors every few seconds.

Jett pulls off his shirt and tosses it over the back of a patio chair, the same one with my discarded clothes. He's wearing black board shorts and I can't help but watch his abs in the moonlight. He walks over to me and takes my hand. "In you go, hot stuff."

I'm shivering from the cold so badly that I don't mind stepping down into the hot tub. The warmth is an immediate welcome to fight off the cold. I sink into the bench seats against the wall and close my eyes.

"Oh my God, this is heaven."

"Not quite," Jett says, sitting next to me. He takes the waterproof remote and flips on one of the televisions that are mounted from the patio's ceiling. He turns the channel until it's on a music station and then slides his arm around my back. I'm lifted into the water and he settles me on his lap, my back pressed against his chest.

"Ah, this is better," he whispers in my ear. His hands slide around my waist and hold my hips in place in his lap while the jet streams fill the water with bubbles. Steam rises, giving the moonlit air a nice glow.

I lean back and let my head rest against his shoulder. "You never answered the main question at dinner," I say, remembering the biggest problem in my life right now.

"What's that?"

I slide my hands on top of his. "What do you want for your birthday?"

His shoulders shrug beneath me and his kisses my neck, doing a damn good job of distracting me. "I don't need anything, babe. His hands slide up my sides, cupping just underneath my bikini top. "I already have everything I want."

I gasp for a breath to steady myself. "Okay then what do you want for Christmas?"

He chuckles, kissing my neck again. "Just you."

"You already have me," I say, twisting around to kiss him. "I need present ideas . . . things that aren't me. I don't count."

His biceps flex and lifts me up again, this time turning me around to face him. I'm practically weightless in the water but it's hot anyway. I grab his shoulders and pull myself on top of his lap.

"Key, I really don't care about presents. I have everything I could ever want—there's a dirt bike track in my backyard and my girlfriend lives next door." His head tilts to the side, his hair all steamy and flattening on his forehead. "My life is literally perfect."

I frown and try not to show how much I love when he grabs my hips and pulls me into him. My boobs press against his chest and I bite my lip, trying to stay focused. "You're getting a birthday and Christmas present from me, whether you like it or not." I press my forehead to his. "It's not fair that your birthday is on Christmas Eve."

He chuckles and kisses me, pulling my bottom lip into his teeth. His thumbs slip under the strap of my bikini bottoms and if I weren't afraid of his parents possibly walking out here, I'd rip them off.

"It is a little unfair, I guess. My parents used to let me have a birthday party in the summer to make up for it. But now I'm older and I don't really care."

I reach down and slide my hand over his erection. This time his eyes close, his head falling back to rest on the edge of the hot tub. I lean forward and kiss his neck, then I drag my tongue up the side of his ear. "I'm getting you two awesome presents this year," I whisper. "I don't care if you don't want anything."

CHAPTER SIX

Jett

Sweat drips down my eyebrow in defiance of the chilly mid-December air. Two hours on a dirt bike, covered in fifty kinds of protective gear will do that do you. My bike rumbles underneath me, the performance racing engine begging to take off.

Team Loco gave me this bike and it's a crazy upgrade from my old racing bike, which was already a pretty fast ride. This new bike does not like idling on the starting line. It wants to haul ass, leaving nothing but upturned dirt in its wake.

It's probably close to noon by now, but we're not stopping any time soon. My first Team Loco race is at Oakcreek Motocross Park this weekend and I need to do good by their name. I need to race hard and fast and prove to them why they chose me out of hundreds of other fast guys in the nation.

And because of this, Dad is making me train my ass off.

"No pressure, son," Dad says, slapping the back of my helmet as he stands next to me at the starting gate on our track. "But you need to shave a few seconds off your holeshot."

"Yeah, no pressure at all," I mutter, but he can't hear it beneath the roar of my bike.

The holeshot is what we call the first position after the gate drops. In motocross, all the racers line up at the starting gate and as soon as the metal bar drops, you take off, pinning the throttle as fast as you can go. The first racer around the first turn has a huge advantage in winning the race, since there's almost always a crash of multiple bikes at that first turn. If you're not fast enough to be first, then you're right in the middle and more likely to crash into a massive bike orgy. Not cool.

So I line back up, wait for Dad to drop the gate, and I pin it.

Then I line back up again, and do it all over again until Dad's stopwatch says something that satisfies him.

"I still think you could do better," Dad says half an hour later. "If you get the holeshot, the rest of the race is easy."

I pull off my helmet. "You wanna try going faster than me, old man?"

He laughs. "Don't tell me the pressure is getting to you?"

I shrug. "I'd just like to see you handle this bike and do better than I'm doing. It's a hell of a lot harder to control something that's so damn fast."

"It can't be that much faster than your last bike," Dad says, stepping back and studying the engine as if that'll tell him what's inside of it. "I had Jake bore out your last one so it's pretty damn fast."

Jake is the best engine and suspension guy in the nation. He also happens to be one of my dad's good friends. I hop off the bike and hold the handlebar, angling it toward him.

"Give it a go if you don't believe me."

Dad smirks and takes my helmet, pulling it over his head.

He hands me the stopwatch, which is stopped at seventeen seconds. He climbs on the bike and revs the engine. "Get a good look at that number," he says, grinning beneath the helmet. "'Cause I'll beat it."

I roll my eyes and walk over to the lever that pulls the gate up and down. Dad rides my bike over to a starting line and nods.

I wait a few seconds just so he's stuck in anticipation and then I restart the stopwatch and drop the gate at the same time.

Fifteen and a half seconds fly by and Dad's at the end of the line. Son of a bitch.

I'm shaking my head when he rides back up, slamming on the front tire brake right before hitting me. He holds out his hand and I give him the stopwatch. He just grins and hands it back to me.

"I guess there's still a few more lessons you can learn from this *old man*," he says, pulling off my helmet and handing it back.

When our riding session is over and every muscle in my body aches, I shower until the water runs cold. It's only two more weeks until Christmas and I know Keanna and Becca are probably still out Christmas shopping, so I take my time.

I head downstairs to get a snack and Mom corners me, hands on her hips. Her belly seems to have gotten twice the size overnight, or maybe it's because she's wearing one of Dad's shirts and it swallows her up.

"Did I do something?" I ask, holding up my hands in surrender.

She nods once and purses her lips. "You still haven't given me any good present ideas, you little punk."

I sigh and roll my eyes, walking around her to get to the fridge. "Mom, I told you I don't *need* anything."

"But what do you *want*?" She stares at me very seriously and I know it's important to her, but I can't think of anything.

"Video games?" I say, cracking open the lid on a bottle of Gatorade. "Maybe clothes? You're good at picking them out."

"You have tons of clothes and when do you ever have time to play video games?" Mom says, sitting at the kitchen island. She opens her laptop, probably going to Amazon or another online place she likes to shop. "Your dad wants one of those new smartwatches," she says, watching me intently.

I scrunch my nose. "I'd break something like that. No thanks."

She groans. "What about money?"

I shrug. "Money is always fine," I say with a laugh. "Mom, I don't need anything. Can't you take some comfort in knowing that you raised a son who is content and happy with his life and doesn't need anything else to make him happy?"

She sighs, resting her chin in her hand. "You've had a shit ton of presents underneath that tree every year of your life," she says. "I can't just stop doing that. I'm your mom and mothers don't understand the concept of not getting their kid anything for Christmas."

"How about I don't get you anything either?" I say, giving her a smirk. She glares at me.

"Oh hell no. I have a list a mile long," she says, laughing as she points toward the fridge, where I see an actual list stuck to the side with a magnet. That must have appeared today because I haven't seen it before. I make a mental note to take a picture of that with my phone next time Mom isn't in here, but for now I shrug. "You don't need anything, Mom. Your life is great."

"Oh, I'm gonna beat you," she says playfully.

I finish my Gatorade and toss the empty bottle in the recycle bin. Mom points at me as I walk away. "You better make a list yourself, or I'll have to surprise you."

When Keanna calls later, I tell her about the conversation with my mom. "It's just so annoying," I say, gripping the phone but wishing I was holding her instead. "I don't want any freaking presents, why can't she just accept that?"

"Jett," Keanna says, her voice soft. "I know it bothers you but you have to look at it from her perspective. When you love someone, you want to give them gifts. It's not like she's doing this to be mean—obviously. It probably hurts her feelings that you don't want anything. She wants to show how much she loves you and you can't fault her for that."

I get the distinct feeling that her speech isn't just about my mom's feelings. I sigh into the phone. "You're right. I'll make her a list."

"She'll like that," Keanna says.

I don't say anything, but I vow to make Keanna a list, too. I hadn't thought of Christmas and my birthday in that way before. If the people who love me want to do something nice for me, why would I stop them? My favorite part of this year will be showering Keanna with gifts, just like I did on her birthday last month. So yeah, I need to give them the same opportunity.

I guess I'm even luckier than I realized.

CHAPTER SEVEN

Keanna

Now that I'm officially graduated, it feels both scary and exhilarating to be free from any kind of education until next August. Becca agreed with my plan to take time off and follow Jett around the country for his races, and in the fall I'll start college, wherever that might be.

I'll probably pick a local college for now. My parents will be paying for it so I don't exactly want to go crazy with applying to ridiculously expensive schools when all I want is a simple degree.

But for now, who cares? I'm free and my life is awesome. I'm going to run with that for as long as I can. My full time is now working at The Track, starting today.

We just opened and our first set of clients are already out on the track with Jace and Park. Jett is somewhere around here, cleaning his bike and getting things ready for the races this weekend. He's been extra nervous lately, which isn't like him. Normally he's excited for the races, but maybe that's because he's always pretty confident he'll win. I've heard enough from our clients and from Jace and Bayleigh lately to know that this weekend at Oakcreek is a big deal. Racers from all over the country have traveled down for it. Now Jett will be competing against all the Texans he already knows, plus a handful of racers he's never seen before. Maybe some of them are faster than he is. Hopefully not.

I make a fresh pot of coffee in the breakroom and fix myself a cup. The front doorbell jangles, announcing the arrival of someone so I quickly press a plastic lid onto my coffee cup and rush up there.

Becca's grin is a mile wide and kind of makes her look like a creepy clown doll. I approach the front desk slowly, setting down my coffee while I eye her suspiciously.

"Why do you look like you're about to murder me and chop me into tiny pieces?"

"Morbid, much?" she says, flipping her hair over her shoulder as she brushes past me. "I am perfectly normal, *thankyouverymuch.*"

I follow her into the break room and watch her make a cup of coffee. "What's going on with you? Where have you been?"

She shrugs. "Oh just maternity stuff . . ." She chuckles while stirring hazelnut creamer into her coffee. "One great thing about having a surrogate is that I can have all the caffeine I want."

It hits me then, and I feel bad for forgetting. "Bayleigh just had the ultrasound, right? How'd it go?"

Becca grins and stirs her coffee like she's the evil villain in a movie. "Can't tell you," she sing-songs.

"You can't tell me the sex of the baby but surely you can tell me how it went?" I ask.

She breaks from her strict look and says, "Well, you're right. The baby is healthy and perfect! But I can't tell you if you're getting a sister or brother until the party. I don't even know myself." She's still sing-songing but I figure having your first baby is the only time it's okay to wander around in a dreamlike haze.

"I'm excited," I say, giving her a hug.

"So are you ready for the races this weekend?" Becca asks. She opens a browser on the work computer and pulls up a baby registry on Target, so she can add new items. That's pretty much all she does lately.

"Yeah, I think it'll be fun to watch a race at somewhere other than here." I pull my barstool next to hers so I can look at baby stuff over her shoulder.

"Races are a lot different than practice," Becca says, using a voice that sounds more mom-like than I've ever heard from her. "Now that Jett is in the public eye, he's going to be the talk of the races. It'll probably be hard on you at first."

My chest starts to ache. "What do you mean by that? It's not like I'm the one racing."

She nods slowly and focuses on the computer. It's almost as if she doesn't want to look at me because of what she's about to tell me next. "It's just hard on girlfriends. You'll have to stay positive no matter what. If Jett loses, he'll be pissed. He'll act like someone you don't even know."

I swallow. It's hard picturing Jett acting any differently than his usual sweet self with a happy attitude. "He won't lose," I say, but even my voice sounds shaky. "He's really good."

She smiles warmly at me and pats me on the arm. "Hopefully he'll win. He's definitely good enough."

The door jingles again and Bayleigh comes in, covered in that pregnancy glow that until now, I'd thought was just an old wives' tale. "What are we talking about, ladies?"

"I was warning Keanna on what to expect during the race this weekend," Becca says.

Bayleigh's face shifts into a quick grimace. "Ah, yeah. This'll be your first time watching him at a serious race." She walks forward and puts both of her hands on my shoulders, looking me in the eye. "Nothing is your fault. Got it?"

"Huh?" I say, lifting an eyebrow.

Bayleigh sighs and looks upward like she's trying to get her words in order. "Jett doesn't handle losing well. He might need space, or maybe a water bottle, or —" She throws her hands in the air. "Hell, I don't know. He's my kid and I don't know. He's never brought girls to the races with him before, so this is new territory."

I look from my mom to my second mom. "I think ya'll are making a big deal out of nothing," I say. "I've seen him ride tons of times. It'll be okay."

The two best friends share a look and then turn to me. "We haven't even started on the track girls."

"Track girls?" I set my phone on the desk.

Bayleigh nods. "My friend Hana's dad owns Mixon Motocross Park and she had one hell of a time dealing with those moto skanks when we were young." She rolls her eyes and Becca nods adamantly. "Jett is famous now—well, more famous than he's ever been—and the girls will be flocking around him like seagulls to a bag of Cheetos. Don't let them get to you."

I shrug it off because I'm pretty sure they're both making way too big of a deal out of this.

"So," I say, smiling and changing the subject. "Do you have any ideas on what to get Jett for his birthday and/or Christmas?"

Bayleigh laughs out loud. "Oh honey, if I knew that, I'd be using those ideas for *myself.*"

"Still nothing on his wish list, huh?" Becca says, shaking her head. "That boy is stubborn."

"Tell me about it," I say at the exact same time as Bayleigh saying the same thing. We look at each other and laugh.

"Oh, I like you," Bayleigh says, putting an arm around me. "You fit in just fine around here."

CHAPTER EIGHT

Jett

Saturday morning feels like the beginning of the rest of my life. On another hand, it could also feel like the start of a short-lived dream that's about to crash and burn. I shake my head and pull on my clothes, telling myself not to think like that. It's four in the morning and we're about to head out to Oakcreek which is a couple of hours away. My first Team Loco race. I stare at myself in the mirror, my hair is all disheveled but my eyes are fierce.

Don't let it go to your head.

That's my dad's famous line, the one he's been telling me nonstop since I got my internship. The worst thing a young racer can do is get a small amount of recognition and then throw it all away thinking they're suddenly famous. I am not famous. I'm barely even worthy of news.

For now.

We all pile into Dad's truck and soon, Mom and Keanna are passed out in the large backseat.

"Girls," Dad says with a snort. He readjusts his rear-view mirror and then focuses back on the drive.

My nerves keep me company on the long drive and by the time we arrive, unload the bikes, and get all the gear out, I'm basically no longer a human being, but just a human-shaped bundle of nervous energy. I force myself to eat and drink but I don't want to. My stomach is in knots.

Mom and Dad set up the pop-up canopy and fold out chairs and Mom insists on helping even though Dad keeps telling her pregnant ass to sit down and relax.

I'm sitting in a chair, snapping up the buckles on my boots when Keanna returns from the concession stand, holding two cups of coffee.

"That was like the longest walk of my life," she says, handing me a cup. She lifts her foot and wiggles her white sparkly flip-flop. "You should have told me to wear better shoes."

"You wouldn't have listened," I say, grinning as I sip from my coffee. It's too hot, but she's put just the right amount of sugar and cream in it, so it'll be perfect in a few minutes.

Keanna glances around, watching the other riders unpack and get set up in the pit area. We've parked near the finish line jump, right between an older guy racing in the over forty age group and a little kid racing in the peewees. I know my friends are around here somewhere, but I haven't sought them out yet. I prefer this kind of pit area when I'm at the races. As a kid, we'd park next to my friends but it's hard to concentrate like that. I'd rather be surrounded by strangers who don't bother me. That way I can keep my head focused on the race.

"This place is awesome," Keanna says. She sips from her coffee and then recoils at the temperature and sets it on the back of Dad's tailgate for safe-keeping. "It's huge."

"That's because it's a real race track," I say. My boots are buckled and I've got everything but my jersey, neck brace, and helmet on. Those things can wait until before I go ride. "The Track is just a practice facility so it's smaller. We don't need room for parking or race fans or anything."

She nods, shoving her hands into the back pockets of her cut-off jean shorts. "It's cool. I like it."

"Maybe we'll own a race track someday," I say, sipping from my coffee. I'd had a protein shake a few minutes ago, but this really hits the spot.

"I thought we were going to own The Track?" she says.

I shrug. "We could do both."

Her whole face lights up and she drags a chair over to me, sitting so that her bare knee touches my gear-covered one.

"You look hot," I say, leaning back and admiring the view. She's wearing a plain black tank top but it dips low and shows off her awesome boobs. She's also wearing a hoodie since it's a little chilly before noon. Her hair is piled up in a messy bun on top of her head, little strands of it falling all over the place. I want to reach up and brush the hair off her neck, then drag my tongue across it.

Shit, Jett. Head in the game. Head in the game.

"What was that look for?" she asks, her adorable eyebrows pulling together.

I shrug. "Just telling myself to stop thinking about how hot you are so my racing won't be affected."

She rolls her eyes but her cheeks turn a glorious shade of pink. "You're dumb."

"Dumb and in love," I say, tilting my head back and downing the coffee.

Dad rolls out my bike and sets it up on the stand. It's all clean and gorgeous—in a non-weird way—and I'm instantly in love.

"How are you feeling?" Dad asks.

"Great." I slide my hand down the leather seat. In the distance, the track announcer is telling us when practice will start. Bikes crank up from all over the pits, the different sized engines making a rumbling melody in the air.

Keanna walks over and touches the black numbers on the front of my bike. "Twenty-four?"

"Yep," I say, pulling the bike off the stand and crawling on. I motion for Dad to bring me my helmet. "Team Loco let me pick my number but if I go pro, it'll change."

Her face lights up in recognition. "Your birthday."

I nod. "Yep."

"I like it," she says, stepping back as I crank up the bike. The motor roars and I hold my helmet on top of the gas tank, motioning for her to come closer.

She leans over and I kiss her, trying not to get all caught up in how much I love this girl. Head in the game and all that.

"So this is just practice?" she says, gazing out over the track.

"Yep. So don't judge me. The best way to ride the practice session is to go nice and slow, get a feel for the track and pick the best lines."

"I would never judge you," she says, grinning as she throws her arms around me. My helmet is so bulky I can't really hug her back. She peers into my eyes. "Be careful."

I press my gloved hand up to my helmet and blow her a kiss. "Always."

CHAPTER NINE

Keanna

A real motocross race is almost nothing like being at The Track back at home. There, it's always busy and the air is a steady roar of dirt bike motors, but here, it's a well-organized circus. Hundreds, if not thousands of people are here and they're just the spectators. There's a ton of races ranging from little kids to guys that are over fifty years old. They even call that race "the over fifty" class.

It's crazy how busy it is, with people going all over the place and bikes riding in between everyone. I'm in awe. This is a huge race—some kind of regional race that attracts people from several states over. I hadn't been nervous for Jett's ability to win until this very moment.

Bayleigh closes the truck door and walks up to me, her lip-glossed lips turned upwards. She's wearing a boho sundress and sandals, her hair pulled in a messy ponytail that looks cute on her.

"Want to head to the bleachers?" she asks, pointing toward the set of bleachers just in front of us. They're facing the finish line jump as well and they're twice as big as the ones we have at The Track.

"Sure," I say, taking my empty coffee cup to toss in one of the big blue trash cans set up around the pit area.

Bayleigh is stopped by two different women on our short walk to the bleachers. They both want to rave and squawk about her baby bump. Both make the same adoring face when Bayleigh tells them she's being a surrogate for her best friend. It is a pretty noble thing she's doing. I know it's a little dorky, but I feel cool by comparison just hanging out with her. Bayleigh knows *everyone* here, from moms to racers to little kids and old people. She smiles and waves and calls them all by name.

Finally, we get to the bleachers and climb about halfway up, taking a seat in the middle. The starting line is toward the right, forty gates all next to each other with a break in the middle for the guy who drops the lever to start the race.

Jett is already there, in the third line from the middle. Jace stands next to him, kicking at the dirt at the front of the gate. A lot of racers or their mechanics are doing the same thing to their own lines, so I guess it's some way to help him get a better start.

A cool breeze temporarily relieves the scorching morning air and I grin, feeling my hair blow all over the place. I'll need to fix this messy bun soon.

Another woman about Bayleigh's age walks up and squeals when she sees Bayleigh. They start talking, but after a quick introduction, I turn back to the gate to watch Jett.

That's when I realize that although most of the racers have a mechanic (or dad, or in Jett's case, since it's the same person) with them, several of the guys also have a beautiful girl standing nearby.

I squint to see better and watch a gorgeous supermodel of a girl wrap her arm around a racer's back and lean up on her toes to kiss him. The racers to the left and right of Jett both have a hot girl on their arm, fawning over their dirt bike and leaning in to whisper, probably telling them good luck.

My stomach twists into knots. Those are all girlfriends, standing by their man. Jett didn't even ask me to go down there with him.

Is it because even though they're several yards away, I can tell they're all super-hot and done up like they're attending a red carpet event instead of a dirt bike race?

Is he embarrassed of me?

I look down at my crappy jean shorts, my plain tank top and my chipped toenail polish. I didn't even put on any makeup today, besides some BB cream that I used for the sunblock. Ugh.

I came here expecting yet another hot as hell day of sweating and feeling sticky and gross. December in Texas doesn't really mean anything as far as the weather. I didn't bother trying to look hot. But it's clear that every other girlfriend puts their looks above comfort.

I glance around the bleachers and suddenly feel like the loser on the playground. Everyone looks nice. I look like a bum.

The gate drops and forty bikers take off, all headed toward the starting turn. Jett's bike pulls in front, barely skimming past the guys in second and third place.

If not for the big number twenty-four on his number plates, it'd be hard to tell them all apart.

Their four laps around the track take no time at all, and soon I'm standing and cheering with Bayleigh while Jett soars over the finish line jump. The checker flag is waving and he turns the bike sideways, doing a little show off move where he points straight at the crowd. At me, but it's not like anyone knows that. Even if the whole world knew that Jett Adams' girlfriend was here in the bleachers, they'd never suspect me, the plain boring slob of a girl.

We scale down the bleachers quickly, eagerly ready to get back to the truck to congratulate Jett on his win. Bayleigh grabs my hand while we walk and squeezes it. "This is really good. He'll be happy."

Jett's already back at the truck when we get there, his bike on the stand and his helmet hanging off the handlebar. I watch him pull off his jersey and toss it on the chair, his tanned skin glistening in the sunlight. The taut muscles in his back twist as he reaches into the ice chest in the back of his truck and grabs another bottle of water.

If I could pause time and stand here, watching how sexy he is for all of eternity, I'd seriously consider pressing the button.

Instead, I settle for taking a photo on my phone. Now Jett, standing there with the sun shining behind him, chugging a bottle of water while sweat drips down his chest is immortalized forever in my phone.

Yes, please and thank you.

"Great job, babe." I go to hug him but then stop, realizing how sweaty he is.

"Thanks." He grins and throws both arms around me, holding me in a rocking bear hug. I squeal. "Gross! So sweaty!"

He just laughs and kisses me on top of the head when he finally pulls away.

I put my hands on my hips and glare at him. "Now I smell bad."

"You smell delicious as always, babe."

Jace walks up and pats his son on the back. "One down," he says, grinning from ear to ear. "Good job."

Jett nods, but I can tell it means a lot to have his dad's approval. Jace readjusts his baseball cap and glances at his watch. "Only three more to go, but you might have time for lunch if you want it."

"Three more?" I say, looking up at him. "I thought you're only racing two classes?"

"Each class races twice," Jett explains, but now I remember that I've heard that before. And although I'm excited for him to be here representing Team Loco, I am *so* ready to go home. I need to get back to our familiar little neighborhood track, where I don't have to dress like a supermodel to feel like I fit in.

Jett pulls on a white T-shirt and it's a devastation to all of womankind to hide those abs. "Wanna grab some nachos?" he asks.

I nod. "I always want nachos."

He slips his hand into mine and although it's a little sweaty, I still get butterflies in my stomach. Jett leads the way to the concession stand which is practically across the entire track. At some point our hands break free as he's caught up saying hi to other racers and shaking a ton of hands. The moment we get to the long line for nachos, I can smell them before I see them.

A flock of moto girls, decked out in pristine sweat-free cute outfits, jewelry and fancy hair. Their flirty gazes are all fixed on Jett. And they're coming straight toward us.

CHAPTER TEN

Jett

"Ugh." Keanna's groan is kept to herself but I hear it and look over.

"Don't worry, the line usually moves fast."

"Huh?" she says, looking at me as if she's forgotten that I'm even here.

"The nachos?" I say, gesturing toward the long line in front of us. "Is that why you groaned?"

Her features soften, her gaze now peering at me as if I were a lost puppy. "No babe. I don't care about the nacho line."

"Hi Jett!" The perky voice of an adoring fan makes me turn around. Three girls around my age are all smiling so big, I'm not sure which one said hi to me.

Behind me, I hear, "That's why I groaned."

All three girls kind of look exactly the same, even though one is a brunette Hispanic girl and the other two are blonde. They must have dressed each other this morning. "Hello," I say, looking down at my wallet like I'm counting money.

"You did so great out there," the brunette says. "It was like watching a professional."

"Thanks," I say at the same time one of the blonde clones says, "He *is* a professional. He's Team Loco now."

I rub my forehead. "Well, it's an internship."

"You'll make it." The other blonde smiles. She reaches out to touch my arm, and although Keanna is standing to my side and back a little, I can practically feel the anger rolling off her in steady waves. Honestly, it's cute. She has nothing—not a damn thing—to be worried about. But I guess the moment she stops being affected by her boyfriend's attention from other girls, I'll have a problem.

It would be *kind of* fun to tell them all to screw off and make sure they know the gallon of *eu de track slut* they doused on themselves this morning is a big of a turn off, I have to maintain professional and courteous contact with all the race fans. It's part of my Team Loco contract and I am *not* going to screw it up on my first official race for them.

I take a step backward, which moves me closer up the nacho line. "Ladies, this is my girlfriend, Keanna." I put an arm around her and smile. "I didn't catch your names."

"That was really sweet of you," Keanna says. She studies her plastic tray of nachos and fishes out one by the smallest piece of the chip that's not covered in cheese. She's sitting on the tailgate of Dad's truck, her legs swaying in the air.

I'm sitting in a folding chair on the ground next her, but under the blue canopy. It's hot as hell, but Keanna insists that she'd rather be in the sun to work on her tan.

"What was sweet of me?" I ask, tilting my head back and eating a soggy cheese-drenched chip.

"Calling me your girlfriend in front of those fangirls." Her voice is a little softer than usual.

I snort. "What else am I supposed to call you?" I lower my voice and give it a British accent while rolling my hand as if I'm introducing her again. "Why, allow me to introduce you to Keanna, my female consort. I am in love with her and we often enjoy canoodling in bed."

She bursts out laughing and covers her mouth with her palm, making sure to keep her cheesy fingers off her face. "You know what I mean," she says once she's calmed down. "Those girls were practically supermodels and I'm just—" she looks down at her lap, her lip curling. "Ugh."

"You are *not* ugh," I say kicking out my motocross boot so it taps the bottom of her flip-flop. "You're the hottest girl here."

"Maybe in terms of temperature," she says, fanning herself with her hand. "But you should have warned me, you ass hat."

My mouth falls open. "How am I an ass hat?"

"You didn't tell me that coming to a motocross race is a fancy event," she says, eating another chip. "I look like a homeless person compared to all these other girls."

I shake my head. "You're the only girl who matters and I know how hot you are so who freaking cares what you wear?"

She sighs. "Again, thank you for saying that."

"It's the truth," I say. But it's obvious by the look on her face that she doesn't quite believe me.

Dad grills me while we wait at the starting line for my second race. This is the two-fifty pro class—a much tougher race than my first class this morning. I'm in here with guys in their twenties who have qualified to race a professional supercross race or two in their time. One of them, Tony Baker, has a dad more famous than my own.

Dad rests one hand on the front fender of my bike after he's tamped down the dirt in front of the wheel. "You can't let up on the holeshot this time," he says. "Do it just like we practiced."

I nod since he won't be able to hear me over my helmet and the roar of all the surrounding bikes. My heart jackhammers around in my chest. I've raced a million times in my life but only once with the Team Loco logo on the back of my jersey and on every graphic on my bike.

This is a whole new kind of nervous. Not to mention, I can't stop thinking about that weird look Keanna had on her face when I kissed her goodbye just now. She looked hurt, insulted even. But why? I had to go race and she knows that, so why did she seem like I had disappointed her?

I draw in a deep breath and try shoving those worries to the back of my mind. Emotional stresses are the last thing I need when I'm in the middle of a race. I must keep my head in the game, stay focused, and win this race.

Engines rev and I lean forward, elbows high and toes barely touching the ground. I stare at the gate until everything else around me disappears. It drops, and I pin the throttle.

Tunnel vision has me seeing only the dirt in front of me. I shift gears and lean back, letting the bike pull me into the lead. I round the first corner with other bikes nipping at my heels. There's a tire right next to me, the other rider gaining on me every second. I slide to the front of the bike, drop gears and dive into the sharp hairpin turn.

There's a loud clang of metal on metal and then I go down. Dirt fills my vision, pain rockets through my shoulder. Exhaust fumes and loud engines overtake all of my senses and for a few seconds, I only know one thing: I crashed.

Dammit.

CHAPTER ELEVEN

Keanna

I blink. *Please, please don't be Jett.* But when one of the three fallen riders jumps up, shakes himself, and grabs the number twenty-four bike, I know the worst has officially happened. Bayleigh curses under her breath but she never takes her eyes off her son.

Luckily, he doesn't appear to be hurt and he yanks his bike back upright and hops on, cranking the engine and taking off faster than any of the other guys who fell over. My heart races and anxiety consumes me as I watch him fly through the track, trying to catch up to the rest of the racers. I've never felt so hopeful and helpless at the same time.

I want him to win so bad but there's not a damn thing I can do. This is all him. The emotional rollercoaster is driving me crazy. He zooms through the track, easily passing all the guys at the back of the line. But there's thirty-something other racers and he has to catch up with every single one if he wants a chance of winning.

My bottom lip draws blood before I realize I'm biting it. My hands hurt from being clenched into fists. A few laps go by and Jett is now in third place, gaining on second.

"Come on, come on," Bayleigh says, squinting so she can see him clearly. I force myself to take a deep breath and then I let it out slowly. This isn't the end of the world, but damn it feels like it.

Jett's bike is just inches away from the second place guy. They hit a sharp turn and Jett pins it, kicking the bike out sideways and then hauling ass through the turn, blowing past the other guy like he was sitting still.

Hell yes!

Now he just has to beat the guy in first place, but unfortunately he's pretty far ahead. They're now so fast and so far ahead, they're passing up guys who are in last place. Jett flies past one of the last place guys and charges toward first place.

The checkered flag whips through the air and Jett's bike soars over the finish line jump, simply and quickly. There's no flair to his jump this time because he's in second place. I let out the breath I'd been holding and tell myself that winning isn't everything. At least he is healthy and in one piece. Second place isn't too bad.

Bayleigh leans over, her hair wafting coconut shampoo in my direction. "Be careful. He'll be pissed." She holds up her hands and wiggles her fingers. "Kid gloves."

Jett's still on his bike when we get back to the truck. His helmet blocks any emotions on his face and he's listening to his dad, who is talking animatedly with his hands. Jett nods, and then nods again. Then he hops off the bike and practically tosses it to Jace.

I hang back, pretending to examine some T-shirts for sale in the booth a few cars down from us. In the corner of my eye, I watch him yank off his helmet, then his neck brace, then finally his jersey. Shirtless and sexy as hell, he paces the few feet of shade underneath the canopy, his hands running through his hair while he stares at the ground.

Bayleigh walks right past him and talks to Jace instead. This must be what she means when she said to use kid gloves—just ignore him completely. I study his movements as he gets a water and sinks into his chair. He's definitely disappointed but he seems a little out of it. He hasn't even looked around for me. Maybe he knows I'm staying away on purpose.

When the lady at the T-shirt booth starts looking a little annoyed that I'm not there to buy anything, I start walking slowly back to Jace's truck.

I can't stop the onslaught of self-depreciating thoughts that flow through my mind as I slowly put one foot in front of the other. If I were hotter, would he be in a better mood? If I were the kind of girlfriend he could be proud of, and I got to stand with him down on the starting gate, would he have done better? Never wrecked in the first place? The lump in my throat is unbearably huge.

Jett's sitting in the chair, elbows on his knees and his eyes watching the ground. I try not to focus on how hot his biceps are—this isn't exactly a time to be sexually objectifying him or anything.

When I'm a few steps away, he looks up slowly. His eyes catch mine and a small smile spreads across his lips.

"Hey, you," he says, his grin getting wider.

"Hey," I say, biting my bottom lip. Two seconds of silence pass but it feels like ages. I'm standing here awkwardly, wondering if I should say something about the race—some kind of trite feel-good saying about never giving up, or if I should just tell him he did good anyway, or—ugh, I don't even know.

I bet the hot motocross girls would know what to say. I bet those girls on the starting line have an entire speech of great things to tell their boyfriends after a bad race. But here I am, the dorky loser with no motivational skills whatsoever, standing with my toes curling into my flip-flops as I internally freak out over what to do.

Jett slouches down in his chair, his head tilting to the side. "Come here," he says, beckoning me with the wave of his hand.

I take a tentative step toward him, still weighing the options of saying something or keeping my mouth shut.

He holds out his hand and I reach forward to take it. Then, swiftly and like nothing is wrong, he pulls me into his lap and wraps his arms around me.

"I'm glad you're here," he whispers into my ear. "I love you."

CHAPTER TWELVE

Jett

I can't prove it, but I'm pretty sure my dad made me work today just as punishment for sucking at the races two days ago. It's Monday, my first day of homeschooling, and here I am stuck at work. In the front office, no less. It's safe to say my first race for Team Loco wasn't the best of my life. I did place first overall in the first class, but the two-fifty pro class kicked my ass both times. I finished second overall after failing yet again to get the holeshot and keep it. Second place out of forty racers isn't the worst thing in the world, but it's not the best. It is *second* best.

"Absolutely!" Keanna says to a client's mother. She's working the front desk like usual and although I'm supposed to be helping her, she's cool if I work on the computer instead. I brought my laptop and set up my online profile for homeschooling through TSU. I have four classes: History, English, Geometry, Biology. They all have the same assignment for my first week. I have to write a short essay introducing myself and my skills and deficiencies in each subject.

Although I'd met with the main professor for homeschooling, each subject has a different teacher who will grade my assignments. They all filter through the main professor. It's weird, but at least it's not normal public school.

"Here's the main schedule," Keanna says to the woman. She leans over the counter and turns the paper around, pointing out various things. I'm guessing the lady is a new client because I've never seen her before. I shift my gaze back to my laptop and try to focus.

I click on the text box for my geometry class and stare at the blinking cursor. I let out a sigh. It's math class. Not writing class. Shouldn't I be able to demonstrate my skills in the subject by answering some freaking math problems?

The bells on the front door jingle and I glance up out of habit, but it was just the sound of the lady leaving. Keanna tips her head back and finishes the rest of her coffee before chucking the paper cup in the trash.

"How's the homeschool life going?" she asks, leaning over and looking at my screen. She smells like some kind of summer angel even though it's the middle of December. Her hand lotion smells like coconut and hibiscus flowers. Even in a plain black T-shirt with The Track's logo on the front, she's beautiful. Her lips are red and sparkly, and she's wearing black leggings with those fuzzy boots she saw at the mall and had to have, swearing one day it'll be cold enough to wear them. I guess that day is today.

I frown and push the side of my laptop, sliding it at an angle so she can see it better. "I have to write an essay about my skills in math."

"Blah," she says, making a gagging sound. "Want me to write it for you?"

I lift an eyebrow. "I can't ask you to do that."

"Sure you can. It'll be a trade." She wiggles her eyebrows.

"A trade for what?" I ask, reaching out and poking her in the stomach.

"You see that key over there?" she nods toward the edge of the counter where one of Becca's colorful keys with a matching girly key fob sits.

"What about it?" I ask.

"It goes to one of the bike storage stalls. There's a bunch of plastic bins in there . . . can you bring them all in here?"

"The Christmas decorations," I say, nodding. A couple years ago, my mom and Becca went to some massive Christmas shopping convention in downtown Houston and came home with enough crap to decorate the North Pole about fifty times over. The stuff they didn't keep for their houses went into bins in storage. We've never taken them out since. I cross my arms. "How do you know about that?"

Her eyes light up. "Becca told me about it and I thought it'd be fun to decorate the front office."

I know Keanna's past life wasn't especially joyful around the holidays and she's been trying to make up for things she's missed out on ever since she became an official member of the Park family.

"I'd love to," I say, grabbing the key. "But seriously, you don't have to write the essay for me. It's only three hundred words so it shouldn't be too bad."

She slides my laptop over to her side of the desk and begins typing. "I don't mind. Really."

When the decorations are all in the front office, Keanna has already finished all four of my introductory essays. I feel a little—okay, a lot—guilty for it because it quickly becomes apparent that she's done an awesome job on it. It even sounds like something I would have written, like she somehow managed to harness my personality and use it to write four boring essays.

"How are you so freaking smart?" I say, looking up from the assignment after she gives me back my computer.

She makes this little grin and lifts her shoulders. "I can't help it. I was born awesome."

I slide my arm around her back and hug her close. "How can I pay you back?"

She tilts her lips up to mine and the eager look in her eyes right before we kiss gives me a massive hard on. "No need to pay me back. We're a team."

I brush her hair behind her ear. "I'm going to marry you one day."

Her lips twist upward and then she shimmies away, eagerly taking off lids from the bins of decorations. I attempt to go back to my work, but I keep getting distracted by her perfect, perfect ass in those leggings. That kind of sexiness should be outlawed. How on earth can I ever get any work done when every dirty thought in the world keeps my sex drive alive and well?

I take a deep breath and glance up. Keanna bends over, taking strands of garland out of the bin. Then she climbs up a stepladder to hang it along the window and now her ass is eye level. I sigh and look back at the computer. This is going to be a lot harder than I thought.

Eventually, Keanna makes the front office look like a Winter Wonderland and even though I'm a guy who doesn't really care about this stuff, I think she's done a great job.

I head back to the breakroom to brew another pot of coffee for my dad who just got into his office after working with clients all morning.

I fix a cup of coffee for Keanna and me, adding extra hazelnut creamer to mine because it's so good. A few days ago, this would have been school time for me. I'd be stuck in third period, listening to some stupid lecture and daydreaming about lunch, which was the only twenty minutes of semi-freedom I got each day. Now I'm free all day, every day.

Why do people even go to normal school when they could be homeschooled?

I stop in the hallway when I hear my name said by a girly yet unfamiliar voice. Keanna's voice fills the air next.

"Excuse me?"

"Well, you know," the voice says, sounding awfully suspicious. I don't know why I stand here hidden in the hallway, other than because my intuition won't let me take another step. "Does he really have a girlfriend or is that just some rumor?"

Keanna snorts. "Does it really matter? I mean you clearly don't know him so I don't see why it matters."

"True, but my brother is about to start taking lessons here so I figure I'll have plenty of time to get to know him."

Keanna's stunned silence is my cue to move.

"Did I hear my name?" I ask, flashing my charming smile. I hand Keanna a coffee and then kiss her on the cheek. I watch her for a beat longer than necessary, making my feelings for her known. Her cheeks flush a deep red.

"Hi," I say to the girl. She looks to be in her late twenties, which is kind of hilarious. I'm not even seventeen yet, so what the hell? "Can I help you?"

She swallows and clears her throat. "Um, nope." She adjusts her purse on her shoulder and then smiles. "Have a good day."

Keanna and I watch the woman disappear in a cloud of dust—okay maybe it wasn't that fast, but clearly she hoped it would be.

"I'm sick of being a heartthrob," I say, sipping my coffee.

"I'm sick of being the heartthrob's girlfriend." Keanna peers up at me over the top of her cup. "Maybe we should make you ugly so girls will stay away."

I pretend to be offended. "Never! This handsome face will stay handsome, *thank you very much.*"

She laughs and turns her attention back to untangling a strand of mini Christmas lights.

"Having fun?" I ask, taking another strand to help her out. "Your decorations look really good, by the way."

"Yeah and I'm just getting started. Tonight will be even more magical."

"What do you mean?" I ask.

"Tonight," she says, watching me like I should know what she's talking about.

I lift an eyebrow. "We're decorating your family's Christmas tree tonight," she says, nudging me with her elbow. "Duh."

"No one told me this." I laugh. "How come no one tells me things?

She shrugs and drapes the lights over the back of the work computer. "Maybe your mom likes me more than she likes you."

She leans over the counter, lifting up on her toes to reach the monitor. It puts her ass on display and I can't help but give it a friendly smack.

"Maybe you're right," I say, admiring the view. "Maybe you're right."

CHAPTER THIRTEEN

Keanna

Christmas is only two weeks away and I still have no idea what to get Jett. Times two. Why does his birthday have to be the day before Christmas? That's twice the pressure to get him something he'll love. Ugh.

Bayleigh has a small list he wrote for her, but I can tell the items are just things he put to make her happy. iTunes gift cards, new motocross goggles, various superhero movies on Blu-ray . . . none of those are quality gifts. I need a gift that will blow him away. Times two.

When I get home from work, our house is like a magical elf gingerbread cookie house. Becca must have spent the entire day decorating. And here I thought my efforts at The Track's front office were grand.

The kitchen has Christmas themed chair covers, a candy cane tablecloth, Christmas dishes set out on display. There are lights hung over every window, every ceiling arch, and every door. The salt and pepper shakers have been replaced with Mr. and Mrs. Claus salt and pepper shakers. The cookie jar, kitchen towels, floor mats—everything has been removed and replaced with something that shouts Christmas.

"Holy crap," I say, jaw open wide as I take in the new kitchen. The decorations extend into the living room and Christmas carols play softly on our house-wide surround sound music system. Becca pokes her head out from the hallway.

"How do you like it?" she says, her expression nervous like maybe I won't be impressed. There's red and silver garland strung around her neck and she's wearing rolls of ribbon on her wrists, a pair of scissors in her hand.

"It looks amazing. I wish I was five years old again so I could really enjoy it."

She steps into the living room and does a little dance. "Woohoo! I'm glad you like it."

She pulls off a piece of garland, cuts it with her scissors, then ties the loose ends together with a red ribbon. "Next year when the baby is here, it'll be even more magical."

"I can't wait," I say, smiling as she leans over and puts the garland necklace over my head.

"I'm sorry you're too old for the real magic of it," she says, her hand touching my cheek for a second. From this close, I can see glitter in her hair, probably from hanging all the glittery wreaths that are now everywhere. "But hopefully all of these Christmas cockles will brighten your holiday anyway."

"Christmas *cockles?*" I say, lifting a brow. "I'm not sure that's a word."

"Sure it is!" She spins around, holding the garland around her neck like a feather boa. "These are the cockles!"

She winks at me and then disappears back down the hallway. She might be a little crazy, but it's the good kind of crazy.

I follow the trail of cockles down the hall and into the den, which is our formal living room that has wide bay windows that look out into the backyard.

This is where Becca has set up the Christmas tree, and it's a spectacular sight. Probably ten feet tall since the roof is extra high in this room. The tree is huge and green and covered in clear lights. All the ornaments are in boxes next to the tree, waiting to be hung.

Becca drops down to the floor and rolls out a tube of green and red metallic wrapping paper. "So what do you think?" she says, holding up a box to me.

I take it and examine it carefully. It's a fancy men's razor, electric and with its own charging/cleaning base. It looks top of the line, but it's not exactly like I'm fluent in men's shaving accessories.

"I love it," I say sarcastically, putting a hand to my chest. "Mom, you really shouldn't have . . . it's the best present ever."

She rolls her eyes and takes the box. "Obviously it's for Park, you big dork."

She positions it on the wrapping paper, then begins to wrap it up.

"I think he'll like it," I say, sitting down next to her. On the fireplace mantle across the room, three stockings are hung and one has my name on it, written in silver sequins.

"Although I am disappointed that I don't get a fancy man's razor," I say, rubbing my chin as if there were facial hair there.

She laughs. "Hopefully those will make up for it." She gestures across the room to the leather armchair that I notice is full of wrapped presents. "Whoa," I say. How many family members do you get gifts for?"

"All of them," Becca says, ripping off a piece of tape and pressing it to the package. "But those are just yours."

My jaw drops. There's at least twenty wrapped gifts of various shapes and sizes. "You're kidding? You can't get me that many presents."

Becca gives me a look that dares me to question her. "I'll get you whatever I want to, missy, and you'll like it."

She pulls off another piece of tape and sticks it to my nose. "You *will* allow me to spoil you, kiddo."

"Yes, ma'am," I say, drawing it out like I'm a kid in trouble. But I can't stop grinning. Presents. For me. The kind Santa could never afford in my childhood.

So far I've bought her some fancy art supplies from the expensive part of the art store that she always avoids because she doesn't like to splurge on herself. But now I'm going to get her a few more things, just so she knows how much I appreciate all that she's done for me.

"It even smells like Christmas in here," I say, rocking back on my heels as I gaze about the decorated room. "I'm excited."

Becca's smile is genuine and I wonder how many years she shared Christmases in his house with Park and wished there were kids to share it with. I'm not really a kid anymore but next year the baby will be here.

"So are you coming to the Adams' house tonight to decorate the tree?"

"Oh no, honey, that's your thing."

"Why not? I don't mind."

Becca reaches for another roll of wrapping paper and I slide it to her. "Keanna, that's not what I mean. Decorating the tree is a big deal to Bayleigh." Becca's eyes glimmer as she thinks about her best friend. "It's tradition and it's for her family, which until now has been Jace and Jett. But now she's including you, and that's a big deal.

My eyes widen and Becca nods. "In Bayleigh's mind, having you help decorate the tree is her way of welcoming you to the family, officially."

"Wow," I say, biting my bottom lip as I gaze up at our own tree.

Becca nods. "And I can tell you this much: no other teenage girl has been invited over to do that at Jett's house."

My cheeks flush and Becca tosses an empty tape dispenser toward me. "Will you throw this away, hun? And then maybe do me a huge favor and get me another roll from my studio?"

"Sure thing," I say, rising and making my way up to the third floor. The entire third floor is just a small room that's Becca's art studio. It's really awesome up here, with a huge window that looks out into the yard.

I quickly find the stash of clear tape and then gaze around the room, admiring my new mother's creations. There are easels and canvasses and half-finished masterpieces set up. As I turn to go back to the narrow staircase, I get an idea. As quickly as if a wave of inspiration just crashed over me, I know.

I have the perfect gift idea for Jett's birthday.

Relief hits me hard and I feel like half a weight has been lifted off my shoulders. All of these weeks of worrying what to get him and the answer was right here above my head. Of course, the other half of the weight is my lack of a Christmas present for him, but at least half my problems are solved.

I breathe a sigh of relief and practically skip down the stairs, nearly forgetting to give Becca her tape.

One present down, one more to go.

CHAPTER FOURTEEN

Jett

"It's here," Dad says, peering out of the front window. He's as eager as a kid on Christmas morning, and yet he's a thirty-six-year-old man and it's still a while until the big day. Every year, Dad has a Christmas tree delivered from Mr. Brown, an older guy who owns a Christmas tree farm on the other side of town. My parents took me there when I was a kid and we'd pick out trees and then bring them home, so it's a tradition. However, a few years ago, we were all so busy we couldn't go get one and when Mr. Brown offered to deliver one that he hand-picked out for us, a new tradition was born.

"Come on, son," Dad says, waving for me to follow him outside.

It's already dark even though it's not quite seven yet, and the air is finally getting cold. I wish I would have put on a jacket, but it's a short walk so I suffer through it.

Dad small talks with Mr. Brown and I help unload the tree. It seems even taller than usual, no doubt because Mom wants to make our first Christmas with Keanna even more special. I swear, if we still lived in the old days where families married off their children, Mom and Becca would have made us get married by now.

Which is funny, because all of my friend's parents are constantly telling them not to settle down in high school because it's not realistic. You know what else isn't realistic? Getting knocked up in high school, marrying your first love and still being together seventeen years later. Yet my parents pulled that off pretty well, so realistic situations can kiss my ass.

Who's to say I can't be just like them? Except maybe the teen pregnancy part.

Keanna and I still haven't had sex yet. I mean, we've done just about everything else, but yeah. I shake my head and focus on the task at hand. The last thing I need to do is think about sex while moving a cold-ass tree with my dad holding onto the other end of it.

We get it set up in the living room, right in front of the window. I crawl under the bottom branches and pour water into the tree stand, making sure the bolts are extra tight.

"Nice butt!"

Keanna smirks at me when I emerge, backward and on my hands and knees. I grin up at her and then rise to my feet. "You liked the view?"

She nods. "Mmhmm . . . very sexy."

I grab her hips and place a soft kiss on her pink-glossed lips. My parents aren't in here right now, but they will be any second, so it's best not to get too heated.

"You look beautiful," I say, stepping back to admire her red strapless dress that stops just above her knees. She's wearing a black crocheted cardigan on top of it and a strand of blinking Christmas lights around her neck.

"Nice lights," I say, touching the strand with my finger.

She grins. "Becca gave them to me. Said it was my *Christmas cockles*."

We share a laugh at Becca's overenthusiastic holiday spirit. "Did I mention how pretty you are?" I say, taking her hand and twirling her around.

"You might have," she says, playing all coy with me.

"Here I am in sweatpants," I say, glancing down at my winter pajamas.

Keanna smirks. "Becca warned me that your mom will probably want to take pictures, so I dressed up. If I'm going to be immortalized forever in one of your mom's family photo albums, then I want to look good."

"You succeeded," I say, giving her ass a squeeze. The soft fabric of her dress makes it a little hard to get a grip. "I should go change."

Mom walks in right as Keanna bites her lip and gives me an appraising look over. "Yep. You should change."

"Jett!" Mom says, hands on hips. "This is a special night. Go put on something decent!" She waves me away and I can hear her fawning happily over Keanna's dress as I head upstairs and grab some khakis and a dark red dress shirt. I figure it'll match Keanna's dress and maybe one day our future kids will look at the pictures of tonight and know their parents were in love from the very start.

Once I'm dressed like a real person and not a hobo, we decorate the tree with my mom's insane collection of red, white, and silver ornaments. A long time ago, she picked a candy cane theme and she's stuck with it ever since. Just as Becca predicted, there are many photos taken but we all have a good time.

I watch Supercross on TV with Dad while Mom and Keanna bake cookies. They had me help them with the Christmas shaped cookie cutters at first, but after it was determined that I'm terrible with anything food related, I was given permission to leave.

Now, they call me back into the kitchen and Keanna hands me an icing piping bag filled with green icing. "You can handle this," she says, flourishing her hand. "Just ice, and then use the sprinkles."

She gestures to a pile of random jars of sprinkles. I nod. "I got this. You won't be disappointed."

I wink at her and her cheeks flush. When the cookies have been decorated and half-eaten, Mom makes coffee and Dad makes a fire in the fireplace and we all gather around, chatting like some kind picture-perfect Christmas movie scene.

I'm cool with it, though. Keanna snuggles up against me while we sit on the floor, a flannel blanket pulled over us. The fire warms up the room and casts a wintery glow around the living room, shining off the ornaments on the tree.

"So what does Jett want for his birthday?" Dad says, throwing his arm around Mom's shoulders while they sit on the couch. "I heard he's being hard to shop for this year."

I hold up a finger. "I gave you a list," I say to Mom, who nods.

"He did." She turns to Dad. "We have a list, honey. It's a *boring* list, but at least it's an idea of what to get him. Keanna's gifts are already bought, since she's a girl with good taste." She flashes a wink to my girlfriend who chokes on her coffee.

"You don't need to—" Keanna says, but Mom waves a hand at her.

"Nonsense. Your gifts are already chosen." Mom's eyes sparkle from the glow of the fireplace. "You're going to love them!"

Keanna's smile is her only reply and I know she's probably a little awkward about this all, so I take over. "We got you guys awesome presents this year," I say, holding up my head. "Keanna knows you two better than you know yourselves. Well, better than I know you, at least."

Mom laughs. "Well, that's good. Jett's usually more of a 'tell me what you want' kind of guy."

"Oh you mean like how you're being to me this year?" I say sarcastically.

Mom blows a raspberry. "It's not my fault you don't want anything."

"If only he'd make a longer list," Keanna says, shaking her head. "I have one awesome gift idea, but I'm still stuck for his Christmas gift."

"Babe, you don't need to get me anything." I tell her.

Dad sips his coffee. "He's right, Key. Jett doesn't really care about gifts."

She shakes her head. "I'm still getting you something," she says, turning to look at me with an intensity that makes it feel like we're the only two people in the room.

If my parents weren't in here, I'd be inclined to let her know *exactly* what it is I'd like from her.

There must be something in my gaze because her cheeks flush and she looks down. It would be wrong to ask for sex as a gift, right?

Yeah. Definitely.

But that doesn't stop me from thinking about how great it will be to finally make love to the girl who has my heart.

CHAPTER FIFTEEN

Keanna

By noon on Tuesday, it's apparent it'll be a pretty slow day. While some riders like practicing in the cold weather, most of them don't. We've only had one client this morning and he had to leave early because his bike broke down right after he started riding. I like the idea of running a business that's not always ridiculously busy—it gives you time to relax and chill for a bit.

Becca and I are getting plenty of chilling done and I'm guessing this is why Bayleigh clears her throat, making me turn around. I'm at the front desk, flipping through a motocross magazine that features Jett while Becca sits next to me, working on the computer. And by working, I mean playing Solitaire.

At first I think I'm hearing things, but then the second throat-clearing makes me look back. Bayleigh's eyes are wide and she secretly motions for me to join her. She puts a finger to her lips and I know she wants me to keep this secret from Becca. O-kay . . .

"I'll be back in a second," I tell Becca, who barely notices because she's focused on her spreadsheets.

In the hallway, Bayleigh takes my hand and pulls me into her office, closing the door. "I'm taking you off front desk duty," she says, turning to dig through her purse. "As you know, this Friday is the gender reveal party."

I nod. Becca has been talking about it non-stop. They're going to announce to all their friends if the baby is a boy or girl. I think it's weird, but whatever makes her happy.

"I need your help." Bayleigh retrieves what she's looking for in her purse and hands me a silver credit card. "I need you to plan the party."

"What!" My eyes bug. "I can't do this . . . I have no idea how."

Bayleigh waves a hand at me. "Of course you do, kiddo. I've already ordered the custom cake but you do the rest, okay? If I plan it, Becca will notice and it won't be as much of a surprise. Right now she thinks we're just doing a small thing with family, but I'm inviting everyone."

Bayleigh's eyes sparkle mischievously. "Which reminds me . . . go to a craft store and get at least seventy-five invitations, the kind you can print on, and we'll make them with my printer. Also, we need party decorations and stuff for seventy-five people."

My hands shake as I stare at the shiny card in my hand. "I . . . I don't know if I can do this. I've never planned a party."

"Check your phone," she says. If she's lacking faith in me, she definitely doesn't sound like it. "I sent you some Pinterest inspiration ideas," she says with a wink. Then she meets my eye and her silliness turns serious. "Honey, you'll do perfectly. I can't imagine a better way to have the party than to have Becca's first daughter plan it. I'm totally here if you need any help, but my plan is to keep her busy and occupied, pretending to plan a fake family-only party, so that when Friday comes and the real party is here, she'll be truly surprised."

"Okay," I say, standing a little straighter. I slide the credit card into my pocket. "I can do this. What's the party budget?"

"No budget. Just whatever we need, okay? Have fun with it!"

It's hard not to go completely crazy given this kind of power and the pressure that goes along with it, but Bayleigh is not only my new mother's best friend, she's Jett's mom. So, I need her to keep liking me and trusting me with stuff. I need to do a good job, and screw the fact that I've never been to a real party in my life.

"I'll make you proud," I say, grinning like I'm not scared out of my mind here.

"I know you will," she says. Now slip out the back door and I'll tell Becca I have you working on the Track's mailing list flyers."

I head out the back door and look for Jett, since he didn't answer his phone. I find him in the gym, headphones blaring and two hundred pounds on the weight rack.

Great, I'm supposed to be fully concentrating on planning this party and now I have to see my boyfriend, sweaty and vascular, looking like some kind of tanned God in a tight black tank top.

"Hey good lookin'," Jett says, winking. He uses that Texas twang voice sometimes just to annoy me.

"I have a crisis," I say, sitting on the end of the weight bench.

He racks the weight bar and sits up. "You don't look very crisis-ed, so I'm guessing it's not bad?"

I heave a sigh and explain to him about the party planning.

"What is Pinterest? Mom is always talking about that."

I shake my head. "Trust me, you don't want to know right now. I have no idea how to plan a party, and when I'm freaking out, my first thought is to ask you for help but I'm betting you can't plan a party, either?"

He laughs and runs a hand through his dark, sweaty hair. "No, ma'am. I wouldn't know the first thing."

My shoulders fall. It's not like I expected Jett to jump up and down and get excited to plan a party, but I don't have anyone else to seek for help. Jett leans over and kisses me, only letting our lips touch so I don't get all sweaty.

"But I know someone who would love to help you."

I look up. "And who is that?"

"Maya."

Maya is Jett's best friend's girlfriend and I haven't talked to her since I was still in school. She's a cheerleader and she's extra girly *and* peppy so she'd probably make an excellent party planner.

"I don't know . . . I don't want to obligate her," I say. Maya and I are friends, but not really close friends. I haven't exactly known her that long and we've always hung out with our boyfriends.

Jett shakes his head. "Nah. D'andre said she was asking for your number the other day so ya'll could hang out." His head tilts to the side. "Of course, I totally forgot to give it to him until just this second because I guess I got distracted."

A special kind of warmth floods through my chest. Maya wants to be my friend outside of school? I push Jett's arm. "Well, what are you waiting for? Give her my number!"

He laughs and gets his phone from a shelf up against the wall. "Texting her now. I'm telling her you need to ask her advice for party stuff that way she'll get back to you soon."

"Thanks, babe," I say, throwing my arms around him. I immediately regret it because: sweat. Ew.

MAYA COMES OVER AFTER SCHOOL AND WE HEAD STRAIGHT TO THE PARTY SUPPLY store, which as luck would have it, is right next to the craft store. After looking around at the stuff they have for sale, we walk across the street to Starbucks and get a coffee so we can go over Bayleigh's Pinterest ideas.

"My aunt had one of these parties," Maya says. "But instead of cake, she had cake balls and everyone had to bite into theirs at the same time. The inside was pink cake so we all knew she was having a girl."

I lift my straw to slurp off the whipped cream from the top of my Frappuccino. "Bayleigh's doing a cake, so I guess everyone will notice when they cut into it."

"This will be fun," Maya says, scrolling through Pinterest. I sent her a link to the board so we're both using our phones to look through it all. "Looks like she wants a country type theme . . . twine, mason jars, sunflowers . . . I love it."

"Yeah, that really fits Becca's style."

An idea comes to me, making me jump. "Oh my God, we should totally make her a canvas for the party . . ." I say while I gaze out over the coffee shop. This has the potential to be a great idea.

"You mean like her professional artwork?" Maya asks.

I nod. "Becca's Inspirations is her business and she paints inspirational quotes on canvases and decorates them to look all pretty. What if we think of a sweet quote about babies, or having children, or being a mother or something, and then make her a canvas?" Chills prickle over my arms as the idea forms in my mind, making me all excited. "It could be a party decoration and a gift."

Maya's smile stretches across her whole face. "That's a perfect idea."

We talk more about party planning and take down notes in a sparkly notebook we find in the clearance bin at the craft store. Soon, we have two baskets full of decorations that fit Bayleigh's inspiration board perfectly, and we've spent so much time together that I'm starting to feel like Maya is my new close friend, and not just the girlfriend of a friend.

"This is really fun," I say while we sort through fake sunflowers in the floral aisle. "I'm glad Jett and D'andre hooked us up."

"Totally." Maya rolls her eyes. "I love my cheer squad but those girls can be vapid and bitchy as hell. It's nice hanging out with someone who isn't a stuck up princess, ya know?"

I laugh. "I can only imagine."

Our conversation goes from crafting to boys to sex and the lack of it—she and D'andre haven't yet done it either—and before I know it, it's nearly seven in the evening.

"I'm starving," I say, as we pile our shopping bags into the trunk of my Mustang. "Want to grab something to eat?"

"I have a better idea," she says, handing me a shopping bag. "Why don't we call the boys and all go out to dinner together?"

"That sounds like a plan," I say.

I can really get on board with this concept of having true friends.

CHAPTER SIXTEEN

Jett

A hot shower does little to soothe my aching muscles. I spent this entire week working my ass off, both in the gym and on the track. Tomorrow is another race for Team Loco and I'm determined to win.

Ironically, it can be said that I've trained my ass off for every race I've ever had, yet somehow, now that I'm sponsored and riding for an official race team, it feels like all those years of training were weak compared to now. Now, it really counts. Now I'm pushing harder than ever before. Let's just hope it pays off.

Tonight is the sex party, a hilarious name which Keanna has strictly forbidden me from saying. But I chuckle to myself as I get dressed because sex party sounds hilarious. She prefers the term "gender reveal party" but yeah, I can still laugh about it in my head.

I'm a little surprised that my mom knows the sex of the baby inside of her and she hasn't let it slip at all. Usually she's terrible at keeping secrets, but this time she's as sealed up as a bank vault.

Keanna is hoping for a boy because she has this weird issue where she doesn't want there to be two girls in the house, because she fears she may never live up to their real daughter as time goes on. She's being ridiculous if you ask me, but I've been supportive of her. I'm hoping for a boy because then I'd have a little protégé to raise up into the next massive motocross star.

Of course, if they have a girl, I'll be raising her the same way. Although motocross is mostly a male-dominated sport, the women who do race kick a ton of ass, and it'd be cool to see more of them out there. So, I guess no matter what this baby is born as, he or she will end up being a motocross superstar.

The Track's parking lot is full, as well as the Park's driveway. It's only six-thirty and the party is supposed to start at seven, but my parents and the Parks have a ton of very caring friends.

Luckily, it doesn't take me too long to find my girl. The Park's house is even more decorated for the holidays than my house, and I hadn't thought that was possible. But in the living room, they've taken out the Christmas decorations and swapped them with baby stuff. Rustic, country living type baby stuff. There are sunflowers everywhere, along with yellow and white decorations. Keanna had explained that yellow is the color you use when you don't know if a baby is a boy or a girl. Which is kind of cool, I guess, because I've always liked green and orange so I'm not sure why blue is supposed to be the main boy color but I guess some traditions never fade away.

I admire Keanna from a distance. She's wearing black leggings, teal cowboy boots and a teal oversized sweater that looks so soft I can't wait to slide my hands over it. Her hair is down and wavy and she's smiling so much it's almost like she's a whole new person. It's nice to see her having a great time with all of these people she's never even met before.

Becca sweeps in and introduces Keanna to an older couple whose names I can't remember. I think she knows them from craft fairs. Keanna smiles and shakes their hands and then the wife of the couple pulls her into a hug. I'm realizing now that this party isn't just for the unborn child that's about to be in the world, but it's also a way for Becca to show off her new daughter to everyone.

"Hey," I say, walking up behind Keanna.

She jumps a little but then smiles when she sees me. "What do you think?" she says, gesturing to the party set up. On the far wall is a decorated table with a two-tier cake. It's one of those marzipan cakes that looks like something from a Dr. Seuss world. It's white with pink and blue question marks all over it.

"Everything looks awesome," I say, wrapping my arm around her waist and kissing the side of her head.

"You really think so?" she asks, her voice soft.

"Yes. It looks like one of those house design shows in here," I say, kissing her again. But I'll need to stop and keep my hands off her because if I linger too close to this beautiful girl and her intoxicating scent, I might get entirely too turned on in this room full of people.

I mean, I know it's a sex party, but it's not *that kind* of sex party. Ha.

Keanna's brows draw together. "What are you smirking about?"

I shrug. "I was thinking about the term *sex party*."

She rolls her eyes. "You are such a child."

I break my own rule and kiss her again. "Too bad you're stuck with me."

The party goes on for a while and Becca and Mom are the center of attention after everyone's been introduced to Keanna.

Finally, Mom silences the crowd by tapping a knife on her wine glass that's filled with sparkling water.

"I think it's time to get to what everyone has been waiting for," she says, throwing a smile toward her best friend.

She takes a silver handled spatula and knife and hands it to Park.

"You sure you trust me to do this?" he asks Becca. He does look a little awkward holding the cake cutting tools. He looks out at the crowd. "I'm sure you guys remember how unskilled I am at cutting cakes from our wedding day."

There's some laughter and then Becca agrees to help him.

Everyone watches excitedly as they cut into the cake. I stand behind Keanna, my hands on her hips while we watch. They make a second slice and then Park shoves the spatula under the piece of cake.

Everyone goes silent while the cake slides up and out, revealing the blue inside.

"It's a boy!" my dad says as everyone starts clapping.

Beneath my hands, Keanna is shaking from how hard she's clapping. Becca's hands go to her mouth and she starts crying and even Park looks like he might shed a tear.

Mom hugs them both and then everyone takes turns congratulating them on their new baby boy.

"Looks like you're getting a brother," I whisper into Keanna's ear.

She looks up and back at me, a grin on her face. "I wonder what they'll name him."

"I think Jett is a great name," I say, smirking as I scratch my neck.

She grins and leans into me, then twists and wraps her arms around my waist.

"I'm really happy for them," she says softly, letting her cheek rest against my chest. Her eyes close and I run my hand down her hair, letting her take a private moment to reflect on the big news.

After the party, I play the role of Perfect Boyfriend and help them clean up. Mom, Becca, and Keanna say they can handle it, but us men know better. So Dad and Park and I help get everything thrown out or wrapped up and put away. There's enough leftover finger foods to snack on for a couple of days and I'm pretty psyched about that. No one loves those mini tortilla roll-ups as much as I do.

When Mom and Dad leave and Becca and Park retire to their room, I let my guard down and grab Keanna's hand while she walks to the fridge. I spin her around then pull her close to me, kissing her soft lips with the intensity that I've been wanting all night.

She moans as I flick my tongue across hers, and her hands claw at me, trying to bring me closer.

"Want to take this somewhere more private?" I whisper.

She gives me this perfect sex vixen grin and then hurries us to her bedroom, closing the door behind us.

This time she attacks me, pressing my back against her bedroom door while her hand slides up to my neck and holds me close.

While she kisses me, I crush my hips into hers then slide my hands over her ass and lift her in the air. She wraps her legs around me and we stay like this, making out until I'm about to explode at the seams.

I walk her to her bed then gently set her down. She doesn't untangle her legs from around me, so I crawl up her bed until her head is on her pillow and I'm hovering over her.

"Jett?" she asks, her voice soft and tentative. Her bottom lip trembles and I lean on my elbows, brushing the hair from her eyes.

"Yes?"

She averts her gaze, drops her legs to the bed. "We've been together a long time and still haven't had sex."

"Okay?" I say slowly. "I am aware of this."

She heaves a sigh and reaches up, touching my face. "I guess I feel like now it's becoming a big deal because we haven't done it yet."

I smile. "You're overthinking this."

She shakes her head. "Am I? I mean, I want it and you want it but we just . . . *haven't.*"

"We will. When the time is right." I roll over to my side and wrap her in my arms. "Of course, the time is always right as far as I'm concerned," I say with a smile in my voice.

She chuckles. "We are *not* doing it tonight."

"Why not?"

She looks up at me and presses her lips together. "Because then you'd forever get to say that the sex party ended up being a real sex party."

I can't help myself, I burst out laughing and have to cover my mouth with my fist.

She rolls over and crawls on top of me. her hair forming a wall around us. "Not. Funny." I try to force my mouth to stop smiling and the goofy attempt only makes her smile bigger.

"Soon," she says, kissing me quickly.

"Soon," I agree.

Then I wrap her in my arms and make out until we fall asleep.

CHAPTER SEVENTEEN

Keanna

I go to the races with a plan. I'm wearing cute shorts (that were actually sold as shorts and not just cut offs I made myself) over black tights and I wear one of Jett's hoodies with his last name and racing number on the back. Only the racers get these things, so it's pretty obvious if I'm wearing it that I'm the girlfriend.

And yes, this wardrobe choice is totally intentional.

My hair is on point and my makeup is flawless. I had to wake up at three in the morning, but it'll be worth it. I also spent a fortune on expensive shine-free, foundation and powder so I'm hoping all the walking around outside won't make me look like a swamp monster.

When it's time for him to race, he kisses me goodbye and I tell him good luck and once again he goes down to the starting line alone and once again, I sit on the bleachers watching all the other girlfriends supporting their men from the starting line. Bayleigh isn't here today because she wasn't feeling well, so it's just me here on the bleachers. I didn't realize how lonely it would be sitting here all alone, and now I'm wishing I would have asked Maya to come with me.

Jett wins his first two races and we spend the intermission together, eating nachos and watching a DVD on his laptop that we set up on a folding table under the canopy. It's a little windy today, so Jett and his dad zipped on the walls to the canopy to keep the chill out.

It also has the added benefit of keeping out the lookie-loos. Now that Jett and I can hang out inside the canvas tent between races, no girls come wandering up wanting to talk to him. No middle-aged women stare at him flirtatiously as they walk by. Nope, we're all alone.

Maybe this makes me a bad person, but I love it. I'm secure in our relationship, but I don't think any girl is a fan of seeing multiple women a day asking their boyfriend to take a picture with them.

After intermission, Jett's dad disappears somewhere with an old racing friend of his. Now that Jace isn't here to help Jett get ready, I hand him his gloves and goggles and helmet. I move the bike stand out of the way when Jett gets on his bike.

All that's left is for me to go down to the starting line with him. But I can't get the nerve to ask. I fidget and kick at the dirt while Jett gets ready. He revs the bike engine and stretches his head to the left and right.

Another racer drives by, his girlfriend riding on the back of his bike. She's wearing shorts and a T-shirt. "She must be really cold," I say.

Jett nods. "She's gonna end up with pneumonia."

I want to say: *I wonder where she's going?* Or *why is she on the back of his bike?*

Of course, I don't. I'm too chicken. But if I *did,* he'd have to answer and then maybe he'd tell me why he doesn't want me on the starting line with him.

He's not embarrassed of me, is he?

After kissing him and wishing him good luck, I make the walk over to the bleachers to watch him race. It's pretty packed today so I climb up only two rows and choose a spot without many people around.

I stare at the finish line jump while I wait for the race to start, because if I look over at the starting line, I'll see the other girlfriends and I'll get pissed.

"Jett Adams? I love him."

The voice came from somewhere to my right, so I glance over. A girl about my age nods to me. "Where'd you get that hoodie? Are they selling them at the Team Loco booth?"

I try not to look smug. "No, actually I got it from Jett."

"Seriously?" Both she and the girl next to her look impressed. "How?"

I don't know why this makes me nervous, but I tell her the truth. "Because I'm his girlfriend."

She laughs. *Laughs.* "Oh my God, you totally had me going for a minute. So, you're like his sister or something?"

I lift an eyebrow. "I'm his girlfriend. It's not a joke."

The girls look at each other and then back to me. "Honey, I'm sorry to break it to you but you're not his girlfriend." Before I can speak, she adds, "I mean, you might *think* you are . . . you could even be the flavor of the week, but—" She sucks in air through her teeth like she's genuinely sorry for what she's about to tell me. Meanwhile, my blood is boiling even in the cold air. "Real girlfriends hang out down there," she says, pointing toward the starting line.

Suddenly, I'm feeling vilified and also like fifty birds just crapped on my head.

I shrug and keep my face neutral. These girls will *not* get a reaction out of me. "I'm not really feeling well so I didn't want to walk all the way back up here after the race started." To finish the lie, I give them a polite smile. "Oh look, the races are starting!"

They seem totally uninterested with me after the gate drops, and they cheer for a lot of riders, including Jett. When he flies over the finish line in first place, I hop off the bleachers and book it back to our truck, squeezing my hands into fists in an effort to calm down. I should really just woman up and ask him why he won't let me go down to the starting line with him.

There's one race left of the day, so there's still time to secure my rightful place at his side. I just need the metaphorical balls to ask him.

Jett's already back at the truck when I get there, and so is Jace. His dad is beaming with the third win of the day, and Jett's in a great mood as well.

He gives me that sexy grin when I approach. His arms open and I jump into them, wrapping him in a bear hug. "I'm proud of you babe, you did awesome."

He nods and kisses me. With the cooler air, he's not as sweaty after a race. "One more win and I'll have kicked this day's ass."

"Hey-hey! My man!"

I release my boyfriend as a group of Team Loco guys walk up and loudly congratulate Jett on his win. They stand outside of our walled canopy so there's no getting rid of them for a while. Jett introduces me to the guys as his girlfriend and I kind of wish those girls from the bleachers were here to witness it.

Jace offers me a hot chocolate while the guys are still talking and I spend some time talking with him while I wait to get my boyfriend back. He really is a cool dad and he seems to like having me around.

And then, just like always—like freaking clockwork—a girl walks up all pink-cheeked and grinning from ear to ear. She asks Jett to take a picture with her. After she leaves, a few more girls do the same thing, but they're all about twelve years old so it doesn't bother me much.

Jace and I talk about Christmas and I give him advice on what to get his wife besides the comfortable pajamas she asked for. The Team Loco guys *finally* say their goodbyes and wish him luck on his last race of the day. As soon as they're out of earshot, I go over to Jett and take his hand.

"If we get home in time, do you think we could get Mexican food for dinner?" I ask.

His eyes go wide. "Oh hell yes, that would be so good. Way better than concession stand nachos."

"Dude, don't knock the nachos," I say, pretend punching him. "Those things are the sole reason I wake up at the butt-crack of dawn and come to the races with you.

"Oh, that hurts, Key." Jett grips his heart and pretends to be in tremendous pain.

"Hi there!" a soft voice says from a few feet away.

Another, more high-pitched voice says, "That was a nice win, Jett."

Jett gives me this sad smile and we both turn to face the three gorgeous women in their twenties who are approaching us. One of them, an Indian woman with long perfect hair, winks and waves at Jace, who clears his throat and then walks back into the canopy.

"We're huge fans," one of them says. I'm not really paying attention anymore. I walk over to the tailgate of Jace's truck and pull myself up to sit on it while Jett does his thing with his adoring fans.

They gush and smile and tell him how great he is and he takes it all in stride. Then, of course, the cell phones come out and one by one, Jett takes their phones and holds it out for a selfie.

One girl throws her hand around his shoulder. It's annoying, yeah, but I know where his heart belongs.

Just before he snaps the final photo, he glances over and gives me a wink. And this might be the first time in the history of the world that a guy has managed to melt someone's heart while being embraced by three other girls.

CHAPTER EIGHTEEN

Jett

The morning after race day, I lie awake in bed, still plagued by the bad feeling about Keanna. Yesterday was weird. On the surface, it was a great day because I won all my races and did a spectacular job representing Team Loco. Keanna and I didn't fight, or argue, or have anything wrong happen . . . so why does it feel like she's upset with me?

I fell asleep worrying about this after talking with her on the phone all night. She didn't seem mad at me, but things felt off and I'm not sure why. I guess I hoped that when I woke up today, I'd feel better.

Well, I don't.

It's Sunday and The Track is closed. Tomorrow is the start of the last week of school before Christmas break so it'll be a slow week and then we'll have the pre-Christmas lock-in and it'll be busy as hell.

My homeschooling is going okay. It's only been a week but so far all of my online teachers enjoyed my (well—Keanna's) introductory essay. So far I've just had one easy assignment per day for each class.

Easy peasy.

The hard part is dealing with this concern over Keanna. How can you fix a problem with your girlfriend when you're not even sure if there is a problem? Is it all in my head?

Maybe she's worried about my birthday and Christmas coming up because I know she doesn't want to get me anything on the list I made for my mom. I wish I could convince her that I don't need or want anything as long as she's by my side. She's all I need and no amount of fancy gifts could ever replace her.

In an effort to make things feel normal for us again, I call her to ask her on a date. Living next door and working with each other is a great way to fall into a boring routine of a relationship and I don't want that to happen to us. My parents always make time for date nights because it's important, and I'm going to do the same thing.

She sounds sleepy when she answers the phone. I glance at the clock. It's eleven in the morning.

"Hey, beautiful."

She chuckles and then yawns. "What's up?"

"I wanted to ask you on a date tonight. Dinner and a movie?"

"That sounds awesome," she says, her voice perking up. I can hear her smile through her words. "That new superhero movie is out and we haven't seen it yet."

"Perfect. I was thinking of going to The Spot for dinner. It's this really good seafood place and a couple of days ago you said you wanted coconut shrimp so I thought it'd be great."

"Yum," she says. It sounds like she's still in bed, maybe stretching out her arms. I really wish I was in that bed with her. "But, Jett?" she asks.

My chest constricts. "Yes?"

"Can we go out for lunch instead of dinner?"

"But dinner is more of a romantic time for a date."

She laughs. "Babe! I don't want to wait until later. I want to see you now."

I grin. "Guess I can't argue with that."

WE OPT TO SEE THE MOVIE FIRST SINCE WE'RE BOTH NOT THAT HUNGRY YET. I HOLD open doors and keep my arm around her, doing everything I can think of to be romantic. I need her to know that things between us are perfect.

She may be smiling on the outside but something feels wrong ever since the races yesterday. I *need* things to get better.

The armrests in the theater lift up, so Keanna snuggles against my chest while we watch the movie. I love the feeling of her leaning on me, like she can count on me. Like I make her safe.

After the movie, we head to The Spot, a kitschy restaurant, the kind with tons of crap all over the walls and big fake fish hanging from the ceiling. The décor may be annoying, but their food is good.

We order fried pickles for an appetizer and Keanna gets her coconut shrimp, which puts a genuine smile on her face.

"This is the best coconut shrimp in the world," Keanna says, holding up the tail of the piece she just ate. "I am in love."

I nod and reach for one of my fried shrimp. "This place is really good. They only use locally caught seafood as well, so it's not that frozen shit."

My phone buzzes so many times it makes both of us look toward my pocket. I pull it out just enough to see the screen. "Social media alerts," I say, rolling my eyes.

This usually happens when a magazine or website posts a new article about me. Suddenly, I'll get fifty billion comment and post alerts from fans talking to me or about me. I slide the phone back in my pocket and reach for another fried pickle. These things are pretty good.

Keanna makes this big dramatic sigh. "My boyfriend is so popular," she says, grinning. "I feel like I should become a movie star or something so you can get a taste of what it's like to date someone so famous."

I take a bite of shrimp and peer at her for a long moment. "I don't see it. You're not really the actress type . . . I see you as more of the person who designs the movie sets."

"Is that supposed to be a compliment?" she asks, but she doesn't seem offended or anything.

I nod. "You're artistic. You did a great job on the party decorations and I think you'd bring a movie to life, ya know?"

"That's really sweet," she says, grabbing my hand from across the table.

For the first time since the races, I'm starting to feel like maybe things are okay again. Looks like my romance paid off.

After lunch, we walk out onto the restaurant's patio. It's a vast deck on a marina, so we can walk for a long ways and look at the water and the boats passing by. In the center of the deck is a circular viewing area. Signs identify the several types of fish in the viewing area, and there's even a vending machine to get a cup of fish food to feed them.

Keanna's eyes light up. "Do we have any quarters?" she says, digging through her purse. She comes up with one quarter but there's a money changing machine next to the food so I use two dollar bills from my wallet to get more.

We have a blast dropping pellets of fish food down to the fish, and soon there's dozens of them all floating around the water, begging for the next piece of food.

Keanna tosses a piece toward an empty section of water and we watch a fish swim toward it, only to have another catfish beat him to it.

"Rude!" Keanna says, tossing more pieces down the fish who got left out.

A little kid walks up with his grandmother, who tells him she doesn't have any quarters. Keanna gives him some of ours and it melts my heart to watch the kid's face light up excitedly. I love that she's kind and generous and not some stuck up motocross groupie like many girls I've known before.

Keanna excuses herself to go to the restroom back inside the restaurant and I stay, feeding the fish with the little boy.

My phone keeps buzzing like crazy, so once my cup is out of food, I decide to check the messages. But I barely type in my lock code when someone approaches me. It's a girl around my age, pretty but with something sly behind her eyes. I instantly know she's the kind of girl who can't be trusted, and even if I were single, I'd know to stay away from this one.

"Hi there," she says, dropping a quarter into the machine and letting it fill up her plastic cup. "Are the fish hungry today?"

"Yeah, they're gluttons," I say, turning back around and smiling at the little boy who is still feeding the fish.

"I can't believe I ran into someone famous while at the marina," she says, not looking at me as she strides up to where I'm standing near the fish viewing area. Ugh.

Of course.

Why can't I ever be approached by normal people? People who *don't* know who I am.

"I'm not famous," I say, using the same old line I've said many times before.

She snorts. "don't worry, I'm not some crazy stalker fangirl or anything."

Yeah, right, like I trust you. Instead, I say, "Good. I've had enough of those in my lifetime."

She turns to me and gives me what can only be described as a sultry, *come-hook-up-with-me* smile.

"Nice meeting you," I say, pushing off from the railing. "I need to get back to my girlfriend."

"You already have a new girlfriend?" she says, her voice higher than before. "Damn, that was fast. Like, super-fast."

I stop. I should probably keep leaving but dammit, now I'm curious. "We've been dating a while," I say. "What do you mean by *fast*?"

She peers at me like she's trying to tell if I'm lying. "The internet says you're single now."

"When did it say that?" I shouldn't care, but I ask anyway.

She lifts a shoulder and tosses more food to the fish. "Today."

So that's what all those phone alerts were about. I put on a casual smile. "You can't believe everything you read online, unfortunately. My girlfriend and I are still very much together."

"Weird," she says. She flips her hair over her shoulders. "Well, good thing I'm not one of your stalker fangirls or I might be disappointed."

I nod once and head back toward the restaurant. I see Keanna walking toward me, weaving her way through the dozens of outdoor tables. She gives me a cute little wave and I wave back, walking quicker to meet her sooner.

"What's that look about?" Keanna says, eyeing me suspiciously when we're finally back together, my hand in hers.

"Oh, nothing," I say, letting out a long sigh.

As we head back to the truck, I remember a speech my dad gave me a while back. It was before I'd met Keanna but when I was still fast enough and winning enough races to get noticed on a more popular level. He'd told me that dating and motocross don't mix well. That fame changes a person, makes them more powerful because they can date nearly anyone they want. He said girls can't handle the jealousy and competition and guys let it get to their head too easily. I'd been warned that dating and fame are hard to manage, and yet I'd thrown away all those warnings when I met Keanna.

Dad's advice doesn't hold true to some aspects of dating and fame—I don't care to play the field anymore. I only want Keanna and she only wants me. But he was right about one thing. It's not easy. I don't like having the public analyze my personal life outside of the races. I don't like getting hit on by girls of all ages, some of whom could be my mother, or grandmother, for that matter.

Dad didn't go back to professional motocross after falling for my mom. Although being a racer has been my dream for as long as I can remember, maybe it's not worth it in the long run. Dreams can change, after all. For now, I guess I'll see what happens.

CHAPTER NINETEEN

Keanna

Since it's a slow week at work, I get permission to come in at noon instead of at eight in the morning. Jett has been doing all of his homeschool work in the mornings, so this is the perfect time to work on my present for him.

With only a few hours of headache trying to make our home printer work, I managed to take my favorite photo of Jett, blow it up into nine pieces of paper, and print it out on canvas transfer papers I found at the craft store.

Then, I got a stretched canvas from the art section that's the exact size of my blown up image. Using internet tutorial videos, I place all nine sheets of transfer paper onto the canvas and then scrape it with a spatula until the image transfers over.

I hold my breath as I peel off the papers, hoping that the canvas image looks as good as it is in my head.

It comes out perfectly. I'm grinning so much as I look over the canvas. Now, my photo of Jett, muscular and shirtless, standing next to his dirt bike, is a work of art.

I stand back and admire my work. But it's not done yet.

My plan is to decorate it with a painted-on quote and then seal it up with some of Becca's clear sealant. That way it'll be waterproof and last forever.

At first I think I'm imagining Jett's voice but then I hear it again. He calls my name.

He's in the house!

"Keanna? Are you upstairs?"

Shit. I rush to move the canvas to the corner of the room and then I take a sheet and toss it over.

"I'll be right down!" I call out, nearly tripping over Becca's art supplies as I scramble to the doorway. I pull it open just as Jett starts up the stairs to the studio.

"Hey," I say, taking a deep breath and trying to look normal. If he gets suspicious of what I'm doing up here he might figure out that I'm planning something for him.

"Done with your school work already?" I say, putting a hand on my hip. If I change the subject, then maybe he won't ask what I was doing.

"Nope." Even from his position at the bottom of the stairs, he looks tall and handsome as hell. "I skipped out on the last assignment because I wanted to see you."

I hold onto the handrail and step down until I'm two steps higher than he is. "That's very bad of you, Jett Adams. I might have to punish you."

He grins. "I think I need a paddling."

He holds out his arms and I jump into them, holding on when he grabs me and heads back to my room. Since my parents aren't here, I don't hold back the squeals when he drops me to the bed and tickles me.

"Stop!" I gasp, squirming to get out of his wiggling fingers. He dives onto the bed next to me and I seize my opportunity to tickle him right on the side of his ribs.

"Hey now! Not fair!" Jett says, rolling out of the way. "I can only tickle you. You can't tickle me."

I roll over onto my stomach and prop myself up on my elbows. "What kind of double standard is that?"

He fluffs the pillow next to mine and lays down. "It's a double standard that works in my favor."

I roll my eyes. "Dork."

It's past noon and Jett's still in his flannel Homer Simpson pajama pants and a black undershirt. I guess he really did come over because he wanted to see me.

"I have to go to work soon," I say, frowning.

"I know. That's why I wanted a few minutes with you." He tucks his hands behind his head and stares at the ceiling. "Plus, we need to talk."

Those formidable words are usually a sign of bad news but the way he says them makes me more curious than worried. "What's up?"

"There's some dumbass rumor online that Jett Adams is a single man again."

He looks over at me, searching my eyes for something.

I shrug. "So?"

"It's no big deal because obviously, we're fine, but it's annoying."

"Are you going to say anything or just let it go?" I ask.

He looks over and leans up on his elbow. "I have an idea, but you'd have to go along with it."

"Oooh, enticing." I wiggle my eyebrows. "What is it?"

He sits up and gnaws on his bottom lip. "Okay, it's kind of stupid. Like—way stupid. This isn't my usual personality at all."

I narrow my eyes at him. "Does it involve social media?"

"Yep."

I sit up, eager to hear about his *so-not-like-him* plan. "You want me to type up a message that tells everyone you're happily dating me and post it to your account?"

He shakes his head, and takes out his cell phone. "I have a better idea. Let's take some selfies."

I make this exaggerated gasp and cover my mouth with my fingers. "*Selfies?* You? Wow, I am shocked."

He laughs and shakes his head. "I know. I'm not a selfie person. But I was thinking, instead of addressing the stupid rumors by telling everyone I'm not single, what if I post a picture of us in bed and send it to Instagram with a caption that says I'm sleeping in with my girl or something? That way it's like a subtle *fuck you* to the people starting rumors."

I grin. I really like his ideas when they involve me. "That's a perfect plan." I take his phone and open the camera. "But take off your shirt."

He lifts an eyebrow and I wave my hand for him to get on with it. "Take it off. It'll look more convincing." Then I run my tongue across my lip. "Plus I just want to see how freaking sexy you are before I go to work."

"Can't say no to that," Jett says, lifting up and pulling off his undershirt. He tosses it to the floor and then lays down in bed, beckoning me into his shoulder. I lean against him and then spend way too much time fixing my hair and trying to look extra cute for a picture that's supposedly taken just when we woke up.

He holds out the camera, we give sexy but sleepy smiles, and he snaps the photo. I enjoy the smell of his cologne as I snuggle against him, watching him upload the photo to Instagram.

He types *I love lazy days with my girl* and puts a heart emoji next to it. I try not to be a vain person, but seeing the picture of us on his Instagram account that has fifty thousand followers kind of makes my whole day.

"You're the coolest girlfriend ever," Jett says after he puts his phone on my nightstand. "I tell you the internet is saying we broke up and you don't even care."

I shrug and run my fingers down his bare chest. I would kill to have half the tanned and toned body he has. "Who cares about rumors? It's not like we know any of those people."

"True," he says, kissing my forehead. "So . . . this is a sexy outfit you're wearing."

I look down. I chose a pair of leggings that are a little too tight and a spaghetti strap pink tank top that I'm not too fond of, that way if any paint or glaze got on it, it wouldn't be a huge loss. Jett slips his finger under the strap and pushes it down my shoulder. He leans over me and kisses the skin where his fingers touched. I close my eyes and revel in his gentle embrace, the soft touch of his lips on my collarbone.

Warm hands slide down to my hips and then his fingers slip under my tank top.

The fabric rises until my breasts are exposed and Jett hovers over me, kissing me while his chest presses against mine. I moan from the intensity of his kiss and then lean back, letting him pull off my shirt. He tosses it right on top of his on the floor and then our tongues caress each other while his hands roam down my body.

I grab his back and pull him into me, feeling his excitement press into my stomach.

When he reaches for my leggings, I beat him to it. I can't help myself, he's so hot and I want him so badly. I slip the leggings down to my ankles and then kick them off, leaving everything exposed except for what's under my panties.

Jett's eyes fill with desire, and he grabs my hips, crushing me against him while we make out. I tangle my hands up in his hair, breathing hard against his neck.

He is so sexy and I want him so bad.

CHAPTER TWENTY

Jett

The way she moves beneath me, her fingernails digging into my back—it's all too much to experience and still walk away. I let my fingers explore her body, but focus on kissing, wondering if just making out will be enough.

"Jett," she whispers, gasping for air. Her hands dig into my hair. "It's time."

"Are you sure?" I ask, pulling back to look into her eyes.

She pulls at my pajama pants. "Yes, I'm sure."

I stand up and although I don't want to leave her, I rush over and lock her bedroom door. Her parents won't be home anytime soon but I am *not* about to get caught in bed with their daughter. That would be embarrassing and fifty kinds of traumatizing.

When I walk back to her bed, she gives me a sultry gaze and wiggles out of her panties. I take in a deep breath and drop my pants to the floor.

"Are you sure?" I ask, not getting back in bed until I know this is okay.

She nods eagerly and waves for me to join her. "Stop stalling," she whines. "You're just being mean now."

"Never," I say, crawling into bed with her. We slip under her sheets and I tug them up around us, knowing it'll help ease the awkwardness if everything isn't on display.

Besides, I have the rest of my life to admire her perfect body. Right now it's all about us.

I pull her face toward mine, and kiss her with everything that I have. Her back arches toward me and I stop, suddenly remembering something very important.

"You said you were on the pill, right?"

"Yep," she says, lifting her head and kissing my shoulder, then my neck. "Take it at the same time every day. You've seen me."

I nod. That's true. I take a deep breath and relax into her embrace, allowing myself to love her in the way I've been wanting to since the day I met her.

Her green apple shampoo smells like heaven when I bury my face into her neck. I let myself enjoy every touch, every sharp gasp of breath, the cute little way she shudders underneath me.

Despite my best efforts, it doesn't last very long, but she doesn't seem disappointed. After, we cuddle in her bed, her fingers tracing soft circles on my chest.

"That was better than I imagined," she breathes, her breath tickling my shoulder.

I run a hand through her hair. "And exactly how many times have you imagined that?"

She giggles into my neck and shakes her head. "*So* not telling you."

I take a deep breath and let it out slowly, reveling in the feel of her in my arms, the way the sun shines through the windows on this perfect winter day.

"I like this," I whisper, kissing the top of her head.

"You know what I like the most?" she says, looking up at me. "It just happened."

I lift an eyebrow. "*That's* what you liked the most?"

"Yeah, it was just us. Just a thing. After all these months of me stressing about it like some kind of crazy person, we finally did it." She draws in a deep breath and lets it out slowly. "All of that talk for waiting for the perfect time . . . and it turns out *this* was the perfect time."

She smiles up at me and I lean down and kiss her forehead. "It was perfect."

"And now that it's over, we can start doing it all the time," she says playfully.

"Oh yeah?" I run my finger up her side, feeling goosebumps lift on her skin. "That sounds like a great way to never get any more school work or riding done."

She frowns in this silly way. "I guess we'll just have to stay in this bed forever."

I close my eyes and wrap my arms tightly around her. "Sounds like a plan to me."

We rest in each other's arms for a while and just when I'm about to doze off, I hear her sigh.

"Seriously, Jett. *How* did I live so long without experiencing that?"

"It was that good, huh?"

She shrugs. "There's something special about being with someone you love. I guess I never realized how special it really is."

I sit up and pull on my clothes, handing hers back to her. It's been an hour or so and we don't want to risk any awkward family encounters.

"It was also awesome in other ways," I say, sitting back on her bed.

She tugs her shirt back over her head. "How so?"

I'm not sure I want to tell her for fear of sounding like some kind of perv. "Well . . . we . . ." I make these God-awful gestures with my hands, but it doesn't help explain anything. "It was a first for me, uh—physically speaking."

She gives me exactly the kind of crazy look I deserve. "Huh?"

I sigh. "No condoms. That was . . . intense."

Her confusion turns to desire. "Oh yeah?" she leans forward on her hands, pressing her boobs together between her arms. "You liked that?"

I nod eagerly. "Oh yeah. Way more than I should have."

"Good," she says, grinning so hard her eyes crinkle. "I like knowing I could give you something no one else has."

"Oh, you have. You *definitely* have."

Even her neck blushes with the way I look at her. It makes me want to go for round two. Instead, I check my phone, which has now blown up with notifications from my newest picture post.

"Wanna see?" I ask her, waving my phone.

"Hell yes," she says, snatching it from my grasp. She falls back on her bed and holds the phone so we can both see.

OHEMGEE, HE STILL HAS A GIRLFRIEND

Wait, is that the same girl or what?

I'm going to cry myself to sleep again. Dammit, I hate everything my life is shit.

"Wow, I feel bad for that girl," Keanna says after reading the third comment. "Maybe you should reply to her and say her life isn't shit.

I shake my head. "I've been advised against that by a few of my Team Loco racing buddies. Apparently interacting with the hyperactive fans is a way to get a stalker. Or, even worse, if you talk to them and then don't keep replying they might threaten suicide and then you have to get the cops involved."

I run a hand through my hair, remembering the story one of the guys told me during my first Team Loco race. He's had to call the police on three different internet girls who had obsessively written him and said they'd kill themselves if he didn't reply. Fearing for their safety, he kept talking to them and it all got really crazy. One of the girls even found out where he lived and broke into his house. I shudder at the memory. I do *not* want that to happen to me.

"Wow." Keanna's lips form a small O. "That's some scary stuff. I say we make you ugly and gross so no one likes you."

I cross my arms. "I don't like that idea."

She laughs and hands my phone back to me. "Fine, stay sexy. I like you better that way anyhow." She takes her sweet time crawling out of bed, giving me a view of her ass in those tight leggings. "I guess I should get to work now," she says, slipping into her closet.

"Fine," I say, sinking back in her bed. "I'll be waiting right here for you to get back."

By Friday, I can't concentrate on helping Dad train our five-year-old clients. Sure, I'm dressed appropriately, I'm standing out on the track in the sun, and I'm even helping kids start their bikes. My body and brain are here at work—but my mind is elsewhere.

Yep, I am lost in a vortex of daydreaming about a beautiful girl with dark brown hair and even darker eyes. Her soft skin, the way she giggles when I shower her with kisses. I am totally and completely consumed by Keanna Park.

It royally sucks that I'm stuck at work.

Somehow, I manage to fake like I'm actually paying attention all day and when my shift is almost over, D'andre shows up at The Track, but he's not in his riding gear.

"Hey man," he says, fist-bumping me. "What do you got planned after this?"

I shrug. The answer is Keanna, obviously, but I'm a guy and I have to pretend like I'm not totally lost to my friends.

"Cool, so you wanna hit up the mall or something?" He takes out his wallet and flips through some twenty dollar bills. "I have two hundred and seven dollars and need to find a Christmas present for Maya."

Damn. I need to get Keanna's present, too, and the longer I wait, the more hectic and horrifically busy the mall will be. I really should go now, but sacrificing a few hours away from my gorgeous girlfriend is going to suck.

"Yeah, sounds good," I say, choosing the logical thing over what my heart wants to do. "I'll meet you in the parking lot in a minute."

I head inside and clock out, then call Keanna and tell her the plan.

"That works," she says, not even sounding disappointed. "I'm actually kinda busy so take your time."

"Cool," I say, even though I don't believe it. "I'm gonna miss you."

"I always miss you," she says, and then she kisses the phone. "Love you."

"Love you more."

At the mall, I find about five thousand things I know Keanna would love. I don't buy them all because that would make me a crazy person, plus I've seen half the stuff my mom got her already and I'm not sure Keanna's bedroom is big enough to house it all.

I get her favorite body lotion from Victoria's Secret, and then throw in a gift card just because.

D'andre goes a little overboard in the same store. He gets Maya three bras that apparently she has already picked out and hinted for. I think it's a little weird getting a girl a bra, but whatever.

I get a few smaller things throughout the store, mostly just stuff that makes me think of her, like a new phone case that's solid pink glitter. But I'm still missing the main gift. The big, awesome, present that will make her mouth drop and her eyes water.

The kind of gift that says I'm the best boyfriend on earth.

I'm about to give up hope on finding such a perfect gift, but then we stop to get some fish tacos and a shiny display case around the corner catches my eye.

While waiting for our food, I walk over and gaze at the beautiful items beneath the glass. And I know. As sure as I've known anything, that this is the perfect gift for Keanna.

CHAPTER TWENTY-ONE

Keanna

It's extra windy today, as evidenced by the creaking and whipping sound on the studio's windows. On the third floor, I almost feel sea sick when I look outside and see all of the trees swaying like crazy in the breeze. Of course, the house is sturdy so I'm not really moving. Maybe I've just been breathing in this clear sealant too long.

I open the studio door to let it vent some fresh air into Becca's small art room.

My canvas of Jett's photo looks amazing; like some kind of shabby chic artwork you'd find in a high end shop.

I lightly touch the corner of the canvas, checking to see if the clear coat is dry yet. It feels like it, so I stand back and admire my work again. I'm not sure how I'll wrap it; covered in wrapping paper, or just presented with a pretty ribbon bow on the corner.

"Wow," Becca says, suddenly appearing in the doorway. I hadn't even heard her walk up the creaky stairs, probably because of the wind outside. "That looks amazing."

I've been keeping this project a secret from everyone, including my mom.

"Are you sure?" I ask, watching carefully for any signs that she's just saying that to be nice.

"Absolutely. I love what you did with this—was it transfer paper?"

I nod. "It's Jett's birthday present . . . Do you think he'll like it?"

She steps forward and lightly touches the side of the canvas. "Oh yes. He'll love it. This picture shows his dedication and hard work."

My chest tightens. Now that the project is over, I officially have his birthday present. Now I just hope he likes it as much as I do.

While Becca points out all the things she likes about the canvas, my brain starts stressing over what to get him for Christmas.

"What's wrong, honey?" Becca asks, her brows pulling in at the center.

I toss up my hands. "I still need a Christmas present for him. I can't think of anything to get."

"Hmm," she says, putting a finger to her lips.

"I need something extra nice. Something worth it." My feet begin to pace the small room.

"It's not the monetary value of the gift, Keanna. It's about the meaning of the gift. Think of something that will be special to him—even if it's cheap."

I heave a heavy sigh. "I'm not even concerned with the cost of it. I have money. What I don't have is ideas."

Becca follows me down to the living room, giving me advice but no real answers for gift ideas. "Try to think of something special to your relationship. Maybe an inside joke or a special memory?"

Her phone starts ringing from the kitchen so she squeezes my shoulder before leaving. "You'll figure it out."

Right. Sure, I will.

There's only a few days until Christmas and if I want to get him a gift, I'll need to do it soon. My phone buzzes just as I'm about to call Maya.

Jett: Shopping with D'Andre is weird.

Me: lol. What are ya'll shopping for?

Jett: Can't tell you. It's a secret.

Me: Uh huh, sure. How much longer will you be?

Jett: At least an hour, maybe more.

Me: Cool, because I have some shopping to do with Maya.

Jett: I TOLD YOU I DON'T WANT ANYTHING

Me: Who says I'm shopping for you? :p

I'm so glad Maya agreed to go shopping with me. Since she already knew that our boyfriends were at the mall, she suggests going to an outdoor mall a little further away, that way we won't run into them.

I haven't been to this place yet and it's pretty awesome. There's a ton of clothing stores that I'd love to spend hours pursuing, but we have a goal. Christmas presents for the boys.

Maya holds up a men's sweater, frowning and then putting it back. "So, I have to admit I kind of freaked when I saw the Facebook drama about Jett being single again."

I snort. "Why?"

"Because I was like, no way. No way would they break up and she not tell me!" Maya laughs. "Then I felt like an idiot for believing it, if only for a short while. Ya know? God, I hate the media."

I run my hand across a rack of men's clothing. None of this would be a good match for Jett, but it is kind of the style D'andre likes so I'm stuck here for the time being. "I'm so over this media and fame crap."

"D'andre said you've been handling it like a pro. Apparently, you didn't even get mad when that breakup rumor hit."

I lift an eyebrow. "How did he know about that?"

"Jett told him."

"Hmm." I didn't realize Jett talked about that kind of thing to his friends. Was I supposed to get pissed? Go on some kind of online rampage? It's not like that would have helped anything. People online are going to say whatever the hell they want, and if it pisses you off, then they'll only be happier.

"Okay, you look upset," she says as we leave one store and walk into another. "What's bothering you?"

I shrug and try to focus on all of the things in this store. "I'm not really so easy going about all of this crap. I actually *hate* Jett's popularity."

Her eyes widen. "You hide it well, girl."

"I know. I have to. I'm not about to be the girl who whines and complains every time I get jealous. That would only drive him away."

"True, but damn." Maya shakes her head. "I don't know if I could do it. I like D'andre because he's safe. He thinks I'm the best girl he could ever get so I feel secure, ya know?"

I laugh. "Probably don't tell him that."

She gives me an evil grin. "Don't worry, I won't."

"When it comes to security, I'm okay I guess. I mean, I know he loves me and I love him. But it's still not cool seeing all these girls swooning over him." My lip curls in disgust. "They touch him every chance they get. Little arm pats, or hand touching. Ugh. It takes everything I have not to go all Hulk Smash on those bitches."

She grids her fist into her hand. "If you need backup, let me know."

We laugh and leave another clothing store. The food court is up ahead, an all outdoors kiosk style place. At the corner is a massive store that's probably the biggest place in this whole shopping center. I've never heard of it before, but it says it's an *outdoors paradise*.

"What's this place?" I say, stopping to gaze into the massive windows. There's all kinds of fake rocks and waterfalls and trees decorating the shop. I see a pair of skis and tents and fake dogs in the window display.

"Some kind of outdoor place," Maya says. "My dad shops here a lot for his fishing gear."

My lips slide to the side of my mouth. It's an interesting place, for sure. Maybe there will be something in there to spark an idea for Jett's present. I turn to Maya. "Can we go in?"

"Girl you know I'm too feminine to care about anything in that place." She glances down at her four-inch heels and then grins. "But I'll suffer through it for you because I'm an awesome friend."

I reach for the door handle, which is a reclaimed tree branch and pull it open. "Good, because my women's intuition is telling me this might be the perfect place to find my dream gift."

CHAPTER TWENTY-TWO

Jett

Keanna gives me this look that apologizes for what Becca is about to do. All I know is that I've just walked into their house and Becca yelled from somewhere out of sight that we have to wait in the kitchen until further notice.

I wrap my arms around Keanna and kiss her hello. "How was your day?"

"Very productive," she says, squeezing me tight. When she pulls away, her eyes flit to the oven. "I have officially gotten you the best Christmas present ever."

"Wrong," I say, shaking my head. "I got you the best present ever, so I guess yours is second best, but not *the* best."

She shakes her head and even her expression is stone cold confident. "You're wrong. I'm right. Get over it."

The oven timer dings and she rushes over, grabbing two oven mitts off the counter and taking out a glass dish that smells like Mexican heaven.

"What's this?" I say, walking over.

"Enchiladas." She sets down the dish and reaches for some plates. "You hungry?"

"Hell yeah," I say, taking out some forks from the silverware drawer. "This smells amazing."

She puts her hands on her hips. "Okay, confession time, Jett. If you're going to be with me for the foreseeable future—"

"Try forever," I say, holding up a finger.

"For *forever*," she says, grabbing a spatula and cutting the enchiladas apart. "So here's the confession—I'm not a good cook but I'm an okay preparer."

"What's the difference?"

She shrugs. "I made these with store bought tortillas, pre-shredded cheese, and canned sauce. I know a perfect girlfriend would have like secret family recipes and stuff, but I don't have anything except the recipes on the back of the box."

I take her hand and pull her across the tiled floor until our toes touch. I tilt her chin up to peer into her eyes. "You worry way too much my dear. You could make a bowl of cereal and I'd be forever grateful."

She makes this sad smile and then turns to grab a bag of tortilla chips from the pantry. "Becca makes all kinds of dinners from scratch. I don't know how she does it."

"She's also like twice your age babe. We have time to learn all that stuff. You don't need to stress about it now."

"Yeah, I guess you're right," she says, looking at the dish of enchiladas. "I guess because I'm out of school already, I feel like I need to be more grown up all the time."

"These are supposed to be the best years of our lives," I say. "We can be adults later."

Becca rushes into the kitchen, her face flushed. "Okay, I'm ready! Come on in," she says, waving for us to follow just before she disappears into the hallway. Keanna and I exchange a glance and then we find her in the new nursery room.

"What do you think?" Becca says, twirling around with her arms open. She's wearing a long black skirt and it flows with her, swooshing around her ankles when she stops.

I gaze around the room. It used to be a junk room but lately she's been transforming it into a nursery. The walls are pale green with little woodlands creatures painted along the walls. There's a crib and dresser and an old rocking horse given to her by her dad. But the grand masterpiece of the room is the tree.

Becca had a vision for it and hired someone to help her see it through. I remember hearing Keanna mention it offhand, but damn, this is amazing. The entire corner of the room is now a fake tree. The kind with a huge old trunk, hollowed out at the bottom to make a secret playroom. The fake branches extend up to the ceiling and run along for several feet, fake tree leaves dropping down.

"Your baby is going to have such a great childhood," I say, walking over to the tree's opening and peering inside. There's a little light hanging from the ceiling in here and pillows and a bookshelf filled with baby books.

"I'm so excited," Keanna says, gushing over all of the pieces of the room. "We still have so much to do but this is great!"

"I know, right?" Becca says.

"Wait, you have *more* to do?" I ask. "What more could you possibly do?"

They both look at each other like I'm just a clueless bum. "Oh honey," Keanna says, shaking her head. "You're so sweet and innocent."

"Babies come with a lot of stuff," Becca says. "I mean, look at our closet. There's not even any clothes yet!"

"You guys are weird," I say, just as the alarm on my phone goes off. I check it and my face falls. "Oh, shit. I can't believe I forgot."

Keanna looks confused for a split second and then recognition dawns on her face. "Your Skype interview."

"Yeah. Shit."

In just fifteen minutes, I'm supposed to be having a Skype interview with some motocross magazine online. They arranged it a few weeks ago, but I totally forgot. Apparently, I'll be talking to the host and they'll ask me questions from fans. It's part of their social media marketing stuff.

"You could do it here," Keanna says. "Just use my computer."

"You don't mind?"

"Of course not. Just don't put me in the video and I'll be fine."

We agree to use her computer and have it facing a blank wall in her room so that my background will look nice and professional. While she sets it up, I scarf down three of her enchiladas and they're amazing, but I know if I tell her that'll just roll her eyes and say they could have been better.

While I wait for the magazine's social outreach coordinator—Brie Mason, according to my email—to call me on Skype, I try to remember our first phone call weeks ago. I've done plenty of interviews over the last couple of months and it's hard to remember what belongs to what.

Keanna's eyes go wide when Bree's Skype call starts ringing. She kisses me on the side of my head and gives me a quick hug. "Good luck!" she whispers just before I answer the call.

Bree is a hipster woman in her late thirties, her hair buzzed on the sides and dyed bright green on top. She wears thick black frames and has an interesting and badass looking tattoo on her neck. She explains to me that they're using a software that allows fans to call in and ask questions. Their video chat will be at the bottom of the screen, while hers will be up top. I'll be the main event though, my face nice and huge on the live stream and the video they'll keep on the site later on.

"Any questions before we begin?" she asks.

"Yeah," I say, feeling like an asshole. "What magazine was this for again?"

She laughs. "*Motocross Girls*"

"Oh, right." I give her what I hope is a charming smile. "That's what I thought."

Inwardly, I cringe. *Motocross Girls*? Does this mean what I think it means?

Yes, yes it does.

Bree's head is about two inches tall on Keanna's computer monitor. "Okay guys, our first question comes from MxGurl14."

Another little square pops up at the bottom of the screen and a young girl appears. Her cheeks are flushed, probably from nerves, and when she talks, her voice is all shaky.

"My questions is: Jett, do you think a girl could ever be a fast racer?"

"Absolutely," I say. "Girls can be just as badass on a dirt bike as a guy can be. I always tell people the key to being fast is to start as young as possible and work your butt off."

She grins and her pixelated cheeks turn red. "Cool. Thanks."

Bree introduces the next caller and this time it's an older girl, probably around my age. "Hi Jett," she says, waving flirtatiously at the screen. "I want to know, what do you look for in a girlfriend?"

"Uh, well," I say, looking toward Keanna's bed where she's no longer sitting since she left the room a few minutes ago. "I'm not currently looking for a girlfriend but when I was, I wanted someone sweet and kind. Someone I can trust."

"You could trust me, Jett," she says, tilting her head.

I don't know what it is about girls and that weird head tilt. I guess they think it makes them look sexy, or possibly like an innocent baby deer or something. Instead, it just makes it look like they're trying too hard.

The next few questions are all basically the same thing. Why did I agree to this interview, again? Was I temporarily insane? Probably.

Right after my internship went through, I got a little too excited about all the hype and attention I got. I would have agreed to anything.

Bree comes back on after about twelve callers. "Okay, it's time for some questions from our staff here at *Motocross Girls*."

Oh thank God, I think.

Bree asks me some questions that are legit motocross inquiries, and I'm happy to answer them.

Keanna stays away, probably to give me the privacy to work on this without distractions, but I miss her a lot. I'm also wondering if there's any more enchiladas left, but I'm betting Park has cleared out the leftovers by now.

"One final thing," Bree says. She adjusts her glasses and then grins. "A little birdie told us that your seventeenth birthday is tomorrow. Is that right?"

I chuckle. "Yep. That's right. I'm the Christmas Eve baby."

"Well, we have a special call for you next." She looks down at her keyboard and then a long window appears at the bottom of the screen. It's a video feed of about three dozen teenage girls. "Some of your biggest racing fans are here to sing you happy birthday."

They all sing the Happy Birthday song. Keanna walks back in just when they're finishing and she breaks into a smile.

"Awesome," I say, clapping. "That was really cool. Thank you."

"*Thank you* for being here with us tonight!" Bree says. She says a few more things and then the call is officially over.

I look over at Keanna. "Well, that was fun and annoying."

She checks the time on her phone. "We still have four hours until midnight, when I want to give you your birthday present. Can you think of anything fun to do?"

"Actually," I say, swiveling in her desk chair until I'm facing her. "I have a great idea."

I DECIDE TO TAKE KEANNA TO SHADY CREEK HEIGHTS, AN UPPITY RICH PERSON subdivision two towns over. It's kind of a long drive, but I know it'll be worth it. It's Christmas Eve *Eve* after all, and everyone's lights will be on. Just before we arrive at the famed subdivision, I pull into a Starbucks and we get massive hot chocolates.

"So are you going to tell me where we're going yet?" Keanna says, blowing into the little hole on top of her hot chocolate lid. "I can't think of any place that's actually open this late besides Walmart."

"We're actually staying in the truck the whole time," I say cryptically.

Her lips move to the side of her mouth and then her eyes light up. "We're driving around to see something?"

I nod. She glances out the window and then gives me a knowing look. "Christmas lights."

"Yep." I steer the truck back onto the main road and take the exit for Shady Creek Heights.

This place has been on TV shows for its incredible Christmas lights display. The subdivision has about thirty mansions, all of which are owned by the super rich: athletes, doctors, and a few lesser famous celebrities and country singers. Every year, the neighborhood chooses a theme and all of the houses decorate according to it. I remember watching on one of those TV shows that participating in the holiday decorating is actually a rule in their homeowner's association. So this place is a big attraction and I'm excited to show her. I haven't been here since I was a kid.

"Oh my God," she says, putting her hand to her window.

We're only at the entrance of the neighborhood, but it's already spectacular. The brick entrance that spans on both sides of the gated entryway has been covered in a solid sheet of multicolored lights. A sign has been placed near the road.

Transiberian Orchestra Christmas! Tune in to channel FM 93.1 to listen!

I turn the radio to the right station and it begins playing one of the Transiberian Orchestra's amazing songs.

The guard at the gated entrance waves us through, saying visitors are allowed thirty minutes to drive through and check out the lights.

The tree-lined road is coved in lights that blink to the music. It is absolutely incredible. I barely remember to breathe as we take in house after house, each of them a beautiful mansion in their own right, but now they've been blanketed in LED lights that move to the music.

Waves of blue lights create a frozen lake that blinking penguins skate across. A holograph Santa walks across the roof of a house, then jumps into the chimney, disappearing in a starburst of lights.

Keanna's jaw drops and so does mine. We become completely overtaken by the beauty and the masterpiece of this neighborhood's Christmas display. Each house's design flows into the next one, creating Santa Claus' workshop, a gingerbread house, a candy cane lane, and a Christmas feast. The last house on the block has turned its roof and lawn into a three dimensional nativity scene, while still staying timed to the music.

It is absolutely breathtaking.

Half an hour later, we've idled through the whole neighborhood, and we make our way toward the exit. Dozens of cars are in front of and behind us, but I hadn't really noticed them until now.

"Wow." Keanna lets out a breath. "I feel like my life will never be the same again, now that I've seen that."

I grab her hand and then take a sip of my hot chocolate. "That was a thousand times cooler than when I came here as a kid, and back then it was still awesome."

"I'm glad you took me," she says. She unbuckles her seatbelt and slides over to the middle seat, leaning her head against my shoulder while we drive.

Once we're back in Lawson, I turn down a back road and we cruise around some more, looking at the random house lights we pass on the way.

"So, we have thirty minutes until midnight," she says, checking her phone for the time.

"What's so fancy about midnight?" I ask.

"It's your birthday, duh!"

I chuckle. "I think you care more about my birthday than I do."

"Well, I'm supposed to. I'm your girlfriend." She sticks out her tongue and I lean over to kiss her, almost missing a stop sign in the process. Luckily, we're in the middle of nowhere so there's no other cars around. "You look really hot tonight," I whisper into her ear before driving forward. "You always look hot," she says, giving me that seductive grin I love so much.

"There's a park up ahead," I say. "We should pull over and make out in the back seat."

She gives me this look. "That's something dumb teenagers do. We have bedrooms to use for making out."

I turn into the park anyway and choose a parking spot at the back. The lights are off and no one is here because it's so late at night. "Well, we are teenagers so . . ."

She leans over and slides her fingers into my hair. Her lips brush against mine. "So get in the back seat."

CHAPTER TWENTY-THREE

Keanna

I pull my clothes back on in the surprisingly roomy backseat of Jett's truck. My heart is pounding from another encounter with Jett and all of his special ways of making sure I feel loved. Jett sits up in the back seat, pulls his shirt over his head and then grins at me. His jeans are still unzipped, but at least they're on now. This whole time I'd been a little afraid that a cop would show up or worse—someone with a video camera. But we didn't take long, and no one so much as drove by. I guess Christmas Eve Eve isn't that big of a late night travel day.

My phone alarm goes off, alerting me that it's now midnight. I slide across the bench seat and crawl into Jett's lap. My head barely misses the roof of the truck, but I duck down to kiss him.

"Happy birthday."

"Thanks," he says, his fingers trailing down my chin. "I love you."

"I love you," I say between kissing him. "We need to get to my house. I have a present for you."

"It can't wait until tomorrow?" he asks.

"It already *is* tomorrow," I point out. "Besides, I'm dying to give it to you."

"As you wish," Jett says. He opens the truck door and a cold burst of winter air fills the truck's cab. We get back in the front seat and as soon as we pull into his driveway, I realize the flaw in my plan.

His present is still on the third floor studio at home. Those stairs are creaky.

But I absolutely have to give him his gift at midnight. It's how I've been planning this whole thing. That way he'll get it now, then go back to sleep, wake up in the morning on his actual birthday and he'll have to wait a whole extra day to get his Christmas presents. It'll give the allusion that he's not getting gifts back to back, although he really is.

I don't know. Maybe it's lame. But maybe I'm just a lame person who enjoys these kind of things.

We sneak over to my house and I open the back door as quietly as possible. Although the Christmas tree's lights are still on, leaving a whimsical glow all throughout the living room, my parents are asleep.

I put my fingers to my lips and motion for Jett to follow me to the stairs. Going up to the second floor is easy because these stairs don't creak, but once you go down the hallway and face the much thinner row of stairs that lead to the studio, it gets a little shady.

"Be very quiet," I whisper, pressing my finger to his lips.

He pulls me into the darkened alcove at the base of the stairs and kisses me deeply, holding me tightly against his chest.

I kiss him back, getting lost in his touch until my head goes all lightheaded and swirly. I gasp for breath and step backward. "How dare you," I whisper, putting my hands on my hips.

"Sorry," he says, leaning in and kissing the crook of my neck. "I couldn't help myself."

I swallow, and try to gain control of my mind once again.

I step up on the first stair and then the second. If the wood creaks, I quickly shuffle to the other side. We walk slowly, Jett grabbing my ass on more than one occasion because it's right in his face, and eventually we get to the top of the stairs.

"I hope you like it," I whisper, my hand on the door. Only now am I getting really nervous. Making this project had been fun and even exciting, but now that I'm about to give it to him, I'm suddenly wondering if maybe it's not as great as I think.

I let out a nervous breath and open the door. Once we're inside, I close it behind us and then turn on the light.

I'd chosen to leave the canvas open, with only a silver bow on top. But I used some scrapbook paper and designed a big gift tag that hangs from the bottom. It says: HAPPY BIRTHDAY JETT, LOVE KEANNA in lettering that's big enough to read across the room.

"Whoa." Jett just stands here, his hand over his mouth.

I bite my lip so hard it starts to sting. "I made it," I say meekly, walking toward the canvas. I touch the side of it and watch him, judging for his reaction. "Do you like it?"

His shocked expression twists into one of excitement. "This is incredible. You *made* it? How?"

He walks forward and runs his hand down the shiny canvas. "Where did you get this picture?"

"I took it on my phone," I say, lifting my shoulders. This picture was taken in his quiet moment of personal reflection. He hadn't known I'd captured it to last forever. "I thought it was a special picture so . . ." I motion toward the canvas.

"This is the greatest thing ever," he says, not taking his eyes off it. "This is so much better than those professional shots of me racing or flying over a jump. This one is like . . ." he shakes his head and looks over at me. "This one is special. Personal."

I grin. "Happy birthday, babe."

He wraps his arms around me and holds me tight. "Thank you."

I WAKE UP THE NEXT MORNING TO THE SOUND OF CHRISTMAS CAROLS BEING PLAYED through the house's surround sound. I glance over at my phone and see that it's only eight in the morning. Ahhh . . .

But as tired as I am and as badly as I want to sleep in, I shuffle out of bed, yawn fifty thousand times, and head out into the kitchen. My new mom is grinning from ear to ear while she pours waffle mix into the waffle iron.

"Merry Christmas," she sing-songs as I pad into the room, rubbing sleep from my eyes.

"Merry Christmas," I say. I drop into one of the barstools on the other side of the kitchen island.

Park walks in from the back door, a bottle of syrup in his hand. "Morning, kiddo," he says, giving me a quick hug while he sets the syrup on the island. His jacket is freezing cold and it makes me shiver.

"Becca wanted waffles and we were out of syrup. It's a good thing some stores are actually open on Christmas day." Park grins and reaches into his jacket pocket. "Merry Christmas, by the way."

He pulls out two scratch-off lottery tickets and hands one to me and Becca.

"Cool," I say, taking the massive thing. It's as big as my head and boasts that you can win up to twenty times. "Thank you."

"He gets me one for every holiday," Becca explains. "That was sweet of you to get one for Keanna," she tells him.

Park winks at me and flips on the coffee pot. "She's my girl now, too."

Warmth fills me and it's not just from the hot air coming off the waffle iron. We scratch the lottery tickets and Becca wins twenty dollars and I win thirty-five. Not bad.

After breakfast, we head into the den, where the presents seem to have multiplied since the last time I was in here.

Although some of the gifts are for Becca's parents and relatives and Jace and Bayleigh, and some are the gifts Park and I got for Becca, most of them are for us.

Park and I open gift after gift, all of which make Becca smile and tear up when she sees our reactions.

"Mom, you should *not* have gotten me so many things," I say, looking up from a small box that contained a dozen gift cards to all my favorite fast food places. "This was way too much."

"Never!" she says, laughing. "I told you, I'm making up for eighteen years of gifts here." She looks around, reaches for another package that's wrapped in silver paper and shoves it in my hand. "So you're gonna open them and like them, missy."

"Yes ma'am," I say, tearing into the paper. It's a new wireless mouse for my laptop, which is perfect since I recently dropped mine on the patio and it shattered. Becca truly thinks of everything.

My new parents love the gifts I got them: home décor for Becca from her favorite boutique downtown, and new subscriptions to three of Park's favorite motocross magazines.

Becca sets up her camera on a tripod and gets a million family photos of our first Christmas together. Overall, it's the most amazing Christmas morning I've ever had, and that's not because of the gifts involved. It's because for once in my life, I'm spending it with family, laughing and joking, and enjoying the morning. Christmases with Dawn were usually spent with her at work, or sleeping late, or telling me that Santa must not have been impressed with my behavior that year.

Bayleigh calls shortly after and insists that we come over as soon as possible. She's making a full Christmas meal for lunch but wants us over before that to hang out.

First, we open presents and although it's a little awkward at first, I feel more at home with Jett by my side.

His parents give me a charm bracelet from a very famous Texas jeweler named James Avery. The silver chain has heart-shaped links and they've added the dirt bike charm, a K+J charm, and one that says family. I tear up the moment I hold it in my hands. It is beautiful and thoughtful and I know I'll wear it forever.

Jett gets me a bunch of fun gifts that he knows I'll like, like a new case for my phone, and a gift card to the bookstore. I also get DVDs of my favorite shows that aren't on Netflix, and an entire stocking filled with my favorite kind of candy. My name is written on the top of the stocking in glitter and he admits he had to get his mom's help to make it look that pretty.

"Have you given her the . . ?" Bayleigh asks him after a while.

He shakes his head. "Not yet."

"Given me what?" I ask, peering at him. "You've already given me way too many things."

"Well, I have one more that's even more special."

"I have one more that's even more special for *you*," I say, poking him in the chest.

"Let's play rock paper scissors to see who goes first," he says, positioning his fist on top of his hand.

I play him and my rock beats his scissors. I squee and reach for the big box that I'd had to get Park to carry over here. It's not that it's too big, but it's way too heavy.

Everyone watches while Jett opens the box, revealing a massive camping backpack, filled with gear. But on the outside, safety pinned to the zipper so he sees it first, is his real present.

A week long hiking trip across the Guadalupe Mountains National Park, all-inclusive with a tour guide of our very own.

"You're coming too, right?" he asks.

I grin. "My backpack is at home."

He throws his arms around me. "This is amazing."

"Tell him the reason behind it," Becca says. I explain to him that I thought a camping and hiking trip would be a great way to destress after all of these motocross races. We'd be in the wilderness, connecting with Mother Nature, and away from all of the fame and annoying parts of the internet.

"This makes my gift look terrible," Jett says, laughing. He reaches under the tree and takes out a small box. "But here you are. Merry Christmas."

I'm keenly aware of our parents watching me intently, but I try to block it out and just focus on Jett. Inside the box is a velvet jewelry box, long and rectangular. I pull open the lid and gasp.

It's a pink gold heart necklace, the heart is made of diamonds and I know without asking that they are real. I remember telling him that pink gold was so pretty and he must have remembered.

Tears flood into my eyes as I thank him, and he fastens it around my neck for me. Becca and Bayleigh coo over how pretty it is, and Jace tells his son he did a good job.

When all of the presents have been opened, we enjoy a Christmas feast around the Adams' dining table, and I eat until I'm totally stuffed.

It occurs to me, that in only a few months, a holiday that used to be meaningless to me has now become my favorite part of the whole year. I can see why Becca is so excited to share it with her future son. I can only imagine how much more magical it would be to experience all of this love and family as a child. But the past is in the past, and from now on, I'm living for a better future.

CHAPTER TWENTY-FOUR

Jett

It had taken me a while to decide on the perfect place to hang my artwork from Keanna. My dad thought it'd look great at The Track, but I wanted to keep it for myself, where I could see it any time. Plus, Keanna said she could always make more motocross themed canvases to hang up at The Track. This one in particular is mine.

I finally decide on mounting it directly above my headboard in my bedroom.

With a hammer and two nails, I hang it up and then step back to admire my handiwork. It looks great. Like the new focal point of my bedroom. I know I'm going to have this for a long time, and one day when I'm old, I'll be able to look back on my glory days.

Today is New Year's Eve, and my parents are throwing a big party at The Track. This has been their tradition for about five years now, and I'm only recently considered old enough to attend and drink the beer. The first couple of years, my parents only invited adults and it got kind of wild and crazy. They spare no expense for this party, calling it a way to 'give back to their clients' at the end of the year to use some of it as a tax write-off, I guess.

But Keanna is excited to attend, and even more so now that Becca and my mom have declared this party to be a masquerade. (I think they've been watching too many fancy shows on Netflix.)

The party theme is open to interpretation any way you'd like to, whether by dressing in a classic Victorian masquerade fashion with the fancy dresses, or by just wearing a mask. Hell, any mask would do, even one of those cheese plastic vampire masks for Halloween.

You can guess which way my girlfriend wanted to interpret it. The fancy way.

She'd spent the last few days scouring the city with Maya in an attempt to find the perfect Victorian-style dress. She'd told me she was going for something black and gold, the classic New Year's Eve colors. I'm guessing she found something suitable because yesterday she delivered my own ensemble for me. A black tux with a gold tie that has some kind of black baroque print on it. It matches the pocket square and I have a very masculine, if not tacky, black and gold face mask.

I haven't seen what she's wearing. Apparently, like getting married, showing your fancy dress off before the big party is a big no-no. I'm excited though, because Keanna is excited. I'm happy to participate in whatever makes her eyes light up, no matter how silly it might seem to me.

After I'm all dressed in what feels like too many layers of fancy clothing, I head out to my truck and drive over to her house. The Track's parking lot is starting to fill up with catering vans and my parent's closer friends who show up early to things like this. Becca and Park walk outside just as I arrive. Park is dressed like normal, but he's wearing a plastic mardi gras mask over his face. Becca is wearing a long red gown that looks like it was salvaged from a vintage shop. Her mask is covered with an array of red and black feathers that go up taller than her fancy hairstyle. "You look so handsome," she says as our paths cross.

I thank her and then go inside, looking for Keanna. Her door is closed, but I go to walk in anyway and I nearly crash into it. It's locked.

I tap on the door with my knuckles. "Keanna? I'm here."

There's silence for a moment and then she says, "Go away."

"What?" My heart hammers in my chest. Have I done something wrong?

Then, on the other side of the door, she says, "No. Don't go."

I lean against the door frame. "You okay?"

"No."

"What!" My panicked reply must startle her because the door unlocks and opens just a crack.

"I'm physically okay." One of her eyes watches me through the crack in the door. I know I could overpower her and shove my way inside if I wanted, but I give her the privacy she desires. She sighs. "I'm just not feeling very great about this dress."

"You've been raving about your dress for three days," I say.

"That was before I overheard your mom saying there's going to be two hundred guests tonight."

"So? It's a fun party, not everyone will be dressed up."

"That's not it," she says, pulling open the door further.

She's wearing a black gown with golden sequins sewn all over it in an intricate pattern. It's all very pretty, in a regal way instead of like what girls wear to prom.

"You look amazing," I say, taking her hands.

She frowns. "How many other girls will be there looking even better?"

I lift an eyebrow. "Zero. Exactly zero."

"You don't know that."

"Of course I do," I say, tilting her head up so I can kiss her. "There are no prettier girls than the most gorgeous girl on the planet."

She rolls her eyes but she smiles a little, so that's good.

"Baby, what's bothering you?" I ask, walking her over to her bed.

She lifts one shoulder and stares at the carpet. "I don't know. I *was* excited, but then I started thinking about all of your adoring fans and wondering how many of them will be here tonight."

She lifts the fabric of her skirt a few inches and then drops it disdainfully. "And how many of them will be dressed in revealing slutty clothes that make me look like some kind of prude weirdo?"

I can't help but laugh. "Baby, you're over thinking this. First of all, you're absolutely beautiful," I say, pointing to my finger. "Secondly, slutty girls aren't my thing, and thirdly—" I take her hand and bring it to my lips, kissing it. "You're the only girl I care about. For now, and forever."

"For*ever?*" she says, pronouncing it like two separate words.

There's a gift in my pocket that I've been saving for midnight. But I can't deny it—I'm thinking of giving it to her now. I gaze into her dark eyes, taking in all of her fear and insecurities. I wish I could wrap them all up, set them on fire, and ensure that she never feels any kind of pain again.

"Forever, Keanna." I kiss her cheek. "This is our first New Years together. Let's make it special."

CHAPTER TWENTY-FIVE

Keanna

The party has transformed The Track into something magical. All of the grassy area between the main building and the track has been covered with those big white tents you see at weddings. There are three tents in all, each the size of a house. They all connect to a wooden dance floor in the middle.

Clear lights and confetti and ice sculptures adorn every square inch of the place. There's a live band playing music, a catered dinner, and best of all: everyone wears a mask.

Some people took the silly approach like Park did, by wearing football mascot masks, or Halloween scary faces, but most people are more elegant, staying true to a classic Masquerade. I love every second of it.

And the best part?

Since we're all in masks, I can't really be compared to the other girls. No one knows when Jett and I enter the main tent, hand in hand. We're just two faceless people in a crowd of hundreds of others.

I can't believe I was so worried. If the masks stay on all night, I'll have no comparisons to other girls. It'll just be me and Jett.

Jett looks handsome as hell in his black, form-fitting tux. His mask is the male version of mine, so we match perfectly. It's taking everything I have not to shove him in a corner and make out all night. That would just be rude to our guests, right?

We sit at a table with other anonymous people and enjoy a dinner of salmon, wild rice and delicious veggies. Then, we walk around and mingle, and Jett eats something off every tray of finger foods we pass.

I spot Becca standing hear Park, her gorgeous red dress like a spotlight on her.

We walk over and she recognizes me too, since we both helped each other get dressed.

"Having fun?" she asks, taking another sip of her champagne.

"Lots." In fact, my cheeks hurt from how much I'm smiling. I can't help myself. It's like a beautiful fairy tale in here.

Jett pulls me onto the dance floor, and although I'm horribly self-conscious and shy, he leans in and whispers, "No one knows who you are."

His words are like a magic spell that brings out the dancer in me. We twirl and glide and hold each other close, our bodies moving to the beat of the music.

My waist starts to vibrate and I realize it's my phone. I had slipped it into the hidden dress pocket before I left my house, just in case I wanted to take pictures of anything. Now that I remember it's here, I take it out and ignore the phone call. It's a random number I don't know, so it's probably a telemarketer.

"Smile!" I say, holding it out and snapping a photo of Jett and me. Though our faces are covered, you can still see in our eyes and smiles that we're having a blast.

My phone rings again, vibrating with some unknown number. It's not even the same area code as the numbers around here I hit ignore and shove it back in my pocket.

Jett spies a tray of pigs-in-a-blanket, his favorite finger food, and scurries off to get some.

My phone vibrates again, only this time it's a text message.

Honey, please pick up.

What the hell? My hands turn to ice as I stare at the anonymous text message. Who else would call me *Honey*? Could it be her?

My throat goes dry. The phone begins to ring again. I catch Jett's attention as he shoves a finger food in his mouth and I point to the phone and then the door, letting him know I'm going to step outside to take this call.

Then my feet carry me as quickly as they can, through the blur of dancing strangers and out into the cool night air. I slide my finger across the answer key, and with a shaky hand, I bring the phone to my ear.

"Hello?"

"Keanna! My dear, how are you?"

My chest aches, but not from nostalgia. "I'm perfect."

I take a deep breath. All of the things I wanted to say in those first few weeks after she left me, all of the anger and betrayal I felt—I'm now just an empty shell of emotion. I can't be bothered to care anymore, so I keep my mouth shut.

"How are you, Dawn?" I ask.

"I'm okay, okay. But, I could use some money, dear."

I laugh out loud, a loud bark of sarcasm. "I don't have any money."

"No, dear, not from you of course. I mean from the Park's. Can you put Becca on the phone? I just need a small loan, or a gift, really. Just a few thousand dollars."

"You don't deserve anything," I say through gritted teeth. "Certainly not a gift."

"Keanna Byrd! How dare you speak like that!"

"My name is Keanna Park," I say, my breath coming out in little puffs of white air. "Don't call me again. You won't be getting any money from us."

"That is no way to speak to your mother," she hisses.

I clench the phone tightly to my ear. "You're right. But you are not my mother."

The cold air helps calm the anger that's coursing through my veins. I turn my phone completely off and then shove it back in my dress pocket. I will *not* let her ruin my New Year's Eve.

How could she even have the balls to call up out of the blue and ask for money? Seriously? She abandoned me. She let another couple legally adopt me without so much as telling me a final goodbye or that she loved me. But I've only ever been a burden to Dawn Byrd. Something she didn't want but couldn't find a way to get rid of until I was practically an adult.

I draw in a deep breath and turn back toward the party tent. I close my eyes and picture balling up all of this drama with my biological mother and throwing it in a trash. Then I tell myself I'll walk back into the party and I won't be pissed off anymore. I'll be over it. Because Dawn is not worth even two seconds of my time.

The tent is even more packed with guests now, happy drunken, dressed up guests. The music plays a lovely song, that has me swaying to the beat as I meander through the partiers, looking for my boyfriend.

Finally, I spot him, standing next to a tall cocktail table near one of the tent's clear fake windows. He's drinking a beer and talking with two guys who have put exactly zero thought into their masks.

As I make my way toward him, I see a girl in a skintight black mini dress, wearing the same black and gold eye mask as mine. I guess that's not too surprising; I'd gotten it at Charming Charlie, a fun girly store nearby.

She saunters up behind Jett, then taps him on the shoulder. Instinct has me annoyed, but I tell myself she doesn't know who he is—she's probably just being nice.

Wait.

What?

The whole room seems to blur into nothing as I watch the scene unfold. The girl, wearing my mask, taps his shoulder and he turns around. Then she grabs his face and pulls him into a kiss. She flings her body against his, grinding against him while she assaults his mouth with hers.

A pained gasp escapes my throat but the music is too loud for my pain to be heard. My legs keep walking somehow, and now I'm standing right in front of them. Jett's face scrunches beneath his mask and he pulls away, his lips turned into a scowl. The girl tries to grab him again but he looks up, almost confused.

Our eyes meet and I lift my mask off my face. A single tear rolls down my cheek as Jett makes the connection. The girl throwing herself on him is not me.

He shoves her back by the shoulder. "What the fuck?" he says, though it's barely audible.

The girl reaches for his hand and he yanks it away, then moves around the table to where I'm standing, still in shock.

"Baby, I'm so sorry," he says, his arm sliding around my waist. "I thought she was you."

"I know." I nod because my voice is too choked up to understand. "I saw it."

The mask girl twirls around, then puts her hands on her hips. Her blue eyes bore into mine and her lips twist into a smirk. "You're not good enough for him, you know."

"Who the fuck are you?" Without realizing it, I'd thrown my body forward to launch at her, but Jett holds me back.

"Don't, baby. It's not worth it."

"You're trash," she tells me, her voice confident. "He'll never be good enough for you."

"Get out of here," Jett tells her. He points to the door like she's a bad dog who lost her indoor privileges. "Go and don't come back."

My chest heaves and my hands are shaky. Without another word, I turn on my heel and rush out of the tent. I need air. Cold air, fresh air. Air away from all of these people.

I bump into a few shoulders but I don't care. Soon, I burst free from the tent and I'm in the dark, running into the parking lot. I make it all the way through the rows of cars until I'm standing near the road. The music is just a soft thumping sound in the distance. I am finally alone.

I pitch forward, resting my hands on my knees. This gravel parking lot has probably ruined my black velvet heels, but I don't care.

Between Dawn calling me for the first time in months, and seeing some bitch take advantage of my boyfriend and then tell me I'm not good enough—the one fear I can't ever seem to shake—I can't handle this.

I need to be alone. I need a moment to breathe.

"What's wrong there, girly?" The slurred male voice startles me. It seems to have appeared out of thin air.

"Nothing, I'm fine," I call out, without turning around. I stand and wipe the tears from my eyes as I gaze out the county road in front of me, the vast endless horse pastures beyond. The moon overhead casts a glow on a small pond in the distance.

"Looks like somethin's wrong," the guy says. He sounds closer.

"I'm fine, really." I wave a hand through the air. "You can leave."

A sweaty hand wraps around my wrist, pulling it behind my back. I stiffen, my entire body going into panic mode. Warm breath hits my ear. "You look like you could use some cheering up, darlin'."

My heart seizes in my throat. Another hand grabs my ass, squeezing it so hard I wince.

"Let me go," I say, my voice trembling. I need to run. But my feet won't move. I am stuck, dammit. I am frozen. *Move.*

I'm spun around against my will and a guy in his twenties, wearing ratty clothing and no mask at all gives me a look that chills me to the core. His grin is pure evil.

"What do we have here?" he says, his eyes roaming down my body. With a death grip on my wrist, his other hand grabs my boob.

"Get off me!" I yell, happy to have found my voice. I strain to move but he holds me against him, the air smelling like stale cigarettes and body odor.

He grabs my dress and pulls it up until my whole hip is exposed. I wriggle and struggle to get away but he's too strong. "You're a hot mess," he says, running his hand up my thigh.

Tears burn my eyes and I pull so hard it feels like my wrist is going to break. Good, I don't care. I just want away from this creep.

His rough hand inches up my thigh and I scream. I scream as loud as I can. His grip lessens and then he's throw backward.

Jett's mask flies to the ground and he plummets his fist into the guy's face, then kicks him right in the stomach, making him fall to the gravel.

"Call the police," Jett tells me, meeting my eyes for just a second before he unleashes on the guy, pounding his face into the ground. He flips him to his stomach and pulls his arms around his back. Jett's knee digs into his shoulder blades and he uses the guy's own arm to choke him.

I take out my phone and wait for it to power up, which seems to take forever. My fingers are shaky but I get the numbers pressed. I tell them I was attacked by a strange man.

Soon, police cars show up and the guy is arrested. It all happens so fast.

Jett talks to the officers and then they talk to me. It turns out the guy was home hobo and also a criminal. He wasn't invited to the party; he had just been passing by when he happened to see me walk to the road. He's assaulted women before. The police ask if I'd like to press charges.

Jett holds my hand and looks me in the eyes. "He shouldn't be allowed to hurt people and get away with it," he says.

I look to the officers. I tell them yes.

CHAPTER TWENTY-SIX

Jett

It feels out of place being so full of *rip-someone's-face-off* anger while wearing a fancy suit. Once the police leave, I can tell Keanna is still shaken up. If I hadn't arrived when I did—well, I can't think about that. I might actually rip someone's face off.

I can't believe my girl got attacked because of some bitch who tried to trick me into making out with her. If that hadn't happened, she would have never run outside, prompting me to look everywhere for her. That homeless criminal would have never gotten his hands on her.

My fist aches to punch something.

"You okay, son?" Dad's brows are pulled together. He's been out here since the police arrived, helping Keanna and me get through the whole ordeal. We'd insisted that everyone else stay at the party, keeping up the fun so that the whole night wouldn't be ruined.

I squeeze my shoulders together then relax them. "I guess. I'm just pissed."

"That's normal," he says, lowering his gaze on mine. "But you need to be strong for Keanna, okay? She'll probably be freaked out for a while."

He has no idea. Now not only does she have to deal with being groped by some asshole, she's also hurt from watching another girl kiss me. But Dad doesn't know that part and I have no intentions of telling him.

I nod once and let out the breath I'd been holding. Staying so pissed off won't help anything. "I need to find Keanna," I say. Dad steps out of the way and I walk over to where Mom and Becca are talking with her.

When she sees me, her sad eyes look straight into mine and she walks into my arms.

"Sorry for all the drama," she mumbles into my chest.

"You have nothing to be sorry about," I say, kissing the top of her head.

Becca and Mom watch me like I'm some kind of puppy or something. I don't think they'll ever treat me like an adult after seeing me as their kid for so long.

"Honey, ya'll take some time alone and if you feel like getting back to the party, we'll be here, okay?" Mom smiles and hands me my face mask. I don't know where I dropped it earlier, I only remember throwing it out of the way. Our two moms leave and then I'm left alone with my girl, near the entrance to the main tent.

"Can we just not talk about this anymore?" Keanna says, gazing up at me. Her eye makeup is all streaked from crying, but she lowers her mask back over her face, and now it doesn't matter. "I want to at least *try* to have some fun tonight."

My hands slide down her arms, my fingers weaving with her fingers. "Of course. It's almost midnight."

"Good," she says, rolling her eyes. "I am ready for this year to be over."

I chuckle. I want to kiss her so bad, but I'm not sure if that's the right move after she was just traumatized. The little box in my jacket pocket is burning a hole in me. This was supposed to be a magical party full of love and romance, where I gave her this gift under a moonlit night of perfection. Instead, it's all kind of gone to hell.

But maybe I can still salvage the night.

"Will you walk with me?" I ask, holding out my elbow like they did in the old fashioned movies.

She links her arm in mine. "I don't see the harm in walking when I have you with me."

I grin. "Nothing will ever happen to you when you're with me."

Her head rests against my arm as we walk through the party, then head outside near the bleachers. I consider bringing her out to the back of the track where we had that picnic one time, but it's too dark and we're not wearing the right clothes for a dirt bike ride. I think the bleachers will have to do.

I glance behind us to ensure that we're alone. The party rages on behind us, everyone keeping inside the tents because that's where the portable heaters and booze are.

"So," I say, swallowing. There was a whole speech I'd had planned out, an entire thing. I've been reciting it in the shower for a week and yet now, it's all gone. Not a single word remains in my memory. I look over at her, hoping to glean some inspiration from her beautiful face.

Only, she's crying.

I stop just short of the first row of bleachers. "Baby, why are you crying? Is it because of that asshole, because he's going to be locked up for a long time. Plus, we've got a restraining order—"

"No. It's not that. It's not him." She lifts her eye mask off her face and sets it on the bleachers, then she dries her eyes with the back of her hand.

"Can we sit?" she asks, gazing up at me with those innocent but pained eyes.

I sit on the bottom bleacher and she joins me, leaning toward me so that our knees touch. My heart thumps like a freaking jackhammer. I have no idea what she's going to say but it's terrifying.

She frowns and looks at her lap. "Earlier, before that girl—"

"Honey, I swear I had no idea she wasn't you at first. It was like two seconds and then I realized it. I shoved her away."

She shakes her head. "No, I know. I saw it all. That's not what I'm talking about."

Okay, now I'm even more freaked out. "Go on," I say. "Whatever's on your mind, I want to know."

She swallows and looks up at me. "Dawn called me today."

My jaw tightens. Of all the days to call the daughter you threw away, she had to pick this day? The last day of the year that I had planned to make special for my girlfriend.

"I know," Keanna says, after seeing my reaction. "And you know the worst part? She just wanted money. No apology, no asking how I'm doing. Just asking for money."

I take in a breath through my nose and let it out in a huff. "You are too good to be born to someone like that."

"I agree with you on that one," she says, making this sad little smile. "Even if I was really poor and alone and couldn't afford a kid. If I *had* one, I'd love it and take care of it. I know I would. I don't know how anyone could put their own happiness over a child's. It's not like I *asked* to be born."

"You are not like her in any way." I bend down and kiss her. To my surprise, she takes my head in her hands and deepens the kiss.

"Now that's more like it," she says, grinning as she pulls away. "Only my lips get to touch yours."

"You seem a little happier now." I take her hand and bring it up to my lips.

She nods. "I don't really want to waste all this time talking about Dawn. I basically told her to fuck off and then I blocked her number, so we're good. I just wanted to let you know that it happened but now I want to forget all about it. Does that make me weird?"

"Not at all," I say. There's a loud cheering coming from the party so I check the time on my phone. "Two minutes until midnight."

"What is it you wanted to say?" Keanna asks, nudging me with her elbow.

I lick my lips. "How'd you know I wanted to say something?"

She gives me a look. "You were stuttering and tripping over your words the whole way over here, Jett. I'm not stupid."

I sigh and look up at the sky, gazing at the bright moon above us. "You are too smart for me," I say, shaking my head. "But, you're right. There is something I needed to say."

I know I shouldn't get down on one knee—this isn't exactly that kind of thing. But sitting on the bleachers feels weird, too.

"Keanna," I begin, as I stand and take her hands to pull her up next to me. "I have a present for you. It's more of a promise, really."

Her eyes widen in curiosity. The moonlight makes her look like a damn angel and in this moment, my chest hurts so bad. I am so lucky to have this girl in my life, to have her be mine. She loves me, and I love her.

Words pour of out me, and they aren't exactly like I'd rehearsed but I think they get the job done.

"You are my soulmate, Keanna Park. I love you and I love everything about you. In less than a minute, we're going to start a new year together, and I want you to know that this is the start of everything for us. Not just one year, but every year, forever." I reach into my pocket and take out the small box. "I know we're too young for actual marriage, so I'm doing something else." I open the box, and Keanna gasps. Tears fill her eyes, but for once tonight, they are good tears.

"This is a promise to you," I say, taking out the pink gold ring. Its heart-shaped diamond sparkles like crazy beneath the stars, and Keanna lifts a shaky hand to me so I can place the ring on her finger. "It's a promise that you'll always be mine, forever and ever, and that one day," I say, gazing into her eyes, "one day I'll marry you."

From back at the party, everyone begins the countdown to the New Year. "Ten . . . nine . . . eight!"

Keanna watches me with a look of awe. She looks at the ring on her finger and then throws her arms around me. "Thank you," she whispers.

"Four! Three!"

She pulls back and we gaze into each other's eyes while the crowd at the party counts down to zero. A roar of cheers bursts out and I kiss her, long and passionately, bringing us into the New Year in the most perfect way possible.

EPILOGUE

Five months later

I burst into the waiting room, startling not only Jett but the random couple in the corner. "Sorry," I say, giving them an apologetic wave. Then I dive straight toward Jett, who'd been sleeping in the uncomfortable hospital chair.

"He's here!" I say, unable to contain my excitement. "He's here, he's here, he's here!"

Jett rises and wraps me into a massive bear hug. Becca had insisted that I be in the delivery room with her and Bayleigh. Park and Jace decided to stand just outside the door so that the room wouldn't be too crowded, and Jett had kindly offered to sit in the waiting room. I think the idea of a baby being born is kinda gross to him.

"His name is Elijah," I say as I take Jett by the hand and pull him toward Bayleigh's delivery room. "And he's perfect. Absolutely perfect."

"Someone sounds like they're already an impeccable big sister," he says, bumping into me.

I can't stop my grin because I am truly so excited for my new family. We enter the room at the same time Park and Jace are leaving, both of them wearing these proud fatherly grins. There is so much more than friendship between these two married couples. It's like we're all one big family.

I poke my head in the room and Becca motions for us to enter. She's standing, holding her new baby in her arms. Bayleigh is in the hospital bed, looking tired yet somehow still radiant. Jett walks over and hugs his mom and then comes to see the baby.

"You're right," he says, watching Elijah with sense of pride in his eyes. "This is one adorable baby."

"Thank you, dear," Becca says. She kisses her newborn on the forehead and then turns to me and smiles. "Last year I had no kids and now I have two."

The way she says it brings tears to my eyes. I lean against her and watch my baby brother, who is fast asleep. He hasn't even been on earth a whole hour yet, and here I am feeling more love than I'd ever known was possible. I know for a fact that I'll never let anything or anyone hurt this little guy.

Later, Park brings in an enormous amount of Chinese takeout and we all sit around Bayleigh's hospital room and eat it, family style.

"So was it easier or harder having a baby the second time?" Jett asks his mom.

She considers it for a moment, her egg roll dangling over the sweet and sour sauce. "You know, I think it was easier. But only because I wanted to do a really good job for my best friend. I wasn't about to let this labor take forever," she says with a laugh. "I wanted Becca to get her son ASAP."

Becca laughs and Elijah yawns from his clear plastic nursery bed.

"Are you already tired, little man?" Jett asks him. He looks up at Park. "We need to get your kid in shape if we want to make him the next motocross superstar," he says with a smirk.

Park nods. "I made an appointment with his personal trainer for tomorrow morning."

Becca swats at her husband. "Oh hush."

"So," Bayleigh says, looking over at Jace. "We have a little announcement for you all."

Jace hurries to finish his bite of food and then gets up and sits next to her on the hospital bed. "Are you telling them or should I?"

They stare at each other for a moment, lost in their own little world. Finally, Bayleigh grins. "I'll do it." Then she turns to us, her smile stretching across her whole face. "We want to have another baby!"

Stunned silence fills the room and then Becca breaks into a cheer. "Oh my God! We'll have babies at the same time!"

"I know," Bayleigh says, a child-like excitement on her face. "I figure our two older kids are all grown up now, so why not?"

"I am so excited," Becca says, clasping her hands in front of her chest.

"Keanna," Bayleigh says, looking at me. She points her fork between Jett and me. "You two need to figure out your wedding dates because I refuse to be pregnant and fat at the wedding, okay? We need to work around it."

My cheeks flush. I glance down at my promise ring, a gorgeous piece of jewelry that probably cost more than most people's engagement rings. "Um," I say, but Bayleigh waves a hand at me.

"Don't play cool, girlfriend. We all know you and my son are meant to be together. Hell, Becca and I have practically planned your whole wedding already."

I turn to the left and bury my face into Jett's shoulder. My cheeks are so red hot right now I'm afraid they'll get a third-degree burn.

"Don't worry," Jett says, patting my back. "The first thing we'll do after we get married is move far *far* away from these lunatics."

"HA!" Bayleigh says. "Keanna's not going anywhere, son. She loves us. Isn't that right, Becca?"

"It's right," Becca says, giving me a wink. "You're stuck with us forever, Jett."
"Yep," Bayleigh says. "Forever."

BELIEVE IN LOVE

A BELIEVE IN LOVE SHORT STORY

CHAPTER ONE

Keanna

There's only one sound worse than the high-pitched wail of my phone's morning alarm when I don't feel like waking up. It's the high-pitched wail of my little brother.

I roll over in bed and pull my pillow around my ears, trying to drown out the sound of his screaming. Elijah is six months old now, and Becca says he's going through a colic phase, whatever the hell that is. I actually Googled colic and discovered it's this weird phenomenon where babies will just cry and cry for no freaking reason. As if babies didn't cry all the time for specific reasons, like they're hungry or need a new diaper or they're sleepy, let's add some pointless crying!

Ugh.

My curtains are drawn, but when it's time to wake up, I can usually tell because the sun will slip through and light up my room like a second unwanted morning alarm. This means I still have time to sleep before the worst day ever. My first semester of community college was not as great as I'd hoped it would be. All I'm taking are Gen Ed classes, the supposedly "easy" classes for a first year college student.

They are so not easy. They were miserable.

Becca says my mom is to blame for my education, or my lack of education, rather. She means my real mom—the biological one named Dawn, the woman who abandoned me at Becca's house two years ago. I've stopped trying to care about the *whys* of my mother's thinking, and now I just don't care at all. She left me with a stranger and promised to come back and then she never did. Becca and her husband Park ended up adopting me even though I was nearly an adult. Now I have two loving parents and none of them have tried to abandon me at a stranger's house.

I also have a brand new little brother, and right now he's driving me insane. The pillow-over-the-ears trick isn't working. If I squeeze my fingers against my ears and then bury my head in my pillow, it helps a little. But there's no way I can go to sleep like this, keeping pressure on my ears.

With a sigh, I lower my hands and the sounds of Elijah's colic crying fills the room again. Why hasn't Becca gotten him yet? Normally she's up and down the hall to the nursery just seconds after he wakes up.

With the crying still loud as ever, I give up on the idea that I might fall back asleep soon, and check my phone. It's half an hour until I need to be up to head to the college. It's hard enough getting up at the normal time, and this baby waking me up is about a million times worse.

As I stare at my phone screen, I try to take a deep breath and relax a little. I'm so stressed for my history and English final today, but staring at the picture of Jett and me on my phone's home screen helps a little.

I really do have the hottest boyfriend ever, even in pixel form.

I smile and look down at my ring, a pink gold promise ring Jett gave me last New Year's. It is so beautiful it usually always makes me feel better when I look at it, and right now is no exception.

Elijah is still screaming. It's seven thirty, so I guess Park is probably at work now. Still, this is so unlike Becca. She's the world's greatest mom. I'm surprised the *Guinness Book of World Records* hasn't stopped by to give her a plaque for her excellent parenting.

With a sigh, I throw my blanket to the side and get out of bed, yawning so hard it hurts my jaw. Even though Jett purposely ended our date night early last night so I could get sleep and be rested up for my finals this morning, I didn't go to bed early.

I'd stayed up all night studying for these stupid exams. I think I'll be okay with English, but history is freaking hard. We have two hundred vocabulary words and fifty dates to memorize. The entire test is fill in the blank, not multiple choice. This is going to suck so bad. Even as I make my way down the hall and toward my parent's room, I'm still filled with anxiety over this stupid test.

I tap lightly on the door, but no one answers. Probably because Elijah is screaming his little baby head off in the room down the hall, so Becca can't hear anything.

I push open the door. "Becca?"

Now I know why she's not taking care of Elijah. She looks like shit. Her nose is all red and her eyes are puffy. She's sleeping with her mouth wide open because I'm guessing she can't breathe through her nose. There's cold medicine on the nightstand and a box of tissues next to it.

I walk in. "Becca," I say louder. "Are you okay?"

She startles, slowly opening her eyes. "Hey," she says just before she starts coughing. Her brows pull together. "Is the baby crying?"

"Yeah, but you look awful," I say, taking a step back. "Are you contagious?"

She shrugs and reaches for a tissue. "I think it's just a cold, so I probably am. This sucks, getting sick three days before Christmas."

I really, really, want to go back to sleep and be as rested as possible for my exams today. But I can't let Becca risk getting the baby sick, especially not on his first Christmas. "You stay in bed," I say. "I'll go take care of Elijah."

She puts a hand on her heart. "You're the best, sweetheart."

"I know, I know," I say as I step back into the hallway, closing the door behind me to keep all of her sick germs inside. I peek out the window and see that Park's truck is over at the Track next door.

My adopted parents own a motocross track with their best friends, who happen to be my boyfriend's parents. They're all big into dirt bike racing and so owning the business was a way to turn their passion into a career. The Track, with its very simplistic name, is situated right between our two houses.

Back when my real mom dropped me off at Becca's house for the night, she'd promised to come get me the next day. But she never came back, and I didn't care because by then I'd met the boy next door. Jett Adams is a dirt bike racer just like his dad was back in the day. He's hot, sweet, and talented on a dirt bike. And now he's all mine.

I smile as I head to Elijah's nursery. The room is decked out in a jungle theme, with little monkeys and bears all over the place. Elijah's chubby face is red from crying, and he doesn't even care when I enter the room. That's the thing about colic—he just wants to cry when he's having a colic episode. On normal days, he brightens when someone comes to get him.

"Hey there, butt face," I say, whispering the last part. I don't know how much babies pick up on when they're this young. I change his diaper and get him dressed in a really cute outfit of tiny little baby jeans and a blue button up shirt. He looks like a miniature version of his dad.

He finally stops crying after a while, and although I'm tired as hell, I make my way to the kitchen and heat up a bottle for him. I sit on a barstool and hold him in my lap while he drinks his bottle. When he's almost finished, I glance at the clock on the wall.

Shit.

It was time for me to get ready for school five minutes ago. Now I'm late. "Oh my god," I groan, as I toss the bottle in the sink.

"Come on, baby, we gotta go." I hoist Elijah up and pat his back to get him to burp. Since Becca is sick, I plan on taking him next door so Jett's mom can watch him today. Luckily, the Track is closed this week since it's the week of Christmas so none of us have to work. If only the college had that same courtesy, but no, they schedule finals three days before the freaking birth of Christ.

Finally, Elijah burps. Warm goo rolls down my fingers and I cringe as I hold the baby up to my eye level. It wasn't just a burp; it was one of those throw up burps. Now white gunk is spilling all over his new outfit and all through my fingers.

I groan. I'm late enough as it is. Now I have to clean up both of us.

In a rush, I jog back to Elijah's room and change him into a new outfit, shoving supplies into his baby bag while he wriggles around on the changing table. Then I go back to my room and grab my backpack, cell phone, and car keys.

"Taking the baby to Bayleigh!" I call out to my mom as I run by. I'm not sure if she heard me, but she's probably too sick to care.

Outside, the cool December air chills my bones as I run the distance between the Adams' house and mine. Elijah is all warm in his jacket as I clutch him to my chest, but I forgot to grab one for myself so I'm kind of freezing.

Bayleigh, Jett's mom, is hanging out in the kitchen when I get to their back door. She smiles and opens it for me since my hands are full.

"Good morning," she says, sipping her coffee. "What's up?"

"Becca is sick," I say, holding out Elijah. "Can you watch him while I go take my finals?"

She sets her coffee mug on the counter and reaches for the baby. "It'd be my pleasure," she says, grinning and making baby faces at him.

"Thanks," I say, as I heave a sigh. "I'll be gone about four hours and then I'll come get him, unless Park gets back sooner."

"I wouldn't count on it," Bayleigh says as she holds Elijah on her hip. "The guys are planning for some race thing next door. It'll take all day, knowing them." She coos at Elijah.

"Are you sure you want that thing in your stomach?" I say with a laugh. Bayleigh is four months pregnant herself. "Babies suck."

She laughs. "They can sometimes suck, but the good parts are worth the sucky parts."

"Hey there," Jett calls out as he enters the room. "I didn't know you were coming over."

He's shirtless, wearing only a pair of flannel pajama bottoms. My boyfriend is so very hot, and it takes all my willpower to pull my gaze away from his six-pack abs. "I'm not here," I say, turning away. "Pretend you didn't me. I'm in a huge hurry."

The smell of Jett's cologne fills the air as he wraps his arms around me. "Yeah, that's not gonna happen."

CHAPTER TWO

Jett

I bury my face into Keanna's hair, inhaling the scent of her green apple shampoo. I can't ever get enough of this girl, and now she's pulling away from me. So not fair.

"Babe, I have to go." She meets my gaze with a serious look in her eyes.

Mom takes Keanna's little brother into the other room, cooing at him and telling him how cute he is. I swear it's like Elijah is the only important one when he's around.

"What's wrong?" I say, sliding my hands around Keanna's back and tugging her close while I kiss her neck. "You want some coffee?"

"No, Jett. Dammit." She pushes me away, an action that makes my chest hurt. With a huff, she tucks a strand of brown hair behind her ear. "I have to go. I have finals today!"

She says it like I'm an idiot for not remembering. But of course, I remember. She's been freaking out about them all week. "I'm sorry," I say, not because I forgot but because I didn't realize she'd be so mad at me. "I'll walk you out."

"You don't have to," she says, rushing to the back door. "It's cold outside and you're half naked."

"You like it when I'm half naked," I say, wiggling my eyebrows.

She's not having any of my joking around today. She rolls her eyes. "Bye."

"I love you!" I call after her as she slips through the back door.

"Love you too," she says back, but there's no heart in it.

I know she's just stressed, so I try not to let it hurt my feelings. Also, there's this part of me that's saying I should suck it up and be manly and stop longing after my girlfriend when she's busy. But I'd be lying if I said I'm not considering running after her just to get a kiss.

I look out the glass door and watch her sprint across the parking lot of the Track next door, all the way back to her house. I keep watching, leaning on the glass, wishing there was a way I could make her feel better.

We'd gone out on a date last night, but she barely touched her food. Afterwards, instead of making out on my bed like we usually do, she'd insisted that I help her study for her finals today. It was a buzzkill to say the least. Maybe that's why I want so desperately to get a kiss this morning. I miss her normally happy and affectionate demeanor. Now these stupid exams have taken over her life. I know she's stressed, but she'll be okay. She knew all of her flash cards. The only time she messes up on a test is when she lets the stress get to her head.

I watch her pick up her backpack from the concrete near her car, a sporty Mustang. She tosses it in the backseat and then disappears inside the car.

I decide I'll rush back to my room, find my phone and send her a sweet text, telling her she'll ace her exam. That'll cheer her up. Smiling, I watch as she puts the car in reverse, going entirely too fast.

Her Mustang slides off the concrete driveway and into the grass. Only it's been raining like crazy lately, and the grassy area next to the driveway is all mud. The rear tire sinks and the car jolts to a stop. It's tilted at an angle, half of the car on the driveway and half stuck in the mud. Even from here, I can tell her back tire is spinning out as she anxiously tries to reverse, but all she's doing is getting stuck deeper.

I don't even stop think that it's cold as hell outside as I slip on a pair of flip flops my dad left by the back door and rush out to save her.

CHAPTER THREE

Keanna

This is so not happening. No, no, no. I slam on the gas again, but my car just revs up and doesn't go anywhere. Only two tires are off the concrete at this point, so why isn't it working? Fighting back tears, I open my door and look out. There's mud everywhere.

The whole grassy section of the yard is now a muddy swamp that's swallowing my car's back tire whole.

Ugh.

My whole body shakes. I am freaking out to epic proportions and I can't even find a way to breathe normally. I'll have to take Becca's car, and she won't mind because she's sick. Park might be pissed about the muddy ruts in the grass, but he'll get over it. Right now, the only thing that matters is getting to class on time. If I'm even five minutes late, I'll be kicked out of class and won't get to take the final. There's no way I'll pass the class without that grade.

I squeeze over the center console and flop myself into the passenger seat so I can get out of the car on the side that's not muddy. On the way over, I bang my elbow, knees, and head in this stupidly small car. Why was I so stupid when I bought this thing? I should have gotten something that could tear through mud with no problem, like a Jeep or a big truck, instead of this showoff sports car.

I really do hate everything today.

Climbing out of the passenger side, I reach in the backseat for my stuff. That's when I hear someone approaching.

My boyfriend, the dumbass who must want to get sick. He's wearing flip flops, his pajama bottoms, and still no shirt. He might as well go hang out with Becca and they can both be sick in there together.

"You trying to get phenomena?" I say as sarcastically as I can manage as I wrangle my backpack from the tiny backseat. Seriously, screw this car. Screw this driveway, and this college and everything. I hate it all.

"I came to help," Jett says, leaning over the safety of the concrete to see the damage done. "I'll grab a piece of wood from the garage and we can wedge you out of there."

He doesn't even seem to notice the cold as he rubs his chin, assessing the situation. "Shouldn't take more than ten minutes."

"I don't have ten minutes!" I say, throwing my hands in the air. "I have to go *now.*"

"Then I'll drive you," Jett says, smiling at me with this little eager grin of his. Normally I think his grin is cute. Right now, I kind of hate it.

"If you had your truck right now, that would be great, but you don't, so go back home."

He frowns, stepping in front of me as I try to push past him. "My truck is thirty seconds away. I'll go get it."

"I don't have thirty seconds," I snap, moving to the right. He takes one stride over, blocking me.

"Babe, calm down. It's going to be okay. I'm not even sure you should be driving right now since you're so upset."

I sigh. "Get out of my way. I need to get Becca's car keys."

Jett puts his hands on his hips. "Keanna, talk to me."

My nostrils flare. Can't he see I'm late as hell? "Go. Away."

He shakes his head, standing there all stubborn and sexy, bare chested in the freezing cold. "You're being an idiot," I say. "A good boyfriend would just leave me alone."

"Maybe," he says, once again blocking me as I try to slip around him. He takes my shoulders in his hands, his eyes crinkling in the corners. "But a *fantastic* boyfriend would figure out what's bothering his girlfriend and try to make it better. I like to think I'm much better than a good boyfriend."

"You know what's bothering me?" I shout, louder than necessary. He flinches, but keeps his hands on my shoulders.

I grit my teeth together. "My stupid ass final bothers me. College in general bothers me because it's too hard and I have no idea what I want to do with my life."

His eyes soften, but I'm so pissed, I don't care. I swing a finger toward my car. "My stupid car is stuck in the mud so I hate it, and I hate this driveway and I hate this house and I really hate being woken up too early by a stupid baby that cries for no damn reason!"

"Keanna, you don't mean that," Jett says softly. His fingers slide down my arms, and when he tries to take my hands, I yank away violently, fixing him with a stare.

"Yes, I do mean it. I mean all of it. And if you don't want to join the long list of shit I hate, you'll get the hell out of my way. How are you going to feel if I fail my final because you made me late?"

"Baby, the class starts in forty-five minutes and it takes fifteen to drive there."

I grit my teeth. He doesn't realize the plan for today is to get there an hour early to study, because if I don't study, I'll fail and if I fail, I'll waste my parent's tuition money and I'll be an utter failure at the easiest possible part of college there is.

"I don't feel like talking right now, Jett. You need to leave."

He steps forward, tilting his head. "Not until you start feeling better." He runs a hand down my hair, a gesture that usually turns me to putty in his arms, but right now I'm just too furious to care. I let the chill in the air turn me as frozen as my heart feels right now.

"Baby, I know you're stressed, but you're going to be fine. I promise. You know this stuff because we studied it all night."

"An exam is a lot harder than studying on a futon," I mutter.

He shakes his head. "You'll ace your exams. Both of them. I promise." He grins. "If not, you can punch me right in the face."

I roll my eyes. "Can I punch you now? Like fifty times?"

He lifts an eyebrow. "Why fifty times?"

"Because I hate everything!" I yell.

He frowns. "You don't hate me. You don't hate Elijah."

"That's not entirely true," I say, interrupting him. "I do hate that baby. He ruined my morning. And I'm starting to hate you because you're ruining my day even more than the baby did."

"Keanna, you can't possibly mean that."

He's right. Deep down, I don't. But that part of my body isn't in control right now. Right now, I'm just hot rage and anger and resentment, all bubbling up and boiling over in my heart. "You need to go," I say again.

"Keanna, we're family. Elijah, Becca, Park, my parents and me. We're all family and we're here for you. I wish you'd realize that instead of shoving us all away."

I press my lips together. I know I'll regret it, but like I said, the good part of my brain isn't in charge right now.

"Yeah? Well my life was a hell of a lot easier when I didn't *have* a family."

"You don't mean that," Jett says, his dark gaze peering into mine.

I press my palm to his cold chest and push him away. "Yes, I do. My life would be so much easier without all of this crap."

CHAPTER FOUR

Jett

My body wakes up slowly. I yawn and stretch out and roll over, keeping my eyes closed until the sunlight from my window gets bright enough to make me open them. It takes me a second to remember it's the week of Christmas so work is closed and school is out. Man, it's rare that I get to sleep in late like this. It feels amazing, even though I do feel a little weird for some reason.

I sit up in bed and rub my eyes. I think about how cool it would have been to get sponsored by Team Loco last year, if only I'd done better in the qualifying races.

Ugh.

I could have gotten out of high school early and then every non-race day could have been *sleep in late* day. I'll probably never stop kicking myself for ruining that sponsorship. Dad says there's still time, I'm still young enough to work hard and find another one.

I really hope he's right, because I don't know what else I'd do with my life without motocross. I guess I'd try to settle down and find a girlfriend—if any girl would have me after the reputation I've earned over the years.

With a sigh, I try to capture the remaining bits of a dream I had just before I woke up. I can't remember it really—but it felt like I was happy. I had a girlfriend, no—she was more than that. She had chestnut brown hair and the most gorgeous smile, and she was mad at me, I think.

I guess that makes sense...even in my dreams, I can't be happy in a relationship. With a sigh, I shake away the feeling and reach for my phone. I have three new messages from three different girls. I don't even bother reading them because those girls aren't exactly hot or appealing.

Before I set my phone down, I stare at the background image. It's just my dirt bike, the same as it always is—but something feels off. It feels—well, like I'm forgetting something. But I don't know what. Maybe I shouldn't have slept so damn late this morning. It's screwing with my head.

My parents are still asleep as I make my way downstairs. I don't bother disturbing them because I'm sure they're also grateful that our family business is closed all week for the holidays.

It's December 23rd, or Christmas Eve *eve* as my mom always says. It's also the day before my birthday. Due to some unfortunate timing on my parents' part, I was born just a few hours before Christmas day. It kind of sucks because people think it's some novelty to be born on a holiday, or they just get me one gift and say it's for both events. Lame.

When I was a kid, my parents would throw me a party in the summer, that way I could enjoy my birthday like a normal kid. Now I don't really care too much.

I just want to ride my dirt bike and be left alone.

So, that's exactly what I do. The family business has three dirt bike tracks in the lot next to our house. We teach motocross lessons and have races on occasion. I head out to the garage and hop on my bike, then take it around the track for a few laps. When I'm out here, just me and my bike on the dirt, I'm perfect. It doesn't matter that I don't have a girlfriend, it doesn't matter that I'm pretty sure I'm broken and will never be able to find the kind of love my parents have for each other. All that matters is the bike, and the dirt. And the air that's all around me as I'm soaring over a jump.

After a few hours, the sun is really beating down, even for December. I head back to the garage and grab a water from the fridge. I hear her footsteps before I see her, and it takes everything I have not to groan.

Emma Clarke walks like she's a princess. I know she does it on purpose. No one naturally takes these little prissy steps to announce their arrival. That is not just a girl thing. It's an Emma thing.

Emma is hot, don't get me wrong, but I'm so sick of her. She's never sick of me, though. She's always around, always dressed in something slutty and wearing a ton of makeup. She refuses to let me go, and sometimes I fear I'll end up settling down with her just because there's nothing else going for me in life. I didn't get that sponsorship, after all.

"Hey there," Emma says, sauntering into the garage. Her blonde hair is pulled back in a ponytail and she's wearing skin tight jeans with a tank top that shows off how well her push up bra works. I don't know who she thinks she's fooling—after having seen those boobs in real life, they are not that big.

"What's going on?" I say, ducking into the fridge to get another water.

"Just wanted to come hang out with my favorite motocross guy," she says, her voice all flirty.

She walks up and slides her hand down my chest, even though I'm pretty sure my dirt bike jersey is covered in sweat. "I freaking love your abs," she says, looking up at me with a desire in her eyes. "You want to go watch a movie in your room?"

That is Emma Clarke speak for want to go *hook up in your room?*

On any other day, I'd probably jump at the chance, because what else is there to do? But today I'm feeling weird. I'm still strung out over that weird dream, I guess. There's this little flicker in my chest that burns with the pain of having lost something. I just don't know what that something is.

"I don't know, I'm kind of tired," I say.

"It's only two in the afternoon, you weirdo." She laughs and takes my hand. "You're not tired! Come on, let's go get you in the shower."

She drags me back to my house. Mom is making a sandwich in the kitchen. "Hi, Mrs. Adams!" Emma cheerfully says.

"Hello," Mom says pointedly, looking at me. She's not a fan of Emma.

Probably because Emma's one of those girls out there for motocross fame. As soon as some other guy comes along who's better than me, she'll be gone. I give Mom this look like I'm helpless and let Emma lead me up to my room.

I mean really, it's not like I have anything else to do. Too bad I can't stop thinking of that girl from my dream. But dreams are just that—dreams, and this is reality.

CHAPTER FIVE

Keanna

My neck hurts. I wince as I try to lift up, but the pain is so bad I just give up and plop back down on my pillow. Well, it's not really a pillow. It's a sweater I rolled up into a makeshift pillow. It's normally pretty cold sleeping in Dawn's car, but last night I got hot because I'm wearing several layers. Pretty much everything I own.

"Mom?" I call out, my voice raspy from hours of sleep. She doesn't reply, so she must not be up front. I honestly don't know how she sleeps in the driver's seat of her car. She claims that years of doing it has made it comfortable for her, but I don't know if she's telling the truth or just pretending she is. My mother is very good and pretending things are fine when they're not.

I sit up in the back seat and rub my neck. Another night sleeping in the car in a parking lot. The car is starting to smell—or maybe I am. I can only get so clean in the bathrooms of department stores and Walmarts.

After rubbing my neck, I look down at my hands. I have no jewelry. Obviously I don't—we would have pawned it for cash a long time ago. Still, I can't stop staring at my ring finger, feeling like something is...missing.

Weird.

After stretching a little, I climb out of the car, squinting in the harsh sunlight. It's cool out here, but not nearly as cool as some of the other places we've been. We're in Texas, I think. Mom and I are nomads. We travel around selling Mom's crafts at craft fairs or wherever she can set up a table. We never stay anywhere very long, but we usually do have a place to stay.

But after the car broke down and Mom had to spend eight hundred dollars to fix it, we no longer had any deposit money to find a cheap apartment. So, we've been in the car for a couple of months now, the awfulness broken up by one or two nights a week when we can afford to stay in a motel. Now we're going on fourteen days of not having a motel. I would kill for a hot shower and a shitty cheap mattress right about now.

I make my way toward the grocery store. It's not a chain, but instead it's some small family owned place. The managers agreed to let Mom set up a table near the front doors to sell her crafts. Normally people tell us no if we're not selling stuff for a real charity, but with it being two days until Christmas, I guess they felt bad for us.

Mom's crafts are beautiful though. She makes windchimes from colored broken glass and other materials we find on the streets, in dumpsters, or at thrift stores. It's rustic and vintage and colorful and rich people pay a lot of money for something they can say was made by a real artist.

"Took you long enough," Dawn says, her upper lip curling as she watches me approach. She's my mom, but she's Dawn in my head. A long time ago I decided a woman who can't provide a normal home for their kid isn't really worth the title of "mom", but of course I still call her that to her face or I'd get a slap across the cheek.

"Sorry," I say, sitting on top of her ice chest as I rub my neck. She has a table set up and it looks quite nice. She's found clothing racks on wheels to use to hang up the windchimes. They sell a lot better when they're hanging up and people can see them in action, versus when they're flat on a table.

Mom sips a cup of coffee, and I eye it enviously. She groans, then reaches inside her pocket and hands me a five dollar bill. "Go get something to eat," she says. "There's a little café inside the grocery store. Pretty good coffee."

I brighten, because we haven't had real food in a while. Stale pop tarts and granola bars do not count as real food in my opinion.

The grocery store is really cute. It has a country store type of vibe, I guess. There's a little café in the corner, with places to sit. It's not terribly cold outside, but I order a coffee and a bacon, egg, and cheese biscuit and sit at a table waiting for it to be ready. It feels nice being inside a real building. I'm so sick of sitting outside selling stuff with Dawn, only to go back into a car at night. I say a little prayer that we sell enough things today to get a hotel tonight, or maybe on Christmas night. That would be nice.

The food is totally divine. I have to force myself to eat slower than I want to, otherwise I'd down my breakfast in two seconds flat and be wishing I had more. I can tell that people around me are avoiding me like they would a creepy homeless person. Sadly, I guess I am homeless, but I'm not creepy. I'm not addicted to drugs or alcohol. I'm just poor as hell.

With a sigh, I stare at my left hand as I sip what's left of my coffee. I've never had a ring before. So why does it feel like I'm missing one?

I shake my head. Ugh, that's so weird. Then my hand goes up to my neck and slides across my collarbone. I don't have a necklace, either, but it almost feels like maybe I dreamt that I did. It'd have a heart on it. I think. I'd like a necklace like that, if someone special gave it to me.

A wave of stress rolls over me. Stress like I've never felt before—not the normal worries of where we'll sleep or what we'll eat—but stress like a normal person would have. School, work, family.

Heh.

What is wrong with me? I shake it off and head outside, where Dawn is selling a beautiful piece to an older couple. This one took her hours to make, using wire-wrapped colorful glass and stones. That thing also had a price tag of eighty dollars on it.

She thanks the customers and then beams at me. "I sold the big one!"

I give her a high five. "Does that mean we'll get a hotel tonight?"

She scowls. "I thought you wanted an apartment."

"I do," I say, blinking. "I definitely do."

"Well, apartments need money, and we won't have any if we spend it all on stupid hotels!"

I frown. "But—Mom. Some places only charge twenty dollars a night. I know they're shitty, but I could really use a hot shower and a real bed."

"Sometimes you're so ungrateful," Mom says, shaking her head. "We only need about a thousand dollars more and we'll have enough for those low-income apartments we found a few weeks ago, baby. You have to pay the first and last month's rent up front, but then monthly it's only three hundred dollars. You can't beat that. So, we'll just tough it out a little longer and hope these people want to buy our stuff for Christmas presents, okay?"

I nod even though I'd rather cry. If we didn't move around so much, we could have a home. A real one. "Okay."

"Good," Mom says, rolling her eyes. "All I want for Christmas is a daughter who won't be grumpy all the damn time."

And all I want for Christmas is a roof over my head, if only for one night.

But I don't say that out loud, of course. I just rub my thumb across my ring finger and wonder why it feels so empty today when it's been empty my whole life.

CHAPTER SIX

Jett

Something is definitely wrong. I can't put my finger on it, and there's a chance I might just be going crazy, but something feels off. Like this isn't supposed to be my life.

It's dark, and the TV has been on a straight Netflix binge of some stupid show Emma likes but I can't for the life of me figure out why. The characters are bitchy, and they're not even that hot. The sole purpose of the show seems to be taking advantage of men every chance they get.

Maybe it's because I haven't been watching the show that my mind is wandering around, wondering why I feel so weird. Beside me, Emma clears her throat. When I ignore her, she does it again.

"Uh, hello?"

"What?" I say, looking over. She's relaxed on the couch in my living room, her feet in my lap. I hate when she does this, but I'm not a jerk so I don't ever make her move her stupid feet.

"It's like really late," Emma says, sitting up a little. She leans forward so her boobs are on display and then she does her classic pout face.

"You want to go home?" I ask.

She rolls her eyes. "It's *late*," she says, emphasizing the last word. "Your parents are already in bed." She folds her arms across her chest. "So why haven't we gone to your bedroom yet?"

"We're not dating," I say. Honestly, I can't really remember what we are, but I'm pretty sure we're *not* boyfriend and girlfriend. The look on her face tells me I'm right.

"No, Jett. We don't date because that's our agreement. But we *do* go up to your room at night." She leans forward and runs a finger down my chest, leaning in so close I can smell her powdery perfume. "So why are you making me wait so long?"

"Maybe you should go home."

She flinches. "But it's almost midnight. I was going to give you your birthday present."

I lift an eyebrow. "Do you really have a present?"

She grins and rubs her hand across my thigh. "It's a present with my mouth," she whispers.

I distinctly remember buying her a fifty-dollar lipstick from the mall for her birthday a few months ago. She demanded that I get her a present even though we're just friends with benefits. My stomach tightens and although I'm a dude with needs, this just doesn't feel right.

I sit up straighter. "You should go, Emma. I'll walk you to your car."

IN THE MORNING, I WAKE UP WITH ANOTHER WEIRD FEELING LIKE SOMETHING IS wrong. My phone glows in the dim light of my bedroom, the screen telling me it's my birthday because a ton of my friends have already texted me.

Still, I feel off. Like there's a huge part of me missing and I can't remember what part it is. Maybe I'm going crazy. Wouldn't that be something for the dirt bike magazines to write about? *Jett Adams goes totally insane on his birthday.*

Mom's in the kitchen making breakfast. The smell of bacon and maple syrup fill the air and make my mouth water. Mom is a great cook and I always get a huge breakfast for my birthday. It's my favorite part of turning a year older.

Dad's in the living room messing with the TV, because apparently the cable has gone out again. "Happy Birthday!" he calls out as I walk by.

Mom pulls me into a hug and pats the top of my head, even though I'm taller than she is now. "Happy birthday, son." Her eyes crinkle in the corners and she stares at me for a minute. "I'm really proud of you."

I'm not sure why. I'm not sponsored, I'm not enrolled in college yet. I'm kind of a loser. But I don't say any of that because I know she'd only disagree with me and list off all these reasons she thinks I'm great even though I'm not. Moms are like that, though. They love you like crazy even if you suck.

I eat entirely too much food for breakfast, but it's worth it because it tastes so good. Just as we're finishing up, the doorbell rings. Most of our close friends come to the back door instead of the front. "I'll get it," I say, figuring it'll be for me.

It's Jacey, my old friend with benefits. I haven't really seen her in a while. Even though she's a little chubby and not as hot as Emma, she's actually nice. That makes her more beautiful, actually.

"Hey," I say, not even faking my smile when I see her. "Want to come in?"

"Sure," she says, holding out a shiny red gift bag filled with blue tissue paper. "I wanted to come bring your birthday present."

"Jacey," I say, feeling a heat rise to my cheeks. "You didn't have to get me anything."

I've never gotten Jacey anything for her birthday, not in all the years I've known her. Now that I think about it, I don't even know when her birthday is.

She shrugs. "It's not that big of a deal. We've been friends for a while, so I care about you, man."

We go to the living room and I'm glad my parents are somewhere else, because opening presents in front of an audience is weird. Inside the package is a shiny new copy of the next Motocross Madness Xbox game.

"No way," I say, grinning wide. "This is amazing. Thank you." I pull her into a hug and she's so warm and smells good. She's the total opposite of Emma in every way.

There's this second where our eyes meet and time feels all squishy and weird. Finally, she breaks the silence.

"I've missed you."

I frown. "I miss you, too. You should come over more."

She chuckles. "I'm not exactly allowed to now that your little girlfriend is always here."

"Emma? She is not my girlfriend," I say, sticking out my tongue. "I'm actually trying to get rid of her."

This makes her laugh, but I think she's faking it. "Why? She's *soooo* pretty," she says, rolling her eyes.

"She's a pain in my ass," I say. I can tell Jacey is happy to hear it, and I realize now that when I stopped hanging out with her to hook up with Emma, it must have really hurt her feelings.

It hits me now, that weird feeling I've had all day. Is Jacey what I'm missing? Is it her? It's obvious she likes me. Could I like her back?

Without thinking, I slide closer to her on the couch. I grab her soft cheeks in my hands and lean over, kissing her softly. She gasps, then kisses me back, harder and more passionately like she'd been waiting her whole life for this moment.

I close my eyes and hope that this will solve that nagging feeling in the pit of my chest, shut it off once and for all.

But it only makes it worse.

CHAPTER SEVEN

Keanna

"That one," Dawn says, narrowing her eyes and motioning toward a man in the parking lot. He's in his forties and impeccably dressed in a way that lets you know he has money. He's also staring at his cell phone as he walks, oblivious to any moving cars nearby.

We're in the parking lot of a fancy part of town. It's like a shopping mall, but every store is a department store or some fancy place I've never heard of. One of the lingerie stores let us set up a table in front. It's officially Christmas Eve, and Mom is making me flirt with potential customers.

Bracing myself for how much I hate this, I walk over to the man. "Hello sir."

He doesn't even look up from his phone. I clear my throat. "Excuse me, sir?"

Now he looks up. Unlike in the slummy parts of town, this man doesn't give me a nasty leer like he's checking me out in every possible way. He lifts an eyebrow, sees the table of windchimes set up a few feet behind me, and grimaces. "I don't want any," he says, briskly brushing past me.

I look back at Dawn and she gives me this look like she'll set me on fire if I don't try again.

"Surely someone in your life would love an artisan custom made wind chime," I push on, walking next to him. Normally I'm supposed to flirt, but clearly this guy doesn't want it. "They're all one of a kind and very beautiful."

"Do you offer gift wrapping?" he says, slowing his gait as he approaches our table.

"We do!" I say, because although we don't exactly offer gift wrapping, I'd bought some gift bags and tissue paper at the dollar store a couple of days ago to use for Dawn's present.

The man's brows pull together as he studies the wind chimes. "I'll take that one," he says, pointing to a pink one made of porcelain.

Mom eagerly rings him up with the app on her cell phone and he pays with a solid black credit card. I wrap up his purchase, tufting the tissue paper to make it look nice.

"Good call on the wrapping," Mom says after the guy leaves. "I never even thought of that. Next year we'll get more."

"I didn't exactly think of it," I admit while I reach for my bottle of water and take a sip. "I bought the wrapping stuff for your Christmas present."

Mom scoffs. "Don't get me anything, Keanna. I'm not getting you anything."

It's embarrassing how much that hurts. I mean, I guess I hadn't expected anything for Christmas. All I really wanted was a hotel room for the night. Now I think about the beautiful turquoise scarf with matching gloves that I'd bought her for Christmas and wonder if I should even give it to her.

I'd used my own money that I earned washing cars at the last apartments we had for a few months. Turns out old pervert guys will happily pay twenty bucks a car to watch you wash it wearing short shorts and a tank top. I decide to give it to her anyway. It's a gift, after all. Maybe the kind gesture will obligate her to show some kindness in return. If we can't get a hotel, maybe we can go out for dinner or something. Later, when the lunch rush has passed and we've sold nearly half our stock, the passing people are clearly getting nervous in their last-minute shopping. The stores close in a couple of hours and there's still a ton of people rushing from store to store, looking for the perfect gift. Most of them are men and it makes me wonder what kind of husband or boyfriend they could possibly be when they wait until last minute to buy gifts.

Mom leaves me alone while she goes to pee inside one of the stores and instead of actively calling out to everyone who walks by like she wants me to, I sit in her chair and rest for a while.

"Hey there," someone says, pulling me from my daydream. In it, I was someone's girlfriend and he didn't wait until last minute to buy gifts. He gave me jewelry and he smiled every time I came over. I don't know why I let my brain slip into silly daydreams like that, but somehow deep down in my chest, it almost felt real. Maybe in another life, I was happy. But not now, because this college frat looking guy is staring at me with a look I know so well.

"What's up, beautiful?"

I sigh. "Just selling these handmade wind chimes for someone who deserves something special. Are you interested in one?"

"Nah," he says, shaking his head. "I'm interested in you, though. You live around here?"

"I don't live anywhere."

He takes my sarcasm in stride. "Well, maybe you'd like to come live with me." His tongue flicks over his bottom lip. "I have a nice apartment."

"You don't even know me," I say, gazing out at the parking lot and hoping he'll get a hint.

He leans forward, the overbearing scent of his cologne making me want to puke. "But I'd like to get to know you. I'll take you to these fancy stores and get you some nice clothes," he says, wiggling his eyebrows. "What's your number?"

"I don't have a phone," I say, not meeting his gaze.

"Well, I'll buy you one of those, too."

"I don't need someone to take care of me," I mutter, folding my arms across my chest. The truth is, maybe I do need someone. Someone better than Dawn. Someone who can help me become something in life. But it's not him, I know that for sure.

Finally, the guy gives up and leaves, slinking away into another store to hassle some other poor woman. But even after he's gone, I can't shake the thought that I really don't belong anywhere. Not here, in the nice part of town. Not with Dawn in her stupid car. Not anywhere.

But for some reason, I can't stop this feeling deep in the pit of my stomach, that maybe somewhere, in another lifetime, I did belong.

But maybe that's just wishful thinking.

CHAPTER EIGHT

Jett

I didn't appreciate my childhood years nearly as much as I should have. Santa Claus brought a ton of presents and my parents were always so happy to wake up at the butt crack of dawn with me to open them all. Now, we all sleep in late and then I drink a beer with Dad while Park comes over and we watch football in the living room.

In the kitchen, Mom and her best friend Becca prepare the food for our annual Christmas dinner when my grandparents will be coming over. I feel bad that they're doing all the work, but when I offered to help, Mom told me not to worry about it. Guess I can't blame her because my cooking skills aren't the best. I'm not even that good at chopping vegetables. I did set the table though, just so I could help out a little.

My parents got me great gifts and I'm happy about them, but it's really not the same as being a kid. All of the magic is gone. I'm wishing now more than ever that I had someone to share the holidays with. Someone besides my family, even if that makes me sound like an asshole.

Though Jacey had liked our kiss, I'd apologized profusely afterward. I felt like a total asshole for taking advantage of her like that. I don't like her in that way. I thought maybe I could, but I definitely don't. That kiss was empty, and it left me feeling more than ever that I'm missing something.

It's been two days since I woke up feeling like my life had been turned upside down and I still don't know what's bothering me. I just feel—less, somehow.

I take another sip of beer, knowing my dad won't let me have enough to actually get drunk. It doesn't matter, because it wouldn't help. Nothing helps.

I feel like I'm missing someone. Someone important, and perfect. Someone I love more than I love myself.

But maybe I'm just crazy.

CHAPTER NINE

Keanna

Christmas morning means waking up with my sweater as a pillow again. When you're poor and homeless, the holidays don't really mean anything. Sometimes we'll go to a food kitchen and get a surprisingly good meal on a holiday. But that's about it.

We're parked in the back part of a Walmart parking lot because this store is nice to people who want to camp out overnight. I grab a few dollars from my wallet and walk inside, going to the McDonald's to get a coffee. Since it's Christmas, I spend an extra dollar and get Mom one, too. The girl behind the counter looks absolutely miserable, with dark circles under her eyes.

"I'm sorry you have to work on Christmas," I say.

She shrugs. "I'm just happy to have a job. I shouldn't have stayed up all night wrapping my three-year-old's presents though..."

She smiles and I smile back. She's right. A job is a job, after all. And if she has a place to live, that's even better for her.

I wake Dawn up when I get back. She takes the coffee I offer her without a word of thanks, but I guess I wasn't expecting one.

"If you gotta pee, you should go now," Dawn says. "We're about to head east. There's a church craft fair this weekend and I've got us signed up for a booth."

The roads are busy on Christmas day. I watch the cars as we drive; see the families packed into each one. There's smiling parents and smiling kids. Some of the kids have little TV screens in the backseat that play cartoons and movies so their drive isn't so bad.

My heart aches for a family. A real one. I'm basically an adult now, but I would love to go back in time and be the kind of kid who has a TV screen in the car. I'd love to be jam packed into an SUV while driving to grandma's house, or wherever it is people go to on holidays.

Feeling sadder than usual, I lean my head against the window and watch the road fly by.

I've always known my life was a little different from most people's. I've always just put up with it, hoping for something better to come along. But right now, I've never felt more hopeless in my life.

I drift off to sleep, only to be awakened by Dawn hitting a pothole an hour later. My head bashes against the glass, startling me awake.

"Ow!" I say, rubbing my head.

Dawn snorts. "Sorry."

I look outside. The sun is starting to go down over a sleepy little town with cute houses dotting the road every so often. We pass a street sign that makes my heart skip a beat.

Welcome to Lawson, TX

I SIT UP STRAIGHTER. WHY DOES THAT NAME SOUND SO FAMILIAR?

"Have we been here before?" I ask.

Dawn shakes her head. "Nope. We should almost be there, though. The church is up ahead and I'm betting we can stay in their parking lot no questions because they're a church."

I rub my forehead as an insane feeling falls over me. I feel like I *know* this place. Like I belong here, or maybe I've been here before.

As we drive, I'm suffocating in the feeling of déjà vu and I don't even know why. We approach a big sign on the road that says The Track. Now my heart is pounding. Why does that feel so familiar?

"Stop!" I put my hand on the glovebox. There's a three story house right next to The Track. I've never seen it before, but something is pulling to me, like an invisible hand begging me to get out. "Mom, stop the car."

She slams on the brakes and slides off onto the shoulder of the road. "Jesus, Keanna!" Dawn says. "You have to puke or something?"

"I need to get out," I say, unable to take my eyes off the wrap around porch of this weirdly familiar house. There are no cars in the driveway and it doesn't look like anyone is home. "I have to go."

My mother stares at me like I've grown an extra head. "Go where?"

"To that house," I say. "I think I've been there before."

She leans forward, looking past me and at the house. "You've never been there."

"I think I have," I say, my hand on the door handle. "I'm going."

Dawn makes some kind of sigh that's mixed with a laugh. "Whatever, kid. I'll go get some fast food burgers and come back to get you. Hopefully you'll have regained your mind by then."

I don't even tell her goodbye. I don't grab my bag from the back seat. I just go, slamming the door behind me and then sprinting into a run as I make my way toward the house.

Mom drives away and I'm all alone on the porch. I knock on the door, but no one answers. And maybe I am crazy, but I twist the doorknob. It's locked.

But I'm still hopeful. Someone lives here, I just know it. I can't describe it and it doesn't make any sense but I know someone will be here for me soon.

I turn and sit on the porch steps, leaning my shoulder against the railing. Someone will come for me. I don't know how or why, but it's a feeling in my gut that I can't ignore.

At some point, I fall asleep. When I wake up, I'm not on the porch anymore. I'm in a warm bed with soft sheets. My eyes are closed, and the soft light from a nearby window trickles into the room. It smells like home in here.

And when I open my eyes, I'm in my bedroom.

And I remember everything.

CHAPTER TEN

Jett

My phone dings. I am groggy as hell from staying up too late watching Netflix last night. At least I think it was last night. I remember being alone because for some reason Keanna didn't want to come over.

I shoot up in bed, my heart racing.

Was it all a dream?

Memories of a dream hit me like an eighteen-wheeler. I had woken up and my life was different. Keanna didn't exist and I was all alone. My mom wasn't pregnant and Becca's baby was never born.

Damn.

It had all felt so real. But as I check my phone, the date is December 23rd, the day before my birthday. I had dreamed that whole thing. It wasn't real. It never happened.

My heart pounds against my ribcage, anxiety pouring over me until I feel like I'm suffocating. That was worse than a dream. It was a nightmare. And it felt like it lasted for days.

I throw on some clothes and slip into some flip-flops that are by the back door. It's only nine in the morning, but I don't care. I have to see her.

Sprinting across the backyard, I ignore the cold air and run up the steps to Keanna's house. My arms ache to hold her. The door opens right before I knock.

Keanna is standing there in her pajamas, cute purple thermal pants and a long-sleeved shirt with an owl on it.

She looks startled when our eyes meet. "Sorry," I say, nearly out of breath from running. "I just had to see you."

Her eyes are wide. She looks down at her hand, then smiles when she sees her promise ring shimmering in the early morning sun. "You okay?" I say.

She shakes her head, looking a little dazed. And then tears fill her eyes. "I had the worst dream," she says, throwing her arms around me.

I hold onto her, inhaling her green apple shampoo. She hugs me tightly and I hug her right back, feeling like it's been ages since we last felt this close.

"I'm so sorry about making you mad yesterday," I whisper into her hair. "I never meant to badger you. I hope your exams went okay."

"I don't care about the exams," she says, her voice cracking. "I just need you."

I pull away a little and cup her chin in my hands. She's full on crying now, and shivering in the cold. I hold her close, rubbing my hands up and down her arms to warm her up. "Baby, what's wrong?"

She shakes her head. "I love you, Jett. I love you so much. I'm so sorry about the things I said, I didn't mean any of them. You're my family, and so are my parents and your parents and Elijah." She buries her face in my chest as the tears begin to fall. "I love you all so much."

I rest my head on top of hers and breathe in deeply. "It's okay baby," I murmur as I rub her back. "You were just having a bad day."

"But then I had the worst dream," she says, looking up at me through teary eyes. "I dreamed I was my old self again, that I'd never met you."

Chills rise across my arms. "I had a bad dream, too," I say, my voice a whisper. Is it possible we dreamed the same thing?

She swallows and throws her arms around my neck. "I'm so happy I have you in my life, Jett."

I kiss her head and then her cheek, and then her lips. "I'm happy you have me, too," I say, flashing her a grin.

She smiles. "Let's never fight again, okay?"

I run my hand down her soft cheek, brushing away the tear that lingers there.

"Never," I say, leaning down to kiss her.

"I love you," she says again.

"I love you more," I say against her lips, and then I kiss her like today is the start of the rest of our lives. Because that's exactly what it is.

BELIEVE IN SUMMER

A BELIEVE IN LOVE NOVELLA

CHAPTER ONE

Keanna

My pencil scratches across the paper, filling in the very last bubble answer on my scantron. Question number one hundred and twelve – answer D.

I drop my pencil on top of the English 101 Final Exam and slowly exhale. It's done. My last final of the first semester of college. I know I shouldn't be disappointed when I look up and see the time on the clock above the dry erase board in this college lecture room.

My last class of the day started at nine in the morning, and the final was over a hundred questions long. I knew I wouldn't get done before ten. It was a total impossibility from the start.

Still.

I guess I had a shred of hope that I might somehow zoom through the exam and finish with just enough time to race home and say one last goodbye to Jett before he hopped in the taxi on his way to the airport.

But it's now 11:28 and he's long gone by now.

Slowly, I slide back my chair and bring my test and answer sheet to the front of the room. There's really no rush now, and even though I've just completed my last final and my first four college classes are behind me, making me one step closer to a college degree, it doesn't really feel like a victory because there's a knot in my chest that's missing Jett like crazy.

I know, I know. I'm pathetic. I just saw him last night. But still. Now that the summer races have begun, he's going to be flying off to some new race every weekend, and I'm going to miss him like crazy. Now that he's a member of Team

Loco's motocross team, he's racing all over the place, not just here locally in Texas. It's the best thing that's happened to his career, but I doesn't mean I have to love it.

Essence puts a hand on my arm as I leave the classroom, startling me from my thoughts. "Perfect timing!"

"For what?" I say, trying to smile back at her and Ashlee, the only two girls I've managed to become friends with in this class.

"We all finished our test at the same time," she says, pushing a wave of her long black hair over her shoulder. Most of the time, Essence looks beautiful with matching outfits and fresh makeup, but today she's dressed in jeans and a T-shirt, and looks like she's missed some sleep. No doubt her bum look today is from spending the week studying for finals.

Her eyes flit from me to Ashlee, who is wearing leggings and an oversized T-shirt. "Let's get smoothies!"

Ashlee rolls her eyes. "How did I know you were going to say that?"

"Because she's obsessed," I say with a laugh. The college has a smoothie cart in the middle of the cafeteria, and they use fresh fruits and probably some kind of magic fairy dust because their smoothies are insanely good.

"I could use a celebratory smoothie now that finals are over," Ashlee says. She turns to me. "You in?"

"Please!" Essence says before I can answer. "Don't give me that boyfriend excuse. You are always rushing off to see him, but this is our last day of classes together, so we should hang out."

"I'm in," I say, ignoring the tightness in my chest. She's right, of course. They invite me to dinner or for smoothies all the time, and I only ever agree to go when Jett is busy and I'd otherwise be home bored.

But what can I say? I'd way rather be with Jett than anyone else.

Sorry not sorry.

Essence takes a long time ordering her smoothie because she can't decide if she wants to go with one of her favorite flavors or try a new one since it's the last day of school before summer break.

Ashlee watches me reach for my phone. "What?" I say, putting the phone back in my pocket without checking it. They're always giving me a hard time for texting Jett in class.

"How long have you been dating him?" She asks.

I give a shrug like I don't know the exact time frame down to the day. "A year or something. Maybe a little longer."

Essence finally chooses her smoothie and then places a twenty on the table. "I'm buying their smoothies too," she says, winking at us.

We thank her and Ashlee and I place our orders. I go with the classic strawberry, kiwi, and banana because it just doesn't get any better than that.

Once Essence has her change, we move to the side while the guy starts making our smoothies. "You know..." Essence says, staring me up and down. "I'm not sure if it's cute or weird that you're so in love with your boyfriend."

I can feel my cheeks wanting to turn red but I beg them to stay a normal color. "Why's that?" I ask, rolling my eyes.

"We're college freshman," Ashlee says. She bumps her hip against Essence's. "We're supposed to party and play the field."

"...And pass our classes," I say sarcastically.

They laugh, but they're not letting me off the hook. My relationship with Jett always comes up with I hang out with these girls. They've been friends since high school and they planned their college schedule together since they both want a degree in teaching. I only had the one English class with them, so I'm more of an outside friend to their duo. Besides being the same age and having one class together, I don't have much in common with these girls. But it's nice having friends. I grew up without any.

When our smoothies are done, we take them to the water fountain outside and choose a seat under an umbrella.

"Ashlee and I had a ton of boyfriends in high school," Essence explains between sips of her smoothie. "But those guys are all just immature idiots, so we made a promise to stay single in college and just date around for fun."

"I don't regret it one bit," Ashlee says. She and Essence click their cups together in a toast.

"Well, maybe that's why I'm different." I stare into my smoothie as I talk. "I didn't have boyfriends in high school. Not really anyone I could trust, either. So when I found Jett, he became both of those things for me and I don't want to let him go."

"Plus, that boy is hot as hell, so I guess I see your point," Ashlee says. Essence nods along, wiggling her eyebrows at me.

Okay, now I do blush.

Essence leans forward. "Keanna, promise us you'll still hang out this summer. We like you and we don't want to, like, never talk again now that we don't have classes together."

"Sure thing," I say, "You should come by the track sometime. It's literally crawling with hot dirt bike guys."

"Oooh..." The girls say in unison.

"That can definitely be arranged," Ashlee says. "Wait... do I not have your number?" Her brows pull together and she takes out her phone. "Girl, we're not even Instagram friends!"

"I don't have one of those," I say. I do have a Snapchat, but I only use it with Jett, so I don't bother volunteering that information. "But you can have my number so you can text me."

"Old school," she says with a nod. "What is it?"

I give them both my number and they save it into their phones, then give me their numbers as well. Essence complains that her house is too small and her little siblings are too annoying, so we'll have to do the hanging out at my house or Ashlee's. They start talking about all the things we'll do this summer – dirt bike races, beach bonfires, shopping trips – and I feel a little excitement sparking in my veins. Now I have three friends, including Maya.

I'm going to miss Jett like crazy while he's off racing, but this can be fun too. Girl time. I could totally see myself having fun with these two.

"There's always some sick parties in the summer," Essence says as she slurps down the last of her smoothie. "But you'll want to bring your boyfriend, otherwise all the guys will be all up on you."

"Highly doubtful," I say with a snort.

"Psh... firstly, you're cute as hell—otherwise we wouldn't hang out with you," Ashley says.

"And secondly," Essence chimes in, "You underestimate the horniness level of guys at parties."

I think back to that drunken asshole at the New Years party a year ago and cringe. Guys can definitely be assholes when they're drunk. Jett had saved me back then, and I know I'll never go to another stupid keg party without him by my side. I like my new friends, but not enough to party alone with them.

"Look at her," Essence says, nudging Ashley. "She's thinking about him."

I roll my eyes, but a deep red fills my cheeks anyway. They both laugh.

"Aww! You are so freaking cute! And so in love," Ashley croons. "I hope one day when I decide to date again, I can find a guy who makes me as happy as Jett makes you."

Essence holds out her hand. "Um, I'm pretty sure that kind of magic only happens once a generation, and this bitch Keanna already got it."

"Sorry guys," I say, holding up my hands. "I couldn't help it."

We sit outside a little while longer, and I let the girls talk while I think about Jett. They're used to this, and since they both love talking and I love just listening, it works out well.

They go on about how settling down is just too hard and they can't possibly imagine doing it at such a young age. I try to put myself in their shoes and understand where they're coming from, but I can't.

I am so very happy with Jett in my life. I like being "tied down" as they put it. Only when they say it, it's in a bad way. I love it. I love knowing that Jett is there for me and I'm there for him and I never have to be truly alone.

Yeah, it sucks on the weekends when he's in another state racing, but at least I know he's still mine. And now that college classes are over for the summer, I can go with him if they don't need me at work.

I take out my phone to text him, and that's when I realize it's been on silent this whole time. I have several texts from him, and a few snaps.

I glance up at my friends, who are now deep in a conversation about the last episode of The Bachelor. They don't even notice that I'm not in the conversation, so I don't feel bad when I check Jett's messages.

Jett: Boarding! This is so boring!

Jett: I hope your exam went well! I love you!

Jett: I have sent entirely too many exclamation marks today....

Jett: Here's! Some! More!

Jett: Haha... I miss you babe. Like... Tons.

I grin and then open up Snapchat. He's sent me a picture of his view out the window of the airplane, and then another one of his face, his lips puckered downward into a frown. His hair is shaggy, even more so than usual, and it makes me smile.

Miss you babe, the caption says.

I bite my bottom lip to keep from grinning like a fool. Essence and Ashlee have made so many great points about why dating in college life is a bad idea.

But I wouldn't have it any other way.

CHAPTER TWO

Jett

I haven't had a window seat the last several times I've flown on a plane, so I treat today like it's special, because it is. Keanna has never flown anywhere, and I keep telling her I'll make sure she gets the window seat when we finally go somewhere together. Today, it's just me. I'm tucked up against the wall of the plane, my forehead resting next to the window. The flight to California is only half full, and I've got the whole row of three seats to myself. This sure beats that time I was sandwiched between two large men who only liked breathing through their mouths.

I snap a picture of the clouds and send it to Keanna. She doesn't read it right away, so she must still be in her exams at the college.

She has a 4.0 GPA and I'm really proud of her, even though at times I feel like maybe she's jealous that I'm not in college and she is. I did at least finish my senior year of high school, even though I did homeschooling which my mom totally hated. Now technically, I could be in college like her, since I graduated early, but I'm not. School isn't on my radar right now. I'm focusing on motocross.

Like my dad says, if you get famous enough as a racer, you don't need an education. Not yet, at least. If all goes according to my plan, I'll race professionally for at least ten years, hopefully fifteen. Then, after a career of professional motocross, I can do anything I want. I'll have the money and just enough fame to get endorsements and side gigs.

I can settle down with Keanna, maybe take over my dad's business and teach kids how to become fast racers themselves. After my racing career is over—and it always ends way too soon because our bodies get old and racing is a young man's game—then I can look into college.

Right now, the idea of sitting in classes and writing essays and shit sounds like my idea of a nightmare. No, thanks.

But Keanna is going, and she just finished her first semester, and I'm really proud of her. She doesn't really have to do anything if she doesn't want to. I already have enough money to take care of us, and her parents are my parents' best friends, and they wouldn't ever kick her out of the house or anything. So maybe that's why I really admire my girlfriend. She does the things she doesn't have to. She goes to college, and works at The Track, and takes care of her little brother.

I smile despite myself and send her another snapchat. This time it's a picture of myself, even though I'm not really a fan of taking selfies. They make her smile, so I do it when we're not together.

As soon as the plane lands, a nervous energy latches onto my insides. Now that I'm here, I have to be in race mode. This Sunday is the start of the Fireframe Summer Nationals, a ten race series that takes place every Sunday for the next two and a half months. Each race is at a different track in a different state, and the first one is here in Anaheim, California. It also happens to be the headquarters for Team Loco, my motocross team.

After being an intern all of last year, I proved myself enough to get bumped up to a real team member. Now I'm a rookie, along with three other guys who are all equally badass on the track, even though I'd rather not admit that fact. Back in Texas, I'm the badass racer.

But these guys are all the badass racer of their home state, and now we're all battling each other in the Fireframe Nationals for a spot at racing supercross in the fall.

Team Loco hasn't exactly said it outright, but my manager Marcus has made it clear that only one of the rookies gets to race for Team Loco in this year's supercross season, so even if we don't like it, that means we're all in a battle against each other, too. We are teammates and competitors.

Supercross is the ultimate professional dream. The races are held in stadiums all across the country, and it's where the famous, most well-known racers battle it out for number one. Supercross season is where even people who otherwise know nothing about dirt bikes come out once a year to watch us race.

And I want it to be me.

I like the other rookies on my team. Zach, Clay, and Aiden are all great guys with a lifetime of amateur motocross championships to their name, just like me. So, no offense to them, but when it comes time for Marcus to choose which rookie gets to race under the Team Loco name this year—I hope it's me.

There's a car waiting for me at LAX. The driver stands there in his pressed suit, holding a sign that says JETT ADAMS. I'm not gonna lie, I feel like a total badass as I approach him like I'm someone worth holding a sign for.

"I'm Jett," I say, trying to sound cool and normal even though this is totally awesome.

"Let me get your bags, sir." The guy takes my suitcase and reaches for my gear bag, which is twice as big.

"I've got this one," I say, holding onto the strap. This bag contains my precious cargo. Team Loco has riding gear and helmets and boots for me already at the track, but this bag has my lucky underwear (the pair I was wearing the day I first kissed Keanna), my laptop and my phone charger. I can't risk letting anyone else touch the bag but me.

I'm dropped off at a five-star hotel in Anaheim, and there's a room waiting for me. I get my key card from the front desk and make my way up to the fifth floor, all the while wishing Keanna was with me. We get plenty of alone time at home, but alone time in a hotel in Cali? That would be fuckin' awesome.

I drop my suitcases and do a sweep of my hotel room. I'm only here for two nights, but I wish it was longer. This place is fucking lit. A huge flat screen television, a balcony overlooking the gorgeous mountains in Cali, and the bathroom is pretty much solid marble with fancy shit inside it. The shower has a built in radio and TV. A TV in the shower. It doesn't get much more five star than that.

I grab a soda from the mini fridge, then drop to the plush mattress and FaceTime Keanna.

She ignores it, and then calls me back on a regular call. "Hey babe," I say. "I tried Face Timing you."

"Trust me, you don't want to see me like this," she says. "I'm crazy ugly right now. Just spent an hour playing in the sand with Elijah and I'm sweaty and gross."

I blow a raspberry. "It's literally, physically, scientifically impossible for you to be ugly."

"Weird... because it's totally happening right now!" she says sarcastically. "I look gross."

"You're always beautiful."

"Whatever."

I chuckle and roll over on my back, staring up at the ceiling in this hotel room. "I miss you," I say.

"I miss you, too. And you've only been gone a few hours, so that's really saying something."

"How was your exam?" I ask.

"It was okay. I think I probably got an A on it."

"Of course you did. You're a fucking badass."

She laughs and it makes me smile. "So, are you at your hotel?"

"Yep," I say. "Tomorrow at five in the morning, we start practice and then the race is Sunday. Then Monday morning I'll be coming home and you better be prepared for a massive hug."

"I'll need more than a hug," she says in this flirtatious way that makes my stomach flutter. "You'll have been away from me for three days, and that's just not okay."

"I'll make it up to you, baby girl."

"Good," she says.

Not five minutes after we've hung up, I nearly piss myself when someone bangs on my door louder than necessary.

"Dude!" Zach Pena says. "Open up, I know you're in there!"

I head to the door and let my fellow teammates inside. Knowing our team manager Marcus, he probably booked us all hotel rooms right next to each other.

Zach is a tanned, dark haired playboy from Tennessee. Somehow all the girls think his twangy accent is sexy, yet I've been mocked for my Texas accent a time or two, luckily not by Keanna. He's got one of those dumbass fidget spinners in his hand and he bumps fists with me as a hello then heads straight to my mini fridge, spinning that thing the whole time.

"Jett, man, what's up?" Clay says, entering behind Zach.

"I should be asking you that, dude. Did you somehow get *taller* since I saw you last month?"

He laughs and runs a hand over his newly bald head. "Nah, man. I hope not."

Clay Summers is the guy I worry about the most on the track. He's slick and quick and trains harder than I've ever trained in my life. He's had shaggy blond hair as long as I've known him, but he just shaved the whole thing off. His new baldness mixed with the tats on his arms make him look a little terrifying.

Honestly, at nearly seven feet tall, he kind of is.

Clay has a rep of being an asshole, both on and off the track. Team Loco took him on a few months before they signed me, and the main thing I've noticed about Clay is that his head is always in the game. I take time off of motocross to be with my girlfriend and my family, but Clay doesn't. He's lived in his own studio apartment in Laguna Beach since he was sixteen, and the only thing he dedicates time to is his dirt bike.

The other rookie on Team Loco is Aiden Strauss, who's still standing in the hallway with my hotel room door open. He's on his phone but he nods at me in a hello. He looks serious, like whatever he's talking about is a big deal. But then again, Aiden is always serious.

His older brother is Mikey Strauss, of former motocross fame. That is until he got thrown in jail for possession of cocaine and performance-enhancing drugs, and lost his professional motocross career along with it.

Like me, Aiden has grown up in the world of motocross, but he's got his brother's reputation to overcome, so he's constantly fighting the media reports that compare him to Mikey. I like him though, he's a good guy.

The guys shoot the shit in my room for a bit, and then we head out to get dinner. I grab a cheeseburger with extra bacon and fries because it's my last good meal of the weekend. Tomorrow, I'll be on protein shakes and lean meat with veggies to help me stay fit, energized, and ready to race.

Tomorrow, the training begins. The practice and bike prep. Then on Sunday, we'll load up in the Team Loco motorcade and head out to the track to start off this season's first race.

I'm not so much nervous, as I am ready to get this thing started. This first race is my first chance to secure the rookie position for the supercross season.

That's just step one to the rest of my life. And I really hope I'll make Keanna proud along the way.

CHAPTER THREE

Keanna

Elijah's eyes light up when I walk into the kitchen on Monday morning. "Bah!" he says from his seat in his high chair. He wags a fist at me. "Bah!"

Bah is my little brother's word for everything he doesn't know how to say yet. Currently he says *mama* and *bye bye* and *moo* and *bah*.

I bump my fist into his. "Right back at you, little man."

"He has a lot of energy for someone who's been awake since four in the freaking morning," Mom says. She gives me an exasperated smile from where she stands at the kitchen sink, her hands hidden by soapy water while she washes out Elijah's baby bottles.

"Four in the morning?" I say with my baby voice as I put my hands on my hips and stare at Elijah. "Why can't you just enjoy sleeping, little man? One day you will be old and you'll wish you could sleep all morning."

"Bah," he says, his chubby cheeks smiling up at me.

"Are you excited for summer?" Mom asks me as I pour myself a cup of coffee.

"Kind of. I'm mostly excited because it's Monday."

"Monday?" she says, lifting an eyebrow. Then it dawns on her. "Ah! Of course. Jett's coming home."

I grin as I pour some creamer into my coffee mug. "One weekend down, nine more to go. Ughhhhhh…"

"Aw, honey, it's not that bad," she says. She moves some bottles over to the counter to dry them off, and I notice a little paint stuck to her hair by her ear. Mom's side business is upstairs in the studio. She paints inspirational canvases and ever since the baby has been born, she finds weird times in the middle of the night to work on them.

"Well, it feels like an eternity to me," I say, sipping my coffee. "I can't stand when he's gone."

"Maybe you can go with him a few times," she offers.

I nod. That's the plan, but I'm always so busy at the track and helping with my brother and Jett's little sister. They all say they can spare me for a few days, but I'm not so sure about that.

I'm about to say something more when the back door flies open and my dad rushes inside, the phone pressed to his ear. He's only thirty six years old, but he seems at least ten years older as he stares straight ahead, his attention focused on the conversation. His brow creases together and he sighs. "I don't know what the hell will happen," he says, heaving yet another sigh. "Let me talk it over with Jace. Okay, Meredith. I'll get back with you."

Mom swings around, her eyes wide. "That was Meredith?"

He nods. "You're not gonna believe this shit."

I'm pretty sure the only Meredith we know is the wife of the guy who owns Oakcreek Motocross park, which is an hour or so away from here. Normally, I wouldn't think twice about a conversation involving some woman I don't even know, but my dad looks seriously concerned, maybe even worried.

He kisses Elijah on the head and then kisses his wife and it makes me melt a little inside, knowing that they can be married for so long and still be so in love.

My mom and dad aren't my real parents. They're Becca and Park—high school sweethearts just like Jett's parents. They're also best friends with Jett's parents and together they own The Track, which is a motocross facility located smack in the middle of our houses. They adopted me two years ago after my real mother asked them to look after me for a week and then never came back. Becca has always been a mom figure to me, so after a while, I started calling her that.

We eat breakfast and I attempt to feed Elijah, even though he'd rather wear his food, and Dad tells us what's going on. Apparently last night the police raided Oakcreek Motocross Park and arrested David Surly, the owner. Then they also arrested the guy who owns Three Flamingos Motocross Park. Dad says they were apparently part of a long investigation by the government and they were finally caught and arrested on charges of money laundering and conspiring together.

David's wife Meredith claims she knew nothing about it, and because of this, the police let her go for the time being. She called my dad in a panic because Oakcreek is having an amateur motocross series this summer and she has no idea what she should do. Canceling all of the races would mean losing a lot of money, but she has no idea how to run the place without her husband.

"Pathetic," Mom says over a sip of her coffee. "If you boys disappeared one day, Bayleigh, Keanna and I would have no problem running the place by ourselves." She looks over at me and winks. "Girl power."

Dad chuckles. "Not to worry, love. Jace and I run a clean business. We pay a shitload of taxes on it, too, but at least we'll never get arrested." He shakes his head. "Idiots."

A little while later, Jace and Bayleigh come over and they meet with my parents to talk about the drama. Apparently Three Flamingos' management team is also freaking out because they too have a summer series to put on and they can't run it without their owner. Not even an hour later, my dad gets another call confirming that the police have seized both properties for the investigation, so no one will be racing there for a long time.

It's actually kind of interesting listening to them talk about it, and I realize that owning a business comes with a shit ton of responsibility. Usually I just work at the front counter and do small things like occasionally take a deposit to the bank. I don't even think about all of the accounting and shit that goes into owning a business. I'm glad my parents and Jett's parents are doing everything by the law.

I get so caught up in the drama discussion, that it actually startles me when our front door opens.

"HelllOooo," a voice rings out. I freeze when I recognize Jett's voice, and then all at once I melt into a puddle of happiness. How the hell could I forget that his plane was about to land? Oh my God!

I throw myself off the couch and jump over mom's feet in my mad haste to the front door. Jett's standing there wearing black basketball shorts and flip flops with a blue lightning bolt Team Loco shirt.

He grins at me in this way that makes my whole body tingle and he opens his arms. I dive right into them. He smells like airplane, but I don't care. I wrap my arms around his neck and kiss him and feel him chuckle against my lips.

"Miss me?" he says.

"You have no idea." I gaze up into his eyes and kiss him again.

"Jett, you won't believe what just happened," Jace says from the living room. Hearing Jett's dad's voice makes me suddenly remember that both of our parents are sitting just twenty feet away and that I just performed this huge display of affection right in front of them. I step back and release Jett's shoulders, feeling a blush slide up my cheeks.

"What's up?" Jett says, snaking his arm around my waist. He kisses the top of my head.

Dad and Jace exchange a humorous glance. "You'll probably want to sit down for this."

It's my third Monday waiting for Jett to get home from his race. He should be in a great mood this time because he's won the last three races in a row, so he's on top of the scoreboards for Team Loco. But honestly, I don't care about any of that right now. I'm stuck at work, and it's slow as hell, and all I want to do is be with my boyfriend.

I check the clock on the wall and wonder why time is going so impossibly sluggish. His plane landed an hour ago, so he should be here soon. I would have gone to pick him up, but my parents are so unbelievably busy with their babies and their business, so I'm working the counter more than usual. The guys are working with the staff at the two motocross tracks that got shut down. Since they always presell race fees for the series, they're all trying to figure out a way to host both track's races here at The Track instead of canceling it all. I'm not exactly sure how that will work since we have our own races and clients to attend to, but luckily, that task isn't on my shoulders. I just stand here, take the money, and answer the phones.

Normally, I'm happy when there's no customers because I can watch Netflix on the shop's computer, or read a book or something. But today, I would love to have a stream of riders coming in here because standing here waiting on Jett is the worst thing ever.

When a black town car pulls into The Track's driveway, I lean over the counter, trying to see if it's Jett. Most people arrive with dirt bikes in tow, so my chances are good. Sure enough, the door opens and my crazy hot boyfriend steps out, looking tired, but still handsome as always. He takes his suitcase from the trunk then jogs up to the building.

"Babe!" I squeal as I run into his arms. I miss him so much when he leaves on the weekends, but our reunions are always pretty wonderful.

"I missed you," he says between kissing me. His suitcase drops to the floor and I'm lifted into the air. I wrap my legs around his waist and he carries me over to the front counter, setting me down on the stainless steel surface. He doesn't let go, though. He holds onto my hips and pulls me toward him while we make out. When I'm sitting on the counter, I'm an inch or two taller than he is, so I slide my fingers through his hair and hold him close.

"I'm so glad you're finally here," I say, closing my eyes when he kisses my neck. He runs his tongue down my skin and I gasp.

"I'm all yours for four days," he says, his voice low and hungry.

He pulls me off the counter, holding onto my hips like he owns me. I love it.

He presses his forehead to mine. "Let's go to the break room," he says, a sly smile spreading over his lips.

My toes tingle at the very idea of it. The breakroom has a couch and a lock on the door.

"I'm the only person working today," I say, pouting my lips.

"Five minutes," he whispers just before he leans in and kisses my neck again, the stubble on his chin sending chills down my flesh.

I moan at the feeling of his body pressed so close to mine and I want him so badly. But I also don't want to upset my parents for skipping out on my job.

"Five minutes?" I say, giving him a coy grin. "That doesn't sound too appealing for me."

"Ten," he says, winking at me. The desire in his eyes is so strong I can practically feel waves of heat rolling off his body. I missed him bad, and I definitely want his body on mine, somewhere private.

I can't help but grin. "Okay."

I take his hand and walk him down the hallway, my heart pounding quicker with every step. I reach for the door handle and then bells jingle in the distance.

It's the sound of a customer coming in the front door.

Jett curses under his breath.

I groan.

"Hello?" Some guy says. "Anyone here?"

I turn around to Jett, who takes my face in his hands and pulls me in for a quick kiss.

"No worries," he says, smacking me on the butt. "I'll still want you like crazy when you get off work."

CHAPTER FOUR

Jett

I consider myself a nice guy. I don't curse in front of old ladies, and I hold the door open for strangers. I don't litter. But right now, I'm about two seconds away from going off on this douche who keeps interrupting me while I'm trying to teach his kid how to perfect his holeshot technique.

The dad sighs for the billionth time since we started this private motocross lesson. "You sure your dad won't be back anytime soon?"

I ignore him for the time being and lean down until I'm eye level with the twelve-year-old kid I'm tutoring today. His dad signed him up for ten private motocross lessons and my dad, the famous (but old) Jace Adams, who taught him the first six lessons. I'm filling in for all my dad's clients this week while he's off helping the other tracks untangle the shitstorm of legal issues they're having. So far, the kids have been fine having me as their tutor, but this guy's dad keeps rolling his eyes and making stupid comments about how my dad should be here doing this.

I'm being polite. I am. I tell the kid to lean forward on the balls of his feet and then try it again. I focus my energy on the kid and not his dad because his dad's a dumbass. Yeah, my dad is the famous Jace Adams from motocross fame like e years ago, He doesn't race professionally anymore, and guess what? I do.

So, if anything, I'm better equipped to teach this kid, but his dad seems to think I'm some teenage moron who doesn't know what I'm doing. As if an entire wall of the main building isn't covered with my first place trophies.

I take a deep breath and push on with the lesson, and when their hour is finally over, I can tell the kid is happy with his progress despite what his dad thinks. I grab a water and check the schedule on my phone. My next client is arriving in five minutes, so that's not really enough time to run up to the main building and say hi to Keanna. I've been home two days and we've barely had any time together thanks to the track being so busy. All we have is tomorrow together and then I'm heading back out to another race.

"Brother!" My mom's voice calls out and I turn around and see her walking up with my little sister in tow. I grin because the baby is freaking adorable –probably the cutest baby on earth—but then I give my mom a look.

"Brother? That's a stupid nickname."

Mom rolls her eyes. "Well, you're her brother," she says. "What else do you want to be called?"

"Jett?" I suggest. "Or something that sounds cool. Not brother. Makes me sound like a clergyman."

"What about big brother?" she asks.

I nod. "I like that one."

Brooke is only a month and a half old, so I try not to take it personally when she doesn't reach out her arms to me when I hold mine out to her. Elijah always wants to come to me when I try hold him, but he's a year old. My sister is still a tiny little infant, so she can't do much but cry and lift up her head when she's laying on the floor. One day she's going to love me though.

Mom hands her to me and I cuddle her close to my chest. She's got that cute little baby smell and I know it makes me a total loser to be totally in love with a baby, but I am. A lifetime of being the only child was fun, but this little kid is now my favorite person. Now I know how Keanna feels about her little brother.

I make faces at Brooke and my mom shakes out her arms. "God, I forgot how tiring it is holding a baby for so long. I'm not as young as I used to be."

I roll my eyes and knock into her shoulder with mine. "Mom, you're the youngest mom around. All my friend's parents are like fifty-something."

She laughs and brushes some of her blonde hair back over her ear. "That's about the only good part of being a teen mom. When you were a baby I had the energy to keep up with you!"

We chat a little bit longer, but then my client shows up so I have to give my little sister back to my mom. She knows the mom of the client, so they stay and talk a while.

After my final client of the day, I grab a water bottle from the break room and head up front to where Keanna is working on the computer.

I step up behind her and kiss her neck.

"Babe…" she says softly. "Why do you have to torture me at work?"

"Kissing is torture?" I say, hopping onto a barstool next to her. "Well then, I better rethink my whole making love strategy."

She rolls her eyes but doesn't take her gaze off the computer. "It's torture when I don't have time to kiss you back."

I'm about to flirt with her some more, but my dad and Park come into the building looking exhausted.

"So here's the deal," Dad says, placing his hands flat on the countertop. "We're taking over both summer series from Oakcreek and Three Flamingos. They usually have races on Sundays, so we're going to do Oakcreek's races on Saturdays and Three Flamingo's on Sunday."

"Damn," I say.

Dad nods and Park says, "They're forfeiting all of it over to us, so we'll be profiting from the races. Since the cops have those tracks shut down, they can't legally do any business anyway, so we're just taking over to avoid disappointing the racers."

"It's going to be a lot of work, but I think it'll be fun," Dad says. "We have Keanna here to kick ass at the front desk."

She smiles. "Just call me the Supreme Front Desk Lady."

Dad throws a pen at me. "It's too bad my damn son had to go get himself a professional job," he says sarcastically. "I could have used you this summer!"

Park tisks, and they both gang up on picking on me. Luckily, I'm used to it.

THE SMELL OF PIZZA CALLS TO ME FROM BECCA'S KITCHEN, BUT I TELL HER I'M NOT hungry. It's just after nine at night and The Track finally closed down for the night. I told Keanna to text me when she was free, and she finally did. So although I'm hungry and that pizza smells good, I just want to see my girl.

I head to her bedroom but it's empty. I walk back into the hallway and to Elijah's room in case she's in there, but the baby is fast asleep and she's nowhere to be seen.

"She's in the shower," Becca says when I walk back into the kitchen.

"No she isn't," I say.

She points up to the ceiling. "She's upstairs. The shower downstairs doesn't have good water pressure and Park's supposed to get someone to look at it, but you know how damn busy he's been." She shrugs. "It might be months before it gets fixed."

"Oh okay… I'll just wait for her," I say. I grab some pizza to eat while I wait, and before Becca gets out, my dad calls.

"Can you run home real quick?" he asks.

I suppress a groan. "What for?"

"I need help moving some pallets into the garage."

I try not to be an asshole about it, but all I want to do is complain. I've barely seen my girlfriend this week, and what's worse is that I head to Florida tomorrow for a race and I haven't practiced at all this week. Literally. I've been so busy taking over dad's clients and helping with the track that I haven't touched my bike once, and now that I know I'm leaving tomorrow, I'm starting to get nervous about it. The other Team Loco guys will have been riding all week. Now I'm rusty.

After helping Dad move a shit ton of heavy crap in the garage, I call Keanna but she doesn't answer. I check my messages.

KEANNA: MOM SAID YOU WERE HERE?

Keanna: Everything okay?

Keanna: I've been up since 4…can't keep eyes open… love you

. . .

I SIGH AND DROP THE PHONE ON MY BED. I WAS GONE TOO LONG AND NOW SHE'S asleep. I missed another night of being with her thanks to being too damn busy at home.

I know she has to be up early tomorrow for work, so although I kind of want to sneak over there and crawl into bed with her, that would be selfish as hell to make her lose sleep.

So instead, I bury down my disappointment over missing my girl and I head outside to the shed where my bike is. Sure, it's almost midnight, but I've got an itch to get out on the track and let out my frustration. Last minute practice is better than no practice, after all.

CHAPTER FIVE

Keanna

The shrill ringing of my cell phone makes me jolt awake, erasing all traces of whatever dream I was having. With heavy eyes, I reach over and look at my phone.

It's a telemarketer. Ugh.

I hit ignore and drop my phone and plop back onto my bed. It's just after midnight and I'm exhausted. I used to be able to stay up late and watch TV with no problem, but now that I'm working at The Track so much, I pass out around nine.

I yawn and turn on my side, ready to go back to sleep. Then a low rumbling sound comes through my windows. It's barely there, but I'd recognize it anywhere.

Someone's riding a dirt bike next door.

I look back at my phone. I don't have any missed texts from Jett, but he probably wouldn't risk waking me up by texting me this late. I crawl out of bed and slip on flip-flops.

I'm wearing spandex workout shorts that barely cover my butt and one of Jett's Team Loco T-shirts that does cover my butt. I take my phone to use as a flashlight as I maneuver through the house and out the back door. The dirt bike is louder out here. The lights on the track are still off, but I can see the bike zoom around in the glow of the full moon overhead.

It's Jett alright—his bike soars over jumps with grace and agility. I watch him ride as I walk through the dew-covered grass to the track next door. I climb up on the bleachers and sit at the very top. The cool aluminum seats send a chill down my legs and I tug on my shirt to cover more of my thighs.

Even in the summer, there's a gentle breeze at night time. It's warm, but it's nicer than the harsh sun in the daytime. I take in the smell of the grass and the exhaust from Jett's bike as he makes another loop around the track.

He seems determined, riding with his whole body attuned to the bike. He's fun to watch in a race, and even more fun when he's the only one on the track. It's like he's one with his bike. I can see why he loves this sport so much.

After half an hour, Jett slows the bike down and rolls over the final jump near the finish line, which is directly in front of the bleachers. He pulls off his goggles and hangs them on his arm. He rides his bike off the track and parks it just a few feet away from the bleachers, leaning it up against a tree.

I know he can't see me and I think about keeping quiet and just watching him for a while. But then I quickly feel like a stalker so I call out, "Hi there."

His helmeted head jerks my way.

"Hi there yourself," he says with a playful tone in his voice.

I get up and walk down the bleachers, stopping on the bottom row. Jett removes his helmet and his gloves, leaving them on the bike seat when he joins me.

His hair is sweaty and he's breathing heavily, but he grins at me. "Hi babe."

I let his sweaty hands grab my sides and pull me up against him. I'm still on the bottom bleacher row and he's on the ground, so we're the same height. I grab his shoulders and make a face. "You're all sweaty."

"I thought you liked me sweaty," he says, winking at me under the moonlight.

"Ew," I say, shaking my head.

He laughs and throws his arms around me. I would scream at the grossness of his sweat all over me, but it's late at night and I don't want our parents thinking someone's being murdered out here. I giggle instead.

"Grossss," I say, letting him pull me on top of his lap as he sits on the bleacher seat.

"You were asleep, so I thought I'd come ride."

I lean my head against his chest and stare up at the stars. You can see them so well here in the middle of nowhere. "Have you ridden at all this week?" I ask.

He shakes his head, then rests his chin on top of my hair. "Nope." He sighs.

"You won the last three races," I say. "You'll win this next one, too."

"We'll see about that."

We're still like this for a few minutes. Jett smells a little like sweat, and although it is kind of gross, it's a smell I've grown used to from being with him at the track. I know that underneath his jersey, his muscles are all bumped and his veins are protruding and he looks like a god. I can handle a little sweat for a boyfriend who is so unbelievably sexy.

"You should probably go back to sleep," he says. He reaches up and brushes hair off my neck before kissing it.

"How am I supposed to go back to sleep if you're doing something like that?" I ask, nearly breathless from the feeling of his lips on my skin.

He chuckles. "You could come sleep in my room," he whispers, kissing me again, this time just above my collarbone.

My whole body tingles. "You know I have to help with the baby in the morning..." I say, but my argument is hard to hold on to.

"I understand," he says, wrapping his arms around me and squeezing into a tight backwards hug. "I'm gonna head inside to shower. I don't suppose you'd want to come with?"

I stand up and turn around to face him. "Well you got me all sweaty, so technically you owe me a shower."

A devilish look flashes across his eyes. Even in the dim light of the moon it's unmistakable. "Come with me," he says, taking my hand as he stands up. "I'll get you the shower you deserve."

I giggle and follow him across the yard to his house. We walk inside quietly and pad up the stairs to Jett's bedroom without making a noise so we don't wake up his baby sister. Usually she sleeps in Jett's parent's room downstairs, but we don't want to risk anything.

Upstairs, Jett has the whole place to himself. His room is larger than my own parent's master bedroom and he has his own bathroom as well.

He slips into his bathroom to crank up the hot water in the shower. I stay behind, looking around his room. Jett has a large bed and then a game room area off to the side, with a couch and a big TV and every gaming console a guy could want. I gaze around, taking in how weirdly clean everything is. Jett's room usually has at least an old T-shirt tossed on the floor, or ruffled sheets on the bed. Something to make the place look lived in. Instead, he has a suitcase and his gear bag next to the door, and all of his main stuff is inside. Since he's traveling every weekend, he doesn't bother unpacking. And we've been so busy at The Track this week, he probably only comes in here to sleep.

I walk over to his desk where there's a framed photo of us. I smile, knowing he has another copy of this picture in his wallet.

"You're in luck," Jett calls out from the bathroom. "Your favorite towel is clean!"

"It better be!" I say, joining him in the bathroom. He hands me the folded pink towel. It's plush like a bathrobe and I brought it over from my house months ago and then never took it back home. Sometimes he uses it and I always tease him when there's a pink towel hanging on the towel rack.

"I think the water is hot enough," Jett says, peaking into the glass shower door. He pulls off his motocross jersey and tosses it toward the hamper in the corner. I watch his tanned skin, the bulging muscles of his arms, as he unzips his riding pants and pulls them down. It's sexy, no doubt, but a little silly because under the pants he wears spandex underwear that go down to his knees and then knee pads and shin guards.

While he takes them all off, I undress quickly, tossing my clothes into his hamper. I'll just steal more of his to wear back home tonight. I know he wants me to stay over, but I can't. As soon as the baby wakes up, I'll need to help my mom get breakfast ready and get Elijah dressed for the day. She's entirely too busy working at our track while my dad and Jett's dad take over the other two tracks. My parents have given me so much in the last couple of years, and I'm not about to let them down when they need me.

"How is it possible that you got hotter since the last time I saw you naked?" Jett says. He's naked now too, his waist creased around where the elastic of his underwear left an imprint. He's already erect and it makes me blush.

"Shut up," I say, moving to the shower. Steam fills the air and covers the glass doors. He's seen me naked a million times, but I'm still self-conscious about it. I slip into his shower and close the door behind me.

Jett comes in a few seconds later, his hands finding my waist and his lips finding mine.

I close my eyes and let the water wash over us while we make out. Then I grab a bar of soap rub it all up and down his chest to get rid of the sweat.

"Once we're clean we can make out," I say, rolling my eyes as Jett pulls me up against him.

"I don't want to be clean," he growls in my ear just before running his tongue down my earlobe. "I want to be dirty."

I laugh as chills trail down my skin in every place he kisses. "Let's get clean first, and then we'll be as dirty as you want."

CHAPTER SIX

Jett

I don't realize how much I miss Keanna until she's right here with me, her breath hitching against my ear, my hands holding her and caressing all the places that make her squirm. I only *think* I miss her when I'm lying in some hotel bed far away. The nights seem long and cold and desolate. The stress of the next morning's race weighs heavy on me and I miss her so bad it hurts.

But none of that compares to the feeling I get when I'm right here with her, knowing I'll be leaving tomorrow. It's almost too much to handle.

She wraps the absurdly pink towel around her as she steps out of the shower. I grab my own towel and step into my room before I dry off. I need the blast of cold air to pull me from my Keanna-induced lovesickness. And damn does it work. I start shivering from the chill of my bedroom, which is always cold since I like it that way.

I rush to towel off and then grab some boxers from my dresser because that's all I prefer to sleep in, and after the hour of riding my bike hard and fast and then my love session with Keanna in the shower just now, I could use the rest.

"Aww, you're covered in goosebumps," Keanna says, running her hand across my bare back as she walks past me.

"It's freezing in here," I say as I tug on my boxers.

She laughs. "Um, yeah. That's why I dried off *inside* the bathroom. Like a normal person."

She sticks her tongue out at me and all I can do is just roll my eyes while I watch her mosey across my room wearing nothing but a towel. She opens my closet door and slips inside, flipping through my shirts until she finds one she likes.

It warms me inside to see her make herself at home in my room, with my stuff. When we first started dating she was so insecure about everything. She made herself small and unassuming. It's taken me over a year to break her out of her shell.

I like this new Keanna. Beautiful, confident, and unflinchingly mine.

She takes a gray shirt from my closet and then steals a pair of my boxers. I don't know why, but they look sexy as hell on her. She rolls up the waistband a few times to make them short and then she crawls into bed with me.

I slip under the covers and move over until I'm lying on her pillow. "You're the hottest woman alive," I say, cupping her cheek in my hand.

"I should go home." She bites nervously on her bottom lip, then looks over my shoulder to check the time on my nightstand. "It's late and—"

"Stay," I say, sliding over until we're both on her side of the bed. I grab her butt and tug her closer to me. "I don't want you to go."

Even as I say the words, I feel guilty. I shouldn't talk her into staying when she wants to go. It just makes me physically sick to think about leaving her. I don't want to sleep here tonight knowing she's just a few minutes away, sleeping in her own bed next door. Tomorrow I'll be in Washington, a couple thousand miles away. There's no walking outside and going to her house when I'm in Washington.

"I'll stay for a little bit," she says, scooting over and cuddling up to me. I kiss her forehead and run my fingers through her hair because I know she loves that. "I'm sorry, babe. I know you need to go home, I just don't want you to leave."

She sighs. "I don't want to leave either. I wish you weren't racing this summer." She stiffens. "I mean—not like that. I'm so happy for you and I'm proud that you're on a professional team now. I just miss you."

I chuckle. "Babe, I'll quit it all in a heartbeat. Just say the word."

She pulls away and leans up on her elbow, looking me in the eyes. "Absolutely not. Racing is your life. You have to keep doing it."

I shrug. "It doesn't have to be my life."

She glares at me. "I won't be the girl responsible for doing that to you. It's just a few weekends. We'll be fine." Then she shoves me in the chest, all while giving me that serious look of hers. "Don't even joke about quitting!"

I take her hand off my chest and bring it up to my lips, kissing her palm. "I need you to know you're the most important thing in the world to me, Keanna. I'll do whatever it takes to make you happy."

"It'll make me happy if you keep following your dreams," she says, laying back down on my shoulder, her eyes facing the ceiling.

"Then I'll keep doing that." I kiss the top of her head. I could really go for another round of love making...get all hot and sweaty underneath my sheets...

But I hold back and try to be a gentleman. This is a sweet moment with my girl, and I don't want her thinking I'm just some pathetic horndog every time I see her.

"My mom was talking about you earlier today," I say, changing the subject to get my mind off sex.

"Oh yeah? What about?"

"She was on the phone with some friend, I'm not sure who it was, but she was all bragging about you getting straight A's in college."

"Aww," Keanna says. She traces the outline of my abs with her finger. "Your mom is the best."

"She's alright," I say sarcastically, which earns me a slap from my girlfriend.

"Your mom is awesome and you know it," she says.

"Yeah, yeah." I'm already regretting changing the subject. "She loves you."

"And I love her," she says. Her breath is warm on my chest as she cuddles closer to me. I wrap my arm around her back and slide my fingers up and down her side, just enjoying the moment before time will surely slip in and take me away from her for another weekend.

My eyes start to flutter closed as my breathing slows and our combined warmth makes me sleepy. Keanna's breath slows too, and she's cuddled so close to me I don't ever want to let her go. I struggle to stay awake because I know she needs to go back home so she'll wake up early for her family. But it's hard. I just want her to stay.

"Jett?" she says, her voice soft. I don't know how much time has passed or if I accidentally fell asleep.

"Hmm?" I manage to say.

She snakes her arm around my stomach and cuddles tighter. "I love you."

I chuckle. "I love you, baby girl."

CHAPTER SEVEN

Keanna

While the summer time is always busier than usual at The Track because kids are out of school for summer, it's even worse on Fridays. I'm guessing it's because the parents who take their kids to ride can only take off work once a week and Friday is the best day for that. Not to mention, Fridays are the days Jett heads to the airport every week. So, in a world where most people love Friday, I'm beginning to resent it.

Try as I might, I can't hold back the yawn that pries open my mouth. It's the fourth one in just a few minutes, and I feel like a terrible employee. I'm working the front desk at The Track today, and we have five people in line right now.

"That'll be twenty dollars," I tell the older man standing in front of me. He reeks like cigar smoke and the coveralls he's wearing are smeared with oil and dirt, meaning he probably just got off work himself before he brought his two kids up here to ride for the day.

He reaches into his wallet and hands me a fifty, so I open the cash register to get his change.

The two boys who are with him are dressed in identical red riding gear, and I'm still trying to decide if they're twins are just brothers who look a lot alike. One of them looks up at me.

"Why is this place called The Track?" he asks as I hand his dad the change.

"Because it's a dirt bike track?" I say.

The other one laughs. "But that's a stupid name. Other tracks are called Oakcreek and Ultimate Motocross."

I shrug. "Don't blame me, kid. I didn't name the place."

The dad smiles at me and then they leave as the next person steps forward in line. It's been so busy, I didn't even recognize D'andre standing there all this time. He's one of Jett's best friends, and he loves riding motocross even though he's not at a professional skill level or anything.

"Hey!" I say, happy for a familiar face. "You didn't have to wait in line."

He shrugs. "I don't mind. To be honest, I don't even want to ride today."

I lift an eyebrow. "Then why are you here?"

He shrugs again and steps to the side, motioning for the two older women behind him to move up. "Y'all can go ahead of me," he says.

The women hand me their money and sign in quickly. They're in their forties and have been riding their whole lives. They come in at least three times a week.

"Have fun, ladies," I say, waving as they walk back outside.

D'andre waits while I take care of the remaining customers, and then he rests his elbows on the counter. I get the feeling he'd rather chat instead of ride right now.

"What's going on?" I ask. "And why bother bringing your bike up here if you don't want to ride?"

He shrugs. He's done pretty much nothing but shrug since he got here. "I don't know, Key. I'm just... blah."

I frown. "It's summertime. You should be happy." Then an idea hits me that's so sad it can't possibly be true. "Wait..." I eye him suspiciously. "You and Maya..."

He shakes his head. "Nah, we're good. Perfect, actually."

I let out the breath I'd been holding. "Good."

Maya is D'andre's girlfriend and she's pretty much my only real friend besides the girls from college, who still haven't texted me all summer. Maya and D'andre make a cute couple and I'd hate to see them split up.

I lean on my elbows from the other side of the counter until I'm eye level with him. "So why are you so sad?"

"Maya just left to visit her family in Maine." He frowns and stares at his truck keys as if they're fascinating. "She's going to be gone for eight weeks."

"Damn." I pat his shoulder. "I'm sorry."

"I don't know how I'll survive without her for so long," he says, standing up straighter. He goes to shove his hands in his pockets, but he's wearing riding pants which don't have pockets, so he just settles for slumping his shoulders. "I'm in love with this girl, Key. I can't stand being away from her."

"Trust me, I know how it is." I grimace. "Jett leaves me every weekend and it's freaking hell. He's actually about to head up to the airport any minute now." I glance at the clock on the computer screen. It's noon and he's leaving at 12:15. My chest aches and that hollow spot that appears when he's gone has already wallowed out a spot inside my ribcage.

"We should hit up a movie this weekend and be miserable together."

I laugh. "Sounds like a good idea. If I ever get off babysitting duty, I'll call you."

He nods, then opens up the wallet he'd set on the counter. "It's ten bucks on Fridays, right?"

I wave my hand at him. "Today's ride is on the house. Go ride until you're not as sad anymore."

He grins. "Thanks, Key."

"Aww man, did I miss D'andre?" Jett asks a few minutes later. His sudden voice startles me since he'd came up from the back hallway and not the front door where I'm facing.

I turn around and see him staring out the window to where D'andre is driving his truck toward the back part of the track.

"Yep," I say, throwing my arms around Jett's strong torso. "And I forbid you to go chase him down and talk."

"Why's that?" he asks with a chuckle.

I press my cheek to his chest, inhaling the scent of his cologne. I'm immediately jealous that anyone on the plane sitting next to him will get to smell the same scent. "Because I want to stay right here holding you until your Uber gets here."

His hands slide down my back until his fingers slip into my back pockets. "Sounds like a plan. I'd rather cuddle with you than D'andre anyhow."

We have to break apart a minute later when another customer arrives. I check him in and then as soon as he leaves, I turn back to Jett, finding him sitting on the stool behind the computer, a dejected look on his face.

"What's wrong?" I ask.

He lifts his shoulders. "I'm not feeling too confident about this race. I got like, zero practice this week." He shakes his head, his neck muscles tight. "I'm just worried about it."

"Well, you won the first three races so you're allowed to not win this one. You'll still be better ranked than the other guys."

His tongue slides around the inside of his cheek and he stares off at nothing instead of looking at me. "I know it won't technically matter, but I have this—like, *dream*—of having a total winning streak for this series. I'd be the first rookie to do it. With something like that under my belt, I'd be open to even better sponsorships and opportunities next year. I could finally be the guy the articles brag about."

I give him a look. "Babe, you're already bragged about in magazine articles."

He shakes his head. "No, I'm always the subject of articles called 'Is this the new rising star of motocross?' or 'Jett Adams is the Rookie to Look Out For'."

He rolls his eyes. "I want an article called, 'Jett Adams is the Best Racer of the Year.' No speculation, no watch lists. Just a definite, real, truth to it."

I lean forward and wrap my arms around him, pulling him against my chest. He makes this pleased noise when his face presses against my boobs, and I laugh. "Baby, you are the best. Think of how many guys would kill to have any article written about them! You've got tons of people talking about you, and it's all good stuff."

He sighs. "I know you're right. But that doesn't stop me from worrying about this stupid race."

"So don't worry about it," I say, running my hand through his dark hair. "Just take life as it comes and see what happens."

His lips quirk up in the corners. "I love you."

"I love you more."

He shakes his head. "No possible way."

We kiss and I hold onto the moment for as long as I can, but soon his phone beeps.

"My car is here," he says, frowning just before he kisses me on the nose. "I'll miss the hell out of you."

"I'll miss the hell out of you *more*," I say with a teasing grin as I walk him to the door where a red Ford Escape is waiting for him. We get one more kiss and one lingering hug, and then he's gone again.

Later, when The Track is finally closed and I've given Elijah a bath so Mom can relax a bit, I dress my little brother in the cutest onesie ever. It's blue and slightly fuzzy, and has monster eyes all over it, making him look like a monster baby. Very, very cute. I kiss his head, which smells like baby powder, and sit in the rocking chair in his nursery, holding him tightly swaddled up in a blanket while I rock him to sleep.

Elijah's bedroom is like a child's dream come true. My parents had it designed with this huge built in fake tree. The branches rise up the walls and to the ceiling where it's covered with silk leaves and little fake birds and animals. The main trunk of the tree is in the corner of the room, with a hole at the bottom where you can crawl inside and have your own playhouse. When Elijah gets older, he's going to absolutely love it. I can already imagine the books I'll read to him while we're inside that tree with little Christmas lights strung up for ambiance. His life is going to be an absolute dream.

It won't be anything like my childhood with my real mother was, I'll make sure of that.

After he's asleep, I snapchat with Jett for a little while before I finally convince him to get to bed. It's not as late in Washington as it is here, but he still needs his sleep so he'll be rested for tomorrow's practice all day.

I'm feeling particularly woozy and lovesick as I brush my teeth and get ready for bed. There's something about that boy that drives me crazy in all the right ways. I love him so much it physically hurts.

There's a light on in the living room, and I walk in to find my mom sitting with her feet dangling off the edge of the recliner while she reads a book.

"Hi, honey," she says, smiling up at me as I walk in the room.

"Can't sleep?" I ask.

She shrugs. "I'm just enjoying some me time, even though I'm exhausted." She slips her bookmark into the book and then closes it in her lap. "How was your day?"

I sit in the couch next to her. "Is there something wrong with me, like...mentally?" I ask. This makes her eyebrows shoot up, so I clarify. "It's Jett... I mean... he leaves every weekend this summer and I know it's coming and I know he'll be back... I should be used to it by now, right? But my chest hurts and my stomach aches and I just hate it when he's gone. I miss him so much. Earlier today I wanted to sneak over to his house and smell the clothes in his closet just to feel like I was near him."

She chuckles and gives me that warm motherly smile that I love seeing. It means she cares about me, not just as a person, but way deep down where it matters. She treats me like real family.

"Honey... you're not crazy. And there's nothing wrong with you."

"It certainly feels like something's wrong," I say with a sigh. I press my hand to my chest. "It just hurts so bad when he's gone."

She watches me with this expression I can't quite place, but it's a nice one, I think. "Keanna, sweetheart. You're in love. That's all there is to it."

CHAPTER EIGHT

Jett

By some stroke of luck, I manage to win the Washington race even though I only got that one night of practice before the race. I chalked it up to sheer luck and nothing more, since normally I train every day leading up to a race, so there's no way I could have actually ridden as fast as I did. Maybe the other guys on Team Loco just had bad days…along with the other twenty one racers on the track.

Whatever the case, I'm happy but still stressed as I go back home and continue taking over my dad's clients and some of Park's clients too. They're too busy setting up the new race schedule and calling in the part time employees who help us run our normal races. Some of them can work all of the extra races, but some can't so we have to hire more.

I'm more nervous than ever for the next race because I didn't even manage to slip in a night ride at home. But somehow, I manage another win.

On the third week in a row of flying into another state on barely any sleep following days of working at The Track instead of training for my own career, I know I'll be screwed. I arrive in Scottsdale, Arizona on Friday night, just in time to go to dinner with Zach, Clay, and Aiden. They pick some local cheeseburger place that sounds okay to me, but as soon as we walk inside, I realize it's just a knockoff of Hooters, complete with skanky-looking waitresses.

"Are you gentleman all sitting together?" the hostess says after we walk in.

"Yes, ma'am," Zach says in his twangy voice. He gives her that cocky smile of his that always makes the girls swoon. "But I'm not sure I'd call us gentlemen."

She gives him a coy grin back and says, "Follow me."

We're seated at a table that's higher than normal, with tall bar stools instead of chairs. As I look around, I notice that even the booths are tall like this. Weird.

Then I realize why.

"Hey there, handsome men," a girl in booty shorts that could pass for underwear and a tight fitting spandex tank top says. She has long brown hair that's wavy and smells like hairspray, which is probably why it doesn't move at all. Her boobs are pretty much right in my face.

That's why the chairs are tall. I'm sure they get a lot more tips when the customers are eye level with their assets.

"What can I get you boys to drink?"

"You could pour yourself in a glass," Zach says. He hasn't even been drinking today—alcohol isn't allowed so soon before a race—but he's already let his womanizing side loose. I guess he can't help it.

Clay snorts and smacks Zach with his laminated menu. "He'll take a Coke, and so will I."

Zach gives Clay an annoyed look, but it's for his own good. He's used to getting all the girls because of his southern charm and motocross fame, but our manager Marcus is constantly telling him to get his head in the game and off of girls. He tends to flirt more than he rides, and it only gets worse with each new interview or magazine that features him.

Of course, that's kind of a benefit for me, since the more he sucks at tomorrow's race, the more I'll be able to beat him. So I just order my drink and don't bother giving him shit as he continues to flirt with our waitress, whose nametag says Princess, and I'm wondering if that's actually her name or some scheme she uses to get guys to be infatuated with her.

"Dude," Aiden says after we're eating our food. He's got a French fry in one hand and his cell phone in the other, the screen glowing and lighting up his face. "All these girls from high school who didn't give a damn about me..." He shakes his head and puts the phone in his pocket.

"What about 'em?" Clay says, not looking up. Clay is the tallest of all of us, and his arms of tattoos and newly shaved head makes him look like he doesn't really belong in this group, but maybe a group of ultimate fighters or something instead. If I didn't know him, I'd be a little wary of being in a dark alley with him. He's not really an asshole; he just seems like one. He's known for never giving autographs unless Marcus makes him, usually for the tiny fans who are around five years old. The truth is, Clay only cares about dirt bikes. Not girls. Not fame. The fact that he's even speaking up now is kind of funny. "They trying to get your attention now?"

Aiden snorts. "I'd say. My inbox is full of nudes."

Zach's head snaps up. "Show 'em!" he says with a mouth full of food.

Aiden shakes his head. "Nah, man. That's invasion of privacy. Some of them aren't even that good, trust me."

Zach rolls his eyes. "Trust *me*, she sent them hoping you'd show her off to your friends."

Aiden shakes his head and keeps eating.

Clay smacks me on the arm. "Are you the only one who doesn't want see them?"

I shrug. "I've got the most perfect pair of boobs waiting on me at home."

"Maybe that's true," he says with a laugh. "But they aren't here now, are they?"

"Man, you know Jett," Aiden says. "He's our old man of the group—only eighteen and already settled down and shit."

"You say it like it's a bad thing," I say, taking a sip of my Coke. "But you see, instead of dating one girl after another, I've got my life already figured out. I got the girl... and the first place trophy," I say with a smirk. I bite down on a fry and the guys all laugh and make annoyed noises.

"Dude, you ain't got that trophy *yet*," Clay says. "Yeah, you won some races, but that don't mean shit."

"Fuckin' Jett over here, thinking he's better than us," Zach says, shaking his head. I know he's just messing with me, so I lean back in my chair and put on a smug grin.

"We should hang out after the race tomorrow," I say. "I mean, I'll obviously get to the finish line first, but I'll wait around for you all to catch up."

They laugh and I'm punched in the arm a couple of times, but deep down it's hard to keep up this confident exterior. I've barely trained in three weeks and soon my luck is bound to run out.

Yet when the gate drops on Saturday morning, I lean forward on my bike, elbows out, feet on the pegs. I pin the throttle and my bike roars into action, a cougar chasing its prey—the finish line. There are no bikes next to me as I take the first turn, meaning I got the holeshot—the first position.

I breathe in and out, and I focus on the track, letting all thoughts of everything but motocross leave my mind. The gears clink down when I slow for a turn, then the engine roars when I soar over a jump. All fifteen laps fly past me as if I'm going through life at warp speed, and then the checkered flag is waving as I fly over the final finish line jump.

Marcus is standing there with the other team managers as I roll my bike up to him, my heart pounding and sweat rolling down my face.

"Congrats little Adams," Marcus says, referring to my father as the big Adams. He pats me on the helmet. "Looks like my newest rookie might take the series win."

I don't tell the family that I've exchanged my flight ticket for an earlier departure, because I want to surprise them on Sunday morning. I was originally supposed to leave at eleven, but I forced myself to wake up early and get to the airport at six-fifteen. It's a three and a half hour flight from Arizona back to Texas, so I arrive just a few minutes after The Track has opened for the day. It's race day, and the place is packed. I pull down the bill of my baseball cap in an effort to hide my face because there's people all over the place, especially teenage girls. Most of the guys love the attention motocross gets them, but like I told the Team Loco guys—I'm settled down. I don't care for the attention at all, not unless someone wants to comment on my racing skills, not my looks.

I slip into the building and go unnoticed for a few minutes because there's so many people in here, visitors, and family members of racers.

The main building is where people pay their entry fee, race fees, and fill out waiver forms for racers. We also have a concession stand with a window outside so you can walk up and order stuff, as well as a daycare and a gym, plus employee only rooms like our break room.

I weave through the crowd and step behind the front counter to where Becca, my mom, and Keanna are working the front desk. Mom's got Brooke swaddled in a blanket that loops around her shoulder like a kind of backpack that holds the baby against her chest.

Mom sees me first, and her expression goes from stressed out to relieved. "Oh my God, Jett," she says, walking over to me. "I wasn't expecting you so soon."

"I took an earlier flight," I say, smiling over her shoulder at Keanna, who looks at me and then turns back to her customers. Weird. I mean I guess I wasn't expecting a full on make out session with all these customers in here, but a smile would have been nice.

Mom takes off the backpack blanket thing and hands the baby to me. "Hold her for a few minutes, okay?" she says, pulling the strap over my shoulder and securing it around my back. Brooke feels pretty securely stuck to my chest, but I keep my arms around her just in case. She's sleeping, her tiny little baby face serene and totally conked out.

"I just need a break," Mom says, looking exhausted. Her hair is in a ponytail, but lots of strands are frizzy around her face, and she has dark circles under her eyes.

"You okay?" I ask.

"Yeah, baby, I'm fine," she says as she grabs my face and kisses my cheek as if I'm still freaking five years old. "I'm just exhausted. That baby gets heavy!" She smiles and then grabs a water bottle from the mini-fridge behind the counter.

I walk over to Keanna and bump against her shoulder since I can't do anything else with this baby in my arms. "Hey beautiful."

"Hey," she says, not looking at me. She counts money at the register and then gives change to the woman on the other side of the counter.

I guess she's stressed out from being so busy, so I try not to let her cold attitude bother me. I check the security of this baby backpack thing, and when I'm positive that Brooke will be safe against my chest without me holding her, I join Keanna and Becca and help sign in the customers.

It's hard to help very much though, because people know who I am and they want to talk about Team Loco and the races and my latest interview with some magazine. I have to balance being nice to them and also trying to make them move along so I can help out more customers.

Eventually things die down as the races begin outside, and my mom comes back for her baby. There's a sweaty part of my shirt from where Brooke was laying, but I tell my mom I don't mind taking care of my sister at all. It's what big brothers do, right?

Eventually, Mom and Becca head to the breakroom and it's finally just me and Keanna. I put an arm around her waist and rest my chin on her shoulder.

"I missed you," I say.

"Good." Her voice is cold.

"Baby..." I tug her closer to me, kissing her neck. "What's wrong?"

"Nothing's wrong."

I gently turn her around to face me, keeping my hands on her waist. I look into her eyes, trying to do some mind reading, but it doesn't work. "Baby, what's wrong? You've barely spoken to me since I got home."

She shrugs and looks away, not meeting my eye.

"Key..." I pull her closer, wrapping my arms around her and resting my chin on top of her head. "Please tell me what's wrong."

She softens a little against my chest, and it relieves some of the fear I feel right now. "I don't know," she mumbles against my shirt. "I just missed you, I guess."

"Well you're acting like you hate me."

She shakes her head, then looks up at me. "It's just hard..." she says, tears filling her eyes. "It's just hard."

A lump rises in my throat, and another one settles in my chest. This is exactly what I've worried about from day one. That Keanna wouldn't be able to handle my racing career. I hold her close and tell her I love her.

She doesn't say anything back.

CHAPTER NINE

Keanna

When I wake up on Monday morning, the scent of Jett's cologne is in the air, which is weird because I'm in my own bed. I open my eyes and yawn, and then I look out the window in front of me. The sun sure seems a little too bright for six in the morning.

I jolt up in bed, and that's when I realize I'm not alone.

Jett grins at me. He's lying on top of the sheets, fully clothed, with a smirk on his face. "Morning."

"What are you doing here?" I ask, as I get out of bed and reach over for my phone and—"Oh shit!" I drop the phone and run to my closet. "I'm late! I'm so late!"

Frantically, I look for an outfit to wear. It's 9:45 and I'm almost four hours late for work. Why didn't Mom come get me? Ugh.

Jet appears in my closet doorway, a cocky grin on his face. "You're not late."

"Yes, I am!" I say, yanking off my sleep shirt so I can put on a bra. "I'm supposed to be at the front office by 6:30. I can't believe my alarm didn't go off."

"I can," Jett says. He's still grinning at me, like he knows something I don't.

I stop rushing to get dressed and look at him. "What is it?"

"I turned off your alarm so you could sleep in late," he explains. "It was kind of boring because I've been lying next to you forever, waiting for you to wake up."

"Why didn't you just wake me up yourself?" I ask. I put on a pair of shorts.

"Because you've been working so hard lately, and I wanted you to just enjoy waking up naturally for once."

"Okay well, I'll tell your parents it's your freaking fault I'm late to work."

"You're not going into work today," Jett says. He follows me out of the closet and then takes my hand. "I called in a favor. Krissy from Oakcreek is working in your place today. My parents are totally cool with it," he says as soon as I start to object. "I told them we need a day off so we can have some time together."

I can feel some of my resentment starting to melt away. The last several weeks have been hell. The Track is constantly busy and Jett is either out of town, or working with clients. We haven't had a proper conversation in days.

"We haven't had any alone time in a while…" I say, smiling up at him.

"No, we haven't." He pulls my hand until I step closer to him, and then he kisses my forehead and holds me close. "Let's spend the day together."

I lean up on my toes and kiss him. "That sounds like a great idea."

I can't exactly say it out loud without sounding like a complaining jerk, but our lives are so different. Jett has motocross. It's his career. I have nothing but college classes in the fall and a part time job at a dirt bike track. He has a future—I have regular life.

It's been bothering me a lot lately. Sometimes I wonder if I'm just not good enough for a guy like Jett, whose future is so bright and exciting. Other times I wonder if I should just suck it up and pretend like I am good enough and enjoy the ride of dating a famous motocross racer. Most of the time, I'm just waiting for him to figure it out on his own and then grow to resent me for holding him back.

I shove all my worries away and try to just enjoy this time with Jett. After I finish getting dressed, he drives us to a café on the outskirts of town and we order breakfast among the smell of bacon and coffee in the air.

"So tell me about your last race," I say while we're eating. I'd been kind of cold to him yesterday when he got home, so he still hasn't updated me on anything.

He's always happy to talk about the races when he's actually won it. If he loses —and by getting even second place, he considers it a loss—he'd rather talk about anything else in the world.

After breakfast, we drive to the beach and Jett holds my hand while we walk along the sand. It reminds me of when we first started dating, all sweet and innocent. We hit up the shops on the strand and look at artwork on display from local artists. For lunch, we grab tacos from a food truck and eat them on the patio of a nearby hotel, pretending to be tourists instead of residents.

Then we go back down to the beach and enjoy the beautiful summer day. We walk for a long time without talking about much of anything. The only sounds are the waves crashing to shore, the call of a seagull flying overhead, and distant screams and laughter from children playing on the shore.

"It's nice to relax," I say after a while.

"Mmhmm," Jett says. I look over at him and he's walking with his eyes closed, face tipped up to the sky. "Everything is calm on the beach," he says. I think he's going to say more, but he doesn't.

"Life has been crazy lately," I say to fill in the gap.

He squeezes my hand. "Life will probably always be crazy, baby doll. But I have you with me so that helps me get through it."

I roll my eyes and he grins. "What?"

"So cheesy," I say, poking him in the stomach.

He blows a raspberry. "I'm sorry my love for you is *cheesy*."

I poke him again and reaches out and tickles my ribs, making me squeal and flail to get him away.

"If you think what I said was cheesy... well..." Jett runs a hand through his wind-blown hair and gives me a look.

"Well, what?" I say.

He shrugs. "You're about to see the ultimate biggest cheesy thing ever."

I lift an eyebrow but he doesn't explain anymore. He just keeps walking.

"Oh, come on," I say, grabbing his hand. "You have to tell me. What's cheesy?"

"You'll see..."

And I do.

At the very end of the beach, where the public part of the sand ends for a row of private beach houses, Jett has pulled out all the stops when it comes to cheesy surprises. His best friend D'andre stands before us, his hands clasped in front of him as if he were a butler or something.

"Hello, lovebirds," he says, winking at me. In a swift motion, he steps to the side and reveals what's been set up behind him with a sweeping of his hand through the air.

A plaid blanket is laid out on the sand. Large candles in glass mason jars are sitting on all four corners of the blanket to hold it down, and they're lit, their flames glowing in the evening sun. A picnic basket is in the middle of the blanket, along with a small cooler, a few pillows, and a Bluetooth speaker.

"I did everything you asked," D'andre say as he fist bumps Jett in their usual hello gesture. "I also brought a speaker. Figured you could play some romantic music or some shit."

"Nice," Jett says. "Thanks, man."

"Anytime." He waves goodbye and then jogs off down the beach, leaving us here at this romantic little setup.

"You arranged a picnic for us?" I say.

Jett grins. "I know... it's kind of lame. But I also thought it'd be fun. I wanted it to be a surprise."

"It's perfect," I say. I grab his sides and kiss him, closing my eyes and allowing myself to really feel every part of his kiss. Jett's soft lips on mine, the slight minty smell of his toothpaste mixed with the salt in the air. The way the scruff of his chin brushes against my face.

"I love you," I whisper.

His hands slide up and down my back. "I love you more."

We sit on the blanket and eat dinner, which is a very cool and very chic meat, cheese, and veggie ensemble that Jett had D'andre pick up from the local French Market in downtown Lawson. We watch the ocean turn from blue to orange as the sun begins to set, and down the beach a little ways, someone makes a bonfire which smells like summer.

After the sun has set, Jett and I listen to music and lay side by side, watching the stars while the ocean gently crashes onto the shore.

"I had fun today," I say, nuzzling against his chest.

"I'm glad." Jett exhales slowly, his gaze fixed on the stars. "I'm sorry things have been hard lately. I hate coming home and knowing you're upset with me."

"I'm not—" I begin, but I know it'd be a lie. I sigh and try to gather my thoughts. How can I tell Jett I worry that I'm not good enough for him? What if my confession makes him realize it for the first time?

"Your life is so much cooler than mine," I say after a while. I can tell Jett is listening intently to every word I say, so I try to choose the right ones to define what I'm feeling. "I'm just afraid you're going to pass me by."

"Our lives are the same, Keanna. I mean…we're two different people with sometimes different schedules, but we're on the same track. Two passengers—same train."

I lean up on my elbow. "What does that mean?"

"It means where you go, I go, and I hope you feel the same way. I meant it when I said I'd quit motocross for you. If you're missing something in your life, let's go find it."

"No…" I smile because even though my heart aches, I just love him so much. "I don't want anything else. I just want you, and your motocross life and my job and my family. I'm just always afraid that I'm not bringing anything worthwhile to the table. I'm just…a loser."

"Don't feel that way, baby. You're an amazing person. You help the Track stay in business, which is a good thing because that place will belong to us someday." Jett grins. "You're the hottest girl a guy could ask for, and yeah, that's sexist or whatever, but trust me, it's a good thing. You keep me motivated and encouraged to work hard. You're always there when I need you, and you're the only person in the world I can spend all day with and still not want to leave."

"Go on," I say with a playful smirk. He laughs.

And then he's on top of me, his body balanced just above mine, his hands on either side of my head. "I love you," he whispers.

"I love you more," I say back.

He kisses my forehead, my nose, and then my lips. "Impossible."

CHAPTER TEN

Jett

I underestimated my parents. I had spent hours agonizing over the perfect way to bring up my idea to them last night while I was lying under the stars with Keanna. I had managed to pull off getting us one day off work by having Krissy from Oakcreek Motocross come and work in Keanna's place, but my plan was bigger than that.

I wanted to get her off work for the rest of the summer.

And then I wanted to stop training Dad's clients.

We both need a break. This is one of those points in the relationship where it'll either get better or worse, and I can't have it getting worse. People say long distance relationships never work out, and right now it feels like we're long distance because I travel so much. If everything goes according to my plan, and Team Loco puts me in the motocross series this year, I'll be traveling even more than I am now. I can't lose Keanna and I don't want to lose motocross, either. So I decided to try to fix this before it becomes a problem.

There was no way my parents would agree to this, not at all. Not in the slightest. I mean, they *need* us, right? So, when I finally approach my parents over breakfast and coffee this morning, I don't expect them to agree. But I don't have a backup plan, so I take a deep breath and hope for the best.

"We have to find a way to make it work," Mom says right after I tell her what I'd been thinking.

Dad nods. "It shouldn't be too hard... I mean... I don't trust anyone else to train my clients, but now that the races are set up, I can probably get back to training them myself soon. And we can hire people to do Keanna's job at the front desk."

"And I should probably look into hiring a babysitter," Mom says, her lips sliding to the side of her mouth. She glances over at Brooke, who is laying in this baby seat thing that bounces up and down. "Becca and I have been talking about finding a really good nanny to look after Brooke and Elijah."

Dad lifts an eyebrow and watches Mom with this incredulous look on his face, one that probably matches my own.

"Seriously?" I say with a snort. "You and Becca are like the most overprotective parents ever. I don't believe you'd trust someone else with your kid besides Keanna."

"Well… I said a *really good* nanny," Mom says with a shrug. "You know… one who has lots of references, and one who loves kids and isn't in it just for the money, and one who can pass a drug test and a criminal background test and—" She heaves a sigh. "Trust me, I'd be researching the hell out of a nanny, but I think we could find one. Plus, she could just watch the kids at The Track in the daycare and then Becca and I can keep an eye on her."

"So, you think this can work?" I ask. My voice sounds a little disbelieving because I'm still not sure my parents can actually live without us for the rest of the summer, but I really hope they can.

Mom looks at Dad and they exchange some wordless thoughts with each other.

"Keanna's been working her butt off lately and it's her summer break. She deserves some time off," Mom says.

Dad nods. "And you need to focus on motocross, not working at The Track. I appreciate it, son, I really do, but I worry your luck will run out soon."

I scowl. "You think my winning streak is luck? Psh…"

Dad grins. "It's not luck. I raised you with the skill to win, but you know what I mean. You don't need to be caught up in work here. Focus on Team Loco."

"So…" I set my fork down on my empty plate. "We're off? Starting now?"

"Yep," Dad says.

I grin so big it hurts my cheeks. Mom rolls her eyes and waves her hand at me, shooing me away. "Go on. Go tell Keanna the good news."

I throw on some clothes and call Keanna, asking her to meet me between our houses. I'm too excited to tell her my plans, and I can't waste an extra five minutes walking all the way over to her house.

She's wearing leggings and a tank top with flip flops, which is otherwise known as my favorite outfit of hers. The tight-fitting clothes put all her sexy curves on display. The only thing better would be having her naked under the sheets with me.

"What's up?" she says when we're only a few feet apart.

I grab her and kiss her, because my good news can wait about three more seconds, then I say, "We're officially fired for the rest of summer."

She lifts an eyebrow. "Um…what?"

"Starting today, you're on vacation." I bite my bottom lip to avoid jumping up and down like a kid, but I can't help it. I'm excited. "My parents agreed that you need some time off, so they're hiring someone to be your replacement and Becca and Mom are even getting a nanny and all that jazz, so you and I are totally free for the rest of summer!"

Her eyes go wide. "But, you said *fired*…"

I shrug. "I was just being dramatic. We're not *fired*, fired."

She exhales, putting a hand to her chest. "Thank God. I thought you meant you were fired from Team Loco."

I shake my head. "No ma'am. We're just temporarily relieved of our work duties at The Track. I think my parents realized I needed to spend more time with my girl or I'd go crazy."

She grins up at me, then reaches for my hands. "This will be fun. It'll take some of the sting away from losing you each weekend."

"You're not losing me each weekend," I say, giving her a playful smile.

She must not notice my smile because her expression turns to concern. "But you said you're not fired. There's still four weeks of races left."

"Yep," I say, squeezing her hands. "And you're coming with me."

THE AIRPORT IS A FLURRY OF NOISE AND FILLED PEOPLE DRAGGING LUGGAGE ALONG behind them. I hold onto Keanna's hand as I walk us through the early morning crowds toward terminal C. When I glance over at her, her eyes are wide and child-like, a whimsical glow on her features from the overhead lights.

"This place is awesome," she says. "All these people, all with somewhere else to be."

"This is the international airport which is way cooler than the other one in Houston," I say. "There's people from all countries here. Not to mention the place is huge."

She squeezes my hand. "This is going to be fun, even though I'm kind of terrified of flying."

"Trust me, you'll love it," I say. "You have to sit in the window seat."

We make it through security and into the boarding line. Once we get on the walkway into the plane, I can tell she's starting to get nervous by the way she clings to my hand, her other one gripping my elbow. Keanna has never been on a plane before. I remember my first time flying, and there's really no way to get over the fear than by suffering through it on your first trip.

"The takeoff is fun," I whisper in her ear as we walk down the aisle and choose a seat. "Landing is sometimes creepy. It gets all jolty and bumpy and then they slam on some huge brake that sends you flying forward."

Her eyes go wide for a second, but then she smiles at me. "Well, if we crash and burn, at least we both die."

I snort. "Way to think positive."

She sits next to the window and I store our bags in the overhead bins. A giddy excitement keeps coursing through my bones because Keanna is here with me. I've been on a plane so many times lately, all of them trips taken alone. I've sat in airplanes by myself, or squished between strangers, always wishing she was here with me. And now she is.

Keanna grins at me as the plane taxis to the runway, and then with a huge burst of power, the plane lurches forward and begins its ascent. Her eyes widen and she grins while looking out the window. As soon as we lift off, she holds onto my arm with both hands and rests her face against my arm. "This is scary and fun at the same time," she whispers.

I kiss her forehead.

"Thanks for bringing me, Jett." She grins up at me, then puckers her lips for a kiss. I kiss her softly, closing my eyes and yearning for more. But this is a public plane and I don't want to give anyone a free show. Plus, there will be time for that at our hotel room later today.

"Get used to it, babe." I lace my fingers through hers, and lean my head on top of her hair. "I'm always going to keep you by my side."

BELIEVE IN FALL

A BELIEVE IN LOVE NOVELLA

CHAPTER ONE

Keanna

It's a beautiful Texas day. Well, as beautiful as it can get in the middle of August. The sun is beating down on us as if its only goal in life is to tan everyone to a crisp. But even though it's hotter than Hades outside, it's still a pretty day. A day that shouldn't be spent in the stuffy library of the local community college, surrounded by people who would all clearly rather be somewhere else.

I gaze at the long line ahead of me. It's amazing how many people don't know how to use a freaking computer. I would be at home today, among the people who *do* know how to use a computer, if some utility worker hadn't made an epic screw up.

Early in the morning, while messing with the cables that run underground, some guy from the cable company accidentally severed the lines that bring internet to our apart of the town. My parents got an email (ironically, which they had to read on their cell phones) apologizing for the inconvenience and saying they hope to have internet restored by next week.

Next week will be too late to register for college classes. Next week doesn't help me at all.

I tried registering for classes on my phone, but the website is not made for that, and it just didn't work. So, I had to do what my mom called the old school thing, and head up to the college during one of their registration days. That means standing in long lines to talk to a counselor who will help you fill out a paper with the classes you want to register for. Then you have to take that paper to the admissions office and pay tuition. Last semester, I did it all online in just a few minutes, all from the comfort of my pajamas.

It's like the freaking stone ages in here. I chuckle to myself as I gaze around at the twenty or so people standing ahead of me. We're sectioned off by last names, and the H through P section is the longest. Go figure. It doesn't escape my notice that most of the people in these lines are older, people in their forties and so who are going back to college. I guess they still prefer doing things the manual way.

I send a text to Jett to pass the boredom.

Me: I miss technology.

Jett: You're using technology right now…

Me: I miss the internet…at my home…

Jett: Are you still at the college?

Me: Yep…waiting in line to register.

Jett: that sucks. I'm almost home…I figured you'd be home too.

Jett had left bright and early this morning to pick up his dirt bike from the only shop around that does the best suspension work. It's nearly in Houston, so it was a long drive. I glance at the time—11:15, and realize I've been here for over an hour.

Me: Help me…this line is never ending

Jett: I'll drop off my bike and head your way

I smile. Sure, I feel a little guilty for making Jett come up here just to keep me company, but that's what boyfriends do. His only other plans today were to ride his dirt bike, and you can ride a dirt bike any time of day. There's only a few hours you get to stand in line with your girlfriend, being bored out of your mind. Ha!

By the time he gets here, there's only two people ahead of me, and both of them turn to watch Jett walk up. He's a force of sexuality, that boy. Wearing black shorts, Adidas shoes, and a Team Loco blue T-shirt, he looks just as good as he smells.

"Hi babe," he says, sliding an arm around my waist as he presses a kiss to my cheek. "This line isn't long at all."

I smack him on the chest. "That's because I've already been waiting for hours."

He grins and takes the brochure from my hand, thumbing through the dog-eared pages. "So, what classes are you signing up for?"

"Just basic stuff. History, Government, English, a stupid PE class called Power-walking." I shrug. "The core stuff. Luckily I have another year of basic classes before I need to figure out what I want to study."

"It's weird," Jett says, handing the brochure back to me. His lips slide to the side of his mouth as he thinks. "I'm like…a little jealous? But mostly not. I mean, you're in college and that's awesome, and I kind of want to be in college, but I'd rather ride a bike for a living, you know?"

He grins at me in this horribly cute way that still makes my toes tingle after all this time.

"Yeah well college is what normal people do. The people without crazy dirt bike skills."

"Are you ready to register?" The woman behind the table's voice startles me. I can't believe I'm already at the front of the line. Being with Jett always makes the time go by faster. I should bring him with me every time I have to wait for something.

When I'm officially signed up for classes, we take my registration papers to the school bookstore so I can get all the textbooks I'll need. Jett looks around in wonder as we trek across the school campus, sticking to the sidewalks that link all of the buildings together even though most people just cut through the grass.

"This place is pretty cool," he says. He steps to the side so a guy walking toward us can get by, then he moves back to standing next to me. "It's like how colleges are in the movies. All these people with backpacks and laptops, walking around being all hip and millennial."

I snort out a laugh. "You're such a dork. *We* are millennials, you know that right?"

"Yeah, but we're cooler than most people. Hey, look at that!" He points toward the art building where large sculptures are set up on display in the courtyard. His eyes go wide. "It's fancy art. How very collegiate."

I roll my eyes. "This is just a community college, you know. The bigger universities are probably a million times cooler than this place."

"I didn't really want to go to college, but being here is making me change my mind."

"Wait until you see all the homework and essays I have to write after the semester starts. You'll change your mind again."

"Yeah, I forgot about that," he says, curling his lip in disgust.

We reach the bookstore, which is a large circular building with a domed ceiling that's mostly skylights. It was built in the eighties so it smells like musty old building in here, but it's still pretty cool. A blast of cold air conditioning hits me as I walk inside with Jett right behind me.

Smooth jazz music plays overhead and the two students working behind the counter are sporting several tattoos and LCC college shirts.

"Babe!" Jett says playfully as he wanders over to a rack of those LCC shirts. "Why don't you have any of this awesome merch?" He holds up a hot pink shirt with the school's logo on the front.

I roll my eyes and shove his hand away. "Because I don't have any school spirit, that's why."

"We're going to change that," he says, taking the pink shirt off the hanger and then reaching for a lime green one. "You're my college girl now, and you should be proud." He throws the shirts over his shoulder and then moves to a rack of LCC school supplies.

Yeah, all of the school stuff is kind of cool, but I've never bought any because all the people I see at the motocross track always wear *real* college stuff. Like state universities, or ivy league schools. Community college feels so lame.

When I think back to being raised by my biological mother and how we were nothing but white trash, I do feel proud that I'm enrolled in at least some college, even though it's not a fancy one. Maybe I do need a shirt.

Jett follows me toward the book section, his arms loaded down with silly LCC things he thinks I need. We go through the list of my four classes this semester and find all the books I'll need.

The total comes to just over five hundred dollars, but luckily, I have a scholarship for a thousand dollars that I earned from a local electric company. All I had to do was write an essay on why I loved Lawson, Texas. Since Lawson is the town that gave me my new parents, my boyfriend, and my future, it was pretty easy to write.

Jett insists on buying the LCC stuff for me, and one of the cashiers can't seem to keep her eyes off him. I've seen that look in girls' eyes before. They think he's hot and they can't help but stare. It used to make me jealous, but now it makes me feel kind of awesome. Jett is the guy every girl wants, and yet he's all mine.

What's even cuter is that if a girl isn't actively flirting with him, he doesn't even notice it. I guess if you're crazy hot, maybe you get used to people gawking at you nonstop.

Jett carries my books and shopping bag in one hand and throws the other one over my shoulder as we make our way back out to the parking lot. "Have I ever told you how amazingly beautiful you are?" he asks.

I give him a sarcastic look. "Maybe once or twice."

"Well, you are. I'm so lucky to have you."

I just grin like an idiot at that comment. Jett has been in an amazing mood ever since his summer race series ended with him taking the first place trophy. He and the other three rookie guys from Team Loco raced in this ten week summer series that took place all over the nation. There were twenty other racers as well, some of them on professional motocross teams like Jett, and some were just private racers hoping for their lucky break. Out of all ten races, they average up everyone's stats, and although Jett ended up taking second place two times, he still got first place overall. Another guy from Team Loco named Clay Summers took second place overall and then Aiden Strauss was third place. It was the first time a single professional race team had their own riders on the podium, so it was a big win for Team Loco in general.

I'll never forget the look on Jett's face at that last race in California, when he stepped up on the podium and they handed him the first place trophy. I've never seen him smile so big, and I've never been so proud in my life.

Now he gets the rookie position on the professional arenacross races this year. The season starts in a couple of weeks and his other Team Loco rookies will be there to cheer him on. As much as I loved traveling with Jett for the last four races of the summer season, now that college is starting, I'll only be able to go to the races that are close by. Luckily, arenacross comes to Houston, San Antonio, and Dallas this season. I'm going to be at every one, cheering him on as he pursues his dreams.

CHAPTER TWO

Jett

Arenacross is a whole different beast from motocross, which is held outside on an open track. It's even different from supercross, which is inside a stadium. They're similar, but arenacross is small. Very small. A tight track with lots of jumps and hardly any room to move around. They're usually held in smaller stadiums, like the one happening this weekend in San Antonio, Texas. There aren't any arenacross tracks at home to practice on, and since most of them are built specifically for one race and then demolished so the stadium can host concerts and stuff, I never get to practice.

I'm not going to say I'm nervous, exactly. I'm just a little ready to get this over with.

My ultimate goal is to race in the actual AMA Motocross seasons. That's the most professional of professional that you can get. Right now, I still have to race these smaller things and prove myself worthy to my team. Team Loco has a dozen other riders who are in their twenties and thirties who come from all over the world, and most of them can probably kick my ass on the track. Dad tells me not to worry about it because I'll get there eventually. I'm confident that I will, but I have to put up with these smaller pro races first.

I throw my suitcase onto my bed and find two old socks left over in there from when I used it last time. Gross. I toss them into the dirty laundry hamper and then get to work packing up for two days in San Antonio. It's only a few hours away, so Keanna and I decided to drive. Airplanes get stuffy and old after a while. I'd way rather spend three hours in my truck alone with Keanna than forty five minutes in a plane with strangers.

When all my stuff is packed, I haul it downstairs and set it by the back door so

I'll be ready to go at nine in the morning. My mom is hosting family dinner tonight to say goodbye to us, even though we're only going to be gone for two freaking days. She's making lasagna though, so I'm not going to complain.

When Keanna comes over for dinner, her parents and little brother are with her. Her parents, Becca and Park, are best friends with my parents. Most of the time this is a great thing because they're all pretty chill as far as parents go.

Other times it can be totally embarrassing.

"There's my future son-in-law," Becca says as she walks by. She ruffles my hair, which is something she's done to me ever since I was a little kid. But now that I'm six feet tall and she's still five foot three, it kind of loses it's meaning because she has to reach up so high.

I tell her hello and I ignore the future son-in-law comment. They always do that—act like we're getting married soon, or sometimes like we already are married. I love Keanna with all of my heart and when I gave her that promise ring that she wears on her left hand, I knew one day it'd be switched out with an engagement ring.

But having your parents talk about it all the time is a little annoying. I know they're just happy for us, but I don't ever want our relationship to feel like something that's been laid out for us without our input. When I officially propose to Keanna, I want it to be because *we* chose to take that step in our lives, not because we feel obligated to.

"Hey," I say, reaching out and brushing my fingers down Keanna's arm.

She gives me this exasperated smile, and it's probably because of what her mom just said.

We all sit around the dining table: my parents, Keanna's parents, our little siblings, and us. Mom's lasagna is delicious as always, and my baby sister Brooke, who is only four months old, looks at it like she wishes she could eat some instead of drinking her bottle.

Keanna's brother Elijah is old enough to eat it, but he makes more of a mess with his food in his high chair that actually eating it.

The parents talk about whatever, and Keanna and I kind of split into our own world. We sit close together at the end of the table, my leg touching hers, my elbow brushing against hers as we eat.

It seems to take forever, but finally dinner is over. The parents all tell me good luck at my races this weekend, and I thank them and then drag Keanna upstairs to my room for some privacy.

KEANNA DIDN'T ALLOW US TO STAY UP TOO LATE LAST NIGHT SINCE WE HAVE TO WAKE up early today, but I still feel like shit when my alarm goes off. My girlfriend is up and ready though, bouncing off my bed as if she's been infused with the sunshine that's filtering in from my blinds.

"No..." I say, rolling over in bed and hitting snooze on my phone's alarm. "Five more minutes."

"Babe!" Keanna says, walking over to my side of the bed. It'd taken only a little bit of begging on my part to get her to spend the night last night. She looks hot as hell wearing my T-shirt over her panties. She puts her hands on her hips. "You said if we leave by eight-thirty then we'll have time to get bagels."

"I did say that," I say, pulling the pillow over my head. I take a deep breath and then sit up even though all I want to do is sleep some more.

There's this bagel place on the outskirts of town and they sell New York style bagels that are freaking amazing. But the line is always long so it's hard to stop on our way if we don't have time to waste.

Keanna brushes her teeth while I get dressed, and I watch her from the reflection in the bathroom mirror. She's wearing shorts and a tank top but she looks adorable. I love her in a ponytail. She always looks so happy and carefree when she hasn't put much time into her looks. When we're forced to dress up for some formal event or dinner, she always tends to freak out and worry about herself all night. Telling her how beautiful she is doesn't ever help.

But on days like today, where all we have to do is drive to San Antonio and check into our hotel, she doesn't stress too much.

There's a heat race tonight, which isn't that big of a deal. It's basically a qualifier race to determine who makes it into the official race tomorrow. They only allow twenty five racers and about seventy five show up to qualify. That starts at six this evening, so we've got all day.

My mom is downstairs with the baby and she offers us coffee, but we decline because the bagel place has amazing coffee. I kiss my little sister Brooke goodbye and she touches my face with a drool-covered little hand.

"Thanks," I say, rubbing my cheek on my sleeve.

"It means she loves you," Mom says.

"Uh huh. Sure."

Mom hugs Keanna and me goodbye and then we're finally on the road. There's nothing better than driving in my truck with my girl by my side.

I reach over and grab her thigh, but she doesn't acknowledge me because she's on her phone. I slide my hand up and squeeze right above her knee where it tickles.

That works.

"Ahh!" she squeals, swatting at my hand.

"Whatcha doing?" I ask.

She scrolls down the screen on her phone. "Just reading all your fan messages on Facebook," she says with a laugh. "San Antonio loves you."

"Well—" I say, starting to make some funny joke, but she interrupts me.

"You didn't let me finish," she says, sticking out her tongue. It's so sexy, I'd reach over there and bite it if I wasn't driving. She looks back at her phone. "They love you in San Antonio, but they might love Clay more."

I scoff. "That tatted up stone wall? Why would they like him? He hates everyone."

She shrugs. "That's probably why. You're too nice to everyone and you have this kind boy next door vibe. Clay is edgy and kind of a dick, and girls like that."

I give her a look.

"*Some* girls," she says. "Not me. I like the sweet guy next door."

"Good thing I am literally next door," I say, winking.

I like my teammate Clay, and he's going to this race as a backup for Team Loco.

Where I have a life and a girlfriend and I help my family run the Track part time, Clay only focuses on dirt bikes. It's kind of creepy how focused he is. But it didn't help him win the summer race, and I know he's been aching to prove himself ever since.

"Maybe the girls need to like him more," I say as we drive down an empty I-10 toward the bagel shop. "He needs something to distract him from dirt bikes, just a little. Enough to make him loosen up a bit."

"Why, so you can keep beating him?" she says with a smirk.

"No..." I grin. "Okay, maybe."

Our hotel is a Hilton that's only a few blocks away from the Alamo, and after the races are over tomorrow, I'm going to make sure we stop by and see it. Clay hasn't checked in yet, and Marcus won't get here until his plane lands around four, so I don't feel guilty spending the first few hours of my racing weekend with my girlfriend.

We head outside to the pool and swim around a bit, and then wander into the hotel's restaurant and order some lunch.

"Can we eat this upstairs?" Keanna says after we place our order. She chews on her thumbnail.

"Sure. Are you okay?"

She shrugs. "Those girls are looking at you and pointing at you and I'm pretty sure they're trying to get the courage to come talk to you."

I don't look back to where the girls sit so as not to give them ammunition. I know it makes her uncomfortable to have other girls talk to me in public.

"I think all the arenacross people are staying in this hotel, so it makes sense that I'd get recognized here."

Her lips slide into a thin smile. "It's fine. It's just...ugh."

"I get it, babe." I flag the waiter down. "Is there any way we can get our food delivered to our room instead?"

"Of course," he says, beaming at me with a toothy grin.

"No, that's okay," Keanna says. "It's fine. We don't have to run away just because you're popular."

"I don't mind," I tell her. Our waiter watches me questioningly, waiting for confirmation on what he should do. "We'll take it to go."

"Are you sure?" Keanna says. Now she looks worried and guilty, and all those other emotions that make her chew on her thumbnail.

I give her a heartwarming smile. "I'm positive. Let's go."

I make sure to take her hand as soon as we leave, in case any of those girls are watching. I know it should be common knowledge by now that *Jett Adams Has A Girlfriend*, but some people still don't know, or they choose not to care.

It is kind of cool getting all this attention from girls and guys and everyone now that I'm mildly famous in the motocross world, but I'd never want Keanna to feel threatened.

Our dinner is pretty amazing, but I don't eat too much or else I'll puke out on the track tonight. After eating and watching some TV, I get a text from Marcus to meet him down at the arena next door. Practice starts in half an hour and then the heat race will start promptly at seven.

"Could I maybe stay here while you practice?" Keanna says. She peers up at me from the hotel bed with puppy dog eyes. "It's just that I have to be there all alone when you're riding and it gets boring. I'd rather just go there right before the official race starts."

I laugh because I can tell it took a lot of guts for her to ask that. "Of course," I say, leaning down and kissing her. "Let me get your pass."

I'm already digging in my suitcase for my lucky underwear, so I reach for the VIP pass Marcus sent me for Keanna and me. Mine says I'm a racer and hers says she part of the pit crew. It's a slight lie, but that's the only way to get anyone access to the pit area of the stadium, otherwise she'd have to stay up in the stands with everyone else.

"Here's your pass," I say, handing her the laminated card strung on a lanyard. "Do you know where my lucky underwear are?"

She frowns. "Did you remember to get them out of the dryer?"

"Dammit." I cover my face with my hands and look up at the ceiling. "No. *Shit.*"

"Baby, you'll be fine," she assures me. "Underwear doesn't make you win races."

I breathe in deeply and let it out slowly. I won every single race this summer while wearing them. I know it's a silly superstition, but it's important to me.

I stand in front of where she sits on the mattress, and put my hands on either side of her legs. "I love you."

"I love you," she says back just before I kiss her.

"See you at the races?"

She nods. "See you at the races."

CHAPTER THREE

Keanna

Our hotel room is really nice. The bed is plush and pillow soft, the sheets made of some high thread count. They even smell like fancy laundry detergent. I stayed in a few hotels with Jett this summer, and they all made me feel the same way, like I was wrapped in luxury. These aren't even five-star hotels or anything, they're just nice and clean.

The bathroom has marble countertops and there's a large flat screen TV on the wall, which I turn on to a movie channel. All of this luxury is fun, but it reminds me of my old life, where I had a mom who would make us sleep in the car when we couldn't afford rent. Cheap motel rooms for the night were a luxury and they were already inhabited by the roaches and mice who lived there full time. I used to long for a shower, not even caring how filthy the motel was, just because I hadn't showered in days.

I'm glad I didn't know about these nice hotels back then. I don't think I could have handled it.

I order a strawberry banana smoothie from room service and lay back in bed and enjoy the peaceful serenity of our room with a balcony that overlooks the city of San Antonio, which isn't like Houston at all. It's sprawling, with shorter buildings, and not much of a big downtown area. The land is hilly and sloping, unlike the flatness of Houston. It's pretty here, in its own way. It's not as busy and filled with people or traffic.

When it's almost time for the heat races to start, I push myself up out of the super plush mattress. It's a chore leaving a bed that comfortable, but I'm excited to watch Jett race.

I stand up, and step right on top of my suitcase which I'd left next to the bed. I jump, afraid to put much weight on it because my laptop is in there.

That's when I squeeze the Styrofoam smoothie cup too hard, and the last few inches of strawberry banana spill out all over the place.

Ugh.

I rush into the bathroom and clean off, but my shorts are pretty much ruined for the day. I kick them off, toss them over the edge of the bathtub and then get a new pair. Luckily, it all went down my legs and missed my shirt, so I leave that on.

I grab my phone and my room key and head down to the lobby. Outside, the stadium looms in the distance. It looks so small compared to the large arenas we've been to in other states. I don't even know if they could host a football game in this one.

I walk toward it, slipping into line with the rest of the spectators. I know I have a pit pass to visit Jett after he races, but for the actual race, I want to sit in the stands so I get a good view. My name is on the will-call list, so they let me in and I make my way down to the section of seats in front of the finish line, which is always the best place to watch a dirt bike race.

The place is buzzing with excited spectators. Children wearing T-shirts of their favorite racer, and parents doing the same. Some little kids play in the aisle next to me with toy dirt bikes. They make the motor sound and have the bikes jump in the air and then tumble downward. I don't know why they like making the bikes crash so much. In real life, that's the worst thing to happen in a race.

The smell of exhaust fills the air as the first heat race lines up at the gate. I scan the number plates of all the bikes, but Jett isn't in this one, so I'm only half paying attention.

I see what Jett meant about the arenacross tracks being different—they're tiny! There's a ton of jumps and turns but it's all jam packed together, and even the track itself is only wide enough for maybe four bikes at a time. At home, our motocross track is huge and it fills several acres. There's hills and long jumps and little jumps and big sweeping turns, with three long straight ways. You can enjoy yourself on a track like ours at home, but here it's all business.

A woman wearing lots of perfume slides across the aisle and sits two seats down from me. She's also wearing a lot of hairspray in her poufy hair, and she reminds me of Dolly Parton. She's as Texas as it gets and it makes me smile.

"Darlin, you here alone?" she asks me after a few minutes of watching the races. She has one heavily painted one eyebrow lifted in concern.

I nod. "Kind of."

She lifts the other eyebrow.

"My boyfriend is racing," I explain, nodding toward the track. "So I'm here with him, but I'm sitting alone."

She takes her Diet Coke bottle from the cup holder in her chair and moves over to sit next to me. "Not anymore, you're not," she says with a grin. "My son is out there, number fifteen."

She points to the starting line and I find him on a Honda. He's wearing a lime green helmet that clashes with his otherwise read and black riding gear.

"Nice helmet," I say.

She nods. "I make him wear it so I can see him out there," she says with a grin. "It's so hard to tell one kid from another when they're going so fast!"

I don't tell her that it's pretty easy for me to spot Jett because he's always up at the front. I just nod. "That's a pretty good idea."

"Moms know best," she says. "My name is Marisol, by the way."

"I'm Keanna," I say.

She cocks her head. "Keanna? I've only heard that name once. You're not that famous boy's girlfriend, are you?" Her eyes go wide. "What's his name…he's the son of Jace Adams."

"Jett," I say.

"No way!" she says. "Are you her?"

"That's me…" It feels so awkward being asked this question by a grown woman. Usually, on the very rare times that I've been recognized, it's been a teenage girl asking me.

She squeezes my arm and beams at me. "That is so amazing! My son is going to be so mad that I got to meet you and he didn't."

I feel my cheeks go warm. "Why would he care to meet me?"

She laughs, and glances out at the track to keep an eye on her son. He's back in the middle of the racers, probably tenth place or so. "Well, honey, he'd say it's because he's a big fan of Jett, but I think he has a crush on you." She winks at me and then gazes back out at the track. "We saw you and Jace's wife once at that track out in Lawson, Texas and he went all googly eyed and wanted to go say hi to you. Never got the guts though." She looks over at me, grinning through her long fake eyelashes. "Of course, I told him he ain't got a chance in hell when you're dating Jett." She winks at me. "Girl, I had the biggest crush on his daddy when I was young. That's about the only reason I went with my dad and brother to all their motocross races. I was hoping to see Jace."

I laugh. "Yeah, I've heard stories like that."

Jett's dad is definitely cute in an older guy way, and I know Bayleigh had to put up with girls throwing themselves at him all the time. Now I'm in the same position with Jett, but I never thought a guy would like *me*. It's kind of flattering.

We finish watching the race, and Marisol's son takes ninth place which is just good enough to guarantee him a spot in the real races tomorrow. She tells me about how he's a private racer and has been hoping to get some sponsorships but they haven't happened yet. They live in Dallas, right in the heart of the city, so he didn't get to grow up riding every day like some of the other guys did.

After two more heat races, it's finally time for Jett to qualify. I watch him ride out to the starting line. Marcus and Clay walk up behind him, and talk with him before the races. Now I kind of wished I would have used my VIP pass to go down there and tell him good luck before the race. But there's not enough time to go down to the pits and then come back up here to get a good view, and I love watching him ride.

"You can tell your boy knows what he's doing," Marisol says as Jett lines up at the starting gate and pulls his goggles over his helmet. "He's got that confident posture. He's a pro already. My boy needs to learn more of that."

"Jett had a good teacher," I say with a smile. It may seem silly, but it's a total turn on when I see Jett on the track, especially compared to other guys. He's a pro. He's good at what he does, and it shows. He never bumbles along the track or looks foolish. He is sleek and skilled and fast as hell. My chest fills with pride as I watch him.

The racers rev their engines and wait for the gate to drop. As it falls, Jett takes off, pulling the lead just like I knew he would.

Marisol squees in delight as we watch him go, pulling a bigger lead every second. Today's race will be easy because he's riding with people who are trying to qualify. Tomorrow, when he's riding with all of the best racers, it'll be more of a challenge. Today though, he almost seems bored. Before long, Jett's got such a huge lead that he's coming up on the racers who are in last place. He passes a few of them, meaning he's over a whole lap ahead of those guys, and I lose sight of the guy in second place as he gets caught up racing around the guys in last place.

Jett is easy to spot though, not because he has a crazy colored helmet or anything, but because of his style on the track. The way he carries himself, the way he throws his whole body along with the bike over the jumps and then ducks down low to sweep through a sharp turn. I'd recognize his racing style anywhere.

He comes up on a section of whoops, which are tiny jumps that are so close together you can't exactly jump them. It's like gliding your bike over a bunch of speed bumps in a parking lot, only they're about three feet tall.

Everything seems to go in slow motion as I watch one of the straggling racers in front of Jett wobble on the whoops. His handlebars yank sideways and then his whole bike flops and he's thrown to the ground. Normally I wouldn't think twice, only he does this right in front of my boyfriend.

Jett's bike is going too fast to slow down or get out of the way. His front tire crashes into the side of the guy's bike and Jett flies forward, tumbling over the wreckage. I jump straight out of my seat as his body seems to float in the air for a second and then he crashes face first into the next jump, his leg bent around behind him.

"Shit!" I stand here, fists clenched at my side, waiting for him to jump up and run back to his bike. He's got a big enough lead that he still has plenty of time to get back on the track and keep his first place lead. But he doesn't get up right away.

One of the guys on the track rushes over and waves a yellow flag, which signals to the other racers that they need to slow down because they're approaching a crash scene.

The first guy who fell in front of Jett gets up and dusts himself off, then goes to pull his bike away from Jett's.

I stare at Jett's helmeted head, watching as he wobbles and tries to climb to his feet, but he's not moving very fast. He must have been dazed. Marcus runs across the track, rushing to his aid, and another track guy picks up Jett's bike and rolls it over to him. Now all Jett has to do is get up and get back on it and start racing again. He's taking so long, and each second that passes is going to be harder for him to secure first place.

But first place doesn't matter right now, I tell myself. He needs to place in the top ten to move on to tomorrow's race. This will be fine.

The track guy tries to give Jett his bike back, but Marcus shakes his head. What? What the hell does that mean?

He's kneeling down beside Jett, who is moving, but barely. I see the paramedics on a golf cart speed down the side of the arena, heading toward Jett.

"Oh shit," Marisol says beside me. "He might be hurt."

I turn to her, eyes wide, because she just said exactly what I've been afraid to admit to myself.

I run down the stadium aisle and toward the VIP area, barely missing crashing into popcorn vendors in my haste. I get to the blue doors that say EMPLOYEE'S ONLY and there's two big muscled guys wearing polo shirts with the stadium's logo on it. They block my way. "You need a VIP pass to get in here," one of them says.

"I've got one!" I say, shoving my hand in my back pocket. But all I feel is my cell phone. Panic courses through me as I check my other pocket, and then all of them again. Where the hell is it?

Of course. The shorts I left in the bathroom of the hotel. They had the pass in it. I curse under my breath and look up at the guys, trying to seem innocent. "Is there any way you can let me in? Please? My boyfriend is racing and he just got hurt."

They both shake their head.

I turn around and walk as quickly as I can to the doors that lead outside. And then I run.

The stadium is round, and a third of the way down is where the entrance is for the racers. They're all parked outside in the parking lot, but they have to get inside the stadium somehow, and this is how I'll do it, too.

There are people all over the place, managers like Marcus, and other dirt bike people who put on the races. I keep my head up and I pretend that I'm totally supposed to be here and hope no one says anything.

There's an ambulance parked back here, and right when I walk past it, two EMTs run up and climb inside. They drive the ambulance forward to the doors that lead to the stadium, and then the back door opens and a female EMT jumps out, lowering a stretcher. I see the two guys from the golf cart pull up, and they're carrying Jett on one of those orange plastic stretcher things. My heart skips a beat and I run toward him.

"Stay back," one of the EMTs says, holding out a hand to stop me.

My heart is racing as I try to catch a glimpse of him, but he's got an oxygen mask on his face, and he seems really out of it. They load him into the ambulance, and I rush forward. "Please," I say to whoever will listen. "I need to go with him!"

"Family only," the woman says, not even looking at me in her haste to get Jett into the ambulance.

It feels a little gross, but I say what I need to say. "I'm his sister!"

She looks back at me, lifting an eyebrow as she gives me a once over. "Please!" I say. "I'm the only family member here with him."

"Get on in," she says.

CHAPTER FOUR

Jett

When I open my eyes, it's bright as hell in here. My head is killing me, but it feels slow as well. Sluggish. This isn't the first time I've woken up in a cold hospital room with all the sense knocked out of me. I get it immediately. I know why I'm here.

Dirt bikes. It has to be.

I close my eyes and try to focus on my breathing, hoping my rapid heartbeat will calm down if only to make that stupid machine shut up. Where the hell am I and what race is it?

That's right. Details come back to me slowly. San Antonio. Heat race.

I couldn't get out of the way fast enough.

"Shit," I say, opening my eyes. I get a bright dose of hospital lights and I lift my head, but I can't sit up much. I'm groggy, heavily drugged from the feel of it.

"Hello!" I call out. There's hospital blankets on top of me, and I smell like sweat. I look down and see my leg is in a cast. Fuck.

A cast. A real one, plaster and all, not just a walking cast or a splint.

This is not good.

A curtain opens and a white coat doctor with graying hair appears with a cheerful smile on his face. I look around find myself surrounded in these white curtain walls. That explains why it's so damn loud in here. We must be in the ER.

"Hello, Mr. Adams," the doctor says in a booming voice.

"Mr. Adams is my dad," I say on impulse, although that doesn't really matter right now.

"How's your head feeling?" the doctor asks.

"Like shit. What's wrong with me? My leg? Anything else? How bad is it?"

I try sitting up on my elbows but I quickly fall back down because the drugs are making me woozy. The doctor chuckles. "Just take it easy, son. You're not in too bad of shape. Just a minor concussion and a fractured tibia."

I sigh and curse under my breath. "A fracture is a big deal, doc."

"You'll be healed up in about six weeks," he says, giving me an assuring smile that does absolutely nothing to assure me.

"Six weeks is a lifetime in my world."

He chuckles again and holds a narrow flashlight up to my eyes. He does a few more checks and says some more shit about how I'll be able to leave the hospital today and that my head isn't that bad. I don't pay much attention. All I'm thinking about how is how I can't race for Team Loco for the next six freaking weeks. This might ruin me. What if Marcus kicks me off the team?

The tail end of something the doctor says catches my attention. "Your sister is here, so she'll be in here soon..."

I look at him. "My sister?"

He nods. "She's here. You do have a sister, right? I'm tired of these dirt bike guys being followed around by stalkers claiming to be family members."

I nod slowly. "I have a sister but—my parents are here?"

"No, just your sister. She told me you live few hours away."

That doesn't make any sense. My sister is a baby. How the hell is she here?

The doctor opens the curtain and motions to someone, and then Keanna appears. She's got a timid smile as she slips past the doctor and approaches my bed.

"Hey," she says. "Good thing I was here because they only let *family* join you." She gives me wink.

I grin. "Thanks, sis."

The doctor tells us someone will be in here shortly to discharge me and then we're left alone.

"Oh my God, Jett," Keanna whispers. She grabs my hand and squeezes it. "You scared the hell out of me." Tears immediately flood her eyes and roll down her cheeks. I reach up and swipe them off, cupping her face in my hand.

"Baby, I'm okay."

She shakes her head, blinking quickly to clear the tears. "You're not okay. You have a broken leg and a concussion. I watched you crash and you didn't get up and it was the worst thing ever."

She takes a ragged breath. "It's just—I'm just glad you're okay."

Seeing her makes me happy, and for about thirty seconds I feel relieved and glad to be with her. Then it all comes back to me, the reality of my situation and how I've just been injured on the first damn race of the season.

"This sucks," I say, covering my eyes with the hand that's not holding onto Keanna. "I'm out for six weeks."

"Marcus is waiting in the lobby," she says. "He's not mad," she adds after my eyes go wide. "He's just really concerned about you. He sent Clay in to race after you left, and he qualified in the next heat race so Team Loco is still being represented tomorrow."

I nod slowly. "That's good."

She squeezes my hand. "Marcus wants you to focus on getting better and then he's putting you right back into the races. He told me to tell you that so you wouldn't be mad."

I chuckle. "So, he's not kicking me off the team."

"No way." She leans down and kisses me. "You're just on a short hiatus."

"Hey now," I say, giving her a playful look. "Sisters don't kiss their brothers like that."

She turns beet red. "Shut up! I had to say it so they'd let me on the ambulance."

I run my thumb across her palm, staring at the ring I gave her. "We should get married. Then you'll have all legal rights to be with my broken ass in the hospital."

She swallows. "What, like right now?"

I shrug. "I don't know. Soon. I mean…that's where we're headed, right?"

Her lips break into a smile that's so sweet it makes my heart hurt. "I hope so," she says quietly. "But you can't just marry me because it makes it easier to get into your hospital room."

"That's not why I'd be marrying you," I say. It's a sweet moment, but a nurse interrupts us by barging in and talking about the discharge procedure. I'm loaded into a wheelchair and rolled outside where Marcus is waiting in my truck to take me back to my hotel.

Every freaking bump on the road sends pain shooting through my head, but I believe the doctor when he says my concussion isn't too bad. I've had worse. My leg aches as well, so the hospital meds are probably starting to wear off.

Clay and Marcus help me get into a wheelchair the hotel has on hand while Keanna looks at me like I'm go into break into pieces if I'm not handled carefully. "I'm fine," I tell her. "I'll be able to walk on crutches after my freaking head gets a little better."

"We're getting you a wheelchair," she says, her face resolute. "I have to go fill your pain med prescription so I'll get a wheelchair, too."

"I'll drive you," Clay tells her as we all pile into the hotel elevator.

"Thank you," she says, giving him a smile. She puts a hand on my shoulder. "You're going straight to bed, mister. No walking around. You need to rest."

"Shit, how the hell am I going to get us home tomorrow?" I say, looking down at my foot. I can't exactly drive with a huge ass cast on my right foot.

"I'll drive us," she says. Despite how she's scared of big trucks and she's never driven mine at all, she says it with confidence and a tone in her voice that says I'm not allowed to argue.

I kind of like it when she gets like this. It's totally sexy.

When I'm in my hotel room, Clay and Keanna head to the nearest pharmacy and my heart immediately beats a little harder in what is most definitely jealousy. I'm glad it's Clay with her though…the other guys on my team would no doubt try to hit on her. But Clay only cares about motocross, so hitting on my girlfriend would be the last thing on his mind.

Marcus gets me a soda and hangs around while we wait for them to get back. I know the procedure—get a concussion, have everyone watch you like a baby for a few hours. It's annoying.

"You got a good girlfriend," Marcus says.

"Trust me, I know."

He laughs. "I've seen so many motocross fangirls in my life, and they're always in it for the wrong reasons. Not that girl, though."

"I know what you mean." I pile the pillows on the bed so I can sit up on them. "She's the best."

"When I was racing, I never had a steady girlfriend," Marcus says. "They were all in it for the wrong damn reasons."

Marcus was a pro racer about twenty years ago, but he only lasted three years before his parents died in a car wreck and he quit to take care of his siblings. My dad knew him a little bit, but Marcus was older than him so they never raced together.

I'm pretty sure he's been single his whole life, or at least never married. You never see Marcus with a girlfriend, and he never talks about dating anybody, but maybe he just keeps that part of his life to himself.

"I'm going to marry her," I say.

Marcus holds out his can of soda to me in a toast. "I bet you will, Adams. I want to be invited to the wedding."

I grin. "You better get us a badass wedding gift."

CHAPTER FIVE

Keanna

I don't know much about Clay, so it's a little weird walking with him to the nearby pharmacy. He's tall, taller than Jett, and a little wider too. Tattoos line both of his arms, some of them colorful and some are just black shadows and shapes. I find myself trying to sneak a glimpse of them without being too obvious.

He used to have hair, which he kept floppy and in need of a haircut. That's how he looked when I first saw him on the Team Loco website. But a few months ago, he shaved it all off and now he looks like a scary bouncer at a nightclub.

"You gotta make me a promise, okay?" Clay asks me as we walk.

"Um...okay?" We barely know each other so it feels weird that he wants promises from me.

He gives me a hesitant smile. "Now that Jett's out of the season for a few weeks, Marcus is going to put me in the races in his spot. There's no denying that Jett is the faster guy here, that's why I got second place and he got first in the summer series. I just—" He runs his hand across his head, almost as if he expected to be able to run his fingers through his hair. He sighs, letting the air out slowly through his lips.

"I'm not trying to upstage him or anything, okay?"

"No one thinks you are," I say. This is a new side of Clay, the timid and slightly worried side. He's always seemed too uptight and serious when I've been around him.

He nods quickly but he still looks nervous. "I don't want Jett to be pissed at me for taking over, you know? If you could just, I don't know, like say nice things about me to him? Let him know I feel like shit and I hate that he got injured."

"I think he knows that, Clay. It's not like you jumped out and pushed him off his bike or anything."

He shrugs. "This is a competitive field. I can already see the articles now...journalists asking me if I'm happy I got another chance to up my race stats and take over as the top rookie..." He shakes his head. "Jett and I are teammates. I want it to stay that way. I'm on his side."

"I'll make sure he knows," I promise.

At the pharmacy, Clay opens the door for me. While I get Jett's prescriptions filled, Clay walks around the store, collecting random items. We make our way to the front desk to pay, and Clay dumps it all on the counter.

"It's on me," he tells me, taking out his wallet.

"What is it?" I say, lifting an eyebrow at the stuff he's chosen.

"A care package for Jett. Magazines I know he loves, candy, junk food, a phone charger because he was complaining that he left his at home, and some Band-Aids."

"Band-Aids?" I ask.

Clay smirks, handing his credit card to the cashier. "Inside joke."

Clay holds the bags of stuff as we make our way the three blocks to the hotel. "Don't take this the wrong way," I begin.

"Uh oh," Clay says. "Those words are almost always followed by something I'll take the wrong way."

I laugh. "It's just that you're actually a cool guy."

He grins. "That wasn't so bad."

I scratch my arm and glance over at his tattoos again. "You just seem like a boulder. Like this mean asshole who doesn't ever know how to smile."

"Okay, that was mean," he says sarcastically.

"I told you not to take it the wrong way!" I say, slapping him on the arm.

He chuckles. "It's cool. I get that a lot. I'm just a quiet guy most of the time. I don't care for small talk or any of that shit, unless I'm with friends."

"So are we friends?" I ask.

He throws an arm around my shoulder. "Looks like we are."

THE NEXT MORNING, I PACK UP ALL OF OUR STUFF EVEN THOUGH JETT WANTS TO help. I have to glare at him and tell him to keep his ass in the bed where he belongs. The last thing he needs is to break his other leg while hobbling around the hotel room packing a suitcase.

"Baby..." Jett says in a whining voice. "I'm not an invalid. Let me help."

"You're recovering from a concussion," I say, giving him a pointed stare. "Your butt stays on that bed until I say so."

"You're even worse than my mom," he says.

I heft the suitcase onto the bed and zip it closed. "What'd she say about all of this?"

He snorts. "She hasn't said a damn thing because I haven't told her."

I put my hands on my hips. "You were in the hospital with a concussion and a broken leg and you didn't call your mom?"

He shrugs. "Why should I?"

"Because she cares about you!"

"It's not that bad of an injury," he says, but he does look a little guilty. "I would have called her if it was something bad."

I roll my eyes. "Give me your phone."

His eyes widen and he grabs the phone off the nightstand, pressing it against his chest. "She's just going to worry."

"No, she's going to be pissed that you didn't call and tell her immediately."

Jett sighs and holds out his phone. "You're right."

I take it and call Bayleigh. I was right, of course. She was not thrilled to hear about Jett's injury a day after it happened. But she tells us to be careful getting home and even offers to drive up to get us. I tell her we're fine, and that leads me to the obstacle I've been avoiding.

Driving Jett's truck.

It's huge, with an extended cab and big tires and it feels like a monster on the road, especially compared to my tiny Mustang back home. It's small and close to the road and I feel comfortable in my own car. I haven't been driving long and Jett's truck feels like a monster I'd have to wrangle into submission. But I'm doing this for him, and for me, to prove we can handle anything.

Jett climbs into his truck just fine by himself, even though I stand around to make sure.

"Baby, it's a broken leg. I'm fine, really," he says, kissing me just before I close the passenger door for him.

My heart pounds as I walk over to the driver's side, the part of this truck I've only ever been near when I'm kissing Jett goodbye from the outside. With a deep breath, I grab the handle and yank open the door, then I climb inside as if I'm totally cool with this.

After all, I do know how to drive. It's a straight shot back to Lawson, just a few hours of interstate and then we'll be home. I can do this.

"You look sexy in a truck," Jett says, winking at me as I start the engine.

"You look sexier than I do in the driver's seat," I say.

He grabs my leg and squeezes it, then reaches up and brushes my hair behind my ear. "Baby, you're a great driver. Don't let the truck intimidate you. You've got this."

My heart warms and I return his smile. Then I put the truck in gear and pull out of the parking lot.

I was right about the interstate. It's not so bad driving on it because there are no turns or red lights. By the time we get back to Lawson, Jett's pain meds have kicked in and he's asleep in the passenger seat. I feel a sense of pride at being the girlfriend who can handle things when he's injured. It feels empowering, too. Like we're both partners here.

When we get home, Jett's dad meets us in the driveway with a pair of crutches that are covered in dirt bike stickers. Jett laughs when he sees them.

"They're lucky crutches," Jace explains to me when I give them both a weird look. "They've got me through a few broken bones and Jett's used them twice."

"Good ol' Crutchy," Jett says, winking at me. "I named them when I was five and Dad had broken his ankle. I wasn't very creative."

I roll my eyes and open the truck's back door to retrieve our luggage, but Jace stops me. "I'll get this stuff, hon."

“Thanks,” I tell him, then I rush ahead to open the back door for Jett.

“You’re the best,” Jett tells me as he crutches on by me and into the house. He leans forward and gives me a kiss, then hobbles into the kitchen. I can hear Brooke crying from another room, which is probably where Bayleigh is.

Upstairs, Jett settles onto his futon, with snacks and drinks next to him and a video game loaded into the Xbox.

“I think you’re all set,” I say, surveying the scene I’ve put together.

Jett leans his head back on the futon and gives me a sultry look. “I’m missing one girlfriend,” he says, patting his lap. “Come here.”

We make out a little bit, but I cut it short because tomorrow is Monday and my first college classes start. I scoot off his lap and sit on the futon next to him, keeping my arm wrapped around his shoulder.

“I love you, but I need to go.”

He frowns, jutting out his bottom lip. “But I’ve heard that kissing makes bones heal faster.”

“I’d love to see the scientific evidence on that,” I say.

He grins and slides a hand up my leg, his fingers sliding under the hem of my shorts. “Let’s do our own research.”

My stomach flutters. I pull him closer and kiss him, parting my lips and letting his tongue do some exploring. His touch sends a fire up my belly, and before I know it, I’m allowing myself to be pulled onto his lap once again, my body grinding against his, his hands feeling up my shirt. I grab his hair and lightly tug his head back, breaking our kiss.

“I have to go,” I say, grinning at him.

“I know,” he says. He grabs my butt and rocks me against him. “You’re free to leave whenever you want.”

I close my eyes and take a deep breath. It’s after ten at night and I have school at nine in the morning. “I love you,” I say just before I climb off him and try to gain my composure.

“Love you more,” he says back, giving me a wink.

Downstairs, Bayleigh stops me before I leave.

“What’s up?” I say, trying to look cool and not like I just made out with her son.

She shifts Brooke onto her hip and gives me a sad smile. “Just wanted to give you a little warning about Jett. He’s just like his dad,” she says, rolling her eyes in this sarcastic way. “When he gets hurt, he’s going to be pissed that he can’t ride, and it might feel like he’s mad at you. But he’s not, okay?”

My brows pull together. “He seemed okay just now.”

“That’s good,” she says. “But six weeks is a long time. If he starts becoming an asshole, just know it’s not you that he’s mad at. He’s mad at himself, okay? Don’t be afraid to put him in his place if he starts being an ass.”

I smile. “I’ll keep that in mind.”

“Good,” she says, patting my arm. “Have a good night. And good luck at school tomorrow!”

CHAPTER SIX

Jett

The weird thing about a broken leg is that it doesn't hurt so much after a couple of weeks. My arms hurt more than anything because they're sick of using the crutches, but my foot feels okay. Too bad I can't actually walk on it yet. I have four more weeks before I can get a walking cast and even then, the doctor doesn't want me riding a bike just yet.

This whole situation sucks balls.

Keanna's taking college classes, so to fill the void, I've been doing her job at The Track almost every single day. All I have to do is sit behind the counter and deal with customers, and it's boring as shit, but at least I feel useful. The worst part is when my friends come in to ride and I know they'll be having a blast on the track while I'm stuck here, immobile and wasting away.

I hit the gym in the evenings, working on arms, chest, and back so I can stay at least a little bit in shape. I do everything I can to stay busy, but it doesn't help much.

By October, I'm fighting a losing battle with depression. All I want to do is hit the track. Feel the bike underneath me, the motor roaring in my ears. I want to travel again and revel in the feel of being the first racer to fly over the finish line jump. But now Clay gets that privilege and I'm stuck at home.

The boredom is driving me crazy. I don't know how Keanna handles working at The Track so much. Just a couple of weeks being stuck behind this counter drives me crazy. I don't want to be inside, I want to be outside, on the track.

It is nice that I get to see my girlfriend more often, but she's stressed with midterms and college essays and reading assignments, so she's kind of in her own world.

On a particularly cold October day, every one must decide to stay home because I'm stuck sitting here in the front office for three hours without seeing a single person. My mom is at home with Brooke, and Dad is giving a lesson. I'm not sure where Keanna's parents are, but she's in class right now, a three hour lecture on history.

I doodle on a notebook until I run out of paper and then I look around the office for something else to distract me. But there is nothing, and that heavy weight of depression that's been lurking around the corner is closer than ever.

I can't ride and that pisses me off.

I'm bored, and that pisses me off.

My leg isn't healed yet, and that also pisses me off.

But none of these things are what's causing the depression. I think it finally hit me, something I guess I've known my whole life but always chose to ignore. This... this boring empty day is exactly what my life would be if I didn't have motocross.

While Keanna is getting an education and making something of herself, I've got nothing. What would happen if I suddenly wasn't able to ride anymore? If I got fired, or injured too badly? I'd become a huge burden on my family. Keanna would have no reason to be with me anymore. She'd have lots of opportunities to meet college guys who are better than me and can give her the life she deserves.

I let these thoughts consume me for the next hour. Anxiety fills my thoughts, followed quickly by anger and depression. Without motocross, I am truly nothing. I can't go off and create my own dirt bike track like my dad did. I have no skills, no talents. Just motocross.

I turn to the work computer and pull up the local college's website. They list all of their academic programs, but nothing really stands out to me. I don't want to study the earth, or do financial accounting, or produce music albums. I don't want to do any of this crap.

A deeper level of panic hits me when I realize that I can't even come up with a backup plan if everything about college doesn't fit me. There's not a single college degree that interests me. Plus, where would I find the time for a fallback education in case motocross doesn't work out?

What the hell have I been thinking all my life?

Only idiots think they can become famous and keep that fame forever. I need money. A career. A backup plan.

I'm so stressed I've developed a migraine. I look under the front desk for some aspirin, but I can't find any. My crutches are next to me, but the thought of hobbling down to the break room sounds like too much effort for my already exhausted brain. I lower my head to the counter and close my eyes, letting the cool stainless steel surface wash over my forehead.

"Babe?" Keanna's voice is soft and tender, just like she is in real life.

My eyes flutter open. I don't know how long I've been asleep, but my migraine is still here, thundering around in my skull. Keanna peers at me, looking overly concerned, just like she's been since the day I got hurt. Her hand touches my back.

"Are you okay?"

I shrug and sit up slowly, the pain in my head rocketing around with the movement. "Just bored."

Her lips press into a thin line. "You look sick."

"My head hurts," I add.

"What about your leg? Do you need some pain meds?"

I nod. "Please."

What I don't ask for is enough alcohol to knock me into a drunken stupor. Being able to forget about all of my flaws sounds like a perfect idea right now.

"Baby, you seem weird," Keanna says a few minutes after watching me down my pain meds. She's sitting on the stool next to me. We can't leave since The Track is technically still open for a few hours, even though no one is here.

I look over at her, a lie balancing on the tip of my tongue. It'd be easy to tell her that I'm fine. That nothing at all is wrong. But she'd know better.

"Just thinking about life," I mutter, taking another sip of the water she'd brought me.

"Baby…" her hand slides up and down my back. "You'll be back on your bike in no time."

"Yeah, until I get hurt again."

Her hand stops moving. "You don't get hurt very often, Jett. It probably won't happen again."

I shake my head. "You don't know that. It's all chance. But it's worse than chance…chance is that you might get hurt in a car wreck. What I do is choose to ride a dirt bike all the time, and that's a much more dangerous thing than driving." I slam the bottle of water down so hard it makes her jump.

"What I've chosen is a career that will most definitely get me hurt over and over again." I look at her, noticing for the first time that she's wearing the dark purple scarf I'd bought her from my trip to Washington. I swallow. "What happens when I don't recover in a few weeks? What happens when I fuck up my knee or my wrist or my head, and I can't ride anymore?"

Her gaze darkens. "Baby…you're just thinking about the worst right now. It's going to be okay."

I shake my head and stare out the window in front of us, looking out at the empty fields across the road. "Underneath this motocross thing, I'm a nobody. A total loser."

"You are not," she says, standing off her stool. "You're an amazing person. So what that your leg is broken? You'll heal and you'll be fine."

I shrug. "I just can't stop thinking about how one day I might not recover fully and I'll be off the team. One day will come where I can't race motocross anymore. What will I do then? You'll have a fancy degree and a good job and I'll be stuck being the idiot loser that you have to take care of."

She laughs. It's a little chuckle at first, but then she bursts into pure, unfiltered laughter. "Oh my God, Jett…" she puts a hand to her chest and forces herself to stop laughing.

I sit up straighter and cross my arms over my chest while I wait for her to stop laughing.

"You think I've got this shit figured out? I have no idea what I'm doing, either. Nobody does. I don't even think most adults know what they're doing."

I frown. "How are you so cool with this? I'm potentially a big failure with no career prospects to fall back on.

She shakes her head. "That's not true. You have this place, The Track. You have experience and skills and fame. You could become a reporter on motocross, or a race announcer, or the manager of a team like Marcus. You could do all kinds of things." She reaches for my hand. "Besides, baby. You still have a lot of racing ahead of you."

"What if I don't?" I say softly, as I stare at her hand in mine. "What if the next crash is what does me in? Stops me from racing forever?"

She shrugs. "What if a meteor crashes through the roof in three seconds and kills us both?"

Everything is quiet for a few seconds. I look up at the ceiling, then exhale. "Glad that didn't happen."

She punches me in the arm. "See? Everything is fine."

I reach out and run my fingers down her chin, taking in how purely beautiful she is and how she has the ability to be calm and serious when I'm freaking out. I breathe in deeply and then pull her toward me for a kiss.

"Sorry I freaked on you, baby doll," I whisper against her lips. "I'm just not having a good day."

"Not every day is a good one," she says, pressing her forehead to mine. "But no matter what, I'll always be here with you. Sink or swim, win or lose."

I grin, and some of my fear washes away beneath the power of her loving gaze. I wrap my arms around her and tug her toward me. She gets off her stool and positions herself between my legs, her hands finding their way around my chest.

"We're soul mates," she says. "Where you go, I go."

"What if where I go is Loserville?"

She shrugs. "It doesn't matter where we are. As long as we're together."

CHAPTER SEVEN

Keanna

I can't believe I thought my college history class would be easy. This is all the internet's fault. My instructor, Mr. Garrett, has high ratings on rate-myprofessor.com, and everyone says he's a super easy teacher and it's not hard at all to get an A. That's the exact reason I chose his class when I signed up.

Now that I'm a few weeks into the semester, I should leave a bad review on all of those former students because they are totally wrong. Mr. Garrett is nice enough, but his entire curriculum involves listening to him lecture on various unrelated history stories and then taking a test over a million vocabulary words. I spent the first couple of weeks of class wasting my time taking notes on his lectures. They literally don't matter at all. I think he just likes to lecture to hear himself talk.

At the end of the week, he gives us a ten page (or longer) print out of just history vocabulary words, and that's what the test is based on. And then the text is the very next day. I wish he would give us the vocab words at the start of the week, so I could spend my hours in class studying instead of listening to him go on and on about history.

I adjust positions on my bed. My legs and back ache from sitting up so long hunched over my study sheet. I straighten my legs and stretch my arms over my head.

There's a soft knock on my door.

"Come in," I call out.

The door opens, and I look over.

And scream.

Jett bursts into laughter and pulls up the hideous Halloween monster mask, revealing his normal face underneath. "Oh my God, I got you," he says, leaving the mask on top of his hair while he crutches himself into my room.

My heart is still racing from the split second of total fear, and I put a hand to my chest, taking a deep breath. "I will get you back," I say.

He winks. "I'd love to see you try."

The bed sinks when he sits down next to me. He pulls off the mask and tosses it to the floor, then leans his crutches against my dresser.

"Still studying?"

"Yeah," I say with a groan. "I'm sick of it, but I only know about half of these terms so far."

Jett takes my vocabulary list and looks it over. "When's your test?"

"Tomorrow."

"What? What kind of asshole gives a test on Halloween?"

I chuckle. "College classes don't care what day it is."

"That's crap," he says, frowning. He slides over to the foot of my bed and holds the list in front of him. "Do you want me to ask you the word or the definition?"

"You don't have to study with me, babe." I reach for the papers back, but he holds them out of my reach. "I'm serious. It's super boring."

He shrugs. "I'd rather be bored with you than bored without you."

It's a simple sentence, but it makes me blush a little. I love that he can still do this to me, make me feel special and wanted even after all these months of dating.

I lean back against my headboard and let him ask me the questions. We study until I've got them all memorized, at least enough that I'll be able to choose the definition off Mr. Garrett's multiple choice test.

After our study session, I make some popcorn and bring it back up to my room, and Jett turns on Netflix. He leans his back against my headboard, his broken foot out in front of him like a large rock at the foot of my bed. I lean against his chest, my feet curled up underneath me. I love the way his arm holds onto my shoulders, and how every time I lean against him, it's like his arm is magnetized to hold onto me. He never forgets that I'm right here next to him.

"So my mom told me we're on candy duty tomorrow," Jett says.

"Try not to eat it all like you did last time," I say, elbowing him in the stomach. He laughs.

"Do you think I can wear this mask?" He pulls it back over his head. It's some kind of hairy monster with a snarling mouth. "Or will it be too scary for the little kids?" His voice is muffled from the mask.

I tilt my head. "You'll be fine. I mean, it's not much different from how your normal face looks."

"Oh, I'm going to get you for that one," Jett says. He dives on top of me and begins tickling my sides. I squeal and fall back on my bed, struggling to get him off me. His creepy monster mask hovers over my face.

"I love you."

I shake my head. "I'm afraid I can't love a grotesque monster like you."

He lifts up the mask, and his normal gorgeous face smiles down at me. "What about now?"

My lips slide to the side of my mouth and I take a long time, like I'm thinking it over. "I guess," I say with a sly grin. "But I mean, I'm not seeing much difference from when you had the mask on."

He kisses me. "Better sleep with one eye open, sweetheart. Me and this mask have a lot of scaring to do."

He winks at me and I roll my eyes. "I can't believe it's already Halloween. Seems like this year just started."

"Are you saying time flies when you're spending it with me?" he asks with that cocky grin of his.

I grab his shoulders and pull him down for a kiss. "Something like that."

Since it's Halloween, the Track stays open a few hours later for a fun party. We turn on the track lights and let people ride, and Bayleigh and my mom decorate the main building in spooky Halloween decorations. Creepy music plays through the track's speakers, and Jett and I sit on the bleachers, handing out candy to trick-or-treaters and the occasional person stopping by on a dirt bike.

Jett wears his scary mask, but I'm dressed up like Tina Belcher from my favorite TV show, Bob's Burgers. A lot of people immediately recognize me, which is fun.

After a group of kids leaves, Jett turns to me, his scary monster face blocking him from my view.

"Your birthday is coming up," he says.

I lift an eyebrow. "Wow, I forgot about that." My nineteenth birthday is in three days. Funny how it hasn't even crossed my mind lately.

"I haven't forgotten." Jett says. His head drops and I imagine he's staring at his feet even though I can't tell for sure because of his monster mask. "I had these awesome plans for it, but now that I can't walk much, they're ruined."

"We don't need to do anything fancy. I'm not really into celebrating my birthday anyway."

The monster turns to face me. "But it was going to be so much fun," he says, sounding all disappointed. "An hour away, there's the annual county fair. It's huge, and there's carnival rides and games and a concert every night. I was going to get us horse rides and cotton candy and wristbands that let us ride every ride as much as we want." He looks back down at the bowl of Halloween candy in his lap. "It was going to be the greatest night ever and now there's no way I can hobble on crutches at the fairgrounds. I wouldn't even be able to get into half of the rides, or get on a horse." He heaves a sigh.

I put my hand on his back. "Baby, it's fine. We'll go next year. I'm serious though—I have no plans to celebrate my birthday. It's not a big deal at all."

"I just want to do something special," he says, his voice muffled. "You may not care about your birthday, but I do. You're my favorite person in the world and if you weren't born, my life would suck. So I definitely want to do something, even if it's just low key."

"Let's definitely stay low key," I say. Some little kids walk up and bashfully yell trick-or-treat, ending our conversation for now. We pass out candy and Jett gets stuck talking to some kid's dad who is apparently a big fan.

Once they leave, and we're alone again, Jett lifts up his monster mask. "What would you like to do for your birthday? Dinner somewhere nice?"

I curl my lip. "Not really. I don't really want to go anywhere."

He looks disappointed, his bottom lip poking out just a bit. "Sorry," I say. "I just want to stay in. College is kicking my ass and work is hard and the baby drives me insane half the time. I just kind of want to sit in a quiet room and be alone with you. We could watch movies or something."

"What kind of movies would you like?"

I shrug. "Eighties romantic comedies."

He laughs and pulls his mask back down over his face. He leans over and lovingly bumps me in the arm with his shoulder. "Sounds like a plan, baby doll."

CHAPTER EIGHT

Jett

I use the wall to balance myself as I climb down the stepladder on one foot. It's much harder than it seems, but I can't put any weight on my broken foot at all. I think it's probably healed for the most part, but stepping on it would break the cast and get me in hot water with my doctor, and probably with Keanna.

When I get to the floor, my broken leg bent at the knee, I hop over to my crutches.

"Jett Adams!" My mom's shrill voice scares the shit out of me, making me jump. I lean against the wall as my crutches fall to the floor.

"Jesus, Mom," I say, turning to look at her. She's got a stack of DVDs in one hand and the other is on her hip. Her eyes narrow at me, her lips pressed into a thin line.

"Are you trying to kill yourself?" She looks from me to the step ladder, then to the window which I've covered with a blackout curtain. She heaves a sigh. "Son, I can do this for you."

"I got it," I say. I bend down and pick up my crutches, then I hobble over to her. She runs her hand down the creases in the brand new curtains, probably wishing I had ironed them first.

Not gonna happen. I wouldn't even know where to find the iron.

"I'll do the rest," she says. "You can't use a step ladder with a cast on one of your feet."

"Mom, it's fine," I say, throwing my arm around her shoulders. She's so much shorter than I am, it's kind of funny, even though she's still glaring at me. "My cast comes off soon, so my leg is already healed by now. They always leave it on way too long anyhow."

She snorts. "Right, okay. I forgot you went to medical school and you know more than your doctors." She rolls her eyes. "Just let me handle the rest of these. You can do something less dangerous."

Tomorrow is Keanna's nineteenth birthday. Since my awesome county fair idea was dead on arrival, thanks to my broken leg, I've taken her movie idea and turned it into something awesome. If all she wants to do is sit at home and watch movies, I can still make it special.

Upstairs in my house, we have a game room, that's basically just a big open room with a pool table and a TV and some leather recliners for watching movies. The TV is mounted to the wall and it's only forty-seven inches big, so It's not nearly big enough for what I want to do.

I'm buying a projector and a screen and Dad is helping me install them. I pick up the DVDs Mom set on the couch and go through them. She was in charge of finding eighties romantic comedies that she thinks Keanna would like, and judging by all the girly images on the covers, I think she probably nailed it. As soon as Dad gets back from Best Buy, we're going to set up the projector screen which will make a ninety inch theater screen on our wall. It's going to be amazing.

I also bought four blackout curtains to replace the existing girly ones with black and white baroque patterns on them that my mom picked out a long time ago. These are solid black and have a reflector type of material on the back and they promise to block out all sunlight.

I've rented a popcorn machine from a local party rental place, and bought a ton of candy and drinks, which Mom is helping me set up on a table as if it were a concession stand.

The best part? My parents and Keanna's parents will be hanging out at Keanna's house all day tomorrow, that way the little kids won't be loud and mess up our day. As soon as Keanna comes over, we're go into have a dark movie theater and a stack of movies. I can't think of anything more relaxing, and I really hope she'll love it. The best part, is that it doesn't require any walking, so my stupid broken leg won't ruin the evening.

"What will you be having for dinner?" Mom asks after she's hung up the other three curtains. The old ones are draped over her shoulder.

"I was thinking some kind of takeout," I say. "Whatever Keanna wants, and we'll get it delivered."

Mom nods. "I'm baking her that chocolate cake she loves. Should be done soon if you want to come eat the leftover icing."

"You know I do," I say, rubbing my stomach.

She laughs. "Do you like the movies I picked out?"

"Hell if I know," I say, casting a glance back at them. "It's not about me liking them, it's about her liking them."

"I've raised you right," Mom says before she heads back downstairs.

When Dad gets back from the store, we set up the projector screen. He thought my movie projector idea was so badass that he wanted to buy it himself, to add an extra level of awesome to the game room. I had planned on buying the projector since it was my idea, but I don't complain. Dad and I hang it from the ceiling and run the wires through the attic. He has to do that part, since I'm stuck with my leg.

We screw the retracting screen from the ceiling and pull it down to cover the existing TV on the wall. Our new massive movie screen looks amazing.

"We can watch the dirt bike races on this thing," Dad says as we sit back and admire our handiwork. Right now it's just playing the DVD loading screen for The Breakfast Club but it still looks amazing.

He claps me on the back. "I can't wait until you're back out there racing."

"Me too, Dad." I cast a scornful look at my leg. "Me too."

I OVERHEARD BECCA TELLING MY MOM THAT SHE WAS PLANNING A FANCY BIRTHDAY breakfast for Keanna, so I decide to let her have some family time on the morning of her birthday. She texts me asking if I want to come over, but I know I'll have her the rest of the day, and I think it's so important for her to be with the people who love her the way she never had when she was growing up, so I tell her to come to my house when she's done. Sometimes it sickens me when I remember that her own mother dumped her off with strangers and never came back. How could anyone do that to their own child? I can understand it happening when the child is an infant and the parent is too unfit to raise them. That's the only thing that makes sense…giving up a child you can't take care of for the greater good. But Keanna was practically a legal adult by the time her mom left her. They'd already spent a lifetime together. That's just cold and unforgivable.

Mom's beautiful chocolate cake rests on the dining table, on a fancy crystal cake stand. My baby sister is now seven months old, so Mom lets her lick some icing off her finger. She doesn't seem to like it, which was kind of hilarious because Mom's homemade from scratch chocolate icing is literally the best thing in the world.

I help Mom decorate the table, but she quickly shoos me away, saying I'm not good at sprinkling confetti, whatever that means. It's just confetti!

But somehow, Mom's right. The table looks amazing when she's done with it. A silver tablecloth sparkles under the chandelier and pink and purple confetti is sprinkled perfectly down the center of the table. My parents' presents for Keanna are wrapped much nicer than how I wrapped mine, and they're sitting next to the cake.

Keanna comes over around eleven, once her family breakfast is done. I meet her at the back door with a kiss and a birthday hug. "Do you feel older and more mature?" I ask her with a grin.

She grins back. "Older, yes. Mature? Never."

I'd told her to dress comfortably for our day of movie watching, so she's wearing pink and black striped leggings that do wonders to the curve of her ass, as well as a long sleeved Ivory Ella shirt with a cute cartoon image of an elephant on it. It's Keanna's new favorite clothing brand, because the company donates money to saving elephants. She only has one of their shirts right now because she discovered the company a month ago, but she'll have more when she opens my presents.

"So what movies did you get?" she asks as we walk from my back door toward the dining room.

"Mom picked them out, so don't worry," I say with a chuckle. "I think they'll be perfectly girly and romantic enough for you."

She gives me this bashful smile. "You'll like them too, Jett. Everyone loves romance."

I pretend to gag, just to keep up my manliness. She punches me in the stomach.

We find my family in the kitchen. "There's the birthday girl!" my mom says to Brooke in her baby voice. "Can you give Keanna a big birthday smile?"

Brooke grins easily, especially when you talk to her in a high pitched voice. Keanna gushes at the baby smile and she bends down and kisses Brooke's fat baby cheek. "Thank you, Brookie!" she says.

"What is she wearing?" I ask as I make baby faces at my little sister. Mom's dressed her in the fluffiest outfit on earth. A pink T-shirt with sparkles all over it, and pink leggings and this pink sparkly tutu thing around her waist. She's wearing socks that have both sparkles and like mini tutus around the ankles. Brooke's hair is covered in a sparkly headband with a flower and rhinestones on it.

Basically, my baby sister has been dunked in a bucket of pink sparkle.

"She's adorable," Mom says. "It's her party outfit."

"I love it," Keanna says. "You're the prettiest baby in the world!" Brooke squeals and holds Keanna's hand in her little baby fist.

"She can probably be seen from space," I say. "That's more sparkle than a craft store."

Dad laughs from the other side of the room, where he's setting out tiny plates and forks. "Your mother never got to dress you up because boy clothes don't sparkle," he explains. "She's making up for that now."

"Damn right I am," Mom says. Brooke flails toward Keanna so Mom hands her over. "Jett's clothes were *so* boring when he was a baby. Oh my God. Monster trucks, monkeys, and alligators and stuff. No sparkle at all."

Keanna's smile is never as big as when she's holding her brother or my sister. Watching her play with the baby gives me all kinds of feelings that, as a guy, I usually try to ignore.

Like how one day if we have kids, she'll be that happy playing with them. I try to imagine being a parent. Taking care of a baby that's actually mine and not just my little sister. Raising a kid to know right from wrong, teaching them how to tie their shoes and cleaning up puke when they're sick. All the things my parents have done over the years.

It's a ton of work. I only like playing with Brooke when my parents are there to make sure I don't screw up. I can't even imagine doing it all alone, and that's exactly what my mom and dad did when they had me. They're my heroes. Someday, I hope Keanna and I will be half the parents they are.

My mom lights the candles on Keanna's cake and we sing her happy birthday. She looks so beautiful sitting in front of the candles, her face glowing from the flames. I kind of wish everyone else would leave so I could be alone with her.

Brooke seems to love all of it, from the singing to the candles to the sound the wrapping paper makes as Keanna tears it off her gifts. My dad gives her a yearly membership to the local car wash place that Keanna loves. They wash your car as much as you want if you're a member. He also gets her one of those hard shell suitcases for when we travel to races together. She'd been borrowing an old suitcase of mine before, but snow she has her own. She likes it so much, I worry she won't like my gift nearly as much as this one.

Mom gives her lots of clothes, all of which are things Keanna beams at and squeals over. While Mom and her are gushing over the clothes, which are apparently exactly what Keanna wanted, Dad and I exchange bored looks. He winks at me. "Get used to it, son. Your mom knows your girlfriend better than we do."

I laugh. "She hasn't seen my gift yet," I say, giving her a wink. "But you have to wait until we get upstairs to get it."

She grins at me.

We finish our cake and then my parents wish her happy birthday one last time before leaving to go next door. Keanna knows I've planned a movie day for us, but she doesn't know that I've transformed the game room into our own personal theater.

"Close your eyes," I say when we reach the top of the stairs. "And prepare to be amazed."

CHAPTER NINE

Keanna

I don't know what I'm expecting when Jett tells me to close my eyes. Well, popcorn, I guess. I can smell it at the top of the stairs. Jett's hand closes around mine and I hear his crutches shuffling as he walks me to the game room.

"Okay, open your eyes."

I do, and I'm faced with a thick red curtain blocking the arched entryway to the game room. I lift an eyebrow. It's obviously a temporary addition to the house because the curtains have been thumbtacked into the wall.

Jett rolls out his hand and pushes it open for me. "Welcome to the birthday theater," he says, then he frowns. "Okay that was lame. I should have thought of a better name."

I step into the game room and my mouth falls open. Jett's turned the space into a movie theater. It's dark in here, with all of the windows blocked out. White rope lighting is taped to the floor, forming a fake center aisle just like in the real movie theaters. It leads to a leather loveseat that's positioned in the middle of the room, right in front of a huge drop down movie screen that definitely wasn't there before today.

The other chairs in the room have been shoved off to the side, making it just a theater for two people: Jett and me.

On the back wall of the room, there's a real popcorn maker, filled up with freshly popped popcorn. There's even paper bags with red and white stripes and a little metal scoop to fill the bags just like at the movies. There's a table next to it with canned drinks in a bucket of ice, candy in dishes, and candy bars laid out—all of my favorites.

"You really outdid yourself," I say, grinning as I turn back to Jett.

He's leaning on his crutches, but he lowers his head down to mine as I wrap my arms around him. "Thank you."

"Happy Birthday," he says. "We get to spend the next eight hours watching romantic old movies on a ninety inch screen. And pigging out on junk food, of course."

"Is there any other way to spend a birthday?" I ask.

He grins. "Nope."

"Actually..." I say, sliding my fingers up Jett's hard chest. I peer up at him, letting my intentions be known with the look in my eyes. "I can think of a better way to spend our time. At least...before the first movie starts."

His eyes fill with desire, and a little grin appears on his lips. Balancing his crutches under his arms, he grabs my hips. "Oh yeah? Like what?"

I push him toward the loveseat, and he hobbles over. Even in crutches, Jett is the sexiest guy I know. His arm muscles only flex more on the crunches, the strength there turning me on. He eases himself into the loveseat and pats the seat next to him. I shake my head.

"That's not where I'm sitting," I say. I lower myself onto his lap.

"Mmm," he murmurs. His hands slide up my thighs. "I'm loving these leggings, by the way. You look sexy as hell in them."

"Does that mean you don't want me to take them off?" I say as I slide my hands up his shirt, then pull it over his head.

He smirks, his hands finding their way up my shirt to unhook my bra. "As sexy as they look on you, my love, they would definitely look better on the floor."

I pull off my shirt and Jett's mouth instantly goes to my breast. All thoughts leave my mind as his tongue flicks over my skin with expertise. I gasp and rock against him.

"I love you, baby doll," Jett breathes against my neck.

I tug on the button of his jeans. "Prove it."

ONCE OUR CLOTHES ARE BACK ON, AND I'M FEELING MORE LOVED THAN I THOUGHT possible, Jett and I settle into the temporary movie theater. I get us popcorn and candy and we snuggle up under the massive movie screen.

Maybe it's the sugar, or the salty popcorn, or the love of my favorite old school romances, but I feel my stress melt away. I'm here with Jett, wrapped in his strong arms and kept warm by a throw blanket, and Molly Ringwald is on the movie screen. School doesn't matter. Chores and work don't matter. Nothing all can weigh me down right in this moment. I am happy and free and relaxed.

Jett's phone vibrates as soon as the credits start to roll on the movie Sixteen Candles.

"Shit," he says as he leans over to take the phone out of his pocket. "I thought I turned this thing off."

"You can answer it," I say, getting up to stretch my limbs and get some more soda.

"It's Clay. I guess I should."

He answers the phone and I use the opportunity to go pee, then get more drinks and candy. When Jett finishes with the short phone call, he smiles up at me.

"Clay won this weekend's race," he says, taking the Dr. Pepper I hand him. "Team Loco is officially winning more arenacross races than any other team."

"That's good, right?" I sit next to him, placing the bag of popcorn between us.

He nods. "If it's not me winning, I at least want it to be one of my teammates."

I get up to put the next movie into the DVD player and settle back next to Jett, which could otherwise be called the greatest place on earth to sit. I love the smell of his cologne. The taste of his lips (salty and buttery from the popcorn) as we kiss every so often. I love everything about him.

"I love that you're here with me," I say, leaning my head against his shoulder. "This is the best birthday ever."

"Oh shit," Jett says, sitting up. "I totally forgot to give you your present! It's over there on the other couch." He nods toward the couch that's up against the wall, then he pushes up on his hands and reaches for his crutches.

"Don't worry about it," I say, putting my arm over his. "Just stay here with me. I'm comfortable."

"But it's your birthday present," he says. "You're going to love it."

"I know I will," I say, snuggling my head against his chest. "I'll get it later. For now, I just want to enjoy all this time with you."

He laughs and runs his fingers through my hair, before resting his cheek on top of my head. "You're the birthday girl," he says. "So I'll do as you say."

CHAPTER TEN

Jett

Silver County Medical smells like plastic and rubbing alcohol. The fluorescent lights are too bright and the staff is too cheery for this early in the morning. I yawn and cover my mouth with my hand. The paper cover of the exam bed crinkles under my weight.

In the chair across from me sits my girlfriend, her head resting in her hand. She's exhausted too. We probably shouldn't have stayed up all night last night binge watching Netflix, but what's done is done. The Flash is a pretty damn good show and we couldn't stop watching it even though we knew I had a 9 a.m. doctor appointment this morning.

There's a knock on the door and then the doctor comes in. He's young, probably fresh out of medical school, and he's smiling brightly as if he did the responsible thing and got plenty of sleep last night. "Ready to get this cast off?" he asks.

"Hell yes I am."

The doctor uses a cast saw thing, which I've seen a dozen times in my life, but it's new to Keanna.

"Is that a saw?" she asks, eyes wide in fear.

"Kind of," the doctor says, showing it to her. "The blade isn't sharp by itself. It vibrates very quickly and that's what cuts off the cast. It won't cut skin."

He turns it on and touches it to the back of his hand, and sure enough, there's no cut underneath the blade. Keanna lifts an eyebrow, but doesn't look very convinced as she leans forward in her chair, biting on her bottom lip.

The doctor cuts into the side of my cast, and the vibrations tickle a little. My skin is warm where the saw cuts through the cast, but it doesn't hurt. Soon, he's halfway down and then he starts up the other side.

"You'll need to take it easy," he warns me as he works the saw through the cast. "Your leg won't be back to one hundred percent for a couple of weeks."

"It's all good," I say, glancing at Keanna who is looking very concerned at my leg. "I'll take December off and then get back to the winter series that kicks off in January."

The cast is pried off my leg, revealing one pasty ass white appendage that doesn't match my other one at all. My leg hair is all matted up and my ankle is weak, but I can move it. Finally.

"Freedom!" I say, pumping my fist in the air.

Keanna rolls her eyes. The doctor laughs, and finishes his examination.

When it's time for me to stand on my own two feet for the first time in forever, Keanna rushes to my side, throwing my arm around her shoulders. She's so cute and loving and caring and I think I might explode from the warm fuzzy feeling it gives me.

We walk down the hallway and back up again, much slower than I'd like, but it's something. I'm walking again. I'm no longer relying to Crutchy to get me places.

Keanna drives us home in her Mustang, and I spend the entire ride home moving my ankle up and down and back and forth. I missed being able to do this. Also, I am in serious need of a tan from the knee down. Now that it's almost winter, I won't be wearing shorts much so this ungodly uneven tan I have will probably last until spring.

My parents are having lunch with Keanna's parents, and they brought the babies with them, so we're all alone.

Keanna insists on keeping her arm around my waist as we walk into my house. I'm a little weak, sure, but I'm fine. Still, I hold onto her shoulders and let her help me because she cares so much and I'm so grateful to have a girl like her on my side, looking after me. I've heard all kinds of stories in my life about how motocross girlfriends tend to dump a guy when he's no longer winning races. Keanna isn't like that, not one bit.

"So what do you want to do with your newfound leg freedom?" she asks me as she pours us a cup of sweet tea.

I sit on the barstool and consider it for a moment. "I want to get on my bike," I say, and that earns me a quick glare from my girlfriend. I laugh. "I know I can't do that right now, so I think I'll go for the next best thing."

Keanna leans on the kitchen island, her elbows squeezing her boobs together as she takes a sip of her tea. "What's that?"

I grin. "Take a shower. A real one. Standing up in the hot water with my leg *not* wrapped in a freaking trash bag."

She laughs. "Probably a good idea. It's no telling how bad your leg smells right now."

I use the handrail to help me hobble up the stairs, and by the time I'm in my room, Keanna is already in my bathroom, running the hot water.

"Baby," I say, leaning against the bathroom door frame. "I love you so much, but when you do all these things for me, I feel bad.'

"Why would you feel bad?" she asks, setting a clean towel on the towel rack for me. "I'm just helping. I'm happy to do it."

"I know. But you don't have to do those things. I should be doting on you."

"It's a two-way street," she says, pressing her hands flat on my chest as she leans up and kisses me. "I'm happy to do things for you."

She starts to step away and I stop her with a hook of my hand around her back. I tug her close and kiss her on the lips, harder than I mean to. She sighs against me, her body pressing all up against mine. Her breasts feel amazing, and I can't help but picture what they'd feel like if there weren't shirts in between us.

The shower fogs up the air around us, casting a steamy glow on the mirror.

"I need your help with one more thing," I whisper into her ear.

"What's that?" she says, giving me this adorably not-so-innocent look.

"It's been a while since I showered without a cast on my leg." I slide my finger down her side and up again. "I think I might need some help."

Her cheeks turn pink and then she gives me a sultry look, as if she's already undressing me with her eyes. "Like I said earlier," she says as she slides her hands up under my shirt and lifts it over my head. "I'm happy to help."

BELIEVE IN WINTER

A BELIEVE IN LOVE NOVELLA

CHAPTER ONE

Keanna

I am not exactly thrilled with the idea of snow. Sure, it's pretty to look at, and I'll happily assemble a puzzle of a snowy house set on a hill surrounded by the white stuff, but when it comes to spending actual time in these frigid temperatures? Yeah, that doesn't sound very fun.

I'm warm blooded. I like Phoenix, Arizona where it's frequently over a hundred degrees outside. I like Texas when the humidity is low and the sun is shining and I'm getting a tan. Anything else makes me shivery and cold and uncomfortable.

Every time I step into Jett's bedroom that he keeps unbelievably cold, I'm always reaching for a blanket to wrap around my shoulders. And that's only like sixty-eight degrees. I can't even imagine snowy weather.

I sigh.

It doesn't matter what I feel about the cold, because that's where we're going. Denver, Colorado in the middle of winter. My parents and Jett's parents first brought up the idea over Thanksgiving dinner. They wanted to go on a vacation for Christmas instead of spending it at home like we always do. They said we could buy each other small gifts that fit into our luggage and we'll take a fun vacation that will be like a Christmas present to ourselves.

I, like everyone else at the table, had happily agreed. And then when it was all planned and ready to go, my mom told me we were going to a ski lodge. I'm still happy about the vacation, but I'm just a little bit wary because cold weather sucks.

We'll be spending a week in a fancy resort in the snowy Colorado mountains. The best part is that since my parents and Jett's parents have babies and we're legally adults, Jett and I are getting our own room next to their two rooms. It'll almost be like we're taking a vacation by ourselves, except we'll be spending all our time with our families.

I chuckle to myself and keep pulling clothes out of my REI shopping bags to relocate them to my suitcase. Mom and I have spent the last few days buying winter clothes and ski clothes and even new pajamas because it's going to be so freaking cold there. I didn't own a proper winter coat, or a warm pair of boots, because here in Texas you don't need them. Most of the time when it's cold here, you only need jeans and a hoody to keep warm.

Ski pants are bulky and huge and they make you sweat when you try them on in Texas. I fold mine up and shove them in my suitcase as well, even though I'm not exactly thrilled at the idea of skiing. It's kind of terrifying to think about, even though Dad swears there's easy slopes that aren't scary.

"Keanna!" Mom calls out from down the hallway. I leave my overstuffed suitcase on the bed and walk out to find her.

"Yes?"

"Baby's room!" she says, sounding frustrated.

When I find her in my brother Elijah's room, she's standing with her hands on her hips and throw up all over her shirt. "Do you mind watching him while I change clothes?" she asks.

I laugh because I've been in her position before. "No problem."

My brother grins in his crib, no doubt happy about puking all over his mom. He's only wearing a diaper, so I grab some wipes and clean him off, then get him dressed in some leggings and a shirt that says Little Brother. I bought it for him so it's my favorite.

"He better not do that on the plane," Mom says when she returns a few minutes later in a new shirt. She picks him up. "God, I hope you're good on the plane."

"I hope so too," I say, making funny faces at him until he laughs. "I'd be super embarrassed to have a crying baby on a plane."

Mom laughs. "Be glad you're not going to be there or I'd tell everyone he's yours."

Tonight, my parents are flying out to Colorado, but Jett and I are staying behind one extra day. Jett got stuck doing a last minute Christmas themed motocross interview in Houston with his race team, Team Loco.

I didn't want to fly without him since every time I've been on a plane it's been with Jett by my side, so I changed my ticket with his for a later flight. We'll join our parents at the resort tomorrow night.

After going through Mom's list of stuff the baby needs, we confirm that she's packed everything we will need for a week of vacation. It's a lot of stuff for one person to go on vacation, but when you have a baby to bring, it's all about diapers and formula and extra clothes. Together, our family of four has seven suitcases. Dad says he can bring my suitcase so that I don't have to worry about lugging it through the airport tomorrow.

I play with Elijah while my dad loads up the suitcases into the back of his truck. Mom and I eat peanut butter and jelly sandwiches for dinner and then I ride with them to the airport so I can drive my dad's truck back home.

The airport is insanely busy. Worse than I've ever seen it on all the times I've flown somewhere with Jett for his races.

"Holy crap," I say softly as we pull into the drop off area of the parking lot.

"Christmas traveling," Mom says with a sigh. "It's completely insane. I thought we might miss some of it since we're leaving three days early."

"Will you be okay driving home?" Dad asks me.

I nod confidently even though driving these big trucks is kind of scary. I've driven Jett's a few times now, so I think I'll be fine. I help them take out their luggage and then it's time to say goodbye.

Elijah reaches for me while Mom holds him on her hip.

"I'll be there tomorrow," I tell him, kissing his little head. Now that he's eighteen months old, he has a lot of fuzzy light brown hair and he makes a ton of facial expressions that are always making me laugh.

"Have a safe flight," I tell my family as I hug them all. It feels silly to be sad that they're leaving. I'll be joining them tomorrow morning, so it's not really goodbye at all.

On the drive home, I get a text from Jett and I wait until I'm at a red light to check it.

JETT: OMG I MISS YOU SO MUCH

I GRIN AND TYPE A REPLY.

ME: YOU'LL SEE ME LATER TONIGHT YOU DORK.

Jett: doesn't matter. Still miss you.

I CAN FEEL MY FACE FLUSH HOT AS THE LIGHT TURNS GREEN. JETT IS IN HOUSTON right now, and it's a little over an hour away. He'll probably get home around midnight because these TV appearances always seem to run longer than you want them to. It's not that big of a deal. I'll wait for him at his house and fall asleep in his bed and whenever he gets home I'll see him.

But then I get a better idea...

Sure Houston is an hour away, but it's not like I have anything else to do right now. The Track is closed all week for our family Christmas vacation and everyone at home is already gone. I'll be bored and alone at home so I might as well do something fun.

I take the next exit and drive my dad's truck to Houston, the radio blaring my favorite songs.

I have to use the GPS on my phone to get me to the Hyatt hotel where Jett said they were recording. At least, I think that's what he'd said. I don't text him anymore because I want this to be a surprise. I find a place in the back of the parking lot to park my dad's impossibly huge truck, and then I try to calm my nerves before walking in. It doesn't help though, because every time I'm about to see Jett, I get excited in this nervous way. All this time of being together, and I'm still fluttery and lovesick over him.

The hotel is very tall with mirrored windows on the outside. The whole place is swamped with people, probably visiting for the holidays. It doesn't take long to see people who look important, dressed in suits and holding cameras, and I follow them down the hallway to where the conference rooms are in the hotel.

The biggest room is set up with Team Loco banners and lots of those studio lights to make the guys look better on camera. There's a sign near the open door that says VIPs only, but I ignore it and slip inside without being noticed. I find Marcus, the manager of Team Loco, standing off to the side talking to a few important looking guys in suits.

My eyes scan the room looking for Jett. There's two large blue couches set up in front of a big banner that has fake snowflakes on it. It must be the background set for where they'll do the interview. A TV crew mulls about, setting up cameras and lighting and tossing cables all over the floor.

A tatted up guy with a shaved head and lots of muscles catches my attention. Clay Summers, one of the Team Loco guys. He's standing with Aiden Strauss and Zach Pena, all of the new guys on the motocross team, except for Jett.

I walk over to them.

"Hey girl!" Aiden throws his arms around me in a hug. He's the only guy I knew before Jett joined this team because his older brother Mikey Strauss was a famous motocross racer before he went to jail for drugs.

I hug him back.

"I didn't know you were coming," Clay says, stepping up next to give me a hug. Unlike Aiden's bear hugs, Clay is kind of standoffish and he barely wraps an arm around me in a quick movement. I don't think he's very comfortable giving hugs to anyone.

I shrug. "I didn't know either. But I got bored and I was already on the road so I figured I'd stop by."

"I think Jett went to the bathroom," Clay says, glancing over the crowd of people. He's tall enough to see a lot more than I can.

"Man, no one cares about Jett," Zach says in his southern Tennessee twang. "She came to see me, right Keanna?"

He gives me this goofy grin and I roll my eyes. "Yep, I totally came to see you."

The small talk goes on for just a few more seconds and then I start to notice it. The attention. All of the women in the room, even the older ones who shouldn't care about young motocross guys, suddenly feel like they're staring at me. It makes me feel important, even though it's kind of stupid. Girls always wish they could date the motocross guys, but they usually just stay away and admire them from a distance. If they really want to know these guys, they should just come say hi.

Still, I think about how it'd be if I were in a different position. If I hadn't met Jett back when I had no idea who he was, I'd probably have trouble talking to him. If the first time I'd ever seen Jett was at one of these TV show things, I'd probably stay a mile away.

Luckily, my life didn't go that way. I realize I've been standing here in my own little world and the guys are still talking to me, telling me stories about what happened earlier today when they did another interview.

"I love you guys," I say sweetly as I interrupt the conversation. "But where's my boyfriend?"

CHAPTER TWO

Jett

Even in the bathroom this hotel is playing Christmas songs. I wash my hands and listen to Rudolph the Red Nosed Reindeer for probably the fifth time since I got here a few hours ago. The entire hotel is decorated with fake snow and Christmas trees and lights hung up everywhere. The windows have Styrofoam snowflakes and every corner is packed with boxes wrapped to look like big presents. This place is so decorated, I'm not even sure I'd recognize it after the holidays are over and the decorations are taken away. But I guess travelers get a kick out of this kind of thing.

I could personally go without the cheesy Christmas music playing nonstop.

I'm about to leave the bathroom when I hear the sounds of girls talking outside the door.

"I saw Clay and Aiden and Zach, but I can't find Jett anywhere," one girl says.

"Are we sure he's supposed to be here?" another one says.

"Facebook says all of them will be here," the first one says. "That means Jett too!"

I take a step back from the door, hoping they leave soon. Ironic, how they're looking for me and I'm right here on the other side of this door. What would they do if I stepped out right now?

I chuckle and back up again so if any guys come in here I won't get face smacked by the door. While I'm stuck in here a few more minutes, I take out my phone and send Keanna another text telling her I miss her.

She writes back after a few minutes.

Keanna: So come hang out with me!

I sigh and stare at my phone. I wish I could. I like doing these fun promotional things with Team Loco, and when I was a kid this was the kind of thing I dreamed about. How it's just hard being away from her. I would have brought her today but she had to take her parents to the airport. My parents left around the same time too, and they're having a guy who works at The Track drive my dad's truck back home.

I send her back a crying emoji and tell her I'll be home as soon as I can.

At the bathroom door, I listen carefully and don't hear anyone. I slowly open it and step outside, looking into the hallway. There's mostly people here who are travelling for the holidays and they don't pay me any attention. To most people, I'm just some guy they don't know about.

To the motocross community, I'm the rookie everyone's keeping an eye out for. *Jace Adams 2.0* as one magazine just called me. My dad cut out the article and taped it to our fridge, saying he's proud of me for carrying on his awesomeness. I asked him if he's always been that damn dorky and my mom confirmed that yes, he has.

I keep my head down and make my way back toward the conference room that the TV show has rented out for our interview. It'll be shown on ESPN and a few extreme sports TV channels all over the country. Just thinking about it makes me all kinds of nervous. I get interviewed all the time, but it's usually when I'm sweating and covered in dirt, fresh off my bike from a race. And those interviews are only shown on the big screen to the people in an arena where I'm racing.

This one is being taped and then broadcasted all over the place. At least it won't be live. Hopefully if I fuck up they'll cut the footage and let me try again.

"Oh my god, oh my god!"

I cringe, knowing that what follows a high pitched cry out to God is usually a girl wanting to talk to me. Sure enough, two of them, probably the girls from the bathroom, rush up to me with big smiles on their faces.

They're a little younger than I am, I think. Maybe sixteen or seventeen. They're both pretty but trying too hard, wearing a ton of makeup and those drawn on eyebrows that I'm not a fan of. I want to take girls like these and tell them that guys don't like all that nasty makeup. It wears off on our pillows and it smells weird. Just be yourself, I wish I could say. Be like my girl who is pretty all the time, even when she's covered in puke from her baby brother. Keanna's eyebrows are normal, not penciled in like she's a cartoon character. That's just one of the many reasons I love my girl.

"Jett! Oh my God," one of the girls says. She's the taller one, with makeup so thick I could probably scratch my name into it.

I chuckle to myself and give them a polite smile. "Hi there."

Just because these girls are all swoony and flirty with me doesn't mean I should be rude. They're fans, after all. They buy tickets to my races and they buy T-shirts with my name on them and they're all part of the reason I still get to live out my dream. So, although I'm not really in the mood to be bombarded by fans right now, I'm still grateful for them.

"Kendra," the tall one says, her lips stretched in a wide grin.

"I'm Monique," the other girl says. "But you can call me Moni."

"Nice to meet you Kendra and Moni," I say, shoving my hands in my pockets. The last time I held out my hand for a normal handshake, a girl grabbed it and licked it. Now I keep my hands to myself.

"We're huge fans," Moni says. "I don't want to like, bother you or anything but, could we get a selfie?"

I can tell she's nervous as hell asking the question, and it makes me feel good on this superficial level that will totally go to my head if I let it. It's annoying being chased down by girls who spout their undying love for you, but it's also awesome when people care.

"Of course," I say, flashing her a grin. "But only if you post it online saying I'm the best member of Team Loco."

"Oh my God, duh," Kendra says. "Absolutely. You're our favorite. We already met the other guys but you're the best."

I take a selfie with Moni and then with Kendra and then I take another one with both of them. Since they're being nice and not insane, I go ahead and wrap my arms around their shoulders for the third photo and both girls freak out about it, saying they're never washing their shirts again.

Kind of weird, but still cool. I want to tell them I'm no one special. I'm just a guy who lucked out and was born to Jace Adams, a guy who used to be a famous motocross racer himself. Without my dad's love of motocross, I'd just be some normal idiot kid without anything special about him.

My life, my fame, my career – I owe it all to my dad.

After a few more fan visits, I slip past the crowded lobby of travelers and make my way back to the conference room. This room is still packed, but it's with the professionals from the TV crew and Team Loco, so at least these people aren't dying for a picture with me.

Marcus nods at me as I walk by, and I give him a wave. Marcus is a great team manager in general, but I think he likes me the best out of the other rookies. I check the time on my phone and see that Keanna hasn't written back yet. It's also only seven minutes until we start filming.

I make my way to the couches that have been set up like a talk show stage for the filming today. Clay and Aiden are already sitting there, eyes closed as the makeup artists cover their face in a shine-free powder.

I'm starting to get nervous just like I always do before something like this. On the track, I'm free. I don't get stressed or nervous or worry about how I look. But in front of a TV camera, it's a whole different thing. I don't want to embarrass the hell out of myself, and deep down, as embarrassing as it is, I want to seem cool enough for my fans to still like me.

I grab a water off the snack table to the side of the stage and drink half of it at once. As I make my way back toward the couches, I see a girl standing facing Zach, her hands in her back pockets exactly the way Keanna always stands.

Wait.

The girl turns to the side and laughs at something Clay says, and that's when I realize it *is* Keanna.

All of my anxieties wash away as I rush up to her, throwing my arms around her waist as I hug her from behind.

She squeals. "Oh my God, Jett." She puts a hand to her chest. Funny how those same words from Keanna melt my heart but make me cringe when random girls say it.

"You scared me!" she says, smacking my arm.

"Sorry, baby." I turn her around in my arms, keeping her in front of me. "I wasn't expecting to see you today."

She grins at me, her cheeks turning pink. "I was hoping you'd be happy and not like... annoyed."

"Why would I be annoyed?"

She shrugs, looking down. "I dunno. I wanted it to be a surprise but then I thought maybe you'd think I'm clingy or something."

I chuckle and kiss her forehead. "I want you everywhere I go," I say, looking her in the eyes.

Her nervous smile turns into a real one and I kiss her quickly because now they're calling us to the couches.

"Want to get ice cream after this?" I ask her as I'm moved to the couch and the makeup lady starts powdering my face.

Keanna curls her lip. "It's freezing outside!"

"Okay so ice cream and hot chocolate?" I say with a wink. "That way it balances out."

She rolls her eyes. "Sure."

Once I'm all powdered and a lady fixes my hair, I take my place at the end of the couch next to Aiden. Zach sits on the opposite end, closest to the lady who's interviewing us. He talks more than any of us, so he's the best one for that spot.

The producer comes up and holds out red Santa hats. "We thought it'd be cute if you guys wear these," she says, handing each of us one. I lift an eyebrow and Keanna laughs into her hand from where she's standing a few feet behind the cameras. Knowing that she thinks it's funny makes me go with it.

I pull on the hat and so do my teammates. Now we look like a bunch of hard-core motocross racers with Christmas spirit.

Our host is Mia Matthews, a leggy brunette who married Dylan Matthews a few years before he retired from motocross racing because of a shattered knee. She's famous in the motocross world for being a host of stuff like this and for interviewing guys on the race track.

She's wearing a black miniskirt and a Christmas sweater, but no one makes her wear a Santa hat, probably because the makeup and hair ladies just spent an hour fixing her hair. She does some vocal exercises and then nods toward the cameras. "I'm ready."

"Everyone ready?" the producer says. "We begin filming in three...two...one..."

CHAPTER THREE

Keanna

As I watch Jett and his team be interviewed on a national TV show, I find myself becoming just as obsessed and giddy as his many adoring fans. It's one thing to watch him on TV, but it's another to watch it being filmed. I'd be terrified to be in front of the cameras that huge, but Jett takes it all in stride. He doesn't seem nervous at all.

Everyone in the room has to be extra quiet and they've warned everyone to keep their phones off and their mouths shut. I stand very still, not wanting to accidently trip over something and make a noise that would ruin the filming.

Jett looks so cute in his Santa hat, and although all the guys on Team Loco are handsome, muscular, and talented, mine is the best one.

I watch him answer questions and chat with the guys, and I know all of the people who will watch this at home will fall even more in love with Jett when they see it. He's so charming and sweet and his smile makes me melt.

Eventually, the show is over and my boyfriend is free to leave that blue couch. He walks right up to me and kisses me on the lips. I wrap my arms around him and breathe in his scent.

"Hey lovebirds," Zach says, smacking Jett on the arm. "We're all going to the bar for a drink. Want to come?"

Jett gives me a questioning look. "What do you think?"

I shrug one shoulder. I don't really want to go, but if he wants to, then I will too.

"Nah, we're good," Jett says, reading my mind. He tells everyone goodbye and then walks me out to my dad's truck, which I'd accidentally parked across the entire lot from where Jett's truck is parked.

"I wish we could ride home together," I say with a pout that turns into a shiver because it's cold out here.

"Me too," Jett says, rubbing his hands up and down my arms to warm me up. "It's only an hour drive, and then you're all mine."

I can't help but grin. "Promise?"

His gaze turns so sexy that I almost melt despite the cold. "Promise," he says, pulling me in for another kiss.

I FOLLOW JETT'S TAILLIGHTS AND I JAM OUT TO SOME UPBEAT MUSIC TO KEEP ME awake. Eventually, we get home and I leave my dad's truck in our driveway then I run over to Jett's house, shivering from the cold.

He answers the door in his boxers.

"Wow, you undress quickly," I say, poking him in the stomach.

He grins. "I was putting on pajamas." He gives me a look over. I'm still in the clothes I wore to the hotel because I didn't think to change. "You're staying over, right?"

"If you want me to," I say, poking him in the stomach again.

"I always want you to stay," he says, sliding an arm around my waist. "But when the house is empty, it means we can make as much noise as we want. So…you better be staying tonight."

"You know I'm not a loud love maker," I say, rolling my eyes.

Jett grabs my hips and tugs me against him to where I can feel the boner beneath his boxers pressing into me. "That doesn't mean I won't keep trying," he whispers against my neck.

I close my eyes, the touch of his lips against my skin sending a shiver down my spine.

Then I grin. "I'll race you to your room."

I shove him out of my way and run through the kitchen and up the stairs, knowing he's right on my heels. I grab the banister at the top of the second floor and swing around, dashing down the hallway to his bedroom.

I make it inside just half a second before Jett does. "I win!" I say, throwing my hands in the air. I'm panting from running so hard, but I won, and that's all that matters.

Jett laughs and closes his door behind us. "You won because you cheated," he says, kissing me on the head as he walks over to his futon. He grabs a pair of flannel pajama pants and starts to put them on.

"Wait," I say, reaching out for them. I toss them across the room and they land in the corner. "You won't be needing *more* clothes tonight. Just *less* clothes."

I lift up my shirt and pull it off, tossing it to the floor. Jett's eyes widen, a smirk appearing on his lips as I pull off my jeans and kick them to the side, too. Now I'm in a pink bra and black underwear.

"Should I keep going?" I ask, taking a step backward toward his bed.

He nods slowly. "You should definitely keep going."

"You first," I say.

He pulls off his shirt with one hand and in the time it takes me to blink, he's now wearing just his boxers. I unhook my bra and let it slide down my shoulders and fall to the floor. Jett hooks his thumbs under the waistband of his boxers.

I turn and pull down the covers of Jett's nicely made bed and slide underneath them. "Hurry up, I'm getting cold."

The lights turn off and I smell Jett's cologne as he slides into bed next to me. I feel his hand, warm and calloused, as it grabs my thigh and tugs me closer. I reach out in the near darkness and touch his chest, feeling over the muscles he's worked so hard to get.

Goosebumps trail down my skin as Jett's hand slides up my thigh, then his fingers wrap around my panties and tug them off. I wiggle my feet to kick them down and to the bottom of the bed.

I reach for his boxers but feel only his erection. "When did you get naked?" I ask.

He chuckles. "I am really fast."

And then his mouth is on mine, kissing me soft and so slowly it makes me want to beg for more. He lowers his body on top of mine, his hands feeling over the curves of my chest, and then down to my butt where he moves me into position. I scratch my nails down his back and hold onto him as he grinds against me, my heart pounding with excitement. "This is way better than drinks at a hotel bar," I whisper against his chest.

He moans softly as he slides into me. "Yeah, baby. It is."

In the morning, I wake up to the smell of coffee. I open my eyes and see Jett looking hot as hell in his pajama pants and no shirt. He holds out a cup of coffee for me. "Good morning, beautiful."

"You had time to make coffee?" I ask, sitting up against his headboard. "And I didn't wake up?"

"You were passed out." He chuckles and sips from his mug. "Guess that's what happens when you're ravished by a sex god the night before."

I grin. "There was a sex god here? I don't even remember that."

Jett puts a hand to his chest. "Oh come on now! Rude!"

"Oooh," I say sarcastically. "*You're* the sex god. I get it now."

He rolls his eyes and sits next to me. We drink our coffee and watch some television until it's time to head to the airport. The place is just as busy as it was yesterday, and Jett and I hold hands as we make our way through all the people and to our terminal. I'm glad I let my parents take the suitcase with my ski clothes in them yesterday because now I just have my carry-on bag and it's hard keeping track of it with how many people are around here.

Still, I'm getting really excited for this vacation. Even though I'm not the biggest fan of cold weather, staying at a fancy resort with my family in the beautiful Colorado mountains will be amazing. Plus, we'll get to spend Christmas morning together, one huge family of Jett's parents and mine.

We make it past security and get on the plane, and my coffee isn't helping much because I'm still tired. I probably shouldn't have stayed awake until three in the morning with Jett last night. We get a row to ourselves and I lean against Jett's arm as I turn on my Kindle and open an eBook to read. It's a four hour flight and I have the perfect book for the occasion.

"I'm getting excited for the trip," I say as the plane starts to take off.

"Me too," he says. "I liked the challenge of getting small gifts for everyone."

We'd all agreed to buy small gifts for each other so they can fit in our luggage. The only exceptions are with my little brother and Jett's baby sister, who have a ton of big toys waiting for them under the Christmas tree at home.

"I got you something awesome," I say, nudging his shoulder.

"It's not as awesome as what I got you," he says back, sticking out his tongue.

"How do you know that?" I've been very secretive about my shopping so he has no idea what he's getting.

He shrugs and gives me this arrogant smirk. "Because I'm awesome."

I roll my eyes and open my eBook. Jett puts in his headphones and plays a game on his phone. Before long, I'm totally into my book, and yet it feels like the plane is slowing down. I check the time. It's only been an hour.

I look over at Jett. "Does it feel like we're slowing down?"

He frowns and checks the time on his phone. "Weird."

The speakers overhead crackle to life. "Attention passengers. This is your captain speaking. I have some unfortunate news. We will be making a stop at the Dallas airport due to weather conditions in Colorado."

CHAPTER FOUR

Jett

The captain tells us what happened over the speakers in the plane. He says a sudden snowstorm has hit Colorado and shut down all flights inbound and outbound for an undetermined amount of time. Keanna's eyes go wide with fear and she sends a text to her mom.

I put my arm around her shoulders. "They're fine, baby. They arrived yesterday before the storm hit."

My parents had called me when they made it to the resort yesterday and said it was beautiful and amazing and they couldn't wait until we got there. Even if it's snowing its ass off there, our family is still safely indoors, so I'm not worried about them.

Keanna looks up at me with worry in her eyes. "What are we supposed to do?"

I shrug. "Hang out in Dallas, I guess. We'll get the next flight out."

Other passengers grumble and complain as we land at the Dallas airport. As annoying as the sudden change of plans is, I'm not too concerned about it. We're still in Texas, and Texas is my home. It doesn't exactly feel like we're stranded here. We could rent a car and drive back home in a few hours if we wanted to.

Keanna and I take a seat in one of the terminals and check the flight status on the big board in the airport. All of the Colorado flights have been cancelled, and a news reporter talks about the sudden storm on the television that hangs from the ceiling. Many displaced passengers are crowded around it, watching the news.

Keanna's parents call her and say they're fine but there's no skiing allowed right now in the snow storm. My mom texts me saying she'll call me later but right now the baby is sleeping and she doesn't want her to wake up.

"What should we do?" Keanna asks me after fifteen minutes of sitting here staring at all of the cancelled flights.

I shrug. "We can get a hotel, try again tomorrow?"

She nods slowly. "Christmas is in two days. We better get there on time."

"We will," I say, taking her cheek in my hand as I lean forward and kiss her.

We decide to stick around longer to make sure we can get a ticket for the next flight out of here as soon as they're announced. Then we'll go get a hotel, but not until we have our next flight secured.

Keanna and I wander the airport to kill time. There's a gift shop with all things Texas. The Texas mugs and shirts and magnets all make me laugh, because who travels to Texas and wants a souvenir of it?

I grab Keanna's hand and we wander around some more. When her carry-on bag gets too heavy to keep lugging around, I take it from her and sling it over my shoulder with my own bag.

"You don't have to carry it," she says, reaching for it back.

"I don't mind."

She rubs her shoulder where the straps of her bag had been digging in. "Thank you."

We find an airport café that looks like the food might be halfway decent, and we eat some lunch.

"This place is awesome," Keanna says as she stabs her fork into her salad. "Not the food, but the people." She glances around at all of the people surrounding us in this airport. Most of them are busily heading to their terminal and some are killing time like we are because of the weather delays.

"So many different cultures here at once."

"It is pretty cool," I say. The couple next to us are speaking Japanese and a few tables down are some uptight guys wearing fancy suits sitting one table away from some hipster kids with English accents.

The airport is where people of all walks of life come to get somewhere else. Keanna and I eat lunch and people watch for a little while, but it gets boring after a couple of hours.

We head back to the terminal to check on the flights. Now the board is red all the way down, the word CANCELLED blinking on nearly every flight that goes out of here.

"The storm must be pretty bad," Keanna says.

I approach a woman behind the ticket counter. "Any word on when we can get a flight to Colorado?" I ask. A few hours ago they'd said new flights will be updated soon, and we could probably leave tomorrow.

She shakes her head, a frown forming on her lips. "We've just been told there won't be flights until after Christmas."

"What?" Keanna says. Her grip on my hand gets tighter.

The woman frowns again. "I'm so sorry. The airline will fully reimburse you for your tickets."

"I don't want a refund," Keanna says. "I want to get to my family for Christmas!"

"Me too!" some older woman says. She's standing in line behind us. "This is bullshit!"

"Yes, it is," Keanna says. She turns to me. "Let's go. I'm just going to keep yelling and it's not this lady's fault that the weather fucked us over."

The woman behind the counter looks relieved and I give her a small smile as we step out of the line. "Damn," I say with a sigh. "This is no good."

"What are we supposed to do?" Keanna says, throwing her hands in the air. Her eyes pool with tears. "Our families are gone. My present for you is there, and I don't have my clothes."

I slide my hands down her arms. "It'll be okay, baby. They're safe and we're safe. We'll just do Christmas when they get back."

She shakes her head, her jaw tight. "This sucks. Christmas is ruined."

"Baby, it'll be okay. We'll make the most out of it."

She shakes her head. "I don't want to be home on Christmas morning if I can't see Elijah open his presents. That house will be too lonely."

"Yeah," I say, realizing I agree with her. Christmas is a time for family. I don't want to spend the rest of the week alone without them. Plus, although my plan had been to just go home, the sign on the rental car kiosk reminds me that I'm not 25 years old yet so I can't rent a car at my age. Getting a four hour Uber drive would be a nightmare.

"I'll be right back," I say, flashing Keanna what I hope is a confident smile.

She shrugs and slumps into a nearby chair. I walk a little ways away and call my mom. I tell her about the situation.

"The babies are too young to realize it's Christmas," Mom says. "We can just wait until we get back home and do it then."

"Yeah, that will be fine, but Keanna is really upset." I glance back at her. She's staring at the floor. "I don't know what to do since we're only a few hours away from home but I can't get there without a rental car."

"Don't go home," Mom says. "This is supposed to be a fun holiday vacation. Stay in Dallas and give her just that."

"A vacation in Dallas?" I ask, lifting an eyebrow. "There's nothing fun to do here."

She laughs. "It's still better than being at home. Find a nice hotel and make it work. Honey, you need to make a Christmas happen in any way you can."

I take a deep breath, realizing my mom is right. Just because we won't be with family doesn't mean we won't have each other. "You're right. I'll do something special."

"I have faith in you, Jett. You're just like your father, and I know you'll figure out the perfect Christmas for Keanna."

I grin. "Thanks, Mom."

Feeling more confident about things now, I head back to Keanna and drop into the seat next to her. She doesn't say anything. I lean to the side acting like I'm relaxing, but it's really so she can't see my phone as I look up hotels in the area. First, I search for five-star resorts, hoping to find something nice with a spa and a good restaurant. We could do a retreat together and try to forget about the world around us. That could be fun.

"What are you doing?" she asks after a while.

I shrug casually. "Just trying to find a cheap hotel that isn't booked up. You know, just so we have a place to stay tonight and then we can head home tomorrow."

She nods, totally believing my lie.

I keep up the internet search and then I see something unusual. Something I never would have considered for a situation like this. It's a five star hotel, but it's nothing like what I had imagined.

I scroll through the website, taking in how awesome it is. Then I search for the best room they have and book us a reservation to last until the last day of our original vacation.

I chew on my lip to keep from smiling, and so far, Keanna is just staring across the airport, totally oblivious that I'm about to rock her world.

CHAPTER FIVE

Keanna

I lift an eyebrow. "What's that look for?" He's being sneaky and excited, and it's written all over his face. "Did you get us a flight out?"

Jett shakes his head. "I'm good, but not that good."

"So what is it?" He's been on his phone for a while but I figured he was just playing online or something. This holiday is so totally screwed up, I can't seem to care anymore right now. I just want to go home.

Jett leans forward, biting on his bottom lip. "I have a plan, and it's going to save Christmas."

I give him a disbelieving look. He laughs. "Okay, well, it won't get us to Colorado, but it's going to save *our* Christmas." He stands and reaches for my hand. "Come on. Let's get out of here."

In the Uber car ride, Jett tells the driver not to say anything about our location because it's a secret. I'm still pretty bummed out about being stuck in Texas, but his excitement is getting a little contagious. I have been stressed about all the snow and being so close to my family for a week straight, so maybe spending Christmas with just Jett can be a blessing in disguise. After all, he's my favorite person on earth and there's no place I'd rather be than with him.

The driver turns into a parking lot that's so huge it's all I can see at first. Just long stretches of parking and concrete. Then I see the building looming in the distance. It looks like a hotel, only impossibly huge. Jett squeezes my hand. "This is going to be fun, I promise."

I look out the window as we pass a sign. Great Bear Lodge. Huh?

"Is this like a ski lodge but for a state where it never snows?" I ask.

Jett chuckles. "Nope. It's perfect for Texas weather. You'll see."

As we drive closer to the hotel, I notice a big colorful tube slide that comes right out of the building and then goes back inside. To the right, it looks like a ten story hotel just like most other hotels, but to the left of the building, there's big walls and colorful shapes and—realization dawns on me. "It's a water park."

Jett nods. "Indoor and outdoor. So now we get to partake in Texas' snow skiing – which is actually water slides."

I laugh. I've never been to a water park, or even an amusement park for that matter. Our driver pulls up to the entrance and lets us out. I throw my head back and marvel at the gigantic concrete bears that line the entryway to the hotel. They must be thirty feet tall. The front façade of the place looks like a massive log cabin, and nature sounds play from speakers above.

Jett and I make our way inside and that's where my mind is totally blown. The lobby is a vast room with a ceiling that arches at least five stories tall. It's a glass dome that shows the sky above, and all around us is decorated like we're in a forest. Sure, the massive trees are fake and the branches hanging out everywhere have plastic leaves, but it's awesome. Nature sounds play in here too, and up ahead is a giant fake bear next to a bench for taking photos. To the left, the wall is glass and it shows the indoor waterpark. I swear it's the size of a freaking Walmart back there. There are slides and pools and a lazy river.

Jett holds onto my hand as he walks us to the front desk. I'm too busy looking around at how amazing the place is to watch where I'm going. Unlike the airport, this hotel is fairly empty. I only see a few families walking around, and no one is at the front desk.

The woman behind the counter is wearing a Santa hat and a necklace of little Christmas lights. That's when I remember that it's almost Christmas. This place isn't really decorated at all. I guess that's because the whole fake forest theme is enough of an attraction without needing to add fake snow to it all.

We get checked in and the woman gives us these plastic bracelet things. "They're waterproof," she says with a smile as she fastens it to my wrist and then does Jett's. "They get you into the water park and into your hotel room. You just press the computer chip to the door and it'll open."

"Awesome," I say, admiring my band. It's silver with the resort's logo on it.

She beams at us. "Have a wonderful stay. Let me know if you need anything at all."

"Thanks," Jett says, throwing an arm around me and nodding at the woman. "You've saved our holiday. Otherwise we'd be staying in some stupid hotel."

"You made the right choice," she says. "Great Bear Lodge is the best!"

We make our way down the main lobby and toward the elevators. On the way, we pass two restaurants, a gift shop, and the entrance to the Fun Center, whatever that is.

"This place is totally awesome," I say, my eyes wide as we take in all the beautiful scenery.

"I'm glad you think so." Jett punches the up button for the elevator. "I was a little nervous that this would be too childish…"

He sets down our luggage and scratches his elbow. "But it just seemed so much cooler than all of the other hotels in the area, plus there's an indoor water park."

"It's perfect," I say, leaning up on my toes to kiss him.

The elevator door slides open and we step inside. I press the seven button for the seventh floor and it makes me smile. That's a lucky number, and maybe this will be a lucky vacation.

Even the elevators are decorated as if we're in a magical forest. There's a fake baby bear cub in the corner, and the walls are painted with trees and other forest characters.

"Maybe it is a little childish," I say with a grin as I pet the top of the fake bear's head. "But I never got to do stuff like this as a kid. So I like it."

Jett squeezes my hand. "I'm sorry the weather fucked us over, but we can have our own holiday. Our own vacation."

I lean against his chest as the elevator rises until it gets to our floor. Jett carries our bags and I take the lead down an impossibly long hallway lined with hotel doors. Finally, I find ours, number 743, and press my wristband up to the lock. A green light blinks and I open our door.

"Holy. Crap."

I'm blocking the doorway, I know, but I'm so surprised I can't seem to move forward.

"Is it awesome?" Jett asks over my shoulder. I not dumbly and then step to the side to let him in.

Our room is nothing like a hotel room I've ever seen before. The ceiling is painted like the sky. The walls continue the forest theme. There is a king sized bed against the wall, but on the other side of the room, is something amazing.

A fake tree like the one in my brother's bedroom, only about fifty million times cooler. It's fat and short, and you can crawl inside of it. The fake trunk has been hallowed out into a bed. There's a wooden sign nailed to the top of the entrance that says *Cub House – No Parents Allowed.*

Clearly, it's a cool little bed for kids on vacation, but I'm still in love with it. I crawl inside and look around at the walls of the fake tree. There's little twinkly lights and fake fairies hanging from the top. There's even a little flat screen television on the wall. So very cool.

I crawl back out and check out the rest of the room. We have a balcony that overlooks downtown Dallas. There's a small kitchenette, a couch, and a large TV on the wall in here. The bathroom is all marble and glass and looks like it belongs at a spa.

I turn to Jett. "This place is amazing."

He sits on the bed, a grin playing on his lips. "It's definitely cooler than the photos online. And those were pretty amazing."

I walk over to him and sit on his lap, wrapping my arms around his neck. "Thank you." I love the way his hands hold onto me like he doesn't ever want me to leave.

"I love you," he whispers.

"I love you more."

I nuzzle against his chest and close my eyes, breathing him in. Leave it to Jett to find the perfect way to fix the holidays that Mother Nature ruined. I love this boy so much it's insane.

I call my parents and let them know we're okay, and Jett does the same with his parents. Apparently, the snowstorm is so bad, they can't even go outside right now so they've been holed up at the resort drinking hot chocolate and watching TV instead of skiing. I think about all of that snow gear I bought and how I shouldn't have ripped off the tags. I won't be using any of it now.

And then something else occurs to me, and I look over at the dresser where Jett dropped both of our carry-on bags.

I have a few books, my phone charger, my laptop, and exactly one change of clothes that I brought in case the airline lost my luggage. My big suitcase with all my clothes in it is in Colorado with my parents.

"Jett," I say with a frown. "I just realized I only have this outfit I'm wearing and one more in my bag."

He laughs. "Yeah, well I only have the clothes I'm wearing. Next time we travel separately, remind me to bring my own suitcase."

I laugh. "Well, there's not a snow storm here, so maybe we can get an Uber to take us to the closest mall for some new outfits."

"I have a better idea," Jett says, wiggling his eyebrows. "Let's go raid the gift shop and look like tourists all week."

I roll my eyes. "My wardrobe is severely lacking in shirts that say DALLAS across the front."

He grins. "Want to go check out the rest of the resort?"

I plug my phone into the charger and decide to leave it there. These next few days are about me and Jett, so the outside world isn't necessary. "Yes," I say, reaching for his hand. "Let's go enjoy our Christmas vacation."

CHAPTER SIX

Jett

I'd really been looking forward to the beautiful sights of the snow-covered Rocky Mountains. I wanted to try out my new snowboard and feel the air in my face. It'd be a new type of speed, similar but different from motocross.

But as I hold Keanna's hand and step into the lobby of the Great Bear Lodge, I realize this is pretty good too. We can go skiing another time, and we can bring the family with us on the next trip. Right now, life has thrown us a curveball and I'm making the best of it.

In the gift shop, Keanna picks out matching pajama sets for both of us. I know I'd joked about wearing this tacky souvenir clothing, but now I'm thinking we should definitely hit up a mall nearby. And soon.

There are only a few people in the gift shop besides the one employee behind the register who looks bored as hell. When my parents first got the idea to take a vacation for Christmas, I thought it was a brilliant thing to do. Apparently, most people only travel on the holidays to visit family in their own homes. It's like we have the whole place to ourselves.

We pick out some silly souvenirs for our family and then I buy a pair of board shorts and Keanna chooses a pink bikini that sends my mind down the dark valley of dirty thoughts.

Back in our hotel room, we change and then head out to the indoor water park. There's an expansive outdoor park as well, but it's entirely too cold to venture out there. Keanna keeps a towel wrapped around her body as we make our way into the park.

Warm air and humidity wait for us on the other side of the glass doors. There are several tall water slides and water jungle gyms everywhere. This place is awesome, even as an adult.

We find an empty table in the sea of empty tables off to the right. There are six people here, and four of them are little kids.

"It's like we have our own private water park," I tell Keanna as we hang our towels over the back of a chair. Keanna pulls her hair into a ponytail and I finally get to check her out in that bikini. She's all curves and faded tan lines from the summer.

"Damn, girl," I say, wiggling my eyebrows. If little kids weren't in the vicinity, I'd be all over her.

She rolls her eyes and puts her hands on her perfect hips. "Lazy river?"

"No way." I shake my head and point at the tallest water slide that has about seven levels of stairs to climb to get to the top. Her eyes widen. "I'm so not doing that. Too scary."

I pout my bottom lip. "It's not scary. I promise."

She gives me a look and I relent. "Why don't we try the smallest one first?"

She still looks hesitant, but she shrugs. "Okay, but if I puke, I'm aiming it at you."

"I'll take that risk," I say, grabbing two tubes from a stack against the wall. "Let's go."

The smallest slide is a yellow tube. It's the one that goes outside the building temporarily before coming back inside and depositing you into a pool of water. It's only three flights of stairs up, and the two smallest kids here are riding it repeatedly. "So…" Keanna says, biting her bottom lip as we stand at the mouth of the slide. "What do I do?"

I laugh. Water parks were a regular part of my childhood and I've done way scarier rides than this. Sometimes I forget that Keanna never had these luxuries when she was growing up.

"Well," I say, setting my tube down. "You sit in the tube, hold onto these handles, and then ride."

"Do I have to like, do anything?" she asks.

I shake my head. "Nope. Want me to go first?"

She nods. I'm a little worried that I'll take off down the slide and she won't follow me, but I decide to trust her. I sit at the start of the slide, give her a wink and then kick off the railing.

The yellow tube seems to glow as I slide down ride, water splashing around. It moves quickly, but it's not too scary and I hope Keanna likes it. Mostly, I hope she's actually behind me and didn't chicken out. I love her, but her fear tends to hold her back from having fun.

A minute later, I whoosh out at the end of the slide and splash into the pool. I dunk down in the water and then flip my hair back out of my eyes.

The next tube slides out and I grin when I see Keanna, her eyes wide, hair wet, a smile on her face.

"Was it awesome?" I ask as I wade over and lean on her tube.

She nods. "So awesome. Let's do it again."

"Can we go to the big one?"

She shakes her head. "Maybe after another small one."

I pull her toward me and smack a kiss on her lips. "Deal."

We ride the yellow slide a few more times and then Keanna wants to try the rest of them. The biggest slide is actually a little bit scary. You climb up a ton of stairs and then you're dropped into a huge funnel that's colored pink and yellow and makes you feel like you're in an Alice in Wonderland movie or something. Keanna and I share one of the figure-8 shaped tubes that are for two people. It goes really fast and Keanna holds onto me, her eyes squeezed shut the whole time.

After we're ridden so many slides our legs hurt from climbing stairs, we decide to take a break. There's a food place at the back of the room so I order us both a drink and then take them back to the table to where Keanna is waiting for me, looking like a soaking wet angel. That bikini is fitting her in all the right places, making my eyes wander to her gorgeous cleavage.

"You look really fucking sexy," I say, handing her a drink as I sit next to her.

"You'd be sexier if there wasn't a cartoon bear on your shorts," she says with a snort.

There's also a cartoon bear logo on her bikini, but it doesn't detract from her hotness one bit.

I throw an ice cube at her. "Punk."

She grins and then gazes out at the water park. A few more people have shown up, and there's lifeguards who work for the lodge here, but mostly it's pretty calm and relaxing. I wonder what my parents are up to in Colorado right now, and then Keanna bends over to pick up her flip-flops and my mind loses focus of anything else besides her perfect ass.

"You're killing me, girl." I take a deep breath and try to look away.

Keanna's brows pull together as she drops her flip-flops closer to the table and then sits back down again. "How so?"

I glance down at my stupid erection, wishing it didn't make my dirty thoughts so obvious. "You just are."

She smiles and lays a hand on top of mine. I settle back into my chair, trying to think of dirt bikes and how much pee is probably in the water slide water in an effort to take my mind off sex.

We relax a bit and it feels nice, almost like summertime in the winter. Outside it's frigid sweater weather, but in here it's paradise.

"I wonder how long we've been here?" Keanna asks. "I'm getting hungry.

I look around the vast water park until I find a digital clock way up high near the ceiling. "We've been here three hours," I say. "It doesn't feel that long."

She leans forward, not realizing how her arms are pushing her boobs together in the best possible way. "Are you hungry too? Or is it just me?"

"I could eat," I say, staring at her assets. "And I'm not talking about food."

She blushes so hard it even makes her chest turn pink. That only turns me on more. She swats my hand. "You can't say things like that in a water park," she chastises me. "There are kids around."

"Fine," I say, leaning forward and lowering my voice. "Want to go back to our room?"

"Absolutely yes," she says. Her tongue flicks over her bottom lip and it does terrible things to the thoughts in my mind. "But after we eat. I'm freaking starving."

A shadow appears to my side and I look over, seeing two girls grinning at me in their bathing suits. "Are you Jett Adams?" one of them says.

I can practically feel Keanna's annoyed stare even though I can't see it. I put a dumb look on my face. "Uh, no?"

The girls exchange a glance. "Jett Adams, the motocross guy? You have to be him."

I shrug and shake my head. "My name is Brian."

I turn back to Keanna, who is watching the girls as they walk away.

"What was that?" she whispers, but she's grinning in a way that tells me I made the right move.

"I'm just preserving our vacation." I wink at her. "It's just you and me, baby. There's no room here for any adoring fans."

CHAPTER SEVEN

Keanna

I watch the girls walk away from us. They're giving each other confused looks like maybe they're crazy or something. I start laughing. That was awesome. I can't count how many times I've been with Jett in public and he's had adoring fans come up and talk to him. I keep my cool and I deal with it, but it always sucks. I always hate it, because it's not like girls are talking to Jett about his motocross skills. They just want attention from him because he's attractive.

But seeing him deny these girls is probably the best thing I've done all day, even topping the water slides.

"I love you," I say when I finally stop laughing.

He winks. "I love you more. And this is our vacation. I don't want anyone getting in the way of it."

I gaze out at the water park in front of us. The building we're in is made of something like clear plexiglass, a big square that's at least ten stories tall to fit in the water slides. There's little splash areas for tiny kids, a huge lazy river, and all of the fun water rides. This place is pretty awesome in general, but knowing it's cold outside makes it even better. It's our own little warm summer oasis in the middle of winter.

I watch a pair of twin boys play on the splash pad with their mother. They're probably about four years old, wearing matching red swim shorts. They're laughing and screaming and having a blast. The mom is having fun too, running around chasing them and splashing them with water.

It makes my heart hurt in a weird way. The scene is cute—a family having fun. Kids being kids. But the feeling it gives me burrows down in my chest and makes my stomach hurt. I never had anything like that.

The closest I ever got to a water park was staying in a cheap motel that had a tiny run down pool I could swim in. I had to swim in my clothes because I didn't own a bathing suit. A couple of times when I was a kid, I got invited to school friend's pool party birthday parties, but my mom never let me go. She said you had to spend money on a gift and we didn't have that.

My biological mom certainly didn't don a swimsuit and splash around with me like one woman here is doing with her kids. My mom didn't play much. She didn't laugh much, unless it was laughing at some stupid joke made by whatever man she'd decided to sleep with that night.

I know I'm an adult now. A college student. An employee and a big sister to my adopted parent's new baby boy. I shouldn't be dwelling on my past, but sometimes it slips into my subconscious even if I don't want it to.

I glance over at Jett, relieved that he hasn't noticed the darkness that's crept over me in the last few minutes. He's leaning back in his chair, his face tipped up to the ceiling where the sun shines in. The warmth we feel in here is no doubt from the heating system, but you can pretend it's the sun if you close your eyes.

"Babe?" I say, reaching out for his hand. "I'm hungry."

Jett chuckles with his eyes still closed. "How are you so tiny when you eat so much?"

I make a face at him even though he can't see it. He sits up and opens his eyes, smiling at me. "I'm hungry, too. Plus, I'm feeling icky now that my skin is dry and feels like I rolled around in pool cleaning chemicals."

I wrap my towel around my still wet bikini, and we walk back to our hotel room. It feels a little weird being half naked in swimwear with wet hair and towels as we walk through the gorgeous forest themed lobby, but other people are doing it, too. I can only imagine what this place looks like in the summer when it's filled with kids and happiness.

The moment the hotel door closes behind us, I drop my towel to the floor. "I call first shower!" I say, rushing into the bathroom.

"So not fair!" Jett says. He throws his wet towel at me and I stick out my tongue. We are really quite mature people.

I turn on the hot water and then strip down, fully aware that Jett is leaning against the door frame watching me.

When I glance over at him, he wiggles his eyebrows. "Can I help you?" I say.

He shakes his head. "Just enjoying the view."

I grin and rinse out my bathing suit in the bathroom sink. "We can make out later. I'm too hungry to function now."

Jett walks into the bathroom and wraps his arms around my stomach while I rinse out my bathing suit. He places a kiss on my neck and I feel chills ripple all over my skin.

"I love you even if we aren't making out," he says softly, resting his chin on my shoulder as he meets my eyes in the mirror's reflection.

I grin and wring out my suit.

The warm shower water feels great as it washes away the sweat and chlorine from a day spent at the water park. But I don't stay in very long because I really am hungry. Climbing up a billion sets of stairs all day really wore me out.

I shampoo my hair with the tiny hotel bottles and then towel it dry. I'm not in the mood for makeup and hair styling, and luckily, my boyfriend doesn't care about that stuff.

Jet showers after me, and I look through the menus for the two on-site restaurants. My phone rings and I feel a little guilty when I see Mom's number on the screen. I should have called her sooner, but I was having too much fun.

"Hey, Mom," I say pressing the phone to my ear as I look over the menus.

"How's it going over there?" she asks. "Bayleigh said you're at a water park?"

"Yeah, it's an indoor water park so it's heated and warm."

"Oh man, that sounds amazing. It is freezing here, Keanna. You have no idea. Absolutely cold as hell."

"Hell is supposed to be hot, I think. What with the fires and eternal burning and everything."

She laughs. "You know what I mean! We wanted to go skiing today but we're snowed in. That stupid storm has covered everything in too much snow and the lodge is making everyone keep inside for the next day or two. Why did we think going to Colorado was a good idea?"

"Temporary lapse of judgment?" I say with a laugh.

"That had to be it," she says with a sigh. "I miss Texas. Even when it's cold there, it's not too cold."

"I miss you guys," I say, glancing out the balcony window at the setting sun. "I think Texas misses you as well. How's Elijah?"

"Oh he's having a blast," Mom says. "There's a popcorn machine in the cafeteria here and he loves watching it spit out popcorn."

"Babies are so easy to please." My stomach clenches as I think about my brother and Brooke, Jett's baby sister. "At least the kids don't realize they're missing out on Christmas."

"That's for sure!" Mom says. "But since tomorrow is Christmas Eve, the lodge has a Santa Claus who will be entertaining the kids. So that'll be fun."

"Oh my God. How could I have been so stupid?"

"What is it?" Mom asks, concern in her voice.

I grit my teeth and stand up, nearly knocking over the chair. "Tomorrow is Jett's birthday!"

"Yep," Mom says. "Not a big deal, sweetie. He knows your present for him is with us."

"Yeah, but it *is* a big deal. I don't want him to have nothing on his birthday."

"Honey, Jett is not very materialistic. He won't mind."

I groan. "Still. I need to do something for him."

I glance back at the bathroom, where the shower is still on, so I know he can't hear me. "Honestly, I kind of totally forgot it was tomorrow. This whole trip has been a surprise so I just wasn't thinking."

"Well, you remembered now," she says with a chuckle. Maybe have room service bring him breakfast with the number nineteen written in whipped cream on the pancakes."

"That's a good idea," I say, but I'm not feeling any better. I'll need to think of some way to truly celebrate his birthday even though the card and gift I got him are currently waiting for me in Colorado.

I flip through the binder of information on the desk in our hotel room. The hotel has that big gift shop we bought our bathing suits at, and they had lots of trinkets and gift items. Of course, none of it is anything I would buy Jett for his birthday, but maybe I can find something that will be special in its own way. Of course, I'll have to get down there without Jett coming with me so the surprise won't be ruined.

And, because fate is being mean today, his birthday is tomorrow and today is almost over. How am I going to pull this off?

I take Mom's advice and dial room service. I order the deluxe breakfast for both of us to be delivered tomorrow morning, and the person on the phone chuckles when I ask for the number 19 to be written on the pancakes.

"I think the cook will be able to do that," she says.

"Thanks," I say. "It's for my boyfriend who is turning nineteen tomorrow."

"A birthday on Christmas Eve? That kind of sucks."

"Yeah, I know," I say. "We're not even supposed to be staying in this hotel, so I don't have his present or anything. I just want something to be special for him."

"I understand," she says. "Actually… hold on a second, I might have something for you."

The water in the shower turns off, and my heart speeds up. I need to get off the phone before Jett comes out here and sees that I'm planning something for him.

A few seconds go by and I'm freaking out, listening to the bathroom as Jett dries off and gets dressed. Finally, the woman comes back on the phone.

"We have a birthday cake that was ordered for Christmas and then canceled," she says. "But the cake decorator made it this morning and we were going to throw it out. It's just plain white icing right now, but he said it's yours if you want it. I know the gift shop sells candles so you could get a tube of icing from the kitchen and decorate it yourself"

"That would be amazing!" I say. "How late are you open? I don't want him to know what I'm doing."

Kitchen is open twenty four hours a day," she says. "I'll tell them to keep an eye out for you."

The bathroom door opens. "Thank you!" I say quickly, and then I hang up.

Jett emerges wearing a pair of jeans and no shirt. He rubs his hair dry with a towel and I can't help but stare at the sexy curves of his chest, the vein in his bicep that bulges as he towels off his hair.

"Everything okay?" he asks, lifting an eyebrow. I am sitting here with my hand on the hotel's phone, and I probably look freaked out about his birthday tomorrow.

I grin. "Yep. I just, uh, called the hotel to see how late the restaurants are open."

"The sign said open until midnight," Jett says.

I shrug. "Yeah, but it's a holiday, so I just wanted to check."

He grins and I feel a little bad for how easily he believes me when I'm lying. But I'm lying for a good cause, so I guess I don't feel *that* bad.

"Ready for dinner?" he asks, pulling a shirt from the gift shop over his head.

"Yep," I say, trying to hold back a grin.

He doesn't suspect a thing.

CHAPTER EIGHT

Jett

While it didn't seem like many people were staying in this hotel, the on-site restaurant is packed. I'm guessing everyone who is here came out for food but not for the water park. Of the two forest themed restaurants, Keanna and I chose the one set in the rainforest for tonight. The other one is themed after a mountainous forest while this one is tropical and filled with colorful fake animals everywhere.

We're seated at a table under a fake tree, where a fake parrot hangs out on a branch nearby, occasionally squawking a recorded message. There's a family of fake elephants to the left, and their ears move every few seconds. It's all pretty cool and would be amazing to see if you were a little kid and still believed in magical things like this.

Keanna studies the menu with one hand tangled in her hair.

"You okay?" I ask. I know she was checking out the menu from the hotel room so I don't know why she looks so lost right now. It must be something else.

She doesn't seem to hear me. "Babe?"

She looks up and gives me a smile. I can't tell if it's a genuine or fake one. "What's up?" she asks.

"You seem weird. Are you feeling okay?"

Her smile widens. "Of course! Just trying to decide between a burger or a club sandwich."

"We'll be here a few days, so you could try out both," I say with a laugh. "I wonder how many days of water park fun we can have before it gets boring."

"Probably as many days of snow skiing you can have before that gets boring," she says.

"Touché."

When our waiter comes by, we order our food and then talk about how cool the restaurant is with all of its decorations. Maybe it's my imagination, but something feels a little off with Keanna. But I can't put my finger on it, so I try to let it go.

Together, we watch the people eating in the restaurant around us, and it seems like maybe half of them are here because they wanted to spend Christmas vacation here with their kids. The other half all look like displaced tourists like we are, staying here because their flight out got canceled.

After dinner, we head downstairs to the main floor. There's an arcade that looks small from the door, but once you get inside, it's freaking huge. There are at least thirty rows of arcade games, seven pool tables and five air hockey tables, and a billion games that spit out tickets you can redeem for prizes.

I get Keanna and me each a game card with a hundred dollars loaded on it. She gives me a look when I hand her the card.

"We could have just share the same card, you dork."

I shake my head. "Let's make it interesting. Whoever's card has the most points at the end of the night wins."

Her eyes narrow mischievously. "What does the winner get?"

I consider it for a moment. "A backrub," I say, wiggling my eyebrows.

She brightens. "You're on."

We hit up the Skee-ball games first, playing side by side for a few games. She's much better than I am at it, so I set off in search of something that delivers more points. I'm pretty good at the basketball throwing game, so I stay there for a while shooting baskets for points. But then Keanna whoops and throws her fist in the air and I miss a basket as I look over at her.

She's standing in front of a tall colorful game. She sticks her tongue out at me. "Five hundred and twelve points," she says. "So suck it!"

"How'd you get that many points?" I ask, going over to her.

She points to the neon sign in the middle of the game that says *jackpot*. "This is my all-time favorite game. It requires no skill at all."

She swipes her card and plays it again. All you do is hit a button that drops a ball onto the spinning circle below. Whatever hole the ball goes into is worth a certain amount of points, and if you get the smallest hole, you win the jackpot. Her ball falls into the fifty points hole and I let out a low whistle.

"Damn. I've been playing basketball for ten points," I say.

"Don't work too hard at these games," Keanna says mockingly. "I need your fingers rested up for my back rub later tonight."

"Oh you are so freaking on," I say, swiping my card on the ball drop machine. I press the button and my ball falls into the hole worth a measly five points. I curse and Keanna giggles.

"I love this vacation!" she says.

I grab her and tickle her sides until she squeals and begs me to let her go. I stop tickling her, but I hold her close and kiss her nose.

"I really thought I'd be better at these arcade games than I am," I say.

She pokes me in the chest. "That's what you get for being so cocky!"

I go in for another kiss, but then a kid runs by us, reminding me we're in public. "I should probably give up now. I'm losing so badly."

"No way, you still have a chance!" She glances toward the door of the arcade and then something weird flashes across her face. She smiles and puts her hands flat on my chest. "I'm going to run upstairs and change clothes," she says. That's a little weird on its own, but the way she says it all quickly is even weirder.

"What's wrong with what you're wearing now?" I ask.

She shrugs. "I'm cold. It won't take long, I promise. You just stay here and try winning more points."

If I didn't know her as well as I know myself, I might just shrug and not think twice. But she's being weird. I'm not sure why, or how I know, but it just feels weird. But I don't want to argue about it on our vacation, so I just shrug. "Okay, see you in a minute."

She kisses me quickly on the cheek and then runs out of the arcade, disappearing around the corner. I try to think of what she could possibly be up to, but maybe it's some kind of girl issue or something and she'd just be embarrassed to tell me the truth.

I play the ball drop game a few more times but I never hit the jackpot or get anything higher than thirty points.

I move around the arcade, scrutinizing each game to see which one might get me the most points, but after a while I realize I don't mind losing to my girlfriend. I'm happy to give her a back rub any day, plus it would make her happy to have bragging rights over beating me at the arcade. Especially since video games are more of my thing than hers.

I find a claw machine and use the rest of my card's value to win her a stuffed unicorn, a stuffed pink heart, and a light up fidget spinner.

When Keanna returns, she's wearing a pair of leggings from the gift shop and the same shirt she had on earlier, underneath my hoodie. She seems like she's in a much better mood from the moment she walks into the arcade, and that lightens some of the anxiety in my chest. Maybe it was just a girl thing. Maybe she's not upset about anything that pertains to me.

Keanna gushes over the silly prizes I won for her in the claw machine, and then we redeem our arcade points for as much candy as we can get. We take our haul back up to our hotel room, and Keanna spreads out the candy on the bed while I find a movie on television to watch.

"You're in a much better mood," I say as I crawl on the bed and lean over the candy pile to kiss her.

"I've been in a good mood all day," she says as she peels off the wrapper of a package of Smarties.

I lift an eyebrow. "You were being weird earlier."

She shakes her head. "No, I wasn't. I'm perfectly happy."

I want to argue that I know her well enough to know when something's wrong, but I don't want to push the issue. Maybe she's still bummed about missing our families for the holiday. I decide to just let it go, and I reach for some sour patch kids.

Keanna grabs the box before I get it. "Not yet," she says, narrowing her eyes at me mischievously. She sits up and moves in front of me on the bed. "Someone owes me a back rub."

I chuckle and kiss her neck, sliding my hands down her back as I move closer to her on the bed. The movie on TV is starting, so I turn up the volume, then slide her shirt over her head, tossing it on the bed beside me.

I sit with my legs straddling hers, her back facing me while she watches the movie. I start out slow, sliding my hands down her back and up again, kissing her shoulder and her neck and then the top of her spine.

She may have won the bet for a back rub, but I've won the ultimate reward: spending the night with her in my arms.

CHAPTER NINE

Keanna

You'd think after a day of swimming and walking all over the resort, Jett would be tired by midnight. I certainly am. I'm doing my best to stay awake though, because Jett has to fall asleep first in order for my plan to work out. We've watched two movies now, and we're cuddled up on this hotel bed, which is so comfortable it's just begging me to go to sleep. Why isn't it making Jett go to sleep, dammit?

When the credits roll on our second movie, I glance over at him and he smiles at me. It's the exact opposite of what I wanted to see. I don't need his smile or his cute gaze. I want to see him passed out.

"I have to pee," I say, crawling out of bed. I lean over and kiss him. "Goodnight."

"Goodnight," he says, which gives me hope that he might finally want to go to sleep, but then he reaches for the remote to select another movie to watch.

When I return, I lay a little farther away from him so that when he does fall asleep I can easily get up without waking him. My eyes keep drifting closed as sleep beckons to me, but I manage to stay awake by counting the stripes in the curtains on the wall.

Finally, when Jett's breathing sounds like it's slowed down and leveled out at a steady rhythm, I glance back and see if he's asleep. He finally is.

I wait a few more minutes just to be safe, and then I crawl out of bed and tiptoe to the closet to get dressed. Then I open the hotel door as quietly as possible and slip outside.

I can't find the kitchen on my own, so I go to the front desk where the woman gives me directions that lead me down the service hallway. The main hallways are cute and forest themed, with little fake animals against the walls, but these hallways are just bare and white. The employees don't get the cute treatment, I guess.

I make my way down the long corridor until I reach the kitchens. I knock on the door and a guy who is about my age opens it.

"Um, can I help you?" he says, his eyes bloodshot.

"I'm Keanna," I say. "Room service said you have a cake for me?"

He nods slowly. "Oh yeah. The cake chick. Come with me."

He leads me into the massive hotel kitchen and to a walk-in fridge. There's a cake box on the shelf between the produce and milk cartons and he takes it down for me. It's just a white sheet cake with pretty a pretty piped icing border. It's perfect.

"Shandra said you're going to decorate it yourself, right?" the guy asks. "Cause I'm just the night cook and I'm not a cake decorator. I would ruin it."

I smile. "Not a problem. I'm happy to decorate it."

He leads me to a long stainless steel table and shows me where the icing is kept. I get a tube of blue icing and get to work. I'm not the greatest at this, but I'm okay. I've piped icing on cupcakes and stuff back at home, and when it comes to a surprise birthday cake in the middle of the night, it's the thought that counts, right?

The guy leans against the opposite table and watches me work. "So what's this for?" he asks.

I explain about how we got stranded and it's my boyfriend's birthday tomorrow.

"A birthday on Christmas Eve? That fuckin' blows."

I nod as I lean over the cake, icing bag in my hand. "Yeah, it does. So I want it to be special for him."

The guy nods. "You're a cool chick."

I look up at him and grin. "Thanks."

On the cake, I write Happy Birthday in the best lettering I can manage. It actually doesn't look half bad.

Then I write a big number nineteen in the middle and put little stars of icing all around it. At the bottom, I write Jett's name, then in the bottom right corner, as if I'm an artist and this is a painting, I make a little heart and sign my name.

Perfect.

With the cake in hand, I thank the teenage kitchen guy and head back. The gift shop is open twenty-four hours a day, and I can't help but stop inside even though I know their selection of items isn't the greatest. I set my cake on the counter and then look around at everything it has to offer.

Lots of clothes, all with the Great Bear Lodge logo on them, or the state of Texas, or both. That's a big no. Jett and I already bought some of these clothes to wear while we're here so clothing isn't a good birthday gift option. There's trinkets like shot glasses and coffee cups, but those are stupid too. There's a whole section of kid's toys and I go through them, wondering if there's something here that I could use to refer to an inside joke or something fun for Jett.

But they all suck.

Then there's board games, which make a lame present. A small shelf of books, but all of them are boring. I make my way around the store three times, and nothing here would be a good gift for Jett. Even if it is just a fun silly thing to get us by until I can give him his real gift—there's nothing good here.

The woman working the gift shop tonight is older, probably around sixty years old. She's been doing a crossword puzzle in the newspaper since I got here, but now she puts the paper down and looks at me. "Can I help you with something, dear?"

I sigh. "I doubt it. My boyfriend's birthday is tomorrow and the gift I got him is several states away. I was hoping I could find something here that would make a good gift."

She nods slowly. "What's his name?"

"Jett," I say.

She frowns. "Well that's no good. We don't have any Jett items here." She nods toward the racks of keychains and stickers that are personalized with common names. That's a problem I know all too well, because there's never a Keanna keychain at gift shops either.

"Well, what does he like?" she asks.

I laugh. "Nothing that has to do with little kid water park hotels."

This makes her laugh too. "Well, you know the best gifts are gifts from the heart. Something sentimental."

You can't get something sentimental in a gift shop I want to say, but I also don't want to be rude. It's well past midnight and I'm exhausted and stressed, so I just smile.

I decide to take one more loop around the gift shop, trying to think of sentimental items as I gaze over the selection.

And then my eyes land on a small notebook. It's brown with the Great Bear Lodge on it, and it has fifty sheets of paper. It comes with a little pen attached to the side, and the pen has a fuzzy bear head on top of it.

"I'll take this," I say, setting it on the counter next to my cake.

"Sentimental?" the woman asks.

I grin. "Not yet. But it will be."

CHAPTER TEN

Jett

I wake up to the delicious smell of breakfast. It takes me a few seconds to remember where I am, because the light filtering in through the windows is not at all how it looks in my own bedroom. Then I remember I'm at a hotel, with Keanna.

Also, it's my birthday, not that I really care. I haven't talked about it at all since our flight to Colorado got canceled. It just doesn't seem important to care about a birthday when everything else is going on.

I open my eyes and find the rest of the bed empty. I blink a few times and sit up, yawning.

"Good morning," Keanna says from across the room. She wheels in a cart from room service. There are stainless steel domes on top of several plates that smell like it's probably maple syrup and bacon. And coffee.

I breathe in the scent of coffee and my mouth waters.

I go to stand up but she holds out her hand. "Nope! Stay where you are!"

I sit back down. Keanna grins at me and pushes the cart of food up to the bed. "Breakfast in bed?" I say as she hands me a tray.

She nods. "For my birthday boy."

I shouldn't be surprised that she remembered, even though I didn't want to make a big deal out of this day. I smile and lean my head up to kiss her. "Thank you, love."

She pours us some coffee and then she takes her tray to her side of the bed. The breakfast is glorious—pancakes, bacon, sausage, scrambled eggs, and sliced fruit on the side. There's even a number nineteen piped on my stack of pancakes in whipped cream.

"You're amazing," I tell her as I dig into my food.

"Nah, I'm just appreciating what I've got."

We eat breakfast in bed and watch some Netflix on the hotel's TV. When I'm finished, Keanna refuses to let me pick up my own tray. She carries it all to the room service cart and then keeps the coffee pitcher while putting the rest of it outside our room.

We head to the balcony with fresh cups of coffee and enjoy the morning view of the town. It's chilly here, around sixty degrees, but with a throw blanket and some coffee, it's really nice out here.

"I like this part of Texas," Keanna says, cupping her coffee mug close to her lips. "The land is hilly and greener. Not as many people, either."

"Dallas is pretty cool," I agree. "I like the landscape a lot. Down at home it's just flat, hot, dry land everywhere."

Keanna peers out at the distance. "If our flight hadn't been canceled, we'd be sipping coffee while looking at snow-capped mountains right now."

I look over at her, my breath hitching at how beautiful she looks in the orange glow of the morning sun. "This is good too."

She smiles and it melts me inside.

"We should do this again tomorrow," I say. "I hate that your Christmas presents aren't here, but breakfast on the balcony will be nice."

"Imagine how I feel," Keanna says, her lips forming a pout. "I have your birthday and Christmas presents and you can't get them yet!"

"I don't need any gifts, baby." I lean over and kiss her lips, which are warm and taste like French vanilla coffee creamer. "I just need you."

She rolls her eyes. "You say that every year but I still don't care. I will always get you a gift because I'll always want to."

She chews on her bottom lip and then gives me a look that's a little nervous. "Actually… I was going to wait until later to do this…"

"Do what?" I ask, curiosity getting the better of me.

She looks like she might change her mind at any time. I nudge her foot with mine. "Come on, tell me. I have to know now."

She sighs, her cheeks turning a little pink. "I guess I'll show you. Stay here." She walks back into the hotel room and emerges a few seconds later with a little shopping bag from the gift shop. She holds it out to me.

"Since I don't have your real present, I wanted to give you something. It's kind of lame but…" She drops it into my hand. "I don't know. Here."

I take the bag, my heart filling with warmth at how cute she is when she's nervous. She doesn't need to be nervous though. I mean it when I say I don't care for presents and I'm just happy with her. Anything she does get me, I love just because it came from her.

I reach into the bag and pull out a little notebook from the gift shop.

"The real gift is inside," she explains.

I open the cover. The first page has been decorated with Keanna's handwriting and little doodles. I read the words she's written and my heart melts a little.

50 Things I Love About You

To: Jett

From: Keanna

I look up and her and she gives me a bashful smile. "I know it's lame," she says quickly. "I just wanted to give you *something* on your birthday and the gift shop does not have very many options."

"I love it," I say. "I love it so much."

I turn the page, then quickly flip through the entire thing. She's filled every page with doodles and artwork in addition to words.

"This must have taken you forever," I say, turning back to the first page.

Reason 1:

You saw past all my flaws on the first day we met.

"It took a while," she says, yawning. "I had a lot of fun, though."

I grin and my heart is beating so fast. All I want to do is read through all fifty reasons as fast as possible. But I also want to take my time, enjoying each one, and the memories they bring up. Like the first one, which takes me back to the day I met her.

She was beautiful and mysterious, and kind of a jerk to me. I smile inwardly. I loved her right from the start, even if I didn't realize it yet.

"Thank you," I say, pressing the little book to my chest. "I love this so much. I can't wait to read them all."

Her nervous smile fades away. "You really like it?"

"I love it. This is so much better than what I got you for Christmas."

She sets her coffee cup on the balcony and then throws her arms around me. I pull her into my lap, holding tightly to her and my new notebook.

"You are the best thing that's ever happened to me," I whisper against her ear. She snuggles closer to me, her arms wrapped around my neck. In this moment, I feel not only one year older and one year happier. I feel complete.

And I know without a doubt that this birthday is the best one I'll ever have.

BELIEVE IN SPRING

A BELIEVE IN LOVE NOVELLA

CHAPTER ONE

Keanna

Awesome. My last mid-term of the semester is complete and I'm pretty sure I aced it. All that studying of historical facts with Jett last night helped solidify the information in my mind, and I was one of the first students in my massive class to finish taking the test. If only everything in life was as simple as memorizing a bunch of dates and definitions.

The warm spring sun welcomes me as I step out of the freezing cold college building. I swear, it's like they use ninety percent of our tuition money to keep the air conditioner running twenty four hours a day. But it's not my problem for the next nine days, because it's finally Spring Break.

I check my phone and find one new text from my adoptive mom, Becca.

If you get out soon enough, come by La Tapitia for some lunch! I'm meeting Bay at 1.

I check the time, and grin when I see I got out at the perfect time to meet them. Jumping in my Mustang that's all shiny and smells good since Jett washed it for me recently, I head toward the best Mexican restaurant in town.

It's a little busier than usual, but I guess Friday before Spring Break has everyone in a go-out-and-celebrate mood. I park across from my mom's car and head into the packed restaurant.

The hostess table at the front has at least two dozen people standing around waiting to be seated. I need to squeeze through them to go find my mom and her best friend inside, but I don't want to be rude, so I kind of stand here a minute. Eventually, the crowd thins as a hostess takes a large group to their table.

I slide up behind two women who smell like they donned a little too much perfume this morning, but they're blocking my way into the restaurant. I should just ask them to move over a bit, but being bold and standing up for myself has never been my strong suit.

"Da-aamn," one of the women says in this overly sexual way that catches my attention. "Don't make it obvious," she says, turning toward her friend, "but check out the guys behind me."

Her friend peeks over her shoulder, then her eyes widen and she grins. "Oh hell yes. We should ask if they want company," she says, primping her hair. "I want the one on the left. No—right. Hell, I don't care. I'll take them both."

Her friend pushes her playfully in the arm. "You have to leave one for me. I'll take either one, they're both hot as hell."

I wonder if they know they're being loud enough for me, a total stranger, to overhear every word. They shift over to get a better peek at the hot guys, and I find a way around them, only to see exactly who they're talking about.

My dad and Jett's dad.

I burst out laughing, unable to hold it back. Knowing the women are totally watching me right now, I walk quickly up to Park, the man who adopted me and pretty much saved my life, and say, "Hey guys! Have you seen that amazing artwork by the door?" I point to the door, which makes it look like I'm pointing to the women who are gawking at them.

Jace and Park look right at them, trying to find the artwork, and the women turn a deep shade of red and turn around.

I laugh. "Never mind, you can't really see it from here. So what are ya'll doing here?"

"My wife said they were getting some Mexican food, and we happened to be nearby so we decided we also wanted Mexican food," Jace explains. He pulls back the chair next to him. "Have a seat, kiddo."

I'm twenty years old, but he still calls me that.

"Where are they?" I ask, secretly hoping those two women will still be watching when the guys they were drooling over have beautiful wives join them at the table.

"Bathroom," my dad says.

A few seconds later, my mom and Bayleigh appear, but the drooling women are gone. Damn. We place our order with the waiter.

"How'd your test go?" Mom asks me.

"Really good," I say. "I think I'll be keeping my 4.0 intact."

She squeezes my hand. "I'm so proud of you."

My mom's hair is darker since she recently dyed it, and I think it makes her look younger than it did when she had it highlighted. I can notice the very fine wrinkles on the corners of her eyes, the ones she hates and always complains about, but they make me smile. Those wrinkles are there because she cares. She worries and she loves and she actually cares about me.

"Where are the babies?" I ask, feeling stupid that it's been like ten minutes and I didn't think about my own little brother. Jett also has a little sister and they are usually always with our moms.

"At the track," Mom says. "Betsy is watching them."

Jace says my name. "So are you excited for this week?"

"I'm excited about the time off school, and the races, but not the driving," I say with a laugh.

Jace nods. "There is too much driving in motocross. It's ridiculous."

"Jett makes it fun, but it's still hours of driving, so it can only get *so* fun before it's awful." I say, curling my lip.

He has three arenacross races this week and instead of being stuck at home in school, I'm going with him this time. The first race is in Dallas, then San Antonio a few days later, and two days after that, we'll be driving to Vegas. You can't fly when you have to haul your own dirt bike. Team Loco, which is Jett's sponsorship team, doesn't have any official races this week, so Jett is racing arenacross both for fun, and to keep up his standing as the man to beat. Right now he's ranked number one in his racing class in the whole region. I can't wait until the nationals race where he'll become number one in the whole country.

"Remember that time we drove from Texas to California?" My dad says to my mom.

Her eyes widen. "Oh my god, that was the worst! I mean it ended up being fun, but the initial drive sucked. You had to get a new truck and everything."

"Wow," I say. "When did that happen?"

Mom smiles like she does when she's recalling something special. "Years ago. We were supposed to fly, and then the airport was closed, and then his truck broke down, so we had to buy a new one, and then all the hotels were booked—"

"It was Christmas," Dad says. He looks at my mom and his eyes soften. "But we made it special, right?"

She melts up against his shoulder. "Yes, we did."

I smile, even though it's a little awkward seeing them in one of their special romantic moments. My phone vibrates from my purse, and I bend down to get it.

"Hello?" I say.

"Heyyy babe," Jett says back. His voice always makes my knees week. Good thing I'm sitting. "How was your test?"

"It was good. How was your practice?"

"It was perfection, as always," he says with a chuckle. I can tell he's a little out of breath which means he just got done riding. He's probably covered in sweat, with the veins bulging on his muscles, which is literally the hottest state he can be in. It's a shame I'm not there to witness it.

"I'm eating lunch with the parents," I say.

"Which parents?"

"All of them."

He laughs. "You poor thing. Have they embarrassed the hell out of you yet?"

"Not yet, but once they realize who I'm talking to, I'm sure they will."

That gets Jace's attention and he turns to me. "Talking to Jett?" he asks.

"Nope," I say quickly. "I'm talking to a platonic girl friend."

"Is that why you're blushing?" Dad says.

"Oh my God, ya'll are the worst," I say.

On the phone, Jett laughs. "I'm sorry, baby. When you get done, come home. I need your help packing."

"Don't worry, " I say, giving the parents the evil eye as they playfully make fun of me for being so in love. "I'll be there soon."

CHAPTER TWO

Jett

Keanna sounded like she was in a great mood on the phone. It's nice to see the stress of the school year evaporate, if only for a little while. I'm so proud of her for doing this college thing. I'm not even in college yet, and honestly, I don't even want to go. Here's hoping the motocross gig earns me enough money to retire early. Keanna is the star in this relationship. She's the smart one, even if she doesn't think so. She's the one who takes care of me and makes my life so much easier.

I put up my bike and head inside to take a quick shower before she gets here. Tomorrow we'll be heading to Dallas bright and early in the morning, so she's coming to spend the night with me tonight. Sometimes I wish she'd just stay over here every single night, but since we're neighbors, it's not that hard to see each other. Keanna says it would be too weird if she stayed every night, because it'd be like she was living with me while I live with my parents. I totally get where she's coming from, even though my parents are pretty damn cool.

As I shower, I think back to the life I had before I met her. I was going down a shitty path in life, much the same as most of the guys I know in motocross. Dating whoever, whenever, hooking up with hot girls just for the fun of it. I know my dad hated it, and I can't blame him. When I met Keanna, I fell hard for the girl. All that other shit in my past just disappeared in an instant, and now, even thinking about the idea of random hookups makes me feel sick to my stomach. How could a guy want to live a life like that when you can have a perfect girlfriend every single day?

I love my parents, but I think it's a little more than obvious that they love Keanna more than me now. I snort out a laugh as I get out of the shower and get dressed. Keanna is the girl who saved me from a reckless and stupid path in life. They have every reason to love her, and I'm glad they do.

After I get dressed, I stare at the open suitcase on my bed. It's huge enough for Keanna to crawl inside and zip up—we know because we tried it out for fun once—and it's black with the blue Team Loco logo on it. I could bring anything I want to, and yet I suck at packing. Right now I have three pairs of jeans, some sleep shorts, a few boxers, and some socks.

I freaking hate packing. I always forget something, from my phone charger to a knee brace or that one time when I forgot to bring my toothbrush but brought two tubes of toothpaste instead. Packing is the worst.

"I'm here," Keanna calls out, her voice faint as it travels from downstairs all the way up to my room.

"In my room," I call back. "I need help!"

I can hear her angelic laugh as she jogs up the stairs. "Let me guess?" she says, appearing in my doorway. "Your suitcase is too vast and big and you have no idea what to put in it?"

"Yep," I say, meeting her at the door. I slide my arms around her waist and pull her close. She smells like green apple shampoo and a little like a Mexican restaurant.

"You're a grown man, you know that right?" she says playfully, her nails scratching lightly down my back as I hold her close to me. "Nineteen years old and you can't even pack a suitcase."

"I can pack it, I'm just not good at it." I make a pouty face and she rolls her eyes.

"Don't worry, I got you."

I slide my hands under her ass and lift her off the floor. She wraps her legs around my waist as I carry her to my bed and sit her down carefully. "I love you," I whisper, my lips against hers.

"Do you love me, or do you love my packing skills?" she whispers back.

I kiss her. "Both."

She laughs and pushes me away. "Let's see what train wreck you've assembled here," she says, going through my clothing. "There's not a single shirt… were you planning on spending all week showing off those abs?"

I lift my shirt and flex the six pack I work so hard to maintain. "Sounds like a plan to me."

She rolls her eyes and stands up, heading to my closet. "I will get you some shirts, you dork."

I turn on my TV and set it to the YouTube app so we can listen to music. "Are you packed yet?"

"Yeah, I left my suitcase downstairs by the back door because it's ridiculously heavy," Keanna says. "I brought those books for Aiden's sister."

"She'll love that," I say. Aiden is also on Team Loco, and he has a little sister who is as obsessed with reading as Keanna is. She had an extra set of some teen romance series after she won an autographed set online, so she promised to give it to her.

I walk up behind Keanna while she takes my clothes off hangers and folds them neatly into my suitcase. I slide my hands up her back and rub her shoulders. I hear her release a soft sigh, see her head tilt to the side as I massage her back. But she keeps working, diligently sorting my outfits for the week. I lean forward and kiss her neck. She freezes.

"Baby, I can't focus if you do that."

"Who needs focus?" I whisper, kissing her again. I grab her waist and tug her up against me.

She giggles. "Let me finish packing and then we can continue this."

I heave a big sarcastic sigh and then rest my chin on her shoulder, watching her continue to fold clothes and ignore me hanging out behind her. "Okay, I guess I can wait."

"Such a horn dog," she mutters, but I can hear the smile in her voice.

"I upgraded to the paid Spotify subscription so we'll have awesome tunes while we drive," I say, trying to change the subject since I'm all ready to strip her clothes off and throw her on the bed. "Should make the trip more fun."

"Awesome," she says. "I've been to Dallas and San Antonio a million times, but I'm excited for Vegas."

"Yeah?" I say, watching her face light up with excitement.

She nods. "It sucks that we aren't old enough to drink, but I can't wait to see the Strip all lit up at night. And I want to try that Vegas Cupcakes place. All their cupcakes are ridiculously fancy and are supposed to be the best ones in the country. I think it'll be awesome. It'll be even better if you win your race."

I grin and watch her work, helping me once again do something I'm not good at. This girl is my angel. Vegas will be really fun because we'll have three days there and I only race one of those days.

Maybe I'll find a place in Vegas that would make the perfect spot…

I grin as my heart fills with anticipation and excitement.

Yes. Vegas.

Maybe I'll do it then.

CHAPTER THREE

Keanna

Jett is being a lot more affectionate than usual. I mean, it's not like he's ever been distant or cold toward me, but lately it's like he's metal and I'm magnetized and he can't stay away from me. I like it, but it makes me wonder. Is he being overly affectionate to make up for something I don't know about?

I try to shrug the thoughts away. I remind myself that Jett is mine, and he's the greatest guy ever, and he's loyal and loving and would never lie to me. It helps a little.

I check the time on my phone—it's three in the morning. I keep falling asleep and then waking up half an hour later, filled with bad thoughts about Jett and worries over nothing. I roll over and look at Jett in the darkness. The moonlight filters in through the window just a little, and I can make out the outline of his face sleeping peacefully next to me. I scoot a little closer and rest my head on his shoulder.

On instinct, his arm goes around me. His breath stays steady, and he remains asleep, but even when totally passed out, he remembers to hold onto me. It warms my heart and I slip back to sleep, telling myself I was stupid to worry about anything.

We arrive in Dallas, Texas around ten in the morning. There's a stadium next door to the hotel we're staying at and that's where the arenacross races will be tomorrow. For now, we have the day to rest and Jett plans on taking it easy to prepare for the race tomorrow.

"This hotel is pretty nice," Jett says as we step off the elevators on the tenth floor.

"Damn," a voice calls out from down the hallway. I recognize it immediately as Zach Pena, a fellow Team Loco racer. "They let anyone in here!" he says, winking at me. "I thought this hotel was for classy people only," he says to Jett.

"You should have known it wasn't the second they let your country ass in here," Jett says, walking up and fist bumping his teammate. We may live in Texas, which is home of the cowboys, but Zach is from a small town in Tennessee and his southern twang puts Texans to shame.

After leaving our stuff in our hotel room, we meet up with Zach and the other two guys on Team Loco, Clay and Aiden. I usually feel like the odd one out when I'm with the guys, but it's been long enough now that I feel included. They don't rag on Jett for bringing his girlfriend, and they're all very nice to me so it works. Still, I think it'd be better if one of the other guys got a girlfriend so I'd have someone to hang out with while they do their thing. I don't really see that happening, though. Zach is a player who hooks up more than he dates girls, Clay only cares about dirt bikes so it's like women aren't even on his radar, and Zach cares more about earning money to help his family back home than meeting girls. But maybe one day it'll happen.

We head over to the stadium next door so the guys can get checked in for tomorrow's races. Since I'm Jett's VIP guest, I get a blue wristband that lets me into the races for free, and it also lets me into the special areas that spectators can't get into, like the starting line and the pits. I'm feeling a little more than special as I wrap the bracelet around my wrist.

I love the smell of arenacross tracks. It's a little weird, probably, but the exhaust mixed with fresh dirt has started to remind me of home. Dirt bikes are Jett's thing, and he is my home. The Track, the business my parents and Jett's parents own, is also home and that place is 99% dirt. So maybe it's not the smell of dirt that I'm attracted to, but the feelings that come with it. For the first time in my life I have a home. I am wanted, and I am loved.

I couldn't say so much about the first seventeen years of my existence. I was raised by a selfish woman who could never hold down a job or keep an apartment. Her relationships were crap and her idea of love was trying to get me to sleep with some creeper old guy in exchange for money. Those days of my life seem so long ago now that I've moved on and joined another, much better family. I used to have nightmares about it, about her. But now my life is happy and my dreams are mostly good.

The guys get into the empty arena and one of the employees lets us walk the track. It's not the same as riding it, but seeing the layout lets the guys get a good vibe for how it'll be to race on it tomorrow.

I hold Jett's hand while we walk around on the dirt, and I stay mostly quiet while he and the guys talk nonstop. It's all dirt bike talk, which is mostly lost on me.

Eventually, we leave and walk back to our hotel, which only half a block away. The parking lot is filled with other racers and people who will set up vendor booths at the races tomorrow. Jett and the other guys say hello to a ton of people as we walk past them. I notice a few girls watching me, their eyes trailing from my face to my hand, which is still clasped in Jett's. I try not to let it make me feel awkward. After all, I'd be jealous if I were in their shoes. Everyone loves Jett Adams, but he only loves me.

Since it's nearly dinner time, the guys want to try out this steakhouse that's right across the road. Once we're there, I excuse myself to go pee and wash my hands. The restaurant is huge, so once I walk out of the bathroom, I can't remember which way I took to get here.

I stand near a large potted plant and casually look around the tables, hoping to spot Jett before too long so I don't look like an idiot.

"That is definitely Jett," I hear someone say.

I look to my right and see two girls, about my age, sitting at the bar. They're turned around and staring toward the left. I follow their gaze and see my boyfriend sitting with Clay, Zach, and Aiden, and let out a sigh of relief. Two of Jett's fans saved me from getting lost. Go figure.

"...so fucking hot," I hear one of the girls say.

"They're all hot," the other one says back.

Curiosity takes over and I stay here behind this tree a little longer, just to hear what they're saying.

"Yeah, but Jett is hotter. He looks just like his dad."

"You should go talk to him instead of sitting here lusting after him," her friend says.

The girl wiggles her eyebrows. "Maybe I will ... I don't see that slut girlfriend of his. Looks like he's free for the taking."

A knot of anger twists in my stomach. Just because Jett has a girlfriend doesn't mean she's a slut. It doesn't mean I'm a slut. Why are girls so freaking mean to each other?

"Ugh, I forgot about that hoe," the friend says, curling her lip in disgust. "Are they still a thing? They can't possibly still be together. She looks like backwoods trailer trash."

"Last time I checked, they were," the first girl says.

Hot tears threaten to spill from my eyes, but I blink them away. Maybe it's because her comment hit too close to home, but I'm totally pissed off right now. I was born and raised as white trash. So what? That's not who I am anymore. And Jett shouldn't be insulted for who he's dating.

I step away from the potted plant and walk right up them. Their eyes widen when they see me, and I make a big deal of looking at what the first girl is wearing. A low-cut tank top and short shorts with fishnet stockings underneath them. Her makeup looks like a kid put it on, trying their hardest to be sexy.

"Take a look at the two of us," I say, standing tall and holding my head high. "Which one of us seems more like a slut? Because it's not me."

Her mouth hangs open like the idiot she is, and with a satisfied smile, I turn and walk toward my boyfriend.

CHAPTER FOUR

Jett

I can feel the adrenaline coursing through my veins. The races start in half an hour, and I'm pumped, mentally and physically. I've officially been racing dirt bikes for most of my life and yet the adrenaline never goes away. It's always there, ready to take over the moment the gate drops and I speed off, competing with twenty four other racers for that coveted first place trophy.

Lucky for me, arenacross is a little easier than professional supercross. Not technically, since the track is still a beast to navigate, but the rest of the racers are a step below me in talent. Only a few of them have large sponsorships like me and the guys from Team Loco, so I have a feeling the top three places will be dominated by our blue and black jerseys. We'll make our manager proud.

Keanna watches me get ready. I gave her my VIP pass so she's allowed down here in the pits with me while all the other spectators have to stay up in the stadium seats. I buckle up my boots, throw on my jersey, fasten my neck brace, and then look around for my helmet.

"Right here," she says, holding out my helmet.

"Thank you babe." I take it and lean over and kiss her.

"Not fair," Clay calls out from a few feet over where he's also getting dressed. "It's one thing to bring your girlfriend here, but another to rub it in our faces how happy you are."

"Dude, no one's stopping you from getting your own girlfriend."

He snorts as he pulls the Velcro tight on his gloves. "Eyes on the prize, Adams. I don't have time for girls when I'm too busy trying to beat you."

Keanna watches him with this curious look on her face, and if I didn't know any better, I'd think she's trying to think of someone to set him up with. I know it bothers her that she's the only girlfriend on the team and often feels left out when I bring her to places like this.

I slip on my helmet and poke her in the side. She's wearing black workout leggings and a blue Team Logo T-shirt and she looks so damn sexy in those tight ass pants. I feel like a pig and a caveman when she's all sexy like that because I know it makes all the other guys jealous, and I don't care. I love it, actually. I've got the hot girl and they've got nothing but jealousy.

I poke her ribs again and she squirms. "That tickles."

"Meet me at the finish line?"

She smiles. "You better be the first one across it."

Aiden jogs up and smacks the back of my helmet. "Ready? I'm about to line up."

"Sounds good," I say. I crank up my bike and let it idle for a minute, and then I turn back to my beautiful girlfriend.

"Twenty laps," I say, taking her face in my hands.

"So longggg," she says with a groan.

"It'll be over before you know it."

"And then boring San Antonio, and then onto awesome Vegas!" Her smile reaches her eyes when she mentions Vegas, and once again I'm feeling like that'll be the perfect time to do it.

"Only a few days away," I say.

She reaches up and kisses the front of my helmet. "Good luck."

"Love you," I say.

"Love you more," she says back.

Keanna waits with the other VIPs, who are mostly older mechanics, managers, and parents, and waves to me as I set up my bike on the starting line. The starting line is a long stretch, and you draw a number to see which spot you'll get. I drew a shitty number so I'm right smack in the middle of the line instead of on the edge like I'd prefer. In the middle, you have to make sure to be the fastest at the drop or you'll get stuck behind other people, and possibly end up in a pile up of bikes at the first turn. Not that I can't pull away from something like that and regain first place during the twenty laps, but it's a lot more annoying.

Soon the air fills with the roar of two dozen dirt bikes, and I steady my attention to the starting gate. It drops, and I pin the throttle, my focus solely on the race now.

With luck and talent, I manage to get the holeshot so I'm out in front of everyone. Now I just need to keep it for the next twenty laps.

Which is exactly what I do. I'm not trying to be some egotistical prick, but when Keanna is here watching me, I have way more drive to race hard and fast. Sometimes when I'm traveling with Team Loco, I can feel myself getting lazy after the tenth lap, but this time I don't stop. I ride hard and I keep the throttle pinned, and before long the checkered flag whips out, signaling that I've won the race. I turn the bike sideways as I soar over the finish line jump, and then my heart beats faster knowing that I'm about to see her again. It's so much more fun having my girl with me at these things. I can't wait until this semester is over and she can spend the rest of summer with me traveling and racing. Hopefully she wants that, too.

Sweat pours off me as I slow down and ride to my slot in the pits, which is right between the other Team Loco guys. Clay is right on my tail, so he was probably second place. I see Aiden and Zach a few seconds later. I park my bike on the stand and rip off my helmet, then grab a bottle of water from a nearby ice chest. I glance around and see her walking quickly toward me.

"You were amazing," she says, her eyes sparkling under the bright stadium lights. "I always love watching you race."

I bend down and kiss her lightly so that my sweat-drenched body doesn't touch her.

Zach comes by and shakes my hand. "Dude, good race."

"Thanks, man."

"Showers and then dinner?" Aiden says as he rubs a towel over his sweating head. "Shower separately, and then eat together, is what I meant just in case you pervs thought otherwise."

Clay snorts. "I'm down. I'm starving."

Keanna shifts on her feet and even though she's smiling, I get the feeling she feels a little out of place with the guys.

"I think we're gonna head back to the hotel," I say, giving her a quick wink when she looks up at me. "You guys go on."

"Look at him," Aiden says sarcastically. "Always rubbing it in with the girlfriend."

I flip him off and he laughs. "See ya'll in San A?"

"Yeah, man. See you tomorrow."

After packing up my bike and all my gear, we head back to the hotel. I head straight to the bathroom to rip off my sweaty riding gear, and Keanna calls my name.

"What's up?" I call back.

"Your phone is ringing. It's Zach."

"Let it ring," I call back.

When I get out of the shower, Keanna is sitting on the hotel's desk chair, her face tight with worry.

"What is it?"

"Your phone has been ringing like nonstop. All of the guys have called you like twice each, and I wanted to answer it because I thought maybe it's an emergency but I didn't want to go through your stuff..."

"Babe," I say, holding the towel around my waist as I lean over and kiss her. "My stuff is your stuff. I hope the guys are okay."

I grab my phone off the nightstand and unlock the screen. I have a dozen missed calls and a few text messages.

"What is it?" Keanna asks.

I click on the first message. Shit.

"Well?" Keanna says, her voice growing impatient.

"Uh..." I don't know what to say. I am temporarily out of words. I turn off my phone and toss it on the bed. "It's um, nothing."

"Doesn't seem like nothing," she says, standing up. "Why do you look like that?"

I bite my lip. "It's ... well, it's about you."

CHAPTER FIVE

Keanna

"D*on't worry, none of us believe any of that shit,"* Jett says, as he reads a text from one of the guys. Their words mean nothing to me. I am already worried and I haven't seen what's going on yet.

"Would you please tell me what the hell is going on?"

Jett turns to me, his eyes slowly meeting mine. "It's nothing, babe. Someone just decided to talk trash about you online."

I groan. "What is it this time?"

"It's nothing."

I hold out my hand. "I want to see it."

With a pained frown, Jett hands me his phone. Someone has sent him a link to a Twitter post. I click it, and the Twitter app opens to a very long thread. I see my name, and my heart pounds as I scroll up to the start of the long post that's bashing me.

And then I start reading, and my entire life flashes before my eyes. Not the good life I have now, with family and a little brother and a great boyfriend. My old life. The life that almost broke me.

We were in Phoenix. My biological mom, Dawn, and me. It was the longest we'd lived in one place in a long time, and I was starting to feel settled down in my school. It was freshman year. I had a couple of friends who would sit with me at lunch. One day they invited me over for a party, and I was eager to go. I'd worn my best jeans and shirt, which wasn't saying much, and stole some of my mom's makeup in an attempt to look prettier. Then I walked the fifteen blocks to the girl's house. I remember her name was Mindy, and she was really popular despite living in a run-down trailer. Where I came from, all the popular people were rich, but not in this case. Mindy was pretty and outgoing and a lot of fun. Later, I'd realize that her popularity stemmed from the fact that she'd sleep with any guy who wanted it, but at the time I had no idea. I was just happy to be included. I was out at a party with lots of people, drinking free beer, and trying to enjoy myself, and it was a lot better than sitting at home where we didn't have a TV or internet or anything fun.

Mindy bumped into me with her shoulder. "I see you staring at him," she'd said, making flirty eyes at me.

I probably turned beet red as I shook my head and said I wasn't staring at anyone. But she knew I was lying. "His name is JJ," she said, nudging me with her cup of beer. "Go say hi."

I did. I don't know why, but I did.

JJ was tall, older, and cute in this rugged bad boy way. I'd only been watching him because he was sitting alone on a couch and looked just as bored as I was. But with Mindy's encouragement, I walked right up to him and sat down on the other side of the couch.

"Hello," I said meekly when he looked at me.

"Yo," he said back.

And that was that, for about ten minutes. Then Mindy sauntered over and sat herself between us, throwing an arm around both of our shoulders. "JJ, this is Keanna. She has a crush on you," she'd said entirely too loudly. I wanted to drop dead of mortification, but JJ just looked at me like he'd suddenly seen me in a new light. "Cool," he said with a nod and a sly grin in my direction.

"My work here is done," Mindy said, just before hopping up and disappearing into the crowd.

"So how do you know Mindy?" JJ asked me.

"We go to school together," I said.

He slid a little closer and kept up the conversation. We talked for a few minutes about nothing in particular, and my heart was pounding a mile a minute.

"You want to find somewhere more quiet to talk?" he said.

And I remember it very clearly because he said *to talk*. Not anything else. Talk. I was a total idiot back then and assumed that what he said was what he'd meant. I said yes. He stood up and took my hand and I was so excited that I guy was holding my hand that I let him lead me down the hallway and into a tiny bedroom at the end of the house. He closed the door behind us and then twisted the lock, securing us from the outside world. My stomach flipped.

Then his arms were all over me, pawing at me like some rabid beast. His tongue was hot and tasted gross as it shoved in my mouth. I froze for a second, not knowing what to do. I'll admit, part of me kind of wanted to make out a little, just to know what it was like. He was cute, after all, and he clearly liked me. But then he got too handsy, and he reeked of alcohol, and I panicked.

"I want to take things slow!" I said, my words rushed and panicked and stupidly shaking from my fear.

He jumped back as if I'd electrocuted him. Then he chuckled and ran a hand through his hair. "Baby girl, I don't take things slow. I think you got the wrong idea here."

"What do you mean?" I stuttered out.

He laughed, a cruel sound that made me feel very small. "I don't want to date you. You're Mindy's friend, which means you're just good for a hookup."

Those words stayed with me for months. Even after Dawn uprooted us again and we moved to another town, I still thought about it all the time. I wasn't the kind of girl worthy of a relationship. I was just a hookup. A loser. Not girlfriend material.

But that wasn't the worst part. Just two weeks after the party, I'd come home from school to find my mom hooking up with a guy on the couch.

"Dammit!" she cursed when I walked into the room. "You're not supposed to be home yet!"

I just ran into my bedroom and closed the door to give her privacy with her guest, and didn't bother telling her that this was the exact time I got home from school every day. I'd only seen them for a fraction of a second, but it was all I needed.

My mom was hooking up with JJ. And he saw me too.

Shame falls over me as I scroll through these tweets, disregarding Jett's plea for me to just ignore it.

Some girl is tweeting the whole story, but she's embellishing it a lot.

Let me tell you something about Jett Adam's girlfriend, she begins in the first tweet. *I happened to meet one of her old boyfriends, and he had something to say about her. Not only is she a big slut, her mother is, too.*

It only gets worse from there. The tweets say that I had been sleeping with JJ, and all of his friends, for weeks. And that my mom also slept with them. I'm called every bad name in the book, and then my reputation is dragged as far down as it can go.

She was begging for any guy to sleep with her, the tweets continue. *And after I asked around online, I got many people to confirm this.*

"This is all a lie," I tell Jett, tears filling my eyes. "You know this is a lie, right? I never slept with anyone!"

Jett's lips are pressed into a frown. "I know, baby. No one believes that shit. It's probably just some fan who is obsessed with me. Please don't read any more of it."

Tears pour down my cheeks. I click on the tiny picture of the person who posted all these tweets and look at her profile. Her name is Tawny, and she lives in Dallas. I zoom in on her picture, and realize that this is all my fault. It's the girl from the steakhouse. The one I called a slut.

Looks like I didn't have the final word, after all.

CHAPTER SIX

Jett

I am full of rage, and wish I could hit something. But you can't hit the Internet, which is filled with anonymous assholes. Whoever this bitch is that started a tirade against my girlfriend is going to pay for it. But first, I have to take care of my girl.

"Baby, no one will care about this shit," I say, wrapping her in my arms and resting my head on top of hers. I can tell she's trying hard to hold back tears, but it's not working. "Seriously."

"It already has a ton of likes," she says, her voice muffled as I hold her close. "People do care. They're already saying you deserve better than me."

I cringe. I was hoping she didn't see that part on Twitter. Someone announced that I should break up with her, and lots of people retweeted it and agreed. I don't understand what makes the fans think they can get involved with my personal life. Those aren't the type of people I want rooting for me on the track. Those people can take their drama elsewhere.

I rub my hand down Keanna's back. "Let's do something to take your mind off this," I say softly.

She pulls away. "I think I'm going to go shower."

"Want me to come with you?" I ask, giving her a flirty look.

She steps back and shakes her head. "I just want to be alone. Just … please … just leave me alone for a while."

It kills me to see her like this, but I know that she's serious when she asks for time by herself.

"Okay," I say. "Take your time."

She grabs some clothes from her suitcase and slips into our hotel's bathroom. I hear the water turn on, and I sit here feeling so damn hopeless.

On my phone, I report the girl who posted all those horrible things about Keanna, and then I block her. I scroll down and find every person who was saying anything remotely rude about my girlfriend and I block them, too.

Then I think carefully about my wording and I post a tweet to my profile.

Anyone who spreads untrue rumors, or says hateful things about me, my girlfriend, or anyone I care about is not a fan of mine. Don't come to my races. Don't buy my merch. Kindly fuck off.

I feel a little better after posting the tweet, and the replies and likes start coming in quickly, so I close the app to make sure I don't get caught up in the stupid online drama. People can be so cruel. I don't understand what goes through some of these girl's heads. Do they think that calling my girlfriend a slut will make me dump her and then ask them out? Never happening.

Even if Keanna and I didn't last forever, I'd never date a rude fan. You can't trust them because they're in it for the fame. I grind my teeth and stand up, needing to get all of this anger out of my system. I don't even like thinking about it. Keanna and I are never splitting up. Not if I have anything to do with it.

I decide to step outside and take a walk down the hotel's long empty corridor. It doesn't help clear my mind any, so I call my dad. He always knows what to do.

"Hey, Dad," I say when he answers.

"What's wrong? I saw you got first place so you shouldn't sound so upset, son."

I take a deep breath. "I already forgot about the race actually," I say.

"Why's that?" Dad is always there for me. Because he's younger than my friend's dads, maybe he understands better. Or maybe he's just a better person in general. Whatever it is, I'm never embarrassed to talk to him about what's going on.

"Have you seen the drama online?"

He snorts. "I rarely ever go online."

My dad's not big into social media, so I guess that makes sense. At least this drama hasn't spread very far yet. Maybe it will just stay on Twitter.

I sigh. "Some bitch got on Twitter and spread a bunch of horrible lies about Keanna. Calling her a slut and stuff. And then other fangirls piled on and they're all attacking her online."

"Damn, people are the worst," Dad says. "How's Keanna?"

"Not good. She wanted to be left alone, so I'm walking the hallways of the hotel."

"You should go to her," Dad says.

I shake my head. "It doesn't work like that. If she wants to be alone, I have to respect that. I just feel so shitty. She's not being attacked for who she is, but for who she's dating. It's all my fault that these girls are targeting her. I hate it."

"I know the feeling," he says after a moment. "You can't let it get to you. Stick by your girl and ignore everything else."

"That's what I'm trying to do."

"That's what you will do," he says. "You've got this, son. Just be strong for her and she'll know you've got her back. She's probably not mad about what the people were saying, but about how you'll react to it."

"I'm not going to leave her," I say quickly.

Dad laughs. "I know. But trust me, that's how girls are. They'll worry that you *will* leave. That's how your mom was. It never hurts to remind them that you're not going anywhere."

"Okay," I say, reaching the end of the hallway. I turn around and walk back toward my hotel room. "I'll do that."

"You're heading to San Antonio tomorrow?" Dad asks.

"Yeah, leaving at six in the morning."

"Drive safe. Your sister misses you."

I snort. "That's because I'm the only one who knows how to play a decent game of peek-a-boo."

"That might be true," Dad says with a laugh. "Good luck tomorrow, Jett."

"Thanks, Dad."

"And don't worry," he says. "This will blow over."

I hope so. I really hope it does. Because I never want to see Keanna looking that upset again.

CHAPTER SEVEN

Keanna

The drive to San Antonio is silent. Jett plays some music softly on the radio but I know neither one of us listens to it. I don't want to talk. I don't know what to say. I thought about trying to fake like everything is normal and A-Okay and fine and put on a cheery smile and deal with this, but Jett knows me better than that. He'd see right through the fake happiness, and that would be worse than just being myself. Right now, myself doesn't want to talk, so I don't. I sit here and stare out the window for the whole drive.

Once we arrive at our new hotel which is also next to the stadium for the races tomorrow, Jett reaches over and squeezes my hand. "I love you," he says.

"I love you too," I say back. It's not a lie, and he knows it.

We take our stuff into the hotel and check in. Our room is on the first floor, which kind of sucks because I like looking out windows of somewhere high up so I can see the whole town below.

Not two seconds after we make it into our hotel room does someone knock on the door. Loudly. Annoyingly.

"Open up!" Clay yells. "We've been here for hours!"

Jett opens the door and the three guys from his team all barrel into our room. "It's been more like half an hour," Aiden says. "But we didn't want to walk the track until you got here."

"Although I think we should get a sneak peek so we have a chance to beat you," Zach says to Jett, then he tosses a wink to me. "Not that it would help."

Jett laughs. "You want to go check out the track now?"

"Yeah, then we need dinner," Zach says.

Jett walks over to me and takes my hands in his. He lowers his voice so only I can hear. "Do you want me to tell them to go on without us?"

I stare into his eyes, feeling guilty for all the concern in them. He knows I'm hurting and he'll do whatever it takes to make me feel better. But this is his race, and we're here for him to advance his career. I can't just let it all go to hell because I feel like shit. I shake my head. "I think I'll stay here, but you go ahead."

He gives me a look like he really doesn't like that idea.

I put my hand on his chest. "Babe, I'm serious," I say with a little smile. "Go check out the track. I'm tired, and I just want to watch TV."

"Okay," he says, pulling me in to kiss my forehead. "Call me if you need anything."

I wave to the guys and as soon as they're gone, the door closed behind them, I rush up and twist the deadbolt into place. And then I rest my head against the cool wooden door and start to cry.

I know I should stay away and take Jett's advice and just ignore all the drama online, but I can't. I am weak, and pathetic. I am just as worthless as they say I am.

I sit on the edge of the crisply made hotel bed and open up Twitter on my phone. It's bad enough that this girl blasted me online with lies and horrible name-calling, but she's even tagged me in some of them. My tears come harder as I scroll through the vile on Twitter.

There are a few people replying, telling me not to worry about those bitches, but their kind words don't help at all. The mean words cut into me, lashing my heart wide open. The few nice things here and there are nothing more than tiny bandages that don't help.

Jett's last tweet makes me smile a little. He's being an amazing boyfriend by standing up for me, which is more than I could have asked for. All of the replies to his post are nice, and I'm wondering if that's because he's blocked anyone who says anything negative. Probably. For the millionth time, I wish I had just kept my mouth shut at that restaurant. I should have let her talk about me to her friend. I should have walked away. But instead, I thought I was standing up for myself and all I did was make this girl dig up dirt on me and unleash it into the world. I'm used to being called a skank, or unworthy of Jett. That's been happening since the day we started dating. And it sucks and it hurts, but for the most part, I'm used to it.

This time it hurts worse. She brought up a person from my past. I've spent the last two years becoming a new person with a new life. I threw away all of the memories of my past the day my biological mother disowned me, and I've looked forward to a new life that's better.

But this just makes me realize something I hadn't thought of before. I can get a new last name and new parents and a new house, but I'll never stop being the girl I used to be. I was born trash and I'll always be trash. I tried to run away from it, but that didn't matter.

Jett will see through this one day, I know he will.

I drop my phone and bury my face into the pillow, letting the tears pour out for what feels like a very long time. Every time I close my eyes, I see that last tweet I read before turning off my phone.

That girl's words are burned into my memory, staring me right in the face.

Jett deserves so much better than some trailer trash whore. We should make it our mission to convince him to leave her.

I can't say I blame them. Yeah, I never actually slept with JJ, but my mom did. I was trash. I *am* trash. I still sit at a fancy restaurant with my family and wonder how they do this knife and fork thing with their food when I've never been taught how to eat all classy like that. I barely know anything about motocross. Jett deserves someone better. He deserves a girl that grew up in the sport and knows all about it. Maybe even a girl that also rides dirt bikes so they can go riding together.

Guilt weighs me down as I sit up and try to dry my tears. I know what they're saying on Twitter is true. Jett deserves better. But I still don't want to give him up. He is the best part of me.

There's a soft knock on the hotel door, and it makes me jump. "Delivery," someone calls out. It doesn't sound like any of the guys' voices, so I hope they're not playing a prank on me.

I wipe at my eyes and try to compose myself and then I open the door just a crack. A huge display of flowers fills the air. I open the door all the way and see a man from the hotel holding the huge bouquet.

"I have a delivery for you, ma'am," he says, handing over the flowers.

"Thank you," I say.

He grins and then turns away before I start crying again. I close the door and set the heavy vase down on a nearby table. Flowers of all colors burst out of the vase. Pinks and reds and purples and even sunflowers. It's absolutely beautiful and I can't believe Jett would do something so sweet. We'll be driving to Vegas in two days, so what am I supposed to do with these?

I take the little card off the flowers and open it up, surprised when I don't see Jett's handwriting on the card. I momentarily panic, thinking these flowers were meant for someone else, but then I read the message.

Cheer up, Sweetheart. The people who matter love you, and the ones who don't can go to hell.

Love,

Clay, Zach, & Aiden

More tears roll down my cheeks, but they are of the happy variety. I can't believe I'm smiling after spending the last hour feeling the worst I've ever felt. Having the approval of Jett's teammates makes me feel a whole lot better. Maybe they'll talk to him and encourage him not to leave me like the people on Twitter are asking him to do.

I lean in and smell the flowers and feel my heart start to repair itself. The world may be cruel, but there are still good people out there. And it sure as hell feels good to have someone on my side.

CHAPTER EIGHT

Jett

This isn't the first time I've lost a race. It's just like the unstoppable adrenaline I get before the gate drops—losing makes me feel like shit. I'll never get over it. I'll never lose a race and be like, meh, oh well. It always sucks.

This time my shitty third place finish wasn't due to me competing with faster racers than myself. They didn't have better agility or speed, or even bikes that were faster. In fact, their bikes are exactly the same because first and second place went to two of my teammates. That's a good thing—Team Loco on the podium—but it still sucks for me.

The reason I lost is because I can't stop worrying about Keanna and the stupid drama that comes with being even mildly famous in a professional sport. It's not like I'm Ryan freaking Reynolds or anything. I'm just a guy who races in a sport most people don't even care about. I can't even imagine the bullshit real celebrities go through. I let the trolls online get in my head. I let it bother me, agitate me, and screw up my racing tonight.

I love Keanna with all my heart, but I tell her a teensy lie when I get back to the hotel after the San Antonio race. I squeeze my wrist and say it's been hurting. An old injury must be acting up again, and that's what made me ride so shitty. I think she believes it.

The guys sent her flowers, which I didn't know about beforehand, and that seems to have cheered her up. I wish I had thought of it, but I'm glad someone did. I know she likes being included in my life, and there's no better way than for Team Loco to show their support of her. I love those idiots. They're really good guys.

Keanna barely says a word while we eat dinner with the guys at a local Mexican restaurant. Then when we turn in for the night, she falls asleep quickly and doesn't wake up. I know, because I can't seem to stay asleep. I keep waking up and looking over at her, wanting to make sure she's okay. I wish she'd let me talk about it. But I guess talking won't help much. The sad fact is that jealous girls online will always be mean to her because they want what they can't have. It's not her fault. It's not even about her. It's about me. I wish she'd realize that.

I finally fall asleep while watching her angelic face while she sleeps.

In the morning, Keanna insists on bringing her flowers to Vegas so she has something pretty in the hotel room. We put them on the floor in the back seat of my truck, surrounded by our suitcases and bags to hold the vase upright. She doesn't say much as we get coffee and breakfast at a drive thru fast food place, but she keeps looking back at the flowers and smiling. I'm glad she seems a little better today.

After a couple hours of driving, I look over at her and grin. "Want to get fake IDs and go gambling once we get to Vegas?"

She rolls her eyes. "Breaking the law is against your Team Loco contract."

I sigh. "Yeah. And plus I'd have no idea where to get a fake ID."

She smiles a little, and it warms me up inside. "How are you doing?" I ask, trying to keep my voice level. I don't want to act like she's fragile and breakable because she's stronger than that. But I also would hate to say anything to make her feel worse. I know it's going to take her some time to get over what happened. I've seen her check Twitter a few times since we started driving.

She shrugs. "I'm fine."

"You don't really seem fine…" I say carefully.

She looks over at me and then unbuckles her seatbelt and slides across the front seat. She rests her head on my shoulder and loops her arm through mine. I love being close to her. I kiss her hair while keeping my eyes on the road.

"It just sucks," she says after a moment. "It just really sucks."

I'm not going to insult her by making up some stupid comment like *it'll get better,* when we both know these things take time to heal. "Yeah," I say. "It does."

Within minutes, she's asleep in the middle seat of my truck, her hair falling over my shoulder. She's not stressed when she's sleeping, so I stay quiet and let her rest for the remainder of the journey.

"Baby," I whisper a few hours later. "We're here."

She sits up and blinks. "We're here already?"

"You slept a while," I say with a laugh.

She yawns. This is the moment I've been waiting for, seeing her face as we pull up to the famous city she's been wanting to visit. The barren Nevada landscape is a beautiful as it is different from Texas. We turn onto the Strip, which is really close to our hotel.

"Here we are," I say, watching her while I drive.

She gazes around, but her expression doesn't change. "Cool," she says after a while. "The mountains are pretty."

That's not even close to the type of response I thought she'd give me. I wanted to see her face light up. I wanted her to smile so big it reaches her eyes. I wanted her to do that cute bounce up and down in the seat thing she does when she's really excited. But even the allure of Vegas doesn't help take away her pain.

I grit my teeth as I follow the GPS to our hotel. I wish I could personally curse out every asshole online who said those things to my girlfriend. I wish I could expose their secrets and embarrass them just as badly as they embarrassed her. I haven't even checked Twitter lately. I know it'll just piss me off more.

Still, I put on a smile and try to make Keanna's day better any way I can. Once again, we check into a new hotel, and she's happy when we're up on the nineteenth floor and she can look out at the city below.

I set her flowers on her nightstand and walk up behind her while she's gazing out the balcony window. I slide my hands around her and hold her tightly.

"I love you so much," I whisper.

"I love you, too."

I lean forward and kiss her cheek. "Is there anything I can do to make you feel better?"

She turns around to face me, and I keep my arms around her. Her hands wrap around my neck and she peers up at me with this sad smile.

"I'm okay. I'll be okay. I'm actually more worried about you."

I frown. "Why would you worry about me?"

She shrugs and looks away. "I don't know."

"Baby, I'm fine," I say, squeezing her closer to me. "I'll win this race. I'm not the least bit concerned."

She nods. "That's good."

Damn. Something tells me she didn't mean she was worried about my racing ability.

We settle into the hotel's oddly comfortable couch and watch some TV. The Vegas arena doesn't open up early and won't let us in to scope out the track like the other two had done, so there's nothing to do but hang with my girl. I'm totally fine with that, because she's the only thing in my life I truly care about.

Clay texts me around dinner time, asking if we want to go out to eat with them.

Me: No thanks, man. I'm spending time with my girl.

Clay: She feeling better?

Me: Honestly, not really. I thought Vegas would be special but it didn't help.

Clay: So make it special

Clay: Fuck the haters and make it special, dude.

I read his text and think it over in my mind.

Me: You're right. Thanks.

CHAPTER NINE

Keanna

Vegas is as beautiful as it looks in the movies. The only thing I didn't expect is that it seems a little smaller when you're walking down the infamous Vegas Strip. But the lights are shiny and colorful and fill you up with just enough whimsy to forget your problems. We'd tried visiting the cupcake place I want to try, but it was closed for a private party. I hope we'll get to go back to it before the trip is over.

Last night, Jett and I had gone with the guys to get dinner at some restaurant that had acrobats performing all around us. After the last two miserable days I've had, I welcomed the distraction. I was able to put on a smile and actually mean half of it. It's kind of like magic, how getting out and doing something exciting makes you slip into a world of happiness that exists separately from your bleak real life. But as soon as we got back to the hotel last night, it all came back to me. Tidal waves of sadness pouring over me in ways I couldn't hold back. But I tried to. For Jett, I tried.

We'd stayed up late watching a movie in the hotel, cuddling in the bed surrounded by its many fluffy pillows. I loved the way his chest felt—strong and warm as I laid against him, but I still hurt.

He didn't ask me if everything was okay, or if I was feeling fine, or anything, so I think I did a good job of hiding this feeling that's grown so big inside of me that I fear it'll explode any day now.

Today is Friday, and Jett's Vegas race is tomorrow. We're supposed to do some sightseeing and find all the fun things you can do here when you're not old enough to drink, but we made a plan to sleep in late first. After all these days of waking up early to drive, it's nice to lay in bed with no schedule looming over you.

Only, I can't sleep in late.

I'm laying here in this comfortable hotel bed, next to Jett, who is perfect in every way, and yet I'm not sleeping. I'm staring at the ceiling and chewing on the inside of my lip. It's been hours since I last checked the drama online. I could tell Jett was watching me all night last night, hoping I wouldn't look at social media, so I didn't. But I can't hold back anymore. It's too tempting. It's so stupid, I know, but it is what it is.

I look over at Jett and he's sleeping peacefully, his breathing slow and steady. Carefully and slowly, I turn toward my nightstand and then wait, to make sure he's still asleep.

I reach for my phone, then open up Twitter. I used to check this thing all the time and never think twice about it. I used to scroll through tweets while waiting in line at the grocery store, or during commercial breaks on my favorite TV show. It's never mattered much until now.

Now, my hands are shaking and my stomach hurts and my heart pounds so hard I am certain it's going to wake up Jett. I close my eyes and take a deep breath, but it doesn't help. I have to see what these girls are saying about me online.

I just got another update from the slut's old schoolmates. She used to wear the same three outfits all the time and they were never washed.

That one is kind of true. Many years of my life I only had one or two good pairs of jeans, and we only went to the laundromat whenever Mom had some quarters. For a while in ninth grade, I knew this girl who would let me spend the night and wash my clothes at her house. We were never really close friends though, I think she just felt sorry for me.

She would sleep with any guy who asked. Figures.

Not true. So not true. Ugh. I keep scrolling.

Oh, and now I'm being told that she once gave a BJ to her high school teacher so he'd give her a passing grade in science. Why is Jett with this hoe? Like seriously???

Also not true.

Even though I know my heart will break as I read through this crap, I can't help it. I can't stop myself. I have to see what they're saying about me. I have to know what everyone will be thinking if they see me at the races with Jett. What if Jett's manager gets word of this? What if Team Loco fires him because of his girlfriend's bad reputation?

The panic gets worse. Jett had to sign a contract with Team Loco saying he'd abide by laws and not make an embarrassment of the team with his actions. Surely that applies to the people he hangs out with too? His manager likes me, but probably not enough to overlook what everyone is saying.

I sit up in bed and throw off the covers, my skin suddenly so hot it's burning. Jett stays asleep as I pace the room, my phone gripped tightly in my hand. I can't do this to Jett. I'm going to ruin his career. It doesn't matter that most of the bad stuff is false, because some of it is true. I am not a nice normal girl with a normal family who deserves Jett and his wholesome image.

The lump in my throat threatens to cut off my airway and I put my hands on the glass of the balcony door, willing myself to take a deep breath. Nothing helps my heart slow down. Nothing makes my hands stop shaking.

I look back at Jett, and I'm glad he's asleep. He doesn't need to see me lose my freaking mind right now.

When my vision gets blurry from all the pacing and hyperventilating, I drop into a chair and look out the window, trying to focus on something outside that will take away this panic. A few moments later, I'm looking at my phone again. I hate myself. I hate how this addiction is too strong to break.

Seriously, we need to start a petition to make Jett break up with her. He is so much better than her and he deserves better.

That one is true.

Jett is better than this. He does deserve better. He deserves more. I look back at my boyfriend and tears fall down my cheek. I can't do it now because it would put a damper on his race tomorrow. I'm not sure how I'll survive doing what I know I have to do. We are neighbors. Our parents are best friends. Breaking up with Jett is going to be the hardest thing I've ever done.

I swallow and grit my teeth to keep my jaw from quivering. I swipe off the tears that are splashing on my shirt.

I guess I've known what I had to do all along. I don't deserve Jett. I don't deserve my family, either. Even though they adopted me, I'm a legal adult now so that's meaningless. Park and Becca just felt sorry for me—that's why they did it.

And Jett—he didn't know about my true past. He didn't mean to get caught up with someone like me. Those girls on Twitter are mean, but they're right.

As soon as we get home, I'll have to break up with the guy I love more than anything. And then I'll have to leave, and let the people I care about go back to a life that's better off without me.

CHAPTER TEN

Jett

"You seem nervous."

I look over at Keanna, who's watching me with a frown. "Like... really nervous," she says. "You'll totally bounce back from that last race. I don't think you should be so worried about it."

Right. Tomorrow's race. That's what she thinks I'm nervous about. I take a deep breath and try to let some tension in my shoulders fall away. Now that she mentions it, I am nervous. My foot is twitching and my hands are tapping the steering wheel and there's not even any music playing on the radio. I probably shouldn't be driving right now with now nervous I am.

There's something in my pocket that Keanna doesn't know about. If she did, she'd probably know why I'm so nervous.

We've spent all day exploring Vegas and stopping at famous stores that have their own reality TV shows. We've eaten the famous cheese fries from that food show we like, and we took a trip through the famous pawn shop on the outskirts of town. The cupcake place was closed, but all in all, we've had a great day of being tourists. I haven't even thought of the race tomorrow because I'm not worried about it. I've raced hundreds of times in my life.

But tonight's event—I've never done it at all.

I know Keanna's hiding some of her pain through a fake smile, but I think she's feeling better. I did my best to make the day fun and eventful, and I've been careful not to mention anything that would make her think of Twitter. We will get through this tough time together and it'll blow over eventually. I think it'll really blow over after tonight.

Things are going to be perfect tonight.

The sun is starting to set, casting a beautiful glow on the city as I drive us back to the hotel. I'm running through the list of things in my head, hoping that the hotel's staff was able to set it all up like I'd asked them to. It was difficult planning something this big in secret, and I did most of it through text and when Keanna took a shower this morning. I want everything to be special for her. I hope I did this right.

I grab her hand as we walk in through the hotel's large lobby doors.

"We should go to bed early tonight," she says. "That way you can be fully rested for tomorrow."

"Mmhmm," I say. "Sounds like a good idea."

Little does she know, we probably won't sleep at all.

My pulse races as we step off the elevator and head toward our hotel room. I'm about to find out if my plan has been put into place by all the people I recruited to help me.

I drop the key card when I go to open the door, and Keanna bends down to pick it up for me. "You okay?" she asks.

"Perfect," I say. I slide the key into the lock and wait for the green light. I look at her as I push open the door. She smiles up at me. I draw in a deep breath. It's show time.

The hotel room smells like roses and vanilla, which is better than I'd imagined it would be. Every piece of furniture is decorated with dozens of scented candles, all lit and casting a romantic glow in the room. The bed has been sprinkled with rose petals, and a beautiful red rose bouquet sits on the table next to her other flowers. Soft music plays from a radio in the corner, and I grin when I see the centerpiece on our small dining table. A dozen Vegas cupcakes, bought in advance by me, and arranged in the shape of a heart.

Keanna gasps, her hands going to her mouth. Then she turns around. "What is this? It's not my birthday."

I can't hold back my grin even though my heart is pounding a mile a minute. I reach into my pocket and pull out the little velvet box that's been patiently waiting all week. I drop down on one knee, so unbelievably nervous, and open the box.

Keanna almost looks scared at first, and then tears fill her eyes, and then she covers her mouth and I can't read her expression.

"Keanna," I say, swallowing quickly to get my voice back. I'm so nervous I can barely function. "You are the best part of me. I love you with all my heart and I want to be your husband for the rest of my life. Will you marry me?"

The next few seconds seem to slow to a crawl. Tears fall down her cheeks, and I think they're happy tears, but I'm not so sure. I'm so nervous that she might say no, and all I want is to hear the yes. My hand shakes as I hold up the ring I picked out months ago. Finally, her hands fall from her face. This is it. Now she'll say yes.

"I was going to break up with you," she says.

My whole world seems to crack in half. "What?" I say, still on my knee, my heart rocketing around in my chest. This can't be happening.

She shrugs and another tear rolls down her beautiful face. "I thought you deserved better than me," she says, looking at the floor. "I thought it would be best to break up with you when we get home, and now you just proposed and I don't even know what to say."

"Oh my God," I stammer. "Why..? I—"

She chokes back a sob. "I want to marry you more than anything, Jett," she says as she wipes away tears. "I just feel like you can do better. I know you can do better."

"I don't want anyone else," I say, the words tumbling out of the deepest parts of my soul. "I only want you. And anyone who thinks differently can piss off. You are my angel and my soul mate and I just want you."

A soft smile breaks through her tears. "Are you sure?"

I hold up the ring higher as if this shiny huge diamond is all the proof I need. "Yes."

She smiles. "Are we doing this?"

I grin back at her. "Well, you haven't said yes yet."

She drops to her knees in front of me and throws her arms around my neck. "Yes," she whispers. That single word wraps up all the pieces of my newly shattered heart and binds them back together. I hold onto her tightly and tell her how much I love her. When she pulls back, I take her hand and put the ring on her finger.

"Thank you," I say. "For the most terrifying few seconds of my life."

She chuckles, her gaze focused on her new engagement ring. She looks just as I pictured she would look when I bought it. "I can't believe you want to marry me," she says softly. "After all the drama…"

"That was nothing," I say. "You and me, we're perfect. We don't have drama. Let others create whatever they want to make their lives more miserable, but when we're together, we're happy. And we're all that matters, babe."

I dry her tears with my thumb and pull her closer, placing my lips on hers. "For better or worse, I want you Keanna. Especially in the worse times. When everything else goes wrong, you are the only person I can count on."

She climbs into my lap and now we're both on the floor, clinging to each other like we can't possibly stand to let go. It's the best place in the world to be.

"Jett," she says, peering at me with those eyes that melt my heart.

"Yes, love?"

"Will you take my phone and delete the Twitter app?"

I laugh. "Sure. I'll delete mine, too."

"Perfect." She wraps her arms around my neck and pulls me up against her. "For better or worse," she says.

I kiss her hair. "And forever and ever."

Don't miss Jett and Keanna's final book: Forever and a Day

THE WORLD OF SUMMER UNPLUGGED

Don't miss the spin-off series!

The Summer Series

Bayleigh's best friend Becca gets her own series (and finds her true love) in Book 1, Summer Alone.

Available for FREE.

The Team Loco Series

Jett Adams joins the famous motocross racing team, Team Loco. Meet his team mates and read their journeys of falling in love.

Book 1, Taming Zach, is Available for FREE.

ALSO BY AMY SPARLING

When seventeen-year-old Jeremy's girlfriend agrees to do the deed, life can't possibly get better. And then the condom breaks.

He loves Elisa as much as a popular teenage athlete can love a girl, but he doesn't want to be a dad. Her parents want a marriage - his parents want an abortion, and Elisa and Jeremy's once-perfect relationship has been reduced to fights and drama.

With a college scholarship on the line and the whole high school mocking him, Jeremy makes a decision that may haunt him forever.

ABOUT THE AUTHOR

Amy Sparling is the bestselling author of books for teens and the teens at heart. She lives on the coast of Texas with her family, her spoiled rotten pets, and a huge pile of books. She graduated with a degree in English and has worked at a bookstore, coffee shop, and a fashion boutique. Her fashion skills aren't the best, but luckily she turned her love of coffee and books into a writing career that means she can work in her pajamas. Her favorite things are coffee, book boyfriends, and Netflix binges.

She's always loved reading books from R. L. Stine's Fear Street series, to The Baby Sitter's Club series by Ann, Martin, and of course, Twilight. She started writing her own books in 2010 and now publishes several books a year. Amy loves getting messages from her readers and responds to every single one! Connect with her on one of the links below.

www.AmySparling.com

Made in the USA
Monee, IL
25 August 2021